GW00319471

PRAISE FOR SHANE M

'One of the genre's most gifted writers.' S
Who Weekly

'Whelan is a born politico: a breezy, know-it-all wiseacre with a glad hand and a seductively confiding tone of voice.' *Seattle Times*

'There is only one Australian crime writer on my list this year—Shane Maloney.' *Examiner*

'Maloney is a born writer...For the first time, in the vicinity of Australian crime-writing, we hear the true national voice of comic futility, a literary voice which is rich, ridiculous and tawdry, which can set itself up with a soaring rhetoric and slide on the banana skin of its own piss-elegance...Maloney is terrific...he could be the Australian Chandler.' *Age*

'The funniest meanstreets-style writing on offer these days.' S*unday Age*

'Whelan's voice...is wonderful. He's at once acerbic, sardonic, ever hopeful...always witty and ineluctably clear-eyed...' *Providence Sunday Journal*

'Maloney is a literary writer who some will feel is wasting his time in the detective business. He takes characters that are stereotypes (the public servant, the minister, the arty type) and depicts them with subtlety and originality and compassionate humor. He also writes a ripping yarn.' *Eureka Street*

'Another take on the venerable detective novel...Murray's tongue-in-cheek narrative and the author's delight in satirizing the down-under art scene keep us fully engaged.' *San Francisco Chronicle*

'All great cities have their literary interpreters...now Melbourne has found a fresh spokesman—Shane Maloney. In his four Murray Whelan novels, that city's grubby inner suburbs and its marble corridors of power act as a central character...Visitors could use *The Big Ask* as a Melbourne street directory.' *West Australian*

THE MURRAY WHELAN TRILOGY

STIFF + THE BRUSH-OFF + NICE TRY

SHANE MALONEY

textpublishingmelbourneaustralia

The Text Publishing Company
Swann House
22 William Street
Melbourne Victoria 3000

www.textpublishing.com.au

First published by Text Publishing *Stiff* 1994, *The Brush-Off* 1996, *Nice Try* 1998

The Murray Whelan Trilogy first published 2001
Second edition 2004. This Edition 2007

Printed and bound by Griffin Press
Designed by Chong

National Library of Australia

Cataloguing-in-Publication-data:

Maloney, Shane

The Murray Whelan trilogy.

ISBN 978 1 921351 15 0.

I. Maloney, Shane. Brush-off. II. Maloney, Shane. Stiff.

III. Maloney, Shane. Nice try. IV. Title.

A823.3

 This project was assisted by the Commonwealth Government through the Australia Council, its arts funding and advisory body.

STIFF

For Christine my kind of funding body

The fiddle at the Pacific Pastoral meat-packing works was neither particularly original nor fabulously lucrative. But it was a nice little earner for all concerned while it lasted, and probably harmless enough. All that changed when Herb Gardiner reported finding a body in Number 3 chiller.

There it was, jammed between a pallet load of best export boneless beef and half a tonne of spring lamb. It was a Friday afternoon so, if Gardiner hadn't found it when he did, the corpse would have spent the weekend locked in with the rest of the dead meat, carcasses parked halfway between paddock and dinner plate.

According to the statement Gardiner gave to the Department of Labour investigators and the police, the Number 3 unit had a history of playing up. He had unlocked the door and gone inside to read the gauge when he saw the body squeezed into the aisle running through to the emergency exit hatch. He recognised it immediately as a leading hand with one of the casual work crews, later identified as Ekrem Bayraktar. He didn't need to feel for Bayraktar's pulse to know that he was dead. He could tell by the waxy pallor of the man's face, by the dusting of fine sugar on his lips where his last breath had turned to frost.

The body was sandwiched into a tight space between roof-high stacks of boxes. It was a narrow gap, but it was just wide enough for most men to pass along sideways even in protective clothing—

obstruction of access to the emergency hatch was illegal. But Bayraktar was big, even by the standards of a place where men were hired to hump heavy loads around. Later at the morgue his naked corpse weighed in at over 135 kilos, big doughy rolls of flesh, soft obese bulk, like a weight-lifter gone to seed.

He was squeezed in so tight that they had to bring in one of the forklifts to move the loaded pallets around him before they could remove the body. Even without the boxes there to support him he remained upright, balanced like a great big stalagmite. It was hard to imagine how he had got himself that far down the passage, or why.

In the business that followed—the calling of the ambulance, the notification of the police and the Department of Labour, the removal of the body, the taking of photographs and statements—it never occurred to anyone to look for the small zip-lock plastic bag of folded fifties and twenties that Bayraktar had taken into the freezer with him. And even if they had known to look, and where, they would not have found anything. There were quite a few little details about that afternoon that seemed to have been missed.

With Bayraktar gone, everything might have ended then and there and no-one would have been any the wiser. It was just bad luck really that his untimely demise coincided with a delicate readjustment then taking place within certain echelons of the Australian Labor Party, an organisation founded to further the aspirations of those who toil unseen in dark and dangerous places. An organisation which, next to itself, loves the working man best.

Perhaps I should begin by saying that this is not a sob story. It's a cruel world, I know, and even in the just city a man can be stiff. Bad luck happens. And it's not like bad luck was something I didn't already know a bit about. Damage control was part of my job, after all. But up until then it had been other people's bad luck, not my own, that exercised my professional interest. Maybe that's why I was so unprepared for what happened over those four October days. So I'm not doing any special pleading, you understand. Considering what happened to others I could name, I got off pretty lightly.

It all started on one of those miserable wet Monday mornings when, come nine o'clock, half of Melbourne is still strung out bumper-to-bumper along the South-eastern Freeway. I had just dropped my son Red at school, and as I swung my clapped-out old Renault into Sydney Road the thought of all those Volvo and Camira drivers stewing away behind their windscreen wipers brought a quiet smile to my lips. Not that I bore them any personal animosity, you understand. It was just that if God wanted to punish the eastern suburbs for voting Liberal, She wouldn't hear me complaining.

I could afford to feel like that because the Brunton Avenue log-jam was miles away. Where I lived, north of town, the toiling masses tended to start their toiling a little earlier in the day, and most of those that still had jobs were already at work. By nine the rush hour had already come and gone. Apart from a few hundred light industrial vehicles and the occasional tram disgorging early shoppers, women in head-scarfs mainly, I had the northbound lane to myself.

Not that I was busting a gut to get to work. No clock was waiting for me to punch it, and I couldn't see the pile of paper on my desk bursting into flames if left undisturbed a little longer. The fifteen minutes it took me to drive to work provided one of my few moments of solitude all day and I liked to make the most of it. As I drove I read the paper.

This was less dangerous than it sounds. I'd already studied the broadsheets over breakfast, and the *Sun* was the kind of tabloid easily absorbed while doing something else—shelling peas, for instance, or operating a lathe. I had it spread open on the passenger seat beside me, and whenever I hit a red light or got stuck behind a slow-moving tram I skimmed a couple of pages. The spring racing carnival had just begun, so the emphasis was on horseflesh, fashion and catering. Just A Dash was favourite, black was big, and interesting things were being done with asparagus. Agreement was unanimous—four years in and the eighties were holding firm as the most exciting decade ever.

The Bell Street lights had changed and I was halfway across the intersection when my eye caught a name buried in a two-paragraph news brief at the bottom of page seventeen. That was when I first encountered the name Ekrem Bayraktar. Not that it meant anything to me at the time. It was the other name that got my attention. I snatched up the page, draped it over the steering wheel and turned my concentration away from the road long enough to constitute a serious threat to public safety. This is what I read.

> Police have identified a man found dead last Friday in a freezer at the Pacific Pastoral meat-packing works at Coolaroo in Melbourne's outer north as Ekrem Bayraktar, 42, a shift supervisor at the works. It is believed that he suffered a heart attack and was overcome by cold while conducting a routine stocktake.

Pacific Pastoral has announced an immediate review of its procedures in light of the incident which coincides with the state government's attempts to gain Upper House approval for its controversial industrial health and safety legislation. Informed sources at Trades Hall believe the matter will be considered when the THC Executive meets late next week. The Minister for Industry, Charlene Wills, was unavailable for comment.

I liked the way a whiff of Labor intrigue had been slipped into an account of some poor bastard's cardiac arrest. But that wasn't what interested me. What had pushed my button was mention of the Minister for Industry. Charlene Wills was a person whose reputation was a matter very close to my heart.

Up ahead I could see Pentridge, the razor ribbon atop its bluestone walls dripping dismally in the drizzle. On my left was an Italian coffee shop and a row of old single-storey terraces that had been tarted up into offices and professional suites. I pulled into the kerb, tucked the *Sun* under my arm and pushed open the glass door of one of the shops, the one with the letters on the window saying 'Charlene Wills: Member of the Legislative Council for the Province of Melbourne Upper'.

With a bit of luck, I thought, I'd have just enough time to call Charlene's parliamentary office and get the lowdown on this piece of tabloid crap before the business of the day wrapped its tentacles around me.

Too late. The daily grind had already walked in off the street and was standing at the desk just inside the front door. He was solidly built, in a knockabout sort of way, anywhere between thirty and forty-five, with a duck's bum haircut and hands like baseball mitts. When I walked in, he shifted irritably and shot me a glance that told me he'd got there first and I could fucking well wait my turn.

All his weight was balanced on the balls of his feet, and the tips of his fingers were pressed down hard on the desk. He was glowering across it at Trish who was in charge of office admin. 'I've had a gutful,' he said.

Statements like that, half-threat, half-plea, weren't unusual at the electorate office. But this fellow's tone was tending more to the threat end of the octave, and as he spoke he began tugging his khaki work shirt out of his pants and fiddling with the buttons. 'I pay my taxes,' he said. 'I know my rights.'

Trish nodded at the bloke sympathetically and, without moving her eyes, casually bent forward as if to better hear him out. Trish was big in the chassis and not afraid to use it, but just in case push ever came to shove she kept the butt end of a sawn-down pool cue sitting in her wastepaper basket. As far as I knew she'd never had cause to use it, but on the odd occasion its mere presence could be a comfort. If this dickhead's manner didn't rapidly begin to improve, we'd all have a very unpleasant start to the working week.

'May I help you, sir?' I said, stepping forward. 'I'm Murray Whelan, Charlene Wills' electorate officer.'

As I spoke the man turned towards me and threw his shirt open, like he was performing a magic trick or unveiling the foundation stone of a major civic monument. Underneath, he was wearing what appeared to be a paisley-patterned t-shirt. As I got closer I realised that he was one of the most comprehensively tattooed human beings I had ever seen. Which, in that part of the world, was no mean achievement.

I tried to look unimpressed as I accepted his tacit invitation to inspect his pecs. He was certainly toting some artistry about. Fire-breathing dragons, dagger-pierced hearts, tiger-mounted she-devils, flame-licked skulls, Huey, Dewey and Louie, you name it, he had it. Innumerable little pictures exploded out of his pants, ran up over his flaccid paunch, covered his torso, and curled back across his shoulders.

The mad swirls of colour stopped abruptly, however, at the V of the man's collar line and, I was prepared to bet, at the point in mid-bicep where the sleeves of a summer work shirt would run out. His hands, neck and face were unadorned. No spider webs embellished his earlobes, no intertwined bluebirds flew up his neck. This was a good sign. Here was a man who knew that some people tended to jump to the wrong conclusion about tatts, a man who had the brains not to let his passion for self-decoration get in the way of his employability. Someone you could talk sense to.

And now that he was dealing with a fellow male, he became a little less highly strung. 'I want this bloke put out of business.' He jabbed his finger at the place right above his heart where a freshly laid-on pair of baroque cherubs, beautiful work, were holding aloft an ornate scroll. I moved his shoulder sideways so I had better light to read by. Inside the scroll were the words 'Gial For Ever'.

'Gial?' I said.

He nodded morosely. 'Gail took one look and shot through,' he said. 'Reckoned if I couldn't even spell her name properly, she certainly wasn't gunna marry me.' Then he brightened up. 'I told that fucken prick of a tattooist I'd have his licence. And I'm not leaving here until I do. Dead set. I'm adam-fucken-ant.'

Three years before, when Charlene had offered me the job of looking after her constituents, a Labor MP's electorate office was, by definition, a backwater. Then the tide had turned and swept Labor into office, first at state, then federal level. The drover's dog was in the Lodge. We were the power in the land. And that sign on the door had become a homing beacon for every dingbat within a ten-mile radius.

When I began at the electorate office, our only customers were ordinary voters desperately seeking redress from bureaucratic inanity or government indifference. Or the harmlessly wan and smelly looking for somewhere out of the cold. But by late 1984 we were attracting such a daily barrage of basket cases and snake-oil salesmen that the sign out front might as well have read 'Axes Ground Here'.

Surely, I was beginning to think, the cause of social progress could be deploying my skills more effectively. Could I not perhaps be managing a small lake or pine plantation for the Department of Conservation, Forests and Lands? A modestly demanding range of foothills even? Something with a little less interface.

'Okay, Mr Adam fucking Ant,' I shrugged. 'Let's see what we can do.' Behind the man's back, Trish had relaxed and was grinning like an ape. I discreetly flashed her a splayed handful of digits and led off towards the back of the office. Five minutes of deeply concerned bullshit should, I figured, be enough to see this particular dipstick safely off the premises. 'Walk this way.'

Adam Ant, or whatever his name was, tucked his shirt back into his pants and slouched after me. 'It's not right,' he mumbled under his breath.

What passed for my office was a partitioned cubicle tucked into a back corner behind the stationery cupboard. Before the election had transformed Charlene into a Minister of the Crown, it had been hers. Back in those days, I'd shared the reception area with Trish and whoever else happened to wander in. But I was fast to grasp the perquisites of political power and had quickly taken advantage of Charlene's increasing frequent absence to commandeer her privileges.

I snapped on the flickering fluorescent light, parked myself behind the laminated plywood desk and indicated the orange plastic of the visitor's chair. As Ant lowered his backside into place, obscuring my Tourism Commission poster of Wilson's Promontory, I squared off my blotter, uncapped my pen with a bureaucratic flourish and tried to look like I gave a shit.

'I'd like to help you, mate. I really would,' I said. 'But you've got the wrong department.'

Ant finished buttoning up the National Gallery, ran his hand through his greasy pompadour and looked deeply wronged. 'I rung up Consumer Protection. They said I should try my local member.'

Typical. Consumer Protection took the cake at pass-the-parcel. I nodded understandingly and went through the motions of taking down the particulars. This was the first instance of a dyslexic tattooist that Mrs Wills' office had ever been called upon to address, I explained. And while the Minister would undoubtedly be sympathetic, in a case like this the powers of an elected member of the state's legislative chamber of review might be somewhat circumscribed.

The *Sun* lay between us on top of my overflowing in-tray, still folded open at page seventeen. If I don't piss this joker off soon, I thought, Parliament will begin sitting and Charlene will be unreachable for the rest of the day.

'I'm not going anywhere, pal,' said Ant. 'Until this thing is fixed.'

'This is a legal matter,' I said. 'Restitution. Punitive damages.' These were words he liked. 'You need the Community Legal Service.' The Family Law Act surely included provisions for the irretrievable breakdown of the relationship between a man, his tattooist, and his intended.

Looking like the height of efficiency, I dialled the CLS and made an appointment, skipping the details in case they thought I was pulling their collective leg. Friday was the earliest the slack-arses could squeeze him in. 'This lot will look after you,' I told Ant. 'Top people.'

The CLS was half a mile down the road. I drew a map, wrote the appointment details underneath, and slid it across the desk.

Ant folded his arms across his chest. 'You're just trying to give me the bounce.'

True. But it wasn't as though I hadn't given it my best shot first. 'Look mate,' I said, marginally more firmly, 'there's nothing else I can do. The legal service will handle it from now on. Good luck. Let us know how you go. I'll keep Charlene informed. But in the meantime my hands are tied.'

He shook his head and settled his technicolour mass even more firmly into the moulded plastic cup of the seat. I opened Charlene's correspondence file and buried my face in it, wondering how long it would take Trish to burst in with an urgent pretext. 'Dear Madam,' the top letter began. 'You are a pinko ratbag bitch.'

Five minutes later I was still pretending to read and Ant was continuing to glare. What did he want me to do? Whip out a bottle of correcting fluid and a blue biro and personally amend his faulty chest? 'I'll call the cops,' I said, lamely.

He snorted derisively. Quite right, too. For a start, we could hardly be seen having someone dragged away merely for demanding that the government do something about their problems. That, after all, was what we were there for.

Also, I found it hard to sound convincing. If I called the coppers on every cantankerous customer we had, they'd have to start running a shuttle bus. And given the ongoing budgetary constraints faced by the various agencies under the jurisdiction of the Minister for Police and Emergency Services, a factional ally of Charlene, that was a poor prospect.

Mainly, however, I couldn't call the coppers on some love-struck dumb-bum with Cupid engraved on his left tit because such an encounter was unlikely to be conducive to an outcome of social equity. Let the coppers catch who they could. I'd gone to school with blokes like Ant, and having to resort to the wallopers in my dealings with them would have been an affront to both my personal morality and my professional pride. Quarrels should be kept in the family. 'Do us a favour,' I suggested courteously. 'Fuck off.'

Ant smiled maliciously and leaned back like he had all the time in the world. Fortunately, at exactly that moment the phone rang. It wasn't Trish but Greg Coates, a deputy director in the Melbourne office of the Department of Immigration and Ethnic Affairs.

Nearly a quarter of the electors of the Province of Melbourne Upper had been born overseas and it wasn't uncommon for constituents with an immigration problem to turn up on our doorstep. No problem. Immigration is a Common-wealth matter, so all we had to do was steer them over to the local federal member.

But, as often as not, the problems were little more than language mix-ups, and it would have been criminal of me to allow an important federal politician to be burdened with such trifling matters. Especially if Charlene could get the credit for fixing them. Which wasn't difficult to arrange since Greg Coates had been a mate since university, and was both a fellow spear-carrier in my faction and a member of the same party branch. So about once a week Greg gave me a call and we cut a bit of red tape together and swapped political gossip.

I swivelled my seat around, pointedly turning my back on the tattooed wonder, and spent fifteen minutes firming up a batch of family reunion applications. Eventually Coates made his way, as if in passing, to the prospect of an early election. There was a lot of speculation about, and what with Charlene being in Cabinet, Coates was always trying to weasel the latest inside info out of me.

I told him what I knew, which was exactly zip, and we finished off with the customary exchange of promises to get together for a drink. When I spun my seat around to hang up, Ant had helped himself to my *Sun* and was pretending to read it, something he wouldn't really be able to do until he developed the intellectual capacity of an eight-year-old.

I was about to get seriously snaky when the phone rang again. This time it was a nice old Greek pensioner whose plumbing difficulties I had been shepherding through the maintenance division of the Housing Ministry. In comparison with the idiocy incarnate sitting opposite me, the institutional oddities at Housing were child's play. I made a couple of quick calls to the appropriate authorities, threw my weight about in a minor way, and called the old bat to reassure her that she'd be flushing again before she knew it.

By that stage, it was too late to call Charlene. Besides which, the day had kicked in with its customary vigour. In rapid succession I had a branch treasurer ring to fish for his postage costs to be reimbursed, a school wanting Charlene for its prize night, and a personal visit from a guy with a Ned Kelly beard describing himself as Citizens For A Freeway Free Future. I took him out to the waiting area and spent half an hour outlining the intricacies of the Western Ring-Road community consultative process. He kept his helmet on for the entire conversation, so I'm not sure if he understood everything I told him.

Just after eleven Agnelli rang.

Angelo Agnelli was Charlene Wills' ministerial adviser at Industry. The Industry Ministry was where government policy rubbed noses with the big end of town. The nose was Ange's weapon of choice and Charlene paid him a princely sum to implement initiatives, expedite the legislative process, keep the mandarins on their toes, and God knew what else. Recently, he'd been making the effort to find the time to look over my shoulder and make tut-tutting noises.

That day, the big bee in Agnelli's bonnet was Joe Lollicato. A couple of years previously, Joe had been elected to one of the municipal councils in the area. And in the last round of local government polls he'd been returned with a handsomely increased majority. To Agnelli, who'd never been elected to anything in his life, this sort of personal popularity was both a personal affront and evidence that Lollicato was positioning himself to seize the party's endorsement away from Charlene.

'Forget Lolly,' I told him. 'Parliamentary ambitions are a fact of life around here. Lolly wouldn't be the first person in local government to start thinking he's on the up-escalator to Canberra. But if Lollicato wants a stab at Charlene's job, and that's a debatable point, he'll have to wait until she decides to go, then take his chances along with everyone else. If he tries anything sooner, he'll find out that a stretch at a suburban town hall, a few half-baked factional connections, and an Italian surname won't be enough to convince a pre-selection panel to dump a sitting member. A minister at that.'

Agnelli refused to be mollified. 'There are plenty of people in the party who'd like to see Charlene taken down a peg or two. Lollicato's a sneaky little prick. It wouldn't pay to underestimate his deviousness. He's got more friends than you'd suspect.'

These were facts that could not be disputed, but they were hardly very specific, just the usual Labor Party love talk. The real reason for Agnelli's antagonism towards Lollicato, I suspected, was cultural. I thought this because sensitivity to ethnic cultural nuances was an essential aspect of my professional capabilities.

Charlene's electorate, the whole area in fact, had Italians coming out of its armpits. Fully a quarter of all the Italians in the entire country lived in Melbourne's northern suburbs, not counting their second and third generation descendants. This was apart from the Greeks, Lebanese, Maltese, Macedonians, Turks and Maoris. All things considered, Melbourne Upper should have been called Wogolopolis. A high level of skill in multi-culturalism was, therefore, an indispensable aspect of my job.

It was, I believed, a requirement I fulfilled as reasonably as could be expected for the descendant of three generations of Irish publicans. I had been handing out how-to-vote cards in Italian since I was a teenager. I knew better than to confuse the Federazione Italiana Lavoratori e Famigli with the Comitato d'Assistenza Italiano. I knew who could be relied on at the vegetable market to buy a book of raffle tickets at election time, and whose brother-in-law was private secretary to the Christian

Democrat mayor of San Benedetto del Tronto. And while I would have been the first to admit to having trouble picking a Guelph from a Ghibelline in a dappled olive grove in the Tuscan twilight, I could, to the extent required by profession, reasonably claim to know my tortellini from my tartufo. 'This isn't some sort of Italian crap, is it Ange?' I said.

Agnelli was obsessed. 'That little shit Lollicato is capable of doing any amount of damage if he thinks he can use it to his own advantage. You see the newspaper this morning?'

'Minister in Pre-Selection Wrangle?'

'Jesus, where was that?' There was real panic in Agnelli's voice.

'Relax, Ange. You mean the dead guy at the meatworks in Coolaroo? I've been wondering about that. What's the story?'

Agnelli's voice took on a gossipy conspiratorial hiss. 'What are you doing for lunch?'

'I was thinking of having a pie,' I whispered back. 'You reckon it's safe?'

'Be serious for a minute, can't you, Murray? I'm trying to put something useful your way. Come into town.'

I swung my chair around. The amazing tattooed nuisance had his boots on my desk, right on top of the in-tray. 'I dunno,' I told Agnelli. 'I've got a lot in front of me at the moment.'

'I'll buy.' Agnelli's salary was nearly double mine and this was his first gesture of generosity with anything but unsolicited advice. Clearly, something was going on.

'Ministry or House?'

'House. And since you're coming in, can you do us a favour and give old Picone a lift. He's having lunch with Charlene and I want to pick a bone with the old bugger first. Give him the two dollar tour and bring him downstairs.'

I took my umbrella off the filing cabinet, turned off the two-bar radiator and gently moved Ant's feet over to the out-tray.

'Anyone calls,' I said. 'I'll be out for the rest of the day.'

October was shaping up as the customary disappointment, dithering between erupting into spring or pissing down all the way to Christmas. For the second week in a row, the predicted break in the damp had failed to materialise and rumour had it that the smart money was out the back sawing gopher wood into cubits and collecting matched pairs of animals.

In the rare intervals between showers, masses of frigid air fleeing north from Tasmania or some similarly dismal polar region swept into town and did their best to give spring a bad name. An hour after Agnelli's call I was copping the full brunt of one of these tornadoes as I trudged my way up the terrace of Parliament House.

Our glorious forebears, febrile with easy money and puffed up with Victorian self-aggrandisement, had built the House on a hill and modelled it on classical lines, all monumental portico and reiterated horizontal emphasis. The result was considered by some to be a commanding vista. Personally, with nothing to deflect the nut-numbing elements but a two-piece ninety-nine dollar del Monaco special, and my pace slowed by the company of a wheezing geriatric, I found it all a trifle overstated. When Ennio Picone stopped for the third time for a bit of a breather, I grabbed his arm and all but frogmarched him up the last dozen steps and into the shelter of the foyer. Gentleman that he was, Picone took it for a courtesy. Gentleman that I was, I let him.

Ennio Picone was one of Charlene Wills' prize constituents, an elegant seventy-seven-year-old with fine hands and a matinee moustache. At one time the leader of a dance band, he had spent thirty years tirelessly orchestrating the social life of the electorate's Italians. He had played at their weddings. He had taught music to their children and grandchildren. And now that they were retired, he organised their leisure—for which their grownup children were profoundly grateful.

Those of us who conducted Charlene's affairs knew that we ignored this little old man's ceaseless vitality at our peril. He warranted special attention. It was my job to see that he got it. I wondered what Agnelli wanted with him.

I walked Picone across the coat-of-arms inlaid in the foyer floor and led him into a spacious, high-ceilinged hall with an iceberg of white marble shaped like the young Queen Victoria embedded in the carpet. Leading off to one side was a corridor and a high double doorway. 'Charlene will be with you as soon as possible, Maestro Picone,' I said. 'She's a bit busy right now.'

I shouldered one of the doors open and casually displayed the interior of the parliamentary chamber. It was quite small, hardly more than twenty paces deep, but utterly fantastic, the plaster and gilt hallucination of an imagination overdosed on allegory. Not a surface in the entire room had escaped being moulded, embossed, inlaid, fluted, scalloped, gilded or engraved. Ant's tattoos had nothing on this joint.

An arcade of ivory columns flanked the walls. Above, a squadron of bare-bosomed Amazons brandished symbolic artefacts—the Spear of Boadicea, the Laurels of Victory, the Sheathed Sword of Mercy, the Chain of—what, of Command? Unicorns capered down the walls, and eagles fluttered on high. Heraldic waffle-work of every description abounded unbound, cascading downwards to the rows of padded leather upon which the Honourable Members of the Legislative Council lounged like so many bull seals on a rocky headland.

Best of all, and this was even more than I could have hoped for, Charlene Wills herself was holding the floor.

Charlene was in her mid-fifties, at the height of her powers and, apparently, enjoying herself immensely. When the Cabinet posts had been dished out after the election, there had never been any doubt that Charlene would get a guernsey. For a start she had the factional support, but on top of that she was popular, visible and had a tone of voice that scared the living shit out of the boys in caucus.

She was using it now, a relentless, piercing monotone capable of reducing even the most fractious party conference to numbed compliance. Her topic was obscure—some amendment to some paragraph of some sub-section of some Act, but she was giving it her usual all. You could tell straight off that she knew her stuff and would waste no opportunity to bore it right up the Opposition first chance she got. She was loyal, conscientious, devoted to her constituents, and I loved her like a mother, which was convenient as I no longer had one of my own. Her colostomy bag you couldn't notice, even if you were one of the very few who knew about it.

Unfortunately I'd seen less and less of her in the previous two years. What with being a senior minister and Leader of the Government in the Upper House, she found it hard to make time for electorate matters and had been forced to leave me more or less to my own devices. It was getting so that I virtually had to fight my way through a phalanx of bureaucrats and ministerial advisers just to talk to her, apart from our regular fortnightly meetings. And she'd cancelled the last two of those.

Which reminded me of Agnelli. I allowed Picone a lingering moment to fully register the sumptuousness of his surroundings, and Charlene's central place in them, then tapped him on the shoulder. 'This way, Maestro.' I made a courtly sweep of the arm. Ostentation is never wasted on Italians.

Parliament, we both knew, was a pantomime. Real power was exercised across the road in the Department of Premier and Cabinet, in Management and Budget, in offices with white-boards and synthetic carpet tiles. But you could hardly impress a constituent with an open plan office and an ergonomic typist's chair, however artfully constructed.

I led Picone along the oak-panelled corridor and down a

narrow staircase into a vaulted chamber of bluestone and exposed brick, the law's subterranean forge. Charlene's parliamentary office was a glassed-in alcove tucked under one of the supporting arches. Two desks took up most of it, each buried under piles of well-thumbed papers, sheaves of documents bound in manila folders thick with registry notations. Shelves crowded with green-bound volumes of Hansard and glossy policy proclamations ran up the walls. What little space remained was occupied by a heavy leather chesterfield and a cheap glass-topped coffee table littered with government brochures and the day's newspapers.

A tinny speaker on the wall was broadcasting Charlene's oration from the chamber above. Underneath it, sitting on a corner of one of the desks like he could think of nothing more deserving of his time than greeting the Minister's visitors, was Angelo Agnelli. It was novel to see him sitting somewhere other than on a fence.

Ange was pushing forty just a tad harder than it was pushing back. He had a full head of photogenic black hair, a chubby boyish face skin-deep in conviviality, and a manner calculated to make people feel that he had their number. Angelo Agnelli collected numbers. Sometimes they even added up.

As we entered he tugged at the cuffs of his expensive shirt and reached up to turn off the speaker. He shook hands with Picone and seated him on the chesterfield with the courtesy of a world-weary Venetian diplomat. Then he took a copy of that morning's *Coburg Courier* out of his jacket pocket and dropped it onto the coffee table. It was folded open at a photograph of a group of old men standing at the end of a bocce pitch trying hard to look sorry for themselves, Picone at their centre. The picture took up the bottom half of page three. Most of the top half was taken up by a banner headline reading GOVT STALLS ON ITALIAN PENSIONER CENTRE.

I could have kicked myself. Timely monitoring of the local press was one of my jobs. I'd only been in the room ten seconds and Agnelli was already one up on me.

'What's this fucking shit, Picone?' he said.

Picone, unoffended, showed his palms and shrugged. 'Ten

months we already wait. People, they say maybe you not so fair dinkum on your promise.'

This explanation seemed to please Agnelli. 'What people? Joe Lollicato you mean! Offered to help give us a little nudge in the right direction, did he? Have a word with the local paper, remind us of our obligations, eh? Nothing to do with wanting Charlene's seat upstairs, of course.' He pointed at the ceiling. 'You want Charlene's help, you better watch yourself, Picone.' Evidently Agnelli had not enjoyed his piano accordion lessons. He could always be relied on to put on a good show, but voter relations were not his strong suit.

Picone knew what was expected of him. He shrugged resignedly and mimed the look of a chastened man. But you could see that he didn't mean it. Why should he? In taking his grievance to the local rag he was merely observing the cardinal rule of those who live in a safe seat: never allow yourself to be taken for granted. If the government drags its heels delivering on a promise, scream like a scalded cat.

Charlene had long since promised her electorate's Italian senior citizenry that the government would build them new club-rooms. And old Ennio knew her well enough to know that she would deliver. Eventually. He just wanted to make sure that he'd be still around to take the credit the day the brand new Carboni Club opened its doors.

And so what if Lollicato had been urging the old farts on from behind the scenes, as Agnelli seemed convinced? Lolly was as entitled to cultivate his garden as any other local politician. Picone was merely playing his little part in the game. A man is never too old for that.

So Picone folded his hands in his lap and humoured Agnelli by not interrupting him while he played the minister's hard man. What more could he be expected do? his face seemed to say. Hadn't he come all the way into town in Murray Whelan's decrepit Renault, walked up all those steps in the freezing wind, pretended to be impressed by this overblown colonial copy of some Palladian palazzo?

'Charlene is very disappointed,' Agnelli was saying. 'She's a good friend of the community. You should be ashamed.'

Then Charlene Wills herself came through the door, her plump frame rounded off by the shoulder pads of her knit suit.

'Maestro Picone was wondering if you would be available to be guest of honour at the Carboni Club annual dinner dance,' I said. 'He thinks it would be an ideal opportunity for the community to thank you for your work in securing funding for the new senior citizens' centre. Isn't that right, Maestro?'

Charlene tossed a bulky buff envelope onto the desk in front of Agnelli. 'Lovely. Delighted. Check the diary, Angelo. You'll stay for lunch of course, Ennio? Hello, Murray. You'll have the file back on my desk first thing in the morning, won't you Angelo? Or my life won't be worth living.' She was already out the door, her constituency on her arm.

The envelope landed with a thud. It carried the logo of the Office of the Coroner and had something scrawled across the front in heavy felt-tipped pen. Upside down I could read the words 'Pacific Pastoral/Ekrem Bayraktar'.

As God is my witness, I should have got up and walked away then and there.

Agnelli scooped up the envelope, flourished it triumphantly, and took off up the stairs like he either had an appointment with destiny or a very full bladder. Once outside, he braced himself against the squall blowing along Spring Street, hurtled down the parliamentary declivity and led me onwards into the city.

Since Agnelli was buying, I was content to let him lead. Especially since his destination appeared to be The Society, where a free lunch was worth having. But he didn't falter as he tore past its tinted windows, and I caught only the barest sparkle of silver cutlery before he darted across the road and headed up a lane.

Conversation was impossible. Apart from maintaining a blistering pace, we were both fully occupied negotiating a passage through mountains of old cobblestones and untidy hillocks of sand. What had been a mere footpath for the previous hundred years was in the process of being converted into a pedestrian access facility harmonised to the heritage aspects of the built-form environment. And judging by the amount of excavation going on, it was putting up quite a bit of resistance. Either that or the city council was financing the exercise by strip-mining the entire precinct for minerals.

This kind of obstacle course was something we were all

getting used to. Ever since Labor's arrival in power the city had taken on the aspect of a vast construction site. The leadership had wasted no time making it abundantly clear to both the business end of town and its own membership that the party's historical antagonism to speculation was a thing of the past. A government that couldn't come up with jobs wouldn't last five minutes. Property development equalled jobs and no sentiment was to be wasted on sentiment. Overnight, ancient landmarks became vast pits filled with tip-trucks and management types in business shirts and hard hats.

In keeping with its resolve on the issue, the government had just given some of the more boisterous elements in the building unions a severe judicial crutching. As a result, there were so many construction hoardings and concrete trucks in the city it was impossible to find anywhere to park. And deep festering pools of bad blood awaited the unwary at the Trades Hall.

So far none of those juicy new jobs had come my way. Meanwhile my sense of historical geography was having the shit shot out of it. The old familiar shape of things was changing so fast that it was sometimes hard to know exactly where I stood.

I had no such problem that day, however. Our objective was clearly Chinatown. The pavers beneath our feet had taken on a decidedly oriental motif and all around us gaggles of almond-eyed citizens nicked in and out of eating houses with dead ducks in their windows and names like Good Luck Village and New Dynasty. At a dragon-entwined archway Agnelli abruptly stopped and pushed open a black lacquered portal encrusted with brass studs the size of the hub caps on a Honda Civic.

I was pleasantly surprised and immediately suspicious. My initial assumption when we entered Chinatown was that Agnelli's generosity would run no further than a cheap dim sum, hardly worth my ten-kilometre drive into town. Instead, I found myself being ushered through a grove of bamboo into the Mandarin Palace, winner for three years in succession of the Golden Chopsticks Award in the *Age* Good Gourmet Guide. Judging by the high standard of grovelling we got from the smoothie in the Chou En-lai suit who handed us the menus, Agnelli was a regular.

It was hard to credit that this Agnelli was the same nervy solicitor who had come tentatively tapping on my door at the Municipal Workers' Union ten years earlier, asking to be introduced around the traps. The legal firm that looked after our workers' compensation cases had just taken him on. He joked that he'd probably only got the job because the senior partners assumed he could speak to some of the plaintiffs in their own language.

In reality, his language skills consisted essentially of what he had managed to pick up in his mother's kitchen in Mitcham. His Italian was dialect, secondhand, and unintelligible to most of his clients, especially the Italians. On top of which, he was an indifferent litigator, not that that's ever been an impediment to a successful legal career. But he took to industrial law like a duck to water. For the following three years he pursued it so avidly that he eventually caught enough to hang out his own shingle.

Poaching the best of his old firm's clients and spreading his briefs generously around the barristers' chambers, he steadily built an impressive network in the law and the unions. Now here he was, factional heavyweight, member of the state executive of the Socialist Left, and if not the architect then at least the master builder of some of the government's most ambitious reforms. Self-approbation burst from him like a fountain from a ruptured pipe.

He sat the coroner's envelope face-down on the floor beside his chair, murmured something in the waiter's ear, and pressed a steaming white hand towel to his florid cheeks. 'How's Wendy?' he said. 'Still enjoying Canberra?'

The family small talk was to demonstrate that he hadn't lost the common touch. 'Fine. She's fine.' I hoped I didn't sound too unconvincing. The truth was I hadn't spoken to my wife in over two weeks and hoped it stayed that way.

'You two certainly make an odd couple,' Agnelli went on. 'There she is, flying about the country in her power suit, shouldering bureaucrats aside, writing policy for the PM's department. Here you are, sitting in a three-metre-square cubicle, doing Charlene's housework.'

Agnelli's line on my personal life wasn't so much tactless as simply out of date. The fact was Wendy and I were over in everything but name. All that remained was the inevitable public brawl over custody of our child, Redmond. As Agnelli might have put it, Wendy was out of my league. And she'd worked so hard getting there I was relieved to see her go.

Wendy had been in Canberra for nearly a year on secondment from the Women's Information Referral Exchange to the Office of the Status of Women Industrial and Technological Change Secretariat. Originally the job had been temporary, four months tops. But life with OSWITCS had proven infinitely more personally empowering than WIRE and her contract kept being extended.

When the offer had first come up, a tribute to Wendy's professional standing, I could hardly have stood in the way of her career, could I? Red would miss her but, now that he was settled into school, it was my turn to experience a stint of prime parenting. It was only for a few months, after all, and she would be commuting back to Melbourne two weekends a month. Sure, I said, go.

Ten months later, the so-far-undeclared reality was self-evident. The weekends at home had become more infrequent, what with the conferences in Darwin and Perth, the in-service skills-enhancement seminars in Cairns, and Wendy's ongoing professional need to piss in every pocket within a bull's roar of Lake Burley Griffin. Separation had merely confirmed what we had probably long suspected anyway. Our lives were going in opposite directions.

Not that anything had been spelt out yet. It didn't need to be. We were both old hands at reading which way the wind was blowing. Wendy still phoned Red most nights. She could never be accused of being an uncaring mother. Absent yes, negligent no. Sometimes it was me who picked up the phone when it rang and we exchanged banalities, but there was little the two of us could find to say to each other anymore.

I took it for granted there was someone else. Bound to be. I even had a mental picture—Senior Executive Service, fleet vehicle, desktop computer, divorced, weekender at Batemans Bay, beard. Not that I minded. I felt no rancour. I just didn't want to know about it. And if Wendy had any ideas about getting Red, she and the Family Court had another thing coming.

'So,' Agnelli was saying, 'she still funding long-term unemployed Tasmanian lesbians to build mud-brick whale refuges?'

What a jerk. You had to laugh. A platter of minced pigeon breast arrived, too pricey a dish to be paid for with domestic chit-chat. While the waiter was shovelling a load onto my plate I fed Agnelli his cue. 'If you want someone killed,' I said, 'it'll cost you more than a feed of sang choi bao.'

Agnelli smiled the thinnest of thin smiles. Ministerial advisers were part of the new breed, technical experts who did not like to be reminded, even in jest, of the sometimes rough and tumble reality of political life in the branches and the machine. Politics for them was just another career option. These guys hadn't got where they were without at least some political credentials—Agnelli's ticket had been punched by Labor Lawyers and his clients in the unions—but their personal writ ran no further than the distance between their ministers' ears.

Top-level access and plush salary packages made them feel important, but they were uncomfortable and sometimes even a little fearful in the rough company of party organisers from down the line. And they never really knew where they were with battlefield sergeants like me, crude types who came fully equipped with invisible networks, tacit alliances, and uncertain ambitions. We who could fill halls with a single phone call. Jokes about having people knocked off and knowing where the bodies were buried made the likes of Agnelli nervous. And he didn't need any reminding that it would take more than a free lunch to get me where he wanted me. Or so I thought.

Agnelli launched his spiel. 'Let's contextualise. Then we can parameter the specifics.'

It was getting so I couldn't tell if people were joking when they talked like that. I gave Agnelli the benefit of the doubt.

'Charlene's held her seat for what, ten years?' he asked blandly.

I plucked a figure out of the air. 'Eleven years, two months, five days.'

The sarcasm was wasted. Agnelli was winding himself up to

something. 'Amazing, isn't it?' he said. 'To think that all but two and a half years of that was spent in Opposition. What a waste of talent.'

'I'll tell her you said that,' I said. 'Sucking up to the boss on your own time.'

Agnelli made a self-deprecating gesture. 'I'm like you, Murray. Strictly an idealist. Goes without saying. It's the others I worry about. The ones who can't wait to get their snouts into the trough.'

Lollicato again, I thought. Boring. When were we going to get to the envelope and, with luck, the story behind the report in the *Sun*?

'Ah, but think how useful a bit of general ambition is to a reforming government like ours,' I said. 'Everybody out there, beavering away, racking up brownie points, hoping to be given the nod.'

'Granted.' Agnelli was working overtime at being agreeable. 'But all that nervous energy needs to be managed, directed, channelled. Problem is, the collective memory is short. Even some of our own people seem to have forgotten that no Labor government has ever been re-elected in this state. Three years ago nobody under forty could remember the last time there was a Labor government here. Now half the reporters in town can't remember when there wasn't one. And the way some people are carrying on, there won't be one for much longer.'

Unbidden, steaming platters arrived, glistening and fragrant. I should have held on to my suspicions more firmly. Instead, I picked up my chopsticks and waded in. 'Not Lollicato again?'

The ma-po beancurd was ravishing. Pungent and slimy. I decided to let Agnelli do all the talking.

'If I was him,' he said, referring to Lollicato, 'I'd be thinking that my best chance of knocking off Charlene would be to undermine her credibility as Minister for Industry. Quietly stir up some sort of business–union conflict then step back and watch the fireworks. Do it all at a distance. That way I wouldn't have her blood on my hands when I get reluctantly drafted to replace her after she's become a liability to the party.'

It wasn't a bad plan, but I couldn't see Lollicato pulling it off.

'Bit ambitious for Lolly, isn't it? He'd be lucky if he could knock the head off a beer.'

Agnelli drew his chair closer to the table, squared off his chopsticks, picked up a fat ginger scallop and dropped it into my bowl. 'Joe Lollicato's very well connected at Trades Hall, don't forget. His brother used to be an organiser with the Meat Packers' Union. And there are plenty in the union movement who are still dirty on the government over those building union prosecutions. They might be on the back foot at the moment, but setting Charlene up for a fall would be a good way of telling the government to stay out of union business.'

It was all quite plausible. 'That's the greatest load of shit I've ever heard, Ange,' I said. 'That rarefied air you've been breathing has gone to your head.'

'Yeah?' he said. 'Where do you reckon that story in the *Sun* today came from? That "informed sources at Trades Hall" crap doesn't seem suspicious to you?'

So this was Agnelli's great revelation. He was buying me this splendid luncheon so I could massage his petty paranoia. 'Typical *Sun* beat up, Ange. Anything to slag the government. They've been churning out that "War Drums at Union HQ" stuff for a hundred years.'

'Notice it wasn't signed?'

'So?' As far as I was concerned, no self-respecting journalist would want their name associated with anything in that awful little rag.

'Anyone at the journalists' association will tell you that's a clear signal the piece was cooked up in the editor's office.' Agnelli suddenly leaned forward, beckoning across the hot and sour sauce. 'Truth is,' he muttered, 'it's not just Charlene we're talking about here. There are bigger things at stake than a one-sided pre-selection brawl. Word is, and mum's the word, the chief has decided not to go to full term. There'll definitely be an election before the end of the year.'

My mind raced, but I merely nodded noncommittally and poured myself a thimble of tea, letting the news germinate, take root, send out branches, bear fruit. If Agnelli was right, and it was just the sort of thing Agnelli made it his business to be right about, then I had no choice. As of now, like it or not, I was on the Lollicato case. Shake the Agnelli family tree, I thought, and out would fall a crop of papal nuncios' bastards.

Lollicato was yet another lawyer, working out of the Broadmeadows Legal Service. A tribune of the people, big on street cred. Years of fronting for first offenders in shitbag cases had given him a sanctimonious edge. And now that I thought about it I could see the signs of creeping ambition. Young Lolly was changing his look. The earrings were disappearing, one by one. Ties were in evidence, even out of court. Such a transformation was not inconsistent with parliamentary aspirations.

If Lollicato wanted a seat, fine. So did half the party. When the time came, he was entitled to make a run, even to play a little rough if that was his style. But if he and his disgruntled union mates were sour enough to run a dirty tricks campaign in the *Sun*, and there was an surprise election in the offing, it wouldn't matter whether his shot at Charlene hit home or not. The *Sun* was the biggest selling paper in the state, pitched well under the lowest common denominator. Kicking Labor was its second nature, and it would jump at any chance to bag us as an infighting rabble of intriguers. Not that this was necessarily an inaccurate picture, but it was one we preferred not to be bandied about in the lead up to the polls. Talk about frightening the horses.

'Get the executive committee to haul him in, clip his wings,' I eventually said.

'Based on what?' said Agnelli. 'We need to make a case first. So far all we've got is a bit of gossip and a plausible hypothesis. Lollicato could just be flying a kite. The real question is whether he and his union mates have got enough clout at Pacific Pastoral to make serious mischief.'

'What's Charlene think about all of this?' I asked.

'Put it this way,' said Agnelli. 'It's your job to see that Charlene knows what she should know. It's my job to see that she doesn't know about things she shouldn't know about.'

He was right. Charlene had to be kept out of the picture, at least for the time being, or we really would have headlines reading 'Minister in Pre-Selection Wrangle'. It was also clear that

Agnelli was expecting me to do all the leg work. But I was not about to volunteer for any cowboy reconnaissance mission.

'I see,' I said, and turned my attention back to the table. Those Golden Chopsticks were indeed richly deserved. It was a pity to spoil a lunch like this with politics. But politics was paying and the bill had just been presented.

When Agnelli eventually broke the silence, he seemed to have changed the subject. 'MACWAM met this morning. They were shitting themselves.'

The Ministerial Advisory Committee On Ways And Means had started off as Charlene's private brains trust, a half-dozen old pals from the universities and the career civil service. After the election it was beefed up to an official body and given the job of overseeing smooth passage of Charlene's raft of reforms. Agnelli's official title was MACWAM Executive Officer. MACWAM presided, but Agnelli executed.

'You know what a pack of nervous nellies they are,' he went on. 'It's taken me two years to get them this far. Now, less than a week before the final vote on the new industrial health and safety bill, they've broken out in a cold sweat. The *Sun* runs a story about some silly dago turning himself into a Paddle Pop and now they think the whole legislative process is about to jump off the rails.' For a former defender of the industrially maimed, Agnelli could seem remarkably insensitive to the fate of individual members of the working class.

I could see where all this was heading, and was surprised at how soon I had resigned myself to it. I clicked my tongue sympathetically, feeding Agnelli his lines. 'So you told them that you wouldn't rest until you were sure that some feral shop steward was not about to declare class war at such an inconvenient juncture in the imminent legislative process.'

Agnelli grinned. He liked having his cleverness appreciated. 'Naturally they felt better immediately. And just to formalise matters, I got them to ask me to commission a full and detailed report before the final reading of the bill on Friday.'

Agnelli was full of more than just fried rice, but he could play a committee like Rostropovich played Shostakovich. Now he was sawing away at my strings. 'You can do it on your ear, Murray,' he said. 'You know the drill. Nothing fancy, couple of pages, max. As long as it's in by Thursday it's all the official sanction we need to cruel Lolly's pitch. How soon do you think you can get out to Pacific Pastoral and take a look around?'

I put up a last, half-hearted, line of resistance. 'A big firm like that won't take too well to me waltzing in off the street and grilling the workforce.'

'Leave them to me, Murray. Relations with the business community are my forte. And take a squiz at this.'

Agnelli was really enjoying himself now. Charlene's buff envelope materialised in his hand and skidded across the table. 'If the deceased happened to have any shit on him, the high moral ground would tend to be cut from underneath Lollicato somewhat, don't you think?'

Inside the envelope was a file containing a sheaf of papers and some photographs. One spilled out. It was of a very fat, very dead body with white stuff around its lips.

'Go ahead, Murray,' said Agnelli. 'Finish the duck.'

It had already gone three when I tossed the coroner's envelope onto the passenger seat, shoved Joan Armatrading into the tape deck and headed north. The sky had cleared to a pearly luminescence but the wind was still keen, entertaining itself by stripping the last of the blossoms off the flowering cherries in Princes Park.

Agnelli was probably being over-paranoid about Lollicato, I decided, but there would be no harm in giving his conspiracy theory the quick once-over. His inference that the fate of the government now rested on my shoulders was a bit rich, but any potential threat to Charlene, however unlikely, warranted a closer look. Guarding Charlene's back was, after all, the prime part of my job. And a couple of days' break from old ladies' plumbing and demented tattooees would be a welcome change of pace.

By some obscure culinary demarcation agreement, Chinese restaurants are prohibited from serving decent coffee. So by the time the stately boulevard of Royal Parade became the narrow funnel of Sydney Road, I was in desperate need of a caffeine fix. And I was in just the right place to find one.

Melbourne's main north-south axis was a clotted artery of souvlaki joints and low-margin high-turnover business. Half the Mediterranean basin had been depopulated of its optimists in order to line Sydney Road with free-wheeling enterprise. Bakeries and furniture shops run by Abruzzesi and Calabresi sat cheek by jowl with the delicatessens of Peloponnesian Greeks and the bridal boutiques of Maronite Lebanese. Signs in Arabic announced halal butchers and video shops displayed soap operas freshly pirated in Damascus and Nicosia. The promise of strong black coffee loitered in the air, and through the windows of the Cafe de la Paix, the Tivoli and the Lakonia I could see men bent over tiny cups of bracing black nectar. But parking spots were few and far between, and it wasn't long before I found myself stuck in a half-mile long snaggle of mid-afternoon traffic with no option but to go with the flow.

At the traffic lights beside Brunswick Town Hall, a Rod Stewart haircut at the wheel of a customised panel van was taking the time to pass encouraging recommendations to a poor cow in skin-tight denims wheeling a yowling brat across the road. Further on, the windows of empty shops had been aerosoled with hammers and sickles and plastered with initials and slogans in languages I couldn't identify. PKK. KSP. KOMKAR. Def Leppard.

At the top of a slight rise, a sandwich board outside the Mighty Ten hardware store read 'Pink Batts Must Go'. I parked illegally in a loading zone and stuffed the back of the Renault with bulky packages of the fibreglass insulation, paid for with a card already well over the limit.

Five minutes further up the road and I was back at the electorate office. I parked in a side street, and nicked into Ciccio's Cafe Sportivo, the Italian coffee bar next door. I was standing at the zinc counter, downing an espresso and considering my next step, when the vanguard of the proletariat marched through the door.

Her name was Ayisha Celik. She was a community development worker at the Australian Turkish Welfare League. Exactly what she developed in the Turkish community I wasn't sure. I knew what she developed in me, and I hoped it didn't show enough to cause embarrassment.

She had skin the colour of honey and her lips were like ripe pomegranates. Her eyes, ringed in black, were as dark and wilful as a peregrine falcon's. Her bosom spoke of silk cushions, fretted screens and tinkling fountains. Inspired by such a vision the Ancients had crossed the Bosphorus and pitched their tents beneath the crenellated walls of Troy. All in all, Ayisha Celik had the kind of looks that make veils seem like a sensible idea in places where hot-blooded men go around armed to the teeth. She made a bee-line for the counter and slapped a clipboard down in front of me. 'Slackin' off as usual I see, comrade,' she accused cheerfully.

Ayisha had arrived in Australia at the age of eight and spoke with the teasing upward-rising inflection the kids taught each other in schools where only the teachers spoke English at home. 'Do us a favour, will ya?' she said. 'Sign this.' The clipboard displayed a ragged column of signatures.

Her words wafted towards me on a warm zephyr of spearmint gum, triggering primal erotic associations connected with Saturday afternoons in the back row of the Liberty Cinema. I wondered, not for the first time, what it might take to arouse reciprocal feelings in her. As usual, nothing presented itself. According to Trish, who specialised in such topics, Ayisha was unlucky in love. I was much heartened by this information. And although she was still in her twenties, a good five or six years younger than me, I liked to think that she at least found me interesting. Not that she gave any sign of that being the case.

Still, it's a free country. I could think what I liked.

I picked up the clipboard and tried to look fascinated by the petition. The Australian Turkish Welfare League was big on petitions. 'Who is it this time? The United Nations? The International Court of Justice? The Water Supply Board?'

Ayisha was in no mood. She had news. 'You know Sivan, our welfare worker?'

Everyone knew Sivan, a laughing beetle-browed man with thick English, another collector of signatures. 'They've arrested his brother.'

'They' could only mean the Turkish military, a regime whose taste for terror had driven thousands into exile. Some, Sivan among them, had ended up in the local Turkish community. Many were professionals and artists, progressives and liberals who were putting their skills to work for the benefit of their fellow expatriates. Others, I suspected, had been quite keen on the idea of armed struggle until an even keener crew of nasties had got the drop on them.

Up until that time, I hadn't had a great deal to do with Charlene's Turkish constituents, but they seemed a sociable enough mob. For Muslims, most of them were about as fundamentalist as the C of E. And if it wasn't for their kebab shops, every Friday night the streets of the northern suburbs would have been awash with gangs of half-plastered school teachers looking for somewhere cheap to eat. All I knew, and all I needed to know, was that they could pretty well be relied upon to turn out en masse for Labor.

'We think it's because Sivan works for a subversive organisation,' Ayisha was saying.

'The League?'

The Australian Turkish Welfare League was two rooms and a secondhand coffee dispenser a couple of blocks up the road from the electorate office. Ayisha, Sivan and a clutch of volunteer social workers ran information programs and cultural activities there for newly arrived migrants, partly paid for by grants from the Ethnic Affairs Commission. If pressed for an adjective to describe the League, subversive would not have sprung to mind. Charlene called it cost-effective service delivery in an area of perceived need. What I called it was damned convenient. If ever I needed translation for the odd Turkish customer that walked in the door, all I had to do was get one of the League people on the blower and have them sort it out in the vernacular.

Naturally, in keeping with their advocacy role, the folks at the League went in for the customary amount of third-worldish polemic. Ayisha, for instance, tended to get about in a red keffiyeh, sounding like Vanessa Redgrave. But nobody in their right mind could seriously believe the League posed a threat to anyone, let alone a fully tooled-up fascist oligarchy twenty thousand kilometres away.

Well, at the time I didn't think so. 'You're petitioning the junta?' It seemed a little optimistic even for the League.

'Not them, you dickhead. Canberra. The Minister for

Foreign Affairs. We want something done about the consulate.' She signalled Ciccio for a coffee. He pretended not to see her. Women were not encouraged at the Cafe Sportivo, especially not a houri in jeans and half a ton of kohl.

The idea that the generals in Ankara kept a close eye on Turkish migrants and refugees in Australia was one of Ayisha's big bugbears. Even allowing for Sivan's emigre paranoia and Ayisha's marked list to the left, I assumed there was an element of truth in it. Dictatorships can be funny that way.

I'd heard other rumours, too. For years there'd been talk that neo-fascist groups with names like the Grey Wolves or the Black Ghosts or the Pink Panthers were active in the area. One time you used to hear the same thing about the Lebanese Tigers. They must have been related to the Tasmanian Tigers, because nobody had ever seen a real one.

The spooks in one of the intelligence outfits probably knew what was going on, or should have, if they were doing what they got paid for, but I couldn't see them losing any sleep over the civil liberties of a bunch of left-wing Arab types. The only time that lot ever came out of the woodwork was when some demented Armenian lobbed a bomb at the Turkish ambassador.

I ran my eye down Ayisha's petition, recognising names from the Community Health Centre and the council depot. Not too many of the blokes at the depot had said no to Ayisha. I borrowed her pen and added my name to the list. As far as I was concerned, all Australian residents were equally entitled to freedom of association and assembly. This was Coburg, not Queensland.

Mainly, however, I signed because of Ayisha. Frankly, if she'd invited me to stick my bum in the boiler of Ciccio's cappuccino machine I'd just as happily have agreed.

That probably sounds fairly wet, but you've got to keep in mind that at that point my conjugals hadn't had an airing in six months. If truth be known, they were beginning to develop a somewhat strident attitude. In fact, from here on in, you might as well take it for granted that my loins were pretty well in the driver's seat, although I wasn't necessarily aware of the fact except when they were shouting in my ear.

'The Kurds are getting the worst of it,' Ayisha was saying. 'Sivan's a Kurd, y' know.' She had a full head of steam up by now, which went well with the full head of raven black hair. 'Torture. Murder. Makes *Midnight Express* look like Club Med. Y' can't imagine.'

I probably could, but it didn't bear dwelling on. 'Petitions aren't going to do much good,' I said.

'Maybe not,' she conceded, stepping down off the high moral ground. 'You got any better ideas? Some fascist bastards are going around spying on us. Either we convince the government to put a stop to it, or we take measures to defend ourselves.' She made a pistol with her fingers and cocked one eye. 'We can't just take it lying down, can we?'

Come the revolution I would flee with her to the mountains, impress her with my ardour. She would lie down with me in a cave on a bed of sheepskins. Then either Wendy or some swarthy Abdul would cut my nuts off with a blunt scimitar. Both of them. Both Wendy and Abdul. Both nuts.

Until then, putting my name on her useless petition looked like it was as close as I'd get. International intrigue was not yet on my agenda. As we spoke she pulled out a pouch of Drum and rolled herself a cigarette. When she lit it, a tiny strand of tobacco stuck to her bottom lip. Only the greatest effort of will stopped me reaching over and pinching it away. I could ask her out, I thought. I could get a baby-sitter for Red and the two of us could go to one of those places where they put a piece of fruit down the neck of your beer bottle. Perhaps not.

She put the petition back under her arm. 'Doesn't look like I'm gunna get any coffee round here, does it?'

'Before you go,' I said quickly, grasping the first available conversational gambit. 'Ever heard of someone called Ekrem Bayraktar?'

Either my pronunciation was appalling or she hadn't. She shook her head.

'Turkish name, though, isn't it?'

'Thousands of people in this city have Turkish names,' she said archly. 'In case you haven't noticed.'

'No need to get snaky,' I said. 'I just thought maybe he was .

one of your clients at the League.'

'Could be,' she shrugged. 'We get so many people through the doors it's hard to keep track. Especially considering how little help we get from the government.' Ayisha was never one to pass up a chance for a bit of lobbying. 'So who is he?'

It was my turn to shrug. I could have told her, I suppose, but the last thing I needed was a diatribe about downtrodden workers being sweated to an early grave by the heartless bourgeoisie. 'Just a name in some paperwork I've been lumbered with,' I said.

Playing the beleaguered bureaucrat was no way to Ayisha's heart. She stuffed her tobacco in her bag and eyed the door.

'Tell you what,' I suggested, like it was the best idea since the withering away of the state. 'Why don't I drop into the League tomorrow. I can ask Sivan. Then the two of us can get our heads together on some funding ideas. There're some Commonwealth job creation dollars coming down the pipeline you might be eligible for.'

She put her hand on my arm. 'Murray,' she said. 'You're a brick.'

Pathetic, I told myself. Trying to buy the woman's affections with taxpayers' dollars. Even if I could get her interested, the last thing I needed right now was an entanglement. Not that I stood a chance. And even if I did, I could already hear Wendy. *Murray's got himself a nice Turkish girl. Bit of a Maoist, but he likes them old-fashioned. Sings the 'Internationale' while she does the dishes.*

I was watching the back pocket of Ayisha's jeans disappear through the open door and telling myself to get real when two plain-clothed coppers blew in with the breeze. What with the Hardcase Hilton across the road, dicks weren't an unusual sight in the neighbourhood. The major crime squad guys tended to the handy, all-weather look of well-off tradesmen and you had to be sharp to spot them. But these two were local CIB in three-piece suits that might as well have been uniforms.

They looked me over like I wasn't there and swaggered down the back to the two green baize tables where the same dozen old *paesani* sat day after day drinking coffee and shouting at each other over hands of cards. I had never seen any money on the tables and there was none there now, just a sudden, un-Italian silence and the hissing of the espresso machine. The coppers looked. The old men looked back. Something half forgotten surfaced in my memory, a blue sleeve with sergeant's stripes, the taste of blood.

Then, as suddenly as they had arrived, the forces of law and order were gone, trailing the knuckles of their authority. Ciccio said something that sent a ripple of quiet laughter running through the card players. The cards swished again. I washed my mouth out with cold coffee dregs and went next door to the office.

Adam F. Ant was still lounging around my cubicle like he owned the joint, his head buried in a copy of *Labor Star*. Who did he think he was kidding? Not even its own editors pretended to read the *Labor Star*. I shoved his feet off the desk and rang Bernice Kaufman, an industrial officer on the top floor at the Trades Hall. Bernice had done me the big favour once, just the once, back at university. Ever since she could be relied on to never pass up an opportunity to patronise me.

'It's about that thing in this morning's paper,' I said. 'The bloke dead at the meatworks.'

True to form, Bernice launched straight into a rave about how only a halfwit would believe what he read in the *Sun*. The halfwit I took to be me. Shorn of its sarcasm, the rest of what she said merely confirmed that there was no truth at all to the alleged interest of the Trades Hall executive in the matter. As soon as I could get a word in edgeways, I told her that, since the death had happened in the electorate, it might be appropriate for Charlene to send her condolences to the dead bloke's work-mates. Did she know anyone who could put me onto the shop steward at the meatworks?

Bernice made her snooty exasperated noise and the phone started playing a particularly frenzied arrangement of 'Für Elise'. While I was waiting for her to come back on, I punched the phone's hands-free button and sprayed transistorised Beethoven all over Ant, hoping art might succeed where reason had failed. Three minutes later when Bernice came back on the line, he was humming along.

'Okay,' she said, 'I've been talking to the Meaties. They reckon your best bet is to contact the shop steward out there. Name of Herb Gardiner. And by the way, they reckon that if there'd been any union issues involved in the death, Gardiner would have been onto them like a shot. Real stickler for the award, apparently. Hasn't said boo.'

In a world of ceaseless change, I found something gratifyingly predictable about being patronised by Bernice. I scribbled the shop steward's name on a sheet of office stationery and shoved it in a manila folder along with the coroner's envelope. While I was writing, Trish came in and handed Ant a phone message slip. He glanced at it and laid it on the desk in front of me. If he made himself any more at home, he'd be on the payroll by the end of the week.

The message slip said Agnelli had rung, wanting me to call back ASAP. It was always like this. Now that I had agreed to buy into this Lollicato thing, Agnelli would be on my back every five minutes. Having to write a spurious bloody report was enough of a waste of time without ceaseless fireside chats. I stuffed the message slip into my jacket pocket and stuck my head around the partition.

Ant had ambled out into the reception area and was flashing his stomach at a pair of Coptic monks. Trish was juggling two phones, relaying something about Supporting Mothers' Benefits to a bedraggled teenage mum in a 'Miami Vice' sweatshirt. A toddler in a wet disposable was pulling a Wilderness Society poster off the wall.

Without the slightest tinge of guilt, I stuck the Pacific Pastoral file under my arm and nicked out the back door. The wretched of the earth could wait, at least until tomorrow.

Off Sydney Road the traffic was
quieter. The streets were lined with weatherboard bungalows,
single-storey terraces and, here and there, the saw-toothed roofs
of small factories. This was Labor heartland, the safest seats in
the country—Calwell, Batman, Lalor, Coburg, Brunswick. Elec-
torates whose names resonated with certainty in the ears of
backroom psephologists from Spring Street to Canberra. In
some booths here we outpolled the Libs three to one. Made you
wonder who the one was.

Red's school lay halfway between the office and home, a
slate-roofed state primary. For its first hundred years it had
specialised in producing ruckmen, armed robbers and appren-
tices to the hairdressing trade. Now it had a library wing and ran
programs in two community languages. I found Redmond in
after-school care with the other dozen or so second and third
graders, Matildas, Dylans and Toulas left behind when the
proper parents swooped at three thirty. They were cutting the
heads off models in K-Mart catalogues. Red flung his schoolbag
on top of the insulation batts and we drove home.

Home was a sixty-year-old weatherboard still in its first coat
of paint, one of a spec tract built cheaply in the twenties. Wendy
and I had bought it soon after Red came along. The sign had
read 'Promises Ample Renovation Opportunity for Imaginative

First Home Buyer,' meaning it was all we could afford. We were both at the Labor Resource Centre at that point, getting paid a pittance to crank out discussion papers. Workforce segmentation in the footwear sector. Industrial democracy in the electricity generation industry. Not the most lucrative of postings.

So far, Ample Renovation had consisted of Wendy planting a native garden and spending a small fortune on *House and Garden* while I did as much as a man can do using only hand tools and y-chromosomes. All up, the Opportunity had been greater than either of us was capable of rising to. The set of architect's plans pinned to the kitchen wall, token of our future there together, had long since turned yellow and begun curling at the corners.

Still, Red and I were making a pretty good fist of domesticity. Not that this was immediately apparent to the untrained eye. On the superficial indices of good housekeeping we probably rated fairly low. But we were comfortable and basic hygiene was maintained. And I doggedly persisted in addressing some of the more ongoing infrastructure issues. My objective that afternoon was to maximise our energy efficiency. First I dredged a knife out of the scrap heap in the sink and made two peanut butter sandwiches, folded not cut. 'Now do your homework,' I growled.

The kid rolled his eyes. 'I don't have homework, Dad. I'm only in Grade Two.'

'Then you can watch TV, as long as it's something educational.'

We repeated this corny dialogue word-for-word every afternoon. It was as much a part of our routine as tinned tomato soup on Sunday nights and always being late for school. Red was the best accident I had ever had. He was clever, biddable, undemanding company, and more mature than his baby face and mop of angelic curls suggested. He had missed Wendy a lot at first and still stacked on the occasional turn, but all in all he had adapted pretty well to our bachelor–boy existence.

He took his sandwiches into the lounge room and turned on the television. I use the word lounge room in its generic sense. It might be better described as a cave with floorboards. It had long come to terms with the fact that it would never be a sunny, north-facing, energy-efficient, entertainment/kitchen area with stylish black and white checkerboard tiles.

While Red watched the Roadrunner, I changed into overalls, ran a ladder up to the ceiling trapdoor in the hall and plugged the lamp from Wendy's side of the bed into an extension lead. Then I spent half an hour hauling the bulky mattresses of fibreglass out of the car and up into the roof cavity. From outside, the roof looked sound enough. But in the confined gloom of the cavity, the sheets of corrugated iron revealed themselves to be a filigree of rust held tenuously in place by inertia and ancient cobwebs.

Squatting low on the dusty rafters, I began sidling along, cutting sections of the insulation and stuffing them into place in the irregular gaps between the timbers as I went. Working at a constant crouch was harder and slower work than I had anticipated, and I soon had a sweat up. Minute particles of fibreglass worked themselves up my sleeves and under my collar, sticking to my skin. In case they were carcinogenic I breathed through my nose. Little fragments of pink lodged in my nostril hairs.

That's the problem with working for yourself. The pay is lousy, the conditions suck, and the boss couldn't give a flying continental about safety. The job should only have taken an hour, but with all the fiddling around I must have lost track of the time. Down below the television droned on, constant and indistinct.

It was just as I was reaching over to jam the last batt into place in the tight angle beneath the eaves that something cold and hard struck me on the back of the head. A wave of nauseating giddiness roared in my ears and I toppled forwards, arms scrabbling uselessly in the air. A vice of jagged metal clamped hard around my neck, pinning me so I could neither sit nor stand. Everything went black.

The next thing I knew, a cool clamminess was washing over my face. I blinked rapidly and opened my eyes. Everything was still black. I felt panic surge, then abate as I realised what had happened. I had lost my balance and punched my head clear through the metal roof, jamming my neck in the hole. The darkness was the night which had fallen unnoticed around me. From the shoulders down I was locked in a painful crouch. From the chin up I was John the Baptist on a platter. By twisting my neck against my rough iron collar, I could just make out the street below, deserted but for a handful of parked cars. Far off on the horizon, the illuminated cranes and rising tower blocks of the city winked and glistened, mocking me.

'Red,' I screamed, at the top of my lungs. At exactly that moment a lashing torrent of rain descended, a pitiless wintry surf. Water cascaded down the corrugations of the iron and ran down the imperfect seal formed by my neck. I crouched helpless, feeling it gushing into my overalls. Over the pounding din I could just hear the 'Dr Who' theme seeping upwards, and above that a higher more insistent sound, the impatient ringing of the telephone.

The choice was between drowning and cutting my own throat. I took the second option. Screwing my eyes shut and gripping a timber cross-piece, I jerked downwards with all my might, nearly ripping my ears off and wincing as I felt my cheeks raked with sharp edges of metal.

The minor haemorrhage that resulted was nothing, however, compared with the cataract that descended onto the newly laid insulation once my head was no longer plugging the hole in the roof. I quickly stripped off my overalls, rolled them into a makeshift plug and stuffed up the hole.

Stuffed up being the operative expression.

When eventually I had staunched the flow of water I climbed down the ladder, bleeding, goose-pimpled and draped with cobwebs. Red glanced up from the idiot box for the merest second, then turned his eyes back to the screen. He had seen his father Do It Yourself before.

'Who was that on the phone?' I shouted above the rain pummelling the windows.

Red shrugged and flipped channels. 'When's tea?' he said, crescent moons of sandwich crusts on his lap. 'I'm starving.'

The refrigerator yielded up a carton of milk, five fish fingers, two potatoes, a carrot and half a tray of ice cubes. I put the fish things in the oven, stuck the vegetables on the gas to boil and dropped the ice into a glass on top of an antiseptic dose of Jamesons.

The whiskey was more warming than the tepid trickle that

issued from the antique water heater on the bathroom wall. I lathered up and listened to the whining of the pipes. The whole room joined in, crying out to be transformed into an airy atrium lined with glass bricks and filled with moisture-loving plants. I finished my drink slowly, waiting for the water to run cold and wondering where I could get hold of a cheap roofer. This was one of the few times I ever wished I had friends in the building industry unions.

At the back of the bathroom cupboard behind a lonesome franger, its use-by date long expired, I found a bottle of mercurochrome and daubed red lines down the scratches on my ears, neck and face. As an omen of the pitfalls that were to confront me over the following three days, I can think of nothing more eloquent than the bedraggled zebra that resulted, staring back at me from my fog-misted bathroom mirror. Tetanus, cancer, involuntary celibacy, a hole in the roof. You name it, chances were I had it.

A couple of fish fingers, and Red's memory came back. 'Oh yeah, Mum said to tell you she's been ringing everywhere but you're never there. She said she'll try again tomorrow. And guess what she's bought me. A Dino-Rider. The one with laser weapons.'

Weapons? Apparently Canberra was doing nothing for Wendy's ideological rigour. After dinner, a little convivial family viewing and the customary buggerising around, I finally managed to badger Red into bed. The week before he'd been content to read himself to sleep, but that night he wanted to be babied. Hard day at the office, I guessed.

He dragged a big picture book out of a batch that Wendy had brought home from a sale at the Equal Opportunity Resource Centre, earnest stuff with titles like *Miranda Has Two Mummies* and *Yes, Raoul Is Different*. Fortunately, that night's choice was one of the less pedagogically strident. *Folk Wisdom of the World's Peoples* was its eagerly redundant title. Red snuggled deeper under the quilt and I opened the book at random: 'Of all of the wise men of Turkey none is more famous than Nasreddin Hoca...'

Above the text was a pen and wash picture of a tubby old

man with a bushy white beard, curly slippers and a turban the size of a load of washing. Red nodded his approval and I read on.

One day Nasreddin Hoca was invited to give the sermon at the mosque in his village. He mounted the pulpit and asked,

'O True Believers, do you know what I am going to say to you today?'

The congregation looked at each other in confusion and shook their heads. 'We have no idea,' they said.

'If you have no idea,' said Nasreddin Hoca, 'what is the use of my talking to you?' With that he descended from the pulpit and went home.

As I read, I glanced furtively down at the child's face, seeking out hopeful signs of sleep's imminent arrival.

The following week he entered the mosque, mounted the pulpit and again asked the congregation, 'O True Believers, do you know what I am going to talk to you about today?'

'Yes,' said the wily ones.

'Well, if you already know,' said Nasreddin Hoca, 'what is the use of my telling you?' And again he descended from the pulpit and went home.

The next week he mounted the pulpit and asked the very same question. 'O True Believers, do you know what I am going to talk to you about today?'

The people of the congregation had considered their reply. 'Some of us do and some of us do not,' they cried.

'In that case,' said Nasreddin Hoca, 'let those of you who know tell those who do not.'

Christ only knew what a child was supposed to make of this drivel. It sounded like a Treasury position paper. Fortunately it also produced a similar effect. A muddy glaze was settling over Red's eyes. I droned on, my tone deliberately monotonous. Halfway through the parable of the walnut and the watermelon, bye-byes arrived and slipped Red silently across the border into the Land of Nod. As I laid the book down and tiptoed out of the room, he stirred a little, scratched his head and began quietly to snore.

The deluge outside had dropped to a steady patter. I climbed the ladder and checked the roof. So far so good. My impromptu engineering was holding up remarkably well. The plug of rolled-up overalls was a sodden mass, but it had swelled to a tight fit and very little water was leaking through. Just to be on the safe side, I sat a bucket underneath, balanced on a plank running across two of the rafters.

Then I screwed the top off the Jamesons and sat down with the Pacific Pastoral file. I looked at the photos first, spilling them across the kitchen table. The corpse had a face only a mother could love, a sentimental Hittite mother with cataracts. Apart from that, all you could tell was that he could have done with a course at Weight Watchers and that he was dead. I turned to the papers.

No wonder Charlene had made a point of telling Agnelli to get them back on her desk pronto. Many strings had been jerked and much red tape scissored to get this little collection of paper together. Preliminary reports of the Department of Labour Accident Investigations Division, photocopies of internal police incident sheets, and draft summaries from the coroner's office did not spontaneously aggregate in the privacy of some filing cabinet and decide to throw themselves across the desk of the first available minister. The regrettable demise of Ekrem Bayraktar three days before had set the hidden hand of some dedicated paper chaser into motion.

But as far as I could tell, it had hardly been worth the bother. This was about as prosaic a stack of forms as death ever filled out. If there had ever been any drama here, it had quickly been reduced to a homogeneous grey soup of bureaucratese, lacking even the frisson of an interdepartmental difference of opinion. The medicos, the police, the coronial and departmental investigators were all in furious agreement.

The bare facts outlined were these. Bayraktar was Turkish. That much I had been right about. He had been in Australia three years, status permanent resident. His address was in Blyth Street, Brunswick, a flat I assumed. No next of kin was listed. He had been with Pacific Pastoral for a little over two years and as a leading-hand storeman had regular access to the plant's storage freezers. Some time during Friday afternoon he had let himself in to Number 3 chiller. He did this on his own initiative, without informing anyone and for reasons not apparent. Everyone was very clear on that point.

Some time later a refrigeration mechanic by the name of Herbert Gardiner entered the freezer to check the thermostat and found Bayraktar's body. Herbert Gardiner? Where had I heard that name before? I shuffled the papers until I found the sheet of Upper House notepaper I had used to take down the name of Bernice's shop steward. Yep, that was him.

Oh Herb, I mused out loud, whatever were your parents thinking when they planted that botanical name on you? Basil and Rosemary Gardiner and their little boy Herb. Hardly a sage choice. I shook my head in wonder and turned back to the subject at hand.

The cause of death was a heart attack, the exact time of which was subject to some speculation on account of the low temperature. Precision in this matter did not appear to be an issue, nor was any negligence or malfeasance on the company's part suggested. All in all it was pretty much an open and shut case. Bayraktar was just another of the three-hundred-odd Victorians who died in industrial incidents every year. The only unanswered question was what the deceased had been doing wandering about in a giant deep freeze full of boxes of boned beef.

No bureaucrat in his right mind would have speculated on that topic in an official document. Ever since the Freedom of Information Act had been gazetted, candour was not advisable in paperwork forming part of the permanent public record. Even the most innocuous remark made in dispatches could eventually be ferreted out by some snooping journalist or tireless special interest group, and end up splashed across the front page. Let that happen and you could kiss your preferment goodbye.

Not that there aren't ways around these things. I found what I was looking for scribbled on a yellow Post-It sticker stuck inside the back cover of the file. The handwriting matched the signature on the preliminary report of the coroner's chief investigator. 'Police et al. concur most likely pilfering,' it read. The boys on the scene, it appeared, had gone into a huddle, put two and two together and concluded that the deceased had been in the process of stuffing a piece of prime porterhouse up his jumper when the grim reaper tapped him on the shoulder.

Here at last was something. Not official, mark you, but potentially useful. If Lollicato and the *Sun* decided they wanted a martyr, they might try painting this Bayraktar joker as another Mother Teresa. But if I could get one of his co-workers inside the place to confirm his reputation as a tea leaf, I would be morally one up on Lollicato. Relatively speaking.

Much more to the point was how much mileage Lolly & Co thought they could extract from the situation. That would depend on the attitude of the dead bloke's workmates. That, and whether there was someone inside to do their stirring for them. And I wasn't going to find that out by burying my nose in a pile of papers. I shuffled the pages together, downed the last dribble of whiskey, scratched my head, yawned, and got up for a pee.

How had Agnelli ever convinced me that the government might stand or fall on this particular piece of nonsense? Now I'd have to drive these useless papers back into town, go out and prowl around some butchery in the backblocks of Coolaroo, and waste an afternoon cooking up some bodgie report. The best part of a couple of days down the tubes. And for what? As if I didn't have better things to do with my time.

Red's feet were sticking out from underneath the covers, cold as iceblocks. As I tucked the quilt back in, he rolled suddenly, sat bolt upright, scratched his head fiercely and slumped back into unconsciousness.

By that stage bed was looking like as good a place as any. I climbed into the matrimonial cot with *Understanding Family Law, A Practical Guide to Financial Planning and Court Procedure*. Ten pages of legal prose later, I succumbed to the elemental drone of the rain on the tin roof above me and slipped into the dreamless sleep of the innocent.

Well, maybe not completely dreamless, or completely innocent. About 4 a.m. there was this cave and this sheepskin.

        The Ministry for Industry was
fourteen floors up an octagonal guano-textured megalith a block
west of Parliament. I bunged the Renault into a basement slot
stencilled Strictly Deputy Director, hit the fourteenth floor at a
jog, and slapped the envelope on Charlene's private secretary's
desk. I was back inside the lift, standing beside an anorexic
youth in orange dreadlocks and green lycra shorts, when the
half-closed doors gave a shudder and parted.

'Morning, Murray,' said Agnelli, his palm flat against the call
button. 'What's with the face? Gone ten rounds with a cheese
grater? What's Lionel Merricks going to think?'

'He can think what he likes. I've never heard of him.' I made
no attempt to leave the lift. The doors quivered, fighting to close.

'He's the chairman of Pacific Pastoral and we're expected in
his office in three quarters of an hour. Didn't you get my
message?'

I remembered the phone slip in my top pocket. 'What
message?'

'The one I'm giving you now. Meet me in the foyer of the
Amalfi in half an hour. I'll brief you then.'

'I thought company liaison was your job. I just came in to
drop off the file.'

Agnelli's head did a 270-degree sweep. His voice came

through a clenched jaw, low and insistent. 'Look, Murray...'

'I'd love to stand around and bat the breeze like this, fellers,' said the bike messenger, 'but I've got a previous at the Stock Exchange.'

I wasn't going to argue the toss in front of Boy George. Reluctantly I stepped out into the corridor. Agnelli took his palm off the button. 'Well piss off then, buster,' he told the closing doors. He turned back to me, oozing sweet reason. 'It'll only take half an hour.'

'Corporate relations are your department. What do you need me for?'

Agnelli licked his lips and started talking twenty to the dozen. 'The manager out at Coolaroo didn't want to know me. Typical middle management flack. So I thought I'd teach the prick a lesson. Went all the way to the top. Merricks is on the City Revitalisation Committee with Charlene. The Committee met yesterday afternoon, so I buttonholed Merricks afterwards and put him on the spot. Asked about the newspaper story and made a noise like industrial unrest. Really put the wind up him, it did. So then I told him I shared his concerns and put our little look-see proposition. He's a bit so-so about the idea, obviously doesn't want the wrong person blundering about out there treading on management's toes. Said it would all depend on the "consultant". "Sure," I said. "I can understand that." Told him the individual we have in mind is a real professional. "Talk to him yourself," I said. "If you're not perfectly comfortable, we'll shelve the idea."'

By this stage he had me bailed up against the wall. 'Ange,' I said wearily, 'You're over-reacting. This whole thing is bullshit. That *Sun* story yesterday was a beat-up. There's no mention at all in today's edition. Do us both a favour, get another boundary rider.'

'Nonsense, Murray. You're wasting your talents out in that electorate office. Handle this one right and you never know. Go on, clean yourself up a bit. I'll see you outside the Amalfi in half an hour.' He disappeared in the direction of Charlene's office.

I pulled a tie out of my pocket and went into the men's. The fluorescent tube above the mirror wasn't pulling any punches.

The cuts had stopped weeping and were beginning to scab up nicely. I'd be able to start shaving again in about a week, but it really wasn't the sort of face you'd want to go stalking the corporate corridors in. I made a lump in my tie and parked it in the general vicinity of the top of my chest. This Merricks joker would have to take me as he found me. And if he didn't, so much the better. I'd be off the hook with Agnelli.

The ministry was a typical public service set up—a rabbit warren of chin-high beige partitions, half the desks unattended. I helped myself to one of the empty ones and ransacked the drawers until I found a yellow pages. There were an encouraging six pages of roofing contractors. I dialled the electorate office and ran a pen down the names while I waited for Trish to answer. When she picked up the receiver, I could hear a dog barking in the background. Every day something new.

'Any messages?'

There were plenty, but none urgent. And the guy with the tatts was back, on the doorstep at nine on the dot. Persistent bastard. I told Trish I wouldn't be in until later and to tell Mr Tattoo that I was at the Police–Community Liaison Task Force and I'd probably be bringing some of them back with me. 'And you won't forget to run off the agenda papers for Wednesday night's branch meeting?' There was a bark, but it wasn't a dog. 'And, listen, if anybody rings about a roof, take the number and tell them I'll call back.'

I dialled again, and again, and again, starting at AAAAce Roofing and working my way through to Versa-Tile. Twenty minutes later all I had were half a dozen engaged signals, an invitation to call back later, four answering machines, two no longer connecteds and a wife who would tell hubby when he came home.

The Amalfi was the city's newest and tallest office tower, a fifty-storey icicle of blue-tinted glass built with Kuwaiti finance and tax-free cash bonuses and designed to reflect the many moods of the sky. Its disposition that morning was decidedly unsettled.

Big corporate tenants occupied the higher floors and various government departments were housed lower down. Each had separate entrances and elevators so the business types on their way to the top could be spared the ordeal of having to rub shoulders with scruffy androgynes in polyester cardigans. The corporate entrance was a marble-clad lobby on Collins Street with imposing brass revolving doors. The government tenants entered via an open vestibule around the corner where a gaggle of furtive smokers clustered around a midden of squashed butts.

The Education Department central bureaucracy had set up shop on some lower floors and Agnelli was standing at the government entrance talking to an official from one of the teacher unions, a factional heavyweight, when I arrived. He immediately broke off the conversation and hurried over. He looked me up and down and opened his mouth as if to make some remark, thought better of it and propelled me wordlessly through the revolving doors into the open mouth of a lift.

'Let Merricks do all the talking,' he said as we shot upwards into the stratosphere. 'And for Christ sake, don't contradict him. These captains of industry are totally surrounded by sucks telling them how fucking brilliant they are. Makes them very sensitive.' He said something else, but my ears were popping and I missed it.

We got out at the forty-ninth floor and found ourselves facing a reception desk of black lacquer, burnished to a mirror shine and bearing an arrangement of long stemmed exotic flowers shaped like the genitalia of some endangered species. Behind it sat a receptionist with a face heavily in hock to the Estée Lauder counter at David Jones and sculpted extensions so long they would have curled up and died at the mere sight of a keyboard. Agnelli she eyeballed coolly. When she got a load of me the ambient temperature dropped a good fifteen degrees.

'Mr Merricks is expecting you.' She sounded as though she could not in her wildest dreams conceive why. She led us across a carpet that murmured soft caresses as we passed, and abandoned us in a corner office with a desk you could land a Lear jet on. Two entire walls were floor-to-ceiling glass.

The view was hypnotic, vast, drawing the gaze irresistibly. Rimmed by the green of sand-belt suburbia, the beaten pewter of the bay extended southward to an invisible horizon. Factories and freeways spread a grubby picnic rug as far west as the light would allow. Immediately below, the Spencer Street switching yards were a model train set, Hornby Double-O by the look of it. Out past the Westgate Bridge and the cubist statement of the Newport power station, oil refineries and smokestacks disappeared into a smudgy haze. But mostly it was sky, lots and lots of sky. A flock of seagulls flew past at eye level. Here and there over the bay celestial conveyor belts of sunlight pierced the clouds with radiant beams as though the Assumption of the Blessed Virgin Mary was imminent.

I sank into one of a matching pair of pale-green kid leather sofas. Agnelli strode over to the window, his hands clasped behind his back, his excitement impossible to conceal. I could feel a lecture coming on.

'Look at that.' Agnelli gestured like a carnival barker. 'Industry. Chemicals. Plastics. Automobiles. Foodstuffs. Biotechnology. Computers. The busiest port in Australia. Anything that gets made in this country gets made here. Compared to us the rest of the country's a fucking pineapple plantation or a gravel pit. Think, from here you can see a quarter of the country's population, the most productive quarter, too.'

Far below I could just make out two figures fishing off a pier. At the periphery of my vision the word MOBIL stood out in letters four storeys high.

'Hard to imagine that most of it is already obsolete.' Agnelli shook his head and frowned, barely believing how badly the place was letting him down. 'Technological change, sunrise industries, value-added—they're the name of the game now. There's a hundred million fucking Japs out there.' He jabbed a forefinger vigorously in the general direction of Africa. 'And every one of them is trying to figure out another way to screw the rest of us. If it wasn't them it'd be the Koreans or the Taiwanese. Believe me, Murray, if we don't pull our fingers out, we'll wake up one afternoon and find ourselves sitting on the scrap heap at the end of the universe.'

He picked up a silver-framed family snap from among the yachting paraphernalia on the credenza and waved it about. 'And this lot, our dear old home-grown business establishment, will just sit back and let it happen if we let them. We've got to drag these inbreds into the twentieth century. Show some leadership. Get them off their well-upholstered bums. Offer them incentives to up their game. Investment incentives. Seeding funds. Venture capital. Fast-tracked planning approvals. That's why we're here today, Murray. Me to reassure our corporate friend that the government is on the ball, you to show him we're not on some anti-business witch hunt. Main thing is, just remember your manners, old chap, and we'll be out of here in a jiffy.'

Agnelli's face suddenly contorted with such patent insincerity that I thought he was bunging on a quick demonstration. 'Ah, Mr Merricks,' he gushed, 'So nice of you to agree to see us.' His gaze was fixed on the door, the picture back in place.

Lionel Merricks was a rather short, ruddy-faced man in his mid-fifties. He progressed across the carpet with impatient vigour, preceded by his hand. The fact that he was in his shirtsleeves, coupled with his slightly flushed appearance, gave the impression that he had just been interrupted giving himself a bracing injection of capital. I realised with dismay as I took his hand that I already felt obligated to him for his time.

'Five minutes, gentlemen.' The voice was fussy, half-English, disappointing. So this was the entrepreneurial class, red in tooth and claw. The shareholders of the country's seventh-largest public company might have found the tone impressive, but I couldn't see why. I stopped feeling apologetic.

'We at Pacific like to think of our workforce as one big family,' Merricks began magisterially. 'And believe me, nobody feels it more keenly than I when there is a bereavement in the family. A situation like this should not be made the pretext for industrial scaremongering. Nor the occasion of a fishing expedition. So if you have information relevant to the conduct of our company's affairs, I would be pleased to see that it is passed on to the appropriate area. Otherwise I see no need for outside involvement. You are not, I take it, suggesting the company is in any way responsible.'

Agnelli nearly fell over himself. 'I can assure you there is no question of blaming the company. It's not even that we're expecting any specific problem, sir.' Sir, yet! 'But it would be in nobody's interest if somebody out there went flying off the handle, would it? What harm could there be in having a quiet chat with some of the men? Test the waters, so to speak. All absolutely unofficial, of course. Avoid surprises, eh?' Chummy, now.

Merricks nodded noncommittally and turned to me. 'You have a union background, I understand, Mr Whelan.' He spoke slowly as if I was a little retarded. After Agnelli's performance he could hardly be blamed.

'I was with the Municipal Employees for a while.' This drew a blank. 'Garbage collectors, street sweepers.' Merricks' expression did not change but I knew I might as well have said 'dung beetles or intestinal tapeworms'.

Agnelli felt the crackle of insolence and quickly stepped back in. 'There would be no disruption of day-to-day activities at the plant. Murray here could be in and out of there in a couple of hours. Isn't that right, Murray.'

Merricks still wasn't having any of it. 'Our corporate culture is an open book. But there are always sensitivities at the shop floor level—restrictive work practices, demarcation disputes. I'm sure you are all too familiar with these matters, Murray. Having an outsider go in asking questions, at a time like this, I'm not at all convinced it's a good idea.'

I nodded absently. No skin off my nose. The sheer scale of the view out the window was mesmerising. It seemed like the whole sky was in the room with us. Out over the bay thunderheads were marching in from the west in mile high battalions. I wondered how helpful the plug of overalls would be once that lot broke. Not the sort of problem Mr Lionel Merricks would ever have to deal with. None of his roofs was ever likely to have a pair of soggy King Gees stuffing its inadvertent apertures. Not the gabled mansard one in Lansell Road, Toorak, or the cantilevered art deco one on the cliff top at Portsea or the mossy slate one on the homestead at Macedon.

'It's entirely your decision, of course, Mr Merricks,' I said softly, 'but do keep in mind that I have already discussed this matter with one of the industrial officers at the Trades Hall. You know what the unions can be like. If they were to form the opinion that your company is being obstructive...'

It was Merricks' turn to examine the meteorological panorama. Conditions looked more and more unsettled by the moment. Across the room Agnelli's eyes had gone wide with caution. The clouds moved closer. The moment continued. Merricks' attention seemed to linger on a tanker idling in the bay, waiting for a berth.

'Very well,' he said at last. 'I'll instruct our on-site management to co-operate. But I must insist that liaison be directly with me. Your findings are to be communicated directly and confidentially to me, and to me alone. I trust I am understood?'

There was a knock on the door and the ice queen opened it all the way. Merricks rose, nodded tersely. 'Understood?' he squeaked.

'I'm sure Charlene will appreciate your accessibility, Mr Merricks,' Agnelli cooed, but Merricks had already disappeared.

I looked at my watch. It was just on eleven-fifteen. Merricks had been in the room precisely five minutes.

I shook my head. 'Not a word, Agnelli,' I said. 'Not a fucking syllable.'

Coolaroo lay on the furthermost northern edge of the electorate, out where the fringes of the city finally frayed into paddocks of shoulder-high scotch thistle and the rusting hulks of cannibalised car bodies. Any further out and the voters chewed their cuds. I drove there straight from the city, the highway slick with drizzle, wanting only to get it over and done with.

Half a kilometre past the Ford factory I turned off into an industrial estate of warehouses and small factories. The road narrowed to a single lane of asphalt and I hugged the margins, wary of the lumbering sixteen-wheelers that were the only other traffic. The Renault threw up a slurry of mud and gravel as it went, the suspension feeling its age in the potholes. If I could have afforded anything else I'd have got rid of the shitheap years before. It was the French, not me, who deserved to be punished. I wasn't the one turning Micronesia into croque monsieur.

The Pacific Pastoral meatworks was a block long and half as wide, three storeys high, ringed by a chain mesh fence and fronted by a wide asphalt apron. I pulled into the employees' carpark opposite and eased into the gap between a panel van with chrome exhausts and a lime-green Kingswood with an luminous Cedars Of Lebanon bumper sticker. Through the swish of the wipers I had a clear view of the faceless brick behemoth across the road.

Nothing said trouble. No cluster of pickets at the gatehouse, no windbreakers and beanies, no hands being warmed at smoking ten-gallon drums. But there wouldn't be, would there? It was all bullshit, a figment of Agnelli's overactive imagination. There was nothing but a brick wall punctured at regular intervals by huge doorways, great yawning maws opening into impenetrable darkness. The shit holes at the end of the universe.

The drizzle stopped. A tip-truck came out of one of the doorways and a maintenance crew in navy overalls started shovelling steaming bitumen into pot holes in the apron. I turned off the wipers. As I stepped out into the carpark, my right shoe sank to the ankle in a puddle of oil-slicked ditchwater. I'd make Agnelli pay for this crap one day, I vowed.

The gatehouse attendant directed me towards one of the cavernous doors, apertures big enough for even the largest refrigerated truck. As I passed the first of the great portals I slowed my pace to squint from the silvery glare of the daylight into the interior, but could pierce the Dickensian gloom for only a few metres. From deep inside I could hear the mash and rev of forklifts and a voice shouting instructions, but the only human life I glimpsed was two spectral figures in white hosing down a floor.

As I neared the far door I felt my scalp crawl. I'm no vegetarian, so I knew it wasn't revulsion at the proximity of so much slaughtered flesh I was feeling. I shrugged off the creepy sensation and stepped into the enveloping darkness.

The place seemed even bigger inside, a maze of alleys and sub-buildings. It was older, less high-tech than I had expected, smelling of stale diesel fumes and wet concrete. Just inside the great door was a steel companionway with a sign pointing upwards, marked Office. I went up the stairs and followed the peck of a typewriter along an open deck running along the top edge of a deserted canteen.

The pecker was a well-upholstered woman of middle years, her sausagey fingers threaded with rings. She finished pecking a sentence and looked up without curiosity. 'Yes, love?' I asked if I was in the right place to see the manager. The sausages wrapped themselves around a telephone handpiece. 'Someone to see you, Mr Apps.' There was something about the way she said the mister part that made me smile.

Deep gullies of tedium had etched themselves into the woman's face as though she had spent reluctant decades trapped behind that big metal desk. Next to her typewriter a dusty monstera was taking a long time dying. On the wall behind, a sign said Thank You For Not Smoking. I wished I still smoked so I could start one up, just to see what would happen. Next to it a corporate mission statement in a moulded plastic frame began: 'We at Pacific Pastoral think of our workforce as one big family.'

Apps exploded out of an inner office. He had a beeper on his belt, a long thin face with twerp written all over it, and hands that dangled somewhere around his knees. One of them snaked up to tug at his collar. His Adam's apple came out for a look, didn't like what it saw, and ducked back in.

'Look here,' he started in, his mouth a pinched slot. 'This is tantamount to harassment. You lot at Export Certification seem to think you can ride roughshod over people. Once, just once, the US Department of Agriculture slaps a rejection sticker on a container of our product. Suddenly half the Australian quarantine service is crawling all over us, demanding right of inspection every five minutes. I thought you lot were supposed to be on our side. Just how many times do we have to go over this?'

I wondered just how anyone might mistake me for an officer of the Primary Industry Department. Had I grown a hat? Did I have a piece of straw sticking out the corner of my mouth?

The big vein in Apps' neck was ticking like a metronome. Without pausing to draw breath he stuck his scrawny wrist in my face and tapped his watch. 'Two o'clock, I was told. And what is it now? Twelve-thirty. Ever heard of courtesy?'

I had but I wasn't going to waste any on this prick. 'Lionel Merricks' office will have rung,' I said. 'Whelan's the name.'

Apps arched his neck irritably like the mistake was mine and shot the woman behind the desk a filthy look. The woman ignored him and resumed torturing the typewriter. 'Why didn't you say so?' he snapped. 'Head office said you probably wouldn't be here for a day or so.'

'If this isn't a convenient time...' I shrugged.

Apps writhed halfway between rage and obsequiousness. 'Full co-operation they said. So full co-operation it is. Our corporate culture is an open book.'

But a repetitive one. And I didn't like the tone he was reading it in. 'So I understand,' I said. 'They explained I'm here to talk to some of the men?'

Apps fished. 'Something about workforce attitudes to this death thing, they said. Bit hazy on the detail.'

I made a vaguely affirmative noise in the back of my throat.

'Everyone seems to think I've got nothing better to do with my time than conduct guided tours. I suppose you want to see where it happened then?'

The place was cold and dispiriting enough without a guided tour of some bloody freezer. 'Er, not really,' I started, nowhere near forcefully enough. My words drowned in the clang of Apps' footsteps on the steel plate of the deck. Co-operation, even of the grudging variety, could be so disarming. I tailed Apps deep into the bowels of the great shed, struggling into researcher mode. 'What's your contingent here?'

Apps bounded ahead, making no effort to conceal his irritation. 'Pretty quiet at the moment, as you can see. Best time for what you want is five o'clock in the morning. That's when the trucks come in from the abattoirs up the bush.'

'You couldn't put a number to it?'

He wasn't giving anything away. 'Varies. It's a seasonal industry. Core establishment—storemen, maintenance, cleaners, clerical—between twenty-five and thirty. But on top of that there's anything up to fifty casuals at a time in the place.'

We passed a safety slogan in English, Greek and Italian. 'Lot of Italians?' I asked.

'Don't take any notice of that, it's twenty years old. First it was Italians and Greeks, then Yugoslavs. Now its all Lebanese, Turks. Vietnamese even. Try to keep up and we'd be changing the signs every five minutes.'

We turned into a sort of truck-width street lined with cool

rooms the size of houses. 'You'll be wanting to interview the first on the scene, I daresay. He'll be about here some place.'

'Gardiner?' I looked about, hurrying to keep up.

'You seem very well informed.' It sounded like a reprimand. 'One of the cleaners, actually. Gardiner's on leave for a few days. They kept him here till nearly eight on Friday night, getting his statement and so on. Bloody red tape. I told him to take a few days off to get over it. He's no spring chicken, as you no doubt already know. He's due to retire next month.'

Here was a fly in the ointment. Gardiner was the only contact name I had. This little excursion onto the shop floor was already enough of an exercise in futility. Without Gardiner to interview, it would be even more so. It struck me that if old Herb was that close to retirement then Apps had probably insisted he use up a bit of his accrued sick leave, save the company a couple of bob in termination pay.

'This is it.'

A heavily padded parka was thrust into my hands. A key rattled, a white-clad wall slid away and the interior of Number 3 chiller yawned before me, sucking warmth.

'This really isn't necessary,' I protested, a wave of cold air wrapping itself around me.

The words 'No trouble at all' formed in the mist now coming out of Apps' mealy mouth. The door slid back into place behind us and Apps disappeared into the gap between towering pallet loads of waxed white cartons.

The chiller was large enough to get lost in. One man had died there already. I stuffed my exposed extremities into the jacket, pulled the hood cord tight and followed Apps. Talk about a snow job. This was the original Antarctic runaround. And not a single dead cow in sight to enliven the view, just row upon row of boxes. The whole place was nothing but a very cold storeroom.

'The men,' I insisted through teeth already beginning to chatter. 'I'll only need to talk to two or three of them today.' My wet sock had begun icing up.

Apps led me down a narrow canyon of roof-high boxes and stopped at a hatch about a metre square set into the wall. 'Emergency exit,' he fumed. 'Working perfectly it was. No question of culpability.'

He shoved a spring-loaded handle with his elbow and the little door swung silently outwards. He gestured for me to take a gander. There didn't seem to be much choice. I stuck my head through the hole.

The hatch opened into a narrow access alley running along behind the row of chillers. A man was standing in the alley, smoking a cigarette. He wore white overalls, white rubber boots and a white showercap. The sudden opening of the hatch caught him by surprise and he half-turned towards me, peering out from under his shower cap with dark marsupial eyes. He was about fifty, stocky in a pounded-down sort of way, Mediterranean, with skin the colour of old parchment. For the shortest of moments a flare of defiance lit his melancholy eyes. Then a curtain of indifference descended. He took a final drag, crushed the butt under the toe of a white rubber boot, turned away abruptly and was gone.

I pulled my head back in and rubbed my hands together. 'Very interesting, I'm sure,' I said. 'Now can we get the fuck out of here before I freeze my arse off.' Apps smirked like there was something obvious I'd missed and led me back out.

The man in the white overalls was passing the chiller door, slowly propelling a trolley of buckets and mops ahead of him. Apps put a hand on the trolley and squinted at the ID tag pinned to his chest. 'Ah, yes, Memo. Go with this man, Memo. He's from the government.'

Memo's round mournful face turned green. 'Poliss?'

Apps was taking the piss, palming me off on the mop jockey. Bugger him, I thought. He didn't know I was just going through the motions. And the sooner I divested myself of management the better.

'Not police,' I said emphatically. 'Government.' Probably a fine technical distinction wherever it was that this poor downtrodden Memo prick came from. Cyprus possibly. I turned back to Apps. 'Anywhere private I can do this? And any chance of a couple of cups of tea?'

Apps' elastic larynx rushed from its hiding place and assumed several curious shapes in rapid succession, but the jerk himself said nothing. He led me and the cleaner into the empty lunch room and pointed to a hot water urn and a pile of polystyrene cups on the counter.

'I'll need to talk to the safety officer next,' I said. 'You do have a safety officer, don't you?'

Apps looked huffy and disappeared. I motioned for Memo to sit and went over to the lukewarm urn. One of the disposable cups was half-full of plain-label tea bags. There was no milk. I made two cups of black tea and pushed one across the table. The cleaner accepted with a dip of his head. His eyes remained fixed on the chipped laminex tabletop. Conversation was not forthcoming.

I suppose I must have looked about as gruelling as a Polish film festival at that point, what with the scarified dial and being as stroppy as buggery at having let myself in for this utter waste of time. Memo, on the other hand, gave no indication of what was going on behind those impassive eyes of his.

'Memo, eh?' I said. 'What's that, Greek? Short for Agamemnon, is it?'

The guy sat there like a stuffed mongoose, not touching his tea, his hands jammed between his knees. He gave the question ample consideration and eventually shook his head.

'Not Grik,' he said. 'Memo same like Mehmet. Mehmet Gezen is my name.' The words were extruded tentatively like this maybe wasn't the answer I wanted. 'From Turkey.'

One of the deceased's compatriots. Good. Aside from a minor detour into the minefield of the Greek-Turkish border region we were headed in the right direction. 'Like the man who died here last week?'

Mehmet seemed to search for the right word. 'Similar,' he admitted at last. But not too similar from the sound of it.

Honestly, I could have got more information out of the tea urn. 'Was he your friend?'

Memo took his time. He took so much that I was beginning to wonder if he had understood the question. At last he spoke. 'Friend?'

'Yeah,' I said. 'Friend. Mate. Pal. Cobber. Buddy. Bosom companion.' Memo shook his head.

So much for the small talk. 'You like it here, Mehmet? Good place?' This was safer ground. Memo cheered up.

'No worries,' he said. 'No fucking worries.'

MACWAM would be pleased to know that a representative cross-section of the cleansing department had no immediate grievances. There was a tap at the door and a pair of blue overalls and a horseshoe moustache rolled in. 'I'm McGuire, the safety officer.'

'Thank you, Memo,' I said, relieved. 'That's all for now.' The cleaner looked confused then scuttled out of the room, as relieved as Stalin's barber.

McGuire pulled a chair out and straddled it backwards. I got straight to the point. 'What's the attitude of the blokes to this death on Friday?'

'They couldn't give a stuff. Bit of a prick from what I could tell. Not to speak ill of the dead.'

'Have any particular mates, did he?'

'Wouldn't know.'

'What about the health and safety aspects? Anyone upset about them?'

He sniggered. 'What is there to be upset about? It was a heart attack from what I hear. He wasn't exactly Twiggy, you know. No-one to blame but himself if you want my opinion.'

'What about safety around the place generally? Any gripes?'

'If you can get this lot interested in their own safety you're a better man than I am, Gunga Din. This joint has more turnover than a rotisserie chicken. New set of faces every time you look around. Ethnics mainly. In for a spot of ready cash, then Arrivederci Roma. I do what I can—put posters up in the canteen, make them wear the right gear if I catch them, but what else can you do? We've had the odd accident, but you could count them on one hand.'

He held up his right hand. Most of the ring finger and the top half of the middle finger were missing. He leered through the gap. 'Got three grand for these babies.'

And this was the safety officer. What a dump. 'Union active in the workplace, is it?'

'Well, it's a closed shop, if that's what you mean. They make sure they collect their dues and the pie warmer gets fixed when it breaks down. Beyond that, you'd have to ask the shop steward, Herb Gardiner. He deals with that lot.' He jerked his thumb upstairs towards the office.

One thing was for sure. This place might have been a shit hole, but it was no powder keg. Agnelli could not have been barking up a wronger tree. Unfortunately for me, he was barking hard and trying to get me to join the chorus. He really had his dick in the wringer over Lollicato and no amount of persuasion was going to convince him to pull it out. My only way out of this wild goose chase would be to find a way to keep Agnelli chasing his tail until the next fleeting enthusiasm came along and he found someone else to buggerise around.

As I shook McGuire's stumps goodbye, I heard the tramp of feet on the walkway above me. I looked up and saw Apps scuttle past, bobbing deferentially to a woman two steps ahead of him. She wore a dark pants suit, her greying hair pinned back with a gold clasp, and she carried a briefcase. When they got to the bottom of the stairs, their backs still turned to me, Apps held the case while the woman slipped her arms into a white dust coat. Then they vanished between two rows of freezers.

Upstairs, the lady with all the rings was sifting through a stack of time sheets. 'If you're looking for Mr Apps,' she said, 'he's down on the floor.' She held up a fleshy wrist and flashed a diamante watch. 'With his two o'clock appointment. The inspector.' Her eyes twinkled like rhinestones. 'Something in particular was it, love?'

'I'm supposed to see last Friday's roster. And milk, you don't know where I can find some milk, do you?'

'Personnel records are confidential, love.' But she got a carton of milk out of the private bar-fridge in Apps' inner sanctum. 'You'll have to see his nibs. And I'm not sure how long he'll be.'

The longer the better as far as I was concerned. 'A cross-section of names, that's all I need,' I said. 'No personal particulars or anything.'

She fiddled with an electric kettle at a sink in a small alcove. 'Sugar too, love? Or just milk?' My novelty value was slight, but at least I was better than nothing. 'What happened to your face?'

'Possum,' I said, pulling a chair up beside the desk. 'I've got an on-site van up the river. The thing must have got in through the air vent and been stuck there all week. Soon as I opened the door it went for me. Half-starved probably.'

Not bad at short notice I thought. She clucked sympathetically, whether for me or the possum I couldn't tell, and put a cup of something brown in front of me. Then she opened her top drawer, took out a glass ashtray and put it on the desk next to my elbow. She dredged a packet of Alpine out of her bag and extracted a cigarette. 'If His Highness comes in, this is yours. Okay?'

I grinned and sipped the weak oversweet instant coffee like it was pure ambrosia. 'No worries,' I said. 'No worries at all.'

She held the end of the cigarette to the glowing element of an electric radiator tucked under the desk near her feet. When it caught she put it to her lips and puffed it into action.

I gave her my most hapless look and nodded towards the time sheets. 'I'm running a bit late,' I said. 'I don't suppose I could...'

She shrugged. 'Long as you're quick,' she said. 'I don't imagine it'd do any great harm.'

I flipped through the sheets. They were dated for the previous week. The employee's name was handwritten in the left-hand column, the daily hours in boxes in the middle, the confirming signature of the shift supervisor on the right. It was perfect.

I began copying the left-hand columns. A couple of dozen names would do, I figured. Enough to keep Agnelli running around Trades Hall like a blue-arsed fly for weeks, trying to figure out if any of them had Lollicato connections. As I wrote I began to whistle under my breath.

The names were a real ethnic grab-bag, heavy on Yugoslavs if anything. Zoltans, Zorans and Dragons, lots of -ic surnames. Some were real puzzlers—Amol Ratna, Zeki Muren. But Italians, if anything, were under-represented. If Agnelli was looking for an Italian connection he would be disappointed.

I was well into the third page before I glanced over at the

signature running down the right-hand margin. It was an almost childish scrawl, half block letters, the mark of a hand that rarely held a pen. E. Bayraktar it read. I rapidly flipped through all the sheets on the desk. The signature appeared on three of them, against more than thirty names.

Agnelli is going to love this, I thought. If he must have his seedbed of simmering discontent, what better place for it than among the deceased's most intimate working companions? I scribbled furiously. The names on Bayraktar's first sheet were the usual cosmopolitan mishmash, but about halfway down the third page they became more decidedly Turkish. Well, they seemed Turkish. Dursun and Orhan and Oguz were Turkish names, I felt almost sure. Kartal Tibet, that was harder to pick, sounded Himalayan. Ahmet Ayik, now surely that was Turkish. And Nasreddin Hoca, that rang a bell.

Ding dong, it went. Jingle jangle. Clang, clang, clang. It rang loud and it kept ringing. Nasreddin. That was a name I'd seen somewhere before. But where?

'These permanents?'

'No, love. That's the casuals. Permanents get paid direct into their bank accounts. Only casuals get weekly cash. Filling out that many different bank transfers every week would be a bloody nightmare, pardon my French. Look at those names. Honestly, you couldn't spell half of them if you tried.'

'That must be a lot of fiddling around for you, making up the pay packets.'

She snorted smoke out her nose. 'I've got enough to do as it is, love. The packets get made up by Armaguard. All part of the service. I send them the forms and they deliver the pays on Friday, all ready for the shift supervisors to take round after lunch. Speaking of which, you'd better hurry up with that lot. I've got to get them finished this afternoon.'

'All finished,' I said, quickly noting down the last half-dozen names on Bayraktar's page. I took the cup to the sink and rinsed it. 'Tell Himself thanks for the welcome and that I'm not sure when I'll be back,' I said. 'Could be any time.' She liked that.

The ashtray had disappeared back into the drawer, butt and all.

'Oh, one last thing before I go. You wouldn't happen to have Herb Gardiner's address on file here somewhere, would you?'

Gardiner's place was in Coburg, back towards the electorate office, a fifteen-minute drive. On the way through Broadmeadows I looked for lunch. Out that far, Sydney Road was already the Hume Highway and all I found were fast-food franchises and used-truck yards. Behind them, tract houses spread across the plain where once the Woiworung had hunted and gathered. Presumably with more success than me. I passed the Colonel and kept going.

By comparison Coburg was almost picturesque, a two-time Tidy Town runner-up. It was a world of fifties cream brick-veneer, ruler-straight lawn edges, garden gnomes, roll-down garage doors, low fences, oleanders and lemon trees. None of your unruly natives were tolerated here, dropping their leaf business on the paths and clogging up the guttering. Herb Gardiner's house was the neatest in his street. A big For Sale sign was planted on the front lawn.

I stepped over the wrought-iron gate and rang the doorbell. As a four-note chime sounded distantly, a white silky terrier hurtled around the corner in a frenzy of yapping. I braced to defend myself, and a female voice screamed in my ear. 'Garn. Git.'

The fanged snowball skidded to a halt, turned and limped away. A woman of about Charlene's age, respectably made up, was standing behind the heavy grille of the screen door wiping her hands on an apron.

'Mrs Gardiner?'

'Vera passed away six months ago.'

'But this is the Gardiner house?'

She didn't want anybody getting the wrong idea. 'I'm The Nextdoors. I pop in now and then to give Mr Gardiner a hand with the housework. If it's about the house, he's up the street I'm afraid.'

I was suddenly acutely conscious of my appearance. I straightened my back, ran my fingers through my hair and tried to look as prospective as possible. If I'd been wearing a hat I'd have taken it off and fiddled with the brim. 'Been on the market long, has it?' I enquired politely.

'The sign has only just gone up.'

'Well, another time, I suppose.'

The screen swung open. 'Herb won't be a moment, I'm sure.'

I wiped my feet vigorously and stepped onto the salmon pink carpet of the entrance hall. The wallpaper was pink, too. A pink on pink fleur-de-lis motif, with a row of miniatures, ballerinas in candy tutus. The telephone table was white though, Queen Anne, to match the antique ivory and brass telephone. I followed the wall-to-wall through to the lounge.

Mrs Nextdoor went into an impromptu pitch. 'As you can see it's too big for one person. Herb's been here on his own ever since...' She tactfully left the sentence unfinished. 'It was the same when my husband went. Herb, I said, you can't live forever surrounded by memories.'

'I can understand that,' I said. And I could.

Herb's memories were pure oestrogen. The lounge was the hall writ large. The sofa was done in pink floral with matching throw cushions. The pelmets above the windows were uphol-stered in the same pattern, with little valances matching the gathered lace of the drapes. Rows of porcelain dolls with painted blushes stared out of a blondwood crystal cabinet towards a print of a sad-eyed clown with a ruffled collar hanging on the rambling-rose patterned wallpaper. There was so much pink I thought my eyes must be haemorrhaging.

On the mantelpiece in front of a bevelled mirror etched with lilies was a big oversized brandy balloon half-filled with rose petal potpourri, but the smell was that of thickly laid-on air freshener. The only visible evidence of human habitation was a scattering of brochures and documents on the pink-tinted glass top of a brass-rimmed coffee table. Beside them sat a copy of *Best Bets*, tell-tale male spoor.

The helpful widow offered me the sofa. 'I'd best leave the formalities to Herb. I'd feel a bit strange showing someone around someone else's house, if you know what I mean.' That was a relief. I perched gingerly on the edge of the crepe de chine.

I decided I'd give Gardiner five minutes. If he hadn't shown by then, I'd take the phone number and call him from the office. To tell you the truth, I wasn't even sure why I was there. Covering my arse, I suppose. Dotting the t's and crossing the i's.

She of the Nextdoor hovered, uncertain of the protocol. 'Nice big place,' she improvised. 'Ideal family home. Too much cleaning for one. Herb's new place is fully serviced. Hot though, Queensland.'

'Queensland?' I improvised back. 'Nice weather.'

'Can't say I blame him, day like today. But I don't know how he'll get on by himself. A man needs someone to look after him.'

Indeed, he did, I admitted. Make that three minutes.

'Anyhow, you might as well have a cuppa while you wait. Fully equipped kitchen.' That about exhausted the conversational possibilities. She opened the door through to the kitchen. Baking smells, good ones, came in and fought with the evil air freshener.

A white cuckoo clock ticked loudly in the silence. My stomach growled back at it. Past two-thirty and I still hadn't eaten. I picked up the form guide, put it down, flicked through one of the brochures. Ocean Towers, Broadbeach. Absolute beachfront. Two and three bedroom apartments from two hundred and fifty thousand dollars, plus on-road costs.

I tossed the glossy folder back down onto what could have been a title deed and looked around. Not a bad swap, a quarter of a mill's worth of sea views and a spa for a crocheted tissue box worth maybe half that, absolute maximum, drizzle running down its windows. Old Herb must certainly have been stacking it away all these years. And why not? A lifetime on your back on the concrete with your mouth full of self-tappers, staring up into the innards of a bung compressor. Make a nice change, Broadbeach would.

My own old man had done something similar when they bought the pub out from under him for a drive-in bottle shop. But instead of the high-rise condo in Surfers he'd gone for the fibro shack on Bribie Island and the aluminium runabout. Horses for courses. Plus it looked like Gardiner had a bit more nous in the financial planning department. That wouldn't be hard. Whelan senior had been through six pubs in twenty years, each smaller than the one before it.

I was thinking about making a break for it when a little tan Toyota Corolla scooted into the driveway and disappeared down the side. The dog yapped a bit, then the front door opened. For a man in his sixties, Herb Gardiner was very well preserved, a bit of a gent in a Fletcher Jones tweed jacket, corduroy trousers and a rollneck navy-blue jumper. He had the nuggetty face of an ex-pug and the lightness on his feet of a man who'd just taken out the box trifecta at Eagle Farm. He wore the crooked grin of a short man on good terms with the whole world. If he was suffering from post-fatality trauma, he was bearing up well.

'And who are you, then?' he demanded with exactly the inflection you'd use yourself if you walked into your lounge room and found a total stranger with a scabby face dawdling on the divan.

As I stood up to tell him, the widow came out of the kitchen. 'He's come about the house,' she said. The apron had disappeared and she'd plumped up her hair. Gardiner shrugged off his tweed jacket, brushed the raindrops away with the meticulousness of a bloke who took good care of his tools, and draped it over the back of one of the pink armchairs.

'Actually,' I said guiltily, 'the union suggested I get in touch.'

'Did they just?'

Fair enough. This one called for a very straight bat. 'It's a courtesy call really, Mr Gardiner. My name is Murray Whelan.

It's about the, uh, incident last week at work.'

Gardiner gave me the stop sign. 'Those scones of yours smell scrumptious.' He sprayed charm all over the widow, splashing some on me in the process. He scooped the brochures up off the coffee table and slotted them into a gap in a blondwood shelf of white-bound encyclopedias. 'I'll make a bit of space. Sit down, Mr Whelan.'

'Murray, please.'

The scones appeared before my bum had even hit the cushion, straight out of the oven. A good three inches tall, they were, on a tray with jam and whipped cream and little linen serviettes. As Mrs Nextdoor bent to lower the tray, Gardiner, master again in his own house, patted her rump. She all but purred. He looked at me across her backside and winked. Here was a man who had it made, and didn't he know it. For the first time all day, I was beginning to enjoy myself.

'Leave you boys to it, will I then?' she said.

'Rightio, pet. Thanks a lot.' Gardiner pulled up his sleeves daintily and reached for the teapot. Under the grizzled hair of his forearm was an ancient tattoo—a faded, languorous mermaid. 'I'll be mother,' he said.

Entertaining Herb's uninvited callers was clearly not what the good widow had in mind when she'd come round to play house, but she copped it sweet. Gardiner would be around for a little while yet. She went out through the kitchen and I heard the back door close.

'So, what's this all about, son?' Gardiner said amiably.

It was long past the point where there was any mileage in playing funny buggers. I put my cards on the table, face up between the apricot conserve and the turf tips. 'I work for Charlene Wills,' I said. Gardiner accepted my credentials with a nod. The local member was well known.

'Dunno if you saw it,' I went on, 'but there was bit of speculation in the *Sun* yesterday to the effect that this business out at Pacific Pastoral on Friday might lead to some kind of industrial problems. The government would prefer that didn't happen. A committee in the Industry Department has called for a report. Since I work in this area they decided I was just the bunny to write it for them. And because you're the union rep and also happened to be on the spot when the body turned up, I thought I'd come straight to the horse's mouth.'

Gardiner took all this in, nodded again and broke open a scone. 'I went through all of this pretty thoroughly with the police and so forth on Friday.'

I hastened to reassure him. 'Oh, I'm not interested in the death *per se*, just any possible industrial implications.'

Gardiner applied butter. 'Who else you talked to?'

'No-one much, yet. Lionel Merricks.' This was nothing but craven big-noting. I wasn't even sure he'd recognise the name.

He raised his eyebrows. 'You don't muck about, do you, son?'

I brushed it aside, modestly. 'Just protocol really. It's the situation on the ground at Coolaroo that interests me. And you'd know more about that than any chairman of the board.'

'What about Apps?'

'Correct me if I'm wrong,' I said. 'But I got the definite impression Mr Apps wouldn't recognise an industrial situation if it bit him on the bum.'

That got a chuckle. Gardiner relaxed back into his armchair, cup and saucer on his lap. 'Bit tense, was he?'

'Yeah,' I said. 'Is he always so stroppy?'

I must've been making a good impression. Gardiner touched the side of his nose and proceeded to slip me the inside oil. 'Couple of months ago a mix-up happened in one of our shipments to America, sub-standard meat or something. There was hell to pay. Threat to the credibility of the export industry, all of that. Apps copped a bit of flack from the higher-ups and he's been like a bear with a sore head ever since. You talk to anyone else?'

'Not really. Some bloke named McGuire, the safety officer. A cleaner called Memo. My impression is that I'm on a fool's errand.'

So far I was doing too much talking. At this rate those scones would get away from me. I smeared one and bit down hungrily. 'What do you reckon?' I mumbled through the crumbs and cream. My mouth filled with heaven, all melting and warm.

Gardiner picked up his cup and settled deeper into his seat.

'Well it's all news to me, son. I've been there sixteen years, ever since I left the service, and in all that time we've had fewer than half a dozen strikes and stoppages. And they were all at the behest of the union, backing up the log of claims and so forth. The slaughtermen, up to their knees in guts and shit all day, now they go out at the drop of a hat, and who can blame them? But our lot, industrial action isn't their style. Most of them would rather have the day's pay and solidarity be buggered. I just can't see it, myself. I certainly haven't heard anything, son. And I would, believe me, I would.'

This was music to my ears. I tackled another scone and moved on. 'So what do you reckon he was up to in that chiller? Bayraktar, the bloke you found?'

'Well, he wasn't working on his tan, I can tell you that much.'

'Fair bit of that sort of thing goes on out there, does it?'

'As much as anywhere else, I suppose.'

'So it's pretty widespread?'

'Stands to reason that a man who works in a meat warehouse would be a mug to buy his own chops. But not everybody's walking out the front door with a side of lamb under their arm, if that's what you mean.'

I'd walked into that one with my eyes wide open, practically called the man a thief to his face. I backed off at a million miles an hour. 'Bit stiff, though. Freezing to death for a couple of kilos of free sirloin.'

'Maybe he was greedy. Had quite an appetite by the look of him.'

'Ever had much to do with him?'

Gardiner wiped his fingers on one of the little floral serviettes. 'Knew him to look at. The ethnics keep pretty much to themselves.'

'Speaking of which.' I pulled the time sheet list out of my pocket and folded it down to the bottom half. 'Know any of this lot?'

Gardiner took a spectacle case out of his pocket, slipped on a pair of half-glasses and tilted the sheet of paper to the light.

'What's this, the Cairo phone book?'

'They were all on Bayraktar's shift last week.'

Gardiner shook his head. 'I'm not much good with ethnic names, I'm afraid.'

I drained my tea and began to get up. 'Well, thanks a lot.'

'Anytime, son. Happy to help. Need anything else, just let me know. But you'd better be quick. I'm due to be demobbed any day now. Only a couple more weeks of 5 a.m. starts and I'm my own man.'

'So I hear.' I took the list back. Not an entirely unproductive half-hour all in all. A free feed, plus old Herb had driven yet another stake through the heart of Agnelli's conspiracy theory, at least the Pacific Pastoral part of it. I changed the subject. 'What do you think you'll get for this place?'

'The agent thinks ninety-five, ninety-five and a half. I wouldn't know these days. It needs a lot of work.'

Apart from the decor I couldn't see where, but then Gardiner probably changed the tap washers once a week. 'That'd make my place worth about fifty bucks. You should see it. Talk about needing work! I was up in the ceiling putting in some insulation last night and the roof fell in on me. That's how I got these.'

'Nasty,' said Gardiner.

'They're the least of my worries.' I fingered my scabs. 'Think I can get a roofer to come and give me a quote? Been on the phone half the day I have.' Well I would be, as soon as I got back to the office.

Gardiner got up and started wrapping the remaining scones in a serviette. 'Here, take these, son,' he said. 'She'll get shirty on me if she thinks we didn't eat them all. And while you're here, give me your details. I've got a mate in the building trade who might be able to help you out.'

'You sure?' I hesitated only long enough to be polite before stuffing the bundle into my pocket.

'Sure I'm sure,' he said. He wrote my address and phone number on a pad by the phone and opened the front door. 'I'm getting as much as I need.' Faint kitchen noises came from back in the house. 'Believe me, son. Believe me.'

Out on the street, the rain had let up. All that remained of the puddles was an iridescent glaze. By the look of it, things were on the improve. When I glanced back, Gardiner was still standing at the open door, the little white terrier nuzzling his hand. I gave a nod and climbed into the Renault, one hand already dipping into the package in my pocket. A quick half-hour drafting up the MACWAM report and I'd have this thing knocked on the head.

Context, I thought. Make that *Background*. Double underline. The words in my head began to shape themselves into a preamble.

Background
A situation has recently arisen in the context of the ongoing legislative process relating to the Industrial Insurance Act such as to suggest it advisable that specific consultations be undertaken in relation to addressing uncertainties which may have been perceived to have arisen as a consequence of press speculation concerning a recent workplace fatality in the Melbourne metropolitan area.

Not bad for openers, I thought, mentally moving on to Implementation. But my concentration was slipping. An image kept surfacing in my mind, a tubby little man in harem pants.

Nasreddin Hoca, he of the hefty turban and curly slippers. He of the bushy beard and pithy parable. Fancy him working at Pacific Pastoral. It was a bit hard to imagine that wry old wiseacre in a pair of white overalls and a shower cap, hefting a side of beef out of a refrigerated semi. Not his style at all. Not unless the arse had fallen out of the obscure epigram business.

If Red's bedtime story book was right and this Nasreddin Hoca guy was a famous Turkish legend, up there in the Mother

Goose category, then wouldn't Bayraktar have known he was signing off against a false name? Interesting.

Since I was out and about, I decided on the spur of the moment to roll past Bayraktar's address. From what I could remember of the coroner's file, it was either 363 or 636 Blyth Street. Either way, the detour would not take me far out of my way. A few extra minutes of solitude in the car would help me finish mentally drafting the report.

Blyth Street is a broad avenue running east-west from the Merri Creek to Sydney Road. I started at the Merri end and cruised past respectable homes with barley sugar columns holding up their porches. 363 was a Shell self-serve, so I followed the numbers up towards Sydney Road.

Once upon a boom the local gentry had lived up this end, in polychrome brick villas and imposing terraces fretted with iron lacework. Things had taken several downturns since then and all that remained to hint at the vanished grandeur was the occasional one-winged terracotta gargoyle or the peeling curve of a bay window. Mostly it was blocks of flats, crummy, identical strata-titles, pockmarking the streetscape. Six feet of red scoria and a dead cabbage palm out the front, letterboxes exploding with junk mail down the side. Bayraktar's joint was bound to be in one of those.

But closer to Sydney Road, things were on the up and up. Skips full of builders' rubble sat by the kerb outside big Victorian terraces, evidence of renovations in progress. Brass plates and Mercedes hinted at solicitors and pathologists. And 636 was no dingy block of flats, flung up in the sixties.

It was a classic two-storey boom-era Italianate mansion, modestly substantial and trying its best to look inconspicuous behind a cast-iron fence, the original by the look of it. A dinky little square tower sat on top, and jutting out above the front door was a coach-porch sort of arrangement. Everything had been painted a matt white with fetching gloss highlights in olive green on the woodwork and the little iron balconies wrapped around the first floor windows. The overall charm was complemented by little security cameras mounted under the eaves at each corner. Taken together with the gunmetal grey BMW parked under the portico they gave the place the discreet and impenetrable air of a private casino on the Cote d'Azur.

Far too fancy a set of digs for a meat lumper, even if he was a foreman. By the look of it, somewhere along the line someone had screwed up the paperwork. I slowed to a crawl and peered out the passenger window at the brass plate on the gatepost. Etched in black were the words Anadolu Klubu, then underneath in smaller letters Anatolia Club.

An irate toot sounded behind me, a glazier's truck in a hurry. Up ahead, the lights at the corner had just gone orange. I hit the accelerator and raced them, turning up the hill into Sydney Road. Past the Patras Emporium and Appliance Discounters I went. Past the Court House Hotel and the Edinburgh Castle, past Barnacle Bill's, past the black walls of Pentridge. Two blocks past the electorate office I pulled into the kerb outside the Turkish Welfare League.

The League was another shopfront opening directly onto Sydney Road. The only other businesses this far up were in the motor trade. Direct-to-the-public retread wholesalers, windscreen replacements while-u-wait, Midas Mufflers. And up here, the road was an industrial-strength drag strip.

Apart from the rent being cheap, there was a certain logic in this choice of location for the League's office. Most of Melbourne's Turks were factory workers, imported by the jumbo load to fill the assembly line at Ford or Repco. So if any Australian-made car less than fifteen years old ever missed the turn and ploughed through the League's plate glass window, it had a better than even chance of connecting with the very bloke who had spot-welded its front assembly into place.

I locked the Renault, a purely symbolic gesture in this neighbourhood, and walked inside. The League's front office consisted of two dented filing cabinets, an ancient Gestetner mimeograph machine, probably the last in captivity, and three battered desks. Paperwork trays overflowed with forms and documents and handbooks from various government departments and philanthropic organisations. Posters from the local screen print co-op covered the walls creating an atmosphere of embattled engagement that not even the damp seeping upwards from the threadbare linoleum could dispel.

A cluster of men was hunkered down around one of the desks, men with faces that were maps of a wide brown land. But not this wide brown land. Not yet anyway. At their centre was Sivan the Kurd.

I didn't know then, and still don't, if you can tell a Kurd from a Turk by looking at him. But for my money Sivan was everything you could have wanted in a manifestation of that proud and embattled race. He had the beak of an eagle, shoulders built for bandoliers, a torso the size of Asia Minor and a crop of grizzled stubble that had me reaching self-consciously for my own lame thirty-hour growth.

He made a rumbling noise, a thick geological growl that began deep inside and came erupting out his toothy grin. 'Murray, my friend.' His arm swept wide. 'Meet Sayfeddin, Gokhan, Bulent.'

A good head for names was indispensable in my line of work, standing at a politician's shoulder refreshing her memory. But to my unending dismay, Turkish names could rarely find purchase on my mnemonics. Greeks I could do—they were all Jim or Con or Nick. Italians, no problem, even since the Johnnies and Joes had taken to reverting to Giovanni and Giuseppe. And no-one ever got fired for calling an Arab Mohammed. It was bound to be in there somewhere. Unless he was a Christian, in which case George or Tony was usually a safe bet. But Gokhan? Bull ant? Sayfeddin? Say what?

'Merhaba,' I mumbled. Yassou. Ciao. Howdy doody. This I could do in a full range of community languages, including Maltese, but I'm a great believer in the unifying influence of English, so that was as fluent as I was going to get.

'Merhaba,' they all replied, looking at me expectantly.

I cocked my head towards the back of the building. 'Ayisha in?' I wanted a quiet chat, not to go live-to-air on Radio Istanbul.

Sivan indicated a narrow corridor opening in the back wall of the room. 'Girl mechanic today.'

The corridor was lined with tourist posters of the Bosphorus and newspaper photographs of heads that looked like they belonged on the banknotes of some very foreign currency indeed. I found Ayisha kneeling on the floor of an office that was a smaller, pokier version of the one out front, her head buried in the innards of an antique photocopier. Bits of machinery were spread in an arc on the floor around her backside. She had her back to the door and didn't see me arrive.

Her hair was wrapped in a scarf, and as she reached purposefully behind her for some part or other, her hands black with toner powder, she looked for all the world like a Heroine of Labour resolutely overfulfilling her norm for Xerox repair under the first Five Year Plan. My heart clenched itself into a fist. Forward to the World October, it silently shouted.

I had been leaning against the door frame, silently admiring her industry for nearly a minute when she pulled her head out of the machine's interior and sprung me. 'Jeeze, Murray,' she said. 'What are you perving at?'

A question very much to the point. I felt heat spread across my cheeks. 'That name I mentioned yesterday,' I countered quickly. 'Find anything out?'

'Nearly scared the shit out of me,' she said. 'Sneaking about like that.' Clearly, she had forgotten to ask. She stood up, demonstratively kneed the photocopier door shut, and palmed the print button. The machine whirred and began ejaculating copies. 'You all right?' She came right up to me and stared at my face, deliberately much too close for comfort.

I tried to hold her gaze. 'Just a few scratches, that's all. It's not contagious or anything.'

'Those faction fights can get pretty rough, I hear.' She patted a sooty palm against my cheek. I felt myself flush under the smear of graphite. It was a wonder she didn't get third-degree burns.

I stepped back abashed, and cracked the back of my head on the door frame. 'You should have seen the other guy.'

Suddenly a hand clamped down on my shoulder from behind and spun me round. 'Trying to seduce Ayisha, eh?'

It was Sivan. He must have been reading my mail. 'It is useless,' he said. 'Many have tried, all have failed.'

'Get stuffed,' said Ayisha. She plonked herself down behind her desk and started rolling a grubby cigarette. 'Murray here wants to know about some guy he thought we might know. Name of...'

'Ekrem Bayraktar.'

Sivan repeated the name, rolling it around in his mouth like he was making concrete out of it. 'Bayraktar means he who carries the flag, the standard bearer.' Sivan had been a school-teacher before the army tore up his diploma and poked matches under his fingernails. What he was saying was all very interesting, but I wanted lowdown not etymology.

'You heard of him?'

Sivan shook his head.

'What about any of these guys?' I handed him the payroll list.

He ran a hairy finger down the names, turned to Ayisha and broke into a broad grin. 'He wants to know if we have heard of Nasreddin Hoca.'

A sly twinkle crossed Ayisha's face. She caught me watching and dipped her head to light her sooty fag. I didn't want her thinking I was a complete drongo. 'The parable of the walnut,' I said, quick as a flash. I pointed to the name underneath. 'What about this guy, Gazanfer Bilge?' Rhymed with pilfer.

Him, Sivan knew. 'Wrestler,' he rumbled. 'Very famous in the nineteen fifties. You know Turkish wrestling? First they put oil on their bodies and...' He advanced, arms spread, intent on demonstrating a key grip. I fended him off with the next name. 'Orhan Gencebay. That Turkish?'

Sivan froze in mid-stride. He rolled the list into a tube and waved it about in front of his mouth. *'Bir tesselli ver,'* he wailed, his voice weirdly high and strangulated. *'Yaradanin askina.'* He swayed from side to side and with his free hand pounded a beat on the edge of the desk.

I rolled my eyes towards Ayisha. She didn't know what was going on either. Sivan threw his arms wide and changed languages, holding the same tune. *'Everybody make mistakes,'* he sang.

I got it now. 'Singer?'

'Bingo,' he said. 'Tom Jones. Molly Meldrum.' He ironed the paper microphone flat on the surface of the desk and dropped back into pedagogic mode. 'You know Turkish music? The saz is similar to the bazouki, the drum is called darbooka, the...'

'Kartal Tibet.' I snatched up the list and read the next name. 'Let me guess, husband of the famous Donna Kebab.'

'Close,' said Ayisha. 'Movie actor, I think. Before my time. More Sivan's vintage.' Sivan was all of thirty-five.

'Commercial crap,' said Sivan. 'Do you know the films of Yilmaz Guney? For example, *The Herd*?'

A mythical sage, an oily athlete, a pop singer, a film star. The early shift at Pacific Pastoral was beginning to look a little top-heavy with talent. I interrupted Sivan's discourse on modern Turkish cinema. 'Ever heard of a place called the Anatolia Club.'

Sivan stopped talking and gave Ayisha a very strange look. 'Oh, very bad place, my friend,' he growled. 'You should not go there.'

'Why? What is it?'

Before he could answer, Gokhan—or was it Sayfeddin— burst through the door. He said something terse in Turkish, a harsh sounding phrase, then abruptly turned and disappeared.

'Shit.' Ayisha was on her feet, slinging her bag across her shoulder.

'What?'

She came round the desk, chewing her bottom lip and took off out the door. My entrails turned to iced water and I took off after her. She shot out the front door like a rocket, turned left and sped up the footpath.

A burly, hard-faced man in a military-style jacket was standing beside the Renault, resting a jack-booted foot provoca- tively on the front bumper. He was levering up the blade of my windscreen wiper. 'Hey,' I demanded. 'What do you think you're doing?'

He turned and lazily raked me with cold contemptuous eyes, sure of his own power. Then he slowly raised his arm and pointed back over my shoulder. Without looking, I knew what he was pointing at. CLEARWAY, the sign beside me read, 4:30–6:00 p.m.

'Fair go, mate,' I pleaded, staring in disbelief at my watch. 4:32, it said. He thrust a pink piece of paper into my hand. Pay the City of Coburg forty dollars, it said. Or else. Further up the street Ayisha opened the door of a newish metallic-blue Laser. She waved gaily and drove off, scot free.

A line of trams was backed up along the centre of the road, leaving the Renault blocking the only other northbound lane. As far back as I could see, traffic sat stalled, horns blazing. For the briefest moment I considered leaving the car where it was and going back inside to ask Sivan what he had been about to say about the Anatolia Club. The Grey Ghost tapped his behaviour modification pad against his thigh. 'I'd shift it,' he said nastily. 'If I was you.'

I took my time, rolling the parking ticket into a ball as I went. I slammed the door, gunned the engine, pulled out around the nose of the tram, threw an illegal u-turn in the face of the oncoming traffic, stuck my arm out the window, gave the by-laws Nazi the finger, hit the gas, and burned rubber. It wasn't forty dollars worth, but it was consolation of sorts.

Up to that point, you'd have to admit, I had been doing pretty well in the amateur sleuth stakes. In barely four hours not only had I confirmed that industrial action was unlikely at Pacific Pastoral, but I had established that something dodgy was going on in the vicinity of their payroll, and that there was more to this dead bloke Bayraktar than met the eye.

So as I parked behind the electorate office and slipped in the back door, I must confess to feeling as pleased with myself as a man might with a squashed-up forty dollar parking fine in his pocket. I even had enough unanswered questions to justify paying another visit to Ayisha's office fairly soon.

Back in my cubicle, I found things exactly as I had left them. The same overflowing in-tray, the inevitable yellow pile of phone message slips, the same tattooed oaf sitting in my visitor's chair with his size tens parked on the walnut veneer.

Our more troublesome sort of customers usually got bored after a couple of hours of the cold shoulder and took their grievances elsewhere. Two full days was a new record. Not that I told Mr Adam F. Ant that. He might have taken it for encouragement. Instead I pretended he wasn't there, sat down and dug out the Pacific Pastoral file. Without the coroner's envelope all it held was a single sheet of paper with Herb Gardiner's name written on it. I added the payroll list and ticked off the four names I knew for sure were phonies.

There were any number of reasons why someone might work under a false name. Minimising tax on a second job was one. Holding down a paying job while pulling the dole was another. Illegal immigrants did it. All you had to do, after all, was fill in a false tax-declaration form and put some bogus details no-one would ever check on the personnel department sheet. Half the uni students in the country were doing it, including some majoring in Ethics. Shit, I'd done it myself a dozen years before, signed on for bar work as F. Engels. It was a bad undergraduate joke, made worse by the fact that I kept forgetting to answer to the name Fred. Not that the boss gave a toss, long as the job got done.

But this was different. One fictitious name was unremarkable. Two would have been a coincidence. Four or more, all of the same ethnic persuasion as the foreman, suggested an altogether different kettle of calamari. Either Bayraktar was turning a blind eye to the legal niceties on behalf of a clutch of his compatriots, or stuffing the odd bit of stray beef up his overalls was not the only means he had found to diddle Pacific Pastoral.

Of course, neither the internal financial administration of Pacific Pastoral nor the affairs of the deceased Bayraktar were any of my business. But things were now developing a momentum of their own at a level well below the threshold of rational thought. An idle mind, as the Brothers used famously to say. Curiosity had me by the short and curlies.

I picked up the phone and dialled Wageline, a telephone service operated by the Labour Ministry to provide information on award wages and conditions. The going rate for a part-time casual labourer in the meat industry was nine dollars eighty an hour. I did some rapid arithmetic on the inside cover of the file. Nine dollars eighty times forty hours equalled close to four hundred dollars. Less tax, I figured on a take-home pay of three twenty-five. About thirty dollars a week less than me. Not brilliant money in anyone's language.

After that, the figures were pure hypothesis. Any company operating a hand-delivered pay-packet procedure was crying out to be ripped off. Bayraktar had keys. He'd been in a position of trust. Suppose, just for argument's sake, that he'd also been in a position to add dummy names to his work team, then confirm their attendance and hours?

The four fake names were due a total of thirteen hundred dollars. Multiply that by, say, twenty-five weeks a year and the figure totalled somewhere in the neighbourhood of thirty-two thousand dollars, a very attractive part of the world. Even if the fiddle was only being worked one week in four, it was still a nice little earner. All in cash, in handy buff envelopes.

What gave this conjecture enormous appeal was not only the possibility that a barely literate migrant was sticking it up snotty-nosed Lionel Merricks to the tune of many thousands of dollars, but that he was doing it using names equivalent to Friar Tuck, Brute Bernard, Frank Sinatra and Robert Redford. If it was true, this Bayraktar deserved a posthumous industry award for having more front than a well-known city emporium.

Diverting as I found all this conjecture, it wasn't plugging the hole in my roof. I closed the file, tossed it on top of the ever-increasing mound that was my in-tray, shot Adam Ant a filthy look, and turned my attention to the swatch of phone messages that had accumulated on my blotter since the previous morning.

Most of the little yellow slips logged calls from missed appointments. Three were from Agnelli. These I threw in the bin. Two were call-backs from roofing companies. The first was engaged. The second, A-OK Allweather, couldn't have been more obliging. A very chatty woman made sympathetic noises, took my particulars and offered to send a man round to assess the situation at my earliest convenience. I suggested seven that evening, asked Ant to switch the light off before he left, and was out the back door before Trish even noticed I'd been there.

As I settled into the traffic flow I began to hum a tune that had lodged in my brain and wouldn't go away. '*Bir tesselli ver*,' I crooned. I was sure I had the pronunciation right. But I couldn't for the life of me remember what it meant.

Tuesday nights meant something special for us Whelan boys. To be precise, it meant the Manager's Special at the Bell Street Pizza Hut. Hawaiian Slice with extra pineapple plus the All-You-Can-Eat Dessert Bar for only $5.95. Lucky me, eh?

The cocktail hour crowd was thin, a handful of birthday revellers in paper hats with balloons tied to the backs of their chairs. 'Grade Ones,' Red sneered dismissively as we slid into our usual booth with its panoramic view of the car park. The party table were tourists all right, lowering the tone of the joint. But to give them their due they had brought their mothers along, some of whom were a bit more interesting to look at than the artificial stag fern that constituted Mr Hut's idea of decor.

The mumsie crowd, faces half-familiar from the schoolyard gate, were jammed into a booth against the far wall, smoking, drinking white wine, and laughing too loud. When Red and I came in they looked up and watched us cross the floor and I nodded a tentative hello in their general direction. They nodded back and returned to their conversation.

One of them, a red-headed looker in the early Bette Midler mould with satellite dish earrings, held my gaze for several seconds longer than was absolutely necessary. A fellow single parent, no doubt about it. The idea that she was probably wondering who had attacked my face with a Whipper Snipper failed to occur to me.

Anyway, just as I slid my backside in next to Red and my eyes motherhoodward, my line of sight was obstructed by an adolescent waitress in a red and white pants suit that made her look like a piece of boiled confectionery. She thrust a laminated menu into my hand and in a single breath intoned that if our order did not arrive within five minutes we would not have to pay.

'Starting when?' said Red.

My heart went out to the poor girl. Some hormonal eruption had given her face the texture of a coconut macaroon. Being forced to dress up in a ludicrous corporate costume was humiliating enough without having to cop lip from every smartarse seven-year-old that walked through the door.

I elbowed Red in the ribs and ordered our usual. The instant the words departed my lips, Red whipped his sleeve back and locked in on the dial of his precision-engineered four-dollar digital timepiece. I left him to it and sauntered over to the pay phone near the door, taking the long way around, as close as plausibly possible to the group of women. The redhead looked up and gave me the eye. True, I swear it.

I fed the phone and dialled Greg Coates at Immigration and Ethnic Affairs. It was just on six, past office hours, but Coates hadn't got to be a Dep. Dir. by flexing off at 4:52. He answered on the second ring. I threw him a speedy pleasantry and cut to the chase. 'Do us a favour,' I said. 'Punch up a name for me on that computer of yours.'

Coates must have been on his way out the door. 'Can't it wait until tomorrow?'

Sure it could. But that wasn't the point. It wasn't as though I was asking for the world. All he had to do was tap a few keys and he'd be through to the departmental database in a nanosecond. If some anonymous global corporation that didn't know me from Adam could commit itself to delivering my pizza in less than five minutes, surely Greggy-boy could bend over his desk and press a couple of buttons for me. Aside from which, standing at the phone gave me a much clearer view of you know who. I gave

Coates a gentle reminder about the nature of mateship. 'You still running for the state admin. committee,' I asked.

Party rules stipulated that a member attend at least three branch meetings a year to remain current. Thus far Coates' total for the year was exactly zero. Not that there was anything unusual about that. If the attendance rules were enforced, half the office bearers in the party would have been out of a job. The reason they weren't was because they had mates like me, branch secretaries who made sure their names went down on the roll, show or no. It was the sort of thing mates did for each other. Like looking up the odd file.

'No need to get stroppy,' Coates said. 'What's the name?'

'Bayraktar,' I said. 'Ekrem.' I gave him what little detail I had from the coroner's file and listened while he made some keyboard noises.

'While you're here,' he said. 'What's your little pal Agnelli up to? He's been working the phones in a major way, I hear, but I can't get a word out of anyone he's been talking to.'

Typical Agnelli, having sworn me to secrecy on his hot election tip, here he was blabbing it to half the town. And since when had he been my little pal? I started telling Coates what Agnelli had said about the early election, and a blaze of sparklers hurtled past my shoulder. The waitress plonked a spluttering cake in the middle of the Grade Ones and a ragged chorus of 'Happy Birthday' twittered across the restaurant. The redhead, bending misty-eyed over the birthday girl, glanced upwards. Our gazes locked. No doubt about it, I was in with a chance.

'Access denied,' Coates said.

'What?'

'Access denied, that's what it says on screen. I got a folio number, so this bloke's in the system, but I can't call the file up.'

This was interesting. 'Why not?'

'Dunno. Probably just a software stuff-up.'

Computer talk was all double-dutch to me. More likely Coates was sticking it up me for getting shirty on him. Fair enough. 'I'll try again in the morning,' he offered. 'If that's soon enough for you.'

By the time I got back to the table Red had all but demolished the pizza. 'Four minutes and thirty-two seconds,' he said dismally. You'd have thought it was him who was paying.

The last of the birthday crowd was straggling out into the rapidly gathering dark with their lolly bags and balloons. I sent Red over to the dairy-whip dispenser and ambled nonchalantly over to where the birthday girl and her mother were packing presents into a shopping bag. Mumsie was about thirty, obviously a child bride. Close up, the red of her hair was shot with henna, an affectation from which I took strange encouragement.

'Hi,' I started in. 'I've seen you at the school, haven't I? I'm Red's dad.' I indicated the fruit of my loins who was engrossed in constructing a half-scale model of Mount Kilimanjaro out of aerated dairy fat.

Henna-head smiled and nodded. So far, so good. 'This is Alice,' she said. Alice looked like a proper little miss. Her mother had a squeaky little voice that sounded like a cheap fountain pen signing a bad cheque. Still, conversation wasn't the only thing I had in mind. I gave the brat a courtly bow. 'Happy birthday, Alice.' A few short years out of circulation, I thought, and I'm reduced to this.

Alice took one look and bolted. 'Daddy, Daddy,' she screamed. Daddy was coming through the door in a camel-hair overcoat and striped scarf, a tenured sociologist or a freelance travel journalist by the look of it. He gave torch-head the kind of self-deprecating look that women seem to go for. 'Darling,' she trembled.

I scuttled over to the dessert bar and fiddled with the sno-cone dispenser. From the icy mirror of its stainless steel my face stared back at me, bathed in sweaty condensation. A face like a freshly ploughed field. The face of a man who had just made an inept play for a married woman in a Pizza Hut at six-thirty on a Tuesday evening, stone cold sober. 'Phew,' I told it. 'That was close.'

'Sure was,' it replied and watched me pull myself a comforting big bowl of sugared gloop.

Red sidled up beside me. 'Nuts,' he said. 'No nuts.' So that was the problem. We took All We Could Eat back to our booth and I watched Red eat one-handed while he did the puzzles printed on his place mat. Join the Dots. Spot the Mistake. Between scoops of ice-cream he gnawed the end of his pencil and furiously scratched his head. 'Want to hear a riddle?' he asked. 'What's white and bites and lives in your head?'

I made like it took some figuring out. 'Teeth?' I hazarded.

Red crowed. 'Ha, ha. Wrong. Guess again.'

I guessed all right, amazed I hadn't thought of it before. That crawling in my scalp earlier in the day at the meatworks definitely hadn't been unconscious revulsion. Grabbing Red's head I shoved him cheek-down onto the laminex. He fought for a second, then went limp, resigned to humiliation. I pinned his head in place and ferreted through his hair. Within seconds I found the first of the tiny white specks. 'Nits,' I hissed.

Jesus wept, how had I not noticed them before? All that scratching in the night. And if Red had them, I had them too. We'd been sleeping in the same bed all winter. We paid the bill, went out into the drizzle and headlights, spent thirty minutes finding an all-hours pharmacy where we could buy flea shampoo for double the recommended retail price, and drove home to our dark and damp house. As we turned into the street, the seven o'clock news came on the radio and a flat-bed truck with A-OK Allweather painted on the door passed us going in the opposite direction.

I put Red in the bath with a foaming halo of toxic dioxins, stuffed the washing machine full of bedsheets and tipped in half a bottle of Pine-O-Cleen. Then I changed into a pair of old jeans and a moth-eaten jumper and braced myself to climb the ladder into the roof. Rain had been falling off and on for most of the preceding twenty-four hours and I guessed at least some of it had found its way past my makeshift plug.

That's when I noticed that the lounge room ceiling had changed colour. It used to be an off-white. Now it was a pale tan, the exact shade a milk arrowroot biscuit turns when you dunk it into a cup of steaming hot tea. Worse, it had developed a slight but distinct droop. Wrestling the kitchen table into the centre of the room I put a chair on top, climbed aboard, reached up and pressed the palm of my hand against the surface of the plaster at the point where it sagged lowest. It felt clammy, but firm. I pushed gently upwards. The plaster strained back against my hand. Right then, Red started screaming from the bathroom at the top of his lungs that he had shampoo in his eyes and unless I rushed in and removed it instantly he would go permanently blind.

Judging by the weight, my ceiling now housed an undercover aquatic recreation facility deep enough to drown a small mammal. But not for long. The exploratory pressure of my palm, slight as it felt, was sufficient to produce an immediate effect on the precarious hydraulic dynamics of the situation. The exact amount of water and sodden plaster that fell on top of my head at that point may never be known. It felt like a lot. And it hit me hard enough to tilt me off balance. I flailed out, looking for my equilibrium, and found the cable holding the ceiling light pendant.

It was handy, but I don't think it had been designed to be swung from. A blue spark jumped, a pop and a fizzle sounded, and the entire house was plunged into darkness. By then I was flat on my back on the floor, the light fixture in shattered pieces beside me, gungy water dripping into my open, stunned-mullet mouth.

The very moment this happened, Red's sight was miraculously restored. Being a clever kid, he immediately noticed that the lights had gone out and, lest this fact escape his rather dim father, decided to bring it to my attention. 'Dad, Dad,' he called. 'Dad. The lights have gone out. Dad, Dad.'

At that point the phone began to ring. General de Gaulle, it is said, permitted no telephone within earshot of his office in the Elysee Palace. Not for him the presumptuous summons of some anonymous jangling bell. I wished I had his singlemindedness. I stumbled through the blackness, dripping and twitching like a half-drowned Labrador, following the siren wail of Red's voice.

'Dad, Dad,' he was chanting. 'Dad. The phone's ringing. Dad, Dad.'

'Shut the fuck up,' I screamed reassuringly in the general direction of my only child as I grabbed the phone. STD pips sounded. Either it was the prime minister calling to offer me a place in Cabinet or Wendy calling from Canberra.

'Oh, it's you,' said Wendy.

I took a deep breath, shook a couple of litres of filthy water out of my sleeve and counted to five. 'Red's in the bath,' I wheezed, calmness itself. 'I'll get him to call you when he gets out, if you'll still be there.' Meaning the office, the flat, wherever she was calling from. A busy woman is always on the hop.

'What do you mean, if I'm here? You're the one who's never there.'

'What do you mean, never here? Never where?' It was all going swimmingly, so far.

'Don't worry about it,' she said in a tone that meant I should do precisely that. 'I know how much he enjoys his bath.' Unlike his cruel father who would drag him out at a moment's notice to come to the phone. 'Tell him I'll see him on Thursday. I'll be down for a few days for the Construction of Gender Reference Group. And maybe you and I should have a bit of a talk then, too.'

'We're talking now, aren't we?'

'You know what I mean.'

I guessed I did.

'You've got to think about Red,' she added, gratuitously. Was I right in imagining the Methodist Ladies College was resurfacing in her voice, that censorious interrogative at the end of sentences? 'And don't worry, I'll be staying at Mum's.'

So, it was out in the open at last. 'Okay,' I said meekly. Let her think I was ready to throw in the towel even before the fight began, that was my strategy. Then when the bell rang, come out fighting.

Wendy was booked on a two o'clock flight and told me she'd go straight to Red's school to pick him up. That's what she thought. Let Red out of my sight and the next time I'd see him would be on a monthly access visit.

I lit a candle and inspected the damage. As well as the roof problem, I now had a gaping hole in my lounge room ceiling and a severely shorted-out lighting circuit. Nothing that several thousand dollars I didn't have couldn't fix. I took the candle into the bathroom, stripped off my clothes, climbed into the tub and sank my fingers into Red's scalp, rubbing until their tips were numb and both of us were limp with hysterical exhaustion. 'Mum will be here the day after tomorrow,' I said.

'I know.'

'She wants you to stay in Canberra with her.'

'I know.'

Knowledgeable little bugger. I wondered what else he knew, but decided to leave well enough alone, for the time being at least.

We sat on the edge of the big bed wrapped in towels and he let me comb the dead nits out of his hair by the light of a lamp plugged into the power circuit. Half an hour of nit-picking produced a dozen white pinheads, a couple of dead insects and a child as limber as a rag doll. I engineered Red into his pyjamas, slipped him into the freshly made bed and waited quietly until he was abducted by the sandman. His locks, drying around his drowsy face in corkscrew ringlets, gave him the aspect of a Botticelli cherub.

I took my own scarified dial out into the black hole that was the laundry, rubbed some of the creosote-smelling flea wash into my scalp, pulled on some clean-dirty clothes and went to work.

Navigating by the light coming in the window from old Mrs Bagio's sleepout next door, I rolled the lounge room rug into a squelching cylinder. It was a tribal kilim, a little something Wendy had picked up in India, way before my time. I dragged it to the back door and pitched it into the yard, managing to snap off her *Grevillea robusta* at ground level into the bargain. Then I used newspapers to mop up the grimy dribble trickling down from above. I did this somewhat reluctantly as the only papers I could find were several dozen back copies of the *National Times* and the *Guardian Weekly* I had been warehousing against the day I got a federal grant to catch up on my reading.

Take my tip. Never use the *Guardian* for this sort of work. The flimsy airmail paper has practically no absorbency. The *National Times*, on the other hand, would soak up practically anything. It was a pity to waste them and I worked slowly, giving the copy the quick once-over in the candlelight as I reluctantly discarded the pages, catching up on a couple of Royal Commissions as I went.

The worst of the wet was just soaking into a ten-page piece on the roots of monogamy when a feature in the finance section from the previous July caught my eye. The article was headed 'Darlings of the Market'. It was a safe bet that this did not refer to the Trash'n'Treasure conducted at the Coburg Drive-In every third Sunday. Below the headline was a row of photographs of well-barbered male faces sporting expressions that suggested butter might safely be stored in their mouths. Among them was a head I recognised from earlier that morning when I had seen it attached to the body of Lionel Merricks. I took the paper over to the window and held it up to the light.

Lionel Merricks, according to the introductory blurb, was one of the new breed of knock-'em-down drag-'em-out financiers who were cutting a dash through the currency desks with their bold visions of an untrammelled tomorrow. Spread across two pages were illustrated profiles of Lionel and his fellow high rollers, the text even more gushing than the crap coming out of my ceiling. I don't know what these guys were doing for the economy, but they excited the hell out of the media. Normally I gave this sort of thing a wide berth. But, now that I knew one of these objects of veneration personally, I read on, fascinated.

Young Lionel, it said, had displayed early promise, making book for the upper sixth at Grammar before doing his patriotic stint as a naval supply officer. A blurry photo illustrated this moment, Lionel all white socks and knobbly knees. Barely out of uniform and here he was, the up-and-coming executive, a divisional GM at Ayers Land and Livestock, back before they merged with ICU Resources to form Pacific Pastoral. Here was the mature Lionel coming aboard the board, here Lucky Lionel in the chair. Finally here were Lionel's visionary plans to haul the ladder up after him and flog off those components of the company currently encumbered by the tiresome necessity of actually growing, making or trading things. The time had come, he declared, to concentrate on the basics. What, I wondered, was more basic than killing animals and cutting them up for food?

Only towards the end of the page did a sour note intrude. The speed of Pacific Pastoral's asset rationalisation, warned the last paragraph, might be hampered by market concerns at the threat to the value of its meat export operations posed by...*continued on page 47.*

Page forty-seven was a sodden mass, somewhere underfoot, lost in the dark. I searched for it briefly and gave up. Finance was beyond me, and the increasing frequency with which we were bombarded with updates on Dow Jones and the All-Ordinaries had done nothing to enlighten me. Three billion, six billion, nine point eight billion. The press was full of these incomprehensible figures. All it appeared to take to be hailed as a major player was to pick a digit, stick a dollar sign in front of it, add a long row of zeros and wait for the applause.

Some financial wizard, this Merricks. An Anatolian fatso who could barely sign his own name had, in all probability, been tickling his till to the tune of two grand a week and hadn't even been noticed. But that was the point though, wasn't it? Not noticing. All the puny fiddles of all the world's Ekrem Bayraktars would never amount to more than a drop in the vast ocean of moolah that Captain Merricks and his crew of Old Grammarians blithely sailed upon.

And if the Premier, Agnelli, Charlene or anyone else thought they could quietly slip aboard the good ship Big Bucks and run their social agenda up the mast when nobody was looking, they were flattering themselves. Merricks and the rest of his class were no fools. They'd been repelling boarders since back before their great-grandfathers had sailed through the Heads with an axe in one hand and a blank title deed in the other. From high in their glass towers, they could see us coming a mile away.

I dropped Lionel Merricks face first into a damp patch and climbed up into the roof for a spot of damage control. The overalls, heavy with rainwater, had fallen out and knocked over the bucket, possibly as far back as the night before. Using rags and plastic bags I made the best of a bad job, trusting in luck, a change in the weather and the speedy return of A-OK Allweather. Afterwards, I stood in the dark with my head in the laundry tub and washed the parasites out of my hair. Then I went to bed and read *Understanding Family Law* until the words began to blur together, turned off the light, rolled over and parked my lustful dromedary in the caravanserai of dreams.

Two uniformed coppers, one male, one female, with the faces of twelve-year-olds and big revolvers jammed next to their kidneys, were standing at Trish's desk when I pushed the office door open the next morning. During the night someone had prised the bars off the outside of the dunny window, smashed the glass, climbed in and ransacked the joint. Why they bothered to do this beggared the imagination. The most valuable items in the place were the photocopier and a four-drawer filing cabinet, both of which were still sitting against the wall beside Trish's desk.

The only thing missing was the petty cash tin, containing a dozen thirty-seven cent stamps and an IOU from the week before when I'd raided it for lunch money. Total value twelve dollars.

'Anything else?' said the girl cop, doodling details onto a triplicate incident sheet. I went up the back to count my paperclips. Everything on my desk had been bulldozed into a heap on the floor, the drawers rifled and my wastepaper basket upended. By the look of it, nothing was missing. Worse luck.

'You think it's politically motivated?' the boy cop said.

'It's got Baader-Meinhof written all over it,' I said.

'Kids, most likely, then,' he agreed.

Well it wasn't the gang from Mensa, that was for sure. It took me a full minute to work out that the thing drawn on the toilet mirror was a dick. While I was still standing there in a pile of broken glass, who should walk in but Adam Fucking Ant. He put a toolbox on the toilet seat and began slipping new panes of reinforced glass into the louvre slots.

'What's he still doing here?' I went out and asked Trish.

'Making himself a damned sight more useful than you,' she said and stuffed a fresh batch of phone messages into my paw. Declining to rise to this bait, I went back to my cubicle and rummaged through the mess on the floor until I found the yellow slip from the day before with A-OK Allweather's number. I dialled, hoping that last night's little timing glitch had not put me in bad odour with them. They were engaged. So was the other mob. No sooner had I hung up than the phone rang. Guess who?

'Well?' said Agnelli.

By that stage, considering the more pressing domestic disasters I was battling, any lingering curiosity about Ekrem Bayraktar and the goings-on at Pacific Pastoral had well and truly evaporated.

'Just like I said it would be,' I told Agnelli. 'Nothing to connect Lollicato to anyone at the Coolaroo plant. And even if there was, industrially the place is as dead as a dodo. On top of which nobody out there has a good word for the dead bloke, who by the way was probably on the fiddle in at least two different directions at once. In short, a total fucking waste of time. All of which will be in an appropriately worded report on your desk at the close of play today, as promised. End of story. Full stop.'

Predictably, Agnelli had to put up a fight. 'Half a day, Murray, is not what you might call an exhaustive approach to the issue.'

I got down on my hands and knees on the floor and began searching the desk debris for the Pacific Pastoral file. If I could find that list of bogus names—Gherkin Marzipan, Cartoon Niblet and the rest of them—I could send Agnelli off chasing his own tail around the Trades Hall while I got on with the more urgent task of repairing my near-derelict hacienda.

'And what about the funeral?' Agnelli was saying.

'What?' I was buggered if I could find the bloody folder.

'Dead bloke's funeral. Mood of the crowd and so forth, always a good indicator in this sort of case.' Agnelli sounded like he'd been watching too much television. The idea was bizarre.

I had six months worth of paperwork spread out across the carpet tiles by this stage. Still I couldn't find the fucking file. Worse, I was starting to listen to Agnelli. And that, believe you me, is never a good idea. 'Who did they release the body to?'

'Stuffed if I know,' said Agnelli. 'Family, I suppose.'

As far as I knew from the coroner's documents there wasn't one. 'Who's doing the honours?'

'Martinelli.'

'I thought Martinelli only did Italians.'

'Martinelli will bury anyone. Believe me, mate,' he said. As if he'd know. 'It's listed for ten at Fawkner. Call me back afterwards and we can discuss the report then.'

That's what he thought. Personally speaking, I had better things to do with my time than go tramping about a cemetery in the rain looking for a scene out of a social realist movie. Things like getting my desk back into some sort of order and finding a roofer and an electrician. I was thumbing through the phone book with exactly that in mind when there was a knock at the partition and Xenophon Xypnitos from the community health centre came in and opened his briefcase.

This appointment had been in my diary for a month, so there was no getting out of it. On top of which Trish's crack about my recent absence had been quite correct. It was about time I got back to doing what I was being paid for. In this case it meant reviewing the terms of reference for a survey of projected needs in the provision of health services to the aged. Charlene had swung the funding and the consultants were being paid a small fortune, the sort of money you don't fork over unless you know the results in advance. I got up off the floor, apologised for the mess and started talking service delivery.

By the time Xenophon closed his briefcase it was just about to go ten. Fawkner Cemetery was only a kilometre or two up the road. I rang Martinelli's funeral home and commemorative chapel and got directions to the plot. The interment, as they called it, was imminent. Questions about who was paying for it were politely deflected.

Before I left I quickly drafted the final version of my report to MACWAM, concluding that there was no evidence of incipient industrial action at the Pacific Pastoral plant. I gave it to Trish to type and put in the internal courier. If Agnelli thought I was going to spend any more time on this crap than absolutely necessary, he was mistaken.

The outlook that Wednesday was for showers, with fresh to strong westerly winds ahead of a change, a gale warning for the bays, and a sheep weather alert in southern and mountain districts. I didn't have any sheep worth alerting. I took my collapsible umbrella instead. Three blocks up the highway a sign read Mulqueen and Sons, Funeral Directors. Underneath it said *Provinciale Servizio Italiano.* Weren't the Irish dying fast enough? Or were they all dead already? They might as well be. Once upon a time party and union rolls in this town read like the Ballymalarkey baptismal register and the sons of Erin cut some ice. But those days were long gone, thanks to the Church and the Left and about a thousand boatloads of Thracians and Piedmontese.

An arrow said Necropolis Next Left. A nice democratic town, Necroburg. Catholics, Orthodox, Muslims, Christadelphians, all bedded down together in the sprawling suburbs of the dead. Along Box Forest Road, the forest of yellow boxes long replaced by the tin sheds of cut-price monumental masons, I found what I was looking for. In a muddy paddock backing onto the railway line a silver-grey Martinelli hearse was drawn up beside the customary dark rectangle. Two pallbearers sat in the cabin catching a quick puff before the mourners arrived.

A singularly dismal sight it would have been, too, if not for an incongruous splash of colour against the yellow clay of the earth. Draped over the coffin was a piece of scarlet fabric. A flag. A red flag. The people's flag of deepest red. That which shrouded oft our martyred dead. On top of the flag was a modest wreath of white carnations. It looked like Agnelli was right, the union would be bunging it on in no uncertain terms.

I cruised once more around the little ring-road and fell in with a cortege just arriving at the grassy area opposite. I parked unnoticed in clear view of the Bayraktar plot. A light drizzle began falling and the pallbearers got into the cabin of the hearse. I turned off my engine and waited.

Teardrops of vapour emerged out of the mist forming on the inside of the windscreen, swelled, and tumbled slowly downwards. I wound down my window and the sound of weeping women came softly across the lawn beside me. Short vertical lengths of pipe had been sunk into the grass to make recessed vases. Here and there, little posies of mixed flowers sprouted straight up out of the turf, cellophane and all. Gradually it came to me that this was where they buried the children. I quickly looked away.

A car had pulled up over near the hearse and two men were getting out. I knew immediately they were not union officials. For a start their clothes fitted them properly, expensive-looking overcoats protecting well-cut suits. Also, the car was a recent model BMW, sleek in the rain. The two were heavy set, and crossed the field of mud with a business-like sense of purpose. There was no doubt that they were compatriots of the deceased. Rather well-heeled ones by the look of the togs and the wheels.

The Martinelli crew had dumped their fags and settled into postures of respectful solicitude by the time the pair reached the graveside. Muted words were exchanged and heads bobbed all round. I bent forward and wiped a hole in the condensation. The pallbearers withdrew a little and the two dark-haired men stood together and faced the coffin, their backs to me. Then, and this part really made me sit up and take notice, they snapped to attention and executed a couple of brisk, well-practised military salutes. They stood like that, elbows rigid, immobile in the soft rain, for perhaps fifteen seconds.

Then, as if at an invisible signal, the arms descended and the shorter one bent and picked the white carnation wreath up off the casket. He handed it up to his companion who read the card then tossed the whole thing like a frisbee onto the green carpet covering the mound of dirt beside the grave. Meanwhile the first guy had grabbed a handful of the flag and was hauling it towards him like a waiter changing a dirty tablecloth. As he swept the fabric into his arms, I caught a flash of white, a crescent moon and a star. Bayraktar was being laid to rest not under the ruby standard of the workers of the world, but beneath the banner of Ataturk.

The flag was swiftly folded and the coffin disappeared into the earth. The mystery men put their erect carriages into the BMW and drove away. It was all over in less than two minutes. Not exactly a state funeral, but honours of some sort, honours I was prepared to bet were not for services to humanity.

Mustapha closer look at this, I told myself. As soon as the BMW was out of sight and the Martinelli hearse had driven off, I put up my umbrella and squelched across to the hole. The box stared up at me silently, not the budget model either, by the look of the silver handles. The card on the wreath read 'RIP— Management and Staff, Pacific Pastoral'.

So much for family feeling. The pricks hadn't even sent someone to the funeral. The union hadn't showed either, but that was arguably grounds for relief. The first sight of that red flag had me worried, if only that Agnelli was about to be proven right. But a union like the Meaties, with probably twenty thousand blokes on the books, could hardly be expected to turn out every time a member fell off his perch. They'd never get any work done. Not that you'd notice. On the other hand, a company the size of Pacific Pastoral sending fifteen bucks worth of carnations to the interment of a man who died on the job, that was just plain lousy. It wasn't as though they knew he was ripping them off, after all. It was just plain contempt, pure and simple.

Bayraktar might have been a fat pig with sticky fingers and some pretty dodgy-looking militaristic friends, but so what? The same could be said of the federal Minister for Defence Procurements. A principle was at stake here. A man carks it *in situ*, the least the management can do is send a representative to stand at the graveside and pay the widow the courtesy of some hypocrisy, should she happen to be there. It didn't have to be the chairman of the board, that would be too much to expect. But they could have sent along the third assistant deputy under-boss. Where was Apps, that gangling streak of officiousness?

Merricks had insisted that I keep him appraised. Well, appraised he would be. Appraised of incompetence in the administration of his Coolaroo plant's payroll. Call me bloody-minded, but one member of Pacific Pastoral's management at least would be made to rue the day he hadn't taken half an hour off to whip down the highway and shed some crocodile tears over the coffin of a recently defunct employee. A quick phone call to the CEO's office describing the discrepancies I had discovered in the administration of the payroll, and the company auditors would be running their fingers through Apps' books before you could say 'performance indicators'.

'Headstones from $395,' yelled a sandwich board at the exit. There were more pressing demands on my finances. An electrician, I figured, would set me back about sixty dollars to get the light working, which would be a lot to pay to have a fuse replaced and listen to a sales pitch about how the whole place needed rewiring. Still, if anyone was going to get electrocuted, I preferred it to be an accredited and fully insured tradesman. The cost of a new roof I didn't even want to think about, let alone the prospect of wringing half of it out of Wendy, present circumstances considered.

Rather than dwell on the ugly subject of money I did not have, I turned my thoughts to the strange obeisances I had just witnessed at Bayraktar's graveside. Some of Labor's all-but-forgotten heroes and heroines were buried here and I could imagine what they might have said if they knew foreign military types were goose-stepping among their headstones. Was that grey BMW, I wondered, the same one I had seen parked under the carport at the Anatolia Club, a place Sivan described enigmatically as somewhere to be avoided?

Since I had to pass the Turkish Welfare League anyway, it would only take a couple of extra minutes to pop in and see what light the encyclopaedic Kurd could shed on the subject. And with a bit of luck Ayisha would be there, too.

I found Sivan pinned down behind his desk, his palms spread defensively in front of his chest. 'Ah, Murray, my friend.' He leapt to his feet, like I was the foreign legion come to relieve the fort. 'Meet Muyesser, Hatice, Huriet.'

Muyesser was a classic crone in a shapeless floor-length skirt and head-scarf who looked like she'd come straight from offering Snow White a poisoned apple. Her two offsiders were younger and not as conspicuously folkloric. They were busy giving Sivan a hard time and had no intention of being taken in by his transparent diversionary ploy. They stopped their hectoring only long enough to nod in my general direction, then resumed talking over each other and waving pieces of official-looking correspondence. Somewhere in the incomprehensible torrent I clearly heard the phrase 'Taxation Department'.

Parked next to one of the women was a stroller out of which a toddler was attempting to writhe his way to freedom. His hair was cropped to the bone, his burning little cheeks varnished to a high gloss with fresh snot. Poor Sivan slumped back into his seat, resigned.

Better you than me, mate, I thought. This situation was a perfect example of why I was such a keen supporter of funding for the League. If Sivan hadn't been here, available to have the shit annoyed out of him in an appropriate community language, these three wicked stepsisters would have been half a mile down the road annoying the shit out of me in broken English. More better this way.

I cocked my head in the general direction of Ayisha's office and raised my eyebrows.

'With a client,' Sivan semaphored over the din.

While I was waiting, I helped myself to the spare desk, dialled directory assistance and got the number for Pacific Pastoral's head office. The call bounced upwards off a series of buffers until it reached the forty-ninth floor. I could hear the well-coiffured hair of the ice queen turn at the sound of my voice, but she put me through without argument. Merricks came on briskly, the great man's time still too valuable to squander on courtesy. 'Well?'

The jabber of Turkish across the room increased in volume. I stuck a finger in one ear. 'Something a little outside my terms of reference has come up,' I said. 'But since you asked to be kept informed, I thought I should share it with you.'

'Yes.' Spit it out, man. Time is money.

'It concerns irregularities that have come to my attention concerning your operations at Coolaroo.'

Merricks took this on board and walked it around the deck a couple of times. 'Irregularities? What sort of irregularities?' His peevishness register had dropped a notch.

'I'm not an accountant, Mr Merricks,' I said blandly.

'But you are implying some sort of dishonesty?'

'As I said, I'm merely keeping you appraised of my observations,' I said. And having a jolly good time of it, too.

'Look here, Whelan.' The strangulated English squeak was back in Merricks' voice. 'I'm beginning to have very serious reservations about this whole exercise. Is your minister aware that you have taken it upon yourself to start tossing about these sort of vague inferences?'

I'd expected the darling of the markets to greet the news that he was being diddled with some degree of scepticism, perhaps even to question my motives. But at least he could have shown a little more curiosity about what exactly it was I was alleging before issuing a barely veiled threat to dob me in to Charlene. I should have known that managerial caste loyalties always took priority. What a pompous arsehole, I thought. Stuff you, Charley.

'Listen, Lionel,' I said, dropping all pretence at deference. 'If you prefer I could always bring this matter directly to the attention of the appropriate authorities. Frankly I don't give a fuck either way.'

Just as I was beginning to think Merricks had hung up on me, he spoke. 'I understand,' he said, his words measured and full of meaning.

The toddler in the stroller had given up trying to escape and was navigating his way around the room by dragging himself along the furniture. He advanced steadily towards me, hand over hand along any object within reach, blowing elastic bubbles of mucus ahead of him as he came. I fended him off with a tissue.

'Do you have a figure in mind?' Merricks was saying.

All I had was a list of Turkish celebrities, and I wasn't even sure where that was anymore. But I certainly wasn't going to tell Lionel Merricks that. I realised I should have taken the trouble to think the whole thing out before I placed the call. It was beginning to feel like a lot of trouble to go to just for the sake of getting a rocket fired up some crappy plant manager I'd only met for five minutes.

But since I was in this deep, I thought I might as well lay it on with a trowel. 'Fifty thousand,' I said. 'Maybe more, depending on what else turns up.'

'Now wait a minute.' Merricks seemed to be struggling with his emotions.

It was then that the kid dragged the telephone cord out of its socket. Ripped it right off the wall, plug and all. The phone went dead in my hand. By the time I had extracted the cord from one sticky little fist and plugged it back in, all that remained of Lionel Merricks was a dial tone. Which was just as well, because one of the women had taken it upon herself to whack the wretched mite so firmly across the knuckles that the only thing Merricks would have been able to hear was a high-pitched wail. Fuck him, I thought. Merricks, not the kid.

Despite the decibels being emitted by the child, Sivan's conference with the harpies was continuing unabated. The expression 'Supporting Mother's Benefit' was now cropping up with some frequency. I decided on a tactical withdrawal in the direction of Ayisha's office. The door was shut. I tapped lightly and poked my head inside. Ayisha was in professional mode, leaning intently forward on her elbows, giving her full attention to something being said in Turkish by a man in a sports coat sitting with his back to the door. 'Sorry to barge in,' I began.

The man stopped talking and swung around, irritated at the intrusion. He had thick curly hair and a self-important, intellectual air. I almost didn't recognise him without his shower cap and white overalls. Away from the harsh artificial light of the meat works, his face had lost its ghastly jaundice. Like this, a cheap tie knotted at his neck and a grace note of grey at his high temples, he could have been a professor of history. But no doubt about it, it was Whatsisname, the cleaner from Pacific Pastoral.

He recognised me immediately, too. And our little chat the day before had clearly made a deep impression on him. Either that or he wasn't quite the full felafel. In rapid succession, he uncrossed his knees, lurched to his feet, and stumbled backwards, knocking over his chair. His eyes filled with betrayed disbelief and began furiously darting about the room.

'Hi,' I said.

The cleaner looked daggers at Ayisha. If she had any better idea than I did what was going on, she wasn't showing it. Getting no response, he came to a rapid decision. He extracted his legs from the tangle of fallen furniture, marshalled his dignity, drew himself upright and advanced towards the doorway. When he was almost on top of me, he clenched his fists and thrust his arms forward, wrists pressed together. 'Yes. It was me,' he cried. 'I killed Bayraktar.'

I didn't know whether to spit, shit, or go blind. This was a joke, right? How could this broom pusher have killed Bayraktar? He hadn't even rated a mention in the documentation. Christ, I couldn't even remember his name. 'Huh?' I heard myself say.

I looked across at Ayisha, but she wasn't laughing. If anything, she had gone a little grey around the gills. I looked back at the guy in the sports coat and searched his face for some clue, some skerrick of explanation as to the meaning of these theatrics. The bland, self-effacing look that had sat so naturally across his features the day before had been replaced with an intensity that was almost incandescent. He pumped his fists forward again, insisting on being handcuffed.

Up the corridor behind me came the wailing of the snotty tot and the background jabber of Sivan's case work. I stepped around the door to enter the office properly, and the cleaner reeled back before me as though expecting a blow.

'Go on,' he challenged. 'Arrest me, Mr Policeman.'

Well, that got a laugh, thank Christ. I was beginning to think all the oxygen had been hoovered out of the room.

The laugh came from Ayisha, a high nervy snigger. Then she said something in Turkish, a curt little sentence, the immediate upshot of which was that her client suddenly looked like a horse had kicked him. The ominous glow disappeared from his eyes, replaced by a rather touching look of bewilderment. His gaze dropped to his hands, as though he now had serious doubts about their ownership. His fingers were long and fine, the skin that covered them shiny with scar tissue. He stuck them rapidly into his pockets and a single eloquent word that needed no translation escaped his lips. 'Shit,' he said.

Too late, pal. 'You killed Bayraktar?' I said. 'How?'

But the fire was dying. The man turned, hauled his chair back upright, sat down with an audible oomph, and covered his face with his hands. Ayisha came out from behind her desk, firing me a questioning look. When I shrugged she went down on one knee at the man's elbow and began whispering in Turkish. First he just sat there with his shoulders hunched, slowly shaking his head. Eventually she extracted a couple of reluctant monosyllables. She persisted, persuading him to lower his hands. Then began a hushed and insistent tide of explanation.

From the man's sideways glances I could tell that at least part of the time he was talking about me. Why they were whispering, I didn't know. I couldn't understand a word they were saying, after all. After a while I began to feel like a bit of a geek, standing there with my back to the door, so I went across and sat down behind Ayisha's desk. Whatever it was she was saying, it seemed to be doing the trick. The guy looked across at me a couple of times in a half-apologetic sort of way, like we were strangers in a pub and he'd just knocked over my beer and we were waiting for the barman to bring me another.

I still hadn't been able to shave, and my whiskers were at that stage where they itch like nobody's business. I sat there trying not to scratch, wondering what the hell was going on. Ayisha's tobacco was sitting on the desk. I opened the packet and rolled myself a cigarette to keep my hands busy. Out of solidarity with Wendy I'd given up smoking when Red was on the way, and my rolling technique was now a bit rusty. The best I could manage was a lumpy little greyhound with lots of brown threads sticking out the end.

By the time I'd finished carefully prodding the loose fibres of tobacco into place, Ayisha and the cleaner—his name was Memo, I remembered, Memo Gezen—had been whispering away in front of me forever. I was beginning to feel a little excluded. So I leaned forward on my elbows and struck a match. It flared dramatically, erupting into the tide of Turkish and bringing it to a halt. 'Don't mind me,' I said.

For want of an equally spectacular follow-up, I put the flame to the end of the fag and sucked in. The smoke hit deep—a dirty, forbidden, anarchic, exhilarating taste. My head spun and the tips of my fingers tingled. 'Feel free to chat among yourselves,' I exhaled.

Ayisha got up and sat on the edge of the desk. 'It's all a misunderstanding, Murray,' she said. 'Memo here thought you were a cop. I've straightened him out. I told him you're okay, and you wouldn't dob him in. You won't, will you?'

If anyone else had asked I might have taken offence. Memo had perked up somewhat by this stage. He was positively cheerful, in fact. Obviously Ayisha had convinced him that she could put the genie back in the bottle. 'So you didn't kill Bayraktar at all?' I asked him.

Convinced that he was safe from immediate arrest, Gezen obviously felt some need to explain his weird behaviour. He fished a packet of Winfield out his jacket pocket, lit one, and gave me a what-the-hell look. 'I locked him in the freezer and he perished,' he blurted, half in remorse, half in defiance.

Perished? I wasn't sure whether to laugh or congratulate him on the improvement in his vocabulary over the preceding twenty-four hours. Terrific word, perished. So apposite. Very Scott of the Antarctic. Gezen's accent was much lighter, too.

Ayisha was off the mark like a bush lawyer. 'It was an accident,' she snapped. 'Besides, the guy was a thug. He deserved to die.'

I held up one hand. 'You don't have to tell me anything, you know that, Memo.'

He nodded, looked to Ayisha for confirmation and nodded again, almost eagerly. He didn't have to, but he wanted to. Something was bothering his conscience and he wanted to clear the air. He had a dose of the Raskolnikovs real bad, and he wasn't going to let either me or Ayisha stand in his way. 'I was angry,' he said. 'Bayraktar, he called me a mountain Turk.'

Hardly grounds for homicide, one would think. I raised my eyebrows. 'Are we losing something in the translation here?'

'It's what right-wingers call the Kurds,' Ayisha explained. 'Memo here's a Kurd.'

Naturally. Any more Kurds weighed in around here and you could start a cheese factory.

'The money,' she said irritably, as though Gezen was a slow child. 'Tell him about the money.'

Now that he had stopped hyperventilating, Gezen was practically garrulous. 'Forty dollars a week. He said I must give him forty dollars a week or he will say I am stealing. I get sack. Jail maybe.' He hastened to add, 'I am not a thief.'

At Pacific Pastoral? Heaven forbid.

'He should have told us here at the League,' Ayisha butted in. 'We'da fixed the prick.' I waved her into silence, lest she break the spell. This was all just too fascinating. 'So you locked him in the freezer and he perished?'

'No,' said Gezen. 'I paid. More than two thousand dollars he took from me. Then, last week, he wants more. Fifty dollars a week. Inflation, he says. And all the time he calls me these insults.' He dragged his chair closer to the desk, going into a kind of confidential huddle as he got to the good part.

'That is when I think I will lock him in the freezer. But not to kill him. That was not my....'

At last his English faltered. He searched for the right word, vibrating with frustration. He used a Turkish word, glancing again at Ayisha.

'Intention,' she said. She'd obviously heard this bit before.

'I meant only to frighten him. Then I would rescue him. Understand?'

Not really, I didn't. Well, sort of. It seemed a rather fraught way to win friends and influence people, but I could see a sort of desperate logic at work. 'But something went wrong?' I said. The roll-your-own was a greasy brown stub in my fingers. As I butted it out Gezen hurried to offer me a fresh tailor-made. Out of courtesy and not wanting to interrupt his momentum I accepted, but didn't light it. It's not like I was really a smoker.

I could see what Gezen was doing. He was enlisting an ally. The Australian, the government official, on the other side of the desk must be made to understand exactly what had happened, must be won over.

'What I do is this. From the beginning I watch him. He does not see me, but always I watch. I see everything. What I see is this. Every Friday, just before knock-off time, he goes to Number 3 freezer. He looks to see that nobody watches, then he goes inside, two maybe three minutes. It is very cold inside, you understand. Ten minutes and a man will die.'

Yes, I recalled. A more than unusually nippy spot.

'So last Friday, after lunch, I move a forklift truck so it is parked against the emergency exit. This is not allowed, but it happens all the time. Nobody notices. Then when Bayraktar goes inside.' He mimed the snapping of a padlock. 'I lock the door.'

Gezen's speech had taken on a vivid present-tense intensity. I remembered the cigarette in my hand and lit it. It was insipid, but I drew deep anyway.

Gezen went on. 'I wait one minute, two, three. Bayraktar will be very frightened. Soon I will open the door. Then the other one comes.'

'Other one?'

'The mechanic, Gardening.'

It was hard not to laugh. He was trying so hard. 'Gardiner?'

'Yes. I do not think he will come so soon. He unlocks the door and goes inside. Quickly I move the forklift away. Still Gardiner is inside, long time, six or seven minutes. Then he leaves and I look inside. Bayraktar is there, perished. Then Gardiner comes back with the boss. Ambulance comes. Police. They ask if I saw something. I say nothing.'

Gezen shrugged, laying his offering at my feet. Take it or leave it. Smoke rose from the cigarette folded into the cup of his hand, the filter squeezed between forefinger and thumb. His fingers were fragile, a pianist's or a surgeon's. He followed my gaze downwards and rolled his wrist, the better to display the translucent veneer of hardened scar. Was this an appeal for sympathy, I wondered, or somehow part of the story.

Ayisha broke the silence. 'People's justice. Self defence. Whadda ya reckon, Murray?'

What I reckoned was that the sooner I got myself out of there the better. Gezen's yarn had less internal logic than a Democrat campaign promise. Trying to follow the who did what to whom part had been hard enough, let alone the other questions that sprang to mind. And Gezen himself, hysterical one moment, sucking calmly on a fag the next. Was he telling the truth or weaving some bizarre, self-justifying fable?

Not only was this impromptu little confession unintelligible, it was unwelcome. My plans for a strategic withdrawal from all this Pacific Pastoral bullshit were rapidly coming undone. I was already regretting my little chat on the phone with Merricks. He had probably immediately called Agnelli, or even Charlene, to bitch about me. If giving cheek to a captain of industry wasn't bad enough, here I was involving the office of a minister of the crown in some sort of ethnic criminal extortion revenge murder mystery caper. Shit, the *Sun* would have a field day.

On the other hand, there was Ayisha. She was sitting on the edge of the desk, her eyes blazing conspiratorially. Excited. Impatient. Come on, they seemed to say. Impress me with your masterly command of the situation. Let's fix this together, the two of us.

Come across as some sort of pen-pushing apparatchik and I could cancel forever my hopes of forging a bedroom alliance here. 'What else do you know about this?' I asked her.

'Nothing. Dead set,' she swore, looking to Gezen to back her up. 'This is the first time I've seen Memo in months.' Gezen nodded confirmation. 'He came in out of the blue about twenty minutes ago. Said the cops were after him. Wouldn't say what for. Said he wanted to give himself up. Then you stuck your head through the door and he chucked a mental and started talking about killing someone. Reckoned you were a cop.' Gezen was trying his best to look chastened, not entirely succeeding. 'You gotta help sort this thing out, Murray,' Ayisha pleaded. 'Memo can't go to prison. It'd kill him.'

I helped myself to one of Gezen's cigarettes and turned the

situation over in my mind. For a start, a confession of murder would be welcomed by nobody. The official coronial enquiry was still months away, but if the documents Agnelli had slipped me were accurate, a finding of natural causes was a foregone conclusion. The cops and the Labour Department investigators were unanimous. They'd look like a proper pack of idiots if it turned out to have been murder. The Department of Labour was probably already busy drafting amendments to the legislation on mandatory aisle widths. Pacific Pastoral had just said good riddance, said it with flowers. In short, unless some new evidence turned up, nobody would want Bayraktar's death to be anything other than it appeared to be.

Maybe Bayraktar deserved what he got, maybe not. The idea that he was conducting a bit of extortion in the workplace wasn't at all inconsistent with what I already knew about him. Maybe Memo Gezen had meant to kill him, maybe not. He didn't seem the homicidal type, if there was any such thing. And if he could live with the consequences of his actions, I certainly could, at least until someone better qualified to judge came along. What the guy needed was a bit of decent legal advice. 'Know any lawyers?' I asked Ayisha.

'There's a firm we refer our compo cases to,' she said, moving around the desk. 'You want the number?'

A workers' compensation specialist wouldn't be an ideal first choice in a case like this, but she had given me an idea. A lawyer was a lawyer, after all. Client confidentiality and all that. 'I know someone,' I said. 'Top gun. He'll be keen to help.' He'd better be, I thought. It was him who got me into this shit in the first place. 'But first, I need some assurances. For a start, this conversation never took place. Not a word to anyone until you hear back from me. Understood?' Their heads bobbed, corks on a rising tide. Ayisha was having the time of her life. 'No more confessing, okay Memo?' Gezen bowed his head sheepishly. 'Act normal. Go to work as usual. Do nothing to attract attention to yourself. Sit pat. Do not contact me. Ayisha will be in touch. Understand?'

'But the poliss.'

'Don't worry about the police,' I said. 'Right now, I don't think they suspect anything. Even if they change their minds, they still have to make a case against you. You'll be okay as long as you keep your mouth shut. Presumption of innocence and all that.'

'Presumption?' said Gezen. 'What means 'presumption'?'

'It means you got away with it, Memo,' said Ayisha, cheerfully defying me to contradict her.

But Gezen still had a problem. 'Why do the police watch me, then?' he said.

The guy's bad conscience was certainly working overtime. I must have done a poor job concealing this thought. Gezen's eyes flared again, the weirdness back in evidence. Then he was up, heading out the door. We found him staring down the passage. 'There,' he gestured.

The three women and their yowling child had gone. Sivan was deep in a phone conversation, bent low, taking careful notes. Gezen jerked his head again. I stepped in front of him, following the line indicated through the plate-glass window, out into the street. Across the road in front of my Renault two dark-suited men were sitting in a parked car, the one in the driver's seat making an elaborate show of reading a street directory.

'That's not the jacks,' I said. For a start the Victoria Police didn't go tooling about in sporty European coupes. Also, I recognised the men. It was the goons from the cemetery.

Ayisha jostled in beside me, the two of us squeezed together in the narrow passageway. I bent closer, feeling her hair graze my cheek. 'Not ours, anyway,' I whispered. 'More like the Turkish secret police, wouldn't you say?' She swivelled her eyes around, knowing it wasn't the cops out there, letting me have my lame little joke.

'What's the Anatolia Club?' I said quietly, a secret conversation, just ours, my mouth accidentally against her ear, in danger of electrocution. She creased her brow into a silent question, her two perfect eyebrows arching like downy black caterpillars. 'I think Bayraktar was a member,' I whispered.

Her jaw hardened and a flare of alarm shot across her face. She repeated the short, sibilant, deeply expressive word that Gezen had uttered earlier. 'Wait,' she snapped. She turned and closed on Gezen, making reassuring sounds in Turkish, propelling him backwards down the narrow passageway until he disappeared into the obscurity of its far end. Then she wheeled and advanced on me. 'Stop pissing about, Murray,' she hissed, not in the least bit playfully. 'This is serious.'

Her face was so close I could taste the mixture of spearmint and tobacco on her breath. Any closer and I would do something I'd regret. 'Take it easy,' I said, backing off. 'I'm on your side, remember.'

Sivan looked up from his phone call, registered our presence, and returned to scribbling notes.

Quickly I described how I had driven past the address in Blyth Street the day before and seen a BMW like the one parked across the road. For good measure I threw in the goings-on I had just witnessed at Fawkner Cemetery. As she listened, Ayisha gnawed her bottom lip and glanced anxiously out the window. 'It's a gambling club,' she said. 'Run by right-wing thugs. Maybe more, even.'

'More? Like what?'

'Rumour is they keep an eye on things in the local community for the consulate.' She shrugged meaningfully. 'You think they're really after Memo?'

She said something else, but I didn't hear it. I was already out the door, feeling the wind cut like a knife. Streams of traffic hummed past in both directions, as I dodged and skipped towards the twin yellow stripes at the centre of the road.

As a rule of thumb, I kept my nose out of ethnic matters, for all the obvious reasons. When it came to complex, bitter and intractable conflict, the Labor party more than met my needs. Tolerance, however, had its limits. Obscure foreign toughs could not be allowed to go cruising around my patch, staking out the offices of a perfectly respectable welfare organisation, without having their activities at least remarked upon. You have to draw the line somewhere.

I was standing on that line now, waiting for a wall of semi-trailers to pass, their tyres raising a slurry off the wet asphalt. Through the flashing gaps between each successive truck I saw the faces in the BMW turn impassively to observe my approach. Blue-shaven faces, hard-featured, don't-fuck-with-me, no-speakada-English, see-this-knife faces. I closed on them, ten metres, five, two, suddenly regretting my bravado. A less confrontational, more oblique, more measured approach might be appropriate. Hi there, I could say. Looking for something? Can I help? Behind me Ayisha was on the footpath, gnawing that lip again.

The BMW trembled gently, flashed an indicator and inserted itself into the latest wave of steel and rubber hurtling down the southbound lane.

'Piss off, you mongrels,' I yelled at its departing bumper bar, fist in the air. 'You're in Australia now.' An ancient Greek in a tram shelter looked up impassively from his cane. 'Not you, mate,' I hastened to reassure him. 'Not you,'

Ayisha stood shaking her head in amazement, clapping and grinning, and I realised where my urge for heroics had come from. In like Flynn, I told myself. Up the Revolution.

Back inside, Sivan was still engrossed in his phone conversation. The inner office was empty. I walked through to the backyard. Gezen wasn't in the outhouse either. Ayisha had slung her coat, a huge quilted thing, over her arm and was back on the footpath, looking up and down the street. 'We've got to talk,' I said.

'Later.' She climbed into a taxi and wound down the window. Her arm came out and I felt her palm, cool on my cheek, brushing past with the forward momentum of the cab. 'You were fantastic. You won't say anything, will you?'

Shit no. Leastways not until I got to a phone.

'Here,' said Ant. 'Hold this.'

Two days before, this Pacific Pastoral caper had been a minor chance to earn a few brownie points with the powers. Now it was a major can of worms. If only I had come straight back to the electorate office after the funeral, I would have been sitting at my desk finishing off Charlene's correspondence while arranging for some super-efficient roofing firm to drop around and seal my drips. Instead, it was already noon and, not only were my drips still dripping, I was standing around with a fluorescent tube under my arm watching Ant balance on an upended milk crate on the top of my desk.

Fixing the flickering overhead light was item four on a list of odd jobs Trish had given the tattooed complainant that morning. The first was replacing the toilet window the burglars had broken. Then came adjusting the automatic closing gizmo on the front door, and eliminating the rattle in the gas wall-furnace. Trish was never one to let a chance go by. 'He's got nowhere else to go,' she told me when I returned from the League and found him hoisting the milk crate onto my desk. 'Apparently his girlfriend, Gail...'

'G.A.I.L.'

'She really has kicked him out. This morning I found him asleep in his car out the front. If you're going to hang around like a bad smell all day, I told him, at least make yourself useful.'

So there he was, making himself so fucking useful I couldn't get at my desk. How a man was supposed to get anything done in that lunatic asylum, let alone have a discreet telephone conversation about manslaughter, was anyone's guess.

I passed the fluoro tube up with one hand and dialled the ministry with the other. Agnelli was such a smart lawyer, he was bound to know some similarly talented criminal lawyer. Between the two of them they could take Gezen off my hands, along with any uncomfortable legal consequences his impromptu confession might have thrown up. Presuming he ever surfaced again. More likely he'd had second thoughts about unburdening himself so freely and was currently sitting with his luggage in the international departure lounge at Tullamarine waiting for the next direct flight to Ankara.

I tried Agnelli's direct line again. It was still engaged. Somehow Ayisha's tobacco and matches had found their way into my jacket pocket. I rolled myself a calming smoke and called A-OK Allweather.

'Yeah?' This time it was a younger woman, bored and snappish.

'Is that A-OK Allweather?'

'Hold, please.' Inane repetitive music blared.

'Rip-off merchants,' said a voice from above. Ant was slipping the diffuser panel back into place. 'I done a job with them once. The specs said four gauge but they used two point six. Said no-one would notice. Twenty years time the brackets'll be completely stuffed. Shit work, mate, take my word for it.'

A deejay screeched in my ear like an enraged mouse trapped in an empty margarine container. 'You telling me you know something about roofing?' Number plates I could imagine, mail bags, a bit of hot wiring. Trish might have been impressed with this odd-job stuff around the office, but as far as I was concerned all it amounted to so far was oiling a sticky hinge and changing a few light globes.

'Gas fitter by trade,' said Ant. 'But I've been around. Metal fabrication. Plumbing. Concrete. Roofs. You name it.'

The mouse went heavy metal. 'What about domestic? Ordinary houses?'

Ant dropped something solid into his tool box and stepped down. 'I might not be Bertram Russell, sport, but I know what domestic means.'

A-OK was still somewhere on the other side of a dozen howling chartbusters. I was sure that I would live to regret what I was about to say, but I was desperate enough to say it anyway. 'Listen,' I said. 'I might be able to put a bit of work your way, round my place. We could nip across now if you like, have a quick look, tell me if you're interested.'

'Get fucked,' said Ant amiably. 'You're just trying to get rid of me.'

'By showing you where I live? You want some paid work or not?'

'What sort of work?'

Fifteen minutes later we were standing on the footpath outside my front gate. The rain had stopped for the time being, but the sky pressed low and menacing. Drips hung from the rust-frayed gashes in the guttering and my ball of rags protruded above the line of the roof like a goitre. Ant clicked his tongue ominously. 'I'll need a ladder,' he said, and headed down the side path, peering upwards and shaking his head. Winding me up for a big slug, I assumed.

As the front door key snicked into place, a sound erupted inside the house. Heavy footsteps pounded in the bedroom. A shadow flashed across the leadlight panel, retreating towards the other end of the house. I twisted the key, cursing the stiffness of the lock. As the door finally flew open, a crash came echoing up the hall, followed by a muffled oath. I flew through the house and shot out the back door.

Ant was sprawled on his back, blood and broken teeth spewing out his mouth. The side fence rocked. I vaulted the rickety timber slats and landed amid the Vesuvius cups of Mrs Bagio's foundation garments flapping on a rotary hoist. Footsteps sounded down the side of the sleepout. A second fence loomed, an obstacle course of old water pipes, Mr Bagio's bean trellis. Up and over I went, rubbish bins breaking my drop. Down a driveway towards the street a car door slammed. I hit the nature strip just in time to see the tail-end of an early model

Falcon 500, a flash of aqua blue, go fishtailing around the corner. But not before I got the last three digits of the rego number.

When I got back inside, Ant was sitting at the kitchen table. A damp towel tinged with pink was pressed to his mouth and he was poking around in a saucer filled with fragments of denture—a palaeontological exhibit, the upper jaw of homo pictorial. He peeled away the cloth to display a mush of split lips and swelling nose. 'Fuck was that?' he lisped. 'Cunt hit me in the face with the screen door.'

It didn't seem like an appropriate time to instruct him on non-sexist language. 'Some junkie low-life, I guess.' I panted. 'Driving some piece of shit.'

'Get anything?'

I doubted it. Whoever it was—not that I'd actually seen them—had not been moving like someone with a television set under their arm. I took a look around. There was no sign of forced entry, no broken window or splinter marks around the locks. Everything seemed pretty much as I had left it when I'd gone to work. I had to laugh, imagining the look of dismay on the face of any housebreaker unlucky or dumb enough to target this place. Across the mouldy-smelling carpet of damp newspapers covering the lounge room floor the stereo was untouched.

A couple of years before, Wendy had come home and found the front door open, the place clumsily ransacked, the portable tape deck missing. It was a nuisance and an intrusion, but the occasional break-in by bored kids or junkie desperados was only to be expected. It was all part of the inexorable process that begins with heritage colours and native gardens and culminates in some Liberal-voting busybody ringing your bell one night while you're eating dinner to ask if you'd be interested in helping set up a local chapter of Neighbourhood Watch. If you found the odd burglary impossible to live with you might as well sell up and lock yourself away in some high-security terrace in Fitzroy or a flat in St Kilda. If you were going to be pillaged like a member of the gentry, you might as well live like one. All it took was about fifty grand, which I didn't have.

The bedroom was a mess, but no more than usual. By the look of it, we'd disturbed the intruder early in the piece. I lingered, shutting drawers and smoothing down the bed covers, slight gestures to re-assert my presence. Discarded socks, mine and Red's, lay scattered on the floor. I began scooping them up. It was like I'd been caught in a car accident wearing dirty underpants.

Having some joker sneaking about the house didn't worry me much—I'd just sent the creep packing, after all. But this was the sort of thing that could easily upset a little kid. It wasn't as though I'd found a steaming turd in Wendy's knickers drawer or anything, but a couple of hours either way and it could have been Red's face being smashed in with the screen door. Better not to mention it. I paired off the socks and tossed them into the laundry basket until I was down to a solitary old black thing with a hole in the heel. 'Just the one sock missing, then, sir?' I could hear the police asking.

I knelt beside the bed and stuck my hand under. What I found wasn't a sock. It was a zip-lock plastic bag containing more marijuana than I had ever seen in my life. There must have been a good two ounces of it, packed down hard. Either Red was more precocious than I gave him credit for, or our unknown intruder had fled with considerably less than he came with. I sat on the edge of the bed and stared at the grass, wondering what to do with it.

Ant stomped up the hall, his ballooning lip curling back to reveal an obscene flash of tongue and gum. 'Where's that ladder, then?'

I quickly stuffed the package into my pocket. The presence in my home of illegal substances was not something I wished to reveal to this tattooed yoik. 'I suppose I'd better call the cops, report the break-in.'

'Waste of time,' Ant grunted. It was clear he preferred as little contact as possible with the sherlocks.

I figured he was probably right. We'd have been sitting around for a good hour waiting for the uniforms to arrive with their clipboards so they could fill in a triplicate incident report for the non-existent insurance claim. I'd give them the dope and the digits I'd memorised from the Falcon number plate. Six months later, assuming the car wasn't stolen, they'd ring me up and want me to take a day off work and hang around the magistrate's court so some whacker with pin-prick eyes could spend six months having his criminal skills honed at the taxpayers' expense. No thanks. I got the ladder.

Ant disappeared into the ceiling, bloody towel in one hand, torch in the other. I rolled one of Ayisha's smokes and stood in the gloom of the hallway, staring up at the trapdoor and hoping to Christ I was doing the right thing, thinking I should have got references.

When he came down his lip was curled back in a sneer, whether from the swelling or with contempt I couldn't tell. 'Rooted,' he snorted. 'Totally fucked. Battens are stuffed. Iron had the dick years ago. You need rewiring too.'

'How much?'

'Just the roof? Sixteen hundred.'

I had no idea if it was high, low, or off the register. I thought long and hard for about ten seconds. Unless I acted soon the place would be down around my ears by the time I got a proper quote. Aside from which, it seemed a bit churlish to quibble with a man who had a notch down the middle of his face in the shape of my back door. 'How soon can you start?'

Ant shoved a fuse into place and the lights came on. 'Soon as this weather stops.'

'Discount for cash?'

'Sixteen hundred is cash. Two men for two days plus materials.'

'Insurance? What if you fall off and break your neck?'

'Drag me onto the street and leave me to die.'

'My pleasure.' We shook on it and drove to a materials yard. Ant told them what he needed and we organised delivery for the next morning. They even accepted my cheque. I was overdrawn, but they weren't to know that. Things seemed finally to be moving in the right direction.

On the way back to the office it occurred to me that the intruder might return to look for his drugs, maybe when Red was in the house. I didn't want that happening, but I could hardly sit around the house waiting for him to turn up. A better idea would be to get to him first, give him back his dope and tell him to fuck off in no uncertain terms. Of course I couldn't do something like that myself. But the man who could was sitting right beside me.

First things first, though. Ant needed new teeth and I needed to figure out who owned that lairy blue Falcon. I dropped Ant at a tram stop in Sydney Road with twenty dollars and instructions on how to find the dental college. You could get free dentures there if you didn't mind being used for practice by the students. I didn't mention the students.

A year or so before, Trish had a boyfriend who worked at motor registration. He'd come to our Christmas party, got legless and barfed taramasalata all over my desk. The two of them had a big break up soon after, not related. When I got back to the office Trish was at lunch. Lover boy's number was still in her teledex.

'I'm calling from the minister's office,' I said. It was half true. 'Trish suggested I call.' It was he who had done the dirty, so I figured mention of Trish might trigger some sense of obligation. 'I don't know if this is your department, but she said that if anyone could head me in the right direction you could. The thing is, Mrs Wills was doing some shopping over the weekend and somebody dinged her car. Stove the tail-light right in, snapped off part of the trim. Pissed off without as much as a howdy-do. Luckily somebody witnessed the whole thing, took down the offender's make and model and half the rego number and stuck it under the windscreen. Naturally Charlene doesn't want to make a federal case out of it, but I was wondering if there's any way to track down the owner?'

'You need the Search Section.' Lothario had better things to do than favours for half-forgotten workmates of old girlfriends. 'Bring in some ID, fill in an application and pay a search fee. You'll be notified in about a week.'

'Oh,' I said. Not the powerless 'oh' of a individual faced with a remote and uncaring bureaucracy. The 'oh' of a mover and shaker realising he is talking to a turkey. There was an almost imperceptible change in attitude, a minuscule drop in barometric pressure. 'It was a Falcon 500.' I said 'Aqua blue, mid-seventies model. Something, something, something, eight six five.'

'I'll have to go downstairs,' he said, just so I'd know how much trouble was involved. 'I'll call you back.'

I hung up, then dialled again, the Turkish Welfare League.

'No, Ayisha has not come back.' Sivan didn't sound particularly concerned. 'I thought maybe she was with you,' he added slyly.

'The client she was with, any sign of him?'

'Client?'

'The curly-haired guy in Ayisha's office about two hours ago.'

'Memo Gezen?' Sivan hadn't seen him, but he knew who he was. 'Leading anti-fascist fighter. Tireless worker for the PKK.'

PKK? I'd seen those initials before on posters along Sydney Road. Clenched fists, upraised Kalashnikovs, armed revolution, Kurdish nationalist guerillas. The full kit and caboodle. 'No, this guy's a cleaner.'

'Very clever disguise, eh? Did you know that since the coup d'etat more than eighty thousand people have been imprisoned? It is the policy of the regime that...'

Many migrants remained politically active in the affairs of their native land. There was nothing unusual in that. Lots of Italians were members, office bearers even, in the Italian Communist Party. The El Salvadorean who repaired our office photocopier was reputed to be on the central committee of the Farabundo Marti Liberation Front. And now that I knew of Memo Gezen's political dimension a whole lot of pieces fell into place.

I cut into Sivan's flow of baleful statistics. 'Look, get Ayisha to call me as soon as she gets back in, will you? And one other thing. Look out the window and tell me if there's a BMW parked across the street.'

'I can't see one. Why?'

'Nothing. Get Ayisha to call me, okay.'

'Sure, Murray. I think you like her, huh?'

I'd liked her a lot more before I'd begun to feel like I was having my string jerked. According to one of the yellow slips on my desk Greg Coates had called while I was out. There was a tick in the Urgent box. Ayisha's tobacco was down to powdery dregs. I rolled as I dialled, one-handed, back to the old form.

'You prick,' Coates said. 'Dropped me right into it, you did.' He was as pissed off as I'd ever heard him.

'What are you talking about?'

'That Turk of yours, Bayraktar. He's hot property. I did like I promised and called up his file this morning. Access was still denied and five minutes later two of our security blokes lobbed on my doorstep wanting to know what my interest was. Took quite a bit of tap dancing before I managed to convince them it was a clerical error. Very keen to interview the man, they were. I think you'd better tell me why you're so interested.'

Coates would have to wait until the waters cleared. Anything I told him would be around the traps like a dose of the crabs before the day was done. Which was only fair enough. I'd do the same for him. 'Nothing to tell. The bloke's name appeared in a story in Monday's *Sun* linking Charlene to a potential industrial conflict. I was just following up.'

'You know where to find him?'

'I've got a fair idea. What do they want him for?'

'Everything short of buggering his dog, from what I could tell. He's got a record as long as your arm in West Germany. Grievous bodily harm, drugs, you name it. The krauts were compelled to show him the door. Then he slipped in under our net. Came in as a temporary resident, supposedly working for some cultural exchange mob called the Anatolia Club. Stated occupation, ceramic artist, believe it or not. He throws things all right, but they're not pots. So, if you know where he is...'

'Try Fawkner Cemetery,' I said.

'He's dead?'

'I understand they're very reluctant to bury you there otherwise. Tell your security blokes they can read all about it in Monday's edition of the *Sun*. Cause of death was reported as a heart attack.'

This put Coates back in good humour. He'd be getting mileage out of this one for years. Nothing like a bit of mutual pocket-pissing to keep the fences mended. 'Look,' I said, while he was so cheery, 'There's this other Turkish bloke I was wondering about.'

'No way,' he said. 'Not until things quieten down. I've got

security clearance to maintain here, pal. And what about a bit of quid pro quo. You never finished telling me about Agnelli's big scoop on the election date.'

'Agnelli's sworn me to secrecy,' I said. It always pays to over-emphasise the value of your information, I find. 'Word from the Cabinet room is it'll be a snap job. Pre-Christmas. Second week in December probably.'

'Shit, that's barely ten weeks away. Sounds like crap to me.'

'I'm just telling you what he said. And from what you told me about the punishing he's giving the phones, I'm not the only one he's telling.'

'He could be making a fool of himself on this one. I know for a fact that the state admin committee is up to its neck in a substantial rejig of campaign structures. It wouldn't be too smart going to the polls with half the party machine in dry-dock. Still, there might be something in it. Worth putting in a couple of calls to check out.'

'Let me know how you go.'

'Don't forget to apologise for me tonight at the branch meeting.'

The idea that Agnelli might be wrong about the imminence of an election wasn't surprising. Everything I had learned since yesterday afternoon about the alleged Lollicato–Pacific Pastoral connection cast serious doubt on his credibility.

Jesus, though, this stuff about Bayraktar was interesting. It certainly backed up Gezen's tale of extortion, as well as the police suspicion of thievery in Number 3 chiller. This connection with the Anatolia Club was a major worry. An organised group of paramilitary right-wingers, possibly connected to a foreign government, running a political and criminal standover operation out of a well-secured building in the middle of a Melbourne suburb. And I'd just blown them a very public raspberry.

The phone rang. It was Loverboy at Motor Rego. 'Got a pen?' he said. 'Its a bit of a mouthful. I'll spell it for you. Car's regis-tered to an Ekrem Bayraktar. B-A-Y-R-A-K-T-A-R. Get that?'

No I didn't. I didn't get it at all.

Bayraktar was dead. I'd seen the photographs and stared down a pit at the silver handles on his Martinelli rosewood deluxe. So who the hell had been thumping down my hallway leaving a trail of cannabis behind in their wake? Was there some essential internal logic at work here that I was failing to notice?

The disordered mass of files and paperwork the previous night's intruder had dumped on the office floor lay in an untidy sprawl across my desk, half hidden under a yellow confetti of phone message slips. On top of everything else that was happening, half the known universe seemed to want to talk to me. I began systematically sorting through the mess, hoping that some superficial restoration of order might help me make sense of what was going through my mind.

Some of the calls were from local party branch members. No doubt they would be wanting to know if there was anything interesting enough on the agenda of that night's meeting to tempt them out for the evening. Others would want their apologies noted. Gavin Mullane, the son of the local Lower House MP, had rung to confirm a four o'clock appointment I had made with him the previous week. Roofing companies were now returning my calls, proving the axiom that it never rains. Old Maestro Picone had left word that he wanted to talk about Charlene's celebrity appearance at the Carboni Club dinner dance. Mundane as it was, this housekeeping was beginning to look pretty alluring compared with the dramas on offer elsewhere in the electorate.

By the time I had finished working my way through the jumble of paperwork, I knew for sure I no longer had the Pacific Pastoral file. The previous afternoon it had been sitting on top of my in-tray. Trish hadn't seen it either, or so she signalled as she sat chatting on the phone with her mother.

I called Agnelli. He was at lunch, so I flashed Trish five fingers and walked down to the shops, figuring a bite to eat and the taste of smoke in my mouth might help the mental processes along. On a bench in the market arcade I ate a bucket of chips and broached a new packet of Winfield, trying to figure out the connection between a dead man's car, the botched burglary of my home and a missing file. Nothing fitted. It simply didn't make sense.

Apart from the question of why anyone interested in Pacific Pastoral would also steal a petty-cash tin and draw a penis on the bathroom mirror in felt-tipped pen, the file itself was useless. All it contained was the list of names from Bayraktar's shift—names on record out at the Coolaroo plant, a few random jottings, and a handwritten draft of the introductory paragraph of my report for MACWAM. Stealing that made no sense at all. The file, I decided, had to be back at the office somewhere staring me in the face.

The Falcon presented two possibilities. One was unconvincing and the other downright scary. Either it had been stolen and its use in the attempted burglary was sheer coincidence. Or Bayraktar's mates at the Anatolia Club had it and I'd got myself stuck in the middle of some kind of internecine Turkish-Kurdish thing.

According to Coates, the Anatolia Club was down on the file as Bayraktar's sponsor, which meant the Immigration Department security boys must have already checked it out. So either the spooks were satisfied it had no connection with Bayraktar's criminal activities or they were running their own agenda. Shit, what was I thinking? They hadn't even known Bayraktar was dead. They were probably too busy framing little old Greek ladies on phoney pension fraud charges to be any help to me.

That left the cops, either the locals or the big boys down-town. And I couldn't see them getting interested unless I turned on a pretty convincing production number. Dropping Charlene's name might help crank up some muted enthusiasm. It might also result in a headline reading 'Labor MP Aide in Ethnic Feud Death Probe'. And talking to the cops wouldn't be much point without spilling the beans on Memo Gezen, which would be a breach of faith. Worse, it would be a surefire guarantee that I could kiss my prospects with Ayisha Celik goodbye forever.

And where did Memo Gezen fit into the picture anyway? This story of his about being stood over by Bayraktar tallied okay, but thereafter the tale had got decidedly unconvincing. The man himself was impossible to read, one minute impassive and compliant, the next wild-eyed, sparks erupting out the top of his head. And to top it all off, there was his connection with militant Kurdish politics.

The problem was I had no tangible intelligence to work with. What I had to do was persuade Greg Coates to change his mind and sling me Gezen's immigration file. Maybe then I'd have some hope of working out what was going on. Another thought occurred to me. Maybe Gezen hadn't disappeared of his own volition. With Sivan on the phone and Ayisha out in the street watching my mock heroics, could someone have slipped in the back way and spirited him out the back door? Take it easy, I told myself, there are enough far-fetched ideas flying around here already.

Halfway back to the office a steady shower began. I tucked my head under my jacket and took the short-cut up the back lane. I was only a few paces into the narrow bluestone-paved canyon of back fences when I heard the throaty rev of a souped-up engine somewhere behind me. In this area, a lowered chassis, fat tyres, and a basso profundo engine timbre is virtually mandatory among large sections of the male population. If I'd looked around every time someone dropped a notch and spread rubber, I'd have had a twisted vertebrae before you could say fuel-injected overhead cam.

But when I heard the crunch of a sump hitting the kerb

immediately behind me, I swung around automatically. A turquoise flash of chrome and duco was roaring towards me, its windscreen a rain-streaked blur. I turned on my heels and took off as fast as my legs would carry me.

The lane opened into a side street a hundred metres away, an impossible distance. On either side were the back gates of shops and houses, all of them closed. Leading with my shoulder I threw myself against the first I came to, a teetering dunny door of a thing. It was more solid than it looked. Bouncing off, I felt my feet slither out from beneath me and came down hard on the weathered bluestone cobbles. I scrambled to my knees and found myself staring between my legs at the oncoming grille, reading off the digits of Bayraktar's number plate, the numbers closing fast.

Across the lane I could see Ciccio's pile of empty Bisleri bottles through the gap where the sheet-metal halves of his back gate were held together by a sagging coil of heavy-duty chain. Catapulting across the Falcon's path, I smashed my head into the gap, hoping to Christ I could force it wider. I felt the whip of steel links against my neck and heard the hinges scream.

Bottles rose to meet me, an avalanche of empties skidding across the wet concrete of the yard. A smear of blue streaked past at the edge of my vision. Then one of the bottles was in my hand and I was back in the lane watching it tumbling end over end, its slow-motion trajectory ending in a milky wash of white as it shattered the Falcon's rear window. The sound of breaking glass came back down the lane towards me, mingled with the rapidly fading screech of tyres as the car disappeared.

My heart pumped hard and fast, fed by the jitter of adrenalin coursing through my veins. This was getting beyond a joke. Back down the lane my flattened pack of Winfields was demonstration of the driver's murderous intent. Don't you just hate it when somebody tries to kill you and you don't know who or why?

Ciccio had come to his back door, wiping his hands, the old card players behind him, craning for a view. I brushed past them, my voice rasping in my ears. 'Corretto.' I needed a drink and pronto.

Ciccio fished around under the bar and came up with a bottle of grappa. He tipped a hefty measure into a strong black coffee and watched me down it in one. It was nearly enough to stop my hand shaking. But not quite. I took the second and third slugs neat.

'Fucka idiots,' he said. 'Orta be a law.'

That was it. Things were getting far too hairy to be tolerated any longer. This sort of thing was well beyond the requirements of my job description. If you wanted a meeting stacked or a booth-by-booth breakdown of voting trends with emphasis on the flow of preferences, I was your man. Needed your how-to-vote cards printed cheap? See me. But being a homicide victim? I didn't have the training.

I took a last shot of grappa, punched a fresh packet of fags out of Ciccio's vending machine and ordered my rubbery legs out the door and around the corner to the cop shop. By the time I got there, my hands had stopped shaking enough to prise the cellophane off the cigarettes. 'Someone just tried to kill me,' I said.

The uniformed walloper behind the counter was an athletic-looking lug in his late twenties with the full-page crossword in *People* open in front of him. He looked up like he resented the intrusion. 'That so, sir?' he said, his eyes taking a long slow cruise over my three-day growth, past my skewiff tie to the damp patches the puddles in Ciccio's yard had left on my pants.

'Yeah,' I said. 'First they broke into my house, then they tried to run me over.' The grappa seemed to have finally settled my nerves. I managed one of the smokes out of the pack and inserted it between my lips.

'And who would this be you are referring to, sir?' Next he'd be saying ''ello, 'ello, 'ello'.

'That's what I want you to find out,' I said.

He took a pen out of his shirt pocket and clicked it emphatically. 'Your name?'

I was thinking about the rego number of the Falcon. The image kept fluctuating in and out of focus. Something, something, eight six five. I must have moved my lips. The cigarette fell to the floor. As I straightened from picking it up, the copper leaned right across the counter, following my progress, wrinkling his nose.

'Have you had a drink at all today, sir?' he said.

'No,' I said. 'Well yes, but…' I couldn't quite find the matches. 'You wouldn't have a light, would you?'

The copper gave me a facetious look and squared off the edges of a little pop-up card on the counter that read Thank You for Not Smoking. Why don't they ever just say No Smoking? I patted myself down and felt a lump in my inside jacket pocket, a trafficable quantity of a prohibited substance. The idea of this visit, I concluded, had been a deeply flawed conception.

Talk about making a bad impression. I had got myself so far behind the eight ball that the only way I'd ever convince this guy of anything would be to tell him the whole story. Even then I couldn't see him believing me, let alone taking any useful action. An unknown assailant, no apparent motive, no injuries, no witnesses, the complainant some half-pissed bozo with a pocket load of wacky weed. I turned on my heels and strode out the door. From now on I would rely on my own ingenuity. It wasn't much to be going on with. I started by botting a light from a passer-by.

Trish had locked the office and stuck a Back in Five Minutes card inside the door. I locked the door behind me, left the card in place and dialled Greg Coates' number. 'Couldn't you stretch a point?' I wheedled. 'Just one little file. Another Turk, name of Memo Gezen.'

'Jesus, not again?' he said. 'Unless it's official, I can't help, at least for the time being. I've stuck my neck out for you far enough for one day. Beside which, if I was you I'd be more interested in what a certain Italian of our mutual acquaintance is up to.'

'Agnelli? What's he got to do with it?'

'Get off the grass, mate. I've been applying the blowtorch to some friends of mine at the state office, and very tight-lipped they were too. All this ringing around Agnelli's doing, he's not peddling gossip. He's lining up support for a career move.'

Somehow this did not surprise me. A lot of lawyers fancy themselves as legislators and Agnelli had all the required qualities—vanity, ambition and untrustworthiness. It had only been a matter of time before his parliamentary aspirations surfaced. 'Yeah? So whose seat is he after?' I couldn't see Agnelli contesting anything marginal.

'This was where my sources got very circumspect. But if I were you I'd try imagining him in a frock and sensible shoes.'

This had to be bullshit. No way was Agnelli dumb enough to make a play for Charlene's seat. No way would the faction allow a popular member to get dumped in favour of a sleazebag like Agnelli. I pleaded for the names of Coates' sources at state headquarters, but got no more out of him. I accused him of having me on, sticking it up me for the business with the Bayraktar file. By the time he hung up I was convinced he was serious.

And the truth or otherwise of what he was saying was not the only issue. Speculation of this sort had a tendency to take on a life of its own. And as Agnelli himself pointed out, some sections of the press would only be too happy to jump on the bandwagon. Let alone the idea that one of her most senior staff members was stabbing her in the back. If I didn't nip this little furphy in the bud toot sweet, it would be all over town before you could say knife in the back.

It took me half an hour, but I finally got through to Agnelli. All it would take for him to put Coates' gossip to bed was a simple denial. That, and an oath on his mother's soul. 'Something urgent has come up. We need to talk.'

'I'm in a meeting right now.' Other voices eddied around in the background. Agnelli put his hand over the receiver and said something. When he took it away the noise had stopped.

'I'll come in,' I said. 'Ten minutes is all I'll need.' I wanted to be looking at Agnelli's face when he talked to me. After we'd cleared the air on his plans for the future, we could move on to the legal issues thrown up by Memo Gezen's confession. 'I can be there in half an hour.'

'No.' Agnelli all but jumped down the phone. He immediately back-pedalled, softening his tone. 'I'll call you back, okay?' Click. The prick hung up in my ear.

Well, fuck you, pal, I thought. I dialled the House again, asked for Charlene and got put through to the party room. She was in the chamber, someone told me, the final reading of the Insurance Bill. The information came as a relief. The impulse to call Charlene had been ill-considered, a knee-jerk reaction. Bothering Charlene with uncorroborated gossip that one of her most trusted lieutenants was planning to do a Macbeth smacked of lack of judgement. Sitting in front of me on the desk was Ennio Picone's phone message slip. I decided to activate the nonna network.

'Maestro,' I cried. 'Many apologies for not calling earlier.' I took my time, confirmed Charlene's appearance at the Carboni Club dinner dance, and made the right noises as the old man went on and on about the catering arrangements. Finally I popped the question.

'Angelo Agnelli,' I said. 'He's got terrible manners, I know, but Charlene finds him useful. Only I think he might be looking around for a new job. Have you heard anything?'

Maestro Picone shrugged audibly.

'Old Mrs Agnelli senior, you wouldn't consider having a quiet word with her for me, would you? See what you can find out.'

If Agnelli's grandmother didn't know what he was up to, Picone would work his way through the family tree until he found someone who did. Right up his autostrada, this sort of thing, keep him happy for days. Naturally he'd want something in return. I'd deal with that when the need arose. He promised to call back as soon as he had news.

While I'd been talking to Picone, Trish had come back, bringing with her a pile of photocopies, the agenda papers for that night's branch meeting. Most of the time chairing branch meetings was a tedious chore, a quasi-official part of my job. But it was also a way of maintaining close links with the local rank and file. And any candidate for pre-selection would need substantial local support. So if Agnelli was planning a challenge, he would sooner or later have to make his intentions known among the natives. Which was something he could hardly do without me finding out.

Trish dumped the papers across my desk in a row of neat but still uncollated piles. An agenda, minutes of the previous meeting, a sheet of draft resolutions, a discussion paper on federal resource development policy. Such was the ammunition with which the membership waged its eternal war against the pragmatism of those it sent to parliament. A ceaseless and often hopeless battle perhaps, but a politics of persuasion, not of muscle-flexing and murder attempts. Not like some places I could think of. Sydney, for example. Or a lane off Sydney Road.

My thoughts must have shown on my face. I looked up to find Trish squinting across the desk at me. 'You look a bit like a bloke who used to work here,' she said. 'He was in more often than you, and wasn't as much of a derelict.' She was right. I was beginning to resemble one of our more unwanted customers. I guiltily stubbed out my cigarette on the inside of the wastepaper basket. 'He didn't try to burn the place down, either,' she jibed. 'Better smarten up, Murray. Your four o'clock appointment's here.'

Gavin Mullane was something indescribably minor in the Miscellaneous Workers. His father had been the area's Lower House MP for longer than anyone could remember, and it had long been agreed within the faction that when he eventually fell back on his parliamentary superannuation Sonny Jim would succeed him. I made myself respectable and went out to greet him. 'Great to see you, Gavin,' I said and took the poor bastard next door for a coffee. Behind his back as we passed Trish made a repetitive stroking gesture, thumb and forefinger touching at the tips.

Young Gavin had grown up in the shadow of his father, an experience that had left him damp. The family tendency was to thin lips, Presbyterian noses, and the kind of unflinching worthiness that could put a doorknob into a coma. The fact that Junior still lived with his parents, though well into his thirties, was perfectly understandable. I could see them sitting around together, reading Hansard and listening to the wireless. Gavin let me buy the coffees without offering to pay.

The idea of dynastic succession among the Labor aristocracy was an affront to my democratic sensibilities, but in Mullane's case I could see its merits. To pass the time until his inheritance arrived, the heir apparent was serving his political apprenticeship as councillor for the north ward of Coburg. Even within the sorry milieu of local government he displayed such a conspicuous lack of talent that it was universally agreed that the sooner he went elsewhere the better. All the way to the back benches of the state legislature if necessary.

Eventually nature would take its course. Mullane senior and his ageing cronies would die off, and the young dauphin would be despatched to the tumbrels. But right now there was no point in rubbing Daddy up the wrong way. Besides which, the old man kept his ear pretty close to the ground in the party room. And who knows what juicy snippets had been dropped at the Mullane family dinner table? On more than one occasion Junior had inadvertently let the cat out of the bag. Mullane waited until Ciccio brought the coffees, then bent gravely across the table. 'Somebody's going to be killed,' he said. 'Soon.'

I froze in mid-sip.

'The way they come down that hill, it's only a matter of time before there's blood on the street.'

With relief I realised Mullane was merely peddling his current pet project, a personal campaign for the installation of a pedestrian crossing at Edwardes Lake, a splotch of recreational water bang in the middle of his council ward.

'You reckon you could hassle Charlene to hassle the Minister for Transport to hassle his department to hassle the Road Traffic Authority, ASAP?'

'No hassle,' I said. 'At least not from Charlene's point of view. She's behind you 150 per cent on this.'

In fact Charlene wouldn't go near the Minister for Transport with a twelve-foot Croatian. And she and the Treasurer had already privately agreed that in an area already so adequately resourced infrastructure-wise, road funding would be better directed to pressing community development and social justice issues—such as the capital construction costs of the Carboni Club.

'The problem will be getting it past those pen-pushing pricks in Transport,' I warned, conjuring an elaborate map of the decision-making process. 'But give her the bullets,' I said, 'and Charlene will fire them.'

Mullane proceeded to crap on about traffic density ratios,

while I waited for a chance to change the subject. 'Heard this talk about an early election?'

'I'm sure the leadership has the matter well in hand,' Mullane said primly. A tendency to mouth platitudes was another family trait he had inherited early.

'Angelo Agnelli reckons early December.'

Mullane opened his mouth to say something, thought better of it and snapped his teeth shut. His was a face not well suited to deception. His jaw worked overtime. Something was trying hard not to burst out. 'I'm not big on idle speculation.' He pushed his chair back and stood up. 'Practical issues, that's what concerns me. Things that are important in people's daily lives, traffic safety for one.'

I headed him off before he started in again. 'Couldn't agree more, Gavin.'

When we shook hands and Mullane turned away, he had the look of a man whose team is six goals up at three-quarter time, a man more pleased with himself than any paltry assurances about some stupid fucking zebra crossing warranted.

By now it was four-thirty, more than five hours since Ayisha and Gezen had disappeared on me. I rang the League. A heavily-accented male answered, one of their volunteer workers, I guessed. Ayisha was not there, he told me. Nor was Sivan. I left my home address and phone number with a message for either of them to call me urgently. It was a painful process of careful enunciation, slow spelling and double checking. Even then I wasn't entirely sure I'd been understood.

The agenda papers still needed collating, and in barely ten minutes I would need to leave to pick Red up. I sweet-talked Trish into helping me, a gesture towards restoring workplace harmony. She locked the front door and I laid the piles of pages out across the reception area floor, passing the finished sets to Trish to staple together. We were just getting up a head of steam when there was a tap on the front window.

Herb Gardiner was outside on the footpath, a spry leprechaun, as cheerful as ever. I unlocked the door, but didn't ask him in. 'Just happened to be in the vicinity, son.' He glanced knowingly towards Trish and gave me a wink.

You get some of these retired or near-retired guys with too much time on their hands. They start looking for an interest. The last thing I needed was the old goat taking me under his wing. 'I'm pretty busy right now, Herb,' I told him.

He eyed the pages on the floor and dropped his voice. 'That your report?'

I shook my head warily, not in the mood for any more confidential revelations of shenanigans at Pacific Pastoral. Gardiner lingered, looking for something to say. He seemed to be expecting me to speak first. It occurred to me that he'd had second thoughts about his comments on the prevalence of pilfering at Coolaroo. Nobody wants to go down in the books as a dobber. He checked out Trish to see if she could hear us. She was noisily punching staples into completed agenda sets. 'What you said,' he started.

I got there ahead of him. 'My report only covers the industrial situation,' I said. 'Anything else, I can be relied on to keep to myself.'

This confirmed what Gardiner was waiting to hear. 'Right you are, then, son,' he said. 'You're calling the shots.' Then he paused pregnantly, expecting me to continue.

What else was there to say? I was tempted to ask if he knew Memo Gezen. From what he'd said before about the ethnics keeping to themselves, I thought it unlikely. And even if he did, what useful information could he possibly have?

Gardiner kept glancing towards Trish, then taking little steps backwards, as if to draw me outside. I didn't have the time for this kind of chit-chat. If I didn't get away soon, Red would be standing in the schoolyard all alone, frightened he'd be left there all night. 'Back at work yet?' I said, clearly a concluding remark.

'Crack of dawn tomorrow,' he said. An idea seemed suddenly to occur to him. 'The reason I dropped in, that roof of yours. That builder mate of mine says he can nip around tonight, take a look. You going to be home?' He said this quite loudly so Trish could hear.

Some inexorable law of mechanical determinism was at work here. Buy something, five minutes later you see a better one at a fraction of the price. If this builder mate was anything like old

Herb himself, he was probably a top tradesman. 'You wouldn't read about it,' I said, 'I've just lined someone up.'

Gardiner sounded a bit cheesed, like he was being pissed around. 'Don't be hasty,' he said, forcefully. 'You might regret it.' Boy, was he toey all of a sudden.

No point in having him think I was ungrateful. 'Thanks anyway,' I said. 'But tonight would have been impossible anyway. Monthly branch meeting. I'll be freezing my arse off in a back room at the Lakeview Hotel until well after ten.'

Poor old Herb shook his head like he couldn't believe what he was hearing. Like he couldn't see why I was passing up an offer this good. 'You sure you know what you're doing?' he said.

I told him that I did, and that I had work to do, edging him out the door. He backed off, looking puzzled, his palms spread. 'Have it your own way,' he seemed to be saying. As I bent back down to the agenda papers Trish cleared her throat noisily and rolled her eyes sideways. Gardiner was still standing outside the window, watching. He jerked his thumb over his shoulder, beckoning me outside.

I didn't have time for this. I turned away, ignoring him. When I sneaked a furtive look a minute later, he was gone.

Red pulled an envelope out of his schoolbag. It had a Health Department logo.

> Your child has been examined today and found to be infested with headlice. Until appropriate treatment is commenced, he/she cannot attend school.

With the note came a glossy brochure. 'Headlice,' it read, 'live equally happily on the rich, the poor, the clean and the dirty, regardless of age, occupation and status.' Genially egalitarian as this made our little visitors sound, if Wendy turned up and found Red off school with a lice infestation, I would never hear the end of it. The high moral ground would rise beneath her feet and become an unscaleable mountain. But what constituted appropriate treatment?

A haircut, we decided, and a second shampoo. The place Wendy usually took him was in High Street, Northcote. Snipz Unisex Salon, children a speciality. Only now it was Voula Modes. It smelled of singed cats and was full of bottle-blond matrons in animal print leotards and cashmere sweaters with shoulder pads and appliqued sequins.

We walked up the hill, me on the outside, half an eye cocked at the slow crawl of outward-bound traffic in the far lane. A window displayed badger-bristle shaving brushes, briar pipes, and a black and white print of Tony Curtis. 'No way, Jose.' Red shook his head and we kept walking, past a newsagency with a good price on Winfields.

The shops changed. Bed'n'Bath and Seconds'n'Samples gave way to an Indian restaurant, a hip record store, boutiques. The next hairdresser was called Hair-o-Inn, a retro horror full of lava-lamps and cone-chairs and other knick-knacks of the sort anyone over thirty had spent their adolescence trying to escape. We stepped inside and a tweenie in black came smirking out from behind somebody's father's kidney-shaped rumpus-room bar. Red gazed about like he was in a museum, flipped open an English fashion magazine, a catalogue of tribes.

'Give him a trim,' I told the coiffeur and nicked back up the street to the newsagent. Midweek Lotto had jackpotted to five million that week and the counter staff were flat chat handling a late rush of systems entries and syndicates. It hardly seemed worth the wait considering that I didn't really smoke. I waited anyway.

Back at the hairdressers, Red's Botticelli locks were a trampled heap on the floor. A sheet flapped like a conjurer's prop and the boy himself emerged from the chair transformed. His upward-tilted moon of a face, his babyhood, was gone. The new face was keenly alert, a face sufficient-unto-itself, a proper boy's face. My son the apprentice jockey, in a flat-top several sizes too small.

'You're going to die,' this stranger accused, glaring at the cigarette in my mouth.

'I'll be dead when your mother sees you,' I told him, grinding the cigarette into the linoleum. Furtively I scooped up one of Red's discarded ringlets, a relic of my baby's vanished infancy. 'For the mother,' I murmured, catching sight of a live louse in the debris.

We shopped, loading the car with groceries. I was jittery, jumping at the clatter of supermarket trolleys, nervously pacing the half-deserted aisles. After the dramas earlier in the day, these rituals of normality should have brought relief. Instead they made me all the more apprehensive. Red's presence only made it worse. The package of grass was burning a hole in my pocket.

A military funeral, Gezen's confession and subsequent disappearance, an intruder in the house, a wild chase over backyard fences, the business with Bayraktar's car. Collectively, they were adding up to a mystery I felt powerless to unravel, but whose lingering menace I felt everywhere around me. In the cereal aisle at Safeway I put my arm on Red's shoulder at the approach of a swarthy stranger. He was looking for the Coco Pops. When no-one was looking I tucked the marijuana deep down behind a rack of muesli. A little bonus for the late-night shelf-stackers.

There I'd been, Mr Clever Dick, bunging on a white knight act, trying to impress Ayisha in front of Bayraktar's heavy-duty crim mates, when all along she'd been hiding the fact that Gezen was not telling the whole story. Then she'd gone and disappeared, leaving me a sitting duck in a game whose rules I couldn't even guess at. What a bitch she was turning out to be.

As the Renault reversed out of its slot in the supermarket car park, a flash of dusty colour caught the corner of my eye. I pulled the steering wheel in an arm-wrenching arc and craned backwards over my shoulder. You're chasing ghosts in the twilight, I told myself. Two blocks from home, I glanced up at a stop sign and found a cube of lurid blue framed in the rectangle of the rear-vision mirror, an aqua Falcon, its windows impenetrable in the halogen wash of the newly lit street lights. I barked at Red to stay where he was and stepped out onto the road.

The Falcon had the same wide-mouthed grimace as before, but in other ways was subtly different. The duco shone with a higher polish, an air-intake duct sprouted from the bonnet, the tyres were comically fat. The plates were personalised. VROOM, they read. The driver's window came down and Van Halen came out, loud. Then a head, Adonis with acne. 'What's eating you, squirrel dick?' it shouted.

It was a good question. Before I could think of a pithy retort, the head disappeared and the Falcon peeled past, its horn blaring the first two bars of Dixie. 'Dickhead,' said Red. I didn't dare ask him who he meant.

Two men in suits were sitting in a parked car at the end of our street, a white Commodore. It was the two CIB dicks from Ciccio's. I parked outside the house and they got out, hoisting their belts up as they came. When they were two houses away I took out a two dollar note. 'Go get some milk,' I told Red. By the will of Wendy he was still too young to go to the corner shop alone. 'You can spend the change.' He grinned wildly and trotted off. With that sort of money he'd be standing at the lolly counter for half an hour.

I hoisted the bag of groceries and held the gate open for the coppers. 'Murray Whelan?' asked the older one. He had a low centre of gravity and a bulbous aggressive nose but his tone was polite. 'I'm detective sergeant Dalziel. This is detective constable York.' York had been working out. He nodded, real friendly like.

'Acting on information, gentlemen?'

York ambled down the side of the house. I put my key in the front door and jiggled it about. 'Do you have a warrant?'

'Do we need one?' said Dalziel pleasantly. I held the door open and let him in ahead of me. I hoped to hell nothing else had been planted around the house while I was away. We went through to the kitchen. Out the window I could see Mr Muscle step across Wendy's rug and stick his head in the toolshed. Dalziel looked around like what he saw confirmed his worst suspicions. 'You don't seem surprised to see us,' he said.

'In my line of work you learn not to be surprised,' I said, dumping the groceries on the bench.

He was walking around with his hands in his pockets, freely scrutinising everything in sight. 'And exactly what is your line of work?'

When I told him, he showed no reaction, but I could hear the gears whirring as he tried to place me in the wider scheme of things. 'People think their local member can wave a magic wand, fix their problems,' I said. 'If they don't get what they want, they blame me. Some of them start throwing threats around. Anonymous tip, was it?' I had the groceries out of the bag and started loading the fridge.

'We're required to follow these things up,' he said. 'I'm sure you understand.'

'What was it?' I said wearily. I prised the top off a stubby and waved it in his general direction. 'Child pornography? Wife beating? Drugs?'

The copper ignored the beer. He tapped the window and waved York back out front. 'Do you have any idea who might make such allegations?'

'No,' I said. 'But when you find out I'd certainly like to fucking well know.'

Dalziel handed me his card. 'I don't think we need disturb you further,' he said. At least he didn't shoot me, which is more than some people can say about the Victorian police.

Being a functionary of the party in power arguably put me on the same side as the police. But as far as I was concerned, no quirk of political circumstance could alter the fact that, by disposition and training, all coppers were bastards until proven otherwise. I had suspected as much as a child, watching my father unlock the saloon bar in the lull after the six o'clock swill. No point in getting on the wrong side of the law, he'd whisper, reaching for the top shelf. My ambivalence was violently reinforced one afternoon in my first year at university.

There was a march. I can't even remember what it was about. It was a demo a minute in those days. This one was nothing major, no Springbok tour or US Consulate job. Just a few banners and Eureka flags. A couple of hundred chanting longhairs. I'd just tagged along for a look. The hard left were a pack of wankers, as far as I was concerned, middle-class kids trying to pass themselves off as otherwise with bad manners and a lot of beer. But there was this girl, Georgina something, that I was thinking of making a play for. She was right up the front, holding the lead banner.

We were almost back on campus, when the ambush happened. Hundreds of blue uniforms appeared at the top of a rise, more of them than us. An inspector with white epaulettes bellowed something unintelligible through a megaphone. An order to disperse, I guess. There was nowhere to disperse to. Then they charged. They went through us like a dose of the salts. Batons, horses, you name it. They'd taken off their numbers, so they could get energetic without fear of being identified. And they really knew how to enjoy themselves.

A big sergeant got me in a headlock while two of his mates took turns giving me the old one-two. I'd lost two teeth and nearly choked on my own blood before their interest flagged and they moved on. Georgina's boyfriend had his collar-bone broken, so from my point of view it all turned out to be for nothing. The next time I saw the sergeant was a decade later. Deputy Commissioner/Operations I think his title was. He was sharing an official dais with Charlene.

But we get nowhere dwelling on past grievances. The dicks were gone and Red was back with a musk cigar and a packet of gum. Big bubbles. No troubles. I stuck him in front of the telly with the chicken pie we had picked up priced-to-clear at the supermarket bakery counter, rolled up my sleeves, and waded into a frenzy of housework. Wendy would be arriving tomorrow. Things needed to be done. The nit scare had been bad enough; having her find the house looking like a half-demolished rat-trap would have been tantamount to self-destruction.

I drained the lounge room swamp, washed dishes, vacuumed floors and hung damp laundry over the clothes horse to dry. While it felt somewhat ludicrous to be window-dressing the house I had shared with Wendy for seven years, it was also imperative that she find no evidence of inability to cope, no pretext for complaint that the child's welfare and comfort were at jeopardy in his father's hands. I did a particularly fine job on the toilet. In my experience, the link between bathroom cleanliness and female psychology cannot be overemphasised.

All this mindless activity gave me time to think. Someone breaks into my house, plants drugs, then calls the cops. The same somebody tries to run me over. It was impossible not to believe it was all connected to Memo Gezen and the toughs in the grey BMW. But how did they know where I lived? And what was all this supposed to achieve? And what if they came back? Was Red safe? Maybe a few days with Wendy might not be a bad idea, after all. Just until I got this business sorted out.

I was on my knees with a brush up the S-bend when the phone rang. Expecting it would be Wendy, I braced myself. It was old man Picone. Agnelli's uncle's brother-in-law, a market gardener from Werribee, had been at a family lunch on Sunday. Over the vitello tonnato he had been told that Agnelli would definitely be in parliament as of the next election.

I called the House straight away. Charlene wasn't in either her office or the chamber. I asked to be put through to the members' dining room. The head steward came on the line, recognised my voice and informed me that Mrs Wills had just had some kind of collapse and a colleague had taken her to hospital. He didn't know which one. I rang the Royal Melbourne, the Women's, the Queen Victoria and St Andrews, which was closest to the House. She hadn't been admitted to any of them. All I got on her home number was the answering machine.

The rain had let up, so I took a Vegemite jar of Jamesons out into the backyard and we incinerated a couple of tobacco bushes together. When I thought about it, Charlene had been burning the candle pretty brightly over the previous two years. The election, the euphoria of winning office after so long in the wilderness, overhauling a moribund ministry, ramming through a hefty raft of reform legislation, it was all bound to take its toll. I should have been looking after her, shouldering more of the burden.

When she'd cancelled the last two of our regular sessions at the electorate office, our fortnightly chance to catch up with each other, I hadn't even asked why. Preoccupied coping with Red, running maintenance on the house, and stewing in my own juices over Wendy, I'd even been relieved. Not that enquiring after Charlene's health would have got me more than a gruff affirmative. She took far too much pride in her reputation as a tough old chook to solicit sympathy. But that shouldn't have stopped me asking.

The whiskey and nicotine must have fired me up. The urge to do something, anything, gnawed at me. This Bayraktar business was a real piss-off. The last thing I needed to be doing right now was looking over my shoulder every five minutes for the boys from the Anatolia Club. But until Ayisha or Gezen turned up I was left hanging. Or was I?

I rifled the phone book. Fifteen Celiks were listed, ten in the immediate area, none with the initial A. There were no Gezens at all, and no listing under Anatolia Club. A gambling club, Ayisha had called it. Perhaps I was coming at the subject from the wrong angle, thinking about the car. Rational thought hadn't been getting me anywhere. Trying to second-guess the dark recesses of the right-wing Turkish mind could easily take forever. It was time for some direct action, even if it was a blind punt.

Under Police was a listing for the Gaming Squad. A machine answered and told me to leave a message. I hung up, collected my thoughts and rang back. Anonymous denunciation was a game two could play. My accent was terrible, more Bombay than Bosphorus, made even worse by the pencil clamped between my molars. Maybe I sounded like a crank, but I didn't imagine they got too many calls from a prisoner at the Anatolia Club, 636 Blyth Street, Brunswick, pleading to be rescued before he was castrated for his gambling debts. And like the man said, they were required to follow these things up.

The odds were long, but with a smidgin of beginners luck, Bayraktar's buddies would at least be getting an enquiring official knock on their glossy green front door within a day or so. Whether it would be enough to teach them a bit of road courtesy remained to be seen. Jesus Christ, I thought, as I hung up. What had started as a strategy to save the government from embarrassment was turning into a very bad vaudeville routine.

Branch meetings started at 8 p.m. As the product of two inveterate meeting-goers, Red had accepted from infancy the normality of spending at least one night a week under a table with his colouring pencils at some discussion group or executive committee or task force. At seven-thirty I told him to get his coat.

'I'm not going,' he said, digging his heels in. This tough new haircut was going to his head.

I offered him a dollar. He was unimpressed. A dirty brown banknote and a glass of pink lemonade were lousy compensation for being bored out of your brain for two hours while your father massaged the grass roots.

But the options were non-existent. My old man was in Queensland, not that he would have been much use even if he was closer. Wendy's parents were getting on, lived in Camberwell and never volunteered. Besides, they voted Liberal. I couldn't see myself calling them up and explaining the urgency of chairing a Labor party branch meeting.

Red began to whine. Great. Here we were fighting on what was possibly our last night of bachelorhood together before Wendy arrived and started making trouble. There was no alternative but to put my foot down and take a firm patriarchal stance. 'Five dollars,' I said. 'Plus a packet of chips.'

Right then the front doorbell rang. Red, looking for an out, flew up the hall and flung it open. 'It's a lady,' he yelled.

It was no lady. It was Ayisha, draped nonchalantly against the verandah post in her quilted overcoat. 'Sivan said you wanted to see me,' she said, as though she had no idea why. 'What's happening?'

This sudden materialisation on my doorstep set me back a pace. To be discovered like this—a tea-towel across my shoulder, hectoring a small child—wasn't going to do my image any good. How would I ever be able to pass myself off as a Gramsci-reading, internationalist sophisticate after this? Aside from which, where did she come off with this casual attitude? I tucked the tea-towel in my hip pocket. 'What's happening?' I snapped. 'You fucking well tell me.'

My attitude took her aback somewhat. 'You okay?'

'No, I'm not. I'm mightily pissed off. I don't appreciate being fucked around. You could have had the decency to tell me what I was buying into.'

Red was all ears, alert to my tension, watching the way I responded to this strange woman. He tucked himself against my thigh, declaring prior possession.

Ayisha cocked her head to one side. 'You've been to the police, haven't you?'

At the mention of the word 'police', I felt an electric charge of excitement surge through Red.

'Where have you been all day?' I demanded, sounding like a jealous husband. 'And what about your friend Gezen?'

'I've been at college,' she said. 'Why?'

'College? What were you doing at college?'

'Accountancy,' she said.

Accountancy? Christ, what about the revolution? At least she was safe. 'You and I need to have a serious talk,' I said. Not with the child there, though. 'But right now Red and I are running late for a meeting.'

Red saw his chance. 'No we're not,' he piped up cheerfully. 'Come in.' Detaching himself from my leg he took off down the hall. Taking his cue, Ayisha shouldered past me and followed him.

'You have been to the cops, haven't you?' she accused. 'I thought you said you'd help.'

I tailed her down the hall. The draped laundry, so homey and efficient only minutes before, looked pathetic. Red had turned on the television and thrown himself onto the couch. Grabbing Ayisha by the elbow I propelled her out of his earshot. She looked around the kitchen, summing up my domestic arrangements. I could see her mentally pigeon-holing me.

'My wife, well my ex-wife, sort of, well, she lives in Canberra and…' I was babbling, shifting from one foot to the other.

'Christ, Murray,' she said. 'What's got into you?'

'Don't come Miss Innocent with me,' I said, recovering my indignation fast. 'First Gezen disappears, then you take off, then I find out about Gezen's political background, then…'

She pulled me up short. 'Gezen's political background? What do you mean?'

'The PKK, or whatever it is, the Kurdish guerillas. Sivan told me. Don't worry, I didn't tell him about the Bayraktar business.'

'Sivan told you Memo was PKK?' That sly grin was spreading back across her face. 'And you believed him?'

'Sure.' But I knew then that I shouldn't have.

'Christ, Murray,' she laughed. 'Memo Gezen's got six kids and chronic back pain and lives in a two-bedroom flat in East Keilor. He's no more PKK than the man in the moon. Sivan's been pulling your leg.'

Of course. So he had. And I'd fallen for it—hook, line and sinker. 'Why would he do that?' I sulked.

'Jeeze, I dunno. Sivan's a born joker. Maybe he thought you were still playing that guess-the-name game you started him on yesterday. He probably thought you knew he was having you on.'

'But when Gezen disappeared this morning, I thought those

guys in the BMW...' To be perfectly frank, I could no longer remember exactly what I'd been thinking.

'Memo didn't disappear,' Ayisha said. 'He went back to work. When he first turned up, asking about getting a lawyer, he told me he was on his lunch break. Then you said for him to go to work like normal, not to draw attention to himself. So when we knew it wasn't the police parked out the front, I told him to piss off quick smart. Out the back door and back to work before he was missed.'

'So why were the Anatolia Club guys in the BMW watching him?'

'Yeah,' she said. 'I've been wondering that myself all day.'

'At college?'

'Yeah.'

'But why did you take off so quickly? Sivan didn't say anything about you being at college.'

'I knew he'd forget,' she said. 'Usually I go on Thursdays and Fridays. But end of year exams are on. I had a three-hour statistics test at midday. I hadn't exactly been expecting all that business with Memo, you know. And we had to go through that story of his twice, once in Turkish and again in English. By the time he'd finished I was running seriously late. Put me right off, it did. Wouldn't be surprised if I failed. Anyway, we all went off to the pub afterwards and I didn't get your message until I got home half an hour ago. How was I supposed to know you'd been looking for me?'

'Don't you want to know why I was looking for you?' I asked.

'Sure,' she said. We'd sat down at the kitchen table by this stage. She didn't have anything better to do with her time. 'That's what I'm here for.'

I gave her the works, everything from disturbing the intruder onwards. I left out the bits about going to the Bell Street cop shop and calling the Gaming Squad. I felt enough of an idiot about having believed Sivan. For once she didn't interrupt or ask questions, but as I spoke she crossed to the stove, lit a cigarette off the gas jet and began pacing about like a caged animal. 'So you see,' I concluded, 'I've been holding off going to the cops with the full story until I had a chance to talk to you. I want to do the right thing by Memo, but I've got a child to think about.'

Through the door into the lounge room I could see Red entrenching himself deeper into the television. 'Turn off that fucking telly this instant,' I screamed. 'We're late already.' I considered ringing ahead, telling them to start without me. How could they? The agenda papers were on the back seat of my car.

'I can't believe it,' Ayisha was saying. 'Attacking you in broad daylight. It's crazy.'

'You think I'm making this up?'

'No, no. All I mean is…' She brushed her hair back off her forehead, as though this gesture might better convey her meaning.

'We'll have to finish this later,' I said. 'I really do have to go.' In the lounge room, Red had made no move.

Ayisha brushed past me into the other room and perched on the arm of the couch. Red's eyes flickered sideways, registering her presence, then re-attached themselves firmly to the screen. A man in a pair of blue rubber gloves was whispering to the camera in a stealthy undertone as he sidled through some shrubbery.

'This the part with the gorilla?' she said.

Red grunted in the affirmative, the mutual-recognition signal of the committed video-head.

'Can I watch with you while your dad goes to his meeting?' She moved onto the couch beside him, slipping her arms out of that inflatable overcoat of hers.

Could she what. 'Uh-huh,' he said. 'The good bit's on next.'

'You can wait a couple more hours before calling the you-know-whats, can't you?' Red moved aside to accommodate her. 'Don't worry,' she hastened to reassure me. 'I know the drill. I've got five younger brothers.'

There was no fighting it. I'd just been boxed in by the fastest coalition in history. A united front, irresistible force and immovable object.

The Lakeview Hotel was a sprawling ranch-style beer barn in the middle of a residential neighbourhood half a mile from Sydney Road. At nineteen I had worked there in the guise of Fred Engels, pulling trays of jugs and the occasional barmaid. Across the road through a line of scraggy she-oaks lay Edwardes Lake, a flooded gravel pit landscaped with bike paths, coin-in-the-slot barbecues and adventure playgrounds.

The branch met in the Function Room. About the only useful function it served was to store a couple of derelict pool tables and provide a rent-free space for branch meetings. As usual Laurie the publican had laid a sheet of plywood over one of the pool tables, turned on the strip radiator bolted halfway up the wall, and set out thirty chairs on the Prussian blue Axminster. Laurie, a party member since before the Split, was an inveterate optimist. At that time of the year we'd be lucky to get a dozen takers, which was the exact number waiting when I bustled through the door at eight-fifteen. 'Okay,' I said. 'Let's get on with it. We don't want to be here all night.'

We did attendances and apologies first, me putting my hand up for Charlene, Greg Coates and half a dozen others. Thirteen attendances and fifteen apologies out of sixty-seven members on the books. It was the usual crowd—true believers, unreconstructed Whitlamites, reliable booth captains, handers out of how-to-vote cards, knife-sharpeners, has-beens and wannabees. Laurie's son Barry, a forty-seven-year-old bachelor draftsman at the State Electricity Commission, took the minutes on a concertina pile of computer paper salvaged from the SEC recycle bin.

The dauphin, Gavin Mullane, was there, keen to push his traffic safety barrow, and to keep a weather eye on the North West Progress Association, a childless couple in their mid-fifties who stole his thunder on local issues whenever they could. Our resident ex-Trotskyist was a teacher named Vernon Tibbett. Vern had squandered his youth selling *Direct Action* outside factory gates at the crack of dawn and was spending the rest of his life making other people pay for it. Behind him sat Sam Righi, administrator of the Broadmeadows Legal Service where Joe Lollicato worked. This was his first attendance in months. He'd be worth pumping later. A couple of fresh faces were paying their neophyte dues before they stuck their hands up for a job. The rest had always been there, nice old codgers who kept the faith, remembered the ancient enmities, and sat in wise silence as befitted tribal elders.

Mercifully, there were no Greeks. The local inventors of democracy had their own branch where they could engage in vigorous dialectics in their native demotic until the goats came home, sparing the rest of us the ordeal. 'Item one.' I moved briskly into the agenda. 'Matters arising.'

Tibbett leaped to his feet. 'Comrade Chair. Point of procedure. I move a suspension of standing orders in order to bring forward agenda item number sixteen, a resolution pertaining to the federal government's flagrant overriding of party policy in respect of the mining and export of uranium.'

'Fine,' I said. 'Seconder?'

Nobody moved a muscle except a rather jolly nursing aide called Maggie Alcott who was a shop steward with the Hospital Employees Federation. She sniffed and rammed her forearms deeper into the sleeves of her chunky-knit cardigan. I gave it a slow count of ten. 'Motion lapses for want of a seconder. Now...'

We sped through the next fifteen items in an hour and three-quarters flat, including twenty brain-numbing minutes devoted to Gavin Mullane's hypothetical traffic lights, 'not two hundred metres from where we are actually sitting at this point in time'. Tibbett's motion was last up.

For all its outward efficiency, my chairing was driven by a growing sense of impatience and anxiety. After all that had happened that day, how had I been so willing to hand Red over to the first baby-sitter that came along? Ayisha's five little brothers, her childcare credentials, what were they but proof of her mother's fertility? You saw those immigrant families all the time, driving along with no seat belts, tribes of kids standing up on the back seat, only the slightest bump away from being catapulted head first through the windscreen. What did I really know about Ayisha Celik except that I was mad keen to pop her in the cot?

The meeting debated Vern Tibbett's resolution for a tedious half hour, amended it into grammatical incoherence, passed it on factional lines and directed me to convey its views to the national secretary and the relevant minister. By the time I thanked them for their attendance and closed the meeting it was twenty past ten on the Dewars Whisky clock above the bar.

After I'd helped Barry stack the chairs and turn off the heater, I went into the lounge bar to conduct the real business of the night. Mullane saw me coming, emptied his glass, nodded goodnight and ducked out the door. As if I'd want to drink with him. The old blokes were drinking in a school. I bought a round and asked after various grandchildren. No-one volunteered anything about Charlene, so the word wasn't yet out. Sam Righi turned towards me and put two fingers up for another round, an unrefusable invitation. I excused myself and went over.

Laurie's beer was watered and there was urgent unfinished business elsewhere, but ever since Greg Coates' remarks earlier in the afternoon a question had been gnawing at the back of my mind. I hoisted the offered beer and once again lubricated my smoke-bruised throat. 'How's life at the Legal Service? Joe Lollicato still running the joint?' I asked, just making conversation.

Righi grinned. 'Not much gets past you does it?'

I fired up a coffin nail. 'Not if I can help it.'

'That Lolly,' he said. 'Talk about falling on your feet. Good luck to him, that's what I say.'

He said it, but he didn't mean it. Righi's bile was too close to the surface to hide. It seemed that Lollicato had had some kind of luck and Righi wanted to put his own spin on the story. 'Lucky Lolly,' I said dryly, as if to say I never liked him either.

Righi was warming up for a full-blooded bad-mouthing session. 'The silly prick'll need a business card the size of a surf-board.'

I egged him on. 'Yeah?'

'He's been looking for a way out for months. Made no secret of it. Then, bang, out of the blue an offer like this.' As he recited, he expanded his hands like an exaggerating fisherman. 'Senior Lecturer, Intercultural Legal Studies, Faculty of Multicultural Disciplines, University of New England, Armidale.'

I whistled and wiggled my eyebrows appreciatively. So Lolli-cato was planning on leaving town. Hardly the move of a man scheming his way into a local seat. 'Look on the bright side,' I said. 'Fancy title, but those academic jobs pay shit money.'

Righi hailed Laurie for another two beers, not his round. Lollicato was just for openers, there was something else on his mind, something he wanted. 'Don't suppose you've had a chance to think about the by-election yet?'

'You've lost me.'

'When Joe moves interstate, there'll have to be a by-election, won't there?' So that was it. Righi wanted Lolly's spot on Broad-meadows Council.

It was getting on for twenty to eleven. A frank and fulsome discussion of Sam Righi's ambitions would have to wait. I tipped my head back and let the bitter liquid wash across my tongue. As the glass came down, the public bar came into view through the servery hatch. It was deserted but for a solitary drinker wrapped tight around his glass at the far end, his back to the hatch. Something about the way he held himself tugged at a loose thread in my memory. Catching Laurie's eye, I pointed with my chin. 'One of your regulars?'

The publican shook his head. 'Been nursing that drink for half an hour. Better finish soon or I'll do my licence.'

I stood up and laid a hand on Righi's shoulder. 'If you have any ideas about likely candidates, let me know. They could do with some fresh blood up there at Broadie.'

The guy in the drive-in bottle shop was shutting up, pulling the chains on the heavy roll-down door. I told him I wanted a bottle of white wine. 'Something in particular, sir?' he asked, like he was the cellar-master at Chateau Lafitte.

'A bottle of Hope Springs Eternal,' I said. 'If you haven't got that, anything under eight dollars will do.' The covered walkway to the carpark led past the public bar. I glanced in the window as I passed, but the room was deserted except for Laurie up-ending stools on the bar top. I shrugged and threw Barry's minutes into a dumpster, planning to write them up properly in the morning. That uranium motion would need substantial rejigging. Buggered if I was going to have the federal Minister for Resources' office screaming its tits off at me because Tibbett thought his line wasn't sufficiently correct.

Righi's little jewel about Lollicato, coming on top of Coates, added to what I was beginning to glean about Agnelli, made it pretty definite that I'd been fed some monumental crap at lunch on Monday. As I crossed the carpark I tried to reconstruct exactly what Agnelli had said, but only fragments came to mind. On recollection, however, it was plain that Agnelli had been feeding me a lot of ifs, buts and maybes, leading the talk in the direction he wanted, encouraging me to put my reservations aside and jump to a lot of conclusions. Conclusions that were now looking pretty dodgy indeed. Clearly, Lollicato did not then have, and maybe never had, serious parliamentary ambitions. Clearly, there had never been any genuine likelihood of an industrial flare-up at Pacific Pastoral. So either Agnelli had been misinformed, genuinely ignorant, or blowing a cloud of smoke in my eyes. The third option seemed most likely.

Agnelli was enough of a player to know that if he wanted Charlene's seat, he would need either to win me over or to keep me busy while he manoeuvred himself into position. He also knew the strength of my loyalty to Charlene and that any attempt to sound me out would have set off my alarm bells. So getting me out of the way while he lined up the numbers was the only real option. And what better way to get me to take my eye off the ball while the deals were done than to send me chasing a red herring? That's what this Pacific Pastoral cock and bull story had been all about. There had been more than one pigeon on the menu at the Mandarin Palace.

Christ, I'd been well and truly suckered. He'd probably even planted the story in the *Sun*. Agnelli hung around the Windsor Hotel, drinking with the political roundsmen, slipping them judicious leaks whenever the government wanted to fly a trial balloon on some contentious issue. Talk enough bullshit, he liked to say, and sooner or later it ends up in print.

The carpark shimmered, a shallow sea of puddles. I turned the Renault into the road. Its headlights found a break in the trees and fanned across the surface of the lake. A lash of wind stirred the darkness and a squall of fat raindrops burst across the windscreen. I headed up the hill and it began raining in earnest, heavy sluicing bucket-loads that whistled at the seams of the windows and buffeted the small sedan from side to side with a force that momentarily stalled the wipers in mid-sweep. The windscreen became a lustrous swarming blanket. I could scarcely see past the bonnet.

I turned the wipers up high and leaned forward, peering between their puny swipes. My knuckles were white as the wheel turned to mush in my hands. I was piloting a submarine up Niagara Falls. Slowing to a crawl, I inched forward. Up ahead was a roundabout, then the road dipped again, cutting across the bottom end of the lake where it overflowed across a weir and ran off into a creek so insignificant it had no name. This was where Mullane wanted his traffic lights.

The downpour was flash-flooding across the asphalt as the stormwater drains overloaded and backed up. As I neared the roundabout, the engine shuddered and it seemed I might stall, hubcap-deep. I changed down, slammed my foot down hard and felt the Renault shudder as the wheels threw great pounding jets of water up against the floor like fire-hoses turned on a rioting mob.

Just as I entered the curve, a powerful beam of light blazed suddenly on my right. Another car had come darting out of the cross street, its lights on high beam, apparently not seeing me.

The idea flashed into my mind that I was driving without lights. I groped for the switch. Of course the lights were on, I realised simultaneously. How else had I been navigating? No, the other car must be able to see me. I was like a rabbit in a spotlight. What was the dickhead doing?

The dickhead was almost on top of me now, an advancing wall of white light, waves sluicing up from its front wheels. Mullane had been right about one thing. There definitely were some maniac drivers around here. I swerved left, pumping at the brake pedal, feeling it suddenly useless under my foot. The Renault glided forward, rudderless. There was a flash of blue and I recognised the Falcon just at the instant the Renault ramped up the sloping brick pavers of the kerb and left the ground, surging forward into a gap between the crash barriers.

I rose with it, my backside lifting clear of the seat, snapping back into place at the strain of the seat belt. Then, as the Renault's front wheels slewed into the soft earth of the roadside verge, I felt myself rise again. The front end of the car had stopped so abruptly that the back was still going, its momentum carrying it into an end-to-end roll, pitching me into an acrobat's tumble, my hands locked around the wheel in a dead man's grip.

This is it, I thought, and screwed my face shut against the imminence of oblivion. The Renault flipped onto its roof, shuddered, and came to rest. The roar of the storm filled my head and luminous shapes bobbed on the edge of my consciousness. Something wet ran up my face, trickling into my nose and gathering in a pool at the nape of my neck. I sneezed, my eyes squirting open with the force of it. I was, I realised, suspended upside down by the straps of the seat belt, my head jammed sideways against the cold vinyl of the roof. Water was coming in from above, from the floor of the car. You can't be this uncomfortable and dead at the same time, I told myself.

My left hand groped for the catch of the seat belt and sprang it open, releasing me down upon myself, a foetal ball. My right hand searched for the door handle, and failed to find it. Gripping the bottom edge of the dashboard, I struggled to haul myself upright, my shoulders shucking themselves free of the seat belt. A scraping noise began. The car was moving, gathering momentum as it slid down the slippery incline of the bank. The steel shell of the roof screeched as it scraped across the concrete path that circled the lake. The Renault tilted abruptly, tottered for a moment, and slid into the water, rear end first.

The lake was enormously wet, enormously dark. It wrapped itself around the shell of the car and sucked it downwards. The door came open and water gushed in, frigid beyond my powers of description, filling the interior. I never felt more alive in my life. As water forced itself into my mouth, blind terror guided my feet against the dashboard.

Then somehow I was outside, breaking the surface, clawing at the air, my breath raspy and asthmatic, my testicles retreating before the icy onslaught. Sheets of torrential rain churned the surface around me. The bottom was somewhere in the darkness far below. My clothes were bonds, dragging me downwards. Breathing came in short hysterical gasps. Cold was crushing my chest. Looming above, dark on dark, was the embankment. Somewhere a light bobbed, moving closer. I kicked out towards the shore.

Some slimy thing brushed my face, then another, and another, triggering yet more spasms, panic and cold in equal proportions. What horror was this? A tendril swept into my mouth, scaly and stiff. I spat it out, but there were more, dozens of them, trailing their tentacles over my lips and ears. My arms flailed the water, swatting, grabbing, my fingers closing around one of the ropy lengths, slippery and elastic.

My upper body rose from the water and solid ground formed itself under my feet. I stood, amazed to find myself in less than a metre of water. The thing in my hand resolved itself into the dangling branch of a weeping willow. Over my shoulder, the Renault had disappeared entirely. My feet mired in unseen mud, sheets of torrential rain lashing my face, freezing water up to my thighs, I emitted an involuntary groan of relief.

The bobbing light approached, above on the embankment. A stocky figure, half umbrella, was braving the storm, sweeping the lake with the beam of a powerful torch. I opened my mouth to shout and nearly bit off my tongue, my teeth and jaws shivering into spasm. A thin, animal moan escaped from deep in my chest. It was all I could manage. The wind threw it back into the darkness behind me. Grasping the dangling ropes of the willow branches for support, I sucked my shoes up out of the mud and began shuffling ashore. The man with the torch, God bless him, would see me soon. Christ, I was cold.

The bank was a shoulder-high redoubt of slippery mud, cascading with rain water. I tried to cry out again, but still all that came was the same wounded animal noise, lost in the roar of the rain, and the castanet clatter of my teeth. One thing I knew for sure was that if I didn't get out of there soon I'd freeze to death where I stood.

The light was less than twenty metres away by then, almost close enough to touch. The figure holding it crouched low under the dome of an umbrella, and peered intently along the beam, methodically playing it back and forth across the roiling water. But it was pointed in the wrong direction, flashing uselessly across the place where the car had gone down. Whoever it was would pass without noticing me, half-drowned, virtually under-foot. I gathered a fistful of willow frond and hauled, dragging myself hand over hand upwards, into his line of sight.

My fingers were stiff with cold, my sodden clothes a dead weight. The branch bent low and snapped. I was back in the water, my feet kicking for the bottom, not finding it. My suit was a sheet of lead swathing my limbs, dragging me under. The light was going now, retreating up the embankment towards the road. I opened my mouth and pushed a yell up from deep inside my body cavity, but water filled my mouth and all that came out was a wheezing cough. Then the current took me.

Rain, flooding into the lake from every direction, had raised the water above the level of the containment weir. A foaming sheet was pouring over the lip of the spillway only yards away. I felt myself being swept along, the pull increasing. The smooth concrete lip of the rim reared out of the dark and struck my shoulder. Suddenly I was toppling over the wall, ricocheting down the open funnel of the overflow chute. White water buffeted me from all sides. Up ahead, at the apex of the funnel, the dark mouth of a stormwater drain yawned. There wasn't even enough time to scream before I was sucked into its swirling vortex.

Turbid with crap of every variety, the torrent surged through the culvert, hurtling me irresistibly, feet-forward into the void. My jaw was clamped shut against the water, but nothing could lessen the elemental roar that filled my ears as I barrelled the length of the stormwater drain, my head bang, bang, banging against smooth concrete walls.

Just at the moment my lungs seemed about to burst, I was spat out like an orange pip and deposited, flailing, into the bed of the creek with no name. My feet hit the rocky bottom with a bone-jarring impact and I immediately pitched face-down into the stream. Again I was swept helplessly forward, along with all the other crummy debris the storm was flushing away—a toxic minestrone of wormy fur-balls, slimy old Wagon Wheel wrappers, dog turds, all the dross of a thousand households. As I tumbled by, the blackberry bushes crowding the banks slashed at my clothes but failed utterly to slow my progress.

Several times I managed to struggle upright, but the creek bed was an uneven tangle of slippery rocks and lumps of masonry, and the pressure of the current was so immense that I was immediately sent flailing onwards, scrabbling to keep my head above the vile wash.

Then a glowing shape loomed ahead of me. An old white

bathtub, upside down, its bottom perforated with rust like a colander, jutted into the stream. I threw my arms over its slippery enamel curve and felt the ground solidify under my knees as the tide fought to drag me back under. Staggering upright, I threw myself headlong up the bank and pitched into a thicket of blackberries. One, two, three steps and I hit a sagging chainmesh fence. I scrabbled upwards, my fingers through the links, putting distance between myself and the eddying whirl behind me, until the dead weight of my body flipped over the top and toppled into a mound of green plastic garbage bags, soft and yielding.

As suddenly as it had begun, the storm was abating. Rain was still falling, but in an ethereal, almost benign, mist. I rolled over and lay face down, listening to my heart race. The slick plastic was smooth against my cheek. The cushioning softness yielded to my shape. My entire existence seemed to have been reduced to a dull pulsating throb that wobbled back and forth behind my closed eyes like a malignant octopus.

I was cold, I knew that from the chattering of my teeth—now a finer, more regular grinding movement than the out-of-control juddering of before. This was like a special machine, something for polishing stones. I could live with this sensation, as long as the ache in my head went away. Yes, I was cold, but first I had to rest, allow the terror to drain away. Every muscle felt bruised, every nerve teased raw.

Distantly, up the hill, I could hear the faint hum of traffic. I knew that if I looked up I would see a littered incline and the back of a row of small workshops and factories that ran along the ridge above the creek. But to do that I would have to raise my head. The view wasn't worth it.

I knew this place. On paper, it had long ago been slated for development as community recreation space, pending funding. I had seen the plans pinned to a board in the town hall foyer— thematic shrubbery, stick citizens at picnic tables. Submissions had been invited from the public. So far the only development had been the erection of a fence along the ridge behind the industrial estate and some signs prohibiting the dumping of rubbish. Ingenuity thrives on such obstacles. Uncivil garbage, rich in diversity, had insinuated its way over the chain link border and down the slope. Paint tins, twisted bike wheels, warped and splintered plywood, garden waste, trash and junk of all kinds littered the slope where I lay.

But at least it was dry land, drier than the creek anyway. And if not quite land then a squelching mattress, soft and warm against my body. I reached over and stroked the pliant, yielding cushion on which I lay, feeling warmth beneath my fingers as though the core of the earth had risen to comfort me.

Not just my face and fingers felt the soft heat, but my chest and thighs too, even through the sodden fabric of my suit. I snuggled deeper, drawing a filthy sheet of old linoleum over me as a blanket. Pain surged red behind my eyes with the effort of movement. Lie still, my brain commanded.

Smell, as well as warmth, enveloped me, the rich pong of rotting vegetation. Lawn clippings, I recognised. I poked a hole in the bag and it gave a fragrant sigh, a gaseous rush of breath. It was full of half-rotten grass, cut wet and packed down hard, dumped by some weekend gardener too lazy or too lousy to drive to the tip and pay his three dollars. Trapped in the airless plastic, the grass had begun to ferment and smoulder with the same febrile heat that causes haystacks to combust spontaneously.

Ignoring the shrill irritability of the poisonous octopus in my skull, I cradled the pillow closer and snuggled deeper into the bloated softness. Its embrace fused with the dissipating heat of my body and soothed the ache at the centre of my being. Shuddering, I groaned softly and drank in the steaming aroma of a hose-drenched summer lawn. Mother earth held me fast. 'Mummy,' I murmured.

The beer garden of the Pier Hotel had been my first proper lawn. Before that, living upstairs at the Carters Arms, I had envied the other kids their backyards, the space for balls and cubbies. As soon as I saw that lawn at the Pier I had claimed it, a mat of couch-grass just long enough for a run-up and a full toss. I hammered in the stumps as a claim of ownership and set the bails on top.

Fine, my father had said. You want it, you mow it. And he'd

pointed into the shed, past the empty kegs and spare pluto hoses, to the rotary mower. At eight it had been all I could do to push the thing, its cylinder of blades and tractor-treaded iron wheels stiff with age and rust. Then, shaking off the months of disuse, it had darted forward, springing into life, tumbler whirring, and thrown an arc of green confetti behind, first rough and itchy on bare shins then soft and spongy under bare soles. A green rainbow in the summer sun, flecked with transient light like tail lights disappearing in the rain, like the sweep of a torch beam across freshly chopped water.

The police would be here soon. The helicopter would be thumping overhead, wompa wompa, sweeping its bloody great searchlight across the dark waters, following the line of the creek. Floodlights and generators. Frogmen, groping the mud, would attach chains to a tow-truck winch and haul the gushing Renault ashore. Orange tape stretched across the embankment, the traffic branch in their white raincoats going door to door. Did you see anything, madam? The Accident Appreciation Squad.

Told you so, I'd tell them. None of this would have happened if you'd pulled your fingers out earlier. A driver deliberately run off the road, a car on its roof in ten metres of water. Hardly a bit of harmless hooning around. Attempted murder, that's what. Questions in the House, there'd be. Charges laid. Red faces all round. Serves them right. Attempted murder. One for downtown, Russell Street. Well out of the local league, this one. Let's hear what Bayraktar's mates would have to say for themselves when the Homicide Squad came knocking on the door at the Anatolia Club.

Three days ago I'd never heard of Bayraktar, now someone in the guy's car was trying to kill me. What for? Crossing the street with intent to ask questions? What sort of fascistic bloody-mindedness was that? Shaking a fist in the street, hardly a killing offence. Talk about over-excitable wogs.

Gezen was the key. All this shit had started the moment Gezen had decided to make a clean breast of it. Double life Gezen. Timid little mop jockey Gezen, eyes that sucked you dry. What was it he had said? 'I see everything.' Maybe that was it. Maybe he had seen something he shouldn't have. Maybe somebody thought he had dobbed them in. Maybe they thought he had told me something he shouldn't have.

Bayraktar could not have been working alone. The man could hardly even sign his own name, let alone fabricate the contents of a tax declaration form. Was he just doing what he was told, someone else doing the thinking? Maybe it was all bull-shit, Gezen's confession, the whole standover story. Gezen had Ayisha convinced, that much was sure. Or was she in on it, too? That rushed and hushed burble of Turkish before Gezen had told his story, what had that been all about? No, Ayisha wouldn't dud her pal Murray, would she? She liked me. Even though my head ached and I felt like shit, she liked me.

Why else would she be curled up beside me now, here on this rubbish tip, her rump tucked into the curve of my belly, her hair tickling my neck, the rhythm of her breathing rising and falling with mine? She wouldn't lie, she whose mouth was finding mine, the rubbery flesh of her lips nuzzling mine, the wet rasp of her tongue mashing my cheek, a whine of desire rising from her throat.

I opened my eyes. A black dog with yellow teeth—a foul-breathed, wet-mouthed, bow-legged roly-poly lump of an animal with an accordion button row of nipples down its belly—was slobbering over my face. I stumbled upright, throwing off the lino. My shoes squelched. My head felt as though it had been cast in some experimental material that would soon be recalled by the manufacturer. The sky was clear and bright and very high up. At the far horizon a few last cauliflowers of cloud raced ahead of the slight breeze. Through the broken glass of my watch I deciphered that it was just about to go one-thirty. Or had been when the watch stopped. I shook my head in disbelief, igniting fireworks behind my eyes. The searing jolt slowly subsided into mere pain.

Unbelievable. Run off the road, car wrecked, nearly drowned, swept away in a flood, and what do I do? I pass out like a baby, face down in a pile of compost for more than three hours. From somewhere uphill came the fading sound of a car engine. The dog licked my hand and stuck its muzzle in my crotch. It wasn't much, but I was grateful for the thought.

'C'mon,' I said. The vibration of my voice triggered another chain reaction in my skull. I began picking my way through the broken glass and builder's rubble. Bile and old beer rose in my gullet. My trouser legs were rubbing the insides of my thighs raw. I shivered, that old spasm back again.

The double cyclone-gate at the top of the rise was locked, but there was enough slack on the chain to slip through the gap. The low row of brick workshops—a panel beater's, a printery, a tiler's yard—showed no light. Daytime places. In one direction the road curved away towards houses, in the other it ran back down towards the lake. I was a blinking neon of unpleasant sensation, sweating cold. The dog frolicked beside me, an imbecile.

'Easy, lover girl,' I urged, needing to hear my own voice. It was high-pitched, all edge. I wondered where the energy was coming from. The lake came into view, a ruffled nap of black velour. I kept on down the empty road, past the bolted roller door of the Lakeview Hotel's drive-in bottle shop. The only sound now was the faint swish of the treetops.

No rescue squad. No nothing. Maybe, I thought, I'm still asleep. At the weir wall, a thin glaze of water curved gently over the culvert, no more turbulent than a blanket tucked tight at the end of a well-made bed. Down the embankment, the weeds flattened by the upturned Renault's progress were already springing upright. The gashes torn in the earth by the impact were no more than a random string of muddy ruts. From the path at the lake's edge I peered into the water, willing the sunken car to reveal itself. Two grand worth of comprehensively uninsured frogmobile, vanished.

Not a single tangible sign existed that anything untoward had happened here. Maybe, I thought, I'm dead. Maybe I'm over there under the water watching myself, the sole witness to my own demise. The dog whined, clamped its teeth gently around my fingers and tugged. If I'm dead, I thought, who are you? Cerberus, watchdog of the nether world? 'Not enough heads,' I said, out loud. 'You need more heads.' I tried to remember how many, but it made my own ache even more.

Across the road, behind mute front gardens, houses slept dumbly on, substantial and warm. I considered opening one of the front gates, knocking on the door. 'Excuse me for waking you. Someone tried to kill me, but I went to sleep. Mind if I use your phone. You couldn't spare a cup of coffee while I wait, could you?' A crap-encrusted madman, mongrel dog in tow. Just the thought of it was enough to make my headache worse. I turned to the lake and vomited, beery dregs and diced carrots. Where did *they* come from? How come when you chuck there's always diced carrots?

A car approached down the hill. I stiffened and hobbled into the shadow of the trees. A little Japanese number puttered down to the roundabout, turned, and disappeared between the houses, reeling its exhaust rattle in as it went. Paranoia, I thought. Proof of the existence of life. And why shouldn't I have been paranoid? Where were the fucking cops when you needed them? I paid my taxes, didn't I? Wasn't I as entitled as the next person to venture forth on the streets without fear for life and property? Hadn't the Gaming Squad got my message?

And what had become of the Good Samaritan, with his torch and his umbrella? What kind of person would see a car go hurtling into a lake, wander around in a storm searching for survivors, then pack up and go home without reporting it? Shit, maybe the police had already been. Come, found nothing and gone.

I felt my scalp, probing for hairline fractures, distrusting my memory. How could a man think in this state, beaten insensible, his head throbbing and surging? Tender lumps bulged at the nape of my neck. I vomited again, retching bile. I puke therefore I am.

Another car approached. It had a light on its roof. 'Taxi,' I croaked. The word hung in the air as if confirming my existence. I raised my hand and fumbled for the wad of notes and coins in my pants pocket. Five soggy dollars, ten, some change. Enough. I waved it above my head. The cab slowed. I saw myself reflected back in the driver's stony glance. A wild-eyed derro, standing in a pool of chuck, waving crumpled bills, a dirty dog. The cab kept rolling, picking up speed. He might as well have got out and kicked me.

'What's the matter with this country?' I asked the mutt. If the dog knew, she wasn't saying. This bitch was turning into a liability. I sprayed a handful of gravel half-heartedly in her direction. 'Garn. Git.' The dog skittered away, then cringed back, creeping forward on her belly. What have I done to deserve this? 'True,' I relented. 'C'mon then.'

C'mon where? When I'd started down the hill towards the lake I imagined myself being rushed by paramedics. I'd be wrapped in blankets. A steaming cup of tea would be thrust into my hands. A lady sergeant with a clipboard would sit beside me in the back of an ambulance. Well, it was pretty clear that no such thing was going to happen. I thought of Red and a spasm of anxiety gripped my stomach. I must call home. Call home then call the police.

Past the roundabout and up the hill was a little strip of shops—a chemist, a milk bar, an appliance repairer. And a phone booth. I began shambling along the footpath, the dog waddling alongside, forgiven and forgiving. The shivers were getting worse and my thighs were red raw. I was tempted to pee in my pants for thermal relief, like a surfer in his wetsuit. As we passed the neat front yards, their trees stripped of blossoms by the storm, I scanned the facades, wondering if I knew anyone hereabouts well enough to wake them up. The houses all but snored. No light showed, no television flickered behind venetians. Were there no insomniacs left in suburbia? There had to be someone. This was my territory, after all. It wasn't as though I was in a foreign country.

Fight the headache, fight the nausea, this was my mantra. Not far now. Think it through. Must call home, check on Red. Tell Ayisha. God, maybe whoever did this to me had also done something to Red. Calm down. They wouldn't harm a child. Why would they do that? But why do anything they'd done? None of it made sense. The Falcon in the rain, it was the same one, wasn't it? Visibility had been close to zero. There must be hundreds of big blue sedans on the road. Maybe it had just been a perfectly innocent accident. Ahead, a man on a horse tipped his hat at me. Marlboro man was riding the range on the billboard wall of the milk bar. I gripped the coins in my pocket and turned the corner. In front of the phone box, nose to the kerb in the six-slot parking area, sat Bayraktar's Falcon.

A sheet of heavy-duty transparent plastic had been stuck over the missing rear window with blue electrical tape. It was billowing softly in and out like a lung. I went rigid and pressed myself against the cowboy's horse. Nothing else moved. Deep in the milk bar a row of bottles stood sentinel, back-lit in a refrigerated display. The Falcon was empty.

I grabbed the handle and threw the driver's door open, not caring any more. Nothing. No perfidious Turk waiting to spring. Not even any litter. Just the key in the ignition and the ozone smell of freshly wiped vinyl. The dog fixed that, bounding past me onto the passenger seat.

The dog was doing my thinking for me. Take the car and I could be home in ten minutes. I would know if Red was safe. If I called the police from the phone box, a prowl car might be twenty minutes arriving. Then would come the explanations, the questions, more explanations. I would have to take them down the hill, show them the vanishing skid marks, convince them I wasn't deranged. Fuck them. This was all their fault anyway. I'd call from home.

I walked around the car. I crouched, joints stiff, and peered underneath. I sprung the hood and peered into the oily pit of the motor. What was I looking for? A bundle of gelignite, a coil of wires, a ticking clock? The engine block was cold to the touch. I got in. The seat was too far forward, squeezing me against the steering wheel. The last person in this seat had been shorter. I bent forward and found the adjustment lever. A smear of drying mud covered the floor. The seat slid back and I turned the key. The big six-cylinder purred into action. Fingerprints, I thought, shrugged and gripped the wheel. Let the cops figure it out.

Streetlights flashed past overhead, a stroboscope that woke the epileptic octopus in my skull, made it real mad. A nauseating sickly-sweet detergent smell came up at me off the upholstery. Keeping off the main roads I made it home in fifteen minutes. I parked halfway along the street and left the key in the ignition. 'Stay,' I told the dog. Dognapping. What would it be next?

The only other cars parked in the street were familiar. No BMWs. Ayisha's Laser was parked out the front where she had left it. Down the side of the house a light showed dimly at the kitchen window. I was standing on the verandah, patting myself down and asking the toxic octopus where I had left my keys when the front door opened. Out of some swamp deep inside me came the croak of a frog. 'Red,' it said.

Ayisha appeared, immersed in a pool of light. She swam towards me out of her halo. Our Lady of the Muddle Headed. 'Fuck,' she said.

Then nothing. Nothing at all.

She had me on the bedroom floor and was pulling my trousers off. I felt a stirring in my underpants. Not now, I prayed, not now. Then I was under the covers, warm and dry. The octopus prised one eyelid open and Ayisha's face came into focus. 'Accountancy?' I said, concentrating on getting my tongue to work.

'Takes skills to get things done.' She was humouring me. She felt my forehead, all the while gnawing away at her bottom lip. 'Program budgeting skills, mainly.' She dispensed the reassuring grimace that passes for a smile among the caring professions. I'd have preferred a cuddle. 'Lie still while I phone a doctor.'

The wet clothes had been replaced by track pants and a windcheater. No undies, I noticed. I levered myself upright and swung my legs over the side of the bed. My mouth still wasn't working properly. 'Pee,' I made it say. Wee wees. Getting this much of me functioning made my head spin. Ayisha slipped a hand under my armpit. I shook her off, wanting to know how far gone I was. I was pretty far gone. At the door I turned not towards the bathroom but into Red's bedroom. An angular jumble of knees and elbows was breathing rhythmically under a familiar blanket. 'I let him watch telly until he flaked out,' said Ayisha defensively. 'That okay?'

She stood outside the toilet door the whole time. I sounded like a brewery horse pissing in a tin bucket. 'Where have you been? I've been worried sick.' You'd think we had been married for years. I must have slept through the honeymoon. 'You're covered in bruises. It's nearly 3 a.m. Your clothes are wet, torn to pieces. What happened, Murray? Tell me, for God's sake.'

Even when the flush drowned out her voice, she didn't shut up, bless her. As I opened the door she put her palm back on my forehead and rolled back first one eyelid, then the other. Confidently, like she knew what she was doing. 'You should be looked at by a doctor,' she diagnosed.

'Look in the cupboard,' I said, my mouth reluctantly responding to orders. 'See if you can find some aspirin.'

She put two tablets on my tongue and lifted a glass of water to my lips. I felt like I'd just played three consecutive Grand Finals at centre half-forward and we'd lost all of them. On the kitchen table the washing sat neatly folded in a laundry basket. The dishes had been done. I sensed the prospects of romance receding.

Ayisha fiddled with the kettle, poured tea. 'I rang the hotel at eleven. They said you'd left. Can you remember what happened after that?'

The tentacles began mooching about irritably again, squeezing any stray brain cells they could find.

'I thought maybe it had something to do with that storm, an accident or something. Jeeze, it was bad. All this water started coming through the roof.' Through in the lounge room I could see a row of saucepans lined up across the floor. 'Anyhow, I rang around the hospitals, but nobody fitting your description had been admitted. I was beginning to think I'd better ring the police. Then I heard something out the front. It was you, collapsing on the doorstep. I thought you were dying, fair dinkum. Freaked me right out, you did.'

Is it me, I thought, or does this woman take the cake? Softly, not enough to upset the octopus, I laughed. Ayisha's tale had filled me with enough strength to totter across to the cupboard and screw the top off the Jamesons bottle. I thought of the wine, nicely chilled at the bottom of the lake. Ayisha gave a cautionary shake of her head. Bloody Moslems, no appreciation of the tonic properties of the sacred waters. I added a tot to both our cups of tea and moulded a wad of her tobacco into a lumpy cylinder. All this physical therapy was doing me good. My thought processes were beginning to fight their way free. I did the attention-grabbing trick with the match again. This is why people smoke. So many cliches, so readily to hand.

'The aqua Falcon,' I said. 'Bayraktar's car. Ran me off the road. Right into Edwardes Lake. I ended up floating down some creek. Then spent half the night trying to get a cab to pick me up.' I slumped back, exhausted from the effort of talking. I tried to get my thoughts into some sort of order.

'Jesus,' she exclaimed. 'This is getting right out of hand. You're gunna hafta call the cops.'

I shook my head. It hurt. 'No point,' I winced. 'Unless I tell them about Memo. And that's not going to do your, or the League's, credibility any good, is it? It was you who convinced him he could trust me, remember.' Frankly, I couldn't give a shit about Gezen by this stage.

She looked at me like I was a gibbering idiot. 'My credibility? Jeeze, Murray. Somebody's trying to kill you and you're worried about my credibility?'

Isn't she fantastic, I thought. The warm tea and whiskey were beginning to work their cure in the pit of my stomach. I started to unscrew the whiskey cap again. Ayisha wrested the bottle out of my unresisting grasp. 'Call the police!' she ordered. What was it about me, I wondered, that brought out the bossy boots in women?

'I would,' I said, 'if I thought it'd do any good. But it's like your bloody petition. The cops won't act without evidence. And when they do move, it'll be too slow. Or too late.' She didn't know about my earlier conversations with the constabulary, of course. 'Shit, I don't even know why this is happening. You got any ideas?'

That shut her up. And thank Christ, too, said the octopus. On the table a saucer was piled with butts, hers and mine. If I survived, I'd have to invest in an ashtray. 'In fact I'm beginning to wonder if it isn't Gezen driving the Falcon. Maybe he changed his mind about confessing and decided he'd eliminate the only other people who knew what had happened.'

She thought I was serious. 'Gimme a break.' She leaped up and lit herself a cigarette on the gas jet. 'Memo's a little flaky, I'll admit that, but you can't seriously think he's a killer.'

I felt old eight legs shift, spread his grey gelatinous membranes and puff a slow balloon of darkness through the water towards me. A cool black cloud of ink, blotting out the light and noise and the jabber of voices in my head. The world was out there somewhere, moving distantly, glimpsed through a red-tinged slit. I made it go away.

Ayisha was shaking my shoulder. 'You okay?' I jerked upright. I must have dozed off. This was fucked. How could I think in this condition? A sob story like Gezen's would have aroused every conceivable sympathy in someone like Ayisha. It was cruel to taunt her. 'You okay?' she repeated.

I was okay. Red was okay. My constant companion the octopus was so fucking okay it was dancing a hornpipe with my frontal lobes. I had some thinking to do. The only tangible evidence of what had happened was the Falcon parked outside in the street. And in itself the car proved nothing. No doubt the only fingerprints it carried were mine, smeared all over the wheel, the doors, the hood. And I could guess why it had been abandoned with the key in the ignition. What better way to dispose of a car than to leave it where it was certain to be nicked by joy-riding kids who would dump it miles away?

No. It would take more than a dead man's car, a hair-raising tale and a half-baked story about extortion and revenge to get the cops fired up. I could be dead by the time they extracted their collective digit. The only thing I had going for me was that whoever ran me off the road probably thought I was already. 'The Anatolia Club,' I said. 'I think I should pay it a visit. Let them know I'm on to them. See what I can find out.' But not alone. 'You reckon Sivan will come with me?'

'I'd like to see you try to stop him,' Ayisha said, grinning. She was close, her presence overwhelming my senses. I could smell her, taste her. She yawned, no longer able to hide her tiredness. I made my play.

'You go home,' I urged. 'Thanks for minding Red. For every-thing. I'll talk to Sivan in the morning, speak with Memo again, sort something out.' I cocked my finger like a gun. 'No single fascist act must go unchallenged,' I quoted from somewhere, unable to remember where.

It wasn't much of a plan, but she nodded approval. She was tired, resigned. The clock on the stove clicked over. 3:35 a.m. Then she was shaking her head. 'But first you gotta see a doctor. What if you've got concussion? You could slip into a coma or something.'

'First thing in the morning,' I promised. The furry muck on my tongue mingled with the taste of tea and whiskey. I held down a retch. My timing was terrible, I told myself. I wasn't in a fit state for anything.

'It's nearly morning now. Got any blankets? I'll stay on the couch. Keep an eye on you.'

'No,' I insisted, wanting nothing more. Her hand moved, erasing the air between us, brushing my objection aside. Lucky I'd changed the linen. I led her up the hall to the bedroom, trying not to collapse on the way.

She stood with her back to the bed while I went through the motions of reaching up to where the spare bedding was stowed, stacked tight on the top shelf of the wardrobe. I tugged at the scratchy wool, high on tiptoes, dizzy from the altitude. The blankets broke free and I teetered before her, a man leaning into a strong wind. Then the wind dropped and I was pitching forward. Ayisha's arms extended effortlessly, receiving me, enfolding me. Her neck and my forehead, I observed as if from a distance, yielded a perfect fit. Motionless, cradling my eggshell head, she was a bottomless well into which I tumbled headlong into free fall.

'Oh, boy,' exclaimed key sectional interests of my metabo-lism, sensing an advantage. 'You can't keep a good man down.' Actually you can, I'm grateful to say. I felt her warmth reach out and enclose me in its embrace. Warmth, yes. Heat, no. There never would be any heat, I comprehended. But even in the finality of that knowledge I could not bring myself to move, but stood there letting myself be cradled in her arms. What energy I had was devoted entirely to not weeping with gratitude.

Then Red walked into the room and I jumped about ten feet into the air. For a long moment he stood there, regarding me with heavy-lidded, vacant eyes. Then he gripped his pyjama pants by the elastic, gave them an upward tug, turned, and somnambulated towards the bathroom.

Nurse Ayisha, herself at the far extremity of wakefulness, scooped up the blankets and draped them over her arm. 'That reminds me,' she yawned. 'Your wife rang just after you left. Said she'd be on the early flight. Said you'd know what that meant. She sounded very nice.'

I'll bet she did.

'And someone called Angelo Annoletti or something. Said to call him urgently when you got home. Bit late now, I suppose.'

Charlene! He must have rung about Charlene! God, she'd slipped my mind entirely since the branch meeting. Morning, first thing in the morning I would call. Later, later, much later. Sleep first. 'Take the bed,' I said. 'I'm used to the couch.' Shameless to the last.

Ayisha bustled me onto the couch, draped me with blankets, turned off the light and left me to die in peace. A blissful shroud of stillness settled over me. The darkness was good. Nobody would find me there. I could hide for a long time, nothing but me and infinite deep space and far, far away, the distant spiralling remnants of long exploded galaxies. The darkness was good. Darkness and the tick of molecular particles, hydrogen, oxygen, coalescing, swelling, tumbling, colliding, disintegrating. Tick, infinite pause, tick, infinite pause, tick.

The fucking roof was leaking. Very slowly, not much, but leaking drip after drip into one of the pots Ayisha had positioned across the floor. I screwed my ears as tightly closed as possible without disturbing the octopus and retreated into the soundproof maze of reason.

Somewhere my thinking had jumped the rails and taken a wrong turn. All along I had assumed that the nexus between me and Bayraktar ran through Gezen. The break-in, the stuff with the Falcon, it had all started after Gezen's confession. Therefore they were connected. But if this was not the case, then the chain of cause and effect I had constructed was missing some pretty crucial links. The longer I thought about it, the more it looked like a badly frayed string of dubious suppositions and unlikely coincidences. Get to the sharp end of the issue, I thought. Ask yourself the fundamental question. Who stands to gain from your death?

Those guys from the Anatolia Club, for instance. Even if they were a pack of right-wing psychos, why pick on me? Why not one of their own benighted compatriots? Had I witnessed something I shouldn't out at the cemetery? If so, were they also trying to bump off the two employees of the Martinelli family? That would be a serious mistake in anyone's language. Besides which, they hadn't even noticed me. And so what if I'd rushed out of the League's office shaking my fist at them? Hardly a killing offence, and it gave them no reason to connect me to Gezen. And even if they could do that, how had they connected Gezen with Bayraktar's death? In fact, I couldn't even be completely sure it was the same BMW I had seen parked under the carport at the Anatolia Club.

Gezen said they were following him, but Gezen also thought I was a copper, his bad conscience playing merry hell with him. Obviously they couldn't have been following him when only fifteen minutes earlier they had been playing parade-ground soldiers over their dead comrade at Fawkner Cemetery. Now that I thought about it, the idea that I had inadvertently stumbled into some sort of internecine ethnic warfare was less than plausible. Worse, I had been guilty of the most blatant kind of ethnic stereotyping. An old trap for new players. Christ, I'd be imagining the mafia after me next.

There must be a logical solution, I told myself. Could something other than Bayraktar's death be the issue? Something I knew but didn't know I knew? Something worth killing me to keep concealed. So who else knew of my interest in the Coolaroo plant? Who might be spooked by the sudden arrival of a snooper on the scene? Who might have access to the dead man's car?

Could Apps, the human jack-in-the-box, have found out that I dobbed him in to the boss for slack book-keeping and decided to get revenge? A drastic solution, but maybe. He was pretty highly strung, after all.

The boss himself, Merricks? He was out. For a start he had authorised the investigation. Mainly though it was the difficulty of imagining him behind the wheel of an aqua Falcon 500 in his Melbourne Club tie. Not his style at all.

There was Agnelli, whose idea it had been in the first place. Agnelli, who might well have reasons for wanting me out of the way for a while. Out of the way in hospital? Out of the way dead? Christ, maybe it was the fucking mafia, after all. And what about the drugs? Planting dope in my house had clearly been part of an attempt to discredit me. And that quantity of grass suggested a criminal connection, which took me back to the Anatolia Club. Shit, it was all too confusing. My head was spinning again.

Then there was the missing file. Had I merely mislaid it? Or had someone been worried enough to raid the electorate office, steal my notes, and leave a mess that made the break-in seem the work of artistically impaired vandals? But why? Unless somebody thought I had more information than I really did. There was nothing in the file. All it held was the list of Bayraktar's phoney names, a thumb-nail draft of the preamble of my MACWAM report, a bit of rough arithmetic and a scrap of paper with the name Herb Gardiner on it.

What was it that Gezen had said? 'Then the other one comes. Gardening. I do not think he will come so soon.' Meaning what? According to Gardiner's statement it was only by chance he had happened to be in the chiller at all. A spur of the moment decision to check the thermostat. 'Six or seven minutes he is inside.' How long does it take to check a gauge?

Old Herb knew I had the list of phoney names. He was interested enough in my activities to visit my office. In a strangely animated state, at that. He knew where I worked, where I lived, and my plans for the evening. His house wasn't a million miles from Edwardes Lake, either. Nor from the public bar of the Lakeview Hotel. And you don't have to be a gangster accomplice of a man to get hold of his car keys. You just have to take them off his key-ring when you find his body in a freezer. None of which explained why a man like Gardiner might want me dead. It was all too fantastic, too paranoid.

Then, in the interminable drawn-out vastness of time between two droplets of water, I heard at last the inexorable clunk of a penny dropping. And at exactly that moment the baying began. The long, full-throated, moon-mad howls of a captive dog.

The sky was crystalline, utterly cloudless, miles high. The night had entered that great silence that precedes the birdsong. Apart from the pooch, that is, shut in the Falcon and yowling fit to wake the entire neighbourhood. The instant I opened the driver's door, she shut up. She just banged her tail on the vinyl a couple of times and sat there looking up at me. Wanted attention, then didn't know what to do with it. Just like some people.

I left the door open while I examined the patch-up job on the car's rear window. It was a work of art. The clear plastic had been cut to a precise fit. The waterproof seam of electrical tape was light blue, not quite a match with the paintwork, but a good try. A triple layer, the edges straight as a die. All very shipshape. I was thinking about a sailor, about fragments of conversation, things seen but not noticed, all rushing to reassemble themselves, like the film of an explosion running in reverse.

In a circle around me the rooftops were smudged with a flush of luminescence, mother-of-pearl buttons about to pop open and expose the daylight hidden underneath. Not everything was clear yet but, with every passing second, more and more details could be discerned, their blurred outlines coming more sharply into focus.

I could hold the pieces together only by the greatest effort of will. The story existed only as long as I kept telling it to myself. If I stopped figuring it out, even for the merest second, the whole thing would dissolve into an incoherent blur of suspicion and conjecture, the fantasy of a concussed brain. Relax, just for an instant, and none of it would make sense any more. I would no longer be able to convince myself, let alone anyone else. But if I plunged headlong into the morass, others would be forced to follow. No more the prey, I would be the one setting the agenda. Time to get pro-active. I turned the ignition key and felt the Falcon's power fill me with certainty.

Back in the house, pulling on a pair of shoes, I had caught sight of myself in a mirror. My hair had dried wet and sprang out on all sides, a tangle of grass and mud, a fright wig. The fright was my face, overgrown, wild-eyed, the welts peeling to reveal pink stripes. Saggy grey track pants, an old maroon windcheater flecked with paint. Le Coq Sportif. If the black lace-up shoes had been a little bigger, if I had a polka dot bow-tie, the clown outfit would be complete.

As I sneaked past the bedroom door I had glimpsed Ayisha, in my bed at last, dead to the world, guarding me against my coma. She lay there utterly vulnerable, totally impervious, her knees pressed to her chest under the covers. How I could ever have imagined her going for me was already beyond my comprehension.

But now I was heading north, my thoughts moving from darkness to light as inexorably as the widening band of grey on the horizon at my elbow. The dog was beside me, her paws kneading the passenger seat. After that piece of Gallic garbage I had been driving, that ride-on lawn-mower, the Falcon went like the clappers, a veritable limousine. Even the lighter worked. I rolled one-handed as I drove. The knack was back.

The radio worked, too, and the dawn shift announcer spoke in soothing nursery tones, which was nice of him. According to the five o'clock news, police and emergency service personnel were still mopping up after last night's record downpour. An empty caravan had been swept into the Elwood Canal. Big deal. The forecast was for clear skies at least until the end of the weekend. The worst was over, or so they said.

We drove in silence from there on, ruminating. Well, I was. The dog was still squeezing the upholstery. The details were hazy but, if you stood back far enough, the big picture could be discerned. The Rolf Harris method. What had happened was this, I reasoned, guessed, extrapolated.

Bayraktar was a semi-literate thug. A payroll scam, the faking of official paperwork, would have been beyond him. Someone who knew how the place worked must have shown him how to do it. Someone who knew the place well. Someone like Herb Gardiner. Every week, a couple of hours after the pay packets had been delivered, they each made separate visits to the same freezer. A convenient place for Gardiner to pick up his split of that week's bogus wages? But last Friday Gardiner changed the routine. He turned up early, and Bayraktar ended up dead.

According to Gezen, Gardiner was in the freezer a long time, six or seven minutes. More than long enough to read a meter. And when he arrived, Bayraktar had already been inside long enough to discover that he was locked in. If, as Gezen believed, Bayraktar was already dead of a panic-induced heart attack, why did it take Gardiner so long to emerge and sound the alarm? Something else had happened in Number 3 chiller. Some variation on the scam, perhaps? A falling out among thieves?

Whatever it was, Gardiner had succeeded in concealing it. Bayraktar had been carried out feet-first, successfully portrayed as an unlucky pilferer, a stiff stiff. The cops and government inspectors were satisfied and the payroll fiddle had gone undetected.

But not for long. All of a sudden there was a fly in the ointment. This Whelan character turns up asking a lot of silly questions. On the job five minutes and he trips over the one loose thread, Bayraktar's phoney pay sheets. He doesn't know what they mean, but he's asking a lot of silly questions. Christ alone knows what else he might discover, given time. He needs to be flummoxed, discredited, scared off. Got out of the picture, one way or another. And the evidence he has already turned up, the list of names Bayraktar has been using, has to be retrieved before he realises its value.

Fortunately, the guy is an idiot. A trusting soul who volunteers his home address and his planned movements. First his office is broken into and the list taken. Then drugs are planted in his house. Then, after a pretty serious effort is made to scare him, he passes up an offer to talk. So things get deadly.

But where did the drugs come from? And why up the ante to homicide? So what if this Murray Whelan got a bit snoopy? Why were the stakes so high? Charges of fraud would be difficult to substantiate. Even more so with manslaughter. Why go to so much trouble to eliminate someone who wasn't even a witness? Why not sit it out, see what develops? Sit it out while taking in the Pacific from the balcony of your Broadbeach condominium. Sit around soaking up those Queensland sunbeams? Why try to kill a man? Why risk the prospect of spending the rest of your retirement in a ten by twelve cell in HM Pentridge with a view of the handball court?

These were questions best put in person. Bang on Gardiner's door, ask him loud, in front of the neighbours. Make a mess in Tidy Town. Put a rocket up the collective arse of the constabulary. And if I was wrong? If good old Herb was no more than he seemed? What then? Then Murray Whelan too could be no more than he seemed—the dazed and delirious victim of a car accident, concussed, confused and in bad need of a few hours sleep.

It was nearly day. Gardiner's house slept in the stillness behind its For Sale sign. Further along the street a solitary window showed the lights of an early riser. I stepped over the wrought-iron gate and into the space between the house and the cream brick of the garage. Behind me on the nature strip, the black dog did what dogs do on nature strips.

Through the slatted glass of the louvre window the garage interior was matt black. I cupped my hands around my face, adjusting my eyes to the gloom. Floor, walls, work-bench emerged from of the darkness. Shapes floated above the bench, dark silhouettes against a white background—a hacksaw, the descending Gs of a row of clamps, the outlines of tools on a shadow board. No car. The tan Corolla was gone. Across the floor a glint of diamonds caught the pale light of the new day.

The door was locked. I kicked it open with my heel and threw the light switch. A pile of glass fragments, the remnants of a shattered car window, had been swept into a neat pyramid beside the cut-down drum of a rubbish bin. Off-cut strips of clear plastic, precise straight edges, lay heaped in the bin. On a ledge above the bench a row of jars held screws and bolts and nuts—self-tappers, counter-sunk, round-head. Above the jars rolls of electrical tape hung on nails, red, green, blue. A damp umbrella leaned against the wall. Beside it, drying on a sheet of newspaper, was a pair of muddy brogues. Tidy Town, Tidy Shed, Tidy Man.

Up until then I had been a tightrope walker, teetering on a thread of conjecture. Now the ground felt solid beneath my feet. Here was evidence. There would be more evidence out at the plant, of the fiddle at least. Then would come motive.

I sat the ball of my thumb on the doorbell and wiggled, waking an electric Quasimodo, sending it into spasm in the darkness inside. 'Come out Gardiner,' I yelled. 'I want to talk to you.' The palm of my hand came down hard, rattling the aluminium frame of the screen door. Yapping exploded behind the door, answered from the nature strip. My dog sounded tougher.

A carriage light above the door went on and the Nextdoor's head and shoulders appeared. She tugged at her dressing-gown cord and held herself back in the shadows, torn between curiosity and her mortification at being caught out in Gardiner's bed. 'What do you want?'

The dogs were going at it hammer and tongs. I had to raise my voice. 'Where's Gardiner?' I bellowed. It felt good, from the pit of my stomach.

The merry widow recoiled from my certainty. 'He's gone to work.'

I rattled the handle. The door was locked, but the woman drew her collar around her throat defensively and stepped back, receding even further into the protective dark. This wasn't what I'd had in mind, scaring old ladies. Her hand was on the white telephone. 'I'll call the police.'

'You do that,' I said.

As I started the Falcon, the dogs were still going at each

other through the barred door. Snap and snarl and gotcha. Lights were coming on all the way up the street. I swung open the passenger door and whistled. Red had been on at me for ages about getting a dog. I liked this one. I liked her attitude.

Seen distantly from the highway, the smoke was no more than an oily grey smudge on the baby-blue face of the new day. It was only as I neared the dozen or so semi-trailers marshalling on the asphalt apron that I could see where it was coming from. Above the tangle of huge refrigerated rigs moving in and out of cavernous apertures, a guttering black snake was uncoiling itself from the roof of Pacific Pastoral.

I left the Falcon in the carpark with the dog on the seat and loped past the deserted gatehouse. Thin grey wisps were beginning to curl around the upper edge of the entry nearest the office. As I passed through the great door, alarm bells erupted, tripping each other off deeper and deeper into the building, loud, serious, metallic. The acrid smell of burning paint filled the air. The bundy clock read 5:23. Gardiner's card in its alphabetical slot showed a clock-on time of 5:01.

Apps was hopping about at the bottom of the office stairs, a spluttering fire extinguisher dangling upside down from his hand. His Adam's apple was doing the cha-cha, and other parts of his body looked like they were trying to secede entirely. The upstairs landing was belching smoke and through the windows of the lunch room I could see tongues of yellow licking the walls.

'I told the stupid cow that radiator was a menace,' Apps whined at the top of his lungs.

First law of management, I thought. Find a scapegoat. On the periphery of my vision, figures were running everywhere. Shouts and engine noises set up a counter beat to the unfaltering scream of the alarm bells. Apps, registering my identity, turned away from the smoke and grabbed my sleeve. 'What are you doing here?' he demanded.

For a moment I wondered if Apps, not Gardiner, had set the blaze. It couldn't have come at a more convenient time for both of them. No, Apps didn't have that much imagination. 'You said I'd find it more interesting at this time of day,' I said. 'You were right.' I jerked my arm free. Apps cocked his head, straining for meaning, scandalised by my costume. He lunged for my arm again. 'I can't be held responsible...'

I danced out of his reach and took off into the plant. Apps could go to buggery. It was Gardiner I was here to see. But where was he? High above, an oily black haze was gathering, rubbery and noxious. The fire was spreading rapidly. An ominous hissing could be heard below the high-pitched frenzy of the alarm bells. God alone knew what lethal gasses were poisoning the air. I jogged away from the fire, deeper into the complex, straining down corridors for a glimpse of Gardiner's stocky figure.

Herb Gardiner was not only methodical, he clearly had a lot of energy for a man of his age. You had to hand him that. At this rate not just the records in the office but half the plant would be a charred ruin before the fire brigade had backed their shiny red appliances out the station door. He should have put up a sign. Herb's Braised Beef. The arson squad would need barbecue aprons and long tongs to make any sense of this.

I jogged on, dizzy from the effort, getting disoriented. This wasn't how I had pictured it. The idea had been to confront Gardiner, shirt-front him with accusations, create a scene. Instead, Gardiner was one step ahead, putting distance between himself and the evidence. With the records gone up in smoke, it would take a confession to convince anybody of anything. I realised Gardiner would probably be making his way to one of the exits, joining in the confusion and excitement of his fellow workers. He would mingle with them on the apron to watch the spectacle, a mask of plausible surprise on his face.

I turned towards the pale rectangle of one of the doorways. A group of figures in overalls, some white, some blue, was moving in the same direction. One of them had a lamb carcass slung over his shoulder. The things people think to save in a fire. I broke into a trot to catch the last of them up. The acrid smoke began to burn my lungs. Abruptly it started to rain. Somewhere far above, the red tracery of the overhead sprinkler system had kicked in. I bent my head and hurried forwards, concentrating on keeping my balance on the now slippery floor. I'd had more than enough soakings recently, thank you very much.

Just ahead of me, Gardiner came out of an access alley and headed towards the exit. I fell into step beside him. He glanced around. 'Hello, son,' he said, his self-possession never faltering.

'Something I've been meaning to ask,' I said, raising my voice against the unearthly din. 'Where does an old bloke like you get his grass?'

Gardiner slowed and looked at me quizzically. I suddenly felt that I had made a serious mistake. The gap to the hurrying crowd ahead widened. Gardiner said something. I leaned forward. 'What?'

Gardiner put his hand on my elbow and his mouth up to my ear, as if he was taking me into his confidence. 'That prick Bayraktar,' he said. 'He was using the place to shunt the stuff around.' As he spoke, he shifted his grasp to my wrist and stepped behind me, twisting my right arm all the way up behind my back. At the same time, he whipped a long heavy-duty screwdriver out of the thigh pocket of his overalls and pressed its blade against my throat.

I felt a flash of pride at having my assumptions proved correct, but the vanity was short-lived. For a man his age, Gardiner was as hard as a rock. The old bastard sure must have been giving the All-Bran a nudge. He jammed the tip of the screwdriver into the soft flesh between my jaw and windpipe. One hard shove and ten inches of drop-forged steel would be sticking out the top of my skull.

The pain in my shoulder forced me into a forward hunch, pushing me down harder on the screwdriver and bringing tears welling into my eyes. Through the artificial rain I could see the last of the workmen vanishing through the exit. I punched wildly sideways and failed to connect. The sharpened metal bit emphatically into my skin. 'A word in private, if you don't mind, son,' said Gardiner.

He angled me sideways and frog-marched me forward. At every attempt to struggle free or grab at him with my left hand, he twisted my arm to the extremity of its socket until the pain subdued me. 'This is crazy,' I gasped, my carotid artery thumping on cold steel. Gardiner shut me up with a jab and propelled me onwards.

Abruptly, with a sideways sweep of one leg, he knocked my feet out from under me. My arm strained at its socket as I went down, and I cried out in agony. As I hit the ground I felt the screwdriver disappear from my throat. It instantly reappeared behind my head, probing the tender spot at the top of my spine. My forehead was jammed hard against the wet floor, my lips kissing the cold concrete, tasting the tomb. Gardiner's foot was in the small of my back, pinning me down. 'Hasn't anyone ever told you that nobody likes a smartarse, son?'

I struggled feebly, immobilised by the pain in my shoulder and the threat of being skewered. The octopus was back, sorely pissed off. This is not what I had expected. But what exactly had I expected, running around a burning building like a chook with its head cut off, not knowing what I was going to do next, all dumb-fuck cunning and rampant glands?

Gardiner on the other hand knew exactly what he was doing. He worked methodically, the necessary materials readily to hand. Pivoting on the screwdriver, keeping its pressure constant, he jerked my arm downwards. The relief was immediate but temporary. He transferred his foot to my neck and I felt the full weight of his body bear down. Then he lashed my wrists together with tape, his movements sure and agile.

'You're a lucky bastard, I'll give you that.' Gardiner liked to chat genially as he worked. 'When that heap of yours went into the water I was convinced you were a goner.' He hauled at the tape, dragging me to my feet and propelling me forwards again, the screwdriver back against my jugular. We continued down the line of freezers, both now soaked to the skin. Gardiner didn't seem to mind. I was shivering miserably.

At one of the freezer doors Gardiner again forced me to the ground and planted a foot firmly between my shoulder blades. Keys jingled briefly, then I was hauled to my feet and pitched into the cavernous interior. I stumbled, hit a wall of cartons and spun around. The door was sliding into place behind Gardiner. He already had one arm in the sleeve of a padded parka and was holding the screwdriver in front of him like a bayonet. His eyes never left me as he transferred the weapon to his other hand and zipped the jacket closed. Icy air wrapped itself around me, sending a chill through my damp clothes. At a very minimum I was going to come out of this whole thing with a severe head cold.

I teetered precariously back into balance, tugging at the tape. I succeeded only in digging it deeper into the flesh of my wrists. Apparently unconcerned at my mobility, Gardiner began to tug on one fur-lined glove then another. As he did so he stamped his feet, dancing about in a little boxer's jig, and waving the steel shaft in small circles, as though inciting me to charge him headlong. I half expected him to suggest I have a go. And so we faced each other, stamping and steaming, dancing partners in a macabre frug.

'Freezing, eh?' Gardiner said without malice, the words propelled out of his mouth on puffs of white haze. 'Thermostat's all the way down. Turn a carton of boned beef into a slab of granite in twenty minutes flat. Fit young fellow like you, all his juices flowing, a bit longer maybe. But you'll be out cold well before that. Didn't take Bayraktar any time at all. But then he was in shocking shape.'

Freezing wasn't the word for it. The gust of air that had entered with us was a shroud of vapour swathing our feet. We'd been in there less than a minute and already the sodden front of my sweat-top was white with hoar-frost and I was shivering uncontrollably. Shouting would be useless. Even if anyone remained outside to hear above the din of the fire alarms, the freezer walls were thick with insulation.

Gardiner's intentions were now abundantly clear. Keep me

prisoner in the freezer until I passed out from the cold, remove the tape and leave me to die. Or even drag my body out to thaw, closer to the fire. Do that to a chicken and you end up with salmonella. Frozen, baked or bombe Alaska. What a choice.

I glanced about. Aside from being even colder, the freezer we were standing in was identical to the one Apps had insisted on showing me. Corridors of waxed cartons led off into the interior. Nowhere to run, nowhere to hide.

'Oh, don't worry,' Gardiner went on, his mouth pursed against the biting air. 'You won't feel a thing, though I daresay it'll be a little nippy at first.'

As he spoke he unzipped his jacket far enough to thrust a gloved hand down his front and pull a pack of cigarettes and a disposable lighter from an inside pocket. He mouthed a stick from the pack, fumbled the lighter into action, lit up, and zipped himself closed. His eyes never left me. 'Sad what can happen to someone who doesn't know what he's doing when he goes wandering around a place like this.'

I stared at the glowing tip of the cigarette hungrily. It occurred to me to ask for one, a dying man's request. But breathing was hard enough. Each intake of air was an icy flame, searing my lungs. 'You won't get away with it.' The shivering was close to uncontrollable, my voice a pathetic reed trembling behind clenched teeth.

Gardiner shrugged indifference, clapping his gloved hands together around the screwdriver, making a muffled, decisive, sound. 'Don't see why not. I did last time.'

My legs jerked spastically under me. The front of my pants was a crackling sheet of ice, a good case for never going out without underpants.

Gardiner was droning on, the words hypnotic. 'Even if you made other copies of those names Bayraktar was using, they won't mean anything without the payroll records. And this little bonfire should take care of those quite nicely. Tell you the truth, I've been meaning to get round to disposing of them for some time. I suppose I should thank you for hurrying me up.'

This was what Gardiner wanted, I realised. To keep me standing here, listening, until my legs gave out underneath me.

If I went down, I wouldn't get up. I pleaded through the wa-wa pedal of my juddering jaw. 'Please. I don't want to die. Not for some lousy little fiddle.'

Gardiner stopped jogging on the spot and drew back in mock outrage. 'Lousy little fiddle? That any way to talk about a man's life work? Best part of a million dollars I've pulled out of this place over the years, I'll have you know. Call that lousy, do you, son?'

I shook my head, or rather it shook me. It was jerking uncontrollably as the intensity of the shivering increased. I was thinking of the escape hatch, wondering how far I would get with my arms tied back, which way to go. It took all my muscular control just to force words out. 'I'll do anything you want.' Except die. I swivelled on my heels, back and forth, preparing myself. If I was going to go, I might as well go going. Swing right, I decided, and see how far I got.

'You should have thought of that before you tried putting the squeeze on someone like Lionel Merricks,' Gardiner said.

My instruction to my legs faltered halfway down. Excuse me. What had the man just said?

'You've got some moxie,' Gardiner went on. 'I'll give you that much, son. Ringing up, bold as brass. Off the record. Confidential. That will be fifty thousand dollars, thank you very much, Mr Merricks. Bloody cheeky all right. But stupid. Lionel doesn't like being stood over, especially not at the moment. Fix it, he told me. Tidy up all the loose ends. But what do you do when I come around to try to sort something out? You send me packing. Not very civil of you, was it?'

Below the waist I danced on the spot, my legs half rubber, half braced to sprint. The shaking was getting worse. In contrast, my thought processes were slowing down, trudging step by tipsy step across an endless plain of snow. It would be nice, I mused dreamily, to hear the end of Gardiner's story, hear where this latest twist led. Then lie down and sleep. I gathered a breath from my diaphragm and pushed it out my nose. 'Wool ship.'

This pleased Gardiner greatly. 'Bullshit, is it?' He examined me afresh. 'I knew it,' he declared gleefully. 'I told Merricks you were just flying a kite. Fifteen years we've been working together, him putting in lame-duck managers, me handling the day-to-day details. Not a hint of a problem. Even the Yanks thought it was just an innocent mix-up. Buggered if we could figure out how you'd got onto us so quickly. Turns out you hadn't, after all.' Then he chuckled, a terrible laugh of self-congratulation, and I knew how far gone he was.

My brain struggled through a blurring haze to make sense of what I was hearing. The only bit I understood was that I was being killed because of a misunderstanding. 'Let me go,' I pleaded. 'We can deal.' My words were a string of staccato grunts, like a spluttering engine about to stall. 'Why Merricks fiddle own payroll?'

Gardiner was contemptuous behind his glowing cigarette, like it was all my fault that he was being put to the inconvenience of having to murder me. 'Christ, son, you really don't know anything, do you? Merricks isn't tickling the till. That's just a private little sideline of my own. Except I picked the wrong man to go into business with, didn't I? My trusty fucking sidekick Bayraktar got greedy and decided to branch out into drug distribution. Had the stuff coming in from the bush by the truckload. Put our whole operation at risk, the silly cunt.'

I wanted him to know I wasn't completely ignorant. 'And extortion.'

This was new to Gardiner. 'That so?' he said thoughtfully. He threw his cigarette to the floor and ground it out with his heel. 'Not any more though, eh son?' He bent at the knees, his gloved fingers pinching uselessly in an attempt to gather up the scrap of mangled butt. His eyes flickered downwards.

I took off. My legs, loyal lieutenants, jerked me to the right and begun to pump. Skidding on icy soles, I veered into a slot between two mountains of stacked boxes. The cold was viscous and resisted my efforts to push my way forward. I moved in slow motion, the air tasting of wet tin and searing my lungs. Wobbling erratically, trying to find my balance, I bounced off the walls.

Somewhere behind me Gardiner laughed. 'Go on, son, run,' he shouted. 'That greedy pig Bayraktar had the same idea. Go ahead. Burst your heart, just like he did.'

I lurched on and turned deeper into the maze of cartons.

Muffled applause tracked my progress. As I stumbled forward I sawed my wrists numbly back and forth, dimly aware they had no feeling. Had the tape cut off my circulation, I wondered, or could this be frostbite so soon? The effort of movement brought dizziness. Careening full-tilt against a wall, I pirouetted through 180 degrees and came to rest. Gardiner was at the far end of the aisle, genially ambling towards me.

Jacking my hands up between my shoulder blades, I pushed my elbows outwards with as much strength as I could muster, quivering with exertion. My pulse roared like the ocean in my ears. The octopus reared. Gardiner advanced, the screwdriver circling casually at his thigh, impatience beginning to crease his natty, bedroom-bandicoot face. My arms exploded outwards and sent me reeling. Tape dangled from my wrists. Gardiner showed irritation then disappeared from view as I turned and shuffled through a dangling curtain of beef carcasses, setting the whole rack swinging.

A dead end blocked my path, the back wall. I cast about for the hatch, hearing Gardiner's footfall moving closer. The hatch was there, chest high. I fell forward and clutched at the handle. The catch sprang open and the hatch swung wide, wrenching my palm with it, super-glued to the metal. Outside was an oven of smoke and noise. Balmy air, thick with smoke and chemical stench, hit me in the face. I sucked at it hungrily, feeding on its warmth.

Gardiner's arm came around my neck and dragged me backwards. My hand tore free, raw flesh, and I hit the floor. Gardiner kicked me hard in the ribs, one, two. My knees came up protectively, curling me into a ball. Gardiner loomed above, framed demonically against the square of the hatch, blocking the blast of heat from the fire outside. 'Good idea,' he grunted, catching his breath. He half turned and made a facetious show of warming one gloved hand. 'At my age you really feel the cold.' Hunching down, he risked a glance outwards. He was impressed by his own handiwork. 'Spreading pretty fast. No time to waste.' He turned his attention back to the job at hand.

Never once taking his eyes off me, he transferred the screwdriver to his left hand and reached back with his right, searching for the handle of the hatch. The little door had swung right back on its hinges. He swiped at the air with his gloved hand, the handle just beyond his grasp. 'You certainly take a lot of looking after,' he grumbled, demonstratively jabbing the screwdriver towards where I lay.

Rivulets of condensation were already beginning to stream down the wall. Gardiner bobbed swiftly at the knees, ducked his head and shoulders out the hatch, and grabbed the hatch handle. As he did so, I came out of my cringe and jerked myself up into a runner's starting stance, all my weight on the tips of my splayed fingers. Gardiner twisted at the waist, hauling the trapdoor inwards, half-turned in profile.

That's when I killed him. Head-butted him in the nuts.

I rammed my skull into his groin with all the force I could muster. The impact caused his whole upper body to jackknife sharply forward. His forehead smashed hard against the outside edge of the hatch. 'Ommfff,' he went, and his head whiplashed back towards the fire. By then I had my arms wrapped around his knees and was lifting him up, shoving him backwards out the hole. I don't know whether he was dead already then or not, because I was too busy anticipating a punctured lung from the screwdriver. But he was already going limp and when he landed on the top of his skull I heard his neck crack, even over the sound of the alarm bells. I stuck my head out the hatch and saw the screwdriver clatter to the floor.

Then I looked up and saw Memo Gezen. He was just standing there, tight-lipped, staring at me. Water ran off his white shower cap and down his long morose face. Gardiner was an inverted L, hanging from the sill of the hatch like an over-sized child on a monkey-bar. I grabbed his ankles and dumped him out into the access alley. His head twisted sideways and his tongue flopped out of his mouth. All the way out. It lay there beside him, twitching on the wet concrete.

I took a couple of deep breaths and climbed out after him. 'Here,' I said. 'Hold this.' I handed Gezen the screwdriver, slammed the hatch shut and turned towards the exit, stripping the remnants of tape from my wrists and tossing them in the gutter as I went.

Out in the clear light of day it was all happening. There were fire engines everywhere. Officers were shouting instructions through breathing apparatus. Hoses had been run out, bulging and writhing like engorged pythons. A trio of ambulances sat side-by-side with their double-doors swung open, stretchers at the ready. The paramedics were doling out blankets to sprinkler-soaked refugees. Nobody paid me the slightest attention.

The big rigs had been pulled clear of all the fuss and formed a solid wall along the far side of the road. Their drivers stood around in groups of three and four, arms folded across their chests, watching the show. I slipped between two of the semis, heading for the carpark. A heavy-set figure swung down from the driver's cabin and blocked my way. 'You'll catch your death,' he said, and thrust a pair of oil-stained jeans and a scrappy navy-blue windcheater into my hands.

I mumbled thanks and began to strip off on the spot. The driver looked modestly away, told me I could keep the stuff, and sauntered back to his mates. The pants were a good three sizes too big, and there was no belt. Breakdown gear. Not that I was ungrateful. I stuck my head through the windcheater, hitched up the daks and waddled across the road. The carpark was deserted. I started the Falcon and headed for the highway. A line of squad cars was coming in the other direction, spraying gravel and flashing their lights.

I steered one handed, my left palm stripped back to a nasty little stigmata by the super-frozen metal of the hatch handle. I'd never killed anyone before. I wondered what I should be feeling. I rolled down my window and let the cool air buffet my face. The day was turning out to be a bobby-dazzler. The night's storm and everything that had happened in it was already receding into ancient history. On the far horizon the towers of the city were just visible. The highway was an arrow pointed straight at the tallest and most dazzling of them, the Amalfi, shiny and freshly washed.

Some of the picture was clearer now, but the picture itself kept getting bigger, the canvas widening and widening. I wasn't sure that I would ever be able to see it all, let alone make sense of it. Merricks, according to Gardiner, was behind all this. 'Fix it, he told me'. So said the dead man. And dead men tell no tales, do they? But what had he meant? That was a question, I decided, best put to Merricks in person.

But not now. Not like this. Not arriving in a stolen car with a rubbish-tip mongrel farting away on the seat beside me. Not in a pair of fat man's dungarees held up with a bleeding hand. Not in a cast-off jumper, not even one with 'Police Co-Operative Credit Union' printed on the front. Not with a three-day growth and wet shoes and compost in my hair. If this keeps up, I thought, I'll end up looking like Jimmy Barnes.

Merricks was not a man I could see making an impromptu confession. My ill-considered phone call to him had not only very nearly got me killed, it had put him on the defensive. Merricks had more resources at his command than I could possibly imagine, someone to be approached only with the greatest care and planning. Assuming I was in a position to do anything of the sort. Assuming I was not in police custody myself. From now on, spontaneity was out. No more bull-at-a-gate stuff. Aside from which, I had more immediate worries.

I punched the radio on, got the time, punched it back off. I was in no mood for breakfast cheer. It had just gone seven. Ayisha, I prayed, would still be asleep. I could be back on the couch before she woke. I parked a few blocks short of the house and left the keys in the car. There was a high school nearby, and with luck the Falcon would be three suburbs away by the end of morning recess. The mutt got out and followed, her nails pitter-pattering along the footpath behind me. They needed clipping. She'd need a decent wash, too. And a worming. And a distemper shot. I'd have to knock up a kennel for her, too, or Red would have her sleeping in the house. A name would be useful as well. I was still alive, so Cerberus was definitely out. Red would want to do the choosing. Voltron, or something like that, no doubt.

Up ahead I could hear a banging noise, hollow and reverberating. As I turned into my street, Ayisha came out of the house in her big quilted overcoat and crossed the road to her Laser. I picked up pace, shuffling towards her as fast as I could, both hands hoisting the waistband of my pants. She opened her bag, fishing for keys, and saw me coming. The noise was getting louder, a demonic bashing and crashing, and I realised it was coming from my house. Ayisha found her keys, got the door open, and slid behind the wheel.

Just as I got to her, the banging reached a frenzied pitch. The whole of my roof was rearing and pitching and seemed about to break up into its constituent parts. Abruptly the noise ceased. The sheets seemed to settle. A low metallic screech began. One by one, the iron sheets started to slide downwards, gathering momentum, catching and dragging each other, until the entire skin of the roof was an avalanche pitching towards the yard below. There was a moment of near silence. Then, with a great crash, the whole lot tipped over the guttering and landed on the garden, burying the prostrate boobialla under an ugly midden of twisted, rusting iron sheets.

Ant appeared on the ridge beam above. He gave a lunatic whoop and waved a pinch-bar triumphantly in the air. He was wearing a blue singlet, tattered jeans, heavy work boots and wrap-around sunglasses. He looked like the original speed-crazed bikie from hell. When he saw me, he waved, pulled his top lip back to display his new choppers, and gave me the thumbs-up. By then, old Mrs Bagio had come out her front door and was standing at her gate with a broom in her hand. Other neighbours were coming outside for a look, too.

Ayisha wound down her window. Her hair was dishevelled and wide black smudges of mascara circled her tired eyes. She looked like a bad-tempered panda. 'You okay?'

'Yeah,' I said. 'I guess.'

She turned on her engine. 'From now on,' she said, 'I think we should keep everything on a strictly professional basis, don't you?' She was looking right through me.

'I, um,' I said. Across the road, the front door opened and Wendy appeared. She was got up in her corporate amazon outfit—full war paint, shoulders that would scare the shit out of a rugby forward, and, of all things, a double string of pearls. Considering she looked like her mother, she'd never looked better. She appeared pleased to see me, too. But only in the sense that a tiger might be pleased to see a tethered goat.

Ayisha was waiting for me to finish. Wendy came out onto the porch. She had Red by one hand and was carrying his overnight bag in the other. A taxi turned into the street and cruised slowly towards us. 'I, um,' I said again. It seemed to be the best I could do. Wendy began clomping across the pile of corrugated iron with Red in tow. She waved to the taxi. The Laser began to move. 'See you later,' said Ayisha. I doubted it.

Wendy was on the footpath by then. 'Hi,' I said. 'I see you got here nice and early.'

Wendy went straight for the throat. 'Don't bother trying to talk your way out of this one, Murray.' She brushed past me, wrested open the taxi door and hurled the overnight bag inside. 'I get the early flight down especially so I can take Red to school myself. And what do I find?'

Ant came around the side of the house, took one look at what was happening and ducked back out of sight. Wendy let go of Red's hand, grabbed hold of her own little finger and shook it. My crimes were about to be enumerated. 'For a start, you're not here. You've left Red in his bed and disappeared. And where you've gone is anyone's guess. Nobody knows, including'—she moved on to the next finger—'the strange woman I find asleep in my bed.'

Poor Ayisha. Talk about *Wake in Fright*. And I thought the

emphasis on the 'my' was a bit unfair considering Wendy hadn't slept there more than six nights in the previous six months.

'Ayisha,' said Red, exasperatedly. 'I told you her name is Ayisha.'

'Yes, sweetheart.' She laid a proprietary hand on the child's head, then snatched it back to tug at a third finger. 'Banned from school with nits, he tells me. And what do you do? You get him butchered.' Red, the little traitor, made no attempt to contradict her. Worse, he went all waifish, averted his eyes and fiddled with a plastic model he was holding, something halfway between a stegosaurus and an armoured personnel carrier. I remembered the dog and looked around. It was nowhere to be seen.

This lack of attentiveness compounded my dereliction of parental duty. For a moment Wendy looked like she was about to rip my arms off with her bare teeth and beat me to death with them. Then her expression turned to one of genuine hurt. 'And my beautiful rug. I carried that thing all the way back from Srinagar.'

'The roof was leaking,' I pleaded lamely.

That just made things worse. She let go of her finger long enough to jerk her thumb back over her shoulder. 'If you think I'm paying for any of this you've got another thing coming. No expenditure without consultation.' Then, having run out of fingers, she propelled Red into the cab, got in beside him, and fiddled with his seat belt. She pulled the door shut decisively and wound the window down. 'Haven't you heard of passive smoking?' she said. 'There are cigarette butts from one end of the house to the other.' Then she touched the driver on the shoulder and they were gone. She hadn't even asked about my face.

I stood on the footpath and watched them drive away. Wendy was right, of course. Leaving Red like that had not been a good idea. Things did not augur well for the tussle to come. Ant slunk out of his hiding place and stood beside me. 'Christ,' he said. 'What a fucking dragon.' Up close, his teeth looked like he'd gone to the wrong address and ended up at the veterinary college.

'I'll thank you not to speak that way of the mother of my child,' I said.

A flat-bed truck pulled up, driven by a dopey-looking teenager in a Collingwood beanie. 'This is Trevor,' said Ant. 'My offsider.' By the look of him, Trevor was on day-release from a youth-training institution. But as far as I could tell he didn't have a single tattoo. Considering I was paying him twenty-five dollars an hour, cash, I took this as a reassuring sign. He and Ant began slinging the old iron onto the back of the truck and I went inside.

Ayisha must have been nervously lighting cigarettes while waiting for me to return from the branch meeting. Lots of her butts were only half smoked. I squeezed one back into shape and fired it up. The smoke hit the pit of my stomach and instantaneously I was ravenous. I poured myself a bowl of Weeties and ate as I smoked. Then I ate another two bowls. Pretty soon I would have to report the Renault running into the lake. There must have been quite a few accidents during that storm. Talk about lucky.

I turned the shower on full-bore and used the last of the nit shampoo to wash the mud and grass out of my hair. The blood on my hands was mostly metaphorical, so I couldn't do much about that. But I kept scrubbing anyway. The real dirt was what Gezen had on me. I wondered how much he had seen, and decided not much. Not that I could imagine him rushing to the police. If he was nervous before, he'd be shitting himself now. Aside from which, we were even. We knew each other's secrets.

Shaving hurt like hell and a couple of the scabs came away and started bleeding. I offered it up as a penance for my own stupidity. Ant and his offsider were back on the roof somewhere above me, stripping the last of the guttering away and pitching it to the ground. They were working to the sound of a radio tuned to some God-awful top forty station. The nine o'clock news came on, and the fire was the lead story. The blaze had taken three quarters of an hour to bring under control. Damage was estimated at more than a million dollars. But that information came later. First up was a police statement to the effect that an unnamed man was dead. Traffic on the Tullamarine, Eastern and South-eastern freeways was smooth. Nothing about Charlene. We were heading for a top of twenty. Wake me up before you go-go.

My ninety-nine dollar del Monte special was a write-off. I found a pair of tan cords, a white shirt and a clean jumper. Just as well nobody had ever been run out of the Labor party for being badly dressed. At least I wouldn't be stalking the corridors looking like a werewolf. The plan, if you could call it that, was to discover as soon as possible what was happening with Charlene. Then I would pin Agnelli down for a full and frank exchange of views. I assumed that Charlene's bad turn would put a temporary dampener on Agnelli's little scheme. And if he hadn't already worked out that stabbing a sick woman in the back might not be good for his image, it would be my pleasure to draw his attention to the fact.

The soggy bills in my suit pocket would just cover a taxi into town. I rang one and went out the front to survey the damage. The roof had been stripped as bare as a departmental budget the night before the end of the financial year. Ant, Trevor and the supply-yard driver were unloading new sheets of iron off the back of a truck. The garden was fucked, but that was the least of my troubles. The dog had reappeared and attached herself to Trevor like a limpet. I whistled and she ignored me. A car pulled up behind the truck, some sort of public service fleet vehicle. Agnelli got out, smoothed his lapels and waited for me to come over. He looked decidedly unhappy.

'You've really fucking fucked it this time, you fucking little fuck,' he said. With a command of the language like that it was a wonder he wasn't in the federal Cabinet. 'Get in. Charlene wants to see you.' As he drove away, Agnelli tooted. His idea of solidarity with the working class. I closed my eyes and slumped down in the seat. Agnelli had woken up the octopus. It had gone and now it was back. It put its suckers on my eyeballs and started dragging them backwards into my cranium.

As Agnelli drove he reached into his inside jacket pocket. 'You seem to have forgotten just how close to the bottom end of the political food chain you are, sport. Talk about Whelan the Wrecker. A trained chimpanzee could have done a better job.' He had a piece of paper in his hand. My report to MACWAM. 'No immediate cause for concern...Press reports having no basis in fact.' He quoted my concluding paragraphs snidely and flapped the page in my face as he changed lanes. 'You're deliberately trying to make me look like an idiot in front of the committee, aren't you? "No cause for concern." Shit, yesterday there was only one dead body, now there's two and for all I know the count is still climbing.'

He stuffed the paper back in his pocket. I took it that I was supposed to be impressed by all of this. The car was overheated and stuffy and I'd had a hell of a night. I closed my eyes, let a gentle torpor settle over me, and concentrated on getting the octopus to go back to sleep. I guess I must have yawned. This did not go down well.

'You think it's a joke, don't you?' Agnelli screamed. 'I've got Merricks on the phone at the crack of fucking dawn screaming government incompetence at the top of his tits, and you think it's a joke. Half the fucking joint burned down and the other half is out of commission indefinitely. If you had one iota of decency, you'd resign on the spot. You'd order me to stop the car, right here and now, and get out. You'd resign and spare Charlene, and the rest of us any further embarrassment.' He slowed down, as if I might take him up on the suggestion and throw myself out of the moving vehicle. 'You, mate, are in more shit than a Bondi surfer.'

A sticker on the front of the glove box thanked me for not smoking. I reached over and tried to peel it off. The sticker was made out of some sort of paper that tore when I pulled it. Thank You for Not, it now read. 'One thing I don't understand,' I said. 'The story in the *Sun* on Monday. How did you do that part?'

Agnelli didn't miss a beat, I'll say that for him. 'I don't know what you're talking about.'

'It's all been bullshit, hasn't it?' I said. 'Lollicato was never planning a challenge at all. You've been feeding me crap from the word go, keeping me busy chasing my own tail.'

Agnelli was suddenly deeply intent on the traffic. He seemed to find it hard to speak while getting his mouth back down below melting point. 'Why would I want to do that?'

'Because you're lining yourself up to challenge Charlene.'

'Ah,' he said, a long, upwardly-inflected exhale. It was, I knew, as close as he would come to an admission.

'And Charlene?' I said.

'Charlene?'

'Yeah, the woman you're busy trying to shaft. How is she?'

He shrugged. 'Ask her yourself,' he said.

We were in Royal Parade by then, going down the long tunnel of shade cast by the avenue of big trees. I closed my eyes, feigning sleep. After a while the silence got to Agnelli. He snapped on the radio. It was the ABC. Crap, crap. Blah, blah. Then we got the ten o'clock news. The Reagan re-election campaign was entering its final phase. The word Armageddon was mentioned. Marcos had ordered the trial of suspects in the Benigno Aquino killing. I couldn't see much coming of that. The Maralinga Royal Commission had commenced. The British High Commissioner was bitching that Britain's name was being dragged through the mud. So not all the news was bad, then.

After five minutes of this, I had almost fallen asleep for real. Then the local bulletin came on. The fire had already been overtaken by more current stories. In a joint state-commonwealth police operation, illegal gambling equipment had been seized from an address in Brunswick overnight. It was also believed that charges relating to immigration offences would be laid in the near future. After that I must have dozed off properly, because the next thing I knew Agnelli had pulled into a vacant space outside the Peter MacCallum Institute. That woke me up quick smart. The Peter Mac is a cancer hospital. 'What are we doing here?'

'Talking to Charlene.' That was as much as I could get out of him.

'She's okay though, isn't she?'

'You're so fucking smart,' he said. 'You tell me.' He led the way along halls that smelled like the 1930s, all wax and boracic soap. Outside her room he softened a little. 'She wants to tell you herself,' he said.

Charlene was in a private room, in a bed with too many pillows, a view of the back end of the Titles Office, and ominous plumbing fixtures. She was propped up with a tube sticking into her arm and another one coming out of her nose. It was the first time I had ever seen her without make-up. Her complexion was parchment, as if her face had ceded priority to more demanding parts of her metabolism. Her customarily rigid helmet of a perm had flopped into a lifeless mat. She looked a hundred. Whatever was happening to her was happening fast.

She was studying a document. Her reading glasses had slipped down to the end of her nose and she looked out over the top of them. A major display of gladioli had been shoved to the back of the bedside table to make way for dispatch boxes. Arthur, her driver, was standing at the foot of the bed scrutinising his shoes.

'Lovely,' she whispered. 'Beaut.' She signed the page, handed it to Arthur, and sank backwards. Arthur nodded to us on the way out, far too emphatically.

Wordlessly Agnelli and I parted and stood one on each side of the bed. Charlene took off her glasses and put them aside. She winced at the effort and tried to hide it. 'Sit down,' she ordered. Her voice was a tremulous echo of what it had been.

The visitors' chairs were made of tubular metal and plywood and had been painted cream sometime during the battle of Balaclava. Mine shrieked when I dragged it across the floor. I cringed and sat down as quietly as I could.

'It's just a few tests,' Charlene said. 'Not the death of Napoleon.' Paradoxically, her fragility made her seem all the more powerful. 'Angelo told you?' she asked me.

'Told me what?'

'Good,' she said. 'Didn't want you getting any wrong ideas.'

'What's wrong, Charlene?' I said. 'You look terrible.' I thought I could tell her that because it was something she would already have known.

'Bit of a growth,' she said. 'An opportunity to reorder my priorities.'

One of her hands lay on top of the bedclothes, like a chook's claw with rings on. She let me pick it up. It was cool to the touch. As she spoke, I rubbed it between my palms. It didn't seem to get any warmer.

'I've decide to retire,' she said. 'The Premier knows. One or two others. Now I'm telling you.' To my eternal shame my first thought was of myself. Charlene read my mind. 'It's all been taken care of,' she said. 'Angelo.'

Agnelli leaped up, strode to the foot of the bed and gripped the metal bed-end. Rehearsing, I realised as he spoke, his new role. 'Charlene and the faction leaders have agreed that I should take on Melbourne Upper,' he announced, pausing long enough for Charlene's silence to constitute a confirmation.

I assumed she would have some pretty good motives for going along with this caper. She lay impassively, giving me no hint what they might be.

'As you know,' Agnelli went on, addressing the chart above Charlene's head. 'There are always those at the local level who find it difficult to reconcile these sort of decisions with both traditional practices and their own personal agendas.'

Charlene fidgeted impatiently under the sheets. 'Cut the cackle, Angelo. You're not in parliament yet,' she said. She inclined her head in my direction and spoke so softly I had to bend closer to hear her. She did this, I realised, to stir Agnelli. 'The truth is, Murray, this close to an election we can't afford another factional brawl over pre-selection. Angelo is what you might call'—here she paused and made a minor show of looking for the right word—'acceptable to both the left and the right.'

'Acceptable?' I said. 'This is quite a surprise.' Agnelli couldn't conceal a look of triumph. 'And it's bound to be messy.' Agnelli temporarily shelved his hubris. I went on. 'Parachuting in some heavyweight with high-level connections and expecting the local branches to endorse him. It won't go down very well.'

'Quite right,' said Charlene ambiguously. 'That's why we want you to smooth over the transition. Help Angelo garner the support he'll need in the electorate. That sort of thing.'

Do Agnelli's dirty work for him? Like buggery I would. 'Ange has just finished telling me how little confidence he has in me,' I said.

'Ah, don't be so thin-skinned,' said Agnelli. 'You think I'd want you if I didn't think you could do the job?'

'Aside from which,' said Charlene, more to the point. 'Someone well regarded in the electorate will need to be right there beside you all the way through the process.'

An immediate answer seemed to be required. I didn't know

what to say, so I didn't say anything. Perhaps Charlene took my silence for a rebuke. She pretended, at least I hope she was pretending, that it was a negotiating stance.

'Angelo has agreed,' she said, 'that in return for my support, and as a personal favour to me, that he will retain you as his electorate officer for at least the next parliamentary term, whether or not we are in government. His agreement is a matter of record. Isn't that right, Angelo?'

'Absolutely,' said the fucking snake who little more than half an hour before had been trying to get me to jump out of his car.

The temptation to tell Agnelli to shove it was strong. But Charlene had obviously gone to some pains to see me looked after in whatever deals Agnelli was busy cutting. And, truth be known, it was hardly an ideal time to be looking for a new job. The Family Court did not look kindly on the custody claims of unemployed fathers. Aide-de-camp to Agnelli wasn't exactly Ambassador to Ireland but it was a job. And a boy must have a job. I couldn't bring myself to say yes, so I just nodded.

'Good boy,' said Charlene and squeezed my hand. 'Forgive me?'

I never found out what she meant by that. A hippo-faced specialist in a white coat had barged through the door with a clutch of chinless interns in tow and turfed me and Agnelli out. That's what you get for not going to the right schools.

If she meant, did I forgive her for leg-roping me to Angelo Agnelli's political fortunes, the answer was yes. The decision was mine and I've accepted responsibility for it.

If she meant, did I forgive her for conniving with Agnelli to send me on a wild goose chase, the answer is I don't know. I don't know because I could never bring myself to ask the prick if Charlene was party to it, so I'll never know if there was anything to forgive. Nor could I ever bring myself to enquire too fully into the intricacies of the deal that saw Agnelli become the party's endorsed candidate for Melbourne Upper. The fact is some things just don't bear too close examination. Sometimes it's enough just to know that you're still on the team. I held my hand out to Agnelli. 'Congratulations,' I said. 'Comrade.'

The rest is, as they say, ongoing context. Let me parameter the specifics for you.

Charlene was out of hospital the next day just in time to usher the workplace insurance legislation safely into law and see the end of the spring session of parliament. Three days later she announced her resignation and a week after that writs were issued for a state election. While all this was happening, I was having a few sleepless nights waiting for the coppers to come knocking on my door. When they hadn't turned up after a month, I knew they probably never would.

We won the election, despite the best efforts of the *Sun*, with an increased majority. We even picked up a marginal gain in Melbourne Upper, but only at the booths in the heaviest Italian areas. Five months later Charlene was dead. We gave her a wonderful send-off and she's buried out at Fawkner Cemetery. Eternally committed to the electorate is probably the way she'd put it. Keeping in touch with the grass roots.

Going out there again, past those rows of tombs lined up like a miniature set from some sword and sandal epic, reminded me of those weirdos with the military salutes standing over Bayraktar's coffin. By then I knew what had been going on, or thought I did. Coates and I had pieced the basics together, and I fleshed the rest out from incidental titbits that Agnelli picked up on the legal grapevine when the Anatolia Club gambling case came up.

Appearances can be deceptive. At first sight the fact that the Anatolia Club looked so much like a small private casino blinded me to the fact that it essentially was just that. And as such had certain requirements in the way of personnel. That's where Bayraktar came in, initially at least.

The proprietors, including the two bozos I'd seen at the cemetery, had imported Bayraktar from Turkey to act as their debt collector. They were former military officers and Bayraktar had once been an NCO, so they might have known him from the army. Perhaps, he'd merely been well recommended by their crim colleagues in West Germany. In any case, he turned out to be a bit of a liability, inclined to shake down the clientele on his own account. Rather than grasp the nettle in the way that Gardiner ultimately did, they suggested he find employment elsewhere. But they let him keep his little flat out the back, a sort of implicit threat to any of their customers tempted to welsh on their commitments.

Temporarily forced to work for a living, Bayraktar had fallen on his feet. First he was recruited by Gardiner to front the payroll scam. Then he began putting the squeeze on likely fellow employees. Eventually he worked out that Pacific Pastoral provided the ideal set-up for shifting drugs about the country-side. When Gardiner eventually got fed up with all these extracurricular antics and gave him the big chill, the crew at the Anatolia Club were probably as relieved as anyone else.

But he had once been a fellow soldier, and honour required that his death not go uncommemorated. His former associates at the club signed for the body, chipped in for a medium-priced Martinelli walnut overcoat and stood in the rain at attention for two minutes. I can only hope someone does as much for me when the time comes.

Not that any of this came out at the inquest. No new evidence was presented to counter the original supposition that the fat boy had taken a heart turn in the midst of laying in his weekend supplies of scotch fillet. The coroner came down on the side of natural causes, and took the opportunity to comment broadly on the importance of maintaining safe work practices in the cool-storage industry. The Department of Labour responded with a press release pointing out that it was in the process of amending the regulations regarding mandatory aisle-widths and expected to gazette them in the not-too-distant future.

The one minor hiccup in the coronial hearing was the unavoidable absence from the witness box of the man who had found the body. Herb Gardiner was, of course, the subject of his own inquest barely a week after Bayraktar's. Based on the fact that he was wearing protective clothing, and on the testimony of the fireman who found the body, as well as the medical evidence, it was concluded that Gardiner had been inside one of the freezers when the alarm went off. Making a late run for the exit, he had slipped on the wet floor, broken his neck, and been asphyxiated by the smoke as he lay unconscious.

Frankly, that last bit was something of a surprise. I'd honestly thought he was already dead when I left him lying there. Misadventure, the coroner said. I couldn't agree more. More proof, if any is needed, that you can't help bad luck. The cause of the fire was attributed to a radiator accidentally left burning all night in the administration area. Speculation that arson was involved was dismissed by both the company and the police as groundless. The insurance was paid out in full.

Herb Gardiner left an estate worth the best part of two million dollars, including a Broadbeach condominium, an Adelaide motel and part shares in a macadamia nut plantation. It just goes to show what hard work, a bit of thrift, and a remarkable fifteen-year-long winning streak on the horses can achieve. His punting record was all carefully documented in papers found in his bookcase—date, course, race, horse, dividend. In case the tax man ever asked, I guess.

With no-one to lay claim to the estate, it all went to the Public Trustees Office, which will meticulously administer it down to a zero sum over a period of 150 years.

On the way back from Charlene's funeral I drove past 636 Blyth Street. It had already changed hands twice since the Anatolia Club was shut down and was being refurbished as a Maltese wedding reception centre. For all I know that's what it still is. I must check next time I'm out that way.

That could be some time. These days Melbourne Upper is just one small part of the territory I cover in my capacity as adviser to the Minister for Ethnic Affairs, Angelo Agnelli, MLC. Fortunately, for me at least, Angelo is also Minister for Local Government, a demanding portfolio that leaves him with insufficient energy to do serious damage to the interests of those valued members of our community who derive from the more non-English-speaking parts of the planet. In fact Local Government is so unrewarding a portfolio that I'm beginning to think poor old Ange must have trodden on a few important toes on his way up the ladder. Mullane senior for one. Apparently Ange promised my job to young Gavin in return for the old man's support on pre-selection. Right now Ange is off in the bush somewhere trying to convince some quasi-autonomous local instrumentality to voluntarily sacrifice itself on the altar of efficiency.

As for me, I try to keep my head down and my tail up, but I'd be lying if I said I was overextended. Ethnic Affairs is mostly about trying to find ways to give a bit of a leg-up to government supporters with funny surnames. Speaking of which, I saw Ayisha Celik the other day at the Ethnic Communities Council Conference. It was the first time we'd spoken since the big event. Somebody started to introduce us. Ayisha cut in, laughing with her eyes, gorgeous as ever. 'You seen a doctor yet?'

'No need,' I said, 'now that the swelling's gone down.'

'Murray had terrible rash last time I looked,' she explained to our host.

'I see,' he said knowingly. 'Like that, is it?' It wasn't, but she didn't seem to mind if he thought so. Then we all stood there silently rocking on our heels for a moment until the other guy got the idea and made himself scarce.

'I dunno what happened between you and Memo Gezen. And I don't want to,' she said. 'But whatever it was, it did the trick. He's gone back to Turkey. Wife, kids, the works. Thanks.'

I said it was no trouble and all for the best and she said congratulations on my new job. Then the coffee break ended and we had to rush off and chair our respective workshops. For a brief moment there I considered pressing my suit with her, but in the end I decided against it. Keeping secrets is one thing that Ayisha is good at. Best not muddy the waters.

Word is she's on the short list for Co-ordinator of the Migrant Resource Centre. She's got the advocacy routine down pat, and that degree in Public Administration she's got should set her in good stead. So if anyone asks, I'll tell them I can't think of a better person for the job, even if she has got herself engaged to some Macedonian mother's-boy from Pascoe Vale.

Gezen's not the only one to have moved. Red lives in Canberra most of the time now. Very good for kids it is. He can walk to school and Wendy even lets him ride his bike to the shops. The woman Wendy is living with has a girl two years older, so he's not short of family life. He flies down one weekend a month, which is all I can afford at the moment, and as much as his social life permits. I get him on the school holidays too, although last time he went to Samoa instead because Wendy was speaking at a conference there on Women and the Future of Work in the Pacific, and it was too good a chance to pass up.

We'll probably get round to formalising the divorce some-time soon. It's not as if there's any great reason to rush. Wendy eventually saw reason on splitting the cost of the roof job, even though it turned out that Ant had charged five hundred dollars above the going rate and was ripping the materials off as well. What decided her was the capital gain of twenty-five grand we made when we sold the old place. I put my half down as the deposit on a nice little fully-renovated zero-maintenance terrace in Fitzroy. It's handy enough for me to be able to walk to work, which is just as well, as it's murder trying to find a park around here.

Of course it's quieter here in Victoria Parade than it was out at the electorate office. We don't get much passing trade. Just to get to see me, you have to sign in with the commissionaire in the foyer, take the lift eight floors and negotiate two secretaries and an administration officer. Not that I don't make an effort to keep my finger on the pulse, mind you. It's all No Smoking up here, so whenever I want a quick puff I have to pop down to street level and mingle with the other desperados. There's always a little crowd steaming away in the foyer of the Resources and Technology Department next door, and it's amazing what little tit-bits of info you can pick up. And sometimes this woman from Information and Publications on the fourth floor is there. Antoinette Aboud her name is. Lebanese, I guess. Fascinating people, the Lebanese. So much history, so little space.

And you never know, do you? There's this safe seat out Springvale way that might just possibly be on the market before the next election. It's right across the other side of town and I'll probably have to learn a word or two of Vietnamese, but at this stage I'm confident of enough factional support at the centre to warrant throwing my hat into the ring. Naturally the locals will have to be squared off. The electorate officer is apparently quite a handful. But I do feel that I do have a certain amount of expertise in these matters. And expertise is the name of the game these days.

Or maybe I'll stick to my snug little office here on the top floor. I've got my own window now, and I can see right across the treetops of the Fitzroy Gardens, past the spire of the cathedral, to the city with all its cranes and new office towers. Almost every day there's something brand new on the skyline. The way this city is going, by the end of the eighties the place will be unrecognisable. For the past few months one high-rise tower in particular had held my attention, a combination media centre and hotel being put up by a consortium headed by Lionel Merricks.

These days Lionel is not nearly so critical of the government as he was in the first few days after the fire. Not after I found the opportunity for a conference with him. I rang for an appointment a couple of times, all very civilised, but never got past the ice queen. I supposed that Lionel wasn't too keen to start taking my calls again. So I hung around outside the next meeting of the City Revitalisation Committee and caught him in the hallway during a coffee break. Rather than face a scene, he agreed to a private chinwag in the stairwell. He tried to browbeat his way out of it, of course. But I felt that this time I had the edge on him, what with my new suit, my face all healed up and a few well-researched facts up my sleeve.

The folks at the Department of Agriculture had been particularly helpful. They explained just how much illicit money you can make if you've got a meat works, an export licence, a low-key, long-term approach, and a certain amount of contempt for the law. You just stick your boneless beef labels on something else. Donkey meat is a big-margin item. Kangaroo, too. But they're a bit risky. You can still make a pretty penny using lower grade beef.

Naturally, it doesn't pay to get caught. The trick then is to pass it all off as a mistake. It helps if your plant manager is convinced it really is one. And since this sort of thing can do a lot of damage to the reputation of a nation's export industries, the official inspectors are loath to come down with a finding of systematic abuse. Fortunately for Pacific Pastoral, the issue never arose. The fire gave them a much-needed pretext to divest themselves of their entire commodity export operations. They flogged the works off to a Japanese feed-lot enterprise based in Queensland, and used the proceeds to finance their move into tourism, media and real estate development, all of which have been a real boon to the state economy. Not that the issue of finance raised its ugly head in my conversation with Merricks. I was very careful about that.

'Herb Gardiner told me everything,' I said first up, my back pressed against the door. 'He felt the need to unburden himself.'

'I didn't even know the man,' Merricks blustered. 'We've got thousands of employees.'

'True,' I said. 'But how many of them were with you on HMAS Wyndham?'

Another thing Agnelli was right about was how insulated the leaders of big business are. I was probably the rudest person Merricks ever had to deal with. He employed others to deal with ill-mannered oafs like me. He lacked the skills required. 'A frigate,' I said, 'That's not a very big boat, is it? Not like an aircraft carrier or something.'

'The Wyndham's not a boat,' he bleated. 'It's a ship.' That's when I knew I had him.

Which was just as well, since I was only guessing about him and Gardiner having met in the Navy. The Office of Naval

Records doesn't give out personnel information and I'd got the name of the ship Lionel served on from the journalist who'd written the profile for the *National Times*. I'd taken a punt and rung her up, telling her I needed some background for an award the government was thinking of presenting to Merricks. It turned out that he'd mentioned the Wyndham in the course of the interview and I put two and two together. It was sheer quantum mathematics that I got four, since I hadn't been able to find out anything about Gardiner's service record either.

With the Wyndham bobbing about in front of us, Merricks' memory suddenly improved and he was prepared to allow that there may have been a mechanic named Gardiner aboard. And he couldn't definitively discount the possibility that the same man had been employed at Coolaroo at the time he was an up-and-coming line manager out there. But I'd have a lot of trouble proving he'd had any direct dealings with the man subsequently, he told me. And the suggestion that the two of them had in some way been co-conspirators in criminal activity was a preposterous idea. One that, if repeated in public, would land me in court.

I didn't doubt that for one minute. But it was a hollow threat. I had no intention of taking on Merricks. The laws of libel are designed to protect the rich, and the idea that Pacific Pastoral might allow its internal records to be used to implicate its own chairman in protracted and systematic fraud was ludicrous. This little chat was just something I felt was needed by way of clearing the air. A personal matter. The last time I had spoken to Merricks, he thought I was trying to blackmail him. In the light of what had happened since, I just didn't want him thinking he had the moral advantage on me.

'Meat substitution isn't really a crime, I guess,' I told him. 'More just a bit of sharp business practice, eh? *Caveat emptor*, and all that. But what about the payroll fraud, the extortion, the drugs? You and Gardiner were diddling the consumers, Gardiner and Bayraktar were ripping off the corporation, and Bayraktar was screwing the employees and dealing dope off the loading-bay. Nice sort of company you keep, Lionel.'

I think he was so genuinely scandalised by then that I omitted dangerous driving and attempted murder. I left him standing on the stairs and shut the door behind me.

And to give Merricks the benefit of the doubt, I think it unlikely he actually suggested killing me when he delegated to Gardiner the job of sorting me out. Perhaps he had a generous cash settlement in mind. Lionel is a broad brush-stroke man, and not, I think, by nature violent. As distinct from Herb Gardiner, who had clearly been driven barking mad by the prospect of fifteen years' slow surreptitious graft in the arsehole of the universe disappearing down the gurgler two weeks before he retired to enjoy his illicit earnings. A person can hardly be blamed for the things done in his name by over-zealous subordinates.

Merricks, in fact, is so tractable these days that Agnelli has been able to wangle some very substantial donations out of him to offset the rising cost of elections. The outcomes of which have ensured my continuing employment. So I guess that pragmatism is not merely a civic virtue, it is also a personal grace. In tending the Garden State, one must always be mindful of the serpents.

And it's not like I have anything to complain about. Not since the bruises healed up, anyway. As I say to Angelo Agnelli on those rare occasions he asks for my advice, '*Bir tesselli ver*'.

THE BRUSH-OFF

For Wally and May, for their forbearance and their grandparents

'I can't think of a single
Russian novel in which one
of the characters goes
into a picture gallery.'
W. Somerset Maugham

The two cops were virtually invisible. Only the bobbing white domes of their helmets, floating like ghostly globes through the thick summer night, and the muted clip-clop of their horses gave warning of their approach. She hadn't mentioned the mounted patrol when we came over the fence.

'Look out,' I whispered. 'Here comes the cavalry.'

'Ssshhh.' Salina clapped her hand over my mouth, trembling with the effort of stifling her own laughter. 'Get down.'

I got down. On my knees in the leaf litter, nuzzling the pompom fringe of her mu-mu. It was the mu-mu that first drew my eye to Salina Fleet. The mu-mu with its palm-tree motif. Then the apricot lipstick. And the terry-towel beach bag with hula-hoop handles. So playful among all those business shirts and bow ties. 'Rode one when I was ten,' I mumbled.

The pub was closed, the crowd from the art exhibition dispersed. And there we were, in possession of two stolen wine glasses and a filched bottle of chardonnay, hidden in a thicket of shrubbery inside the locked gates of the Botanic Gardens. This, I already suspected, was a decision I might come to regret. For now, however, I was game for anything. Ten or twelve drinks and I'm anyone's.

'Rode a what?' Sal whispered.

'Rhododendron,' I repeated. '*Rhododendron oreotrophes.*' It was written on a little plaque hammered into the ground beside my foot. I said it out loud, just to see if I could.

'Ssshhhh!' Again her hand closed over my face. 'You'll get us arrested, Murray.' Beneath the press of her palm, I opened my mouth. My tongue tasted her skin. The horses passed, so close we could have reached out and stroked their flanks. I stroked Salina's instead.

'Quick.' She grabbed my hand and dashed across the path, a wood sprite disappearing into a tunnel of undergrowth where the overhanging branches were too low for any horse to follow. Her legs flashed white, darting ahead.

Playing hide and seek in the Botanic Gardens was not where I'd imagined our acquaintance might lead when Salina and I were introduced at the Ministry for the Arts earlier that evening. I was the new minister's political adviser. She was the visual arts editor of *Veneer* magazine. The two of us should probably have been discussing post-modernist aesthetic theory and its impact on social policy. I fixed my eyes on her bare legs, took a deep breath and plunged into the darkness.

'You like it?' Sal whirled, showing her secret place. A fern gully. Dark, moist, prehistoric. Round and round she spun, noiseless, abandoned, crazy, even drunker than me. She grabbed my hand again and took off, leading me on at breakneck speed. The path forked and twisted, becoming a maze. She let go, disappeared. The night was tropical, full of sounds, water running, the hypnotic thrum of a million cicadas, bird calls, a high-pitched squeaking like a gate swinging on its hinges in a breeze. I plunged on, running headlong downhill, the momentum irresistible.

A grove of bamboo reared up, the canes as thick as my arm, a kung fu forest. She lay there on a bed of leaves, waiting. I threw myself on my back beside her, and she rolled onto me, straddling my thighs. She could scarcely have been unaware of the effect this produced. '*Pinus radiata,*' I said. '*Grevillea robusta.*'

We did not kiss. It would have seemed soppy. My hands

glided up her ribs, thumbs extended to trace her anatomy through the fabric of her dress. Belly, sternum, ribs. Nipples as hard as Chinese algebra. Her neck arched, her mouth hung open. Dirty dancing in deep dark dingly dell. Above, high above, the sky was a pale blur, immeasurably distant, framed by branches festooned with hundreds of brown paper bags that rustled gently in the still night air.

My shirt was open. Her dress was runched up around her waist. Fingers tugged at my belt—hers or mine I couldn't tell, didn't care. 'Where is it?' she gasped. 'Where is it?'

'In your hand. It's in your hand.'

'Not that, stupid. A condom.'

If she didn't stop doing what she was doing with her hand, I wouldn't need a condom. I didn't have one. What sort of boy did she think I was?

Warm liquid trickled out of the sky and splashed the ground beside us. Rainforest soma, warm and dank. Salina arched her neck again, staring up to where the paper bags shifted and shuffled, fluttering from branch to branch, chattering among themselves, a hundred squeaky gates.

'Bats!' she shrieked.

Hundreds of them. Fruit bats, flying foxes, roosting high in the tops of spindly Moreton Bay figs. She leaped to her feet and we ran, she convulsed with the giggles, me stuffing myself back in my pants.

We exploded out of the fern forest into a circle of lawn. The night sky, drenched with humidity, shone like a sudden spotlight after the jungle depths. We rolled together on the grass, kissing now, all the imminence of the previous moment gone, the compact implicit, a slow build-up ahead of us. Sweet, sweet, sweet. I came up for air. 'You think any of these are rubber trees?'

Salina pulled the wine from her bag and we drank from the bottle, getting sensible, keeping un-sober. 'My place,' she said. A loft. In the city. Safety tackle, more booze. I pulled her to her feet. 'Let's went.'

Easier said than done. Melbourne's Botanic Gardens are

approximately the size of Uganda. At the best of times, finding your way out takes a compass, a ball of twine, and access to satellite navigation. We sat down and drank some more. She watched me graze her lowlands, then we started up the hill, hugging the dark fringes, cutting through the densest thickets.

Here and there we stopped, pressed against each other in beds of flowering succulents, stamen brushing pistil, inhaling nectar. Pissed to the eyeballs. My fingers were sticky with liquidambar. My aching prick was as hard and smooth as the trunk of the ghost gum, *Eucalyptus papuana*, planted here by Viscount de Lisle, Governor-General of Australia, 1961–65.

Eventually, unpollinated, we found the fence at the top of the hill and followed it. An open-sided rotunda capped the crest, its cupola resting on columns topped with stag ferns cast in concrete. My sentiments precisely.

Below was the river, its banks hidden by trees. The occasional swish of a car wafted up from Alexandra Avenue. In the distance, tipping the foliage, the neon sign above the Richmond silos told the hour. NYLEX 3.08. The pub had closed at one. Time was meaningless. Across the river, the lights of the city glowed. A loft, she'd said.

'Princes Bridge.' She cocked her head towards where the fence was concealed in a border of hardy perennials. Princes Bridge was the nearest point we could cross the Yarra. Bliss was a twenty-minute walk away. Never again, I swore by the sacred name of Baden-Powell, never again would I be caught unprepared.

We climbed the fence and began our way across the treed lawns of the Queen Victoria Gardens. The heehaw of an ambulance siren washed through the night towards us, echoing the pulse of my horny urgency. As we headed for the bridge, the sound grew louder, insistent in the stillness, urging us forward.

At the floral clock, where the trees ended and the lawn met the broad boulevard of St Kilda Road, the sound abruptly stopped. We stopped, too, and stared.

Across the road sat the National Gallery, its floodlit facade looming like the screen of a drive-in movie, a faceless wall of austere grey basalt. Extending along the foot of the wall was a shallow ornamental moat, walled by a low stone parapet. In the moat stood a gigantic multi-hued beast with three legs and a head at each end.

This sight was not, in itself, remarkable. The gallery with its moat and its sculptures was a prominent civic landmark. A tourist attraction, a cultural resource. We'd both seen it a thousand times before. But neither of us had ever seen it like this.

An ambulance was drawn up at the gallery's main entrance, a dark mouse-hole in the blank wall. Both of the vehicle's rear doors were flung open. Its light was flashing. Giant shadows, thrown up by the spinning flare, played across the facade of the building like characters from a half-glimpsed puppet show. Like the figures in Plato's cave. Two men were kneeling on the parapet of the moat. Their heads bobbed. Their arms jerked rhythmically. A little cluster of figures moved about the ambulance, engaged in some obscure task. The sudden silence, the lack of passing traffic, was absolute. The tableau was compelling in its mystery.

Drawn irresistibly, we crossed the road. It was a pointless detour, a distraction. Stupid.

The paramedics parted as we arrived, as if to display their handiwork, as if our mere presence entitled us to a view of the proceedings. Except they weren't parting for us, but were clearing a way to wheel a stretcher towards the yawning doors of the ambulance.

On the stretcher was a body. Alive or dead, man or woman, it was impossible to tell. All I could see were legs, clad in wet black jeans. Then my view was blocked by a gallery security guard. His trousers, too, were soaked. Water trailed across the footpath. Someone had been pulled out of the moat.

There was a kind of bleak formality to the scene. Sombre work was being undertaken by those trained to its demands. The climax, whatever it was, had already been played out. We had no business here, gawping at its aftermath. I turned away, embarrassed, a little ashamed of my curiosity. Besides, I had more vital concerns. That loft in the city was only ten minutes away.

But Salina had slipped between two of the uniforms. 'Hey, Marcus,' she called, like it was all an elaborate joke being staged for our benefit. 'What's going on?'

Then I saw what she had seen. A pair of cowboy boots, tooled leather toes pointing at the sky, jutting from the end of the stretcher.

Things happened very quickly after that. A police car disgorged two uniforms, one male, one female. A security guard, some toy copper with pissant insignia, grabbed at Sal, caught one of her hula hoops. I pushed forward, but one of the cops got there first. She had Salina by the arm, holding her back. 'You know this person?'

In the staccato explosions of light, I saw Salina's face as it bent above the stretcher. Saw it change, frame by frame. Recognition. Shock. Panic. Her eyes were wide with dread. 'He's my...' The words hooked in her throat.

'His name?' The policeman was in no mood to be stuffed about by a half-drunk dolly bird. One of the security guards had handed him a wallet, and he was reading a plastic card.

'Marcus Taylor.' Salina's tone was defiant now, as she fought for control. The officer nodded, acknowledging her right to be there, conceding nothing else. The stretcher was almost all the way into the ambulance. Even without looking, I knew who he was, this Marcus Taylor.

'He's my boyfriend,' said Salina. Then she corrected herself. 'Fiancé. He's my fiancé.'

The policewoman drew her back, making room for them to close the ambulance door.

Salina turned then and looked at me like it was all my fault. 'Bastard,' she swore.

I'd been given the brush-off
before, but this was a bit rich. I could see that the woman was
upset, but she could hardly blame me for what was happening.

Twelve hours earlier I'd never even heard of Salina Fleet,
or this Marcus Taylor who was being fed feet-first into the
ambulance. Twelve hours earlier, the idea of romping in the
rhododendrons with a blonde cultural critic in a pom-pommed
mu-mu was as remote as my chances of being appointed ambassador to the Holy See. Seeing a floater being pulled out of the
moat of the National Gallery had not been pencilled into my
diary.

Half a day earlier, I wasn't even on this side of town. I was
stuck in a stifling room behind a shopfront in Northcote, being
given the hairy eyeball by Leonidas Mavramoustakides. It was
the last Friday in January 1989, the stinking hot end of an overheated decade, and I was waiting for a phone call. I wished it
would hurry up and come.

Mavramoustakides was once a major in Greek army intelligence. That was twenty years earlier, during the military
regime. He still cultivated the style. Crisp white shirt, hairline
moustache, dark tie, gimlet eyes. The dye he used to keep his
hair jet black was beginning to run in the heat and little dribbles

of it were trickling down beneath his collar. But I wasn't going to tell him that. Not with the attitude he was taking.

He was sitting behind a tiny imitation baroque desk made of plywood. Most of it was taken up by a voluminous white marble ashtray, and by two pompously over-flowing correspondence trays, one weighted down by a small plaster bust of Aristotle. Mavramoustakides crushed the tip of his cigarette cruelly into the ashtray, put his elbows on his desk and smiled a mirthless smile. 'If we don't get your co-operation,' he said. 'We can make things very uncomfortable for you.'

It was difficult to conceive just how he proposed to do this. I was already about as uncomfortable as humanly possible. The air of the minuscule room was thick with stale cigarette smoke. My shirt was drenched with sweat and stuck to the back of a vinyl chair. My teeth were caked with grounds from the cup of muddy coffee in front of me. And Jimmy Papas, Mavramoustakides' overweight sidekick, looked like he was about to lumber to his feet and smack me across the chops with his fat hand.

'Remember,' warned Mavramoustakides. 'We are more than half a million Greeks in this city.' The way he said it, you'd think he was claiming personal responsibility for the fact. 'You can't afford to upset that many people.'

Actually there were only 326,382 Greek-speaking residents of Melbourne and scant few of them paid any attention at all to Leonidas Mavramoustakides. The only reason we were having this conversation was because he and Jimmy Papas were getting to be a pain in the neck. They'd been ringing around and writing letters and two weeks earlier Papas had confronted my boss, Angelo Agnelli, at Kostas Manolas' daughter's wedding and threatened to make a scene. Angelo, naturally, had immediately agreed to an appointment. Then, naturally, he found he had an unavoidable engagement elsewhere and deputised me to solve the problem.

'Piss off, Leo,' I said, staring at the phone, willing it to ring. 'You're talking crap and you know it.'

We were in the editor's office at *Nea Hellas*, a Greek-language tabloid with an ultra-conservative political line and a weekly readership of about ten thousand. Leonidas Mavramoustakides owned and edited the paper and Jimmy Papas was its business manager, a job that consisted largely of convincing delicatessen owners and fish-roe importers to buy advertising space they didn't really need. This task was proving increasingly difficult, which explained why the two of them were getting so pushy.

'We only ask what we entitled to,' growled Papas, doing to his worry beads what he'd like to do to my testicles. '*Neos Kosmos, Il Globo, El Telegraph*, all these papers get government advertising. How come we don't get our share? If we don't, our readers will not vote Labor at the next election. You tell your boss Agnelli that.'

A little respect would not have been out of order. For me, and for my boss. The Honourable Angelo Agnelli was a Minister of the Crown, the Minister for Ethnic Affairs. Ours was a Labor government, democratic in temper, so obsequiousness was unnecessary. Just a little less contempt, that was all I asked. The kind of scorn that Mavramoustakides displayed was the prerogative of colleagues and associates, not superannuated torturers.

'Get real, Jimmy,' I said. 'None of your readers vote for us anyway. Most of them can't even read.'

The function of the Minister for Ethnic Affairs was to spread a microscopically thin layer of largesse over every ethnic community in the state. My task, as his adviser, was to help wield the butter knife. On a day like this, dealing with pricks like this, it was a job whose appeal was limited.

Fortunately, before I could say something undiplomatic, Sophie Mavramoustakides stuck her head around the door. 'Phone call for Murray Whelan,' she chirped, in the manner of a hotel bellboy paging a guest. 'You want me to put it through?'

Sophie had a hair-do like a haystack and a lot more va-va-voom than she could burn off working as a typist at her fascist father's rag. She splashed some of it over me. She was wasting her time. I was single but I wasn't suicidal.

Only Trish at the office knew where I was, so this was the call I'd been waiting for. But the last thing I needed was Leo and Jimmy breathing down my neck while I got the news. I unpeeled myself from the plastic chair and indicated I'd prefer to take the call in private. Mavramoustakides grunted. My preferences were beneath his dignity. He'd wanted to talk to the organ grinder, not be fobbed off with the monkey. As far as Leo was concerned, I could go climb a tree.

Sophie, utilising as much of her bottom as possible, led me upstairs to the chaos that passed for the *Nea Hellas* production room, indicated which phone I should use and returned Eurydice-like into the Stygian realm below.

Nea Hellas was on the Northcote hill, one of the few elevated points in the otherwise flat expanse of Melbourne's inner-northern suburbs. The view out its first-floor window swept in a broad arc across the baking rooftops of houses and factories, all the way to the glass-walled towers of the central city, a shimmering mirage on the far horizon. Above, an unbroken blue sky beat down with the full power of a forty-degree summer afternoon. Below, a metropolis of three million lay prostrate beneath its might.

For much of the decade, the state of Victoria, of which this city was the crowning jewel, had been ruled by a Labor government. For a while things had gone well. More recently, the auguries were less auspicious. The previous year's election victory had been snatched from the jaws of defeat only by the narrowest of margins. In politics, as in our city's notoriously fickle weather, nothing is certain. When things change, they change quickly. From the direction of Treasury Place, at the foot of the towering office-blocks, wraiths of heat haze ascended to the remorseless heavens like smoke from a sacrificial altar.

It must have been the weather. All this Greek shit was going to my head. I picked up the phone. 'Break it to me gently,' I said.

For the past sixteen months, since the '87 stock-market

crash, the Economic Development Ministry had been haemorrhaging money. What had started as a trickle had become an unstoppable torrent. The government was losing money faster than it could raise or borrow it. A gesture was required. A head must roll. Bill Hahn, the Deputy Premier, had drawn the short straw. The fag end of January met the timing requirements perfectly. Half the population was too shagged out from the heat to be interested in politics. The other half was busy folding its tents and returning from holidays. When the Premier called an unscheduled Cabinet meeting earlier that afternoon, the agenda was only too obvious.

'It's over,' said Trish. 'Angelo's just come back.'

Behind her voice I could hear the mechanical whirr of a document shredder. Which could mean only one thing. There had been a major reshuffle. Angelo Agnelli was no longer Minister for Ethnic Affairs. 'Don't keep me in suspense.' I tried to make it casual. 'What happened? Did he get the sack or did he get a new portfolio?'

Trish was Agnelli's private secretary. I thought I could detect a suggestion of distance in her tone, a hint that old alliances could no longer be taken for granted. The flux was running, changes were afoot up there in the ministerial suite. 'You're going to love this,' she said. She could afford to be flippant. She'd be okay. Whatever happens, they always take their secretaries with them. 'He's been given Water.'

'Christ!' I said. 'Minister for Water Supply. The very thought of it made my mouth go dry. I looked about the *Nea Hellas* production room for something to slake my sudden thirst. The only cup in sight contained the congealing dregs of ancient Greek coffee. My future was suddenly as black as that bitter beverage. I touched it to my lips. At least it was wet.

I'd been at Ethnic Affairs for four years. Employing me as his principal adviser had been one of Agnelli's smarter moves. In a state whose two major ethnic power blocks are the Greeks and the Italians, giving the job to a man with an Irish name was a masterstroke of impartiality. And since I'd once been party organiser in Melbourne Upper, Agnelli's electorate, home to the highest concentration of migrants in the country, it wasn't as though I didn't have some pretty solid credentials in the field of dago-wrangling. But Water Supply? All I knew about Water Supply was it happened when you turned on a tap.

'And the Arts,' said Trish.

Water Supply and the Arts. My heart plummeted. Not only had Agnelli failed to win substantial promotion, he'd managed to put me in very ticklish situation. Local Government I could do. Community Services, no problem. But Water Supply and the Arts? I knew as much about rocket science.

'The Arts?' I repeated dismally. 'That means I'm fucked.'

Now that I had embraced my fate, Trish could afford to allow a little more of the old warmth back into her voice. 'Yeah,' she said cheerfully. 'I reckon.'

The odds that Agnelli would retain me as his adviser on hydraulic affairs were low. But the very idea that a man named Agnelli might employ someone called Whelan to advise him on cultural matters was inconceivable. The fact that Ange had been born in the Queen Victoria Hospital, not five kilometres from where I stood, was immaterial. What possible assistance could an Australian bog-wog provide to a man through whose veins surged the blood of Tintoretto and Tiepolo? A man sprung from the race of Boccherini and Vivaldi. Dante and Boccaccio. Bramante, Caravaggio, Raphael, Michelangelo, Donatello, Leonardo and all those other fucking turtles. 'What do you know about Water Supply?' I begged, no longer bothering to conceal the desperation in my voice.

Trish and I went back a long way. She was a tough cookie who had run the electorate office in Melbourne Upper in the days before Agnelli got the pre-selection. If it walked in off the street, whatever it was, Trish could handle it. 'Can't be too complicated,' she said. 'Dams don't go on strike. Pipelines don't stack committees at party conferences.'

She had a point. Water seeks to find its own level. Even as Minister for Water Supply, Agnelli would still need a man with my skills. Someone to write his speeches. Fend off lobbyists. Crack the whip over the bureaucrats. Sniff the air. Test the water. Help him go with the flow. Maybe he'd keep me on, after all.

'He wants to see you,' said Trish. 'Now.'

It wasn't as if I didn't appreciate the political realities of the situation. The government was skating on thin electoral ice. A Cabinet re-jig was essential if we were to keep the show on the road. But what was good for the party could hardly have come at a worse time for me personally. Not to put too fine a point on it, with the interest rate on my mortgage nudging 16 per cent, I was no candidate for early retirement. It wasn't just the money, either. Family matters needed to be considered.

'Oh, another thing,' added Trish. 'Wendy called. She says to ring her urgently.' Wendy was the mother of my ten-year-old child Redmond. They lived in Sydney where Wendy ran equal opportunity for Telecom. 'Not in trouble with the ex again, are you, Murray?'

'*Malacca fungula*,' I said. A Mediterranean expression meaning 'Don't be silly'.

Trish, who'd picked up a smattering of Southern European at the Electoral Office, pretended to laugh and hung up. Pressing down the phone cradle, I quickly dialled Wendy's mobile. Trust Wendy to have one, the latest toy of the corporate high-flier. At five dollars a minute, *Nea Hellas* could cop the tab.

'Yes.' Wendy's phone manner was brisk, but she wasn't fooling me. Somewhere in the background was the gentle lap of Sydney Harbour, the flapping of yacht sails in the breeze, the lifting of shirts. Wendy was probably at Doyle's, finishing a long lunch. I could see the sucked-dry shells of pink crustaceans piled before her. 'Oh, it's *you*,' she said. 'About time, too.'

Four years before, I'd assumed the prime parenting role while Wendy took a temporary secondment to the Office of the Status of Women in Canberra. Before I knew it, she was the big cheese in gender equity at the Department of Education, Employment and Training, our marriage was finished, and I'd become the non-custodial parent. By the time she got her fancy new job in Sydney, Red's access visits had dropped to four a year. One was scheduled to begin that evening. But not before I was subjected to the customary lecture on my deficiencies as a parent.

'I've got all the details already, Wendy,' I told her. 'How many times have I not been there to meet Red's plane?' A couple, actually, but they weren't my fault and the kid had agreed, for a price, that they'd be our little secret.

'He won't be arriving,' she said. 'His orthodontist appointment was changed and there isn't another flight until two tomorrow afternoon.'

'Orthodontist?' I said. 'What does he need with an orthodontist?' Red's teeth were fine last time I'd looked. This was clearly a pretext to cut short my son's first visit in more than three months.

'Just a check-up,' said Wendy. 'But this guy's the best overbite specialist in the country. You don't want second-rate treatment for your child's teeth do you?' I let that one go by. 'Besides which, school doesn't start until Tuesday, so he can stay until Monday evening.'

'I'll be at work on Monday.' I was trying to make a point, but as soon as I spoke I knew I'd walked into a trap.

'Well, I suppose there's always another time. He'll be very disappointed, of course.'

If I missed this chance, it might be months before I saw Red again. 'I'll take Monday off,' I said quickly. The way things were shaping up, I probably wouldn't have a job to go to anyway. Not that I had any intention of sharing that hot little item with Wendy.

'I daresay the place won't fall down if you're not there for a day,' said Wendy. Telecom, of course, ceased to function every time Wendy stepped out of the room. 'And don't forget to see that he wears a hat in the sun. He nearly got burned at Noosa. Richard had to keep reminding him to put one on.'

Just like Wendy had to keep reminding me that she had

successfully recoupled and I had not. And that her salary allowed her to take Red to fashionable resorts for his holidays, when the best I seemed to be able to do was take him to the cricket or the movies. And the cricket wasn't even on this weekend. 'Two o'clock,' I said. 'I'll be there to meet him. Tell him I'm looking forward to it.'

'Two o'clock is the departure time, Murray,' she said. 'The plane doesn't arrive down there until 3.20.' Her maths were topnotch. 'It's an eighty-minute flight.'

I knew that. 'Three, then,' I said cheerfully and hung up. I know when I'm licked. I went back down the stairs, past travel posters of old women with faces like hacksaws standing beside piles of picturesque rubble.

The air in Mavramoustakides' office, what there was of it, was thicker than ever. And not just with cigarette smoke. Sophie came out the door blowing her nose into a tissue, looking like she'd just been betrothed to a donkey. She flounced back upstairs.

'Okay,' I announced. I hadn't driven all that way in the heat to trade pleasantries. 'This is the deal. You report the government in a more balanced way and *Nea Hellas* gets a regular advertising contract with a major government campaign.'

Mavramoustakides looked like he'd never for one moment doubted his newspaper's capacity to strike fear into my heart. Papas wanted details. 'What campaign?'

I'd brought a bone with me, hidden up my sweaty sleeve. I pulled it out and tossed it. 'Keep Australia Beautiful,' I said.

Leo and Jimmy lit up with a mixture of avarice and incomprehension. As far as I was concerned, Australia the Beautiful could look after itself. I was more interested in keeping my job. That, and a three o'clock appointment at Tullamarine airport the next afternoon.

We sealed the deal with a handshake beneath a poster of Mount Olympus. The gods, if I had bothered to look, were laughing.

Melbourne's weather teeters forever on the brink of imminence. If it is warm, a cool change is expected. A day of rain bisects a month of shine. Spring vanishes for weeks on end. Summer arrives unseasonably early, inexplicably late, not at all. Winter is wet but not cold, cold but not wet.

So far, that summer, all we'd had was heat. Through a city limp and surly beneath its oppressive demands, I steered my butter-yellow 1979 Diahatsu Charade towards my waiting fate. Past the airless bungalows of Northcote and the tight-packed terraces of Collingwood, through the reek of molten asphalt and the baked biscuit aroma of the brewery malting works, I drove to Victoria Parade, a boulevard of canopied elms marking the northern boundary of the central business district.

Laid out by city fathers with Parisian fantasies and strategic interests, Victoria Parade was where the young gentlemen of the Royal Victorian Mounted Volunteers would have drawn their sabres if ever the working-class mob had come storming up the hill from its blighted shacks on the flat below. As it turned out, the tide of history had run the other way. It was the slums that had fallen, captured by the gentry. And me, for my sins, rapidly becoming one of them.

The Ministry for Ethnic Affairs occupied the top three floors of a brick-clad early-seventies office building overlooking the elms. I drove around the block and parked on an all-day meter beside the Fitzroy Gardens. The Charade was a step in the direction of anonymity I'd taken after a demented constituent ran my previous vehicle into a lake one dark and stormy night several years before. It was less conspicuous than my old Renault, but it didn't do a thing for my image.

Short of walking around the block in the blazing sun, the quickest way into the Ethnic Affairs building was via its basement carpark. Suit jacket hooked over my shoulder, I advanced down the ramp into the half-darkness. The carpark was small, its twenty-odd spaces reserved for the building's more important tenants. Agnelli parked there on the odd occasion he drove himself to work. The Director of the Ministry. The Commissioners of the Liquor Licensing Board. Senior managers from the private companies which occupied the building's middle levels.

Taking up two spaces at the bottom of the ramp was a huge silver Mercedes, top of the range, an interloper among the familiar collection of managerial Magnas and executive Audis. At the far end of the garage, next to the lift, was a luminous white blob, Agnelli's official Fairlane. Beside it, wiping the windscreen, was Agnelli's driver, Alan.

Not Alan, I realised, as my eyes adjusted to the gloom. Alan was in his mid-fifties, a fastidious ex-corporal who spent his off-road moments burnishing the Fairlane's duco and picking dead insects out of its chrome work. But, apart from sharing his general height and build, this guy bore no resemblance whatsoever to Alan. Nor was he cleaning the Fairlane's window. Palm cupped, he was scrutinising the car's interior with what I instinctively took to be no good intent.

He was somewhere around my age, mid-thirties, and he affected the style of a spiv. His dark hair was sleekly combed, his trousers and tie black and too narrow. The sleeves of his white shirt were rolled to mid-forearm. He carried himself with the loose-limbed posture of a man who wants it understood that he is handy at close quarters. The only thing missing was the jemmy in his hand. As I drew near, he leaned insolently against the Fairlane's door and tracked my approach through the twin mirrors of aviator sunglasses with an air of casual menace.

I had neither reason nor inclination to respond to the implicit challenge of his stance. Carpark monitor wasn't my job—if I still had a job. The security of Agnelli's vehicle was Alan's responsibility, not mine. Unfortunately, the stranger was between me and the lift, making no effort to move aside. To get past, I'd virtually have to brush against him.

As I closed the last few paces between us, the man's features became more distinct. I realised, with dismay, that I knew him. Nearly twenty years had passed, but it was impossible not to recognise Spider Webb. Mr and Mrs Webb may have called their little boy Noel, but at school he was always the Spider.

Despite his nickname, there was nothing arachnoid about Spider. No spindly limbs or jutting canines. On the contrary. He had an athletic build, high cheekbones and fleshy, petulant lips. He would almost have been handsome if not for his ears. You only had to look at Noel Webb to know why they called them jug ears. Chrome-plated, his head wouldn't have looked out of place in a trophy cabinet. Wing-nut would have been a better nickname. But Spider, despite Noel's dislike for it, was the one that stuck. It suited him. There was something predatory about Spider, cold-blooded, self-serving. He'd been like that at sixteen, and he was still like that. You could read it in his pose. We'd been friends once, or so I thought. Then things had happened, violent things that gave me no reason whatsoever to want to renew our boyhood acquaintance. Especially since Spider had clearly fulfilled the criminal promise of his youth. I hoped to Jesus he didn't recognise me.

As I approached, he massaged a piece of chewing gum loose from its pack, tossed it into his mouth and rolled his head like a prize-fighter readying himself for a bout. I resigned myself to our reunion, waiting for him to speak.

But Spider said nothing, gave no explicit sign of recognition. It had been a long time. With luck, he might not remember me. If he didn't speak, I decided, neither would I.

Back to the wall, I sidled past, head up, eyes straight ahead. We were almost exactly the same height and so close that my own face stared back at me from the mercury pools of Spider's sunglasses. Stereoscopic reflections, I thought, of a man not quite succeeding in mastering his loathing.

Spider straightened a little to allow me passage but still he said nothing. His face had slackened into a sphinx-like inscrutability. Only the muscles of his jaw moved, flexing almost imperceptibly around his gum, a gesture of contemptuous amusement at the discomfort of a stranger. Still an arsehole after all these years.

I pressed on. As I crossed the final few paces to the lift, I heard a dismissive, barely audible grunt and felt hidden eyes boring into my back. Then the lift doors yawned before me and out stepped Alan, a polystyrene cup in his hand, his gaze darting towards the Fairlane. Nodding, I stepped into the lift. As the doors whoomphed closed behind me, I felt a shudder of what could have been either relief or foreboding.

If ever there was a bird of ill omen, it was Spider Webb. Loosen up, I told myself, pushing the button for the top floor. It's only a job. It's not the measure of your worth as a human being. There's always the slow descent into alcoholism and penury to look forward to.

The door slid open to a re-enactment of the evacuation of Saigon. Boxes of documents littered the corridors. Base-grade clerks from the Translation and Information sections bustled about, pushing trolleys in and out of rooms. Trish stood feeding files into the shredder. I recognised one of mine, *Current Issues in the Macedonian Community*. It was a slim document and held no state secrets, but that wasn't the point.

Agnelli had been at Ethnic Affairs long enough to generate more than enough stuff-ups to provide ammunition to his political enemies. Especially those from his own party. So before his replacement arrived everything short of the potted plants would be fed into the shredder. By the end of the day, some of my most skilfully wrought briefing papers would be reduced to a pile of fly-specked tagliatelle in the ministerial dumpster. I prayed that I wouldn't be in there with them.

Back when she ran the electorate office, Trish had been a rough diamond, well-upholstered and ready for anything. She was efficient, smart and knew her stuff. Eventually, Agnelli was persuaded to overlook her rougher edges and reward her loyalty with a promotion. A monster was born. Within a month of being made his private secretary, she'd joined Gloria Marshall and taken a course in fire breathing. Success, in accordance with the fashion of the day, had gone straight to her shoulders. She glanced up from the papery gnashing of her task and tossed a nod in the general direction of Agnelli's shut door. 'Take a number and wait,' she commanded.

I took it into my office and had a cigarette with it. Ours was a smoke-free environment, but what the fuck—as of now I didn't work here any more. Out the window, across the wilting greenery of the gardens, glass-walled towers quivered in the heat haze, molten swords plunged into the heart of the city. In the gaps between, ant-sized men plied construction cranes. Hardier men than the likes of me.

The building boom sustained by Labor's rule was at its peak, a relentless reordering of the skyline that was the most tangible evidence of the government's success. Everywhere the old was being jackhammered away and replaced with the spanking new. So headlong was the charge of money into real estate that slow-footed city shoppers risked being knocked down in the rush to build yet another office tower or luxury hotel. Anything more than twenty years old was obsolete. Yesterday's skyscrapers were today's holes in the ground. Tomorrow's landmarks had lakes in their foyers and computer-monitored pollen filters and the city council was putting little lights in the trees so we'd think it was Christmas all year round.

Not that I, as I pondered my options, had anything to

celebrate. My attachment to Agnelli, like his loyalty to me, was contingent on the political realities. By-passed for promotion this time, Ange would need plenty of runs on the board if he hoped to impress the Premier next time around. My employability depended on how useful he thought I could be in achieving that outcome. This we both understood.

Anybody working in politics who claims to be without personal ambition is a liar. That I hadn't yet quite formulated the nature of my own particular aspirations was beside the point. The fact that I'd placed my political loyalties at Agnelli's disposal for the previous four years didn't mean I had no interests of my own. If Agnelli thought I'd go quietly, he could think again. At the very least he should find me a new position appropriate to my skills. Try to throw me out with the dirty bath water, and he'd soon find that I had plenty of influential friends in the party who'd take a dim view of that sort of behaviour. Plenty. I tried to think of several.

While I was waiting for a name to come to mind, I finished my cigarette. Our smoke-free environment, naturally enough, provided no ashtrays so I took the butt into the executive washroom and stuffed it down the basin plughole. The executive washroom was what we jokingly called the small private bathroom off the minister's inner office. Supposedly for Angelo's exclusive use, it was also accessible from my office. Since it had an exhaust fan, I'd sometimes slip in for a quick concentration-enhancing puff when no-one was looking.

The door leading into Angelo's office was open a crack and I could hear his voice. He sounded keyed up. 'A new broom,' he was saying. 'Energetically wielded.'

I was history.

'Money is the key.' Just the sort of thing you'd expect to hear Agnelli barking down the phone. 'All the policies in the world won't save us if we don't go into the election with a decent campaign fund.'

Party matters were the subject, so he wasn't speaking to a bureaucrat from one of his new ministries. Whoever it was, my employer was warming to his topic. 'It's time to start getting serious.'

'The finance committee's doing everything it can, Angelo.'

Ange wasn't on the phone. He had a visitor. I knew the voice. Duncan Keogh, one of a number of assistant state secretaries from party headquarters. Keogh was a smarmy popinjay, a twenty-seven-year-old smarty pants who could barely remember when Labor wasn't in power. He approached politics as though its exclusive purpose was to provide a career structure for otherwise unemployable graduates of Monash University.

Why, I couldn't help but ask myself, was Agnelli closeted with a mid-level machine man like Duncan when he should have been more concerned with the pressing business of the day, the outcome of the Cabinet reshuffle?

'Duncan,' I heard my boss say wearily. 'You're our third finance committee chair in eighteen months. I'm not saying you aren't competent, otherwise I'd never have supported you for the appointment. But you just don't have the sort of clout you need to be effective.'

Keogh needed more than clout. He needed a brain transplant and a personality upgrade. He was a non-performer who had inveigled himself into the finance committee chair by singing some bullshit song about new blood and fresh ideas. Agnelli had bought it, against my recommendation, and seconded Keogh's nomination. Duncan's subsequent performance had been conspicuously ordinary. With any luck, Agnelli had summoned the twerp to tell him he'd better start delivering, that he should either shit or get off the pot.

'Cabinet-level influence is what you need, Duncan. And that's what I'm proposing to give you,' he said. 'With you in the chair and me setting the agenda, we can move our fund-raising efforts to a whole new level.'

I didn't like the direction this conversation was taking.

Raising the cash needed to run election campaigns was a chronic headache. Last time we'd gone to the polls, we had to mortgage party headquarters to cover the cost of the how-to-vote cards. And, lacking the conservatives' traditional allies in big business, we were forced to scratch for cash wherever we could find it. But rattling the tin for money was a task best undertaken at a very long arm's length from the positions occupied by people like Angelo Agnelli. It was a job best done by more anonymous members of the party apparatus. Collectors of membership dues. Organisers of mail-outs. Conductors of wine-bottlings and quiz-nights. Men like Duncan Keogh. Not Cabinet ministers.

'I'll still be the chairperson,' said Keogh. 'Right?'

I could hear his tiny mind ticking over. Letting Agnelli pull the strings, he was thinking, would be a good idea. He would win a big friend and move a little closer to the centre of the action. Agnelli could do all the work and Duncan would still get to put 'Chairperson, Finance Committee' on his CV.

'Absolutely,' said Angelo. 'So, how much have we got in

the kitty right now?'

'Just over four hundred thousand,' said Keogh. 'Union affiliations and membership levies, mostly. Half in Commonwealth bonds, half on deposit at the State Bank.' A safe player, our Duncan. If this was his idea of a fresh approach, no wonder our finances were in such a parlous condition.

'We're going to need a shitload more than that,' said Agnelli. 'A million five, minimum. What about corporate donors?'

Keogh cleared his throat nervously. 'Barely a pat on the head, so far. About ten grand all up. But we're setting up a sub-committee to look at a strategy to improve that figure.'

'A committee!' Agnelli snorted derisively. 'The skyline's full of cranes. Fucking sunrise industries left, right and centre. People making money out of our polices hand over fist. And ten grand is the most they can cough up. What's wrong with these pricks?'

Keogh was really on the ropes now. 'It's a sensitive area. Either they give or they don't. Mostly they don't.'

Another voice weighed into the discussion, soothing, placatory. 'Duncan's right, Angelo,' it said. 'This is a sensitive area. Go blundering around putting the hard word on the business community, you'll end up being accused of peddling influence.'

For the life of me, I couldn't put a face to the voice. But whoever he was, he was talking sense.

'See,' said Keogh, vindicated. 'It's not as easy as you seem to think.'

But the other speaker hadn't finished. 'That's not to say that there aren't ways of approaching these matters. Take your new portfolio, for example, Angelo.' The voice was of a man used to being listened to, someone at ease in a minister's office. 'Your accounts department alone employs, what, four or five hundred people.' He was speaking, he wanted it understood, hypothetically. 'That's a lot of office space. Property developers pay sweeteners to private corporations to secure long-term leases on their new buildings. If some of them were to get the idea that the Water Supply Commission was thinking about moving house…'

'Jesus,' groaned Keogh. 'We're treading perilously close to the line here.'

'You don't think the Liberals wouldn't be even more cosy with their business cronies if they had the chance?' said Agnelli.

The more I heard of this, the faster my disquiet turned into outright anxiety. Knowing Angelo as well as I did, it didn't take too much mental exertion to figure out what he was up to. He'd decided to do a bit of lateral thinking.

Like the weather, campaign finances were something that everybody complained about, but nobody did anything to fix. Angelo, evidently, had decided he'd be the one to grasp the nettle. Even the most outstanding performance in Water Supply and the Arts could only earn him a limited number of brownie points with the Premier. But if he succeeded in filling the party war chest, some big favours would be due next time the hats went into the ring. Obversely, the consequences of failure did not bear thinking about.

'We're all agreed, it's a sensitive area,' said the voice, conciliatory again. 'And there's no rush. The election is two years away.'

'Quite right,' said Agnelli, getting the hint. 'First things first. What sort of interest is the State Bank paying us, Duncan?'

Keogh rustled some paper and named a percentage. It was about ten points lower than what I was paying them on my home loan.

'Shit,' said Agnelli. 'My cheque account pays more.'

'The money could definitely be working harder,' agreed the other man, business-like now. 'Managed properly, 20 per cent or higher isn't out of the question. That's another $50,000 a year, straight up. And no favours required.'

The intercom buzzed. 'Premier's Department on line one,' squawked Trish's voice. 'About the swearing-in of the new Cabinet. And Murray has just arrived.'

At the sound of my name, I scurried back into my own office and lit another cigarette.

Agnelli was heading straight into the kind of troubled waters he paid me to steer him away from. Why hadn't he discussed his foray into fund-raising with me first? And who was this guy in his office? Knowing exactly who Agnelli was talking to, about what, and why, was what I got paid for. At least it had been, I reminded myself. Angelo's problems were not necessarily mine any more.

Sitting behind my artificial-woodgrain desk, gazing between my shoes into the reception area, I tried to concentrate on my own immediate predicament. What I needed was a bit of instant expertise. Just enough to make Angelo think I might still be of some use, despite the changed circumstances. A couple of tantalising scraps of inside info on the Amalgamated Tap Turners and Dam Builders Union could go a long way. I opened my teledex and started scanning, hunting for a contact who could provide a crash course in the finer points of H_2O.

At that moment, Agnelli's door opened and Duncan Keogh strutted out, a pocket battleship in an open-necked sport shirt that strained at the thrust of his barrel chest. The shirt had a design like a test pattern and looked like Duncan had bought it at one of those menswear shops with a rack outside on the footpath. Any two shirts for $49.95 plus a free pair of pants. He was probably under the impression that he'd got a bargain. Not for the first time, I thought that maybe the Australian Labor Party should consider instituting a dress code.

Close on Keogh's heels came a man who didn't need any fashion advice. His lightweight summer suit was so well tailored it made Keogh's clothes look like he was wearing them for a bet. He could have been anywhere between his late forties and his early sixties, depending on the mileage, and he had the self-assured air of a man who didn't muck around. What he didn't muck around doing wasn't immediately apparent, but he'd made a success of it, whatever it was. His tie was red silk and so was his pocket handkerchief. He was fit, well-lunched and towered over Keogh like a gentleman farmer walking a Jack Russell terrier on a short leash.

He was laughing at something Keogh was saying, but only

with his mouth. His eyes, up there where Duncan couldn't see them, were saying dickhead. Whoever he was, I liked him. He looked like he'd be a handy man to have on a lifeboat. While the others were singing 'Abide With Me', he'd slip you his hip flask of Black Label. He and Dunc went into the lift, doing the doings.

'Who was that?'

Trish, standing at the shredder, pretended she couldn't hear me, giving nothing away until she knew whether I was in or I was out. Jerking her head in the direction of Agnelli's door, she gave me leave to enter.

The great panjandrum's inner sanctum was as dark as a hibernating bear's cave. The air conditioning was on high and the heavy drapes were drawn against the glare of the day and the wandering gaze of the clerical staff in the Ministry for Industry and Technology next door. Through the cool gloom I could just make out the shape of Agnelli himself, a ghostly presence in shirt sleeves etched against the cluster of framed awards and diplomas on the wall behind his desk. Seeing him there like that—surrounded by his Order of the Pan Pontian Brotherhood, his Honorary Master of Arts from the University of Valetta, the little model donkey cart presented with gratitude by the Reggio di Calabria Social Club—made my heart go out to him. Three years at the epicentre of political power and his office looked like a proctologist's consulting rooms.

His back was turned and he was reaching up to unhook one of the framed certificates. His University of Melbourne law degree. He studied it for a moment, then laid it carefully in an empty grocery carton sitting on his desk. Across the room I could read the box's yellow lettering. Golden Circle Pineapple, it said. This Way Up.

Shivering at the sudden drop in temperature, I stepped forward. Agnelli turned to face me. 'You heard?'

I nodded. 'Water Supply and the Arts.' I showed him my palms. Ours not to reason why, ours but to do and die.

Angelo indicated I should sit at the conference table, then crossed to the drapes and tugged them half-open. Harsh daylight swept away the conspiratorial shade. He got a couple of cans of beer out of his bar fridge, kicked his shoes off and sat down opposite me. So, he seemed to be saying. Here we are. Two men who know what's what. He slid me one of the cans— my poison chalice, I took it. And so it was, as it turned out. But not in the way I thought at the time.

He shrugged. 'I won't say I'm not disappointed.'

Power had improved Ange, the way a couple of drinks do to some people. It had smoothed down his more abrasive anxieties, made him more mellow, less in need of having constantly to assert himself. But his forties were well upon him, and he could no longer pass for a child wonder. His smooth black hair still came up well in print, and his cheeks still bulged with chipmunk amiability, but the good fairy of middling high office had scattered ashes at his temples and given him slightly more chins than were absolutely necessary. His heart remained where it had always been, though. Marginally to the left of centre, and closer to his stomach than his brain.

'This will mean some changes, of course,' he said.

I popped the tab off my can and waited for the bullet. Agnelli's gaze loitered in midair, among the dust motes playing in the beams of sunlight, as though they might offer him the right form of words.

'Tell me, Murray,' he said, at long last. 'What are the Arts?'

This was very disheartening. Why go through the pretence of having me fail the job interview? I sucked on my can. Bitter, beer, but fortifying.

Agnelli's question, it turned out, was entirely rhetorical. He didn't want my opinion. He wanted an audience. The axe was too brutal. There must needs first be a little armchair philosophising. A deep and meaningful on the complexities inherent in public intervention in the cultural sector.

'Let me bounce this off you,' he said. A little bouncing before the big bounce. 'The Arts are the measure of how far we have come and how far we have yet to go. A resource to be developed, an economic as well as a social asset. When I hear the word culture I think excellence and I think access...'

I wasn't sure where this was going, but at least he wasn't reaching for his revolver. 'Not bad,' I shrugged. 'Bit vague.'

'Then you'd better sharpen it up for me,' he said.

'You want me at Arts?' I must have sounded a little incredulous.

'If you don't mind.' Ange had a way of making you feel like it was your decision, even if he was making it. 'For the time being. Until things settle down.'

'And then?'

'And then we'll see.' No doubt we would. If, he was making it clear, I didn't botch it.

So, here I was, my fortunes again leg-roped to Angelo Agnelli. Less than a minute before, I'd been merely apprehensive about my future. Now I had real cause for concern. 'I'll line up a departmental briefing, then,' I said, by way of acceptance.

'Fine.' Ange tossed his can at the waste basket, scored. 'You know Lloyd Eastlake?'

I shook my head. 'Should I?'

'He chairs the Cultural Affairs Policy Committee.' In theory, policy committees shaped the party platform and guarded it from the expediency of ministers. In practice, they were ineffectual talking-shops and magnets for inconsequential schemers. That did not mean, however, that due lip-service did not need to be paid. 'Bit of a mover, from all reports,' Agnelli said. 'Well connected in the unions. Not factionally aligned. Seen quite a few arts ministers come and go.' That wouldn't have been hard. The arts ministry changed hands more frequently than a concert pianist with the crabs.

'There's some sort of art gallery thing he's invited me to this evening. The Centre for Modern Art.' The policy committee chairman wasn't wasting any time cosying up to the new minister. 'Reckons it could be a good opportunity to start developing links with the cultural community.'

'Could be,' I agreed tentatively. No skin off my nose what Agnelli did with his Friday nights.

'I told him I couldn't make it, got a family function it's more than my life's worth to miss.' In other words, he planned to spend the evening on the phone, doing his factional arithmetic, figuring out where his esteem in the eyes of the Premier had turned to water. 'I told him you'd represent me. Standard booze and schmooze, you know the drill. He'll pick you up in front of the National Gallery at 6.30.'

Luckily, Red's deferred arrival meant I had a free evening. Not that disrupting my personal arrangements had ever unduly concerned Agnelli. 'This Eastlake and I don't know each other from a bar of soap. Do I wear a white carnation and carry a furled umbrella, or what?'

'I told him to look for someone who can't believe he's still got a job.'

I backed off, not complaining. Stroking the relevant policy committee chair was one of a ministerial adviser's chief chores, after all. And the Centre for Modern Art, whatever that was, had to be a step up from the Maltese Senior Citizens' Association annual dinner-dance, the sort of delegated duty that normally occupied my Friday and Saturday nights.

'Anything else I should be aware of?' I was steering him towards the conversation I had just overheard.

'Matter of fact, there is.' Agnelli ambled back to his desk and resumed his packing. 'See if you can't get me some tickets for *Don Giovanni*. You have heard of *Don Giovanni*, haven't you?'

'Shit, yeah,' I said. 'Big in the concrete business, isn't he?'

'It's a small portfolio, Murray,' said Agnelli, signalling that our interview was at an end. 'Let's not make a meal of it.'

I drained my beer and beat a path to the door, grateful for small mercies. I might not yet have Agnelli's confidence on this fund-raising caper, but at least I was still in work. My fist was closing on the door handle when something crossed Agnelli's mind. 'Lots of rich you-know-whats involved in the arts, aren't there?'

What was that supposed to mean? 'I've heard rumours,' I said. 'Would you like it covered in the briefing?'

Agnelli turned back to his packing. 'Piss off,' he said, not entirely without wit.

I did, too. I immediately rang the Arts Ministry to confirm that the director was in, stuffed a couple of taxi vouchers in my pocket and went downstairs to Victoria Parade. The Charade could stay where it was until I'd scouted the parking situation at Arts. Besides which, I'd probably be offered a drink or two at this modern art joint. No point in risking the prospect of being invited to blow into a little bag on the way home. A Silver Top cab arrived. 'Hut,' said the driver, a wizened Ethiopian. 'Very hut.'

The city centre swarmed with schoolkids making the most of the dying days of their summer vacation. We skirted the soaring steel skeleton of the half-completed Karlcraft Centre and crossed the Yarra, glassy beer-bottle brown under the baked enamel sky, and found another Parisian boulevard, St Kilda Road. On one side it was bounded by the expansive parkland of the Domain, on the other by the brutalist boxes of the Arts Centre, squatting on the bank opposite Flinders Street railway station like a gun emplacement guarding the strategic approaches of the town.

Once upon a time, the riverside had been a jumble of run-down warehouses and obsolete factories, an eyesore enlivened only at night when a huge neon sweet unwrapped itself over and over again in a blaze of coloured lights. But the electric lolly was long gone, replaced by Arts City. Here—in the National Gallery, the Concert Hall, the State Theatre, the Ballet Centre—the blue-collar Labor constituencies to the north and west of the city paid for the Liberal voters of the leafy eastern suburbs to have their self-esteem massaged.

Not, I thought, the proper attitude to be taking. Think centre of excellence, I told myself. Think vibrant treasure house of national identity. Think better than unemployment.

Behind the National Gallery, even newer cultural edifices were rising from bulldozed construction sites. A new HQ for the symphony orchestra, studios for the ABC, a resplendent cultural precinct rising from the flattened ruins of ancient industry. Soon, according to the architects' models, little stick figures would sip cappuccinos here under little stick umbrellas before ambling into the Concert Hall to soak up a bit of moral improvement. Of the uncouth past, only the mouldering 1920s edifice of the old YMCA survived, crouching behind the Concert Hall as if it hoped to dodge the wrecker's ball.

Haile Selassie deposited me in front of the National Gallery and I headed straight for the moat. Its shallow ornamental pools flanked the entrance forecourt, separated from the footpath by a low wall of square-cut stone. Originally intended to mirror the building's blank facade, its austere lines were now a little cluttered with an embarrassment of artistic riches. First had come a trio of dancing water fountains. Then an iron and polypropylene sculpture modelled either on the inner workings of a spring-scale or a trash-can fish skeleton from a Hanna Barbera cartoon. Then a gravity-fed spiral based on the anatomy of a mollusc. Finally, an enormous ceramic creature, a kind of bifurcated llama that straddled the water like an aquatic mutation of Dr Doolittle's pushmi-pullyu.

But the moat was still cool. Resisting the temptation to strip off and plunge my head into it, I pulled my tie down a couple of notches and splashed a handful of the wet stuff over my face. It smelled faintly of soda ash. I trickled a second handful down the back of my neck. Then I lit a pause that refreshes and took in the scene, servant of the master of all I surveyed.

The facade of the gallery rose behind me, a smooth basalt cliff, unbroken by windows. 'We need the space for hanging,' explained the Premier who commissioned the building, or so legend has it. His idea of a joke, in those days of capital punishment. Henry the Hangman, they called him. But that was twenty years ago, a benighted age, a time of human sacrifice. We're more civilised now. We know that the dark forces are better propitiated with social justice impact statements and ongoing consultative processes.

It was just past three o'clock and, despite the heat, the place buzzed with activity. Air-conditioned coaches lined the kerb, disgorging tourists. Elderly matinee-goers swarmed blinking into the daylight. A queue snaked towards the ticket window at the gallery's arched entrance, clinging to the shade. Gelati vans did a roaring trade, dispensing ice-cream that tasted like it came from cows with silicone tits. Frazzled mothers pushed grizzling toddlers past a banner advertising the current blockbuster exhibition. In the midst of all this activity, a glistening supermarket trolley lay abandoned on its side, a found object, far from home.

Beside me, ranged along the parapet of the moat, was a gang of pubescent boys, their sprayed-on jeans and rat-tail haircuts indicating that they, too, were out of place. Marauders from distant suburbs, they were scavenging for submerged coins, their arms plunged shoulder-deep into the water. Egged on by his friends, one swung his legs over the edge and lowered himself waist-deep into the water. Wading out to the middle, he bobbed swiftly to the bottom and surfaced with a twenty-cent piece in each hand. His mates roared uncouth approval. I, too, applauded this community-based initiative in the redistribution of cultural wealth. But I did so silently. These facilities, after all, were now within my purview.

The kid was about twelve, by the look of him, a couple of years older than my son Red. Little kids are easy. An ice-cream cone, a roll down a grassy hill, that's enough to satisfy them. But then they get older, their threshold shifts. They start wading about in public fountains, cheered by their hoon mates. They get drunk and steal cars. But not just yet. Not at ten, I told myself. That was something to look forward to.

Last time Red came to stay, I'd taken a week of leave and we'd headed down the coast. We bought every useless gewgaw in a dozen bait-and-tackle shops, slept in cabins in caravan parks, lived on chips and Chinese takeaway, and fished off beaches and jetties from here to the Cape Nelson lighthouse. But the initial enthusiasm had soon waned. I was trying too hard and we both knew it. After four days we came back to town where Red could do what he'd wanted to do all along. Hang around outside the nearest skateboard shop with his dopey friend Tarquin Curnow.

This time around, I'd made no special arrangements, except to check that Tarquin would be in town. Tark was an utter dill, gawky and buck-toothed with year-round bronchitis and a tendency to play up when his mother wasn't looking. But his company took the awkwardness off Red's visits and for that I was grateful. Splashing a last handful of water over my face, I doused my fag, slung my jacket over my shoulder and hied myself hence to the cultural coalface.

The Arts Ministry was across an elevated walkover that

connected the rear of the National Gallery to the Ballet Centre, home of the national silly dance company. A gaggle of ballet-school students were clustered around the doorway, anorexic girls with their hair in chignons, lithe boys with flawless skin, none of them older than twenty, all of them smoking. Fifteen years of mandatory package warnings, a total ban on television advertising, a Quit campaign, and the fittest, brightest, most privileged young people in the country were tugging away like racetrack touts. If I hadn't just put one out, I'd have been tempted to join them.

'I was just sooo embarrassed,' I heard one of the boys say as I passed. The others all giggled. Scratch the bit about brightest. On the top level, the lift opened directly into the Arts Ministry foyer, an expanse of parquetry with beige walls and rows of little track-lit pictures. The receptionist was fielding a phone inquiry. 'What's it in conjunction to?' she was saying. Off to the side was a glass door marked 'Minister'. I pushed it open and went in.

On the other side of a glass partition, two men faced each other across a small conference table.

The one I recognised was Ken Sproule, senior adviser to the man Angelo Agnelli was replacing, Gil Methven. Ken's boss punched in a heavier weight division than Angelo and had come out of Cabinet that day holding Police and Emergency Services, one of the big ticket ministries. That made Ken Sproule one of the big boys, too. He was a tough cookie with more suspicion than imagination, an indispensable quality in any major player's personal fixer. And for all the factional differences between our respective masters, he had yet to do me serious personal injury. Which, in our party, is tantamount to bosom friendship.

Spotting my arrival, he beckoned me inside. 'Ah! The changing of the guard,' he rasped. He wore a short-sleeved business shirt and a no-nonsense polyester tie. He gestured grandly towards the other man. 'Phillip Veale, meet Murray Whelan, aide de camp of the infamous Angelo Agnelli.'

Phillip Veale stood up and surveyed me with benevolent curiosity. Where Ken Sproule was fidgety and thrusting, Veale was suave and reticent. He was somewhere in his fifties, smooth-skinned, silver-haired, pink with the exertion of carrying just a tad too much good living. A man without angles or apparent malice who wore his two-toned business shirt, French cuffs and matching tie with all the assurance of a mandarin's robe. Which well he ought, since Phillip Veale had been Director of the Arts for as long as anyone could remember. Ministers came and went, but Phillip Veale abideth forever. We shook hands, his skin soft but his grip firm.

'I'm looking forward to working with the new minister,' he said, managing in some intangible way to impart the impression that the change could only be an improvement.

'And Angelo is keen to get started,' I reciprocated. 'Would Monday morning be convenient for a briefing?'

'Perfectly,' Veale said, not entirely able to conceal the humour in his eyes. 'Shall we say nine?'

This exchange of niceties brought Ken Sproule's dial out in a big smirk. I was the sheepdog type of ministerial assistant, there to keep the departmental flunkeys all trotting along in more or less the same direction. Ken was primarily a backroom mathematician, one of those blokes who can't see a head without wanting to sink his boot into it.

'And perhaps while I'm here,' I suggested. 'We can go over the minister's diary.'

'Of course,' said Veale, backing out the door. 'It's been a pleasure working with you, Ken.' For sure.

'I think you've won a heart,' said Sproule as the door closed.

I sat down, leaned back in my chair and took in the surroundings. The office was an airy, glass-walled space, a definite step up from the vinyl and laminate world of Ethnic Affairs. A row of floor-to-ceiling windows opened onto the Arts Centre tower and overlooked a rooftop garden at the rear of the gallery, a rectangle of lawn upon which sat an enormous white ball, as though God were about to tee off. The furniture was pale and waxy, crafted from some rare and expensive timber, soon to be extinct. Sproule followed my gaze out into the fiery afternoon light. 'Not bad, eh?' he said. 'For the booby prize.'

'I'll think of you, Ken,' I said. 'Arm-wrestling the Police

Association while I sit here contemplating the finer things of life.'

Sproule went over to the minister's desk and cleared a drawer into his briefcase. 'A word to the wise, Murray. Those wogs you've been duchessing at Ethnic Affairs have got nothing on the culture vultures. Tear the flesh right off your bones, they will.' Ken had climbed into the ring with some hard-nosed bastards over the years, and he spoke with genuine awe.

'Going soft?' I said.

Sproule gave me a pitying look. 'The first thing you should know about this job, pal, is that in this town the arts are a minefield. Everything from the pitch of the philharmonic to the influence of landscape painting on the national psyche is a matter of public debate. We've got more experimental film-makers, dramaturges and string quartets than you can poke a conductor's baton at. And every last one of them has a direct line to the media. You've never seen so much colour and movement in all your life. Tell you, pal, it's more than a can of worms, it's a nest of vipers.'

The purpose of this sob story, I took it, was to deflect any blame that might arise from unfinished business left by the departing team. 'In other words,' I deduced. 'A time bomb is about to blow up in Agnelli's face.'

Sproule was innocence itself. 'Keep your wits about you, that's all I'm saying. Within a week you'll be Mr Popularity, up to your arse in invitations to opening nights and gala exhibitions. The glitterati will be lining up to wine and dine you so they can piss in your pocket about how much public money their pet project deserves.'

So what was new? Fending off lobbyists was a ministerial adviser's bread and butter. Sproule had finished his packing. I shook his hand, formally accepting the helm. 'Good luck with the coppers,' I said. 'See you round.'

'Not if I see you first.'

The instant that Sproule was gone, Veale reappeared with a folio-sized leather-bound diary and a well-stuffed manilla folder.

We ran through the ministerial appointments for the next week, a predictable round of flag-showings and gladhandings. Nothing so pressing that Trish couldn't take care of it when she arrived with Agnelli on Monday morning. Only one engagement was listed for the weekend. *Karlin. 11.30 Saturday.*

'A small brunch,' explained Veale. 'To mark the acquisition of a rather significant painting by the Centre for Modern Art. The former minister agreed to say a few words of blessing. Given the changed circumstances, Max Karlin will doubtless understand that the new minister is unable to attend.'

'Max Karlin?'

'He's hosting the occasion.' Veale didn't have to tell me who Max Karlin was. His name was in the paper every five minutes. A millionaire shoe salesman who had lately expanded out of footwear into property development. The half-completed Karlcraft Centre I'd passed on the way was his baby, a multi-storey retail and office complex rising on the site of his original downtown shop. 'Karlin's been collecting Australian modernist painting for more than twenty-five years. It's one of his pictures the CMA is buying.'

It suddenly occurred to me that this little luncheonette might serve a useful function. The conversation I'd overheard in Agnelli's office had been replaying itself in the back of my mind, still ringing alarm bells. If Agnelli had indeed decided to re-invent himself as a bag man, Max Karlin would strike him as an obvious mark. Hard experience had taught me that Agnelli did not respond well to direct disagreement. But if I got the two of them together and kept a close eye on what ensued, I might be able to confirm how serious Agnelli was about his new sideline. And once I was clear on that point, I might stand some chance of putting an end to any such foolishness. If Agnelli had a high enough opinion of my abilities to keep me on the payroll, the least I could do was curb his more suicidal impulses.

'Angelo is very interested in the visual arts,' I said. 'I'll let him know about Mr Karlin's invitation. Just in case.'

Veale was inscrutably professional. 'Very good,' he said,

closing the diary and handing me the manilla folder. It contained an avalanche of snow so deep it would take me weeks to dig myself free. Organisational charts, committee membership lists, advisory board structures, policies, draft policies, potential draft policies, terms of reference, annual reports, strategy plans, treaties with foreign potentates, fixtures for the staff association cricket club, a list of recent grant recipients. Heaving a heavy sigh, I took unenthusiastic possession.

'Anything here on the Centre for Modern Art? I'm going to some sort of exhibition there tonight and I really don't know much about the place.' Precisely zip, in fact.

Veale dealt me the relevant document. 'Lloyd Eastlake's not wasting any time taking you under his wing, I see.'

I thought Veale must have been reading my mail until I opened the CMA annual report and scanned its list of office-bearers. Eastlake was the chairman. 'I haven't met him yet,' I said. 'But I've been told he's very well regarded.'

'Very,' said Veale. His arid neutrality betrayed a hint of sniffi-ness. 'Lloyd Eastlake chairs so many committees it's a wonder he finds time to make a living. The CMA. The Music Festival. The Film Development Corporation. The Visual Arts Advisory Panel. The ALP policy committee, of course...'

All political appointments, in other words. This Eastlake, who-ever he was, was clearly making the most of his opportunities. On the league ladder of policy committees, Cultural Affairs was about as low as you could go. A clout-free zone. A sheltered work-shop for no-hoper Upper House backbenchers. Old farts from the Musicians' Union who once played the saxophone in three-piece wedding combos and now spent their declining years haunting thrash rock clubs trying to sign up roadies. Eastlake, alert to the perquisites of his chairmanship, had clearly set about making himself Labor's man in the garden of culture.

'A retired union official?' I asked. 'With a taste for trad jazz and the French New Wave?'

'Financial services, actually,' said Veale. 'Started as a car-penter. Joined his father-in-law's building firm back in the fifties, turned it into a major player in the housing industry, then sold up to concentrate on investment consulting.' An ex-chippie made good. No wonder he got up Veale's aristocratic nose.

A large colour-field painting hung on the wall behind the minister's desk. It was hard-edged, all surface, a bled-out pink with a broad stripe of yellow running right through the middle. Not unlike many in the party. Veale saw me looking over his shoulder and turned to follow my gaze. 'Taste in pictures is such a personal matter,' he said, as though he'd never seen the thing before in his life. 'Does our master have a liking for something in particular?'

Human blood, I nearly said. 'Perhaps something to match his mental processes,' I suggested.

'Nothing too abstract then, I take it,' said Veale, cocking a jovial eyebrow. I had a feeling that he and I were going to get along like a house on fire.

Veale left me alone with my homework. I took it over to the big desk and started in. As well as the National Gallery, the State Theatre and the Concert Hall, all of which I could see out the window, Arts was the overseer-in-chief of everything from the State Library to a regional museum so small the brontosaurus skeleton had to stick its neck out the window. All up, the annual budget topped forty million. Not in the major league by any means, but enough to have some fun with. And enough to generate some pretty vocal squabbling, if Ken Sproule was to be believed.

The list of recent grant recipients revealed some familiar names. The Turkish Welfare League had scored a thousand dollars to run traditional music classes for Turkish Youth. In my experience, your average Turkish youth preferred heavy metal to Anatolian folk songs. Doubtless the dough would go to pay a part-time social worker. At the other extreme, the Centre for Modern Art had copped three hundred grand for a 'one-off extraordinary acquisition'. I wondered what you could acquire for that sort of cash.

I closed the folder. Plenty of time for that sort of thing later.

Reminding myself of more pressing realities, I rang Agnelli and caught him on the way to Government House for the swearing-in of the new Cabinet. I told him about the Karlin brunch invitation, making it sound like a minor formality, and asked for his okay to decline. Right on cue, at the magic words 'Max Karlin', he was dead keen.

'It's important that we maintain continuity of appointments during this transition,' he said.

'You're the boss,' I told him.

By then, it was just on five o'clock. I was feeling a little parched in the back of the throat, but it was ninety minutes before I was due to meet this Lloyd Eastlake bloke. I was flicking absently through the Centre for Modern Art annual report when Phillip Veale's well-barbered mane appeared around the door. 'Drinkie winkies?' he mouthed.

I could tell immediately that I'd have to pull my socks up in the duds department if I ever hoped to cut the mustard in this culture caper. Aside from Phillip Veale's two-tone shirt, I counted three bow ties, a pair of red braces and a Pierre Cardin blazer. And that was just what the women were wearing.

All up, about fifteen people were milling about the conference room, enjoying what Veale described as the ministry's customary end-of-week after-work convivial for staff and visiting clients. In no time at all, a glass of government-issue fizzy white had been thrust into my hand and the director had waltzed me about the room and presented me to sundry deputy directors and executive officers. The natives seemed affable enough and bid me welcome with the wary amiability of practised bureaucrats.

Three drinks later, I was cornered by a large woman wearing a caftan and what appeared to be Nigeria's annual output of trade beads. 'Does the new minister have strong interest in anything in particular?' she asked. Her name was Peggy Wainright and she'd been introduced as the executive responsible for the visual arts.

'The visual arts,' I said. 'Naturally. And puppetry, of course.'

My lame wit fell on deaf ears. The woman grabbed my elbow and began to drag me through the throng. 'In that case,' she said. 'You simply must meet Salina Fleet. She's the visual arts editor of *Veneer*.'

'*Veneer*?'

'The leading journal of contemporary cultural criticism.' In other words, an art magazine. Peggy was shocked I hadn't heard of it. 'Very influential.' In other words, an art magazine with very few readers.

One of the occupational hazards of working at Ethnic Affairs was the tendency it encouraged to categorise people on the basis of their names. In the case of, say, Agnelli or Mavramoustakides this was not difficult. Fleet was pure Anglo. Fleet as in First, as in Street. The Salina bit was definitely an exotic ring-in. I allowed myself to be propelled forward, already a little curious. 'Here's Salina now.'

Salina Fleet was a gamine blonde with apricot lipstick and dangly white plastic earrings, her slightly tousled hair growing out of a razor cut. Her limbs were bare and lightly tanned and she was wearing a mu-mu with a fringe of pom-poms and a palm-tree motif. Slung over her shoulder was a terry-towel beach-bag with hula-hoop handles. A surfie chick from a Frankie Avalon movie. She was about thirty, old enough to know better, so her intention was clearly ironic.

'Salina's on the Visual Arts Advisory Panel which makes recommendations on grants to artists and galleries,' said Peggy, by way of introduction. 'This is Murray Whelan. He's on the new minister's personal staff.'

Salina Fleet turned from pouring herself a drink, cocked her budgerigar head and gave me a long, intelligent and frankly appraising look. 'Really?' she said. She reached into her beach-bag and drew out a pack of Kool. 'How interesting.' You had to admire her attention to period detail. I didn't know they still made Kool.

'The new minister has a strong interest in the visual arts,' added Peggy. 'And puppetry.'

'Really?' said Salina. A flicker of mischief played between her eyes and the corners of her apricot lips. 'How interesting.' She took a cigarette out of the pack.

'You're not going to smoke in here?' said Peggy Wainright with alarm.

'Mind if I have one of those?' I said. I hated menthol cigarettes.

Salina did some jokey huffy wiggly stuff with her shoulders. 'I suppose we'd better be good boys and girls, then.' She nodded towards a sliding glass door that opened onto a narrow balcony overlooking the trellised white tower of the Arts Centre. 'Coming?' She was certainly a live wire.

We took our drinks outside, just us smokers. It was like stepping into an oven. 'Hope you don't mind.' Salina broke out the camphorated stogies and we both lit up. 'Peggy's a dear but she's never off duty.'

'Frankly I'm relieved,' I said. 'For a minute there I thought I'd have to pretend to know something about art.'

'Pretence is essential in the art world.' Salina exhaled a peppermint-scented cloud. Her fingernail polish was apricot, too. Perfect.

'Any other tips for a novice?' I was trying to pretend that my cigarette didn't taste like fly spray.

'The most important thing is always to keep a straight face. As long as you do that, anything is possible.'

I accepted this advice with a grateful dip of my head. 'Salina?' I said. 'Unusual name.'

Too late, I realised that this must have sounded like a very lame come-on line. Do you come here often? What star sign are you?

She didn't seem to mind. 'Literary,' she said. 'Lyrical, at least. The result of having an academic for a father.'

The literary/lyrical reference was over my head. Troilus and Cressida. Tristan and Isolde. Starsky and Hutch. Salina and…?

She came to my rescue. '*Out in the west Texas town of El Paso,*' she began to recite:

'I fell in love with a Mexican girl
Night time would find me in Rosa's cantina
Music would play, Salina would whirl.'

Either Salina's father lacked all academic rigour or he was hard of hearing. I knew the song. Marty Robbins was on every juke box in every bar I'd ever worked in. As a publican's son who had paid his way through university pulling beers, I had an acute ear for bar-room gunfight references in popular music. The Mexican maiden who did the whirling at Rosa's cantina was called Felina, not Salina.

'Your father's academic discipline,' I asked. 'What did he teach?'

'Three-point turns, mainly,' she said. 'And reverse parking. He was chief instructor at the Ajax Driving Academy. I followed in his footsteps. I teach cultural studies, part-time, at the Preston Institute of Technology.'

PIT used to be a trade school for the motor industry. Not much call for that sort of thing any more. Not unless you were a Japanese robot. 'Really?' I said, like she might be having me on. 'How interesting.'

'Salina's a bit prissy,' she said. 'You can call me Sal. But never Sally.' No, she definitely wasn't a Sally. And I didn't care if she was having me on. At Ethnic Affairs, the only women who flirted with me either had moustaches or fathers with shotguns.

'Her name was McGill,' I said. *'And she called herself Lil.'*

'But everyone knew her as Nancy,' she replied. 'The Beatles' *White Album* is on my students' required reading list.'

Having a cigarette was one thing. Standing in a blast furnace was another. We ground our butts underfoot, toe to toe. *'Let's twist again,'* she said.

'Like we did last summer,' I closed the couplet.

As we slipped back into the air-conditioned relief of the conference room, Phillip Veale materialised at my side. He pinged a fingernail on the rim of his glass. The crowd fell silent and turned our way. It was a jolly little speech, delivered in administrative shorthand.

'Welcome to those just back from summer hols. A new year awaits. Exciting developments. Fresh challenges. Not least of which, a new minister, Angelo Agnelli, whose commitment is well known.' Veale's ambiguity raised an appreciative chuckle from the assembly. 'A minister so keen he's already sent his right-hand man to join us.' Eyes darted my way, measuring my response. I tried to look sly. 'So,' Veale raised his glass, staring directly at me. 'The king is reshuffled. Long live the king.' It was blatant flattery. Always the best kind.

I glanced about for Salina Fleet but she must have slipped out under cover of the formalities. Pity, I thought. Still, I had no cause for complaint. Semi-secure employment, congenial surroundings, a drink or three, a little light buttering-up. A man could do worse.

Outside, the late afternoon sun was turning the harsh concrete of the Arts Centre a glowing fauvist orange. Warning-light amber.

It had gone 6.15 and the drinks crowd was thinning to a hard core. I took one last snort for sociability's sake, slung my hook and headed downstairs. By rights, if my day had gone as planned, I should have been at the airport, meeting Red's flight from Sydney. Instead, I was headed for the front of the National Gallery, under instructions to find a total stranger named Lloyd Eastlake so we could go look at some modern art together. Half an hour, I'd give it. Tops.

A slab of shadow had fallen across the forecourt of the gallery. The mouse-hole curve of the gallery entrance dozed, a half-shut eye in a blank face. The crowds were gone, the tourist buses departed, the gelati vans pursuing more lucrative business at the bayside beaches. Later, theatre goers would begin to arrive. For now, apart from a trudging trickle of home-bound pedestrians and a pair of teenage lovers having a snog on the moat parapet, the place was deserted.

Out on St Kilda Road, the tail end of the rush-hour traffic crawled impatiently towards the weekend, raising a desultory chorus of irritable toots. I propped on the edge of the moat, trailing my hands in the cool water, and waited for Lloyd Eastlake, Our Man in the Arts, to arrive. At least he wouldn't have any trouble finding me.

A slow five minutes went by. Romeo and Juliet broke off their tonsil hockey and wafted away, hand in hand. The passing trams became less crowded, less frequent. A silver Mercedes pulled into the Disabled Only parking bay in front of the gallery entrance, its interior concealed behind tinted windows. It sat there for a long moment, too late for the gallery, too early for the theatre. Then the back door opened and man in a suit got out. Well-heeled, self-assured, brisk. I recognised him instantly. The man I had seen coming out of Agnelli's office earlier that afternoon.

He crossed directly to me. 'Murray Whelan?' he said, not much in doubt about it. 'I'm Lloyd Eastlake.'

He was quite handsome in a conventionally masculine way. Close-up, I pegged him for a well-preserved fifty-five, fit as a trout even if the good life had tipped the bathroom scales a smidgin over his ideal weight-to-height ratio.

Shaking off the moat water, I accepted his offered handshake. His grip was competitively hard, as though advertising the fact that he had once worked with his hands. But not for some time. The nails were manicured.

'Don't let the National Gallery trustees catch you paddling in their pool,' he warned. 'They think its a bloody holy water font.' He indicated the open door of his car. 'C'mon. This'll be fun.' Flash wheels but still one of the boys.

The interior of the Mercedes was so cool it could have been used to transport fresh poultry. I followed Eastlake into the back seat, sinking into the soft leather upholstery. Agnelli's Fairlane was impressive in a high-gloss velour-seat sort of way, but it had a utilitarian aspect that never let you forget that it was public property out on loan. This car said private wealth, personal luxury, a separate reality.

As I pulled the door closed behind me, the big car purred into life. 'Centre for Modern Art,' said Eastlake. 'Thanks, Noel.'

My eyes darted forward to the driver. He was wearing a white shirt and a chauffeur's cap. The cap fooled me for a moment, made me think that the Mercedes was hired. Then I registered the pair of fleshy flanges protruding from the sides of the man's skull, and the wire arms of the aviator sunglasses hooked over them.

'Certainly, Mr Eastlake,' said Spider Webb. 'Coming up.'

'You're not one of the sanctimonious ones, are you?' Eastlake sprawled back, observing me with good-natured amusement, misreading the nature of my reaction to his driver. His red silk tie was patterned with little pictures of Mickey Mouse. The sort of tie that says the man wearing it is either a complete dickhead or he doesn't give a flying fuck what anyone thinks of him. 'You don't take a dim view of a man because he's earned himself a few bob?'

His few bob's worth of German precision-engineering purred gently and Spider eased it into St Kilda Road, joining the traffic stream headed away from the city centre.

'Not at all,' I said. 'It's just that you're the first Labor Party member I've ever met with his own chauffeur-driven Mercedes.'

'How do you know?' said Eastlake agreeably. 'You'd be surprised how well off some of the comrades are.'

Doubtless he was right. If Labor really governed for everyone, not just for its traditional blue-collar base, then a millionaire should feel just as much at home in the party as any boiler maker ever did. If the Prime Minister had no problem with that concept, why should I? A decade in government at state and federal level had smoothed over a lot of the old class antagonisms, ideological and personal. Getting real, we liked to call it.

We veered left and headed up Birdwood Avenue into the manicured woodland of the Domain. A late-afternoon haze had turned the sky to burnished steel, bleeding the shadows out from beneath the canopies of the massed oaks and plane trees. Geysers of water sprang from sunken sprinkler heads in the lawn and hissed across the roadway. Not that I could hear them. The cocoon of the Mercedes was a world apart.

'Old loyalties run deep,' said Eastlake, catching my mood. 'I'm a Labor man, born and bred. You don't change your football team just because you change your address.'

This Lloyd Eastlake was not at all what I had expected. A wheeler-dealer ex-carpenter with a penchant for modern art. A party player with a back-stairs fast-track to ministerial ears. I toyed with the idea of asking him how his meeting with Agnelli had gone. Shake the tree, see what fell out. I decided to sit, not give anything away until I had a clearer sense of the lie of the land.

'You'll have to tell me all about the Cultural Affairs Policy Committee,' I said, making myself comfortable, putting both of us at our ease. 'I'm on something of a steep learning curve here, as Angelo no doubt told you. And what's the story on this Centre for Modern Art?'

Eastlake took a blank card out of his wallet and scrawled a couple of telephone numbers on it with a small gold pen. Private numbers. High-level access. 'Call me next week and I'll bring you up to speed on the policy committee.' He tucked the card in my breast pocket. My backstage pass.

'As for the Centre for Modern Art, it's a bit of a pet project of mine, to be frank.' He reassumed his relaxed posture and proceeded to expound. 'The National Gallery is all Old Masters and touring blockbusters. And the commercial galleries are little more than the unscrupulous peddling the unintelligible to the uncomprehending. The CMA's mission is to fill the gap, to provide public access to the full range of modern Australian art, from its originators through to the creative work of contemporary young artists. Being relatively new, we don't yet have our own collection, but we're working on it.'

Art really turned the guy on. I could sense the genuine enthusiasm. For art, and for the games that went with it. The pleasures of collecting. And of getting someone else to pay.

'Quite successfully too, judging by the government's $300,000 contribution to your acquisition fund.'

Eastlake looked at me sideways, crediting my homework, sensing criticism. 'Good art costs money,' he said. 'Do you have any idea how much government money the trustees of the National Gallery have got over the years? The nobs are never slow to stick their hands out, believe me. The old masters are more than happy for the public to pay for their Old Masters. Isn't it time that someone else got a fair suck of the sausage? Newer artists. Or the forgotten ones the art establishment has written out of history?'

He wasn't going to get any argument from me on that point. He saw that and got down off his high horse.

'I started off as a carpenter, you know.' He slipped into an avuncular tone. 'It's a cliché, I know, but when I first began to succeed in business, I felt that people were contemptuous of me. Not that I particularly cared what they thought, but I didn't want anyone thinking they had the edge on me just because of my background. I'd always had a bit of an interest in art, so I cultivated it. I started going to exhibitions, asking questions, buying pictures. Eventually, I got invited onto exhibition committees and boards of directors. Not the National Gallery, of course. I'm still a bit beneath its dignity. I don't entirely flatter myself that it's because my taste and judgment are held in high esteem. I know it's partly because of my business and political connections. But nobody looks down his nose at me any more. Art is an even greater status symbol than having a chauffeur. Isn't that right, Noel?'

'That's right, Mr Eastlake.' Spider was smarmily obliging, sharing a little private joke with the boss.

I raised my eyes to the rearview mirror and found him observing me, stony faced. He tilted his head upwards and literally looked down his nose at me. Making a point. He'd recognised me all right, back in the garage, and knew that I'd recognised him. There was no mirth in the gesture. None whatsoever. I stared back into his mirrored eyes until he returned them to the road.

'The thing to keep in mind'—Eastlake had resumed his briefing mode, oblivious—'is that most arts practitioners, the creative people, are Labor supporters.'

We passed the squat pyramid of the war memorial and turned down an elm-lined side road. The Mercedes cruised to a gentle stop outside a small white house standing by itself in the middle of the park, complete with a front veranda and an old-fashioned rose garden.

'We've arrived,' Spider announced. Eastlake opened the door and stepped out. As I made to follow, Spider slung his elbow casually onto the seat back. 'Haven't we?' he said, pointedly. 'Mate.'

'Hello, Spider,' I said.

He didn't like to be reminded. 'Bit of a snob these days, Murray? You didn't say hello this afternoon. And a bit of an art buff, too. Moving in all the best circles. Haven't turned into a poofter, have you?'

'Even if I had,' I said, feet on the footpath, 'you'd be safe.'

The Centre for Modern Art looked more like the lawn cutter's residence than the cutting edge of the avant-garde. Its function as an art gallery was betrayed only by a rather inconspicuous sign on the gate and people spilling out the front door with drinks in their hands. Clearly Labor voters to a person.

Eastlake led me up the garden path, nodding hellos. He surged into a narrow hallway with a polished-wood floor, track-lighting, and white walls hung with pictures of dwarfs with enormous penises. Through archways opening on either side I could see people milling about, drinking, chatting and pretending to look at crucified teddy bears and scrap-iron dingoes. 'I'm just the front man here,' Eastlake was saying. 'The real work is done by the our director, Fiona Lambert. You'll like Fiona.

Everyone does. Bright as a button. Darling.'

Darling? Eastlake and I were getting on pretty well, but it seemed a little early in our relationship for this degree of affection.

'Dahling!' The word echoed back from the far end of the hall. A woman of export-quality glamour elbowed her way through the crowd towards us. She was somewhere in her late twenties. Her skin was extraordinarily pale, translucent almost, and lustrously moisturised. She was wearing a little black dress with spaghetti straps, its colour exactly matching her finely arched eyebrows and the precisely engineered bob of hair that framed her face. It was a face with too much character to be called pretty, but it was still well worth looking at. Her legs were bare and went all the way to the floor where they ended in a pair of low-heeled brilliantly shiny shoes, one black, one white. If it hadn't been for the slash of postbox red at her mouth, she could have got a job as a pedestrian crossing. But not one I'd ever cross. She was so far out of my price range she might as well have been the Hope diamond. She offered Eastlake one of her cheeks.

'Fiona, darling.' He pecked the air beside her ear. 'I've brought you a present.' He meant me.

Fiona Lambert inspected me with shrewd green eyes, and politely showed me some teeth that must have cost daddy a pretty penny. Her LBD was cut low to display a divine declivity, dusted with barely visible pale-yellow freckles. Not that I noticed.

Eastlake was right, she was as bright as a button—as neat, as highly polished, and just as hard. He introduced us, explaining the change of ministers and embellishing my credentials somewhat. Ms Lambert smiled non-committally and extended her fingertips. The handshake was slight, barely making contact, but there was a firmness of muscle there that made me think of ballet points and horses. I felt like a politician's yes-man in a cheap suit.

Eastlake promptly bailed out. 'Why don't you induct Murray

into the mysteries, Fiona darling, while I get us a drink.' He merged into the throng, waving ineffectually at a disappearing waitress. More people were arriving. I felt conspicuously over-dressed in my workaday collar and tie. The only other men in suits were very old and slightly bewildered. The rest of the crowd was haphazardly casual, the women with stylishly eccentric spectacles, the men meticulously louche.

Fiona Lambert put her hand lightly on my elbow and steered me out of the hall. We went into a room hung with minimalist paintings so well executed I had to look twice to make sure they were really there. The room was filling and there was a slight crush of bodies. Fiona Lambert stood disconcertingly close. Sooner or later I would be asked my opinion of the stuff on the walls. There was bound to be some sort of formula, but I didn't know what it was. A heavy bead of perspiration broke from under my arm and trickled down inside my shirt. 'Lloyd was somewhat vague about the occasion,' I said, groping for small talk.

'Primarily, it's an opportunity for some of the more promising newcomers to show what they can do.' Fiona Lambert was nothing if not well-bred, and she knew her job. 'More of a social thing, really. So our friends and supporters don't forget us over the summer.'

'You make it sound like the night football,' I said. Might as well play the part.

She forged a mechanical little smile. Her attention was elsewhere. A couple were walking through the door, making an entrance. He was well into his sixties, gnomically stocky and almost completely bald. His heavily lidded eyes and well-tanned skin made him appear simultaneously indolent and cunning. He was wearing a sixty-dollar white t-shirt under a nautical blazer. He looked like a cross between Aristotle Onassis and a walnut. She was fortyish, twice as tall and whipcord thin, with leathery skin and a helmet of red hair that had been worked on by experts. The man's eyes scanned the room until they found Fiona Lambert.

'Speaking of friends and supporters,' she said, her fingers fastening around my elbow. 'Come and meet the Karlins.'

As we crossed the room, Lloyd Eastlake sailed into our orbit with a glass of champagne in each hand. He spotted our destination and arrived first, thrusting the drinks ahead of him. 'Max and Becky Karlin.' He smooched the air beside the woman's earhole. 'Meet Murray Whelan, trusty lieutenant to our new Arts Minister, Angelo Agnelli.'

Karlin bent slightly forward at the waist and offered me his hand. My fingers disappeared into an encompassing embrace of flesh and Karlin pumped them softly, as though gently but firmly extracting some essential oil. He fixed me with oyster eyes, my hand still encased in his paw. For a moment I thought he was going to ask me what size shoe I wore. 'You tell your minister that this con man is robbing me blind.'

'Con man? Robbing you?' Eastlake reeled back in mock outrage. 'Six hundred thousand is not what I'd call robbery.'

Karlin let go of my hand and waggled a chubby finger in my face. 'Don't trust this fellow,' he clucked dryly. 'Do you know what he has done to me?'

I made no attempt to reply. My job, I could see, was to play the straight man while these two went into a well-rehearsed double act.

'What I have done,' said Eastlake, 'is agree to pay you one of the largest sums ever paid by a public collection for a work by a twentieth-century Australian painter.'

Karlin flapped his jowls in dismay. 'This talk of money, it insults the picture's true value. Isn't that right, Fiona?'

Fiona Lambert gave every indication of having seen this little song and dance before, but she played along. 'Its a wonderful painting,' she said.

'Fiona,' said Karlin in an aside for my benefit. 'Fiona is our greatest living expert on the work of Victor Szabo. She was very close to him before his death.'

Fiona was suddenly very interested in the track-lighting. I'd get no help from her. The name Szabo meant nothing to me. I was out of my depth and sinking fast. Meanwhile, Eastlake and Karlin continued their Mo and Stiffy act.

'Max here is cranky because his bluff has been called,' Eastlake told me. 'For years he's had what is arguably Victor Szabo's best work hanging in his office, a picture called *Our Home*. But Fiona realised its significance, identified it as the perfect cornerstone for our permanent collection here at the CMA. Max likes to be thought of as a philanthropist, so he couldn't refuse outright to sell us the picture. He just asked a price so high he thought he'd scare us off.'

So, this Victor Szabo was a painter, evidently one big enough to warrant a six-figure price tag. Karlin was finding this all very entertaining, this story in which his taste and acumen were the starring characters. 'I'm practically giving it away,' he told me.

Eastlake was getting to the bit he liked. 'But I called Max's bluff. I told Gil Methven that a picture of this significance really ought to be in a public collection. He agreed that the Arts Ministry would provide half the funds if I could raise the other half. Which is exactly what I did. So Max had no option but to agree to the sale. Now all he does is bitch about how he's being swindled.'

'Bah,' Karlin waved a thick finger in the air. 'Money was never the issue. I love that picture. It's like one of my children. Twenty years ago I bought it, long before most people had ever heard of Victor Szabo.'

Most people? 'I'm afraid I'm not very familiar with Szabo's work,' I confessed. 'Is the painting here?'

'We take possession on Monday.' Fiona Lambert made this a question, arching her eyebrows at Karlin.

He nodded confirmation. 'Until then,' he said, 'it remains my private pleasure. At least until the formalities are completed.'

Eastlake explained. 'Max is holding a little going-away event for the picture, brunch tomorrow. Gil Methven was going to do the honours but what with the Cabinet reshuffle, the short notice and so on...'

It was my turn to flash a little rank. 'Oh, I think I can

persuade Angelo to attend,' I said. 'He's particularly keen to meet'—here I gave my attention entirely to Karlin—'such a prominent supporter of the arts.'

Karlin merely smiled indulgently. 'Yes, fine.' Across the room Becky Karlin and another lizard-skinned bat were scrutinising what was either a visual discourse on the nature of post-industrial society or the wiring diagram for a juice extractor. Nodding a brisk farewell, Karlin took off towards them, a politely hunched Fiona Lambert on his arm.

'You did well to wangle three hundred grand out of Gil Methven,' I told Eastlake admiringly. I didn't want the policy committee chairman taking my little exercise in one-upmanship amiss. 'Spending the taxpayers' money on modern art is not exactly a sure-fire vote-winner, you know.'

'Couldn't agree with you more,' he said with unruffled equanimity. 'But wait until you see this particular picture. The public will love it. It'll become a national icon, just you wait. You think a hardhead like Gil Methven wouldn't have considered the political implications?'

'Just as long as it's not twenty metres wide and made of bullock's blood and emu feathers,' I grudgingly allowed. 'Angelo's in the hot seat now.'

'Believe me.' Eastlake snaffled a couple of fresh glasses off a passing tray and thrust one into my hand. 'Agnelli will love it. He'll think he's Lorenzo bloody Medici. And the public will lap it up.'

Eastlake could afford to be optimistic about the judgment of the people. He'd never have to face it. I didn't tell him that, though. Instead I let him wheel me around the room and introduce me to more names than I could hope to remember and more glasses of Veuve Clicquot than I could reasonably be expected to digest on an empty stomach.

In due course, I found myself standing alone, contemplating one of the pictures. It was a portrait of the Queen constructed entirely out of different varieties of breakfast cereal. Corn Flake lips, Nutri-Grain ears, Coco Pops hair. I had, I decided, done my duty for the day. It was getting on for 8.30. Time to scout for an out.

I sidled through the nearest door and found myself in an enclosed garden, a green rectangle of lawn bordered by high shrubs, a cool refuge from the clamour inside. A lavender-hued dusk was beginning its descent. The slightly overgrown grass was littered with dead marines and ravaged canape trays. Little clusters of people sprawled about languidly with their shoes kicked off. At the far end of the lawn, near a pile of rusty iron-work from the Turd of a Dog with a Square Arsehole school of sculpture, stood Salina Fleet, *Veneer* magazine's spunky visual arts editor.

The palm trees on her mu-mu swayed. Pom-poms brushed her bare thighs. A lipstick-smeared wineglass sat athwart her bosom. All up, she looked a damned sight more edible than the wilting sushi circulating inside. Unfortunately, she was not alone.

Her companion was a male. He was somewhere in his mid-thirties, with lank unkempt hair, heavy-rimmed Roy Orbison glasses and an attempt at sideburns. The sleeves were sheared off his western shirt and he was wearing grimy, paint-speckled jeans. A creative type, no doubt about it. And judging by the intense way he leaned into Selina when he talked—he was doing all the talking—more than a casual acquaintance. He was reading expressively from a tatty piece of paper, as though reciting a poem.

Salina, I noted with some pleasure, didn't appear to be buying it, whatever it was. My hopes soared. The guy was probably some mendicant artist, putting the hard word on her for a grant or a favourable review. But then she stepped closer and put her hand on his forearm. The gesture was so intimate, her demeanour so affectionate, that I mentally reached for the chalk to scratch myself from the race.

The guy jerked his arm away as if stung. No soft soap for him. He spun on his heels and strode towards the doorway where I was standing. Salina watched his progress across the lawn, less than impressed. She shook her head ruefully and drained her drink.

Here was my chance. The bar table was just through the door. I dived back inside and hit the waiter for a quick two glasses of shampoo. As he wrestled the wire off a fresh bottle, the artist-type came bustling up beside me, his eyes glinting through his spectacles with madcap determination. He slapped his hand down on my shoulder. 'Excuse me,' he said, his voice piping with emotion.

Before I could respond, he pushed downwards. Using me for support, he hoicked himself up onto the bar. His tooled leather boots skidded on the wet surface. A loaded tray of empty glasses careened over the edge and hit the floor. They shattered with an almighty crash. Every head in the room turned our way.

'Shut up, everybody,' declaimed the weedy cowboy. He brandished his piece of paper at the upturned faces like he was Lenin addressing the Congress of People's Deputies. 'And listen. You're all being conned. This whole edifice is built on a lie.'

He made a gesture so expansive he had trouble arresting its momentum. And when he took a steadying sideways step, it was immediately obvious that he was drunk. Not legless perhaps, but a good three sheets to the wind at the very minimum. His voice was pitched high with nervous exultation at his own boldness. 'The people behind this place don't care about art.'

Backs turned dismissively, and the hubbub of conversation resumed. There's one in every crowd, the murmur said. Just ignore him.

Seeing his audience's attention begin to slip away, the would-be Demosthenes raised his voice against the resumption of normality. He succeeded only in sounding hysterical. 'Listen, everybody,' he pleaded. 'This is important.'

I almost felt sorry for him, standing there in all his horrible vulnerability, flapping his skinny arms about, his pearls cast before swine, a teenage barman in a clip-on bow tie tugging at his trouser leg. Not sorry enough to forget my mission, though.

Salina Fleet, drawn by the ruckus, was standing in the

doorway observing the spectacle with wide-eyed alarm.

Taking advantage of the waiter's distraction, I filched the still-unopened champagne bottle, grabbed a couple of glasses and began in her direction. 'You'll see,' the cowboy warned. 'You can't dismiss me so easily.'

And, as if to prove his point, and to me in particular, he promptly staggered forward and toppled off the table. He landed on top of me.

It isn't every day I get strafed. I folded like a cheap banana lounge, flat on my backside, glassware skittering, dignity out the window. The demented speech-maker's face pushed into mine, flushed with humiliation and too much to drink. 'Sorry, mate,' he mumbled, scrambling to his feet and rushing for the door. Salina Fleet, seeing him coming, pursed her mouth into a furious slit and folded her arms in an emphatic gesture of disavowal.

The hands of solicitous strangers dragged me to my feet. 'Watch out!' squealed someone. 'Blood!'

My new-found friends all jumped backwards as if jet-propelled. The offending bodily fluid was mine. The stem of a broken wineglass had nicked my forefinger. The cut was small and there wasn't a lot of blood, but that wasn't the point. Who knows what fatal contagion I may have been harbouring?

Whipping a cocktail napkin from my pocket, I hermetically sealed the offending digit. The traumatised bystanders cast me nervously apologetic looks. Fiona Lambert arrived, the scandalised hostess. 'How ghastly,' she clucked. 'Are you all right?'

'Fine,' I said, bravely displaying my ruby-tinged bandage. 'Who was that guy, anyway?'

'Nobody important,' sniffed Fiona, dismissively. 'These would-be artists, they're always complaining about something. Are you sure you're all right?'

Lloyd Eastlake closed from the other side, trapping me in a social pincer. 'You okay?'

Nothing was damaged but my prospects. Salina Fleet was nowhere in sight.

'Let's get out of here,' said Eastlake keenly, clamping my biceps. He was quite shaken, a lot more disturbed by the amateur dramatics than I was. He scanned the room as though my inadvertent assailant might be about to launch another attack from the cover of the crowd. 'People are going across to the Botanical,' he said.

I'd read about the Botanical Hotel. It was a chichi watering hole and noshery on Domain Road, not far away. Before Fiona Lambert could object, he clamped her arm, too, and marched us out the front door.

Night had fallen over the parkland, filling it with the drone of cicadas and the heady fragrance of damp lawn. A straggling gaggle of exhibition-goers meandered through the trees ahead of us, blending into the twilight in the general direction of Domain Road. To my relief, I could make out the bird-like silhouette of Salina Fleet among them. The tormented artist was nowhere in sight. Perhaps my prospects were salvageable.

Eastlake noticed the way I was gripping my forefinger in the roll of my fist. 'Wounded in action,' he said. 'You need a Band-aid on that. Doesn't he, Fiona?'

A Band-aid would be useful, I admitted. The cut was small but it was bleeding profusely. I couldn't walk around all night clutching a bloody cocktail napkin. 'Fiona's place is practically on the way,' insisted Eastlake. 'You've got a first-aid kit, haven't you, Fiona?'

Fiona looked like she'd prefer to save her medicaments for a worthier cause. 'Only if it's no trouble,' I said.

Domain Road delineated Melbourne's social divide. It was the point where the public parkland ran out and the private money began. Marking the border were the playing fields of Melbourne Grammar, a school for children with problem parents. Beyond, were the high-rent suburbs of Toorak and South Yarra. Toffsville.

We crossed the road and walked half a block, turning into the entrance of a pink stucco block of flats. A dog-faced dowager with a miniature schnauzer under her arm was coming out. Eastlake held the door open for her, and the old duck nodded regally but didn't say thanks. It was that sort of a neighbourhood, I guessed.

We climbed a flight of steps to the second floor, where two doors with little brass knockers faced each other across a small landing. One of them had a Chinese ceramic planter beside it, sprouting miniature bamboo. Fiona began to rummage in her handbag, searching for her keys. The bag was an elaborate leather thing with more pockets than a three-piece suit. After she'd been rummaging for what seemed like an eternity, Eastlake said something about dying of thirst, tilted the Chinese pot, slid a key from beneath it and unlocked the door.

Irritation flickered briefly across Fiona Lambert's face, whether at Eastlake's presumption, his casual breach of her security, or merely at the time she'd wasted searching her bag, I couldn't tell.

Fiona's domestic style was tastefully relaxed—what *Vogue Living* would describe as 'a professional woman's inner-city pied-à-terre'. The building dated from sometime in the forties and the best of the original features had been retained—the ornately stepped cornices, the matching plasterwork chevron in the centre of the ceiling, the onyx-tinted smoked-glass light-fitting, the severely square fireplace, the rugs—well-worn but far from threadbare, geometric patterns in black, turquoise and dusty ivory. Aztec jazz.

To these had been added a huge box-shaped sofa, heavily cushioned and covered in cream cotton duck, plain and inviting, a dining-table of honey-coloured wood with matching bentwood chairs, and a marble-topped coffee-table piled with art books. The only lapse into period was a pair of low-slung tubular-steel armchairs, the kind that look like they're too busy being design classics to offer much comfort.

'Make yourself at home,' she said, her hospitality perfunctory at best. 'I'll get your Band-aid.' Eastlake had charged ahead into the kitchen where he was making ice-cube and bottle-top noises. I crossed to the window. The view was of the darkening expanse of the park, and the lit-up towers of the city centre beyond. A tram clattered by, its wheels chanting a mantra. Location, location, location. Eastlake's car stood at the far kerb,

Spider beside it, his jaw working mechanically.

Eastlake reappeared, bearing iced drinks. 'Gin and tonic,' he said. 'Nature's disinfectant.' Fiona handed me a Band-aid. 'Bathroom's down there.' It was perfectly preserved, all green and cream tiles and curved edges, the bathtub big enough to float the Queen Mary. I unwrapped my finger and found the bleeding already stopped.

When I wandered back, Fiona was sprawled on the sofa, almost horizontal. A monochromatic odalisque, bare legs stretched out before her, feet on the coffee table. 'What a week,' she groaned. 'Cheers.' Ah, the gruelling lot of a gallery director.

The heat of the day had permeated the flat, and an air of lassitude filled the room. We sipped without conversation. Lowering myself into the design-benchmark chair, I faced Fiona across the coffee table. The seat was very low and her toes nearly touched my knees. I couldn't help but see her knickers. White cotton. She yawned and ran the bottom of her glass over her forehead. Maybe that's how it works around here, I thought. Averting my eyes, I scanned the title on the spine of one of the art books. *A Fierce Vision: The Genius of Victor Szabo 1911–77* by Fiona Lambert.

On the wall behind her, lit to good effect, hung a large painting in an understated frame. A highly realistic bush scene, pared down to the most basic elements of sky, earth, trees. The work of someone who knew his subject and hated it with a vengeance. Above the mantelpiece hung a smaller painting, clearly by the same hand. A reclining nude.

Lloyd and Fiona exchanged knowing glances, expecting me to say something. Let someone else make an idiot of themselves, I thought. Besides which, I'd already seen enough pictures that day to last me quite a while. Art would keep. My appetites at that point were more basic. 'If I don't eat soon,' I said, sociably, 'I won't be answerable.'

The phone rang. Fiona went into a little study opening off the living room. 'Hello.' She listened for a moment, then reached back with her foot and hooked the door shut. I stood up and sucked my piece of lemon, beginning to get impatient, not sure why we were still here. Pacing to the window, I saw Spider leaning against a tree, a mobile phone pressed to his ear. Wanker.

Lined up on the mantelpiece was a row of framed photographs. Family snaps. Incidental mileposts in life's little journey. Me, Mummy and Toby the pony. Provence on a hundred dollars a day. I took my drink over and picked one up, a five by eight colour print. This Fiona was a good ten years younger. A real little chubby-bubby. Her hair was longer, still brown, her dress a shapeless shift. She was smiling at the camera, close-lipped as though hiding braces. An old man had his arm around her shoulder. He was maybe sixty-five, barrel-chested, with a round face and a bare scalp, tufts of grey hair sticking out above his ears, grinning like a wicked old koala. The background was blurred, providing no clues to the setting.

I held the frame up. 'Her father?'

Eastlake nearly choked on his G & T. 'Christ no!' he spluttered, glancing furtively back at the closed door of the study. 'That's Victor Szabo.' He took the photograph out of my hand, regarded it with ill-concealed amazement and returned it to its place on the mantel. His eyes swivelled upwards, to the nude, and his mouth opened to say something. The study door opened and Fiona reappeared, frowning.

'Bad news?' said Eastlake, turning quickly to face her.

She made a dismissive gesture and shook her head. 'Nothing.' She yawned—it looked forced—and tugged off her earrings, plain pearl studs, one black, one white. 'I'm sorry,' she said. 'I really am, but I'm exhausted.' She was trying hard to sound tired, but there was a tight brittleness in her voice. 'Would you think I was terribly rude if I begged off dinner?'

Frankly, it suited me fine. Eastlake made some dissuading noises, thankfully to no avail, I expressed more gratitude for the first aid than was warranted and two minutes later we were back in the street. 'Think I'll give it a miss, too,' said Eastlake, looking at his watch.

The night was young and I was half-cut and fancy-free. A hundred metres up the road women with backsides by Henry Moore were entering the most fashionable wet-throat emporium in town. As soon as Eastlake began across the street towards the Mercedes, I hastened to join them.

Shuffling down the footpath towards me was my nemesis, the flying cowboy. All the stuffing had gone out of him. He was lost in thought, mumbling to himself. 'Jus you wait,' he was saying, repeating it under his breath. As poignant a solitary drunk as ever I had seen. I gave him a wide berth and went into the pub.

So much fashionable architecture had been inflicted on the Botanical Hotel that it could have passed for the engine room of an aircraft carrier, all distressed boiler-plate and industrial rubber. Business was booming. Salina Fleet was in the far corner of the bistro section, at a raucous table crowded with faces from the CMA back lawn. Down boy, I told myself. Read the mood. Take it slowly.

I ordered a beer, examining myself in the bar mirror. Uglier men were stalking the earth. The barman was one of them. 'Grolsch?' he said. I thought he was clearing his throat. He handed me a tomato sauce bottle of pale brown liquid. *Grolsch Premium Lager*, read the label. *Brewed in Holland.* 'That'll be four eighty,' he said.

That explained the balance of payments deficit. Time was when you could get paralytic for four dollars eighty. On Australian beer, at that. I put my hand on my hip pocket and discovered my wallet was gone.

There was a limited number of places I might have mislaid it. Mentally retracing my steps, I got as far back as that low-slung designer chair in Fiona Lambert's apartment. I went back down the street, took the stairs two at a time, and rapped on Fiona's little brass knocker. Five minutes, ten at the most, had elapsed since Eastlake and I had left, so it wasn't like I'd be waking her up. There was no answer. I rapped again, the sound reverberating down the stairwell. Either Fiona Lambert was a very sound sleeper or there was no-one home. Somewhere inside, the phone began to bleat. When it finally rang out, I raised the edge of the Ming Dynasty shrub tub. The key was back in its hiding place. I let myself in.

Streetlight lit the living room. The remains of our drinks sat on the coffee-table condensing dribbles of water. My wallet was on the floor, just where I hoped it would be. As I bent to pick it up, my eye was caught by the picture hanging above the mantel, the nude. I stood and studied it.

Its subject was the younger, plumper Fiona Lambert, the one in the photograph. The artist's approach was clinical, lurid and without a shred of sentimentality. Superbly confident, the picture captured not just Fiona's likeness but her narcissism as well. The pose was blush-makingly provocative, anatomically explicit. The artist just had to be bonking her teenage ears off.

I did some quick mental arithmetic. At the time he painted the picture, Victor Szabo must have been at least sixty-five. The old goat.

Five minutes later I was back at the Botanical with four dollars eighty worth of Dutch courage in my hand, making eye contact with Salina Fleet.

She waved me over, making space at the table. 'What did you say your name was, again?' she demanded, her way of being smart. I didn't doubt I was already tucked away in Sal's mental Filofax, cross-referenced against future contingency. Everyone was talking at once, bellowing into the general din. Art scene party time. 'Saw you at the CMA,' she half-shouted. 'Thought you were gone.'

'So did I,' I said. 'When that guy landed on me.'

She laughed and bit her lip at the same time, a cornered look in her eyes. I rapidly changed the subject to the only other thing I could think of. 'Got sidetracked by Fiona Lambert.'

She relaxed. 'The Black Widow, we call her.' I bent closer, the better to hear her, and the bare skin of our forearms touched. A little spark of static electricity shot between us. 'Better watch yourself there.'

'Why?'

She was even tighter than me. Not that we were drunk. And so what if we were? The waiter came and stuck a menu in front of my face. It was the sort you read right to left. Everything on offer was either char-grilled, stir-fried, snow-pead, or came with sheep's cheese. What I really wanted to taste was the waxy fruit of Salina's apricot lips.

'Go on,' I urged. 'Tell me.' Keep her talking until we found some common ground, that was the strategy. 'Why do you call Fiona Lambert the Black Widow?'

A thin-lipped, imperious-beaked bloke was squeezed in on the other side of Salina. I'd met him at the CMA but his name escaped me. When he heard Fiona Lambert's name, he pricked up his ears and leaned over. 'They call her that,' he whispered in an accent that sounded like it came from the same place as my beer, 'because of the rumour that Victor Szabo died, shall we say, on the job with her.'

He had a bracket like a Borgia pontiff in a Titian portrait. To hear him properly, I had to lean even closer to Salina, so I kept up the questions. 'They were lovers, were they?'

'She modelled for him, slept with him, buried him, wrote the book on him, is curating his retrospective,' said Salina with what sounded suspiciously like envy. 'She practically invented him.'

'And now he's about to be the next big thing, eh?' I said.

'Bigger than Sir Ned Kelly himself, if the Black Widow has anything to do with it,' confirmed the Pope's nose.

By that stage, I could've eaten a nun's bum through a cane chair. We moved on to the Koonunga Hill cabernet shiraz. Food arrived, cross-hatched from the grill, and I sawed into my fillet of salmon.

'A brutal deconstruction of mordant reality,' declaimed Salina.

'Beg pardon?' I chewed.

'A sundering of the constituent components of antipodean materiality.' She sucked in her cheeks and tried to look severe and authoritative.

'Eh?' I popped a french fry into my mouth.

'The insertion into a distinctively Australian sensibility of the universalising impulse of an internationalist form.'

At last I got it. She was doing a Fiona Lambert impression. Quoting, I took it, catchphrases from her book on Victor Szabo.

'An unflinching critic of the mundane,' piped up the schnoz, getting in on the act.

'*A Fierce Vision*,' we all chortled in chorus.

Holding it up with the best of them, I was. Who'd've known that three hours ago I'd never heard of this Szabo bloke. This art business was turning out to be a piece of piss. While we ate, Sal and the other guy kept up a running patter about Szabo. He was quite a mystery man from what I could glean—a refugee from Europe, a misanthropic recluse who had done most of his work in the fifties and sixties while holed up in rustic squalor. 'A total output of what, fifty or sixty paintings,' Sal said at one point. 'Not exactly prolific.'

'Forty *known* paintings,' the accent corrected her. 'Now that he's getting better appreciated, who knows how many more will emerge?'

The conversation soon meandered elsewhere, and I was happy to go with it. I would have been happy to go anywhere, given the encouragement I was receiving under the table. At the salad, Salina's hand brushed on my knee. By the tiramisu, it was lodged between my thighs.

When the liqueurs and coffee arrived, I knew I was going places. 'Have you ever been exploring?' she asked, dipping her forefinger in Sambuca and offering me a taste. 'In the Botanic Gardens at night?'

It would have been churlish to refuse. What I didn't realise—could not possibly have realised—was that the expedition that followed would lead me much further than over an iron railing and into a thicket of *Rhododendron oreotrophes*. Further than an exploratory probe in the depths of the fern forest. Further even than the searing flare of an emergency light beside the moat of the National Gallery.

And, before it was over, more than one body would be wheeled into the back of an ambulance.

But right then, in the dead of the night, the itch of crushed leaves still on my skin, all I could see was Salina Fleet's contorted face.

'Bastard!' She said it again.

Not an accusation this time. Not thrown in my face, but muttered under her breath. Her eyes followed the movement of the gurney into the back of the ambulance, the trail of water across the pavement left by the lifeless black legs. Her head shook with the movement of it, emphatic in denial. Despite the heat, she was trembling.

Abruptly, slow motion became fast forward. The flashing light went off. Doors slammed. The ambulance began to draw away. I moved towards Salina, wanting nothing except to comfort and to calm. The policeman blocked my path with a hand to my chest. He gestured towards the rear of the departing vehicle. 'Friend of his, are you?'

Salina was moving out of reach, being led towards the police car. She wasn't looking back. The air was humid, cloying. I shook my head. 'Not really.'

The cop was about ten years younger than me. His shirt had two stripes on the sleeve, and he had a howitzer on his hip. 'Don't you think you've had enough, mate?'

I looked down and saw that I still had the bottle of wine we'd pinched from the hotel. We'd been swigging out of it as we crossed the lawn and I was holding it by the neck. Barely a tepid mouthful remained in the bottom. The Botanic Gardens suddenly felt a very long way away. The taste on my tongue was bile, not apricots.

Beyond a pair of security guards, Salina was being helped into the back seat of the police car. The cop followed my line of sight. 'You with her, are you, mate?'

Salina stared back towards me. She was calmer, regaining control, her face as bloodless as marble. Guilty and contrite. She gave a little rueful shake of the head. Goodbye, Murray, it said.

I shook my head slightly, mirroring her movement. 'Not any more,' I said. It seemed like the right thing. Only later did it feel like cowardice.

More police were arriving. Another two squad cars and an unmarked Falcon. A security guard, fishing in the moat, pulled a pair of thick-rimmed glasses out of the water. Another had the discarded shopping trolley from earlier in the afternoon and was dragging it out of the gutter. The car with Salina went.

There were maybe six cops, as many security guards. I was the only civilian. I dropped the wine bottle into a rubbish bin. It was empty and the bottle hit the bottom with a blunt thud that went straight to my temples. 'Go home, pal,' ordered a honcho in an Armaguard uniform. 'The show's over.'

I could, I supposed, have identified myself, claimed some

small entitlement to information. A pretty picture that would have made. A crumpled suit, grass stains on my fingers, a gutful of souring wine, trying to throw my rather limited weight about. And for what? To find out how come my hot date had been cut short?

Snatches of radio chatter and snippets of half-overheard conversations gave me more than enough clues to satisfy my immediate curiosity on that point. The body in the cowboy boots had been found by a security guard. He'd come outside for a cigarette and noticed a dark shape lying on the bottom of the moat, in the shadow of the retaining wall. He thought it was a roll of carpet. Idiots were always dumping things in the moat. He shone his torch into the water and saw what it was. He called another guard and they attempted resuscitation. It was no use. The guy could have been lying there for hours. An empty scotch bottle was found beside the body.

I trudged across Princes Bridge to the dormant railway station, laid my cheek upon the rear-seat upholstery of the only cab at the rank and murmured my address to the driver, a Polish scarecrow in tinted plate-glass hornrims. 'Hot,' he said. 'Wery hot.'

'Gdansk, it ain't,' I agreed.

Chauffeured for the third time that day, the pulse of the passing streetlights throbbing at my temples, the grog finally catching up with me, I succumbed to a headachy doze. And in my waking sleep, I found myself thinking unbidden thoughts of a time long gone.

My father had just taken the licence of the Olympic Hotel, his fourth pub in ten years. Apart from the name, there wasn't anything sporting about the Olympic, not unless you counted the horse races droning away on the radio in the public bar. Mum hadn't been dead long when we made the move, and Dad had taken me out of St Joseph's and put me in the nearest government secondary school. It was a haphazard choice. He said he wanted me near him. More like he didn't want to keep paying the fees.

That was okay with me. Compared to where I'd been, Preston Technical was a breeze. Nobody gave a flying continental about academic results. Soon as they got to fifteen, most of them were straight out the door and into apprenticeships or factory jobs. Plenty of work for juniors in those days, the sixties. But not much teenage entertainment. Not unless you could get your hands on some piss. Not unless you knew how to handle the kid whose father owned the pub.

At St Joey's the only real source of fear was the Brothers, pricks with leather straps, a weight advantage and the high moral ground. At the tech we had the Fletchers, fifteen-year-old twins and their older brother, ferret-faced thugs who hunted in a pack and made the Christian Brothers look like the Little Sisters of Mercy. There was an older Fletcher still, but he was in Pentridge prison. The initial charge was manslaughter but the magistrate believed him when he said that if he'd been seriously trying to hurt the bloke he'd have worn his kicking shoes. So he got off with reckless endangerment and grievous bodily harm. Five years.

The Fletchers lived on the Housing Commission estate, prefab concrete boxes built in 1956 to accommodate the Olympic athletes and already falling to bits when the welfare cases moved in after the Games were over. When you rode your bike to school through Fletcher territory you needed steely nerves, strong thighs and tough friends. That's what they told me at school, anyway. But I was the new kid. I didn't have any tough friends. Not until I was adopted by the one they called Spider. Then I had a friend. Just my luck.

General Jaruzelski woke me long enough to dump me on my doorstep and extract his fare. Then I was face down in my own empty bed, dreaming again. But not of Spider Webb, or the Fletchers, or the bad business with the stolen bottles of bourbon. This dream was more promising.

A wood nymph was tugging at my toga. One more fold and I would spring free and plunge into her grotto. But my toga was tangled and there was a thyme-drunk bee in my ear. Buzz buzz, it went, buzz buzz. I swatted it and it stung my eyes. Daylight poured into the wound and pierced my brain with a red-hot poker. The camp-fire ashes of a thousand marauding armies filled my mouth. Buzz buzz, said the persistent bee. Then a voice started shouting about the weather. Hot. Again. As if I didn't know that already.

Untangling myself from sweat-drenched sheets, I swung my feet onto the floor, slammed one hand down on the clock-radio and picked up the phone with the other. What prick would ring me at 7.04 on a Saturday morning?

Agnelli.

'Urgghh,' I said. The glass of water beside my bed had been there so long it had formed a skin. When it hit my tongue, sea monkeys hatched, spawned, died, and shed their exoskeletons down my throat. I fumbled for a match and fumigated my oesophagus with cleansing smoke.

'You heard about the National Gallery last night?' My boss was wide awake, keyed up.

'What?' I grunted, my head throbbing from the effort. Had I missed something? 'Somebody swipe a Picasso?'

'Some idiot drowned himself in the moat. I've had three different reporters on the phone since 6.30, wanting a comment.'

Even in my fuddled state, I got the point immediately. To the press—reduced to reporting the weather—a body in the moat of the National Gallery would be a story straight from heaven. In a city without distinguishing landmarks—no opera house, no harbour—the Arts Centre was the closest thing to a civic icon. Its picture was on the cover of the phone book, in every tourist brochure and glossy piece of corporate boosterism. Melbourne, City of the Arts. Look. See. Naturally a death in the moat would be a sensation. And if a political angle could be found, so much the better.

But what political angle? By covering my head with a pillow and closing my eyes, I could just about see to think. 'Why call you? What's it got to do with you?'

'According to the journos who rang me,' Agnelli said, 'this

whacker committed suicide in protest at the lack of government support for the arts.' At least it wasn't because his girlfriend was rolling around in the hydrangeas with the responsible minister's major-domo.

'What makes them think that?' There'd been no mention of a protest motive at the death scene, not that I'd heard. And I couldn't see any immediate point in informing Agnelli that I was there when they dredged up the body.

'He left a note.' There was more than a hint of anxiety in Agnelli's voice. 'A manifesto, the press are calling it.'

I realised why Agnelli was aerated enough to have called me at this ungodly hour. Two years before, a Picasso really had been swiped from the National Gallery. It was held hostage by hijackers demanding more government funding for the arts—a motive so cryptic as to bamboozle the police utterly. The ransom negotiations were conducted on the front pages of the daily press. In a series of manifestos, the Arts Minister was described successively as a tiresome old bag of swamp gas, a pompous fathead, and a self-glorifying anal retentive. Subsequent insults were so erudite they had millions rushing for their dictionaries. Eventually, the painting was recovered, abandoned in a railway station locker. But the thieves were never caught.

So it wasn't hard to infer whence Agnelli was coming. Public ridicule and ministerial amour-propre make a poor mix, and mere mention of the word 'manifesto' was bound to set a cat among Agnelli's pigeons. I took a deep breath and started again. 'Just exactly what does this manifesto say?'

'Jesus Christ, Murray, that's what I want you to find out.'

'Has this alleged suicide note been released?' By ratcheting the terminology down a notch I hoped to quiet the quivering antennae of Agnelli's ego.

It didn't work. 'Not according to the journalists who rang, but the general gist is being bandied about. And I'd rather not find out the details by seeing them on television. No surprises, Murray. I thought we were clear on that. No surprises.' Meaning that I should pull my finger out and have something reassuring to contribute to the overview. Pronto. 'I'll pick you up behind Parliament House at eleven. You can bring me up to speed on the way to this Max Karlin brunch thing.'

I told him I was on the case, buried my head in the pillow and tried to get back to sleep. It was a waste of time. Twenty litres of used booze were backed up in my southern suburbs, leaning on the horn. On top of which, a pounding noise was now coming from outside in the street.

Reaching across the mattress, I eased a chink in the curtains. Sunlight stabbed my frontal lobes. Across the narrow street, a guy in shorts and a carpenter's belt was fixing a For Sale sign to the facade of the house immediately opposite. The letters on the hoarding were as big as my hand. *Inner City Living*, they read. *A Gem from the Past. An Investment for the Future.* No room to swing a cat, in other words, but the market is buoyant.

From the front, the house was identical to mine, a single-storey, single-fronted terrace. The whole street was the same, all twenty houses. A cheese-paring speculator had built them as a job lot back in the 1870s. Workingmen's cottages they were called at the time—as distinct from the grander two-storey terraces in the surrounding streets with their cast-iron balconies and moulded pediments.

This neighbourhood was once considered a slum—such an affront to the national ideal of the suburban bungalow that whole blocks of it had been bulldozed in the name of progress. But those days were gone. Thanks to the miracle of gentrification, dingy digs in dodgy neighbourhoods had become delightful inner-city residences with charming period features in cosmopolitan locales. It was truly amazing what a lick of paint, a skylight and an adjective or two could do for real estate values.

This was the fifth time in the two years I'd lived there that a house in this street had been put on the market. I couldn't help but wonder what this one would fetch at auction. Mine had set the bank back nearly a hundred and fifty thousand dollars. A pretty penny—and a bargain at that—for two bedrooms, a kitchen–living room and a back yard the size of a boxing ring. And, with my variable interest rate bobbing around at 16 per cent, a very good reason to get out of bed and go to work.

I padded to the bathroom, fine grit beneath my bare soles, wind-borne detritus of our island continent's blasted interior. A reminder to give Red's room a quick dusting before he arrived. As I crossed the lounge room, I reached into the bookcase, pulled out the dead weight of *101 Funniest Australian Cricket Stories* and tossed it onto the couch where Red would see it when he arrived. He'd sent it to me for Christmas, a boy's idea of the right sort of gift for his dad, and I treasured every page, even though I'd never read a word of it. Just as well Wendy hadn't done the buying for him, or I'd have got *Cooking for One*.

Not that it wouldn't have been handy, I reflected as I rinsed the forlorn breakfast bowl that had been soaking in the sink.

Next Christmas he'd give me *Home Maintenance Made Easy*. And it, too, would go into the bookcase unopened. Right beside *The Rise and Fall of the Great Powers*. That one I bought myself. Got bogged down in the War of Spanish Succession. One night soon I'd try again, get right on top of Metternich.

Red gave me what he thought a boy should give his father. But he needn't have worried about my home maintenance needs. I had none. After seven years with Wendy, fruitlessly wrestling with cross-cut saws and counter-sunk wood screws, all I wanted was to change the odd light globe. That's why I'd bought a renovated house.

So what if all the bench tops were apple-green and the cupboards burnt-orange? So what if all my furniture came from the Ikea catalogue and looked like it was designed for Swedish dwarfs? So what if the walls were still bare after two years? I could walk to work whenever I wanted. Red had a room of his own when he came to stay. And perhaps my new-found friends in the arts could recommend something suitable to adorn my vacant hanging space. Home is where the heart is, after all. Even if it did get a little lonesome from time to time and the shelves in the fridge could've done with a good wipe.

My heart and I went into the bathroom, stood under a hundred icy needles of cold water and started making plans. The first item on my agenda was to forget about last night as soon as possible. Salina Fleet had been a bad idea, even without the business at the moat. In fact, the business at the moat may have been a blessing in disguise. A Salina Fleet was not what I needed at this juncture in my life.

What I needed was groceries. A ten-year-old kid can go through a hell of a lot of groceries in three days.

Hit the oracle, make a few calls, raid the supermarket, meet and brief Agnelli, take in Max Karlin's brunch, then out to the airport to pick up Red. After that, maybe the local swimming pool. Cool down, then take in a movie. Play it by ear.

My first call was to Ken Sproule. Half past seven on a Saturday morning was not the ideal time to go shopping for favours, but I remembered that Sproule had a two-year-old daughter. If he wasn't out of bed already then two-year-olds weren't what they used to be.

As a rule of thumb, personal networks are always preferable to official channels. Sproule would understand implicitly why I was calling. His boss Gil Methven may have been Police Minister for less than a day, but Ken was fast on the uptake and I preferred to be steered informally around police procedures than to go dropping Agnelli's name into the loop at this early stage.

Sproule was up all right, monitoring *Cartoon Connection* and cutting toast into fingers. He was thankful for the distraction and when I drew the map he laughed out loud. 'Agnelli's only had the job twelve hours and already artists have started killing themselves.'

'Maybe the guy hadn't heard about the reshuffle,' I said. 'Maybe he couldn't stand the thought of Gil Methven staying in the job.'

We went on like this for a while until Sproule was in a thoroughly good mood, then I asked him to suggest the least conspicuous way for me to find out what was in the suicide note. Surprisingly, he volunteered to make the calls himself. Under normal circumstances getting someone like Sproule hitting the phone on my behalf would have taken a fair amount of horse-trading. But the idea of a corpse in the moat of the National Gallery stimulated his morbid curiosity. 'Fifteen months in that job, the only bodies I ever saw were in the last act of *Hamlet*,' said Sproule. 'I'll call you back in a couple of hours.'

It was closer to a couple of minutes. 'Something just occurred to me. The name Marcus Taylor rings a bell. Don't quote me, but I think he might have applied for a grant.'

'Did he get one?'

'That's the part I can't remember.'

'If I'm not here when you call back,' I told him, 'try the Arts Ministry.'

I hiked over to Ethnic Affairs via a cup of coffee, picked up my car and drove to Arts, twiddling the radio dial across the eight o'clock news bulletins. The top-rating commercial station had already picked up the story. *Melbourne's arts community*, it said, *was deeply shocked by the apparent suicide of the promising young painter Marcus Taylor*—the young part was encouraging, given that Taylor had looked to be about my age—*in protest at lack of government support for the arts*. Salina, identified as a prominent art critic, was quoted as describing Taylor's death as a shocking waste.

As I passed the National Gallery, a television news crew was shooting background footage of the moat. The vultures were circling.

The ministry was locked, but Phillip Veale's name worked magic at the stage door of the Concert Hall. Keys were immediately conjured up and I was escorted to the top floor of the Ballet Centre and admitted to the deserted offices. The list of grant recipients was where I had left it. And Marcus Taylor's name was on it. Professional support, $2000.

Not exactly a king's ransom, but as a free gift it was a damned sight more generous than a poke in the eye with a burnt stick. By the standards of Joanna Public and her overtaxed consort, it might even teeter dangerously close to the edge of government extravagance. A layabout artist could be drinking red wine out of the public trough for six months with a cheque like that.

Swinging my feet up onto the desk, I let a contented smile settle over my lips. From a PR point of view, Agnelli now had an ace up his sleeve that could be played if the media decided there was mileage to be had from the starving-artist-versus-government-indifference issue. Not that it was likely it would ever come to that. My advice to Ange would be to keep his head down for a couple of days and wait for the whole thing to blow over.

I picked up the list again. While I was on the job, I might as well do it properly. So far, all I knew about this Marcus Taylor was that he tended to histrionics, had a poor sense of balance and had ruined my plans for the previous evening. Quietly aching parts of my own anatomy told me that much. Information of an official nature might be more useful. You can't have too much information. Beside the names on the grants list were reference numbers. Everything I had seen so far of Phillip Veale suggested he ran a tight ship. Somewhere in these offices would be a file containing Taylor's application form.

A cluster of glass-walled boxes, the last word in office design, occupied the whole top floor. At intervals, the layout was punctuated by small sky-lit enclosures, carpeted in white gravel, containing sculptural objects. Ministry management, slaving over a hot memo, needed only raise its jaded eye to find inspiration in an artful agglomeration of whitewashed driftwood or fluorescent space junk. The central registry, down the back beside the lunchroom, held a less encouraging sight—the latest in filing systems, securely locked.

But the offices of the executive staff were wide open. Within half an hour I was sitting at the desk of the Deputy Director Programs, thumbing through an overstuffed file containing the recommendations of the Visual Arts Advisory Panel. Attached to Marcus Taylor's application form was an envelope containing a set of colour slides and an assessment note from Peggy Wainright. She was the one, if memory served me right, in the kinte cloth headdress and Ubangi jewellery.

I took the file back to the minister's office and started reading. I'd got as far as lighting a cigarette when the phone rang. 'What do you want first?' It was Ken Sproule. 'The forensics or the hysterics?'

The coroner's office, alert to the attention a death like this would draw, had been working overtime.

'One of two things can happen when you drown,' explained Sproule. 'Either you take a great big gulp and fill your lungs with fluid. Or you thrash about sucking in air and fill your plumbing with froth and foam until you choke. This bloke did the first. He also had a blood alcohol content of .35 per cent, which means he was pretty whacked when he hit the water. On the medical evidence, opinion is currently divided as to whether the death was accidental or intentional. It's up to the coroner to decide. The balance of probabilities, however, tends to favour suicide, given the note found near the body.

And so to the nub of the matter. 'What's it say?'

'Nothing you might call brilliantly lucid. Lots of crossing out, spelling mistakes, abbreviations. But then the guy was a painter, after all. It's a wonder he could read and write. But he had a chip on his shoulder about something, that's for sure. Listen to this.

'*You so-called experts of the art world,*' Sproule quoted. '*You curators and bureaucrats who hold yourselves up as the arbiters and judges. You big-spending speculators and collectors who do not even know what you are buying. You are all allowing yourselves to be deceived and defrauded.*

'*I take this action to arouse public attention to this pretence, perpetrated in the name of art. Those with their hands on the levers of power are the most corrupt of all.*

'*You who have seen fit to dismiss my work yet do not recognise what is before your very eyes. Who is embarrassed now?*'

As I rapidly jotted this down, it was as though I could hear again the hysterical voice of the figure on the table at the Centre for Modern Art. And I could see, too, the hang-dog look on his face as he passed me in Domain Road, trudging towards his death.

'In short,' concluded Sproule. 'The immemorial whine of the failed artist. I dunno where those journos got their bullshit line about a protest against lack of funding. The stiff didn't say anything about the government. Not so much as a whiff of swamp gas.'

Back at the electorate office, I'd heard plenty worse from disaffected punters every day of the week. And none of them had killed themselves, even if they sometimes made me wish they would. 'Anything else of interest turn up? Personal background, psychiatric history?' Perhaps the artistic temperament was more fragile.

'No criminal priors. Always the possibility he was a registered nutcase, I suppose,' said Sproule, optimistically. 'We won't know for a few days yet. What about the grant application?'

'You were right,' I told him. 'No reason for him to be feeling sorry for himself on our account. We gave him $2000 last November. Nothing more life-affirming than free money.'

That about covered the political aspect, such as it was. Any journalist trying to claim that Marcus Taylor had a legitimate grievance against the government would be drawing a very long bow indeed. 'The story will blow over in a couple of days,' said Sproule. 'If the press try to shift any shit our way in the meantime, we'll be ready.' On that up-beat note, he rang off.

Sproule had come up with a pretty fair haul. Any other

useful background would be in the grant assessment file in front of me.

This is Taylor's fifth application for a Creative Development Grant in the last five years, wrote the Visual Arts Executive Officer. *He is a proficient draughtsman whose work is executed in a highly technically competent manner. There is, however, general critical agreement that it lacks originality and vision. Very derivative. Applicant has been unable to secure representation by any commercial gallery. Recommend reject application.*

Poor prick. It was enough to make anyone want to slash his wrists. According to the application form, he'd shown his work only a couple of times in the previous year, at group exhibitions in regional civic centres—only a short step away from hobby painter shows in shopping malls. DOB 1953, Katoomba, NSW. An unfinished fine arts diploma at Sydney Tech. Address: care of YMCA building. Although he claimed to be painting full-time, his principal source of income was cited as unemployment benefits. The grant was sought to pay for materials.

Despite the executive officer's negative recommendation, the panel had approved a small grant, less than a quarter of what Taylor had asked for. Reading between the lines, I detected a kiss-off, a few crumbs of conscience money to get rid of a nuisance. Either that, or Taylor knew someone on the panel prepared to go into bat for him. I flicked to the front of the file and read the membership list. There were only two names I recognised: Salina Fleet and Lloyd Eastlake. Salina, presumably, had persuaded her fellow panel members that her boyfriend's talent was worth throwing a small bone at.

A sad story but a closed book. When I met Agnelli in two hours, I'd be able to advise him that Taylor's potential nuisance value was negligible.

Tossing the file back where it belonged, I shut the office door behind me and headed down three floors to the carpark. Now that I knew a little more about Marcus Taylor, I found myself increasingly sympathetic to the poor bugger. The man was obviously a social misfit. Spurned by the critics, ignored by buyers, barely qualifying for an official handout, snubbed by a gallery full of art-lovers, dumped by his girlfriend. Talk about suffering for your art. The only thing missing was the garret.

Or was it? The address he gave on his grant application was the YMCA, the ruin next door, so close it would've been cheaper to hand-deliver the letter than pay the postage. And certainly faster. But the YMCA had been derelict for years, slated for demolition as part of the Arts City development. Surely he wasn't living there? Shit, I could just see it: Drowned Artist Squatted in Shadow of Lavish Arts Bureaucracy.

I rode the lift to street level, walked through the parked cars, turned left and looked up. In its heyday, the Y must have been an impressive pile. Seven storeys tall, V-shaped, city views. But the tide had long since gone out, and now it had nothing to look forward to this side of demolition. Peeling grey paint and a hundred grimy windows. But apparently still in use. Although the street-level doors were bricked up, a set of stairs led to a first-floor entrance, a heavy door painted with the Ministry for the Arts logo: a pair of tragi-comic masks surmounted by dancing semi-quavers above a crossed pen and paintbrush.

The door was locked. As I turned away, it abruptly swung open and a hunched spine backed out. It belonged to a spotty youth with an armload of music stands. He propped the door open with the stands, went back in, re-emerged with a violin case in each hand. 'Do you mind?' He held the cases out from his sides and nodded at the music stands. I tucked them up under his armpits, holding the door open with my shoulder. 'If you're looking for Environmental,' he said, pleased to be the bearer of bad news. 'They've already left.'

'I'm looking for someone who lives here,' I said.

He gave me a queer look. 'Bit late for that. Nobody's lived here for years. It's cheap storage now. Rehearsal rooms. Office space for low-budget arts organisations. Artist studios.' He stood there, waiting for me to close the door.

'I might just look about, then,' I said.

'I'm afraid I can't allow that,' he said pompously. 'Tenant

access only at the weekend.'

What was he going to do? Deck me with a Stradivarius?

'Won't be long.' I stepped sideways into the building and the door swung shut behind me.

An ill-lit vestibule faced an ancient cage-type elevator, its oily cables caked with grime. Exhausted linoleum covered the floor. Stairs ran up and down on either side of the lift and a poky corridor extended back into the building, punctuated by doors at regular intervals. The whole place had been painted with mushroom soup at the time of the Wall Street Crash and not swept since the Fall of Singapore. About twenty tenants were listed on a directory board, the names spelled out in movable letters, subject to availability. Th*' Orph*us Ch*ir, J*llyw*gs The*tre *n Educ*tion Tr*up*, Comm*nity Ar*s *nform*tion *esource *ntre, Let's D*nce Victor, Environ Men*l Puppets, Ac*ss Stud*os.

This last item, third floor, struck me as the best prospect. The elevator seemed a bit iffy, so I took the stairs. The third-floor corridor was a dingy passage indistinguishable from those on the floors below, a receding horizon of peeling lino and numbered doors with smoked-glass panels. I started knocking, raising an echo but nothing else. The whole building had a forsaken air. 'Hello,' I called, tentative at first, then hiking up the volume. My voice came back at me, unanswered. I'd worked my way nearly the full length of the corridor, knocking and trying door handles, before one of them gave.

What I found could not have looked more like an artist's studio if the Art Directors' Guild had whipped it up for a production of *La Boheme*. Every inch of the place was crammed with canvases, crinkled tubes of paint, jars of used brushes, stepladders, casually discarded sketches, stubs of charcoal. Paint spills Jackson Pollock would have been proud of lay thick on the floor. Mounted on an easel in the centre of the room was an example of the resident artist's work.

The subject was the quintessential suburban dream home of the nineteen fifties. Cream brick-veneer, red tile roof, green front lawn, cloudless sky. The style was photo-realist, hyper-realist, super-realist, whatever they call it. An exact rendering, anyway. Sharply vivid. Perfect in every detail, a real-estate agent's vision splendid. Crowning this ideal, a lovely finishing touch, was a lawn-mower, a spanking new Victa two-stroke, sitting in the middle of the lawn. Although its topic was utterly banal, the picture was oddly disturbing, as though this commonplace scene contained within it a secret of some deep malevolence.

But I wasn't there to immerse myself in art. I tore myself away and continued my search. Half-concealed behind a heavy curtain was a hole in the wall, a short cut into the adjacent room. This was furnished as living quarters, rough but not entirely squalid. There was a small enamel sink, a trestle table with a gas camping-stove, a microwave oven and a rack of op-shop crockery. A futon on a slatted wooden base. A vinyl-covered club armchair. A brick-and-board bookcase filled with large-format colour-plate art books, filed by artist, Australians mainly. Brack, Boyd, Nolan, Pugh, Williams. Empty bottles, six wine, two vodka. An overfilled garbage bag, a little on the nose in the heat. At the window, a metal two-drawer desk and typist's chair. Home sweet home. But whose?

Moving quickly now, feeling like a burglar, I crossed to the desk. It was covered with loose sheets of doodled-on tracing paper, drafting pens, erasers, crayons, chinagraph pencils, note pads. Nothing to indicate the occupant's name.

I slid open the top drawer. A bulldog clip of receipts from Dean's Artist Supplies. An art materials price-list. Envelopes containing colour transparencies of artworks, pictures of pictures, each labelled with a name. Familiar names from the bookcase. Beneath this clutter, held together by a paperclip, were three photographs. The first was old, the print dog-eared, square, black-and-white, a Box Brownie snap. A pretty teenager, full-faced, her hair permed for home defence. The next was also black-and-white, but glossier, a fifties feel. A man and a woman standing at a scenic lookout, a row of mountain peaks arrayed along the horizon behind them. The Twelve Apostles, the Seven Sisters, the Three Musketeers, somewhere famous. It was the same woman, now a twenty-year-old sophisticate in twin-set and pleated skirt, the man in baggy trousers and a beret. The pair of them relaxed, joky, hamming it up for the camera. Lovers. I had no idea who they were.

The last print was colour, curved corners. A young man with shoulder-length hair and wire-rimmed glasses standing in a row of corn, hoe in hand, bare to the waist, the original ninety-pound weakling. Beside him, leaning on a fork, an older man, barrel-chested, high-scalped. The face unshaven, bags under the eyes, but the same comic tufts above the ears, the same brazen stare as I had seen on Fiona Lambert's mantelpiece. Victor Szabo.

The hippy could have been Marcus Taylor. He had the same elongated face, the same feral intensity. It could have been any-one. I held the photo motionless, observing from a great height, staring down like a bird floating on a thermal, waiting for some-thing to reveal itself.

Nothing did. I was asleep on my feet, miserably hungover. I opened the second drawer, working quickly, feeling furtive. A stamp album, most pages still empty. The few stamps it held were all Australian, low denominations. All bore the Bicentenary logo of 1988. Last year's issues. Hand-written anno-tations in tiny print. Whoever lived here was no great philatelist. A new hobby, perhaps, the interest unsustained. Wedged into the back of the album was a bank passbook. I slipped it out of its plastic cover, flipped it open and read the name.

Marcus Taylor. Bingo.

The dead have no privacy. I thumbed blank pages, looking for a balance. Thunk. Whirr. Somebody had started the eleva-tor. It shuddered and lurched upwards, the sound magnified in the deserted building.

Startled by the sudden noise, I dropped the bankbook. It fell down the gap between the desk and the wall. I began to go down on my knees to retrieve it until it occurred to me that this was probably the police, come to examine the deceased's effects. I felt like a tomb robber. Not that I was doing anything wrong. It's just that I would have been hard put to explain exactly what I was doing. It was, I rapidly concluded, one of those situations where discretion was the better part of anything else you might care to mention.

Dumping the rest of the stuff back into the drawer, I stepped out the door. Down the hallway, the lift groaned and shuddered to a halt, a vague shape behind the grille. Immediately in front of me, a rubbish bin propped open a door marked Fire Escape. The layout of the building suggested these stairs opened onto the adjoining lane. I took them two at a time, scattering litter.

Three flights down, where the street exit should have been, the wall had been bricked up. Half a flight further, they ended at a large door. *Environ Mental Puppet Company*, it said. Beyond, a broad corridor lined with age-speckled white tiles extended towards the vague glow of daylight.

I pressed on, and had taken perhaps a dozen steps when a sudden draft of air stirred the grime at my feet. A pneumatic woomph sounded in my ears. I swung around just in time to see the door slam shut behind me. It was some sort of fire door, steel, fitting snugly into a metal frame. There was no handle on my side.

'Hey,' I shouted, and banged the palms of my hands against the flat metal plate. 'Hey.' There was no answer.

I balled my fist and banged again. The heavy steel reverberated with a dull echo, but there was still no answer. Either a draught in the stairwell had slammed the door shut or somebody was playing funny buggers. If I wanted out of this dump, I'd have to find another way.

Giving the door one last futile kick, I turned and headed along the corridor. Its white-tiled walls, even in their grimy state, reminded me of a hospital or a science laboratory, a place of bodily messes and antiseptic solutions. Even the air seemed to have a faintly pervasive chemical odour, as fusty as the cracked porcelain of the tiles. I soon discovered why.

The wide passageway opened abruptly into a cavernous basement, also lined with decrepit white tiles. Sunlight, struggling through a row of frosted windows high up in one wall, illuminated the room with its pallid wash. Occupying almost the entire space was a gigantic cement pit.

Great scabs of peeling green paint clung to its walls like clumps of dried lichen. Overlapping the edge of the huge trough, at the far end of the room, was a tangle of corroded pipes. Attached to the decaying metalwork was a sign. DANGER, it said. NO DIVING. POOL CLOSED. Lying on the bottom of the empty swimming pool, right in the middle, was a body.

Numerous bodies, actually. But the one that grabbed my attention was the whale. It was life-sized, aqua blue and made of fibreglass. Scattered around it was a pod of papier-mâché dolphins, several dozen polystyrene starfish mounted on bamboo poles, innumerable cardboard scallop shells, piles of flags and pendants embroidered with sea-horses, and a pair of hammerhead sharks made of lycra and chicken wire.

But none of these were as compelling as the whale. Painted across its deep-sea dial was an idiotic anthropomorphic grin. I was buggered if I could figure out why it was smiling, though. It was high and dry, and so was I.

The only other exit was a roller door, big enough for a truck and battened down with more locksmithery than Alcatraz. Through the narrow gap at the bottom, I could just make out the surface of a laneway. Blasts of hot air were already rising from the asphalt. I rattled the roller a few times and gave a yell, but there was nobody outside to hear.

Next door was a long-disused changing room with vandalised lockers and ancient urinals full of desiccated deodorant balls. I tore a length of iron pipe from the wall of a shower recess. When I bashed it against the fire door, it produced considerably more noise than anything I'd been able to raise with my bare hands. Loud enough to make the blood in my temples throb and showers of sparks shoot into my eyes. But not loud enough, apparently, to be heard by anyone else in the building. I bashed away for a fair while, but all I got was a tired arm and an even more aggravated headache. The door was thicker than a Colleen McCullough novel. I could have banged away all day and not got a result.

I carefully explored the whole place again. The only potential exit was the windows. They appeared to be unlocked. They were also six metres up a sheer wall.

It had just gone 9.15 a.m. The situation was beginning to give me the shits. This whole spur-of-the-moment garret-rifling expedition had been of questionable value in the first place. And taking off like a sprung burglar had only made things worse. At this rate, I'd be locked in all weekend. I slumped down beside the wall and lit an aid to clear thinking, my second last.

Bone weariness and enraged irritation fought for control of my body, equally matched. I jumped up, sat down, jumped up again. That little smartarse with the armful of violins had done this. Finally, I collapsed back against the wall and drew what comfort I could from my cigarette. If I'd been the Prime Minister, I'd have cried from sheer self-pity.

Agnelli had got me into this mess, waking me up with his paranoia, sending me to hose down imaginary threats to his public image. Nor was the Premier blameless. If he hadn't decided to reshuffle the Cabinet, I wouldn't have been compelled to change jobs. And if that hadn't happened, I wouldn't have a hangover and be locked in the storage facility of a marine-fixated puppet company.

Who was I trying to fool? Sleuthing around in a brain-dead state for no good reason, it was my own damned fault that I'd managed to get myself in this situation.

In a little over ninety minutes I was due to meet Agnelli, brief him on Taylor's suicide note and escort him to Max Karlin's brunch. A side trip to the supermarket in the interim was beginning to look unlikely. Not that Red would need any groceries, not where he'd be. Standing in an airport lounge waiting in vain for his father to arrive. 'I was only two days late,' I could hear myself grovelling down the phone to Wendy. 'You didn't have to tell the airline people to put him on the next plane back to Sydney.'

When my cigarette was smoked down to its stub, I ground it out on the dirty cement floor and began gnawing at my fingernails. For the first time since the previous evening in Fiona Lambert's flat, I thought about the cut on my finger. Peeling away the flesh-toned plastic strip, I examined my wound. The skin was wrinkled and bleached, the cut shrivelled to a tiny slit. My finger looked like a sea slug, horrible little mouth and all. Very appropriate, I thought. The way things were going, I might as well be part of the flotsam and jetsam in the bottom of the pool.

Hard against the wall immediately beneath the windows was a work bench littered with piles of fabric, tangled chicken wire, bits and pieces of half-made piscine puppets. Maybe I could find enough timber among all this parade-float junk to rig up some sort of ladder. If I got as far as window level, I could perhaps find a handy drainpipe to climb down. On a building this old, the plumbing was bound to be external.

But the only timber at the bottom of the pool was bamboo, flimsy shafts with polystyrene starfish jammed on the end. I went around the back of Willy the Whale and stuck my head into his rear-end aperture. More parade paraphernalia had been dumped inside—jellyfish costumes of green and blue lycra, papier-mache fish masks, plastic sheeting cut up into seaweed shapes, bicycle helmets with fin attachments. Beneath all of this, I found two lengths of aluminium tubing.

Thick as my wrist and about three metres long, they were painted a mottled greyish-blue and tipped with rubber. This was promising. Grabbing a pole in each hand, I backed out the whale's bum, dragging them after me. First came the poles. Then a set of rubberised fishing waders. Then a bulbous blob covered in blue and grey fabric. Then some kind of bodysuit covered with strips of coloured plastic. Then a tangle of foam-covered wire.

I hauled the whole rigmarole up beside the pool and examined it. Metal plates in the insoles of the waders were riveted onto matching plates welded onto the aluminium struts. The bodysuit, complete with foam-rubber midriff, was sewn securely onto the waders. The result was a octopus costume on stilts. The artistry was truly execrable, but the engineering was superb. So much so that it was impossible to detach the poles. Great. Just what I needed. An Oscar the frigging Octopus suit.

Propped against the wall, the aluminium shafts reached only halfway to the windows. My ladder project was shaping up as a dead end. At this rate, I'd be here for the rest of my life. I returned to the fire door, picked up the iron pipe and pounded away in futile rage. Then I spent fifteen minutes trying to lever the bolts off the roller door. I smoked my last cigarette and realised I was hungry. If this Prisoner of Zenda crap went on much longer, I'd be reduced to drinking my own urine. Eventually, like a dog to its dinner, I went back to Oscar.

All my previous stilt experience had been on jam-tin-and-string models when I was about six years old. Octopus costume aside, these babies were the real thing, fully three metres tall. Even if I managed to get myself upright, I'd still need to be standing on the bench to reach the window sill. A fall from that height would do nothing to improve my general well-being.

On the other hand, I had to do something. The Environ Mental Puppeteers might not be back for days. The jerk with the violins said they'd left already. He didn't say where to. Maybe they were on an international tour. Taking the best of the worst of Australian artistry to the world.

Oscar was mostly foam rubber. A big foam rubber cocoon. So if I fell, as long as I didn't topple over the edge into the pool, the damage would probably be limited. A fractured skull, a broken neck. Nothing I couldn't live with. In a wheelchair. If only I had a few more cigarettes. Just one, even.

I sat on the floor, took my shoes and pants off, stuck my legs into the trouser part of the waders and hoisted the engorged champignon bit up around my waist. The toes pinched, but the fit wasn't too bad. Tugging the straps of the overall part over my shoulders, I wiggled my arms down the sleeves and into the washing-up gloves sewn on the ends. A cowl sort of thing fitted over my head, held in place by velcro tabs. The rubbery waders made my legs tacky with sweat and a necklace of tentacles dangled to my knees. I felt vaguely fetishistic. Christ alone knew what I looked like.

So there I was, disguised as a giant cephalopod, flat on my back beside a dehydrated aquatic facility in a derelict cultural resource centre, with absolutely no idea of what to do next. When I'd taken on the job of adviser to the Minister for the Arts,

I somehow hadn't imagined myself in such a position. If this didn't work, I swore, I would make it my personal mission as a senior government functionary to see that the Environ Mental Puppet Company never again received a penny of public funding.

Now that I was togged up, there was nothing for it but to proceed. Grabbing a leg of the bench, I dragged myself upright. Then, flailing my many appendages, I swept the tabletop clear and climbed aboard. By extending the blue poles behind me and pressing my palms flat against the wall, I could form a reasonably stable triangle.

Thus I advanced, palms splayed out before me. Little hop, inch. Little hop, inch. Palming myself along like Marcel Marceau trying to get out of that fucking invisible box of his. The trick with stilts, in case you ever need to know, is to stay in motion. Much like a bicycle. Or politics. Stand still and you're stuffed. Keep moving or you take a dive.

By the time I was five metres up, my priorities review committee had urgently convened. Second thoughts were in the majority. I was bathed in sweat, my arms were aching from the effort, and my sea slug was throbbing. But it wasn't just the prospect of crashing to the floor in a welter of shattered vertebrae and ruptured organs that was urging me to reconsider my strategy. A structural flaw in the plan had became obvious. The transom was rigged to open only part of the way. Even if I managed to get as far as the sill and push the window open, the gap was too narrow to admit a man with a blue rubber mattress strapped to his midriff.

Just your head and shoulders will be enough, I told myself. Even in a precinct teeming with cultural offerings, the spectacle of a man in an octopus suit sandwiched into a window frame could not pass unnoticed for long. Eventually a passer-by would see me, realise I was not an art object and mount a rescue effort.

Grunting, I pressed on. Finally my fingers closed around the metal of the window frame. Pushing the transom open with my beak, I wriggled forward. Somewhere far below, my stilt feet lifted off the floor. My head and shoulders poked through. My position was as tenuous as the Liberal Party leadership, but at least now I had an outside chance of hailing somebody.

Immediately across from my vantage point was the saw-toothed roof of a warehouse, closed for the weekend. Below me was the narrow street I had glimpsed from beneath the roller door. It was an access lane to the warehouse. Not much hope of passing traffic at this hour on a Saturday morning. Not that I knew the hour, not with any precision. My watch, along with my wrist, was encased in latex. But I knew that if I didn't get noticed soon, I might as well throw myself from the window and be done with it. If I didn't meet Agnelli I wouldn't have a job. And if I wasn't at the airport on time my life wouldn't be worth living. Except that I couldn't even get far enough into the window frame to defenestrate myself.

My only hope was the building next door, the Ballet Centre. Its parking levels were faced with vertical steel slats. By pushing myself out the window as far as possible and swivelling sideways, I could just make out a row of parked cars. Eventually somebody would come to collect one of them. Then all I had to do was shout loudly. And hope that whoever heard me would have the sense to stick his head over the edge of the parking deck and look sideways.

As luck would have it, I didn't have to wait long. My vigil had scarcely begun when a figure appeared, an indistinct shape bobbing between the cars. 'Hey,' I yelled, and waved my tentacles.

The shape passed out of sight, then appeared again, partly obscured by a concrete column. He was bending, his head in the boot of a car. Then he stood up. He was hard against the periphery of my vision but there was no mistaking that rear profile, that head like a wing-nut.

'Hey,' I bawled. 'Over here. Noel. Mate.'

At fifteen, Spider was a seasoned drinker, or so he claimed. A man with established tastes. Southern Comfort, he reckoned, was cough syrup. Cat's piss. A man of his experience knew what he wanted. Bourbon. Jack Daniels. In return, I need never worry about the Fletchers again. The Fletchers kept a respectful distance from Spider. He'd done boxing. 'You look after me,' he said. 'I'll look after you.'

Southern Comfort would be easier, I argued. Or Bundaberg rum. The pub sold a fair bit of those. But protection never comes cheap. So, in the end, bourbon it was. Jim Beam. A 'breakage' off the top shelf, syphoned into a Marchants lemonade bottle while I was polishing the mirrors in the saloon bar and Dad was downstairs tapping a keg. Not Jack Daniels but I hoped Spider wouldn't notice the difference.

The handover was to be in the Oulton Reserve, the local football oval, after training on Thursday night. Not that either of us was in the team, but going to watch the Under-19s train was a good thing to tell a father. What could be more innocent? It was all pretty innocent, I suppose. Until the Fletchers turned up.

'Hey, you,' I bellowed desperately, wrenching the sound up from the bottom of my lungs and waving a blue rubber glove.

'Over here. Noel.' At least I thought it was Noel. He'd moved out of sight again.

'Spider!' I tried, hoping to trigger a primal reaction. 'Help! Heeelp!' The cry was as loud as I could make it. My head spun from the effort. It sounded pretty loud to me, but so did the trucks shifting gears on City Road. Oblivious to my impassioned cries, the figure was moving away. 'Help,' I bawled.

It was a waste of breath. The head bobbed down, a door slammed, a moving vehicle flickered momentarily in the shadows behind the screen of steel slats and the carpark was still again.

It remained that way for what seemed a very long time. Nobody else came. Nobody else went. Not in the carpark, at least. Down below in the laneway, a minibus drove briskly by, a cricket team of teenage boys hanging out the windows. I waved my tentacles at the flash of upturned faces, but all I got in return was the collective finger.

Unless somebody saw me soon, I'd be spending the rest of my life on my knees before Wendy with gravel rash on my forehead. No, to do that I'd have to get down first. I didn't even have a cigarette to console me. And even if I did, I wouldn't be able to get my tentacle up to my beak to inhale. I decided I had better prospects at floor level, banging on one of the doors.

To descend from my perch, I had to turn around, press my back to the wall, and execute a controlled slide. Controlled being the key word. Halfway down, the foot of one of the stilts caught in a snarl of chicken wire lying beside the work bench. Off balance, I pitched forward. Suddenly, I was standing upright, clear of the wall, with no way of maintaining my balance but by taking the next step. Then the next. Then the next.

I was stilt-walking. Look Mum, no hands. No place to go, either. Arms helicoptering madly through the air, I tottered forward—towards the rim of the empty pool.

Then Willy rose and swallowed me whole. One moment I was looking down at him from a great height. The next I was in his belly, staring up at a gaping hole in his back. There was a sharp but momentary pain in my left ear. Plunging over the edge, I had crashed straight through the whale's thin fibreglass shell. Luckily, Oscar's copious contents helped break my fall. I had landed on a pile of stuffed squid. I was winded, upside-down and my legs were twisted together, but otherwise I was intact. Willy, for his part, was now the only whale in captivity with a sunroof.

All but hysterical with relief, I jettisoned my ludicrous padding and crawled out the whale's backside. I could have been killed. I was lucky to be alive.

I clambered out of the pool and put on my trousers and shoes. My hands were palpitating so wildly I could barely tie the laces. I breathed deeply to calm down and gave myself a quick once-over. No broken bones, but my explosion through Willy's carapace had done something to my ear. It was bleeding profusely.

I found a crumpled rag and clutched it to my earhole. Then I picked up the iron pipe and began bashing the fire door. I guess I must have lost it there for a while. I was stir crazy. Cabin fever had me in its grip. I may have even been howling. I wanted out and if need be I'd bludgeon my way through three inches of steel plate. I bashed until my arm went numb and bells rang in my brain.

Eventually, worn out, I collapsed against the door. Through the metal, I heard the grind of a bolt being drawn. 'Yeah, yeah,' a woman's voice was saying, irritably. 'Take it easy.'

The door swung backwards to reveal Salina Fleet.

But not the Sal I'd been fumbling in the forget-me-nots. Nor the freaked-out Salina lit by the ambulance light at the moat. This Salina was very sober and very proper. A woman who had made up her mind about something. Gidget was gone. This Salina wore calf-length culottes, a fawn blouse and black button earrings, not a hair out of place. This Salina was so composed she could have read the Channel 10 news.

She took a step backwards. In my panting, dishevelled state, I must have been quite a sight. And not a welcome one. 'What are *you* doing here?'

Snooping through your deceased boyfriend's personal effects did not, somehow, seem like the appropriate answer. Already it was clear that what had occurred between us last night was ancient history, a dead letter. The fire was well and truly out. Our little nocturnal nature ramble was a temporary lapse to which neither of us would again refer. Nothing had happened. Nothing ever would.

'The minister wants a report,' I said, self-importantly. 'On under-utilised Arts Ministry facilities.' Hand pressed to ear, I must have looked like a harmonising Bee Gee. 'I was sent on a tour of inspection. A tenant got hostile and locked me in. You didn't see him, did you? A guy with an armful of violins.'

Salina shook her head, and cocked it sideways in disbelief. To think, her eyes seemed to say, I nearly took this lunatic to bed.

'What about you?' I asked. The pretence begun, I had no option but to continue. 'What are you doing here?'

She cast her gaze downwards and adopted a sombre tone. 'Marcus's studio is upstairs.'

I nodded understandingly and stepped forward, moving us onward from the doorway. 'He was the one at the exhibition last night, on the table, wasn't he?' I said. 'I'm sorry. I didn't realise, I mean...'

She maintained her aloof solemnity. 'No need to apologise. You weren't to know.'

'I mean I'm sorry about Marcus,' I said, gently correcting her. As far as I knew, I didn't have anything to apologise for.

'Thank you.' She spoke formally, bowing her head slightly. Rehearsing, I realised, the role of the grieving widow graciously accepting condolences.

'It was on the radio. You were mentioned, too.'

'Ah.' This information did not entirely displease her. 'So soon?'

She turned and began back up the stairs, as if trying to put an interruption behind her. She was carrying a folio case, the sort art students and advertising types use. Evidently she had just arrived at the YMCA and my banging had distracted her from her objective. When we reached the ground floor corridor, she stopped at the open door, anticipating my departure. Up in the harsher light, there was a fragility to her. She'd probably got even less sleep than me. The strain was showing. I reached over and touched her arm. 'You okay?'

She jerked away, then softened. 'I'm fine. Really I am.' She squeezed out a pained little smile.

I didn't want her thinking I was coming on to her. We stood uncomfortably in the doorway, each waiting for the other to move. I could feel her impatience growing. 'Here to collect some personal things, are you?' I asked.

She nodded, relieved at the explanation. At the same time, she shrugged the fact into wounded insignificance, as though I was trampling on a small private grief.

It was 10.30. That gave me just enough time to get to Parliament House to meet Agnelli. But not with a bloodied rag gripped to my auditory apparatus. I needed water and a mirror and the only place I knew for sure I'd find them was Marcus Taylor's room. 'I'll give you a hand,' I said. 'The artists' studios are on the third floor, aren't they?' I started up the stairs. 'According to the board at the front door.'

Helping myself to the dead boyfriend's personal facilities was not, I knew, the most sensitive move possible. On the other hand, all this holier-than-thou stuff was beginning to rankle. I'd be buggered if I was going to be made to feel like the guilty party here.

'No. Don't.' Salina dashed after me. 'I'll be okay, really,' she protested.

The door of Marcus Taylor's bedroom sat open to the corridor. 'This it?' I said. I headed directly for the small enamel basin. Drying blood caked my ear but a little water confirmed that the damage was only skin deep. My eyes were sinkholes and I had the complexion of a piece of candied pineapple.

Over my shoulder in the mirror, I saw Salina come in and glance around anxiously. As far as I could see, there was no evidence of feminine habitation in the place. For rough-and-ready accommodation, the joint had a certain masculine sufficiency. But I couldn't imagine a woman here. A forest floor was one thing, but this was the pits.

'Don't mind me,' I said. The tin cabinet behind the mirror held shaving gear, out-of-date antibiotics, Dettol, cotton-wool, a roll of adhesive bandage. Salina laid the folio case flat on the futon bed. 'Just a few private effects, is it?'

For some reason, she resented this remark. 'Now that Marcus is dead,' she said, defensively, 'people will be curious about his work. The least I can do is see that it is presented to the world in a favourable light.'

Without turning, I held my hands up in a placatory gesture. 'Hey,' I agreed. 'You don't have to explain yourself to me.' The sharp bite of antiseptic brought tears to my eyes.

Suddenly, all of Salina's freshly cultivated reserve was gone. She slumped down on the edge of the bed and began tearing the wrapper off a pack of cigarettes. 'I should have seen it coming,' she said, her voice thick with self-recrimination. 'Marcus was so depressed and moody lately, drinking a lot, complaining that everyone was against him. I did what I could, even used my influence to get him a grant, but it didn't make any difference. You saw what he was like last night. I told him I was sick of his self-indulgence. Now I keep thinking that's what pushed him over the edge. It's all my fault.'

Black smudges ringed her eyes. Exhaustion and rattiness engulfed both of us. She lit a cigarette, sucked at it hungrily, openly trawling for sympathy. Considering what had almost happened between us, I owed her that much.

Tearing the adhesive tape with my teeth, I patched my ear as best I could. Then, compelled by a weariness as irresistible as gravity, I sank down on the other side of the bed. 'Don't blame yourself,' I said. 'Perhaps it was an accident. He was pretty drunk. He could have fallen in. Perhaps he didn't mean to kill himself.'

She tried without success to make her bottom lip quiver.

'Oh, no,' she said firmly. 'It was definitely suicide. The police showed me a note he left, asked me to identify the handwriting. It was definitely his. His style, too. That litany of complaints. I told them I thought he was probably a manic depressive. He certainly had a tendency to self-dramatisation. That's why I did-n't take any particular notice last night. More of the usual crap, I thought. Told him I'd had enough, it was over between us.'

I helped myself to one of her cigarettes, drawing sustenance from it, oblivious to the vile taste. A scarifying sunlight poured in the window, the window at which Taylor must have conceived his own death, his artistic auto-da-fé. It was a strange feeling, sit-ting there amid the scant domesticity of a dead man I had never really met.

'He was illegitimate, you know,' Salina blurted, offering the fact as if in mitigation. 'A lot of unresolved emotional trauma bubbling away. And his work. He felt the rejection of his work deeply.'

She was veering dangerously close to the maudlin. I sensed that, now the facade was down, she'd keep talking until she got it all out. Not that I was insensitive or anything, but my time was not entirely my own. If I didn't start disengaging, I'd be there all day.

'Forget the souvenirs.' A few scraps of paper weren't worth the aggravation. What she needed was to go home and sleep. 'Come back another time.' Grinding my fag underfoot, I hauled myself into the vertical and held out my hand.

Salina remained where she was. She shook her head. 'You've been sweet,' she said. 'But if you don't mind, I'd like to be left alone.'

I'm not an entirely insensitive person. I nodded and turned to leave, stepping towards the curtain covering the hole into the studio. 'I'll go this way.'

Sal was on her feet in a flash, interposing herself between me and the curtain. 'I feel so bad,' she said. 'About last night.'

She stood very close and put her hand on my arm. Sliding it downwards, she found my hand and squeezed it. Then her head was against my chest, looking upwards into my eyes. Her body moulded itself to mine. She sighed deeply.

Her change of mood was abrupt and disconcerting. But, like I said, I'm not an entirely insensitive guy. I put my arms around her.

Her hand snaked up my back. She stood on tiptoes and pressed the back of my head down towards her closing eyes and opening lips. I kissed her. Compassionately at first. Then, at her insistence, the other way.

Then she peeped and I could see it in her eyes. It wasn't me that Salina desired. Nor was it my pity. She wanted my complicity. Complicity in what, I couldn't tell. But whatever it was, I didn't want any part of it. I prefer to save my cynicism for politics.

Putting my hands gently on her shoulders, I prised my face free. Salina stared up, not comprehending. 'It's okay,' she reassured me. 'My relationship with Marcus was all but over anyway. We weren't even sleeping together. Hadn't been for months.'

The last thing I wanted was the sordid details. I took a step backwards. 'I'll leave you to it,' I said, sweeping the curtain aside. 'Make sure you get everything before you go.'

I don't know why I said it. Taylor's lonely death, his relation-ship with Salina, had nothing to do with me. But my remark wasn't just sanctimonious. It was superfluous. There was nothing for her to get. The paintings that were strewn about Taylor's studio in such ill-ordered profusion just an hour before were gone, stripped off their stretchers or roughly cut from their frames. The easel in the middle of the room was empty, the suburban dream house vanished. While I'd been downstairs impersonating a seafood dinner, someone had cleaned the place out.

Salina stared at the looted room. On her face was the same appalled expression with which she had responded to Taylor's drunken speech at the Centre for Modern Art.

I didn't have the time, the energy or the inclination to keep up with Salina Fleet's emotional gymnastics. Stepping around the discarded struts of timber and upended jars of brushes, I continued into the hallway and down the stairs.

Marcus Taylor's work, it seemed, was finally in demand. Suicide was beginning to look like the smartest career move he ever made.

'It's about time!'

Agnelli cleared a pile of briefing papers off the back seat of the Fairlane and made room for me. We were due to meet at eleven. It was 11.09. Under the circumstances, I thought I'd done well.

'Jesus,' he said, as I finished giving Alan the address of Karlin's brunch and slid into the back seat. 'What happened to your ear? You look like Vincent bloody Van Gogh.' I wasn't going to begin to answer a remark like that.

And Agnelli didn't really want to discuss my aural health. His own welfare was preying on his mind. Ministerial impatience suffused the car's interior like oxygen in a bell jar. 'Those journos have been on the blower again. Now they're talking about allegations of corruption in the arts bureaucracy.'

We glided out the back gate of Parliament House and Alan turned the Fairlane towards West Melbourne. 'Those with their hands on the levers of power are the most corrupt of all,' I quoted.

'Who?' said Agnelli. 'What?'

'I think I've got it right.' I fished my scrawled copy of Taylor's note from my pocket.

Agnelli seized it, avid for the worst. A policy crisis, accusations of pork barrelling, being caught misleading parliament, these he could take in his stride. They were but grist to the mill of everyday politics. But a suicide note, a city landmark, a potential media feeding-frenzy—this was a volatile combination. Agnelli's most defensive political instincts were aroused. His lips moved as he read.

'This is the sort of story the press are going to milk for every possible angle,' I said. 'They're just rattling your cage, trying for a reaction, hoping to drum up a political angle where there isn't one.'

Agnelli corrugated his brow and peered down at the note as though he'd been dealt a very bad hand in Scrabble. 'This is garbage. Who is this guy anyway?'

'An unemployed artist,' I said. 'Possible psychiatric history.' Salina called him a manic depressive. I should have pressed her for details. 'We'll know for sure in a couple of days. The guy was broke, depressed about his work and shit-faced drunk. There's even a school of thought that the whole thing was an accident and the note just a circumstantial furphy. But given the location and the fact that he was a painter, a certain degree of media interest is inevitable. My bet is they'll swarm in the direction of the most obvious cliché—anguished artist dies of broken heart, his talent unrecognised in life.' Particularly with the nudge in that direction that Salina Fleet was already giving them. 'The whole thing will have blown over by this time next week.'

'Maybe.' Agnelli's brow unfurrowed slightly. 'But keep a close eye on it anyway. This sort of drivel is tabloid heaven.'

'If absolutely necessary,' I tossed in the clincher, 'we can discreetly let it be known that shortly before his death Taylor was allocated a small but generous Arts Ministry grant.'

A foxy light came into Agnelli's eyes. 'Now why didn't I think of that?'

The idea that I was being devious was doing wonders for Agnelli's morale. 'And to think I had reservations about offering you this job,' he muttered.

While I pondered that point, he moved on to the topic of our imminent destination. 'So what about this Max Karlin? The Jew from Central Casting, eh?' Two years in Ethnic Affairs had done nothing for Angelo's rougher edges.

'I met him briefly last night,' I said. 'Quite the philanthropist apparently.' This was intended as a fairly obvious prompt for Agnelli to come clean about his self-appointed fund-raising role. It didn't work. He kept his cards pressed silently to his chest. 'I told him how delighted you'd be to meet such a prominent contributor to the public good,' I tried.

'And so I will be.' Agnelli remained impenetrably bland. 'Better give me my starting orders.'

Madness, I told myself, sheer insanity. Here I was, stage-managing an encounter between a minister in an increasingly fragile government, a man to whom I owed my employment and my loyalty, and a wealthy businessman about whom I knew next to nothing. All with no better objective than having my fears confirmed that Agnelli was planning a new career as a bag-man.

'Essentially this is just a low-key meet-and-mingle,' I told him. 'Karlin is something of an art collector and the Centre for Modern Art has recently copped a fairly decent Arts Ministry grant to buy one of his pictures. Lloyd Eastlake, who chairs the CMA, is keen to see that the government gets its share of the credit. Understandably so, since he was also on the Arts Ministry committee that recommended the purchase.'

Eastlake's name was another obvious cue, a little reminder to Agnelli that he had not yet told me about the threesome in his office the previous afternoon. If Angelo wanted to limit my role to strictly arts matters, that was his prerogative. He was the minister. He was perfectly entitled to make all the unwise decisions he liked. But the least he could do was take me into his confidence.

Agnelli pricked up his ears, but not in the way that I hoped. 'What's Eastlake's connection with Karlin?'

'Aside from them both being on the board of the Centre for Modern Art, I don't know. Eastlake showed me his art gallery last night, but he didn't take me into his confidence.' I paused pregnantly.

My delicate condition was of no interest to Agnelli. He was too busy figuring the angles. 'We're funding this picture deal on Eastlake's say-so, right? How much is Karlin getting, and what are we getting in return?'

'Our kick-in was $300,000, towards a total purchase price in excess of half a million dollars. What we, in the form of the publicly owned CMA, are getting in return is a painting by Victor Szabo.'

Agnelli whistled lightly under his breath. 'For that sort of dough we could get a Matisse.'

'Possibly,' I said. 'But Matisse wasn't Australian.'

'And Victor Szabo was?' Ange was probably finessing the point. I suspected he knew even less about Victor Szabo than I did.

'Szabo's background was, er, European, of course,' I ventured. 'But the CMA seems to feel that his contribution to the development of Australian art warrants the price.'

'That may well be,' said Agnelli. 'But he's not exactly a household name, is he? And we're the ones footing the bill. Big-ticket art buys are hardly a guaranteed vote-winner, you know.'

My sentiments precisely, I told him. But the fact that Gil Methven, neither a conspicuous risk-taker nor a notorious art lover, had okayed the deal suggested that the decision was unlikely to be controversial. 'Eastlake raised half the total purchase price from corporate donors. Not only does that spread the risk, fallout-wise, it also gives us the "government in partnership with private enterprise to promote culture" line.'

Agnelli's mental gears went into overdrive. 'Corporate donors? Who exactly?'

I shrugged. 'Dunno, yet. They'll probably be at this brunch, though. Maybe you could take the opportunity to put the hard word on them for a contribution to the party.'

He didn't rise to the bait. 'Good idea.' He straightened his tie and concentrated on assuming his most commanding demeanour.

Fine, I thought. Have it your own way, pal. Just don't come

crying to me when you get into strife, expecting me to clean up the mess.

Max Karlin's corporate headquarters was a backstreet Cinderella, one of a hundred work-worn industrial facades tucked away in a factory precinct abutting the Queen Victoria market on the north-western edge of the central business district. We might have missed it completely if not for the logo of Max's chain of shoe stores, Karlcraft, above the entrance and the expensive wheels parked bumper to bumper at the kerb outside. From here Karlin had built his retail empire. From here he now oversaw his ultimate creation, a vast hub of shops and offices that would one day be the Karlcraft Centre.

Max, looking like an admiral in his navy blazer, materialised on the pavement as the Fairlane drew up. I made the introductions. Glancing at me only long enough to look askance at my mangled ear, Karlin swept Agnelli inside.

The external shabbiness of Karlcraft House belied the maxim about flaunting it. Max had it, all right, but he kept it discreetly out of sight, waiting until the moment you stepped through the door to clobber you with it. Everything about the building's interior was calculated to obliterate any distinction between substance and style. Here was a lush world of working wealth where good taste was a capital asset.

'Darling,' I heard. 'Smooch, smooch,' as the rest of the already assembled guests mingled in the foyer. Women with tennis tans and pre-stressed hair milled about, drinks in hand, chatting with men in oversized shirts buttoned to the neck and tasselled moccasins with no socks. Pouty waitresses, meanwhile, lurked in doorways with trays of glasses, like cigarette girls at the Stork Club refusing to be impressed by anyone less than F. Scott Fitzgerald. Nobody could keep their eyes off the walls.

They couldn't help it. Neither could I. Max Karlin had filled his company offices with paintings whose authorship and authority were unmistakable, even to a yob like me. Definitive works by the who's who of modern Australian art hung everywhere. Each picture seemed so perfectly to exemplify the style of its creator that I almost had to stop myself saying the names out loud. Here a Tucker, there a Boyd, a Dobell, a Perceval. A pair of Nolans faced each other across the lobby. Halfway up the stairs on either side were a Whiteley and a Smart.

I ran out of names long before Max ran out of pictures, but by then I had the message, loud and clear. When it came to aesthetic judgement, there were no flies on Max Karlin. And anyone with the dough to lavish on ornaments of this calibre had to be worth an absolute mint.

As the big boys advanced up the stairs ahead of me, there was a polite cough at my shoulder and I turned to find myself facing Phillip Veale. His eyes flickered over my suppurating ear with a droll twinkle. 'Body art?' he said. 'It's all the rage, I hear.' In the interest of weekend informality, he'd shed the French cuffs for a pastel-yellow polo top with a crocodile on the tit. 'But not as enduring as this kind.' He tilted a glass of kir royale at the nearest wall. 'Impressive, aren't they? It's not every day that Max opens his collection to the public. And only in the worthiest of causes. Today it's the CMA acquisition fund. The donation is a hundred dollars a head.'

I blanched and nearly tripped over the bottom stair.

'You and I needn't worry,' he smiled, dryly. 'The help get in for free. As for the rest'—he indicated the beau monde around us—'they're only too happy to pay. It makes them feel special.' Offices led off the foyer, their doors open to display well-hung interiors. Veale cocked his head towards the nearest. 'A quiet word in your Vincent-like, *s'il vous plaît*.'

The office held Perry White's desk, cleared for the occasion but for four phones and two computer terminals. Apart from the desk and a big caramel landscape by someone whose name hovered on the tip of my tongue, we had the room to ourselves. 'This dreadful moat business,' Veale clucked. 'The minister's heard, I take it.'

'Had the press on the phone at dawn.'

'They have his home number?' Veale was aghast.

'It's in the book,' I told him. Angelo's idea of democratic

accessibility. 'He told them to piss off.'

'Quite properly so,' said Veale. 'All press enquiries are to be handled by the Acting Director of the National Gallery. Not that he'll have anything to tell them, apart from confirming that it was gallery staff who found the body. You, of course, know that already.'

In other words I was not the only one who had spent the morning appraising myself of the facts. 'The dead man was a client of the ministry, I understand,' I said.

Veale's eyebrows went up. Evidently not all the facts were yet in his possession. 'Really?'

'Got a little grant in the last funding round. Two thousand.'

A departmental director could hardly be expected to be aware of every teensy-weensy item of expenditure. But he knew how to draw an inference. 'Ahh,' he exhaled.

'And he was living at the old YMCA. One of our facilities, isn't it?'

'Temporarily. Pending demolition. The rooms are made available to certain worthy causes and individuals. But nobody *lives* there.' The sheer squalor of the idea seemed to appal him.

'At any rate, this Taylor had a studio there,' I said. 'It'd be interesting to know if he had any other connection with the ministry.' This was unlikely, but I was far enough ahead of Veale to have him on the defensive. A good place for a departmental head, however efficient and congenial, to be. 'Indeed,' Veale hastened to agree.

Come Monday morning, deputy directors would scuttle. In the meantime, Veale's prompt attention to the sensitivities of the issue should not go unrecognised. 'I don't believe you've met Angelo yet,' I said, leading him back into the foyer.

'Plenty of time for that on Monday.' He made a self-deprecatory gesture that suggested he would not be entirely upset to be found minding the shop on his day off. We went up the stairs to the mezzanine.

Agnelli and Karlin were getting on famously, a couple of well-rounded high-achievers basking in the cloudless skies of each other's company. They stood shoulder to shoulder in front of a painting while Karlin laid on a monologue. Agnelli jiggled with pleasure at his every bon mot. Ange's hands, I was relieved to see, were firmly in his own pockets. Beside Agnelli, very close, stood Fiona Lambert. And at Karlin's right hand, with the look of a successful matchmaker at an engagement party, stood Lloyd Eastlake.

Veale and I went into a holding pattern, waiting for a suitable break in Karlin's soliloquy. 'This Szabo purchase,' I said to him, passing the time. 'Inheriting such a large grant allocation, sight unseen, may tend to make Angelo a little uncomfortable. If he could meet one or two of the corporate participants in the project, I'm sure it would reassure him immensely.' Not chatting. Pimping. In the hope of catching Agnelli *in flagrante*. Madness, I told myself, sheer insanity. Stop it.

'It looks as though he's beaten us to it.' Veale nodded towards the official entourage. 'Obelisk Trust, contributor, if memory serves me right, of $150,000. Various other donors gave smaller amounts. Fifty thousand here, twenty there.' He dropped his voice, confidentially. 'Clients of Obelisk, I daresay, keeping in good with their line of credit.'

I'd heard of Obelisk Trust—vaguely—and felt it somewhat remiss of me not to know more. It was some kind of financial institution, that much I knew, part of the free-wheeling money market that had erupted onto the scene since deregulation and the floating of the dollar. Merchant banks, brokerage arbitrageurs, futures dealers, entrepreneurial wheeler-dealers—the media was giddy with them. You couldn't turn on the television without some egg-headed pundit leaning earnestly into the camera and whispering about the FT-100 or the ninety-day bond rate. It was all so hard to keep up with. Fluctuations in share prices and currency exchange rates were reported with greater frequency than the weather outlook. Reading the paper was like trying to watch a sport without knowing the rules.

Veale responded to my blank look. 'Lloyd Eastlake,' he said. 'Obelisk Trust's executive director.'

Wheels within wheels. Hats upon hats. 'Handy,' I said. And precariously close to conflict of interest.

Veale's voice took on a slightly miffed tone. 'As far as the Centre for Modern Art and the Visual Arts Advisory Panel are concerned, all procedural guidelines have been rigorously observed.' No funny business on any committees in Phillip Veale's jurisdiction. Not on paper, at least. 'As to the Obelisk Trust, I have no reason to assume other than that Lloyd Eastlake conducts himself with the utmost probity.'

One hand washes the other. While we stand by, holding the soap. But there was no point in ruffling Veale's feathers. 'So where's this Szabo picture,' I said, gawking around. 'It must be quite something.'

Veale loosened up again. 'You mean at six hundred thousand dollars it had better be.'

'The last picture I bought was on the lid of a box of short-bread. Five dollars fifty and I got to eat the biscuits.'

Karlin, Agnelli & Co had ambled along the mezzanine into a spacious boardroom hung with more pictures. A horseshoe-shaped table ran down the middle, invisible beneath a sumptuous buffet of fresh fruit and architect-designed pastries. The aroma of excellent coffee perfumed the air, making my mouth water. 'I doubt if anyone ever expected a Szabo to fetch such an amount,' Veale was saying. 'Arguably, his contribution to Australian art might have gone largely unremarked if not for Fiona Lambert's tireless work in developing his reputation and bringing him to public notice.'

'And what better measure of a man's significance,' I said, 'than the price of his work.'

Veale pursed his lips, pitying me my cynicism. I conceded him the point, sort of. 'Ironical, though, isn't it,' I remarked. 'So many artists never get to enjoy the fruits of their own success.'

'True,' conceded Veale. 'I never met Szabo myself, but I used to know his dealer, Giles Aubrey, quite well. I doubt if Karlin paid Giles more than five or six thousand when he bought the picture back in the early seventies.' A steal. Only a year's take-home pay for one of Max's employees at the time.

Much of the crowd had followed the official party into the boardroom and were tucking into the mille-feuilles and moka blend. I helped myself to a hair of the dog out of a bottle marked Bollinger, poured one for Veale, and sniffed at a tray of dainty pink-and-white sandwiches. 'Caviar?' I wondered.

'Strawberries,' said Veale.

Christ. Strawberry sandwiches. Now I'd seen it all. But I hadn't. Not by a long chalk.

'Ladies and gentlemen,' Karlin began, his voice barely above conversational volume. As if by magic, the chatter of voices and scrape of forks across plates faded. It was Karlin, at least as much as his artworks, they had paid to be near. His entrepreneurship, luck and taste were legendary. Famous, at the very least. Stand close enough, listen attentively enough, and perhaps some of it might rub off.

'Welcome to today's open-house in aid of the CMA's acquisition program.' Karlin's public voice was both smooth and gravelly, a combination of wet cement and washed silk, conveying a mixture of amenability and conviction. The expression 'If madam would just care to try this on' sprang to mind.

Karlin pressed on. 'And an especially warm welcome to our new Arts Minister, the Honourable Angelo Agnelli, who has made a special effort to be here, which I think speaks volumes for his commitment to the visual arts…'

Just in case anyone didn't quite know which one he was, Ange took a half-step forward, smiled bashfully, and let the gaze of the congregation fall gently upon him. There was a shuffling that might have been applause. Ange nodded, recognising in all humility that it was the office, not the man, to whom acknowledgment was due. But conveying, nonetheless, a distinctly personal pleasure at finding himself among like-minded people. A photographer circled, flash popping.

Karlin allowed Ange his moment of grace before continuing. 'Because, thanks to the vision of the government, a great painting hitherto seen only by a fortunate few will soon hang in the

Centre for Modern Art where it will be accessible to all. I refer, of course, to Victor Szabo's *Our Home*.'

As he delivered this phrase, Karlin moved slightly to one side, offering the painting on the wall behind him to the perusal of the assembly. Unfortunately, Phillip Veale was in my line of sight, obstructing my view, and all I could see of it was a bit of blue in the top right-hand corner. As Karlin continued to speak, informing us that the occasion was tinged with regret at the departure of a cherished possession, I popped the last of the strawberry sangers into my mouth, craned my neck over the bureaucrat's gelati-hued shoulder and feasted my eyes.

My jaw froze in mid-chomp. You could have knocked me down with an ermine bristle. The picture I beheld, hanging on the wall of Max Karlin's boardroom, was strikingly familiar. So much so that I thought my eyes were playing tricks with me. It depicted a cloudless Australian sky and a swathe of vivid perfectly manicured lawn. In the middle of the lawn sat a Victa Special two-stroke motor-mower. Behind it was a red-roofed double-fronted brick-veneer house, brooding with malevolent intensity.

I might not know much about
art, but I've been a member of the Labor Party long enough to
recognise the aroma of rodent when it wafts my way. So, when
the speechifying was over, I introduced Veale to Agnelli and left
them exchanging pleasantries while I examined the Szabo at
closer range.

An expert might have detected subtle differences—the
demeanour of the brushstrokes, the gradation of the colour, the
intangible aura of genius—but on face value I was buggered if I
could tell this picture from the one I had seen scarcely two
hours before in Marcus Taylor's studio.

Eastlake noticed my close interest and joined me. 'Following
in the footsteps of Van Gogh?' he said. This joke was beginning
to wear thin.

'Angling accident,' I said. 'You should see the fish.'

He inclined his head towards *Our Home*. 'Come on,' he
beamed. 'Admit it. It does have a certain *je ne sais quoi*, doesn't
it?'

'Oh, I dunno,' I shrugged.

But Eastlake was right. And not just about there being
nothing in the painting to provoke outrage. He'd been right that
people would genuinely warm to it. It did for suburbia what

nineteenth-century Australian painters had done for the bush—made it a worthy subject for art. And, by inference, made heroes of those who dwelt there. *Our Home* was the Parthenon of tract housing, with a bit of laconic satire chucked in for good measure. And an edge of the mysterious, so you knew it was proper art.

'I used to build houses just like this,' Eastlake confided with a proprietary sentimentality.

And millions grew up in them. I dipped my head in acknowledgment of his superior judgment. 'How does it get from here to the CMA?'

Administrative detail didn't interest Eastlake. 'In a crate, I imagine.' His contrivance at being both amiable and patronising could easily have grated. But compared with the unremitting dullness of most of the business types I met, Lloyd Eastlake's candour was disarmingly refreshing. 'Fiona handles that sort of thing.'

Fiona Lambert was across the room, thick as thieves with Becky Karlin and a helmeted honeyeater I recognised from the CMA. 'That guy who got up on the table last night and tried to make the speech,' I started. 'The one who fell over.'

Eastlake's attention was elsewhere. Max Karlin had detached Agnelli from Phillip Veale and was leading him out onto the mezzanine, steering him towards one of the offices. The holy of holies, I took it. Eastlake made a must-rush noise and headed after them.

I should have too, I suppose. Monitoring what passed between Agnelli and Karlin had, after all, been the whole point in bringing them together. To have my suspicions confirmed, wasn't that why I was here? But now something else was exercising my mind, something that took me instead down into the melting heat of the street, to the row of up-market cars lining the kerb, to crack open the seal on the refrigerated interior of Eastlake's big silver Merc. 'Morning,' I said, 'Noel.'

Spider didn't turn. He just sat there, fish-faced behind his shades, contemplating the sporting section of the *Herald*, his hat on the ledge above the dashboard. Even when I slid in beside him he didn't look around. A knob low on the instrument panel might have been the cigarette lighter. I put my thumb on it and pushed until it clicked into place. Agnelli didn't let me smoke in the Fairlane.

We sat there, me side-on, Spider gazing into the V of his paper. Profile was definitely Noel Webb's better angle. Made him look less like a plumbing fixture. 'So,' I said. 'Long time no see.' Long time no answer, too. More than long enough for me to get a smoke out and tap it on the side of the pack. Pop went the lighter. Spider's hand shot out. He held the glowing element short, so I had to bend across to fire up, offering the nape of my neck. A gold pinky ring glistened on his little finger, fat and square, set with a crescent of tiny rubies, a real tooth-breaker. Quite the primitive, Spider. 'This job suits you,' I said. 'You've got the silent menace bit down to a tee.'

Spider tossed his chin in the general direction of the Karlcraft building. 'Won't you be missed?' he said, unimpressed. 'Big shot.'

'Never too busy to catch up with old friends,' I said, absently flicking a molecule of ash onto the car's pale grey carpet. 'Funny, isn't it?' I stretched my legs out and leaned back against the headrest. 'Twenty years since we've seen each other, now our paths cross all the time. Down at the Ballet Centre carpark this morning, for instance.'

Spider very slowly closed his newspaper, folded it neatly in half and laid it beside his hat. 'MOAT DEATH PUZZLE,' read a column-wide headline on the front page. He turned his mirrored face towards me, at last. 'I dunno what you're talking about.' His delivery was flat, sneering. 'And neither do you.'

The big car's interior felt suddenly very claustrophobic. Noel Webb had been a tough kid. And if he was acting the hard man maybe it was because that's exactly what he was. Spider wasn't the sentimental type. Never had been. And any tenuous connection between us was long gone. My feet were getting colder by the second.

For nearly an hour I'd waited at the Oulton Reserve, clutching that contraband bottle of bourbon under my duffel coat, its neck sticky and warm in my hand. Footy practice ended, the oval emptied, and still I sat, half of me ashamed, the other half defiant. Ashamed for the theft, for I'd never before stolen from my father. Ashamed for my reason for doing it, to buy friendship. Defying my father to catch me out, defying Spider Webb to doubt that I could deliver. As I waited, I took little sips. The liquid was fiery and harsh, but it kept me warm. Kept me waiting.

When Spider finally arrived, he came out of nowhere, looming out of the leaden dusk. 'Got it?' he said, sinking down beside me. I hesitated then, kept the bottle hidden beneath my coat, wanting some spoken confirmation of our pact.

'You haven't, have you?' His scorn was wounding. 'You didn't have the guts, did you?'

That's when the Fletchers exploded out of a clump of tea-tree edging the football oval. Georgie, the big one, had a steel fencing picket in his hand. The twins trotted at his heels. Like Attila and his horde, they swept down upon us.

Twenty years is a long time. People change. But if Noel Webb had, I couldn't see it. Maybe I'd underestimated him, though, pegging him for a car thief. Maybe he'd graduated to something more sophisticated.

'Nice car,' I said, running an eyeball over the walnut inlay. 'Been Mr Eastlake's chauffeur long? His status symbol, that's what he called you, didn't he?'

'What's it to you?' Annoyance had crept into Spider's voice, evidence that communication might be possible.

'Probably nothing at all,' I agreed. Probably nothing more than ancient adolescent resentment, octopus-induced irritability, and a suspicious mind. But if I stirred the pot a little, something more might come bubbling to the surface. 'It's just that there are points where your employer's activities and my employer's interests overlap. And proper attention to my employer's interests requires that I keep myself broadly informed. I rather hoped you'd understand that, us both being in the service sector.'

He snorted contemptuously. 'Haven't you got anything better to do with your time?'

As a matter of fact, I did. It was nearly 12.30. Red's plane was due in little more than two hours and, apart from picking up a pack of cigarettes, I still hadn't done any shopping. 'I guess I can always ask Lloyd,' I shrugged. 'Just thought I'd ask you first, not wanting to embarrass an old friend and all.'

'I'm shitting myself, Whelan,' Spider said, brimming with schoolyard disdain. But he tilted his head a fraction and I knew his eyes had gone to the rearview mirror.

The Mercedes had power windows. Mine made a little whirring noise and let in a wilting gust of heat. I stuck my head out, looked back at the stragglers drifting out of Karlcraft and whirred it back up. 'Have it your own way,' I said. 'Mr Eastlake will be along soon.'

Spider puffed his cheeks and blew a long steady breath, like I was a deliberately obtuse child, trying his patience. Then, shaking his head as though reluctantly coming to a decision he already regretted, he leaned across in front of me and casually opened the glove compartment. The lid fell down to reveal a shiny, chrome-plated pistol.

This was not something I saw every day. In fact, I'd never seen one before. Not for real. It wasn't so long ago that not even cops carried guns. And now that they did, they certainly weren't guns like this. This was an automatic, chrome-plated with a cross-hatched grip. I'd seen enough movies to know that. Whether it was the current release Baretta .44 with Dolby sound and merchandising tie-in, I neither knew nor cared. Guns did not interest me. They scared the shit out of me, but they didn't interest me. Beside the gun was an unopened packet of Wrigley's Arrowmint gum. Spider let my gaze linger for a moment on the pistol, then he picked up the chewy and snapped the glove box lid shut.

I got the point. Noel Webb was no mere opener of doors, no low-grade flunkey. Nor was he just there for his good looks, his obsequious manner and his masterful grip on the steering wheel. He was there because Lloyd Eastlake's taste in fashion accessories ran to keeping a bodyguard.

If an arsehole like Noel Webb thought he could intimidate me by showing me his penis substitute, he could think again. It took more than a flash of metal to impress Murray Whelan. On the other hand, I'd just as soon not have anything to do with guns. Spider unwrapped his chewy and proffered the pack. Take it or leave it.

I was shagged out, hungover, lied to, pissed off, ear-mangled and behind schedule. It was none of my business if Brian Eastlake thought he needed an armed minder. Nor was the fact that he'd seen fit to give the job to Spider Webb. As to the matter of the vanished duplicate of *Our Home*, it suddenly seemed unimportant. The main game was being played by the big boys upstairs in Max Karlin's office, not down here in the gutter with a pistol-packing dipstick. Instead of keeping my eye on the ball, I was chasing a chimera. My duties didn't run to this kind of crap.

'See you, Spider,' I said wearily and opened the door.

Webb already had his nose back in the paper. 'Not if I see you first.'

I wished people would stop saying that to me. A man could get paranoid. At least he hadn't said anything about my ear. For obvious reasons. Even with one in tatters, mine weren't half as conspicuous as Spider's.

I turned back towards Karlin's office. Agnelli's Fairlane had pulled away from the kerb and was heading down the street. Wonderful. Agnelli was going without me, the prick. Not only had he probably bitten Max Karlin for a little campaign donation, he was leaving me in the lurch. My Charade was back at Parliament House, a dozen blocks away.

My best shot at a cab was back towards the Queen Victoria market. A shopping list marshalled in my head. Bending beneath the glare of the burnished sky, I made haste through the empty sun-blasted streets. The market closed at 12.30 on

Saturday and it was already that.

The century-old fresh-daily aroma of the open-sided sheds advanced to greet me. Hot sugared doughnuts, bananas on the turn, the rustling exhalations of onion skins, the pungency of soy sauce and live poultry. All mixed together, emulsified with forklift fumes and baked under the grill of sheet-iron roofs. Then came the sound—the murmur of shuffling feet, the shouted offers of last-minute bargains, the street-sweepers' hard-bristled brooms, the play of hose-stream on steaming gutters.

The top shed stalls were already closed, their mountains of lush produce reduced to a range of grey tarpaulin foothills. Downhill, across a street shrill with the beeping of reversing trucks, I found a late-closing Chinaman prepared to risk his vendor's licence with the offer of dew-misted nectarines and fat knuckles of ginger. At a premium, I bought mangoes, mandarins and firm tomatoes. Red liked avocados. I bought six. From a Greek woman clearing a till behind the last glass counter in the delicatessen section, I inveigled fetta, ham and walnut bread. Then I schlepped my supplies to the cab rank. Every other bastard in Melbourne had got there first.

There was still two hours until Red's plane touched down. The dusting could wait. An overloaded plastic carry-bag in each hand, I began up the hill towards the State Library.

A little knowledge is a dangerous thing and if you really want to live dangerously the State Library is a good place to start. Even on a quiet Saturday afternoon, its obliging staff can take your vaguest apprehensions and turn them into a swarm of disturbing possibilities.

The domed reading-room was hushed and serene, bathed in the cool submarine light that filtered down from its huge cavernous hemisphere high above. The long tables radiating from its centre were like the spokes of a wheel, an imperceptibly moving cog in wisdom's silent mill. I delivered my victuals into the custody of the cloakroom attendant and moved from the general to the specific, starting with *Art Sales Index*, the annual digest of works passing under the hammer in the world's major sales rooms.

International art prices were going systematically batshit. In the preceding five years, total world turnover on everything from archaic bronzes to zoological watercolours had doubled then doubled then doubled again. And it wasn't just the Yasuda Fire and Marine or the Getty Museum. The whole world was at it. Firms of English auditors were snapping up Soviet constructionists, Brazilian livestock agents were trying to corner the Flemish rococo and a former signwriter from Perth had just paid £43 million for Van Gogh's *Sunflowers*. For that sort of money, you'd want the ear as well. Almost overnight, scraps of pigmented fabric of virtually no intrinsic value were being transformed by the logic of the marketplace into commodities whose prices could have fed all of Africa.

Not to be outdone by New York and London, domestic prices were hot on the heels of the global trend. According to the gazette of Australian auction records, modest little pictures by well-known Australian artists that could've been snapped up any time in the previous two decades for a couple of grand were suddenly fetching five or ten times that amount.

Victor Szabo's name appeared infrequently, in some years not at all. But then, according to what I'd heard at the Botanical Hotel, his life's work amounted only to forty or so known paintings. Eleven of these had been offered at auction in the previous few years, six more than once. The prices had risen slowly at first, barely keeping up with the general trend. Then, more recently, the pace had quickened. This improvement was in line with a general tendency of the market to seek out previously underrated artists as the value of the big names went stratospheric.

One hundred thousand dollars was the top price listed for a Szabo. Nothing remotely like the figure Karlin was charging. Either there was more to *Our Home* than met the eye or somebody was being taken for a walk.

A Fierce Vision: The Genius of Victor Szabo 1911–77 by Fiona Lambert was a handsomely produced coffee-table job published two years previously. Plentiful text, lavish illustrations and a one-paragraph biography of the author on the inside flyleaf. Exhibition curator, gallery director, BA(Hons). Fluff.

Flipping through, I found what I was looking for. *Our Home: Oil on canvas, 175 cm x 123 cm, 1972. Private collection.* I pored over the plate's glossy surface, searching for some previously unnoticed detail that would spring out and distinguish this image from the one I had seen in Marcus Taylor's studio. It was useless. The two paintings had converged in my memory.

Two pictures, two dead men. One an artist of growing repute, dead ten years. The other an unknown loser, dead twelve hours. Two things linked them. One was a picture of a house with a lawn-mower in the front yard. The other was a dog-eared photograph among a suicide's pathetic collection of personal effects. Something about all of this didn't feel right. Disturbing possibilities rattled around in my brain, nagged at me. The missing painting. Salina's emotional game-playing. Spider's menacing evasions. Something was cooking and it didn't smell right. It smelled of egg on Angelo Agnelli's face. I decided to keep sniffing.

Taylor, Marcus was listed nowhere in Lambert's index. I waded into the body of the text. *The literalness of Victor Szabo's work deploys a multi-layered, almost compulsive, disjunction of a myriad of identities,* it began. *Its vocabulary welds the specificity of circumstance to the logic of allegory so as to create a bridge between the depersonalised formalism of abstraction and the narrative poetics of an uninhibited quest for the archetypically mundane.*

Well, she wasn't going to hear any argument from me. I read on. It didn't get any easier. In comparison with art criticism, the mealy jargon of bureaucracy sparkled like birdsong. Not even in the mouth of the Leader of the Opposition did words convey so little. Scanning and skipping, attempting to draw a thread of comprehension from the furball of Fiona Lambert's prose, I jotted the few biographical facts I could garner on a library call-slip with a pencil someone had mislaid on top of the catalogue cabinet.

The bare bones, as far as I could make them out, were that Szabo had been born in Hapsburg Budapest, had studied art in Paris in the thirties and arrived in Australia as a displaced person after the Second World War. Isolated from the local art scene by circumstances and temperament, he found work as a railway fettler in the Blue Mountains west of Sydney, sketching and painting intermittently. By the late fifties he had moved south and was living on the outskirts of Melbourne, painting full-time, occasionally exhibiting his work, even sometimes finding a buyer. His trademark realism and suburban subject matter began to emerge. Painting constantly, he destroyed most of his output, retaining only his most highly finished pictures. Antisocial and reclusive, he made contact with the outside world only through his dealer, Giles Aubrey. Eventually he fell out even with him. His talent, Fiona Lambert put it, could no longer endure the constraints of the relationship.

About this time, '77 or '78, Lambert herself appeared. And not a moment too soon. Up until that point in the story, no woman had been mentioned who was not another artist, an artist's wife, or a critic. No wonder, if Fiona's version of Victor Szabo's life story was to be believed, the old coot expired in her arms. Sheer astonishment at his change of luck.

If there was some clue to connect Szabo and Taylor, it certainly didn't lie in Fiona Lambert's text. I flicked through the illustrations again. Sketches, draughtsmanlike renderings of landscapes, architectural details, life-studies in charcoal, the finished paintings.

Two of the sketches, dating from the early fifties, were female nudes. Where had he found his models, I wondered, this New Australian railway labourer? One was a rear view, roughhewn, a few broad strokes outlining the curve of a back, a fall of hair, the droop of buttocks. The other was a pencil sketch, highly finished, face and shoulders turned in three-quarter profile.

The resemblance was unmistakable. It was the woman in the photograph in Marcus Taylor's desk drawer. In the souvenir snap she was more carefree. But the woman in the sketch knew he would go soon, her artistic European lover. That happy time when the camera had captured them together on the mountaintop lookout was already fading fast. Her belly was distended, her expression resigned. Marcus Taylor's birthplace, according to his grant application form, was Katoomba, Jewel of the Blue Mountains, gateway to the original Australian bush.

Before I left the library, there were a couple more publications I wanted to consult. *Veneer: A Journal of Contemporary*

Cultural Criticism appeared quarterly. I went straight to the list of editorial credits. *Veneer*, said the tiniest possible type, *acknowledges the financial support of the Visual Arts Panel of the Victorian Ministry for the Arts.* I attributed no significance to this fact. I was just interested, that's all.

The second book I consulted had printing almost as small. It was thick and yellow and lived in a metal bracket under the pay phone in the foyer. Under Art Dealers, between Atelier on the Yarra and Aussie's Aborigine Art was a listing for Aubrey Fine Art. I dialled the number and asked for Mr Giles Aubrey.

There was a moment's silence, then a sound that could have been eyebrows being raised. 'Giles Aubrey has not been associated with us for quite some time,' said a snooty male voice.

'You don't know how I can contact him?'

'Not really. He sold the business and retired several years ago. This is the current proprietor speaking. May I be of assistance?' Meaning, can I sell you a picture, and if not piss off.

'It's a rather delicate matter,' I said, 'concerning the provenance of an item bought some time ago, when Mr Aubrey was in charge. Before beginning legal proceedings, I'd prefer to speak with Mr Aubrey. If, however, that's not possible, what did you say your name was...'

'Just a moment, sir.' After a few seconds, he came back with a phone number. The first three digits, denoting the local exchange, were unfamiliar. Somewhere in the eastern suburbs gentility belt, I assumed.

'That's Eaglemont, is it?' A locale of faintly arty pretence.

'Coldstream,' said eyebrows, eager to send me packing.

Coldstream, of course. Eltham, Kangaroo Ground, Christmas Hills, Yarra Glen, Coldstream. Out where the Food Plusses and the Furniture Barns gave way to plant nurseries and pottery shops. A bushland bohemia of mudbrick and claret in whose sylvan glades colonies of free-thinking artists once made their abode, sculpting wombats out of scrap metal, listening to jazz, swapping wives and growing their beards. Where shadow Cabinet ministers in turtle-neck sweaters once went to have their portraits painted by polygamous libertarians. Long before art was an industry, when it was a talisman against the triumphant philistinism of encroaching suburbia, these scrubby hills on the urban fringe were its Camelot.

Not a lot of Camelot left out there any more, not since art had decamped to the inner city, gone post-modern, started pleading its multiplier-effectiveness and cost/benefit ratios before the Industry Assistance Commission. Not since the bird-watching suburban gentry had parked their Range Rovers in its driveways and paved its bush tracks with antique-finish concrete cobblestones available in an extensive range of all-natural designer colours. Only the artists' half-feral children remained, gone thirty, still barefoot and stinking of patchouli oil. And old Giles Aubrey, retired to some bend in the river.

His phone rang a long time, long enough for me to rehearse my approach, long enough for me to think he wasn't going to answer. 'Giles Aubrey speaking.' A voice with rounded vowels and clipped diction, the sort of voice that would once have been called educated, that suggested I forthwith state my business and heaven help me if I was a fool.

Anyone hoping for Giles Aubrey's assistance would need to play it deferential, keep their wits about them. I apologised for disturbing him at the weekend, inferred that I was calling at the express instructions of the Minister for the Arts, and wondered if he might spare me a few moments of his unquestionably precious time to provide some background on Victor Szabo. 'The minister is currently reliant on a limited number of sources of expertise. Ms Lambert, Szabo's biographer, has been very helpful, naturally.'

For all the archness in his voice, Giles Aubrey deigned not to rise to the temptation of petty rivalry. 'Exactly what is it you wish to know, Mr Whelan?'

'It's more the personal aspect. Family details, children, that sort of thing,' I told him.

'I'm not sure I follow you.' His voice quavered with age, but he was following me all right.

'Victor Szabo is still largely unknown to the general public.'
I was groping my way here. 'So naturally there will be a great deal of interest in his background when it is announced that a government-funded gallery is spending six hundred thousand dollars on one of his paintings.'

'That much? For one of Victor's? Really?' Behind the patrician disbelief was something else. Vindication, perhaps. 'Which one, may one ask?'

I told him. There was a long silence and when finally he spoke it was as if recognising the arrival of something long anticipated. 'Oh dear,' he said. 'Oh dearie, dearie me.'

Coldstream was a good ninety minutes away. 'I'll be in your area a bit later this afternoon,' I said. 'Perhaps I could drop around?'

'Very well.' His acquiescence was immediate, total. 'Some things *are* better discussed face to face.' The last house, he told me, bottom of the hill.

But first things first. The fruit of my loins was making his descent. I hiked my purchases up to Parliament House, tossed them into the Charade and made the airport with seconds to spare.

Tullamarine was thick with Italian families, there to meet the Alitalia flight from Rome, cooling their heels while customs frisked their grandmothers for contraband salami. Red's flight was running ten minutes behind schedule—which gave me a chance to read what the Saturday paper pundits had to say about the Cabinet reshuffle.

Rearranging the deck chairs on the Titanic was the recurrent phrase. Since these were the same luminaries who'd confidently predicted our defeat at the previous election, I tried not to take offence. We had, after all, won by two seats. The *Herald*'s Moat Death Puzzle story ran to five paragraphs, covered only the bare bones and took the anticipated line. A side-bar profiled famous artistic suicides.

All up, I'd been waiting at the gate lounge for half an hour by the time the flight landed and the last of the exiting passengers streamed through the door. Red was not among them.

It was definitely his flight. Definitely. The airline woman at the service counter verified it, ratting her glossy nails across a keyboard, consulting her monitor. Unaccompanied child, Redmond Whelan. Ticketed, confirmed and boarded. Might I have simply missed him in the crowd, she asked? There were quite a lot of families on the flight, returning from holidays. Had he perhaps proceeded directly to claim his baggage?

'He wouldn't do that,' I said, anxiety mounting, and turned with a sweep of my arm to prove my point.

'Tricked ya!'

Red stood behind me, grinning from ear to ear.

We embraced, his cheek on my sternum, the bill of his baseball cap obscuring his face. It was a solid hug, but brisk. Even a ten-year-old has an image to think about.

'So,' I said, holding him at arm's length the better to examine him. Every time I saw Red, he'd changed in some subtle, inexpressible way. His face still had the same cherubic quality as always, but the body below was whippier, carried less puppy fat. His eventual shape, I allowed myself the conceit, would owe more to me than to his mother. 'How you been?'

'Good.'

'How was the flight?'

'Good.'

'How was your holiday?' Three weeks on the beach at Noosa Heads with Wendy and her barrister boyfriend. I didn't want the details.

'Good.'

So far, so good. 'Good,' I said.

Quite the frequent flier, Red travelled light. A backpack and a Walkman were his total luggage. Everything else he needed— several hundred comics, a skateboard and a change of clothes—was waiting in his room at my place. *Our* place, I thought, brimming with the fact.

Back when Red was seven and his mother was in Canberra securing her future in the affirmative action major league, the boy and I had lived together for the best part of a year. Wendy had returned home at regular intervals and phoned frequently, but for weeks at a time it was just the two of us, living the life of Riley. Okay, so we ate out often enough to have our own table at Pizza Hut, slept in the same bed to cut down on housework and missed the odd day of school. But I always ordered pizzas with a high vegetable content, insisted Red brush his teeth at least once a week and kept him relatively free of parasite infestations. And it was only by unavoidable accident that Wendy discovered him home alone one morning when she arrived earlier than anticipated. The olive-skinned beauty in my bed and the Hell's Angel on the roof with a crowbar had a perfectly innocent explanation, if only she'd stuck around to hear it.

'What did the orthodontist say?' I asked as we headed for the carpark.

Red indicated the problem, open-mouthed. 'E ed I eed a ate.'

'Why do you need a plate?' Aside from further enriching some overpriced gum-digger, I was already sending Wendy five hundred dollars a month. Not that I begrudged a penny.

'E ed I ot a oh a ite.'

'You haven't got an overbite,' I said. 'Your face is the same shape as mine. I look okay, don't I?'

Red eyed me sceptically. His gaze lingered on my bandaged ear. He didn't say anything, but I could already sense them gift-wrapping my birthday copy of *First Aid for the Home Handyman* at the Sydney branch of Mary Martin.

'You think Tark's home today?' This was Red being sensitive, not wanting me to think it wasn't me he was here to visit. Tarquin Curnow was his best mate in Melbourne, possibly the world, and doubtless the two of them had already been on the phone, cooking up plans for the weekend. Whenever Red came to stay, he headed directly to Tarquin's place and the two of them hung out like Siamese twins.

I took no offence. Tarquin Curnow had been Red's friend since kindergarten, and the clincher when I bought my house was that it backed onto the same lane as the Curnows' big terrace. Tarquin's parents, Faye and Leo, were old friends and better ones than I deserved, especially Faye who tended to worry about my unattached status. It affronted her sense of the natural order. I was beginning to share her sentiments.

The temperature had long hit the forty-degree mark and my shopping was beginning to go whiffy by the time we tracked down the Charade and blew the carpark. We headed straight for Tarquin's place. Not much point in going home just to put a piece of cheese in the fridge. Faye's would be just as cold.

The Curnows' front door was opened by a four-year-old girl in a pair of faded pink cottontails. Ignoring me, she took one look at Red, pirouetted on the hall-runner and bolted into the shadowy interior. 'He's here. He's here. Red's here.' This was Faye and Leo's youngest, Chloe. No wonder Red liked it here. If Chloe had a basket of rose petals, she'd have strewn them in his path.

At its far end, the hallway opened into a haphazardly furnished room, part kitchen, part lounge, scattered with the customary detritus of family life and heavily shuttered with matchstick blinds. The blinds made about three degrees worth of difference, so the room felt like it was in Cairo rather than Khartoum. Torpor blanketed the house. Tarquin unfurled himself like a praying mantis from a beanbag in front of the television and the boys scooted upstairs in conspiratorial glee. Chloe dogged them optimistically.

Leo was upstairs, napping. Faye was standing at the sink in a shortie kimono thrashing a handful of greenery under a running tap. I opened the fridge. 'I'll have one, too,' said Faye.

The fridge was a cornucopia of everything from anchovies to zucchini. I deposited the ham and fetta, ripped the tops off a couple of stubbies of Cooper's Pale Ale and sank into the nearest beanbag, beginning to unwind at last.

A ferociously modish cook, Faye was a journalist by profession. She wrote for the *Business Daily*—one of those papers that runs stories with titles like 'GDP Gets OECD OK' and 'Funds Pan Mid-Term Rate Hike'—while Leo did something obscurely administrative at Melbourne University. Neither of them were what you might call high fliers and the contrast between Faye's billion-dollar subject-matter and her modestly anarchic personal circumstances never ceased to amuse me.

'So.' She added a baptised lettuce to the profusion in the fridge, dried her hands on her kimono and lowered her big-boobed frame into a cat-scratched armchair. 'You still got a job, or what?' The question was both personal and professional. Ever solicitous of my personal welfare, Faye also wanted the good oil on the Cabinet reshuffle.

'Pending satisfactory performance indicators,' I told her.

'Arts Ministry, eh?' she whistled appreciatively. 'That explains the ear. Trying to wow the art crowd, eh?'

'And not succeeding.' I gave her a quick rundown of the previous evening, all the way to the scene at the National Gallery moat. The business about the dead body interested her only mildly—she wasn't that kind of journalist—but my unconsummated experience with Salina Fleet elicited a sympathetic cluck. 'Not having much luck lately, are you, Murray?'

'How come I never seem to meet anyone sane?' I asked, relaxed enough now to feel philosophically sorry for myself.

'What about Eloise? You can't say she's not sane.'

Eloise was Faye's most recent exercise in dinner-party matchmaking. A waif-like book editor, she laughed so nervously at my little jokes that the beetroot and orange soup came out her nose. Then she burst into tears on her doorstep when I tried to do the right thing.

'She was pleasant enough, I suppose,' I said, not wanting to sound ungrateful. 'Just not my type.'

'And what is your type, Murray?' Faye was beginning to regard me as major challenge. She was constantly inviting me to meals and seating me beside some loudly ticking biological alarm clock. So far, she'd tried to pair me off with a workaholic paediatrician who left when her beeper went off during the osso buco, a lecturer in linguistics who couldn't stop talking about Pee Wee Herman, and an up-and-coming corporate lawyer with the inside-running on the bottom-line, real-estate wise. And then there'd been Jocasta, about whom the least said the better. The name, I think, speaks for itself.

'I don't know,' I said. 'Someone I don't have to impress or compete with. Someone who isn't assessing my genetic material over the entree. Someone nice. Goes off like a rocket.'

'Someone you can inflate when required?' said Faye. 'You don't want much, do you?'

The boys erupted down the stairs, towels over their shoulders. 'Can we go to the pool, huh? Huh, can we, huh, can we?'

'Even better,' I said. 'Let's go up the bush, find a waterhole.' Coldstream, I supposed, might technically qualify as the bush. Red looked keen.

'Do we have to?' whined Tarquin. He'd be a politician one day, our Tark. As a matter of principle, he never did anything without being pressured into it first.

'I'd take Chloe, too,' I said, winking at Tarquin, 'but the seat belt's broken.' That sealed the deal. A boys-only expedition into the wild.

'You stay and help Mummy,' Faye told the crestfallen girl. 'And we'll all have a picnic dinner tonight in the gardens, okay? You can invite your friend Gracie, okay?'

I went upstairs to the Curnows' bathroom and removed the bandages from my ear. It was scabbing up very nicely. I'd certainly come out of my ear-sundering experience better than Vinnie Van G. In two or three days, with a bit of fresh air, my lobe would be good as new.

Smeared with sunscreen, the boys and I piled into the car. 'Stay in the shade, careful of submerged branches, and don't get lost,' suggested Faye helpfully. 'And watch out for snakes.' I passed her my squishy fruit, terminating her bushcraft advisory service before Tarquin could chicken out.

We tooled out the freeway, singing along with the radio, the windows wound down. Hits and Memories. Ah bin cheated. Bin mistreated. When will ah be loved. 'Were you a mop?' Red wanted to know. 'Or a rotter?'

Within half an hour we'd cleared the built-up area and entered open countryside, paddocks of stubble the colour of milky tea. At the turn for Kangaroo Ground, the road ran between two vineyards and the boys let me think I'd conned them that there really were kangaroos bounding between the rows of vines. The road crested rolling hills and dipped into lightly wooded valleys, winding through tunnels of dappled darkness. At the top of a bare rise stood a peeling weatherboard church surrounded by moulting cypresses, a dilapidated sign out front: 'EEK AND YE SHALL FIND'.

'That reminds me,' I said. 'I've got to drop in on someone for a few minutes.' Acquired with parenthood, the habit of compulsive deception is not easily shed.

'Aaww,' the boys groaned in unison, but the wind buffetted the sound away.

At the Christmas Hills fire station, a zincalum shed, volunteer fire-fighters awaited the worst, stripped to the waist in the shade of a concrete water tank, moving only to fan the dust raised by our passing. At the far end of an unmade road, as instructed, I found Giles Aubrey's house in a tinder-dry forest of stringybark saplings.

The architectural style was the local specialty, Mudbrick Gothic. Clay-coloured adobe walls set with clerestory windows, the whole thing slung low into the slope. Somewhere down below, the river wound between the trees. We went around the side, looking for the door. Dry leaves crackled under our feet and bellbirds pinged loud in our ears. 'Careful of snakes,' I reminded the boys. It would be typical of Tarquin to get himself bitten.

'I trust you're not referring to me.' The man who spoke was sitting at a garden table beneath the shade of a pergola on a wide terracotta-tiled terrace. Behind him, glass doors opened into a house filled with pictures, rugs and books. In front of him, spread on old newspapers, was a punnet of tomato seedlings.

He was a desiccated little old rooster, with alert rheumy eyes and a complexion hatched with spidery blood vessels. The draw-string of his wide-brimmed straw hat sat tight under his neck and he wore a pair of canvas gardening gloves. Stripping off the gloves, he stood up and put his hand out, laying on the charm. 'Giles Aubrey,' he announced. 'And you are?'

It was Red he addressed and for a moment it looked like the kid was going to disgrace me. Then he took Aubrey's hand and pumped it gravely. 'Redmond Whelan,' he said. That about exhausted his supply of etiquette.

'Well, Redmond Whelan,' said Aubrey, relinquishing his hand. 'If you two boys go down that path, you'll find a very good place to swim. No matter if you haven't got a costume. It's my secret spot.'

The boys, braced to run, waited on my okay. 'It's quite safe,' Aubrey assured me. 'And I'm well past being a risk to anyone.'

I nodded and the boys bolted down the hill. Aubrey picked up a duck-headed walking-stick and pointed to the tray of seedlings. 'Would you be so kind as to bring those.' Walking gravely with the aid of the cane, he led me to a vegetable patch down a set of steps made from old railway sleepers. The earth was hard packed, the lettuces going to seed. A steep track ran down the slope and sounds of splashing and laughter wafted up through the trees. Aubrey lowered himself to his knees and jabbed the dirt with a small trowel.

'I heard about young Marcus on the radio,' he said. 'Tragic. Didn't quite make the connection at first. He used to be Marcus Grierson. Grierson's the mother's name, of course. Had a bad feeling about it, all the same. Then when you rang and mentioned the painting, it all fell into place. Szabo means 'tailor' in Hungarian. Rather predictable that way, Marcus was. Now I suppose the genie is out of the bottle. It was all in this suicide declaration they mentioned, I take it?'

Well, well, well. 'The note did make some allegations,' I said. 'But we'd like to hear what you have to say before we take the matter any further.'

'To lose one's reputation'—Aubrey tamped the ground around the seedlings, taking his time—'at my age.' Tomatoes planted this late in the season would probably not ripen.

'If you could start at the beginning.' The impersonal bureaucrat, that was the approach to take.

Aubrey gripped my knee and levered himself upright. His weight was so insubstantial I could barely feel the pressure. The horticulture was for my benefit, a demonstration that age had not wearied him. 'I'll put the kettle on.' Hospitality required certain rituals. He watered in the seedlings and we went back up the slope.

Aubrey's domesticity was an eclectic mixture of quality heirlooms and superseded modernity. Earth-toned paintings, over-framed. A French-polished sideboard bearing blobs of runny-glazed hand-wrought pottery. Persian rugs. Well-used Danish Deluxe armchairs. Giles Aubrey had once danced on the cutting edge.

A place for everything and everything in its place. The tea things were already laid out. 'Shall I pour?' he said. 'Gingernut snap?'

I sat my cup on my knee, cleared my throat and waited. Confession, too, had its protocols.

'The early seventies could have been a very good time for Victor Szabo,' he began. 'There was a growing appreciation of his work, thanks mainly to the popularity of the American photo-realists.' He gave a resigned shrug. The cultural cringe must have been an occupational hazard in Aubrey's line of work. 'But Victor was a difficult man, a perfectionist, neurotic and unpredictable. And a drunkard. He'd work on a picture for months, then go on a bender and burn it. What he did produce was good work, but I was lucky if I could get three or four paintings a year out of him. I had him on a retainer, not uncommon in those days. A hundred dollars a week to cover his living costs and materials, recouped from his sales. Costing me a fortune, he was. He was renting an old farm house, up at Yarra Glen. It's gone now, a housing development.' He was meandering off.

'Marcus?' I said.

'Turned up in mid '72. Just twenty, he was. Victor was quite awful to him, denied ever knowing his mother, even though Marcus had pictures of them together. Denied he was the boy's father, even though the resemblance was unmistakable. Marcus didn't want anything, mind you, except to be an artist. He'd sought Victor out contrary to his mother's wishes. I think he'd rather imagined himself as Victor's protege. Brought his folios with him, laid them at his father's feet. Quite competent he was too. Skilful, anyway. That appealed to Victor's ego, I think. So he let Marcus stay on as a kind of unpaid slave. I'd go up there and find Victor raging around his studio with a paintbrush in one hand and a bottle in the other, Marcus on his hands and knees on the kitchen floor preparing his canvases for him. Marcus was there for nearly two years and his presence seemed to have a good effect. Victor didn't drive, but Marcus had an old station wagon and every few months he'd turn up at my gallery in South Yarra with three or four pictures in the back. Never quite enough for a exhibition. I suppose I should have suspected something, but Victor had cost me so much money by then I just didn't want to think about it.'

The tea had gone tepid. I glanced out the open door, cocked an ear to the river, heard no sound of the boys. Aubrey levered himself up and picked up his walking stick. 'Perhaps the bunyip got 'em,' he said.

Just beyond the vegetable garden, we stopped at the top of the track. The river was immediately below us, shallow over a gravel bottom. Red and Tarquin lay side by side, face-down on the pebble bottom, letting the water ripple over them. Their naked skin showed white against the dappled brown gravel.

Aubrey took in the sight with a sigh. '*Quam juvenale femur!*' he exclaimed.

My grip on the third declension had only ever been tenuous, but I got his drift. Old Giles was a leg man. 'Your suspicions,' I said. 'When were they confirmed?'

'When I arrived unannounced one day and found Victor passed out drunk and Marcus working in the studio. He admitted then that most of what he'd delivered in the preceding year hadn't been Victor's work at all, but his own. Victor had no idea what was going on. Marcus begged me not to tell him.'

'And one of those pictures was *Our Home*?'

'The best of them, by far.'

'But you sold it to Max Karlin anyway.'

'Karlin had already bought it. I should have told him, I know. But the subject matter, the execution, everything except its actual authorship was classic Victor Szabo. And I did insist that Marcus stop it. Even offered him his own exhibition. Embarrassing it was. Pretentious art-school abstract expressionism. The only thing that sold, I bought myself out of pity. Victor wouldn't even come to the show. Soon afterwards they had a big blow-up and Victor turned him out. They never spoke again. Two years later I sold the gallery and retired.'

'So you and Marcus Taylor were the only ones that knew that *Our Home* was a fake?'

Aubrey winced at the word. 'As far as I know. I was afraid it would all come out at Victor's death. The will was a bitter blow to Marcus, but when he didn't say anything at the time, I put it to the back of my mind and it's been there ever since.'

'The will?'

'Marcus harboured hopes that Victor would eventually acknowledge him in some way. But he didn't even mention him. Not a word. Left everything to that Lambert woman. Marcus was devastated.'

What a depressing little saga. Father-and-son relationships are notoriously vexed, even at the best of times. This Victor Szabo sounded like a worst-case scenario. Marcus Taylor must have been lugging around enough psychological scar tissue to sink anybody, the poor prick. Fortunately, my own son had already won his Oedipal battle. Half of it anyway. I couldn't vouch for his mother.

'He was susceptible to women, Victor, and Fiona Lambert was scarcely a third of his age. Not that he had a lot to bequeath, just a few pictures and a growing reputation. But she made sure she milked that for all it was worth.'

'The Black Widow.'

Aubrey snorted derisively. 'Don't believe a word of it. She made that up herself. Shameless self-promotion. Victor died of liver disease, the result of poor personal hygiene and a surfeit of cheap wine.'

I struggled to assimilate the significance of what Aubrey was telling me. The news that the CMA's Szabo was not a Szabo at all was dynamite. It had the potential not merely to embarrass Fiona Lambert, the self-declared expert, but to expose to ridicule the competence of the government which had funded the purchase. 'Legal proceedings are inevitable, I suppose,' said the old man, wilting on his cane.

'That's not for me to say. May I suggest we keep this conversation confidential at this stage?'

He nodded penitently, as though receiving conditional absolution. There were other questions I should have asked Aubrey while I had the chance. But his tale of Taylor and Szabo had pricked my parental conscience. Down below, Red and Tarquin were swinging off an overhanging branch into dangerously shallow water. So I thanked Aubrey for his candour, assured him of my discretion and left the shrivelled old bird standing there, Tiberius among his tomatoes.

Shedding my clothes on the sandy bank, I hit the water running, scattering Red and Tarquin before me like startled cranes. Thigh-deep in mid-stream, I plunged to the bottom, luxuriating in the water's cool embrace.

Was it really possible to drown yourself in water this deep? Could any sense of grievance, any urge to self-dramatisation, be strong enough to overcome the body's fundamental instinct for survival? I kicked forward, propelling myself along the dappled gravel, holding my breath by sheer force of will. Could anyone really master that reflexive lunge for air that was propelling me so inexorably upwards? I broke the surface, scattering water, gasping.

No, Salina Fleet was wrong. Marcus Taylor hadn't killed himself. His death was an accident. It just couldn't have come at a better time, that's all.

Forty kilometres downstream, the Yarra berthed oil tankers and container carriers in the biggest port south of Singapore. Closer to its source, at the height of summer, it was little more than a series of shallow pools strung out along a narrow bed that meandered through the low hills.

We went exploring. The banks rose steeply on either side, thick with pencil-straight stringybarks and scrubby undergrowth, punctured with granite outcrops. Giles Aubrey had no immediate neighbours and within minutes we might have been in some trackless wilderness. Here, in the eternal bush, man and boy could test their masculinity against the challenges of raw nature.

'Ow,' said Tarquin. 'That tree scratched me.'

Pushing on intrepidly, we clambered over boulders and along bridges of fallen tree-trunks. 'But aren't there snakes?' insisted Tarquin.

'Keep your eyes open,' I said, drawing on my inherent knowledge of bushcraft. Pioneer blood flowed in my veins. My father's grandmother had once run a pub in Ballarat. 'Make plenty of noise as you go.' The advice was superfluous. If Tarquin managed to get himself bitten, it would be nothing short of miraculous.

'What do you do if one bites you?' Red wanted to know.

Snakes weren't exactly my forte, not in the zoological sense anyway. But the habitat did seem custom-made—sun-warmed rocks, cracks and fissures everywhere, plentiful frogs and other creatures coming down to the water to drink. I owed it to the boys to pass on the time-honoured lore of the bush. 'You have to get somebody to suck out the poison,' I explained. 'That's the standard treatment. Except if you get bitten on the backside.'

'What happens then?' said Tarquin, apprehensively scrutinising the riverbank.

'You put your head between your legs,' said Red, racing me to the punch line. 'And kiss your arse goodbye.'

Where a massive red gum overhung the water, I lingered in the shade and smoked a cigarette while the boys scouted ahead. A crystal stream bubbled at my feet. Dragonflies flitted hither and thither. The scent of eucalyptus perfumed the air. Kookaburras carolled distantly. Luxuriating in the tranquillity of the bush, I banished all thoughts of work—of Agnelli, of the press and Marcus Taylor, of Spider and the duplicate Szabo. I let my eyes close.

'Help!' came a scream from around the bend. 'Come quick.' Red. Not mucking around either, by the sound of it.

It was black, thick as my wrist, coiled at Tarquin's feet. Red was circling at a distance, stick in hand, bellowing for help. Tarquin stood frozen with fear. He must nearly have stood on the thing. 'Don't move,' I yelled. 'If you die, your mother will kill me.'

Grabbing the stick from Red's hand, I lunged forward and smashed downwards at the repulsive black spiral. At the same time, I shoved Tarquin out of harm's way. The snake bucked under the blow, bounced upwards and revealed itself to be the inner tube of a bike tyre.

'Tricked ya!' Red and I cackled simultaneously, high-fiving each other in the time-honoured Australian tradition.

'My ankle,' writhed Tarquin, prostrate on the ground.

'You've broken my ankle.'

It took me nearly an hour to carry him back downstream and up the hill to the car, slung over my shoulder fireman-style. His foot wrapped tight in my shirt, he whimpered right up to the moment I lowered him onto the back seat. 'Can we have an ice-cream on the way home?' he said.

'Shuddup, Tark,' said Red. But he didn't mean it. I suspected he was in on it all along.

It was well past eight when we arrived back in town. A note from Faye instructed us to proceed to the Exhibition Gardens, five minutes away, where a picnic awaited us. While the boys rummaged for frisbees and skateboards, I nicked home, changed into shorts and a t-shirt and put a bottle of pinot vino in a plastic carry-bag.

The shadows were lengthening as we walked to the gardens. The doors and windows of the houses had been flung open to admit the buttery dusk. Cooking smells and guitar-riffs emerged, and the old Italian and Greek remnants of the former demographic had come outside to hose down their footpaths and sit fanning themselves on their minuscule front porches. *Arms for Afghanistan*, said the fading grafitti. *Legs for Tito*.

Faye had not been the only one to think of dining alfresco that evening, and the lawns of the gardens were liberally peppered with picnickers and amorous couples. From the direction of the tennis courts came the pock-pocking of furry balls beating an intermittent rhythm to the chorus of innumerable cicadas.

Chloe appeared from between the trees to guide us to the others. She had a girl the same age with her, shy with big eyes. They led us towards a vast Moreton Bay fig, at the foot of which a blanket was spread. It was all very *Dejeuner sur l'Herbe*. Leo, tall and darkly bearded, lay propped on one elbow, plastic wine-glass in hand. Faye was removing containers from a cooler and laying them out. Seated between them, knees drawn up, glancing over her shoulder to keep a weather eye on the girls, was a woman I didn't know. She was not unlike the woman in Manet's painting except, of course, that she was not nude. Her loose summery dress only hinted at what she might be like underneath. More your full-figured Gauguin sort of thing was my guess.

Apart from me and Leo, there was no other man in sight. Bloody Faye, I thought. Playing go-between again, setting me up.

'Murray Whelan,' beamed Faye, butter not melting in her mouth. 'This is Claire Sutton.'

Claire Sutton had a mass of chestnut hair, pulled back into a bushy ponytail, and a high round forehead. We nodded perfunctorily. Lowering myself to the ground, I shot a sideways glower at Faye.

'I've just been telling Claire that you work in the arts,' she persisted. 'Claire's in the arts, too.'

'Uh-huh.' With Faye on the job, that could mean anything from riding bareback in a circus to running macrame classes. I passed my bottle of wine to Leo who, as usual, was handling the drinks. Faye's spread of salads and cold-cuts was straight out of the culinary pages of the colour supplements, much of it mysteriously so.

The children rushed the food, Tarquin suddenly began hobbling again. 'Guacamole?' said Red. Sydney was doing wonders for his education.

'Zhough,' said Faye. 'A Yemenite dip of coriander, cumin and garlic. What's wrong this time, Tarquin? You put it on the chicken.'

'He made me go rock climbing.' Tarquin jiggled up and down on one foot, dangling the other in front of his mother. Red piled a paper plate with everything in reach. Leo stood with the bottle squeezed between his thighs, straining at a corkscrew.

'I'm not really in the arts.' I met Claire eye-to-eye for the first time. She was, I saw, just as ambushed as me. 'The politician I work for has just been given that portfolio.'

The shy-eyed girl, obviously Claire's daughter, climbed across her to reach for a bread roll. 'Off you go and play,

Gracie,' she said. Claire had a wide mouth, a slightly turned-up nose and watchful brown eyes that hinted they might, if she so decided, laugh. 'I used to be a conservator'—she flicked me a quick glance to see if I knew what that meant—'at the National Gallery. But now I've got a print and framing business.' This was an exchange of credentials rather than conversation.

'Artemis, it's called,' enthused Faye. Tarquin limped off, ankle in remission, plate in hand. 'In Smith Street. Try the tapenade.'

I'd driven past Artemis, on the way to Ethnic Affairs. Awning over the footpath. Window full of pre-Raphaelite maidens. The tapenade was black stuff that tasted like a cross between sea-weed and Vegemite. I rolled it round on my tongue. 'Artemis?' The reference escaped me. Something literary, perhaps.

'Amazonian moon goddess,' said Faye. 'A mixture of olive paste, capers and anchovies.'

'Red or white?' said Leo. 'Capinata? Frittata? Aioli?'

Amazonian moon goddess? My heart sank.

'It's a joke!' Claire rushed to her own defence, spilling crumbs into her abundant decolletage, brushing them away self-consciously as she spoke. 'A pun. Arty Miss. My former husband's idea of being smart. He registered the business in that name and it stuck, even if he didn't.'

The deficiencies of ex-husbands were, in my book, a topic best avoided. 'Guess what I had for lunch, Faye? Strawberry sandwiches. Went to this brunch at Max Karlin's corporate HQ. His art collection is unbelievable. Must be worth millions.'

'He might not have it for much longer,' said Faye, unable to resist shop talk. 'From what I hear, this Karlcraft Centre project of his has turned into a bottomless pit. He's hocked to the eye-balls against the prospect of future commercial tenancies, but by the time the building is completed, there'll be a glut of down-town office space. Unless he can get some long-term tenants locked in pronto, he risks going belly-up.' Faye loved to talk like that. 'Word is that his creditors are getting pretty jumpy. Try the mesclun, Claire. Chloe, Grace, come and get a drink.'

The mesclun was a mixture of nasturtiums, dandelions and marigolds. 'Do I eat it?' whispered Claire behind her hand, making common cause against our mutual tormentor. 'Or put it in my hair?'

When I arrived, I'd wanted nothing so much as to succumb to the torpor of the evening. Now I wasn't so sure. Perhaps it was the wine. 'You've excelled yourself, Faye,' I said. 'Who are his creditors?'

'Various financial institutions. Guarantee Corp, Obelisk Trust. Walnut pesto?'

'I've heard of Obelisk,' I said, trying very hard to avoid looking down the front of Claire's dress when she reached for the crudites. 'What is it exactly?'

'Dip your pita in it. It used to be the Building Unions Credit Co-operative. Then a guy called Lloyd Eastlake took it over, restructured it into a unit trust and changed the name to Obelisk. It's what the Americans call a mutual fund. Manages a pool of funds on behalf of its investors. Unions mainly.'

'Claire mounted our Jogjakarta trishaw-drivers, you know, Murray,' said Leo.

Blow-ups of Faye's arty holiday photos lined the Curnows' hall, flatteringly framed. 'The ones inside the front door?' I said, admiringly. 'You did that?'

'Mounting street-vendors is my bread and butter.' Claire permitted her eyes a small smile, beginning to relax.

Before I could ask her if she'd mind taking a look at my etchings, the kids swarmed over us, Indians storming the fort. We ate. Ravenous, nothing in me but a coffee and a berry sandwich, I fell on the food. Faye and Claire talked kindergarten politics.

When we'd eaten, Leo got out a bat and we played cricket with the kids, using the No Ball Games sign for stumps. Claire hit a six off my first ball. In time, the shadows meshed together and the night fell gently from the sky. We crept through the velvet darkness, feeding cautious possums pieces of leftover fruit.

'Well?' Faye hissed into my ear, behind a tree. 'Thirty-three. Owns her own business. Not bad looking.'

What did she expect me to do, jump the woman on the spot?
'Where's the father of the child?'

'Left them a year ago. New cookie.'

'Coffee?' said Leo. 'Sambuca? Port?'

We walked back to Faye and Leo's, slapping mosquitoes. I
swung Grace up onto my hip. She took it as her due and twined
her arms around my neck. Her sleepy head nestled in the crook
of my shoulder. A daughter, I thought, would be nice.
Eventually.

'She's not usually so trusting,' said Claire.

'I wouldn't trust Murray as far as I could throw him,' said
Faye.

Cleopatra was on television. We sprawled in the dark before
the flickering set, draped with drowsy children. The girls,
curled like kittens in their mothers' laps, were soon rendered
unconscious by Richard Burton's narcotic vowels. Elizabeth
Taylor, fabulously blowzy, seethed and ranted. Leo lay bean-
bagged on the floor, Tarquin using his shins for a pillow. Red
slumbered against my shoulder. 'This film,' observed Claire, 'is
longer than the Nile.' She made, nevertheless, no move to leave.

What were the poor people doing tonight, I mused. Max
Karlin, for all his outward trappings, was teetering on the brink.
Desperate to find those elusive big-ticket tenants, those precious million-dollar customers willing and able to sign on the
line, ten floors for ten years. Multinationals. Public utilities.
Government departments needing accommodation for hundreds of pen-pushers, sitting there at their desks sending out
those millions of water bills.

By the time the credits rolled, Claire and I were the only
ones still awake. Perhaps all that on-screen sensuality had given
me the wrong idea, but her posture seemed more than accidentally provocative. She lay draped languidly at the other end of
the couch, errant corkscrews of hair framing her face. The fabric of her dress moulded to her body. She could not possibly
have been unaware how wanton she looked.

She wasn't. From behind lowered lids, she was measuring

my reaction. No longer concealing my interest, I ran my gaze lazily over her body. Then watched her reciprocate.

Our eyes devoured each other. The time had come to act, to grasp the transient moment. Gingerly, I prised Red's sleeping head from my lap. My hand edged towards Claire's extended leg.

Red's eyes sprang open. 'Tricked ya!' he yawned. His arm flung out in a stretch and connected with my sore ear.

'Ow,' I said. Faye woke with a start, activating Chloe.

'Huh? snuffled Leo, inadvertently letting Tarquin's head fall to the floor. 'Is it over?'

'My ankle,' groaned Tarquin. 'You kicked my ankle.'

Instantly, there was more barging around going on than Cleopatra ever dreamed of. 'Is it time to go home yet, Mummy,' pleaded Grace, rubbing her eyes.

'Yes, darling,' sighed Claire. 'I guess it is.'

Sunday's dawning came sticky with humidity, heavy with the prospect of rain. By dawning I don't mean the sun's rosy-fingered ascension. Nor do I mean the day's first blossoming when I reached for my winsome sleep-mate while thrushes warbled outside my window. I mean eight, when I shucked off the sheets, checked that Red was still asleep in his room and padded to the corner for the papers. I'd slept as deeply as the heat allowed, but my choice of dreams could have been better. Again, I'd been visited by Noel Webb.

Again, we were sitting in the wintry twilight on a park bench in the Oulton Reserve, Spider's contempt ringing in my ears, the three Fletcher boys looming over us.

The Fletchers were weedy runts but they'd been raised on a diet of belt buckles and brake fluid and they had us at unfavourable odds. They were sharpies, an amorphous tribe of terrifying reputation, precursors to the skinheads. In an era when every adolescent male in the world yearned for longer locks and tighter pants, the sharpies wore close-cropped hair and check trousers so perversely wide they flapped like flags. Rumoured to carry knives, they were less a gang than an attitude of casual violence looking for somewhere to happen. And now they had found me.

The moment I most dreaded had arrived. And Noel Webb, my as-yet-unpaid protector, was edging away. Flanked by his twin brothers, Geordie, the seventeen-year-old, thrust his face into mine. 'What are you looking at?' he snarled. His denuded skull occupied my entire field of vision.

A craven bleat issued from my mouth. 'Nothing.'

The twins snickered. 'Nah-thing, nah-thing.'

They acted like idiots, but that didn't make them any less dangerous. The kid their brother kicked to death wasn't much older than me. Trying to fight back would only provoke them. Not that fighting back entered my mind. My guts had shrivelled into a queasy lump and my legs were jelly. The contraband booze beneath my coat was my only hope.

But before I could get it out, offer it up in supplication, Geordie grabbed the crook of my elbow and jerked me upright. The twins closed from either side, pistoning their bony kneecaps into my thighs. 'Ow,' I said. Piss weak. A heel swung behind mine and swept my leg away. Wayne and Danny were pressed so close that I stumbled first against one then the other. Pinning my arms, they buffeted me sideways, setting me spinning like a top, biffing and slapping me as I turned, yelling encouragement to each other.

A circle of faces flashed before me. Fletcher faces. Noel Webb's face. Denied his mercenary price, Spider had gone over to the enemy. Or worse. A set-up all along. The tough men of the district had found some fresh meat. Round and round I spun, all the while attempting to wrestle the bottle from beneath the folds of my coat. Dizzy, strait-jacketed, sweaty with panic. That's when I woke up.

Both the Sunday papers had given the Suicide in the Moat story a run on page three. Both featured Salina Fleet in her widow's weeds, wistfully gazing at one of Marcus Taylor's sketches like it was the shroud of Turin. I took fresh croissants back to the house for Red's breakfast and rang Ken Sproule.

He'd seen the paper. 'As predicted,' he said. 'Angelo can stop peeing his pants.' Despite his crack at Agnelli, Sproule had thought it worth keeping his own ear to the ground. 'This suicide stuff's a load of crap. They found bruising to the back of the skull consistent with a fall. The cops tend to think he was walking along the parapet, tripped over, knocked his head and fell in.'

'What about the manifesto?'

'Could mean anything. Or nothing. The fact that it was found on the body doesn't necessarily make it a suicide note. But an anguished suicide makes far better copy than a clumsy drunk. Particularly with the girlfriend pushing that line. You watch. By this time next week, he'll be a great unrecognised talent and his work will start turning up in the auction houses. Not a bad looker, the girlfriend, eh? She's on some committee at the ministry, you know.'

'While you're on the line,' I changed tack, 'I met Lloyd Eastlake last night. What's a hot shot like him doing on a minor policy committee like Cultural Affairs? He fits that scene like a pacer at a pony club.'

'Parliamentary ambitions,' Sproule said. 'Same reason anyone gets themselves onto a policy committee. If you're not a union official, it's the best way to get yourself noticed, find out how things work. My guess is that Eastlake has targeted the arts to build a profile as something other than just another penny-ante money man.'

'He didn't look too penny-ante to me.'

'That's because you've led a sheltered life, Murray. That chauffeur-driven stuff might impress his investors, but it doesn't mean much in the big picture. For every Alan Bond or Robert Holmes à Court, there's a hundred Lloyd Eastlakes. They're a sign of a buoyant economy, springing up like mushrooms after rain. We need them to make the system work. But don't confuse Eastlake with serious money. You could probably count his millions on one hand.'

'Not a bad result for a humble chippie, though.' I ashed my cigarette in a saucer, sipped cold instant coffee from a cracked cup and wondered what I'd be doing if I had even a lousy one million dollars. 'So why does he want to get into parliament?'

'Why does anyone? If we psychoanalysed every parliamentary candidate we'd have full nut-houses and empty legislatures.'

An operator like Ken Sproule could never be taken on face value. He could be poisoning the wells. He could be giving me the good oil. But he was right about one thing. In our line of work, it was best not to think too much about people's motives.

'Tell me something else,' I said. Since Ken was in a talkative mood, the least I could do was listen to him. 'What's the story on this Centre for Modern Art acquisition? Three hundred thousand dollars was a pretty generous grant, wasn't it?'

'Piss off,' said Sproule. 'If I start to background you on last year's grants, you'll be pestering me every five minutes.'

'Don't be like that, Ken,' I said. 'Angelo's got to live with this decision, so I might as well know the reasoning behind it.'

'What's to tell? The CMA applied for funding. The Visual Arts Advisory Panel recommended the application be approved. Gil Methven accepted the recommendation. End of story.'

'I might have lived a sheltered life,' I said. 'But I didn't come down in the last shower. Eastlake is chairman of both the CMA and the Visual Arts Advisory Panel.'

'So what? Eastlake absented himself from the chair and left the room while his panel voted on the grant.' This was no more than the standard procedure for fending off any suggestion of conflict of interest.

'Eastlake's committee could only recommend the grant. Ultimate approval lay with the minister.'

'You trying to make a point here, Murray?'

'It's a big grant. Lloyd Eastlake must have done a lot of arm-twisting to convince Gil to approve it.'

'Gil agreed to provide half the funds if the CMA could find the other half. He didn't think they'd be able to raise that sort of dough for an unknown artist. But Eastlake came up with the money and Gil had no option but to keep his part of the bargain. The Centre for Modern Art is Eastlake's main hobby horse, but he wears a lot of other hats. Not much point in putting the chairman of the Cultural Affairs Policy Committee offside, not with the friends Lloyd Eastlake has in the unions.'

'His financial clients?'

'Eastlake has been dealing with the unions since back when he was in the building game,' said Sproule. 'What with all these mergers and amalgamations, some unions have found themselves sitting on sizeable assets, as well as having to manage their members' superannuation funds. They need financial expertise. The word got around that Eastlake had the magic touch and he ended up holding the kitty for quite a few of the comrades. You ever heard of Obelisk Trust? That's Eastlake.'

'And Obelisk donated the CMA's half of the purchase price for this picture they're buying?'

'Correctomundo.'

'Helping an art gallery to buy a painting hardly seems the ideal way for an outfit like Obelisk to target its sponsorship money,' I said. 'Isn't Eastlake just using union money to buy himself a bit of kudos with the art crowd?'

'Possibly. He's also engaging in a bit of mutual pocket pissing with Max Karlin. Obelisk has a lot of money riding on the Karlcraft project and paying top dollar for one of Max's pictures could be construed as a gesture of confidence in the project, a way of shoring up the commitment of other investors.'

At last we were getting to the nub of it. 'In other words, the Ministry for the Arts has just spent three hundred thousand dollars of public money to massage one of Lloyd Eastlake's investments.'

'Not just Eastlake's, pal. We're all in this. The Karlcraft Centre project is currently employing a small army of construction workers, most of them union members. It's spending money on everything from cement to door knobs, doing its bit for the local economy. When it's up and running, it'll revitalise much of the central business district, create hundreds of retail jobs and generate millions in government revenues. Putting the arts to work lubricating that process is a job well done, wouldn't you agree?'

Who was I to demur? I told Ken Sproule I owed him a lunch and rang off. 'Wakey, wakey, hands off snakey,' I called through Red's door. 'We aren't going to get much quality time together if you sleep all day.'

He got up and went straight around to Tarquin's place. By the time I'd finished breakfast and read the papers it was getting on for ten o'clock. I found the card with Eastlake's phone numbers on it and looked at it for while, thinking about the story Giles Aubrey had told me.

Like old Giles said, the genie was out of the bottle. Routine police procedures to identify Marcus Taylor would inevitably connect him with Victor Szabo. Shit, it had taken me about five minutes. Aubrey was in a confessional mood. Sooner or later, the whole thing would start to come unravelled. Spending public money on art was risky enough. Spending it on a fake would make us look like idiots, unfit to govern. Angelo would be directly in the firing line. A way would need to be found quietly to scotch the whole thing. I called Eastlake on his mobile and told him I'd appreciate an opportunity to talk to him about the Szabo acquisition at his earliest convenience.

'I understand,' he said. 'Looking out for Angelo's interest PR-wise.' Exactly. Eastlake said he was on his way to the Toorak Road Deli and suggested I join him there.

I went up the back lane and stuck my head in Faye and Leo's kitchen door. Faye had her hands in the sink and Leo had his head in the fridge. 'Where's the cake?' he said. The boys were on the floor glued to the television. There were no cartoons at that hour and they were reduced to watching a rural affairs documentary on mad cow disease.

'That reminds me,' I told Red. 'You'd better ring your mother.'

'It's right in front of you,' said Faye. 'So, Murray, what do you think of Claire? Tarquin, turn that TV off. We're going in ten minutes.' The Curnows, it transpired, were about to leave for Leo's mother's seventieth birthday party and would be out all day.

'Come and ring your mother.' I dragged Red out the back door. 'Then I'll show you where the rich people live.'

The rich people live in Toorak. Skirting the city centre, we crossed the river and headed into its leafy precincts. In hushed cul-de-sacs and meandering avenues, we peered and craned like tourists at the mansions of the filthy rich. Sydney, I informed Red, had plenty of fat cats and flash rats. But for your genuine, copper-bottomed blue-blood, you couldn't go past Toorak.

Cruising past the French Provincial farmhouses and Californian haciendas, the ivied walls and gravelled driveways, we drove the Charade down Toorak Road, a street where all the shops are boutiques and even a carton of milk costs more. The Deli was at the city end, a see-and-be-seen place with Porsches at the kerb and fourteen different kinds of freshly squeezed juice. Eastlake's Mercedes was parked across the road, between a red convertible Volkswagen with an Airedale terrier on the back seat and a Volvo station wagon with P-plates and surfboards on the roof rack.

Spider Webb was standing beside the Merc, looking into the window of a menswear shop called Pour Homme. We parked further down the block, outside one of those places that sells Groucho Marx lamp stands, pink neon telephones and musical birthday cards. A clip-joint for rich kids. Red lit up at the sight of it, so I peeled off ten dollars. Take your time, I told him. And if you shoplift, don't get caught.

The Deli was somebody's gold mine. Cappuccinos to the gentry. *Pain au chocolat* with the accent on the accent. Mobile phones in clear view. Blondes with perfect hair and beesting lips. Jewish husbands with melancholy expressions and big gold Rolexes. Lawyers in leisure-wear.

Lloyd Eastlake was in his element, sitting in a prime booth wearing tennis whites with navy piping. Sitting opposite him was a well-groomed woman in her late forties with big sunglasses and a brittle mouth. The sunglasses were pushed up on top of hair that had the panel-beaten finish rich women spend a fortune acquiring in the taxidermy salons of society hairdressers.

Eastlake saw me enter and waved me over. 'Murray Whelan,' he said. 'My wife, Lorraine.'

So this was the boss's daughter whose hand had given young Lloyd his leg up in business. Lorraine looked like she'd been repenting ever since, consoled only by the diversion of spending as much of his money as possible. She was just leaving.

'I hope I'm not interrupting your game,' I said sociably, an obvious tennis reference.

'Lorraine doesn't play,' said Eastlake. 'Do you, darling?'

'Nice to meet you,' said Lorraine. She'd forgotten my name already. As she headed towards the exit, a ruddy faced man with real estate written all over him moved to fill the vacuum. Eastlake deflected him with an easy gesture, signalled for more coffee and told me to sit down. 'You don't look too happy,' he said genially. 'Angelo not paying you enough?'

'Sorry to be the bearer of bad news,' I said, getting straight down to it before some social fly buzzed over and landed on us. 'I think we've got a problem.'

'Have we?' His expression brightened with amusement at my earnestness.

'You and me both,' I said. 'The Szabo isn't authentic. I'm afraid you've been had.'

His eyes narrowed, assessing me anew. 'You've been hiding your light under a bushel.' His tone was still playful on the surface, but there was a cool undercurrent. 'Didn't know you were such a scholar.'

'I was up Eltham way yesterday and I met someone called Giles Aubrey. He used to be Victor Szabo's dealer.'

At the mention of Aubrey's name, Eastlake leaned forward, beginning to take me seriously. 'Giles Aubrey,' he said. 'There's a blast from the past. So, tell me, what's the old bugger been whispering in your ear?'

'He said *Our Home* was painted by someone else.'

'Oh, did he just?' Beneath the flippancy was a tinge of irritation he couldn't quite hide. 'Did he say who?'

'Szabo's illegitimate son,' I said. 'Marcus Taylor.' Eastlake gave me a blank stare. 'The guy they fished out of the National Gallery moat.' It all sounded a bit far-fetched. 'Anyway, that's what he told me.'

Eastlake drew back and deliberately widened his eyes, like I was pulling his leg. When he saw that I was serious, the amusement drained from his expression. He pursed his lips and rubbed his chin, as though digesting the significance of what I had just told him.

A waiter arrived and put cappuccinos in front of us. Eastlake studied me carefully, as though attempting to discern my reliability. Then he made up his mind. Picking up his spoon, he leaned forward. When he spoke, it was in hushed, confidential tones. 'Can you keep a secret, Murray?'

I didn't reply, but he was welcome to continue.

'I'm not the one being had,' he grinned. 'You are.'

Eastlake built a floating island of sugar on the froth of his cappuccino and watched it slowly sink. 'Giles Aubrey is a bitter and twisted old man,' he said. 'And he's been spinning you a line. I don't suppose you happened to mention to him how much we're paying Karlin for the picture, did you?'

'I might have said something about it,' I allowed.

'And that's when he came out with his story?'

'He was very convincing.'

'Aubrey can be, by all accounts. You wouldn't be the first he's taken in. Lots of authentic Szabo embroidery, I imagine. This bit about the suicide in the National Gallery moat, this whatsisname...'

'Marcus Taylor.'

'That's a nice topical touch. Aubrey saw the story on the news, no doubt, and grabbed the opportunity to make a little mischief.'

'Why would he want to do that?

'Ancient history,' said Eastlake. 'Old wounds. Aubrey genuinely believed in Victor Szabo, but he never succeeded in making anything of his career. Szabo probably even cost him money. Seeing the sort of figures Szabo's pictures are currently fetching must really piss him off. But the money, I suspect, is the least of it. He's jealous of Fiona Lambert getting all the credit for securing Szabo's posthumous reputation. It was Fiona who found *Our Home* in Karlin's collection, pegged it as a benchmark work and suggested that the CMA acquire it. Casting doubts on the authenticity of *Our Home* would be the perfect way to undermine her reputation.'

This made a certain amount of sense. Perhaps Aubrey had seized on my phone call as an opportunity to exact a little belated revenge on Fiona Lambert. But that still didn't explain everything. 'The drowned guy, Taylor,' I said. 'He left a note. A manifesto, the press were calling it. Angelo thought they might beat something up. So I went to his studio yesterday morning, just before Max Karlin's brunch, and took a look around. He'd painted a perfect copy of *Our Home*.'

Eastlake slowly sipped his cappuccino, studying me over the rim of his cup. 'You're quite the eager beaver, aren't you?' he said. 'But I'm not sure what you're getting at.'

'Neither am I,' I admitted. 'It just seemed like an odd coincidence, given what Aubrey told me later.'

'It's not unusual, you know, for younger artists to make copies of landmark paintings. Just proves what I said. *Our Home* is a masterpiece.'

'But Taylor also had a photograph of himself with Victor Szabo. Doesn't that tend to corroborate Aubrey's story?'

Eastlake indulged me, amused by my persistence. 'I've got a picture of myself with the Prime Minister. That doesn't make me his love child.'

Put like that, my concerns were all starting to feel a bit farfetched. 'Looks like I've been wasting your time,' I said, burying my face in my own coffee.

'On the contrary,' said Eastlake. 'You did the right thing coming to me. We *have* got a problem. The art world thrives on gossip. Giles Aubrey's malicious inventions could do a lot of damage.'

'Aubrey can say what he likes,' I said. 'But he can't prove

anything. By his own admission, Taylor was the only other person who could confirm his story—and he's dead.'

'You miss my point,' said Eastlake. 'We're talking perceptions here. The value of a work of art is a fragile abstraction. If word gets around that doubts exist about the authorship of *Our Home*, similar speculation could easily arise about the integrity of other works in Max Karlin's collection. Suggest that one picture isn't what it's purported to be, people might wonder about the others. A person in your position, close to the Minister for the Arts, has a certain credibility. What you say gets heard, passed on, amplified.'

'I think I understand the situation, Lloyd,' I said pointedly, resenting the implication that I needed to be warned not to go blabbing Aubrey's story all over town. 'But I'm more concerned about potential embarrassment to Angelo than the market value of Max Karlin's art collection. In either case, the question is to make sure Aubrey stays quiet. He agreed to keep the story to himself yesterday, but who knows how long that will last.'

Eastlake had already figured this out. 'Call his bluff. Make him put up or shut up. If he took Karlin's money knowing that *Our Home* wasn't authentic, that's criminal fraud. Mention the prospect of prosecution and I bet he'll fall over himself to sign a statement confirming the picture's authenticity.'

A more informed discussion with Giles Aubrey was certainly on the agenda. 'I'll go and see him tomorrow,' I said.

'You do what you think advisable, Murray.'

Business done, I accepted a second cup of coffee and eased back into my surroundings. The Deli's cafeteria decor was obviously not its prime attraction, no more so than the quality of its profiteroles or the freshness of its juices. The customers were there for each other. As we were talking, Eastlake had been fielding social signals from the other booths. Spotting his opportunity, the beetroot-faced realtor table-hopped over, cup in hand. 'Hey, Eastie,' he said, wagging his tail. 'How's that new Merc of yours running?'

Eastlake introduced us, first names only. Malcolm was

wearing a Gucci shirt that might have done something for a man twenty years younger. 'Seen Lloyd's new car?' He jerked his head back towards the street. 'High performance automobile like that and he gets a chauffeur to drive it. That's like having the butler fuck your mistress. What do you drive, Murray?'

'Something smaller,' I said. Then, since the subject had come up, 'Good drivers easy to find, Lloyd?'

'Noel?' Eastlake was back at ease, expansive. 'I didn't find him,' he said. 'He found me. You know the Members' carpark at Flemington?'

Malcolm squeezed in beside me, ready to catch any gems of wit and wisdom Lloyd Eastlake might care to drop. The Members' carpark was where the silvertails held their chicken and champers picnics on Cup Day. Not a place you needed to be a regular race-goer to know about. I nodded. Go on.

'Last spring racing carnival, it was. I was out there with your predecessor, Ken Sproule. Terrible man for the gee-gees, Ken is. We've had a pretty good day and we're both well over the limit. So we get to the car and Ken decides he's not going to let me drive, not in my condition. It's starting to rain and there we are, standing next to the car…'

'That was the 450 SLC, right?' chipped in Malcolm. 'The two-door coupe.'

'…arguing the toss about whether I'm in a fit state to drive. Anyway, this bloke comes along, he's doing the rounds, working for some car-detailing firm. They go around during the afternoon, checking for dents, rust spots, that sort of thing. They put their card under the wiper—flaking chrome, cracked light, whatever—and a quote for the job.'

I could just see it. Spider Webb prowling the toffs' carpark with a twenty-cent piece in one hand and an eye to the main chance.

'So Ken gets an idea. This bloke can drive us into the city, take the car overnight, cut and polish it, drop it off at my place in the morning. It's either that or walk through the rain to the main gate, get a cab, come back the next day for the car. So I said okay. Next morning, there's the Merc in my driveway, spic and span, never looked better. It hadn't been running at its best, and he had a few ideas about that. Ended up looking after my wife's car as well. When I moved up to the SEL, I needed a driver and put him on full-time.'

Malcolm loved it, the adventures of the cavalier millionaire. 'Hundred and fifty grand's worth of vehicle and you handed the keys to a complete stranger?'

Not a bad story, but it sounded like pub talk to me. And a funny way to hire a bodyguard. Through the Deli's plate-glass front window, Spider was visible across the road. He was sipping from a polystyrene cup and lazily chewing gum at the same time. Blank-eyed, bored, watchful. Drip dry. 'This is the guy with the ears, right?' I pushed mine forward by way of example. The wound was healing nicely. 'Thought I saw him down near the Arts Centre yesterday morning.'

A pair of social lions prowled over, her in an Alice band, him in a track suit, faces from the CMA opening. Eastlake tossed me their names. 'You remember...' I remembered I had someone better to spend my time with. Offering my seat, I said hello, made my excuses and went to find Red.

His ten dollars had bought a roll of mints and a small electronic game in the shape of a spaceship. The mints weren't bad. I was trying to wheedle a couple more out of Red when we crested the Punt Road hill and hit the tail end of a string of traffic that ran all the way to the river.

Throwing a hasty left at Domain Road, I cut past the Botanic Gardens and through to St Kilda Road. The traffic was lighter there, although the Arts Centre had attracted quite a crowd. Had Marcus Taylor's famous death, I wondered, prompted a renewed interest in the Old Masters? The gelati vans were back in force and delinquents on skateboards were surfing the steel waves of the sculpture on the lawn next to the Concert Hall. Red was drawn like a magnet to the sight. On impulse, I pulled into a vacant parking space.

A juggler had set up shop beside the sculpture in front of the State Theatre, a hideously ugly brown lump. The sculpture, not the juggler. The juggler was dressed as King Neptune and had three carving knives and a flaming firebrand aloft simultaneously. I thought I knew how he felt. Just as he finished, an octopus on stilts appeared through the crowd. 'Check this out,' I told Red. 'It's harder than it looks.' Especially since one of the stilts had a bend in it. Red wasn't interested in some promenading fish. His interest lay with the skateboarders. I told him to run ahead, that I'd join him in a few minutes.

Jumping up onto the parapet of the moat, I threaded my way past parked backsides and headed towards the entrance of the National Gallery. The parapet was a little less than a metre across, about the width of a standard table. Not exactly an acrobatic challenge. But then Marcus Taylor didn't have a great track record when it came to tables. It would, I could see, have been quite easy for someone with a few drinks under his belt to slip and knock himself out on the hard grey basalt. But what was Taylor doing walking along the parapet? He was coming from the other direction and the most direct way to the YMCA did not lie along the front of the building.

I went the way I'd have gone if I was Taylor, skirting around the back. At the stage door of the Concert Hall, I found the same guy on duty who'd let me into the Arts Ministry the previous morning, and got him to unlock the YMCA. The same air of scrofulous melancholy pervaded the place, but not the same silence. As the lift juddered open at the third floor, Lou Reed advanced down the corridor to meet me.

He was coming from one of the formerly locked rooms. A woman in bib-and-brace overalls stuck her head through the open door and watched me advance, her eyes narrowing. 'If you're a journalist,' she said, 'you're a bit late. I already told that lot who were here yesterday everything I know. Which is nothing. The guy was a hermit.' She had a stick of charcoal in her hand. Behind her I could see big sheets of parchment paper taped to the walls. They were covered in black squiggles that might, given a couple of million years, have eventually evolved into horses. Or dogs. Or giraffes.

'If I look like a journalist, I can assure you it's not intentional.' I nodded towards Taylor's end of the corridor. 'I'm a sort of friend.' Well, Taylor was in no position to contradict me.

'Oh,' she said, scowling. 'I didn't…' She was going to say she didn't know he had any, but stopped herself in time. 'Didn't have a lot to do with him. Like I said, he kept to himself.'

'There was a painting he was working on last time I was here,' I said. 'I was sort of interested in it.'

'Help yourself,' she said, turning her back in disgust. 'Everyone else has.'

When I opened Taylor's door I discovered what she meant. Taylor's rooms had been plundered of almost anything of value. The camp stove had been nicked, the microwave oven, the desk lamp, even jars of used paintbrushes. Most of the books had gone from the brick-and-board case. A half-dozen back copies of *Veneer* remained, a thin tome entitled *The Necessity of Australian Art* and a dog-eared copy of *A Fierce Vision*. I thumbed through it. A sheet of tracing paper marked the plate of *Our Home*, the principal details precisely transferred to a pencil-drawn grid. Using such a template, a competent draughtsman could easily have enlarged the image to actual size and transferred it onto canvas. It told me nothing I didn't already know, that Marcus Taylor had whipped up a pretty fair version of *Our Home*. Whether it was his first or second attempt, why he'd done it, and where it had gone, were all questions that remained unanswered.

Taylor's dog-eared little collection of photographs was still in the desk drawer. When I compared them with the sketch in Fiona's book, there wasn't much doubt that Victor Szabo's life-drawing model was the woman in the photo. The young hippy that could have been Taylor could still have been Taylor. Szabo was still definitely Szabo. I put the snaps in my pocket.

The cheap plastic-covered stamp album was still there, too, with its paltry contents of low-denomination recent releases.

Stamp collecting was a hobby that had never captured my imagination. But waste not, want not. If Red didn't fancy the album, some other child might. That little girl, Grace, for example. Philately might not get me everywhere, but it would give me an excuse to go calling on her mother.

The bankbook was still slotted into the crevasse between the desk and the wall where I'd dropped it in my haste to flee. I hooked it out with a bent coat-hanger and found myself looking at the most interesting thing I'd seen all day.

Critically unappreciated he might have been, but Marcus Taylor was clearly finding a market for something he was doing. Over the previous six months, he'd made a number of deposits. The sums varied from twelve hundred to four thousand dollars, totalling nearly twenty thousand. Not a bad little nest egg for a man whose grant application form said that his sole income was unemployment benefits.

I pondered its meaning. But not for long. Red would be wondering what had become of me. I dropped the bankbook back behind the desk. It felt like evidence. Of what, I didn't know. Sticking the stamp album under my arm, I headed back along the side of the National Gallery. A gang of young hoons was stampeding down the footpath, pushing a shopping trolley full pelt. One of them was crouched inside the cart, gripping the sides for dear life, screaming insanely at the kid doing the steering.

'Help!' he was screaming. 'Murder! Murder!'

There was only one S. Fleet in the White Pages with a CBD address. Little Lonsdale Street. The western end, down towards the railway yards. Funky. Low rent. About the right place for a loft. Fifteen minutes walk from the Arts Centre. A five-minute drive.

'Wait here,' I told Red, parking around the corner. 'I won't be long.'

'Shoosh,' he said. His head was bent and his thumbs were furiously manipulating the liquid crystal blips of his hand-held electronic game. 'I'm going for the record.' The stamp album, understandably, had failed to impress. It lay discarded on the back seat.

'Ten minutes,' I said. 'Then we'll go have some fun, just you and me.' He didn't look up.

The Aldershot Building was six floors of faded glory, a Beaux Arts chocolate box dating from the boom of the 1880s. Barristers from the nearby law courts might once have had their chambers here, wool merchants, pastoral companies, shipping agents, stockbrokers. Then the boom had gone bust. The mercantile bourgeoisie moved out and the wholesale jewellers and sheet-music publishers moved in. In time, as the pigeon shit mounted on the curlicued plinths of the facade, these became two-man tailor shops and fishy photographers, doll doctors and dental technicians. Eventually, the strict prescriptions of the fire department had driven away even these modest entrepreneurs.

But the Law of Unintended Consequences supersedes even the Prevention of Fire Act and the tenants squeezed out by the prohibitive cost of overhead sprinklers and CO_2 extinguishers had been replaced by bootleg gayboy hairdressers, speakeasy desktop publishers and loft dwellers—all of them on handshake leases with blind-eye clauses. At the Aldershot, no-one was really there and if they were they were just visiting.

Flyers for dance clubs were taped to the wall of the small ground-floor vestibule. Among them, beside the lift, was a much-amended hand-written list of tenants. Salina Fleet was on the sixth floor. I took the lift, a modern job not more than forty years old with cylindrical bakelite buttons that stuck out like the dugs on a black sow. It opened straight onto the corridor. Salina's was the first door along.

She didn't answer at first. I knocked, waited, knocked again. A reggae beat was coming from somewhere, emanating from the very bones of the building, dreams of Jamaica. I knocked again and was about to turn away when the door opened a chink and Sal peered tentatively through the gap.

'Oh, it's you.' Her mouth gave me a jumpy, automatic smile and her eyes tried to find their way around me into the hall. They were cold and glistening like she'd just been polishing them and had to put them back in to answer the door and they weren't warmed up yet. Her once-fruited lips were thin and pasty. Unconsciously raising a little finger to them, she tore off a half-moon of nail.

'Don't worry,' I said, harmlessly. 'I haven't come to take you up on your offer.'

The skin was drawn tight across the bridge of her nose, accentuating the bird-like cast of her face. It was a face about five years older than when I'd first seen it. She didn't open the door any further and she didn't invite me in.

'Sorry to drop by out of the blue,' I said. 'But I've heard that they're pretty well decided that Marcus's death wasn't suicide. Thought I should let you know.'

She accepted the news as though already reconciled to the possibility. Her neck flexed in a tiny bob, pecking an invisible grain of wheat. 'Part of me hoped so, in a way. I can't blame myself for an accident, can I?'

'I was a bit abrupt yesterday,' I said. 'If you'd like to talk about it.' I looked at the floor. 'As a friend.'

She reached out through the gap in the door and put her hand softly on my chest. 'You're a sweet guy, Murray. Really, you are. But I'd rather be alone.' She gave me the most bathos-drenched look ever practised in front of a mirror, sighed heavily and stepped back.

She'd tried that one before. Last time, it had nearly worked. Before the door could shut, I had my foot in it. Through the crack, I could see a bed. On the bed was a suitcase. 'Going somewhere, Sal?'

'How dare you!' she spat through the gap, putting her shoulder to the door. 'You can't just force your way in.'

My thirty-kilo advantage sat inert against the door. 'Talk to me,' I said. 'Please.'

The pressure on the door diminished somewhat. 'This official, or what?'

'Or what,' I said.

She backed away silently, letting the door fall open. Her lack of pretence at hospitality was refreshingly unrehearsed.

What Salina called her loft was a large high-ceilinged room that might have once been a typing college classroom or the workshop of a manufacturing milliner. Chipboard partitions had been installed to create separate kitchen and bathroom areas, the floor had been sanded back and the place stocked with oddments of retro furniture of the Zsa Zsa Gabor On Safari variety. The wardrobe was a metal shop-display rack on castors, half empty. The bed took up the rest of the space, unmade beneath a scattering of clothes and a small, half-packed suitcase. The ashtray contained about five thousand half-smoked green-tinged butts.

'Nice,' I said.

My opinion was a matter of supreme indifference to Salina Fleet. 'What's this all about?' she demanded.

A little of the old Sal had returned. She was wearing Capri pants with a pink gingham shirt knotted at the midriff and hoop earrings. She was still in mourning, though. The Capri pants were black. A bit of bluff might have got me through the door, but it wouldn't get me any further. She'd backed herself against a window sill and folded her arms tight. She wasn't going to take any bullying.

I wasn't going to give her any. By way of emphasising that my intentions were honourable, I turned my back to the bed and perched on the arm of a zebra-patterned sofa. 'Suicide or accident, Marcus Taylor's death is a hot story. You're not the only one the press have been talking to. All sorts of stories are flying around. My job involves keeping one step ahead of the pack.'

That was only part of it, of course. In the final analysis, it wasn't the Protestant work ethic that was gunning my engine. It was my frail ego. I had the distinct impression that my string was being jerked. By whom and to what end was not yet apparent. But I didn't like it. Not one little bit. 'You being on the Visual Arts Advisory Panel, I thought you might be able to advise me.'

'Stories?' Feigning nonchalance, she put a cigarette in her mouth and flicked a disposable lighter. 'What stories?'

'Let's start with yesterday first. You went to the YMCA to get a picture, right? But someone had beaten you to it.' Her lighter wouldn't fire. She kept flicking the wheel with her thumb. I got out mine, walked over to the window and lit both of us up. 'Right?'

'I told you.' She exhaled Kooly. 'I went to get some personal things.'

'Toothbrush? IUD? Little things that slip easily into a folio case.'

'And to make my private goodbyes to Marcus.'

'By coming on to me?'

'I was upset. Vulnerable.'

We wouldn't get far heading down this track. I took myself back to the zebra. 'Tell me about Marcus. How did you get involved with him?'

She shrugged. 'How does anybody? We met last winter. At an exhibition. He tried to lobby me for a grant. He was hopeless—insecure and arrogant at the same time.' All the things that women can't resist. 'I was on the rebound. We ended up in bed. You know how it is.'

I nearly did. 'And so he got his grant.'

That was below the belt. 'It was a committee decision, based on artistic merit.'

Now we were getting somewhere. 'Good artist, was he? As good as his father, Victor Szabo?'

'Where on earth did you get that idea?' Apparently the suggestion was ludicrous.

'Like I said. Stories are flying around.' I took the photos out of my pocket and showed her the snap of Szabo with the kid that might have been Taylor. 'Like father, like son. And from what I've heard, there wasn't just a taste for the booze in old man Szabo's genes. Marcus inherited a dab hand for the brush. He could knock out a passable version of almost anything, I understand. Not that I'm any judge, but what I've seen of his work certainly confirms that view.'

Her eyes widened. 'You've seen it?'

'It?'

She didn't say anything for a while. She was too busy giving me the slow burn. It could have popped corn at five paces. Lucky I was wearing my asbestos skin.

When that didn't work, she tossed her head back and studied the way her cigarette smoke rose in a lazy coil towards the ceiling. I studied it, too. Ascending effortlessly in a solid unbroken column, it reached higher and higher, an ever lengthening filament of spun wire, stretching up towards the embossed tin panels far above. Then, just as its destination seemed within reach, it wavered, broke into an ephemeral mass of swirling spirals, and dissipated.

'There was never any misrepresentation on my part,' she said abruptly. 'I want that clearly understood.'

'Absolutely.'

She started pacing then, stalking the right approach. 'If this thing gets taken any further, I want protection.'

Protection? From whom? What the hell was she talking about? 'I understand,' I said. 'You don't want to be the one that takes the fall?'

Her point taken, Salina moved into negotiating mode. 'Damn right,' she said. 'Marcus's image production was a perfectly valid form of post-modern discourse, right out there on the cutting edge. His pastiche-parodies of actual artworks effectively deconstructed the commonly held notions of value, authenticity and signature. They were a critical response to the pre-eminence of the so-called famous artist.' She paced, delivering a dissertation. 'His pictures were never mere copies. If his images were subsequently misread as such by others, that's not my problem. It was not my role to impose a monopoly on meaning. Legitimate appropriations, that's what they were. There was never any attempt on my part to pass them off as originals.'

Sometimes, not often, but sometimes, it's as simple as that. *Eek and ye shall find.* Unless my grasp of art-speak was even more tenuous than I feared, Salina Fleet had just told me that Marcus Taylor had been knocking up fakes and that she'd been marketing them for him.

'And these "appropriations"'—I hooked my fingers around the word and rolled it over my palate, savouring its supple resonance—'included a "pastiche" of Victor Szabo? A "parody" of *Our Home*, perfect right down to the engine number on the motor-mower?' She nodded. I was on the right track. 'Like you say, a perfectly valid form of artistic practice. So where is it now?'

That pulled her up short. 'Christ!' she gasped. 'You mean you don't know. I thought...'

'You thought what?'

But the shutters had come down. She'd been trading on the assumption that I knew something I didn't, that I knew who had the duplicate Szabo. Her hands were shaking. She crossed to the door and flung it open. 'Get out,' she hissed. 'You bastard.' It came to me that she was very much afraid. When she wasn't acting she was quite convincing. 'Out. Out.'

'Who do you want protection from? I can help.'

'Just leave,' she commanded icily, her mouth again tearing at a fingernail. 'I refuse to comment further without a lawyer present. If you don't get out, I'll start screaming.'

She didn't give me much alternative but to do as she asked.

'Under the circumstances,' she said, as I stepped past her. 'I think it best if I resign from the Visual Arts Advisory Panel.' Since trafficking in dodgy artworks was hardly an ideal qualification for membership, that sounded like a good idea. I didn't get to tell her so. She'd already shut the door.

Fifteen minutes had elapsed since I'd abandoned Red to his computer game. A couple more wouldn't hurt. I called the lift up, pushed the ground floor button and stepped back out. Otis elevator smacked his big rubber lips together, growled and slunk away. I leaned against the wall and lit a cigarette.

It had burned to the filter when Salina came out her door. She'd put on a pair of gold sling-back sandals and was carrying the small suitcase. She saw me and stopped. She was about to say something unpleasant when the lift arrived. It made a clunking noise and its doors slid open. Standing inside was Spider Webb.

Old blank face himself, shades and all, flexing his jaw like a punch-drunk pinhead. He registered first me, then Salina, ten metres beyond. I registered her, too. She looked like a trapped animal. I stepped in front of the lift, blocking Spider's way. He stood there, legs apart, sizing me up. The doors began to close. I stepped inside and the doors slid shut behind me.

None of the buttons were depressed. He'd been coming to this floor. Where else? I punched the ground floor button with the side of my fist and we began to descend. I turned to face the door, the way you always do in a lift. 'You really get around, don't you?' I said.

His hand shot past me and hit the red emergency stop button. The lift slammed to an immediate halt, throwing me off balance. Before I could get it back, Spider had his forearm against my chest and my back pressed against the wall. 'What the fuck you playing at?' he snarled, breathing Arrowmint all over me.

Under the circumstance, I assumed the question was essentially rhetorical. I kicked him in the shins. He stepped delicately sideways as though avoiding a spilt drink and rammed the ball of his open hand into my solar plexus. I got a little irrigated in the visual department at that point and would have liked a little sit down, if at all possible. 'Ummphh,' I said. 'Whodja ooatfa?'

Spider's face was pushed so far into mine that when he opened his mouth I read the maker's mark on his silver fillings. Any closer and we'd have to get engaged. All I could see of his eyes, though, was my own reflection in those fucking mirror shades. Five times in three days I'd seen him, and still I hadn't seen his eyes. A regular Ray Charles, he was. By the look of the reflections staring back at me, he was doing a pretty good job of putting the wind up me. 'You know what's wrong with you, Whelan?' he said.

By then I knew better than to even attempt an answer. I just stood there, nurturing my inner cry-baby and waiting for the liquidity in my bowels to abate. Spider adopted the softly solicitous tones of a psychotic sergeant major. 'You get in over your head. That's what's wrong with you. You gotta learn to take the hint. Lay off where you're not wanted.'

He slammed one of Otis's buttons and the lift resumed its descent. Spider stepped back then and stood, legs apart, casually waiting for it to reach the ground floor. 'You fucking ape,' I said. 'I'm supposed to be impressed, am I?'

Actually I was, deeply. In my line of work, it's reasonably rare to be strong-armed by a gun-toting thug. That sort of thing usually only happens in federal politics. 'I'll go to Eastlake. I'll have your job.' It sounded pathetic, but it was the best I could do. Fuck the macho shit.

The lift hit rock-bottom and the doors slid open. 'You wouldn't do that,' said Spider, cheerfully. 'Not to an old mate.' He made like a head waiter, ushering me out of the lift ahead of him. 'And you shouldn't leave your kid sitting by himself in the car like that. You'll get done for child neglect.'

We stood there, looking at each other. Him in the lift, me outside. Then he smiled. The kind of smile that could stop a clock. He was still smiling when lift doors slid shut.

I turned then and ran. I ran out the front door of the Aldershot Building, down the hill and around the corner. At the intersection up ahead, Salina Fleet was getting into the back of a cab. She must have come down the fire stairs. I hit the Charade at a sprint.

'You should have been here, Dad,' accused Red bitterly, his eyes downcast, his little hands twitching ceaselessly. 'I got 20,000 points.'

Russell Street Police Head-quarters was straight out of Gotham City, a brick wall with a thousand blind windows and an RKO radio mast on the roof. Calling all cars.

As a functionary of the incumbent government, albeit an insignificant one, I could not but regard the police as my colleagues. Benign and efficient upholders of the rule of law. Our boys in blue. In other parts of our great nation, the rozzers were thick-necked bribe-takers, rugby-playing racist bully-boys, brothel creepers. But nobody said that about the Victoria Police. Defenders of widows and orphans they were. Protectors of the innocent.

But not necessarily of a ministerial adviser with spiralling suspicions, insufficient grounds for the laying of charges and a child's safety to think about. Quite a lot to think about, as a matter of fact. We drove past Russell Street and kept going. 'How about a movie?' I said. Something we could do together. Somewhere cool and dark where we could hide and I could start drawing some mental maps.

'*Die Hard*?' said Red. '*Young Guns*?'

Whatever happened to Pippi Longstocking? Maybe the movies weren't such a good idea. We kicked around a few other potential game plans. We decided to go exploring again.

We covered a lot of territory that afternoon. We covered school, friends, holidays. We covered Wendy. My former consort had taken up with a prosecutor from the New South Wales Crown Law Department. His name was Richard. You didn't need to be Clifford Possum Japaljarri to connect the dots there. 'What's he like?' I asked.

Wendy was a go-getter. It was her go-getting that had got rid of me. In our marriage of equals, some were more equal than others. We didn't fight. We weren't unfaithful—not that I knew about. Wendy was just moving faster than me, aiming elsewhere. It took me nearly ten years to figure that out, her a little less. If this Richard could make her happy, fine. A happy Wendy would be a sight to behold.

'He's okay, I guess,' said Red, an endorsement so insipid it brought a smile to my lips and nearly broke my heart. This Richard might be around for years. Wendy could shack up with whoever she liked, but if Dicky Boy started calling himself Red's stepfather there'd be hell to pay.

Equipped for high adventure in sandshoes and sunscreen, we followed the same route as the previous afternoon. Out the freeway, past the roadside flower vendors, the orchards and stud farms, the go-cart tracks and vintage car rallies. At the Sugarloaf Reservoir, we bought sandwiches and sodas and ate them in the sausage-scented smoke of the public barbecues. The crowds were out in force, clannish Croats and cacophonous Cambodians and stubby-clutching Ockers. Swimming was prohibited and once we'd walked across the weir, thrown rocks into tomorrow's drinking water and watched the spillway fishermen not catching trout, we struck out for more challenging terrain.

The humidity was 110 per cent, the air as thick as Faye's tapenade, wet as a sauna. The sky oozed over us like a clammy slug, threatening to rain, not delivering. At the Christmas Hills fire station, the sheds sat empty. The brigade was out on a call. A troop of Scouts were filling their water-bottles at the tap. Red disdained them from behind the window of a feebly air conditioned Japanese hatchback.

A kilometre short of Giles Aubrey's private road, we parked in a turn-around and skittled on foot down the wooded incline towards the dull sheen of water. A cascade of rocks and leaves dribbled down the slope ahead of us. The river was slow-moving and not much cooler or wetter than the surrounding air. We stripped to our togs and rushed in, thrashing and splashing and laughing.

Half an hour later, rock-hopping our way upstream, we disturbed a full-grown brown snake. In a single fluid motion, it slithered across our path, long as a broom-handle, flicking its tongue. Watching it go to ground in the fissure between two boulders, Red backed against me. 'Wow,' he whispered, awed and not a little afraid. 'Tark will be pissed he missed this.'

A tad more respectful of our environment, we pushed on. Red was still keen, if a little less gung-ho. Even when he charged ahead to blaze our trail, he kept me in sight, looking back over his shoulder to make sure I was keeping up. It grew darker. The clouds were engorged eggplants, roiling and stewing, close enough to touch. A dry stick of lightning forked across the sky.

We waded out of a narrow ravine onto the dry sand-bar downhill from Giles Aubrey's place. Red, spying the rope where he and Tarquin had played reckless Tarzans, ran ahead.

Halfway there, he pulled up sharp, eyes riveted to the ground. 'Dad,' he called sharply, poised between backward retreat and stark immobility. 'Come quick. Snake attack.'

A man lay face-down on the exposed river-bed beside the eroded wall of the bank. One arm was bent behind his torso, the other twisted behind his neck. It was not a natural position and he wasn't moving.

I took Giles Aubrey by the shoulder and rolled him over. He was as light as balsa and dead as a dodo. His face had been pressed flat against the dry quartz sand of the river-bed and was flecked with grains of mica, diamond dust against the blotched pink parchment of his skin.

How long he had been lying there was impossible to tell. He wasn't warm but neither was he particularly cold. How he had got there was easier to determine. A small avalanche of leaves and pebbles lay scattered around his sandalled feet. He had come tumbling down the near-vertical incline of the riverbank, a drop of perhaps ten metres. The fall had been a nasty one and from the ungainly contortion of the limbs, I guessed that death had come on impact.

Red had found a stick and mounted guard. 'Can you see the snake?'

'He fell.' I pointed up towards the vegetable patch, showing what had happened.

'Yuk,' said Red, disappointed. 'Gross.'

Gross indeed. Leaving Aubrey's body where it lay in sand scuffed and churned from the boys' play the previous day, we climbed the embankment and back-tracked to where his descent would have begun. The old man's duck-headed walking stick lay on the ground at the top of the bank. His prostrate form lay immediately below. Picking up the cane, I silently pointed out the skidmarks that traced a path down the slope. Red nodded gravely, as though absorbing some important moral lesson. This is what happens if you go too close to the edge.

A crack like a gunshot split the air, the temperature dropped ten degrees and the atmosphere condensed itself into raindrops. One by one they began to fall, so slow you could count them. They were as big as golf balls, so fat and heavy they raised craters in the dust. Then all at once it was pouring. Rain churned the earth, turning it to mud.

We dashed for the shelter of the house. Red beat me. We were both already saturated. When I came through the door, he was at the phone, offering me the handpiece. I assumed it had been ringing when he burst inside, the sound drowned in the downpour. I put it to my ear. 'Hello,' I said.

There was no-one on the line, just a ringing tone, terminating abruptly in the faint hiss of an answering machine tape. 'Thank you for calling,' announced a patrician voice.

'Regretfully, I am unable to respond personally at this time. Please leave a message.' Short, to the point, polite, confident. Phillip Veale.

I hung up slowly, my brow furrowed into a question. 'Last number re-dial,' Red explained to the family idiot. 'They always do it on *Murder She Wrote*.'

'What makes you think it's murder?'

Red shrugged. He didn't. He was just following correct television procedure. 'Now dial 911,' he told me.

'Triple zero in Australia,' I informed him, dialling. 'It was an accident. He was very old and he fell over. And don't touch anything else, okay?'

As I finished giving the emergency operator the details, I became aware of a noise. A repetitive thunking. A low-pitched pulse, barely audible over the drum beat of the rain on the roof. Hanging up, I cocked my ears and tracked the sound. It was coming from the stereo, one of those Bang & Olufsen jobs like an anodised aluminium tea-tray. Aubrey must have had a thousand records, the edges of their covers squared off in perfect order in a set of custom-built timber shelves. I lifted the stylus arm onto its cradle and picked the record up by its edges. Faure's *Requiem*, von Somevun conducting. A little light listening for a sticky Sunday arvo. I slipped the record into its sleeve.

In Aubrey's wardrobe, I found a gaberdine overcoat. By the time I'd scrambled down the bank, it seemed like a pointless gesture. His clothes and hair were drenched and little rivulets of rainwater were forking and branching around his twisted limbs. The correct procedure, probably, was to leave him where he lay. Let him lie there, open-mouthed amid the puddles until appropriately qualified people arrived and did what appropriately qualified people do.

But I'd taken tea with this man, eaten one of his gingernut snaps. Not to have picked him up out of the dirt would have felt like a calculated act of disrespect. Of myself as much as of him. Besides which, the river was beginning to rise. Rain-pitted water was inching towards the body. The cause of his death was patently obvious, written in the clearly visible trajectory of his fall down the riverbank. I stood for a moment looking down at the second wet body I had seen in as many days. Then I draped the coat over Aubrey and carried him up to the house. I think the coat weighed more.

'What you told me yesterday,' I asked, as we trudged together through the smell of wet earth and the drumming of rain on leaves. 'What was true and what was lies? And what did you talk about with Phillip Veale?' But Giles Aubrey made no answer.

If moving the body was a problem, nobody told me. Nobody told me much at all, really. I'd only just finished laying Aubrey out on his bed when the ambulance arrived. The two-man crew ignored the rain which had eased to a steaming drizzle. I didn't really know the man, I explained. My son had found the body.

'These old people,' said the driver, not unsympathetically. 'They do insist on living alone.'

The label on a bottle of pills on the bedside table bore the name of a local doctor known to the paramedics. She was phoned and agreed to come immediately. She would, I was told, sign as to cause of death. A nearby undertaker was also called. Procedures were in motion. Red and I were superfluous. We'd walked halfway back to the Charade before I realised that they hadn't even asked my name.

Our drive back into town was subdued. My attention was focused on Sunday drivers, poor visibility and slippery roads. 'You handled that well,' I told Red. 'Not many kids your age have seen a dead body. How do you feel?'

He fiddled with the radio, unfussed, immortal. 'Life's a bitch,' he said. 'Then you die.' The catchphrase in my mind remained unspoken. 'Did he jump? Or was he pushed?'

We made it to the movies, after all. Not *Die Hard* but *Moonwalker*. First we ate cheap Chinese, then we sat side by side in the dark and watched Michael Jackson scratch his crotch for ninety minutes. My mind floated free, searching for a thread to cling to in the maze of possibilities, to bind the fragments of fact and conjecture together.

Marcus Taylor makes a minor scene at the Centre for Modern Art. What were his words? 'This edifice is built on a lie.' Six hours later, he's dead. A note found in his pocket raves about corrupt hands on the levers of power. 'You do not know what you are buying.' A picture vanishes from his studio.

Salina Fleet, my lucky break turned sour. She claims to be Taylor's lover and blames herself for his suicide. Then she plays down the relationship and accepts without surprise the proposition that his death was accidental. Volunteering the information that she was selling his 'appropriations' and demanding protection, she realises she's said more than she should and clams up. Then she flees in fear. Not from me. Her bag was half-packed before I arrived. From Spider Webb.

Spider, me old mate. The hot-shot bodyguard warning me off. Off what? The sixty thousand dollar question. Or the six hundred thousand dollar question? The common link between Salina and Spider—Taylor's vanished painting, *Our Home* Mark 2. And Lloyd Eastlake? Where did he come in to the picture? Or didn't he? And Giles Aubrey, with his incredible tale of undetected fakery. Was he, literally, the fall guy?

By the time Michael Jackson transmogrified into a flying saucer and went into orbit, I knew one thing for sure. It was something I'd known before we came into the theatre. As long as Red was in town, as long as there was the slightest chance that Spider Webb's implicit threat was real, the only business I'd be minding was my own.

Back outside on the street, the drizzle had stopped and the cloud ceiling had lifted. 'Look,' said Red, pointing upwards. 'Michael Jackson.'

I looked where he was pointing, to where the moon glowed like a candle behind a paper screen. It hung low in the sky, immediately above the towering steel skeleton of the Karlcraft Centre. 'This edifice is built on a lie,' I heard Marcus Taylor saying.

'Tricked ya,' crowed Red. As we crossed the street to the car, I reached out and took his hand. He wasn't such a big boy that he wouldn't let me hold it.

My new desk was real wood. My new chair had adjustable lumbar support. The new morning was washed clean from the night's rain. The outlook for Monday was a mild, blue-skyed twenty-eight degrees. My shoes were shined and just enough phone-message slips had accumulated to confirm that I was a man worth knowing.

But turning up at 8.45 a.m. on my first official day at my new job with a pair of ten-year-olds in tow was hardly the ideal way to strike fear into the hearts of the Arts Ministry pen-pushers.

Red was with me because his flight back to Sydney didn't leave until 9.20 that evening and, for a few hours at least, our quality time had to take a back seat to my day job. Tarquin Curnow came along because of a deal I'd cut with Faye and Leo the night before.

The predicament we faced that morning was a common one for the time of year. All over town, parental noses were due back at the grindstone. But the school term had not yet resumed. For another week, mothers and fathers would be forced to improvise child-care arrangements. Fortunately, Leo was employed at the university, a place where the concept of work is still pending definition. We agreed that if he could slip away at lunchtime and mind the boys for the afternoon, I would keep them occupied for the morning. Exactly how, I wasn't sure.

'You two can play computer games on my Macintosh,' said Trish, who'd already set up Checkpoint Charlie at Agnelli's door. 'Just keep the noise down and don't get in my way.' Trish was still adopting a wait-and-see attitude towards me, but she'd had a soft spot for Red ever since he was a baby.

The cool change had made it possible to sleep comfortably for the first time in a week. And I hadn't wasted the opportunity by dreaming of Spider Webb. One of the first lessons you learn in a political party is patience, to defer to *force majeure*, keep your powder dry and bide your time. I'd decided to bide mine until precisely 9.30 that evening, the moment at which Red's plane would be airborne and cruising north at an altitude of 10,000 metres and a speed of 500 knots. As of then, and not before, Spider Webb and the mystery of the missing painting would be at the top of my agenda.

In the meantime, while the boys sat in a corner of the ministerial reception area defending the galaxy from space invaders, I had a different fish to fry.

But first I had to catch it. Since my original idea of putting Angelo Agnelli and Max Karlin together and monitoring developments had proved abortive, the time had come to start asking direct questions about my boss's move into the world of campaign finance. I went to my new desk, picked up my new telephone and rang Duncan Keogh at party headquarters. 'Murray Whelan here, Duncan,' I said. 'Calling from Angelo Agnelli's office.'

That was as far as I got. 'Jesus,' cut in Keogh, irritably. 'Every man and his dog in on it now, are they? Tell Agnelli not to be so damn impatient. A day or so isn't going to make any difference. If we withdraw the term deposits before maturity there'll be penalties. As to the cash account balance of'—he shuffled some papers around—'of $207,860, that was invested in Obelisk Trust on Friday afternoon, just as Angelo instructed. Tell him he'll have to be satisfied with that for the time being.'

My new chair was ergonomically correct, but that didn't stop me nearly falling out of it. In itself, the idea of getting a better rate of return on party savings was a good idea. Dickhead Duncan should have done it himself, months ago. And if Obelisk paid the best rate, so much the better. Keep it in the family. But a 6 per cent boost in interest wouldn't fill the coffers to the extent Angelo had been talking about. If he was moving this fast on basic housekeeping matters, what was he doing on the door-knocking front? What favours was he offering where the big donations were to be found?

As I struggled to digest what Keogh had just told me, Agnelli himself appeared at my door. He pulled his cuff back and tapped the face of his wristwatch. 'Veale's briefing,' he mouthed. 'Coming?'

'Angelo's here with me now,' I said down the phone. 'I'm sure he appreciates your efficiency.' Abruptly hanging up, I made a face like a man who'd just disposed of a nuisance. Agnelli, leading off in the direction of the conference room, showed no interest in who I'd been talking to.

The Briefing-of-the-Incoming-Minister ceremony was a textbook exercise. Veale and a brace of deputy directors laid bare the ministry's policies, resources and processes in a professional and lucid manner. Agnelli nodded sagely throughout. I took notes. 'Any questions?' said Veale, after an hour.

The question I most wanted to ask Veale remained unasked. The mystery of Giles Aubrey's phone call would have to wait for a more appropriate occasion. I asked a few little ones instead, just to show I was on the ball. About the Library Services Review Working Party and the International Festival Economic Impact Task Force. About the advisory panels that recommended grants. I picked one at random. 'The Visual Arts Advisory Panel, say. What's the procedure governing selection and appointment of members?'

'Individuals with expertise are nominated by the panel chairperson.' One of Veale's deputies answered for him. 'Subject to the minister's approval, of course.'

Which would be given without a second thought. No

minister had the time or inclination to vet the membership of the hundred and one committees needed to keep a healthy bureaucracy ticking over. He or she was guided by the judgment of the relevant chairperson. In this case, Lloyd Eastlake.

That about wrapped up the briefing. Ange took me into his office and spread a copy of the tabloid *Sun* across his desk. 'Seen this?' he demanded.

I'd scanned the newspapers over breakfast and found nothing about the floater in the moat. For one dreadful moment I thought I'd missed something, that Agnelli was about to bore it up me for dereliction of duty. But he had the paper open at a section I never bothered to read, the social page. *New cultural supremo Angelo Agnelli lends his presence to charity bash in aid of the Centre for Modern Art*, said the caption. The photograph showed Ange standing between Max Karlin and Fiona Lambert, *Our Home* in the background.

'How's that for an auspicious start?' glowed the new supremo. 'Lining me up with Max Karlin was one of your better ideas.'

For a moment, I was tempted to inform Agnelli that I'd overheard his conversation with Duncan Keogh, that I knew he'd ordered the investment of a fair whack of the party's fighting fund in Obelisk Trust. State my concerns and do my best to convince him that he was headed into dangerous waters. But my years of handling Agnelli had taught me that direct contradiction was a tactic unlikely to succeed. You can't push on a rope, I reminded myself.

'Nothing about corruption in high places, I see.' Agnelli cast yet another admiring glance at his photograph and closed the paper. 'Looks like that body in the moat business is dead in the water.'

The press was quiet on the subject, I admitted. 'At the moment.'

'Speaking of water,' Agnelli went on. 'I'm off on an inspection and orientation tour of catchment resources and storage facilities. The Water Supply Commission is laying on a helicopter.

Won't be back until tomorrow morning.' A joy ride into the hills, in other words. Come lunchtime, he'd be assessing the water quality of Lake Eildon from a pair of water-skis behind the official reservoir-inspection vehicle. 'Think you can see to it that the wheels don't fall off the Arts while I'm gone?'

Bugger the Arts, I thought. With Agnelli out of the office, the coast would be clear to escape and make the most of what little time Red and I still had together. It could be months before I saw my boy again. 'I've got more than enough to keep me busy,' I said.

'Not too busy to write a speech for me, I hope,' said Agnelli. 'I see from the diary I'm booked to open some art exhibition at the Trades Hall tomorrow evening.' By profession, Angelo was a lawyer. Early in his career, he'd specialised in industrial accident compensation cases and he still saw himself as the worker's friend. 'I'd like to say something about ordinary working people enjoying the benefits of high culture,' he instructed. 'And put in lots of jokes.'

I'd just fed Agnelli into the lift with my assurance that his speech would be a masterpiece when Phillip Veale's secretary buttonholed me in the foyer and told me the Director would like a word. Veale looked up from behind his paperwork with the unfussable equanimity of a kung fu master. 'Shut the door, please, Murray.'

When I turned back, he was perching on front of his desk, pinching the crease at his knee so the action of sitting down did not abrade the fabric of his trousers. 'The minister was satisfied with this morning's little show and tell, do you think?'

'A polished performance,' I admitted. 'It will be interesting to see the impact of Angelo's plans for a comprehensive organisational restructure.'

Veale acknowledged my little drollery with a sigh of resignation. Another minister, another restructure. At the briefing, he had been genial but proper. No ironic inflections, no knowing asides. A man with a finely honed sense of the correct demeanour. Now, pressing his fingertips together, he assumed an attitude of hesitation, as if pondering the most tactful approach to a ticklish issue. He let me share his equivocation for a moment. 'A word of advice,' he began, feeling his way. 'If I may be permitted?'

Sure, I indicated. Fire away.

'As a relative newcomer to the administration of the Arts, you, no doubt, will be learning the ropes for some time. And you will, I fully understand, be keen to cultivate diverse sources of information. In doing this, it would be wise to keep in mind just how small and incestuous the arts world can be. Egos are involved, many of them remarkably fragile. Hidden agendas abound. Insinuation and gossip proliferate.'

So far, he wasn't telling me anything I couldn't reasonably be expected to know already. I wondered where this little chat of ours was going.

Veale got to the point. 'Giles Aubrey rang me on Saturday. He told me that you had approached him seeking information of a confidential and sensitive nature. He enquired as to your official status. I told him that you were a member of the Arts Minister's staff.' One of several, the inflection suggested. Not necessarily an important one.

He paused, expecting that I might want to explain myself. Instead, I had a question. 'Did he tell you what I wanted to talk to him about?'

A chastising tone entered Veale's voice. 'As I told you, Giles and I knew each other quite well, at one time. But it's been some time since we've spoken and I, for my part, had no wish to encourage further conversation. Frankly, I found it hard to understand what you hoped to gain by subjecting yourself to the gossip and insinuation of anyone as notoriously self-serving as Giles Aubrey.'

Ah so. I should have realised that Aubrey would check my credentials before talking to me. That explained the phone call. Unfortunately, by the sound of it, he also used the opportunity to re-open an old wound of some kind. Veale now had me on the back foot, and for no good reason.

It was my turn to sound miffed. 'I can assure you,' I said. 'I approached Giles Aubrey on an entirely professional basis, to consult him regarding the valuation of a painting. If he suggested otherwise, he was misleading you. In any case, my contact with him was brief. He died yesterday. A fall, apparently.'

That took the starch out of Veale's shirt. 'Oh,' he said.

A contemplative muse brushed her wings across his features. His thoughts began to turn inwards. Sensing the private nature of his reflections, I made some vague bridge-repairing noises about appreciating his point and quietly withdrew. The sound of crunching eggshells rose from underfoot.

It was past 10.30. The boys were beginning to tire of massacring aliens on Trish's computer. Casting a quick eye over my telephone message slips, I reached for my jacket, ready to go. Just then, reception buzzed to say that I had a visitor, a Mr Micaelis. Assuming him to be an early-bird hoping for an unscheduled appointment, I went out to tell him he was out of luck.

Micaelis was somewhere in his mid-twenties, dark-suited and smelling of Brut 33. He had the slightly put-upon look of the second son of a migrant family. His older brother drove the family truck. His younger brother was studying medicine or architecture. The big plans for him had run as far as accountancy or town planning. Accountancy, judging by the tie. He didn't seem the arty type.

'How ya going?' he said cheerfully. 'Reckon you could spare us a minute?' He handed me his card. It was embossed with a little blue star and a French motto. *Tenez le Droit*. Detective Senior Constable Chris Micaelis, the lettering said. Victoria Police. Well, well. 'Ello, 'ello, 'ello.

We went through the door marked Minister and into my office. Trish shot me a knowing glance as we passed. She hadn't lost any of her street smarts. She still knew a debt collector when she saw one.

Micaelis declined my offer of a refreshing beverage and parked his carcass into the furniture indicated. 'S'pose you know what this is about,' he said.

'S'pose you tell me,' I said.

'This death thing at the weekend.' The cop's studied casualness, we both knew, wasn't fooling anyone. 'Understand you were there when the body was recovered.'

For the briefest moment I wasn't sure if he meant Taylor or Aubrey. Micaelis registered the flicker of hesitation. 'Ms Fleet gave us your name,' he said. Let there be no false delicacy here, he meant. We know that you and the girlfriend were together.

I would share my full concerns with the police in due course, when Red was safe from Spider Webb's threats. In the meantime, I would play it straight, answer any questions put to me and find out what I could. 'That's correct,' I said. 'Salina and I were, uh, strolling in the gardens. We saw the hubbub at the moat and went over. Just as we arrived, they were wheeling the body into the back of an ambulance.'

Sherlock the Greek nodded encouragement. 'Knew Taylor then, did you?'

'Never met him. First time I ever saw him was on Friday evening at an exhibition at the Centre for Modern Art. He was drunk and made a bit of a spectacle of himself, as you're probably aware. I saw him again about 9.30. He was walking alone down Domain Road, even drunker by the look of it. Next time I saw him he was dead.'

Micaelis nodded non-committally. 'And Salina Fleet? Know her well, do you?'

'Not really. I met her for the first time on Friday afternoon here—she's on one of our advisory panels. She was at the exhibition at the Centre for Modern Art—the same one that Taylor was at. I went to the Botanical Hotel afterwards to eat and ran into her again. The pub closed about one and she and I went for a long walk in the gardens. We saw the activity at the moat and went over. She was shocked and upset and that's when you blokes came on the scene.'

Micaelis studied the back of his hand as though consulting his notes. 'So between 1 a.m. and 3 a.m. she was with you.

Strolling in the park?'

It was clear what he thought that meant. He was almost right. 'It was a hot night,' I told him, deadpan.

'Seen her since?' he wondered.

'I saw her early yesterday afternoon,' I told him. 'I dropped in briefly to her place in the city to see how she was feeling.'

'Mmm,' he said, as though I had merely confirmed a known fact. 'And how was she?'

'Naturally she was upset at Taylor's death. She seemed to prefer to be alone.'

Micaelis gave this some consideration, getting up and going over to the window, his hands plunged into his pockets. He rocked on his heels and jiggled a ring of keys deep in the recesses of his pants. 'You don't happen to know where we might find her just at the moment, do you? She didn't come home last night.'

'Perhaps she's staying with a friend,' I suggested.

'Any idea who?' he said pointedly.

'I don't know her that well. Have you tried her work?'

Micaelis didn't need me to tell him how to do his job. '*Veneer* magazine? Not what you'd call a full-time job. They're between issues and haven't seen her for several weeks.'

Nothing in the cop's attitude suggested concerns about Salina's safety. This reaffirmed my decision not to mention Spider's appearance at the Aldershot Building. I went fishing. 'We've been getting mixed signals up here about the cause of death,' I said. 'Do you know yet if it was suicide or an accident?'

'The exact cause hasn't yet been determined,' said the detective senior constable. 'You know the police.' He shrugged absently, as though referring to a slightly eccentric mutual acquaintance. 'Like to have all the facts before making up their minds.'

'But there's something in particular about this situation?' I persisted, pushing it. 'Some reason you want to talk to Salina?'

'Routine procedure, that's all,' he said. 'You'll let us know if Ms Fleet does contact you, won't you?'

The boys were hovering outside my glass door, angling for my attention. No doubt they were bored and keen to make tracks. Micaelis looked at them, then at me. In certain matters, the Mediterranean male mind is an open book. Even as I watched, I saw Micaelis put two and two together and get a resounding five. A married man, I was, having a bit on the side.

'If anything else occurs to you that you think we should know about,' he said.

'I won't hesitate to contact you,' I told him. And I definitely would. In just a little less than twelve hours.

Opening the door, I ushered him to the foyer. The boys ran interference. 'Guess what, Dad?' said Red, tugging at my sleeve. 'Tarquin crashed the computer.'

Trish looked daggers at me over the Macintosh, stabbing at her keyboard, desperately trying to recover her zapped files.

I fed the cop into the lift and we got out of there fast.

I gave the boys three choices. *Gold of the Pharaohs* at the Museum of Victoria, *Treasures of the Forbidden City* at the National Gallery, or an early lunch. The vote went two-nil for a capricciosa with extra cheese and a lemon gelati chaser.

We drove across Princes Bridge and headed through the city towards Lygon Street where the pizzerias and gelaterias were thicker on the ground than borlotti beans in a bowl of minestrone. Just past police headquarters, where Russell Street becomes Lygon, we hit a red light beside the Eight Hour Day monument. On the diagonal corner, on the tiny patch of lawn outside the Trades Hall, stood a newly erected hoarding. Art Exhibition, it read. Combined Unions Superannuation Scheme Art Collection. Free Admission. Opens Tuesday.

This was the event for which Agnelli had commanded me to write a mirthfully uplifting speech by the next morning. Since I was so close, and since I still had to keep the boys for another hour and a half, I decided to kill two birds with the one casual suggestion. 'See that place, Red.' I pointed to the age-stained Corinthian columns of the Trades Hall's once-grand portico. 'I used to work there before you were born. C'mon, I'll show you.'

A mutinous grumble erupted from the boys. 'We'll only be

ten minutes,' I exaggerated. 'Besides which, it's only 11.30—they haven't lit the pizza ovens yet.'

The Trades Hall had been built in the 1870s, a palace of labour, and a rich example of high Victorian neo-classical architecture. A brick annexe had been added in the 1960s, an erection of expedience, its design informed by the contemporary precept that nobody gave a rat's arse about architecture. We went around the side, drove up a cobblestone lane and parked in an undercroft between the old and the new sections of the building. Little had changed in the thirteen years since my career had begun there as Research Officer for the Municipal Workers' Union. The patina of grime that clung to the walls was perhaps a little thicker. The odours that wafted from the outdoor toilets were perhaps a little ranker. But the same threadbare red flag still dangled ironically from the flagpole. When I told the boys that it was here that the party that ruled the nation was founded, they rolled their eyes and complained about the smell.

'C'mon,' I urged, spotting a small sign that indicated our destination lay on the top floor. 'Want to see the bullet holes from the gun battle where the ballot-stuffers killed the cop?'

'Go ahead,' said Red, unenthusiastically. 'Make my day.'

The story of how, back in 1915, gangsters fought a running battle with police along its first-floor corridor had long been part of Trades Hall mythology. So much so that in the three years I'd worked there I never heard the same version twice. The only point of common agreement was that the bullet-riddled banister had been filched by a souvenir hunter back in the sixties. Which gave me plenty of scope. 'They ran up these stairs,' I improvised freely. 'Firing from the hip.'

We went up a flight of stone-flagged steps eroded in the middle from the innumerable goings up and comings down of the uncountable conveners of the manifold committees of the dedicated champions of labour. On the wall at the first-floor landing was a carved wooden honour board, its faded copperplate listing every General Secretary of the Boilermakers and Gasfitters

Union from 1881 to 1963. I touched Red on the shoulder and pointed. R. Cahill, 1903–09. 'Redmond Cahill,' I said. 'Your great grandfather.'

'So where's the bullet hole?' Red said, unimpressed. If I could take the trouble to invent a spurious ancestry, drenched in labour tradition, you'd think the kid could at least pretend to be interested. 'This way,' I lied, leading them along a deserted corridor. The place was so quiet that a regiment of mercenaries could have fired a bazooka down its by-ways without risk of hitting anyone.

The Trades Hall hadn't always been so quiet. In its original form, it was built to accommodate the trade-based guilds whose members had made Melbourne the richest metropolis in the southern hemisphere. In time, it had come to house more than a hundred different unions. The Confectionery Makers' Association, the Brotherhood of Farriers, the Boot Trade Employees' Federation, the Tram and Motor Omnibus Drivers—no trade was so small, no occupation so specialised that its members did not have their own union. Eventually, over a period of a hundred years, every nook and cranny of the place had been colonised. Its once-imposing chambers became a rabbit warren of jerry-rigged offices filled with men in darned cardigans and its hallways bustled with women in beehive hairdos and sensible shoes.

But those days had long gone. The inexorable march of progress had been through the joint like a dose of salts, amalgamating and rationalising the old organisations into industry-based super-unions with names like advertising agencies and a preference for more up-market accommodation. The AWU-FIME, the AFME-PKIU and the CFMEU had ditched the old dump for more modern digs elsewhere. Apart from the Trades Hall Council, which occupied the new wing, there were few remaining tenants.

The labour movement was not, however, entirely unmindful of its heritage. Bit by bit, as the dollars could be scrounged, the place was being restored to its vanished glory. Plasterers' scaffolding cluttered the stairwells and the smell of fresh paint hung in the air. An art exhibition was about to be staged. Somewhere. If only I could find it. The signs had petered out.

Reaching the top floor, we came face-to-face with a pair of knee-high white socks. They were attached to Bob Allroy, the Trades Hall's pot-bellied long-time caretaker. He was standing on a ladder, hanging a banner above a set of double doors. CUSS Art Exhibition, it read.

'Here's the only man still alive who personally witnessed the murdered policeman's death agony,' I told the boys. By now they'd figured out that my impromptu guided tour was just a pretext and were looking decidedly cheesed-off.

Bob Allroy climbed down from the ladder, wheezing. He was one of life's casualties, never the same since a bag of wheat had fallen on him in a ship's hold in 1953. His entire life since had been more a gesture of working-class solidarity than an affirmation of his usefulness. 'Oh, it's you,' he grunted, recalling my face but unable to summon up a name. He opened one of the doors and I helped him drag his ladder inside. 'Unbelievable, eh?' he panted.

Sure was. The last time I'd seen this room it had been a maze of cheap chipboard and second-hand Axminster, a lost dogs' home for officials of the Society of Bricklayers and Tilers. Now it was a spacious reception room with buffed parquet flooring, hand-blocked wallpaper friezes and freshly antiqued skirting boards. Portable partitions had been erected at right angles to the walls to form a series of shallow alcoves and rows of paintings sat stacked against them, face to the wall, waiting to be hung.

'Art exhibition,' explained Bob, not entirely approvingly. 'The girlie from the cultural office is off sick, so guess who's been roped into doing all the work?'

Bob Allroy wouldn't work in an iron lung and we both knew it. 'Doesn't officially open till tomorrer,' he warned, in case I was thinking of stealing a free look. I wasn't there for an unscheduled squiz, I reassured him, but to rustle up a bit of quick background for a speech I had to write.

Bob moved to one of the windows and licked his lips, his liver-spotted nose drawn like a lodestone to the revolving brewery sign atop the John Curtin Hotel, clearly visible across the road. The girlie from the arts office, he thought, would be back tomorrow. Better be, if everything was to be ready for the official opening. In the meantime, I'd better see Bernice Kaufman, next door in the admin office. She might know something about it.

This was a definite possibility. There was very little, by her own admission, that Bernice Kaufman didn't know all about. She hadn't been President of the Teachers' Federation for nothing. A couple of minutes with Bernice and, chances were, I'd know more than I'd ever need to about the CUSS Art Collection. More than enough to write Agnelli's speech. Not the jokes, though. I'd have to write the jokes myself.

Bob Allroy ascended his ladder and began screwing light globes into a reproduction etched-glass gas lamp hanging from the ceiling. 'Don't you kids go nowhere near the art,' he warned. 'That stuff's worth a lot of money.'

Seconding that motion, I told Red and Tarquin to amuse themselves for a minute while I did something important. Then I scooted across to the Trades Hall Council, where Bernice Kaufman was holed-up behind a wall of paperwork in an office marked Assistant Secretary. She could spare me a couple of minutes, but only just. 'I don't want to miss my ultrasound appointment,' she said.

You had to hand it to Bernice. In the time it took to say hello, she'd just happened to draw attention to the fact that she was pregnant. You get to be thirty-five, Bernice had discovered, and your superwoman rating starts to slip if your credentials don't include motherhood, preferably of the single variety. Being the hardest-nosed, most multi-faced Ms in town doesn't cut much ice unless you've also got cracked nipples and a teething ring in your briefcase. So Bernice had scared just enough body fluids out of an organiser from the Miscellaneous Workers' Union to secure herself membership of the pudding club. Not just an ordinary member, of course. Being knocked up would never be the same now that Bernice had a piece of the action.

'Put that cigarette out,' she barked. 'Haven't you heard of passive smoking?'

There was, believe me, nothing passive about Bernice Kaufman. I dropped my fag and ground it mercilessly underfoot. The baby was not due for another five months.

When I explained what I wanted, Bernice didn't believe it. 'I don't believe it,' she said. 'Ministerial adviser for the Arts? Agnelli must be crazy. You're a cultural illiterate.'

'That's why I've come to you, Bernice,' I said. 'I'm after some on-the-job training.'

When I'd convinced her that I really did need background information for Agnelli's speech at the exhibition opening, she reached into a drawer of her filing cabinet and pulled out a thick folder. She was, it transpired, ex-officio company secretary of the Combined Unions Superannuation Scheme. 'CUSS manages several million dollars of union members' money. And while the art collection is only a small percentage of our total assets —its current value is estimated at approximately half a million dollars—it is an important element in maintaining a broadly diversified portfolio. Frankly, the way the financial markets have been performing lately, art is probably our most effectively appreciating investment.'

My amusement must have been too apparent. Bernice changed tack, handing me a page from the file. 'Here's the content guidelines, as laid down by the CUSS board of directors. Keep it. Feel free to quote.'

The emphasis of the collection, read the blurb, was on works that presented a positive view of working life and reflected the outlook and aspirations of ordinary working people. 'Angelo's speech should point out that it includes works by some very prominent artists.'

It did, too. The one-page catalogue Bernice handed me was leavened with the sort of household names guaranteed to reassure the rank and file that its pension funds were not being squandered on the avant-garde. *Potoroo 2* by Clifton Pugh, I read. *Dry Gully* by Russell Drysdale. *Man in Singlet* by William Dobell.

'Did a mob of you go round Sotheby's and Christies with a chequebook or what?'

I didn't take Bernice's withering glance of contempt personally. She thought everyone was an idiot. 'The collection was initiated by the board of directors a little over a year ago, essentially as an investment vehicle. Since purchases of this nature are a specialised skill, we retain an expert consulting firm, Austral Fine Art, to advise us. Austral identifies suitable works for inclusion in the collection, buys and sells on our behalf, takes care of insurance and so on. Up until now, the works have all been held in storage. But a few months ago we decided to put them on show, so our members could better appreciate the investment we made on their behalf. In fact—and this is a point Angelo might also care to make—this is the only time the entire collection has ever been seen by the public.' She put her hands on the edge of the desk and wearily pulled herself upright, levering for two. 'And now I really must go. Can't keep the doctor waiting.'

I walked her to the lift. A waddle was already in evidence. 'So, you'll soon know if it's a boy or a girl—or would you prefer not to find out until the actual birth?'

Bernice might've been up the duff, but she hadn't lost her marbles. 'Information is power, Murray,' she said. 'Don't you know anything?'

Pocketing the pages of bumph she'd given me, I headed back to the exhibition room. Apart from Bob Allroy's ladder and toolbox abandoned in the middle of the floor and the unhung painting lining the walls, it was empty. An icy wave of panic gripped my innards. I should never have let the boys out of my sight. 'Red!' I called. 'Tarquin!' The sound echoed back at me from the deserted corridor.

Suddenly, arms spread wide like music-hall song-and-dance

men, the boys sprang from behind the far partition. 'Tricked ya!' they shrieked.

Even as the words left their lips, Tarquin tripped backwards over Bob Allroy's toolbox and slammed full pelt into the step-ladder. The flimsy aluminium tower skidded sideways, rocked on its legs and began to topple over. I rushed forward to arrest its fall and collided with Red. Tarquin, useful as ever, stood open-mouthed. For a moment time seemed to stand still.

The ladder didn't, though. With an almighty metallic clatter, it collided with the upper edge of one of the pictures leaning against the wall, smashing the frame into gilded kindling and squashing the canvas into a buckled heap. The result looked like a piano accordion that had been kicked to death by an electricity pylon.

'Wow,' said Tarquin.

'Shuddup.' I fell to my knees beside the catastrophe. 'Shuddup, shuddup, shuddup.' My heart was so firmly lodged in my mouth that further conversation was impossible.

The picture's frame was utterly demolished, the joints burst asunder, the side panels reduced to four separate pieces of ornately useless timber moulding. The internal framing was a flattened rhomboid from which the canvas dangled in crumpled folds.

Sweaty-handed, I smoothed the tangled mass into the rough approximation of its original rectangular shape. What I saw filled me with a mixture of unspeakable dismay and utter relief.

The mangled picture was a small oil painting. It depicted a solitary stick-figure stockman. He was perched on a gnarled tree-stump beside the mouldering bones of a bullock. His drought-ravaged gaze extended across a blasted landscape towards a featureless horizon. There was no signature. There was no need.

Nobody else did red dirt and rust-rotted corrugated iron like this. Nobody else would dare. It was the trademark, instantly recognisable, of an artist whose rangy bushmen and desiccated verandas had once adorned the walls of every pub and primary school from Hobart to Humpty Doo.

'*Dry Gully*,' I groaned. 'By Sir Russell Fucking Drysdale.'

Red and Tarquin meekly dragged the ladder upright, more abashed by my obviously panic-stricken state than by the damage their game had inflicted. 'Doesn't look too bad,' offered Red lamely.

'Shuddup,' I informed him.

But my boy was a smart lad and there was truth in his statement. The canvas sagged and buckled over its skewiff skeleton, but the actual paintwork appeared to have survived intact. Apart from some very minute cracks, arguably ancient, there was no visible evidence to suggest that the phlegmatic boundary rider had been struck from a great height by a plummeting pile of scrap metal.

And, in light of the fact that the actual art part was still intact, the destruction of the frame suddenly seemed less disastrous. It was just a few pieces of gilded timber, after all. If I acted quickly, it might just be possible to re-assemble the whole thing into some passable semblance of its previous condition before Bob Allroy returned. Particularly since Bob's toolbox was sitting conveniently to hand on the parquet floor.

'Quick,' I ordered the boys. 'Watch the door.' Then, grabbing a pair of pliers and a screwdriver, I bundled up the buggered item, sprinted down the hall to the Gents and locked myself in a vacant stall.

In less time than it took to wedge the ruptured joints of the frame back into place, the futility of my task was obvious. Even in ideal working conditions and with the right tools, the job would have been beyond me. With the timber of the internal stretcher snapped clear through, it was impossible to get any tension in the canvas. The more I fiddled, the more hopeless it became. On top of which, barely a minute had gone by before Red came knocking on the cubicle door. 'Dad! Dad!' he hissed. 'He's back.' There was no option but to face the music.

Holding the picture before me like an icon at a Russian funeral, I advanced down the corridor towards the scene of the crime, its perpetrators in single, guilty file behind me. As we neared the exhibition room, Bob Allroy stepped out the door and pulled it shut. Without so much as a glance our way, he turned on his heels and scurried down the stairs.

'Can't we just leave it here?' said Red, trying the locked door of the exhibition room. 'And run.'

We could. But Bernice knew that I'd been there. And, faced with a demolished painting, Bob Allroy would soon remember that the only other people to visit the unopened exhibition were that guy who used to work downstairs for the MEU and his two kids.

The time was precisely 12.30. Through a window at the top of the stairs I watched Bob cross the street and enter the John Curtin Hotel.

The days when the industrial arm of the labour movement bent its collective elbow in the front bar of the John Curtin Hotel were long gone. But tradition died hard in some men and Bob was one of them. At least an hour would pass before he completed his liquid lunch and returned for his ladder and toolbox.

'Who's Sir Russell Fucking Drysdale?' said Tarquin.

'Shuddup,' I suggested. 'And follow me.'

Scooping up the bits and pieces of *Dry Gully*, I sped non-chalantly down the stairs. The undercroft was deserted.

'Are we keeping it, then?' said Red, incredulously watching me wrap the picture in an old beach towel.

'Shuddup,' I muttered, throwing a left into Victoria Parade and stomping on the accelerator. What I needed was an art conservator with while-you-wait service.

Artemis Prints and Framing was just down the hill from Ethnic Affairs, at the Victoria Parade end of the Smith Street retail strip. Technically, being on the west side of the street, it was located in Fitzroy, a suburb well on the way to total gentrification. But Smith Street, both sides, was universally regarded as Collingwood, an address that could never successfully shed its more raffish working-class associations. As though clutched in the jaws of this ambiguity, Artemis was slotted between a health-food shop called the Tasty Tao and a second-hand electrical goods retailer whose refrigerators were chained together to discourage shoplifters.

It took me exactly seven minutes and fifteen seconds to get there, including parking time.

It was a quiet drive, despite near-misses when I ran the amber lights at two intersections. The boys were concentrating on perfecting their air of contrition and had kept recriminations to a minimum. I bustled them into the Tasty Tao with funds for soymilk ice-creams and instructions to wait at the table on the footpath out the front and stay out of trouble. 'But what about our pizza...' Tark started, until he was silenced by a shot across the bow from Red. I took the towel-wrapped bundle of canvas and kindling out of the Charade and pushed open the door of

Artemis Prints. A buzzer sounded out the back.

The exposed-brick walls were hung thick with decorator items for the local home-renovator market. Aluminium-framed posters from art museum blockbusters. Georgia O'Keeffe at the Guggenheim. Modern masters. Klimt and Klee. Rustic frames around labels from long-defunct brands of tinned fruit. On the rear wall, beside a curtained archway, hung a selection of sample frames, their inverted right-angles like downturned mouths. Claire, I was pleased to see, carried an extensive range.

She was behind the counter, even more voluptuous than I remembered, serving a teenage girl in skin-tight stone-washed denim jeans and a chemise that showed her navel. Definitely the Collingwood side of the street, probably the Housing Commission high-rise flats. More your Joan Jett fan than your Joan Miro aficionado. 'How much for the non-reflective glass, but?' she was saying.

'It's five dollars more,' said Claire. On the counter between them was a block-mounted poster of a cigar-smoking chimpanzee in a tartan waistcoat riding a unicycle, the glass repaired with tape. Hi-jinx in the high-rise. 'But you get a much better result.'

Claire looked over the girl's shoulder and acknowledged my arrival. Her expression was bland, but her eyes twinkled, inviting me to share the joke. 'I'll be with you in a moment,' she said. 'Sir.'

The teenager gave the non-reflective glass a moment's lip-chewing consideration and decided to go the full distance.

'I think you'll find it well worthwhile,' said Claire. 'You get a clearer view. It'll be ready to pick up tomorrow.' She was, I sensed, doing it hard. All dressed up for the customers in a lick of make-up, pleated chinos and a sleeveless white blouse. Her chestnut hair, much more ravishing in the daylight, was piled high and held in place with combs.

'So,' she said as the girl left, eyeing my towel-wrapped bundle like it was an unnecessary but not unwelcome pretext. 'Don't say you want me to mount your street vendors too?'

Second thoughts had been assailing me from the moment I walked through the door. A few flirtatious glances over a bowl of tapenade were one thing. Bursting into the woman's shop with a filched artwork under my arm was another. Desperado dipstick and his defective Drysdale. I smiled helplessly and mustered my resolve.

'This may seem a little presumptuous,' I started. 'That is, this might not be the sort of thing you normally do. And even if it is, you might not be comfortable doing it in this particular instance. You really don't know me, I know, but it's sort of an emergency and, well, if you don't feel comfortable, I'll understand perfectly and perhaps you could refer me somewhere else...'

At this babble, Claire's lips curled with undisguised amusement. 'An emergency!' She moved aside the cracked chimpanzee to clear the counter. 'As you see, emergencies are our specialty.' If I felt the need to make a bit of a production number, she didn't mind playing along.

'It belongs to friends,' I said, laying my bundle before her. The painting was, strictly speaking, stolen property. If unforeseen difficulties arose, I didn't want Claire implicated as an accessory to a crime. A little white lie seemed best. 'Don't ask what happened.' I cast an accusing backward glance over my shoulder.

Claire followed it out her front window to where the boys sat flicking bits of ice-cream at each other over the pavement table. She gave me a comprehending nod. Detailed explanations weren't necessary. What was parenthood, after all, but a lifelong mopping-up operation?

'And your friends don't know about it yet?' The way she said this suggested that such things were not unknown in her profession. 'You'd like to get it back before they notice it's gone?'

'Exactly.' I began to unfold the towel. She helped me. Her hands were neat and sturdy and when her fingers brushed mine, I felt myself blush. 'The painting itself doesn't seem to be damaged,' I said, keeping my face down. 'Just the frame. All it needs is a few staples, a bit of glue.'

The last flap of towel fell away, revealing what appeared to be the aftermath of a tropical cyclone. Drysdale's lonesome drover, if anything, looked even more despondent. Claire let out an appreciative whistle. 'Is this what I think it is?'

'I'm afraid so. A Russell Drysdale original. But, like I said, the picture itself doesn't seem to be damaged. A few staples, a nail or two...'

Under the counter was a black apron. Claire slipped it on, along with a pair of white cotton gloves. Minnie Mouse. 'Interesting,' she said. 'The only other Drysdales I've seen were on masonite board.' She began to separate the pieces of wood, wire and canvas. Ominous diagnostic noises came from the back of her throat.

'Like I said, the picture itself doesn't seem to be damaged.' I smoothed at it uselessly, trying to be helpful. 'A few staples...'

She smacked my hand away. 'Let me be the judge of that,' she said. 'There's quite a lot of work needed here.'

'Um,' I said, moving my shoulders from side to side and shuffling from foot to foot. 'The thing is...' I looked at my watch.

'How long have I got?' she said, not looking up from probing the debris.

'Half an hour.' I winced sheepishly.

'You have got to be kidding.' But she was already gathering up the ends of the towel.

Through the arch at the back of the shop was a narrow work-room dominated by a long tool-strewn table. Racks of moulded framing occupied one wall. In the other was a window over-looking the side fence. Stairs ran to an upper floor. Clearing away a half-cut cardboard mount, Claire laid the battered picture face-down and snipped away the tangled hanging wire with a pair of pliers.

'You don't know how much I appreciate this,' I said, Mr Sincere.

'Let's just say it's a long time since I've had the chance to work with an artist of this stature.' She removed the stretched canvas from its frame and held it upright. Squeezing the opposing corners gingerly together, she forced the canvas to bulge a little. 'Particularly when he's been hit by a bus.'

Out of its frame, the stretched canvas looked pathetically small, hardly much bigger than a couple of record covers. The edges, long concealed by the boxing of the frame, were a stark white contrast to the murky grey of the rest of the fabric. Claire wrinkled her nose. 'Hmmm,' she said. 'Had this long?'

I looked at my watch. 'About seventeen and a half minutes.'

'Your friends, how long have they had this?'

'Six months or so, I think. Why?'

'Just wondered.' She turned the painting face down and began rummaging through the racks of framing material.

'Hello, Red's dad.' A child's voice came from somewhere behind me. It took me a moment to locate its source. Claire's little girl Grace was peering out shyly from behind the door of a cupboard built under the stairs. Delighted to have surprised me, she opened the cupboard door to reveal a tiny table spread with scrap paper and coloured pencils. 'This is my play school,' she said. 'Mummy made it for me.' Her eyes tracked me across the room as I accepted her invitation to take a closer look.

'Your mummy's very clever,' I said, meaning every word of it. Taking this as a personal compliment, Gracie plumped herself down at the table and began drawing exuberantly with a felt-tipped pen.

'That's the sort of encouragement I like to hear when I'm working,' said Claire. 'Keep it up.'

She withdrew a length of moulded framing from the rack on the wall and matched it with a section of the broken frame, holding the two together so I could compare them. Apart from a slightly deeper gilding on the old frame, they were nearly identical. 'It'll be quicker to build a new frame than repair the damaged one. This moulding is a fairly common style, so it's highly unlikely your friends will ever notice the difference.' I couldn't see Bob Allroy spotting the switch.

'But first I'll need to take the canvas off the stretcher, replace the broken struts, then re-attach the canvas.' With a definitive smash, she tossed the broken frame into a metal rubbish bin full of off-cut shards of glass.

'Is all that possible in half an hour?' I was getting toey, nervously glancing at my watch, as useful as a scrub nurse at a triple by-pass.

Claire shrugged casually. 'We'll soon find out.' She was enjoying this. Not just the professional challenge, either. She began extracting the tacks that held the canvas on the stretcher.

I paced. A compressor sat on the floor, its hose leading to a pneumatic guillotine on a side bench. Pricy items. Staple guns. Sheets of glass. Tools. Racks of unframed prints. Two metal folio cabinets, not cheap. Cardboard mounts. A whole wall of shaped timber. Add the rent, the rates, utility bills.

Claire, pulling tacks, read my mind. 'Not exactly what I imagined when I left the National Gallery. I saw myself sitting in a trendy little gallery offering the works of interesting young contemporary printmakers to a discerning clientele. The trouble is, ten other places within half a mile had exactly the same idea.'

'Is that why you left the National Gallery, to start this shop?'

'Other way round,' she said.

Gracie tugged at my sleeve and handed me a piece of paper. Two blobby circles in felt-tipped pen, one circle with a hat and currant eyes.

'That's me, isn't it?' The child nodded. Who else? 'Why, thank you. It's lovely.'

Claire looked up, the table between us. 'Sleazebag,' she muttered. In the nicest possible way. It was all I could do to stop myself vaulting the table and giving her a demonstration.

'Other way round?'

'I'd been at the gallery six years, ever since I graduated. That's where I met'—she flicked her eyes towards Gracie, back at her drawing—'Gracie's father, Graham. He was an administrator. We were together for a couple of years and when Gracie was on the way I applied for maternity leave. No-one had ever done that before. Women who got pregnant were expected to quietly fade away. They said there was no provision, knocked me back.'

'That's discrimination,' I said. Reviewing the National Gallery's employment practices would, I resolved, be my number one priority when I got back to the office. If changes hadn't already been made, they would be damned soon, if I had any influence on the proceedings. We'd see how soon they smartened up if their conduit was squeezed a little.

'I wanted to make an issue of it, but Graham didn't like the idea. He thought it might adversely affect his career. He encouraged me to set up this business, put some money into it. After Grace was born, he got a job offer from overseas. Now he's Director of Human Resources at the Hong Kong Museum of Oriental Antiquities and I'm sticking non-reflecting glass over chimpanzees and framing other people's holiday photos.'

She wasn't bitter, just telling a story. She dropped her voice a register, whether for my benefit or the child's I couldn't tell. 'We don't see him any more.'

'Great,' I said. 'Great progress you're making.' She only had about half the tacks out. Now that she was handling the painting proper, her technique was meticulous, painstakingly slow. The time was 12.58. My feet were inscribing an ever-decreasing circle on the workroom floor.

'For Chrissake,' she said, moving around to my side of the table for no apparent other reason than to accidentally brush her rump against me. 'Stop prowling around like a caged animal. You're making me nervous.'

Jesus, what did she have to be nervous about? I was the one with the crisis on my plate. Maybe, I thought, I should temporarily remove my twitchiness elsewhere. Make more efficient use of my time by taking Red and Tarquin around to Leo while Claire got on with the job, unencumbered by my stalking presence. 'Go,' she said. 'You're no use to me in your current state.'

'The heat's off,' I told the boys, bustling them and their

dripping stumps of half-sucked carob-chip ice-confectionery into the car.

The Curnows' place was less than a kilometre away through the backstreets of Fitzroy. Even though I knew it would take me scarcely ten minutes to deliver the boys and return to Artemis, I still had to fight the urge to speed. This painting demolition rigmarole had certainly shot the shit out of my quality time with Red. The one o'clock news came on the radio and I leaned across and hiked up the volume.

Prince Sihanouk had walked out on the Cambodian peace talks. Again. F. W. de Klerk had been elected head of the South African government. Fat lot of difference that would make. Emperor Hirohito had died. Not before time, the old war criminal. Police had refused to rule out suspicious circumstances in relation to the death of the man whose body had been found in the moat of the National Gallery. The weather bureau had amended the forecast top upwards to thirty and the All Ordinaries was steady at 1539.4.

This news—the foul play, not the All Ordinaries—was not entirely unexpected. Salina's disappearance was bound to have raised suspicions, even if none had existed before. The ripples thrown up by Marcus Taylor's drowning were spreading outwards in ever-widening circles. An image of Agnelli on the placid waters of Lake Eildon crossed my mind. I couldn't help but wonder what boats might get rocked before this affair was over.

Leo accepted delivery of the boys with a wave from the Curnows' front door. 'See you after work,' I told Red. 'About six o'clock. We'll have our pizza then, okay?'

'Okay,' said Red, easy-going as ever.

I was back at Artemis Prints at approximately 1.10.06. Enough time for a quick gasper. While I sucked, I perused the offerings in the front window. The least I could do, all things considered, was buy something. The Pre-Raphaelite maidens weren't exactly my cup of hemlock. I settled on a Mondrian print. Remembering my little something for Gracie, I dashed back across the road to the car and retrieved Marcus Taylor's stamp album from where Red had tossed it behind the back seat.

The buzzer rang as I went in the door. When Claire stuck her head around the curtain to see who'd come in, I was standing by the counter like a waiting customer. 'Psst,' I said and beckoned her over. She came cautiously, a questioning look on her face.

'I haven't thanked you properly.' I said it deliberately low so she had to step closer to hear me. Then I took my life in my hands. I put my arm around her waist, drew her to me and kissed her gently on the mouth.

Her lips, soft and dry, yielded tentatively. I inhaled the scent of her hair, apple shampoo, dizzying. She leaned into the kiss, accepting it, returning it. We shifted on our feet, neither of us breathing. Her hands found the small of my back and pressed me closer. The kiss went on. And on.

Suddenly, she broke. We stepped back from each other, both swallowing hard, blinking. 'Your friends,' she said. 'How much did they pay for this painting?'

Her eyes shone with anticipation. 'I dunno,' I shrugged. I'd already done the mental arithmetic, speculated on the cost of restitution. Wondered about insurance. Forty-odd paintings in the CUSS collection, total value half a million dollars. Average price, say $12,000. Drysdale one of the stars. 'Maybe twenty thousand dollars. Why?'

'Take a look at this.' Claire tugged at my hand, drawing me into the workroom. At the parting of the curtain, her touch fell away just as Gracie looked up from her colouring-in. The stamp album was still in my hand. I held it out to the child. 'Do you like stamps?'

'Stickers?' She grabbed the book avidly, her diffidence forgotten.

Claire stood at the work table, hands on hips, inviting inspection of her handiwork. The replacement frame was finished, indistinguishable from the original. It sat empty. Next to it was the repaired stretcher, a cross-braced timber rectangle, naked of fabric. Beside them was the unstretched canvas of *Dry Gully*.

Ochre red and russet brown, it looked like the freshly-flayed skin of some desert reptile. Then there was another piece of canvas, the same size as *Dry Gully*. This one was a rather amateurish seascape that seemed to have been roughly cut down from a larger picture. Finally, propped open with a thick ruler was a reference book, *The Dictionary of Australian Artists*.

'I thought there was something odd about this picture.' With all the exaggerated staginess of a conjurer about to execute a marvel of prestidigitation, she proceeded to show me what. First, she turned *Dry Gully* over and invited me to examine the condition of the canvas. Before, when it hung on the stretcher, it was a dusty parchment colour. Now, it was a fresh-looking chalky white. Attached to the fabric, right in the centre, was a small piece of paper on which was printed an image, some words and a number. As I bent forward for a closer look, Claire whisked the canvas away. 'One thing at a time.'

She pointed to the other canvas. 'When I took the Drysdale off the stretcher, I found this underneath.' To demonstrate what she meant, she turned *Dry Gully* face down on the table and placed the fragment of seascape over it, also face down. The two canvasses fitted together perfectly. *Dry Gully*'s obverse side now appeared the same dirty cream colour as when it was still stretched. 'Two canvases,' said Claire. 'One on top of the other—creating the impression that the painting in front is much older than it really is.'

'Why would someone do that?' I asked.

She now removed the false back and allowed me to examine the little square of paper. It had serrated edges and bore an image of the Sydney Opera House surmounted by the head of William Shakespeare. Australia Post, said the inscription, 43 cents. UK–Australia Bicentenary Joint Issue.

'Big Bill in Tinsel Town,' I said. 'What does it mean?'

'It means that if Russell Drysdale painted this picture,' Claire said. 'He did so posthumously.' Her index finger settled on the biographical entry in the reference book. 'By 1988, he'd been dead for seven years.'

'You mean it's a forgery?'

Jesus H. Christ. What was it about me? I'd only been in this culture caper three days and the fakes were jumping out of the woodwork at me. First *Our Home*, now *Dry Gully*. Was no representation of the Australian landscape, no work of art safe now that I was in the field?

Claire's professional curiosity was piqued, but she wasn't jumping to any conclusions. 'Not necessarily. It's certainly not an original, but as to being a forgery—well, that depends.'

'Depends on what? Surely it's either genuine or it isn't.'

Claire sucked in her cheeks and held the counterfeit Drysdale up to the light, as if trying to penetrate its secret. 'I'm no expert, but this seems to be a very competent attempt to replicate Drysdale's work. But the fact that it's been done with a considerable degree of skill does not, in itself, make it a forgery. Owners of valuable artworks sometimes have high-quality copies made—to reduce their insurance premiums, from fear of theft, in case of accidental damage. They lock the original away, hang the copy and let people think it's the original. Perhaps your friends did that.'

'What, like a duchess who keeps her diamond tiara in the safe and wears a paste imitation?' Except there were scant few duchesses around the Trades Hall.

'Exactly. Or maybe your friends are just engaging in a little harmless pretension. Bought themselves a replica and told people it was an original.'

What sort of friends did she think I had? 'Not these people,' I told her. 'Not their style.'

'I don't suppose you happen to know if it came with a certificate of authenticity, do you?'

'What's that?'

'A letter provided by the seller giving details of the picture's origins and attesting that it is what it's purported to be.'

I told her I couldn't imagine my friends buying anything without all the paperwork being in order.

'You don't happen to know where they bought it?'

'It was arranged privately, I believe. Through a firm called Austral Fine Art.'

She swung a phone book down from a shelf. 'Never heard of them. But there's no shortage of art dealers in this town.' There was a page of them, including the Aubrey Gallery. But no Austral Fine Art.

'Forgery isn't my area, I'm afraid,' Claire said. 'My only experience has been with inaccurate attribution and genuine mistakes. The National Gallery has a Rembrandt self-portrait that turned out not to be a Rembrandt at all. We changed the caption to "School of Rembrandt" and left it where it was. But deliberate misrepresentation, that's another matter altogether.'

I was deliberately letting her walk me the long way around this, covering all the bases. I already had a grim feeling that I knew what it meant. But I wanted to be absolutely sure I wasn't jumping to any conclusion just because it was the obvious one. 'What do you think the stamp means?'

'Yes,' she said. 'Interesting isn't it? It's obviously some sort of personal mark. A secret signature, if you like.'

'If it's secret, why is it in such a prominent place? Surely that would increase the chances of the deception being discovered?'

'True,' she agreed. 'Perhaps whoever did this intended

that it be discovered.'

'But why would a forger want to be discovered? Wouldn't that defeat the purpose?'

'It would if the motive was financial gain. But in some cases I've heard about, the forger was less concerned with money than with fooling the experts. After the critics and curators have waxed lyrical about the unmistakable hand of the master being visible in every brushstroke, the forger pops up and reveals that the picture in question was painted not by Van Gogh in Arles in 1889, but by Joe Bloggs in Aunt Gertrude's garden shed last December.'

How did the declaration found in Marcus Taylor's pocket go? *You so-called experts…You speculators and collectors who do not even know what you are buying… You are all allowing yourselves to be deceived and defrauded.* There was another line, too. Something about taking action to draw public attention. Since the note was found on his body, the assumption had automatically been that the action he meant was his suicide. But if he hadn't, in fact, killed himself, what could he have been referring to?

'Gracie, sweetheart,' I said. 'Can I borrow back that sticker book for a minute?'

Gracie, having found the stickers already stuck down, was feeling gypped enough. She warily surrendered the album. 'I suppose so,' she said. 'Just for a minute, but.'

The stamps dated from the previous year. Beneath each, inscribed in minuscule block capitals was a name. Some I recognised as belonging to artists. William Dobell was below a stamp commemorating the Seoul Olympics. Runners breasting a tape, 65 cents. Margaret Preston got paired with a possum. The British–Australian joint issue with the high culture theme bore the inscription 'Drysdale'.

The CUSS catalogue that Bernice Kaufman gave me was still in my pocket. I unfolded it and checked the names against those under the stamps. There was a stamp corresponding to every artist in the collection. Thirty-eight names, thirty-eight stamps.

The album was Taylor's register of production, his output ledger.

Claire, naturally, was regarding my behaviour with a degree of incomprehension. 'What's all this?' she said.

'Just a minute.' Using *The Dictionary of Australian Artists*, I checked two of the names. Noel Counihan and Jon Molvig. I wouldn't have known their work if it was up me with an armful of impasto, but their names rang a bell. According to the reference book, they were both dead. I tried a name I didn't recognise. It wasn't listed. Nor were three others that were unfamiliar. By the look of it, the CUSS art collection contained only works by dead or undiscovered artists.

If this meant what it looked like it meant, the whole lot were what Salina Fleet would probably call referential images at the cutting edge of post-modern discourse. Fakes.

'For Chrissake, tell me what's going on!' Claire was getting impatient, irritated by my lack of communication. 'This is a joke, right? You're playing an elaborate trick on me, aren't you?'

'I wish I was,' I said. 'Mind if I use your phone?'

'Only if you tell me what's going on.'

Gracie was all ears, galvanised by her mother's response to my evasiveness. When I thrust the stamp album towards her, she went all shy and refused to take it back. I put it on her little desk instead.

'I will,' I told Claire. I put my hands lightly on her upper arms, a conciliatory gesture. She shrugged them away. 'I promise. Just as soon as I find out myself. In the meantime, do you think you can put that picture back together the way it was?'

'Aren't you going to tell your friends?'

'Tell them what? "You know your Drysdale? Well guess what? It's not really a Drysdale at all. And here are the bits and pieces to prove it." I've taken it without their knowledge or permission, don't forget. Right now, the only option is to stick to the original plan and get it back where it belongs before they notice it's gone. That way, I'll have enough breathing room to figure out how to break it to them, or have them discover the truth themselves.'

She was, I could see, far from persuaded. But she was also curious enough to put her better judgment temporarily on hold. 'Phone's on the counter,' she said.

I went out into the shop and dialled the Police Minister's office and asked for Ken Sproule. 'Is that criminal intelligence?' I said. 'What's this I hear on the news about Taylor's death being down to suspicious circumstances?'

The methodical whoomph of a pneumatic stapler came from the workroom.

'I'm as much in the dark as you are,' claimed Sproule. 'Now that it's become a police operational matter, it's strictly arm's length from us here in the minister's office.'

'Come off it. You must have some idea. What's this about the girlfriend shooting through?'

Sproule's ears pricked up audibly. 'How'd you hear about that?'

'So you do know something, then?'

Ken got fatherly. 'A word to the wise, Murray. Don't go dipping your bib in here. The cops are notoriously sensitive to any suggestion of political interference in the operational side of things. Do yourself a favour and keep well clear.'

'Since when does asking a question constitute political interference? Don't be a prick. Tell me what's going on.'

'What's going on is a routine police inquiry into a sudden death,' said Sproule in tones that brooked no contradiction. 'Tell you what,' he softened slightly. 'If I hear anything relevant I'll let you know. Can't say fairer than that, okay?' Okay as in end of issue. Okay as in never.

'Well I certainly wouldn't want to do anything that might jeopardise an ongoing investigation, Ken.'

Sproule, for some reason, thought I was being facetious. 'Don't get your wig in an uproar, Murray...'

But I was already hanging up. The stapler had finished its whoomphing and Claire had appeared in the archway, attentive. 'I never did ask about your job,' she said. 'What exactly is it you do?'

It was time I came clean, told her the truth. 'It's hard to explain,' I said. 'I assist the minister.'

The parodic Drysdale was in its new frame, indistinguishable from its pre-accident condition. 'Brilliant,' I said, wrapping it in the beach towel. It was 1.35. Every minute's delay increased the chance of the picture's absence being discovered. And now there was potentially a great deal more at stake than a bit of embarrassment over some accidental damage. 'How much do I owe you?'

This went down like an Elvis impersonator at La Scala. 'You owe me an explanation, for a start.'

'You'll get one, I promise.' I started for the door. 'Soon as I can.'

Soft soap didn't cut any ice around here. Claire blocked my way, hands on hips. 'How soon will that be?'

'I want to see you again. Soon and a lot. But I can't do it today. I've got to get back to work, then I have to take Red to the airport. I won't see him again for a couple of months and I want to spend a little time with him, just him and me, this evening. Let me take you to lunch tomorrow. I promise I'll tell you everything then.'

The curtain was closed, Gracie not in sight. I put my hand on the back of Claire's head. She didn't resist but she wasn't so enthusiastic any more. I gave her a big wet one and bolted out the door, feeling like a fool.

With a good run of green lights, I was back at the Trades Hall in six minutes and at the open door of the exhibition room in another two. My towel-wrapped package was under my arm. Bob Allroy was up his ladder, back turned, his hand in the etched-glass mantle of a reproduction light-fitting. Bob was one of the few men still in regular employment capable of making a day's work out of changing a light globe. I crept across the room and slipped the picture back in place.

'No touching,' Bob growled from above. 'It's moran my job's worth if anything happens to them pictures.'

Returning *Dry Gully* to the collection was one thing, finding out how it got there in the first place was another. That was a question for Bernice Kaufman.

The receptionist was still out to lunch, so I went straight through to Bernice's office. It, too, was empty, as was that of the neighbouring Industrial Officer. But the big fat suspension file labelled Combined Unions Superannuation Scheme was still sitting there, right where Bernice had left it. Lowering myself into the inflatable ring cushion on her chair, I began thumbing.

For all her ferocious efficiency, Bernice was unlikely to win any Institute of Management awards for the neatness of her record-keeping. The CUSS file contained everything but the kitchen sink—minutes of sub-committees, auditors' reports, back copies of the members' newsletter—all of an unedifyingly general nature.

Naturally enough, there was a lot of accounting stuff, including a collection of monthly statements from Obelisk Trust. As of the thirtieth of the previous, CUSS had a balance of slightly more than $6 million in its Obelisk account, half equity linked, half property trust, the first yielding 19.2 per cent, the second 22.8 per cent. Even to a man unschooled in the finer points of finance, these seemed like passably tolerable rates of return. But it wasn't where CUSS kept its cash reserves that interested me so much as where it got its art.

I hit that particular jackpot when I opened a well-stuffed manilla folder and found a sheet of paper bearing the elegantly understated letterhead of Austral Fine Art, Pty Ltd. It was the cover page of a document, dated five months earlier, confirming a number of purchases made by Austral on behalf of the Combined Unions Superannuation Scheme and listing the price of each work. Austral's address was a postoffice box in South Yarra and Drysdale's *Dry Gully*, at $60,000, was its single most expensive acquisition on CUSS's behalf.

Bulldog-clipped to the letter was a swatch of pages, also on Austral letterhead, each headed *Provenance and Certificate of Authenticity*, and consisting of a simple one-paragraph statement, signed at the bottom. The one I wanted read:

Sir Russell Drysdale: Dry Gully *(1946)*
This painting is the work of the late Sir Russell Drysdale
and is from his estate. Austral Fine Art unconditionally
guarantees the authenticity of the above named work.

The signature on both the letter and the certificates was an ornate arabesque, executed in fountain pen and utterly illegible. But the name and title typed below it were decipherable at a glance.

Fiona Lambert, it read, Managing Director.

'Interesting?' Bernice Kaufman loomed in the doorway, her voice dripping sarcasm.

'Ah!' I jumped to my feet, beaming. 'You're back.' I gestured towards the unattended reception area. 'Hope you don't mind me waiting for you in here.'

Bernice's proprietary eyes raked every file, folder and item of correspondence for evidence of unauthorised tampering. 'Forget something?'

I hastened around the desk, relinquishing the Assistant Secretary's throne to its rightful owner. 'I've got an angle for Angelo's speech I'd like to run past you. Get your input.' I tumbled my hands around each other, meshing my fingers like gears. 'How about he emphasises collaboration between the arts industry and union movement?'

'If you were qualified in any way at all for your job,' she advised me primly, 'you would know that the union movement enjoys extensive links with the cultural sector. The Operative Painters and Decorators have, for a number of years, been at the forefront of raising artists' awareness of health and safety issues. Many unions have engaged artists to create works in collaboration with their members. The Building Workers' Union had a poet-in-residence last year.'

A concrete poet, presumably. 'Good points,' I said eagerly. 'Exactly the sort of thing Angelo's speech should mention. What about those consultants you mentioned, Australasian Fine Art, do they have union affiliations?'

Another silly question. 'It's Austral, Murray, Austral. And a CUSS board member with extensive links to the visual arts recommended them, if that's what you mean by union connections.'

'Which reminds me,' I said. 'I'd better get the names of the board members. Make sure Angelo does the acknowledgments right.'

Bernice flicked through the CUSS file and handed me a list. The Secretary of the Trades Hall Council chaired the board. Most of the other names belonged to prominent union officials. Some of them didn't.

'Lloyd Eastlake,' I read out loud. A knot formed itself in the pit of my stomach.

Bernice nodded confirmation. 'You know him?'

'He heads up my policy committee.'

'In that case,' said Bernice, 'I don't have to tell you what an asset he is. It was Lloyd's idea for CUSS to get into art in the first place. Frankly, the rest of the board was lukewarm. But they soon changed their minds. Not only did Austral acquire works by blue-chip artists at very good prices, they found buyers who were prepared to pay considerably more than the works had cost us. The board was so impressed with the investment potential that it immediately upped its level of commitment. It also decided to take a long-term view, to build up the collection rather than just buy and sell on spec.'

'So you must have quite a lot of contact with this Austral crowd? Mind if I take notes? Can I borrow a pen?'

Bernice handed me writing materials. 'Typical,' she clucked. I poised the pen. 'As company secretary,' she went on, 'I am, of course, responsible for the overall administrative framework. But Lloyd insists—and I agree with him on this point—that he handle all direct liaison with Austral himself. That way, individual board members can't try to push their personal tastes. You can imagine what sort of a dog's breakfast we'd end up with if that was allowed to happen.' Not, she felt, that there was any need for Angelo's speech to concern itself with such detail. 'Downplay the investment aspect. Emphasising the cultural benefits to our members would be more appropriate.'

'I agree,' I said. The investment aspects didn't bear thinking about, given what I knew or suspected about the actual value of the works in the room upstairs. Novelty was about the most value they could claim. 'By the way,' I asked. 'How was the ultrasound?'

Bernice's hand went into her bag like a shot. 'See for yourself.' She handed me what appeared to be a polaroid photograph of meteorological conditions over Baffin Bay taken through the screen door of a low-flying satellite during a lunar eclipse.

'A boy,' I guessed, pointing to what looked like an isthmus extending into the north-west quadrant.

Bernice radiated ambivalent pride. 'Sometimes you surprise me, Murray.'

There were plenty more surprises in store for Bernice Kaufman before her bonny bouncing little numbers man was dragged screaming into the delivery room. But she wouldn't be hearing them from me. Not right away. Not until I'd had a chance to ponder the meaning of the amazing information the past hour had brought to light. 'Thanks, Bernice,' I said. 'You've been incredibly helpful.'

For a brief moment, Bernice's insurgent maternal hormones escaped into her voice box. 'Anytime, Murray,' she sighed wearily. 'Now piss off. I've got work to do.'

Pocketing Bernice's cheap ballpoint pen, I backed out the door and headed downstairs, deep in thought.

Arts was supposed to be a cushy posting. Everybody knew that, for all of Ken Sproule's talk about the culture vultures ripping your flesh. Freebies to the opera and holding the minister's hand at gala soirées were supposed to be the name of the game. Not Spider Webb, dead bodies, police investigations, missing pictures and forgery rackets.

Was it really possible that Lloyd Eastlake knew the paintings in the CUSS collection were fakes? Surely not. A measly half a million dollars worth of pictures was small beer compared with the sort of dough he handled every day at Obelisk Trust. He had too much at stake to engage in such risky business, even if he was that way inclined.

But the moral, legal and financial dimensions were not the only ones to be considered. There was a much more important aspect to all this. The political one. The resignation of the Deputy Premier and the Cabinet reshuffle had been designed to counter a growing perception that the government was financially incompetent, no longer a fit custodian for the public cookie jar. What would happen to voter confidence when it was revealed that the government's appointee as head of the Arts Ministry panel that handed out grants to artists couldn't tell a fake from a fish fork? And that one of its members was brokering forged artworks?

Admittedly, this was not the sort of issue upon which a government stands or falls. But nor was it something you'd want to read about in your morning paper. Not if your boss was the minister responsible. Not if it was your job to see that precisely this sort of thing didn't happen.

Things were starting to get seriously complicated.

Going to the police on this CUSS forgery business was out of the question. Nothing would be gained and much might be lost. A quiet word in the right ear at the right time and the unions could bury their own dead. And, in any case, I was holding firm to my decision not to talk to the cops until Red was safely up, up and away.

But that didn't mean I couldn't make some discreet enquiries of my own in the meantime. The problem was where to start. This needed some nutting out. I drove back to my new office, nutting all the way.

Trish thrust a wad of telephone message slips into my paw as I came in the door. Mendicant terpsichoreans and lobbyist librarians. String quartet convenors and craft marketers. Festival creators and design innovators. People whose calls I was paid to return. 'Thought you'd taken the day off,' she said.

I went into my calm new office, sat at my new desk, looked out my big window and I asked myself the same question I'd been asking myself all the way from the Trades Hall. The inescapable one.

Was Lloyd Eastlake knowingly involved in the faking of the CUSS art collection? And if so, did that mean he was implicated in the death of Marcus Taylor?

Realities were at work here that experience had ill-equipped me to deal with, but that I would very swiftly have to learn to manage if I wanted to keep my head above water.

Back in Ethnic Affairs, I'd encountered my fair share of wealthy men. Some of the richest men in the state were migrants. Not that you'd often find them snoozing in the library at the Melbourne Club. Their own communities knew them as employers and entrepreneurs, as the patrons of social clubs and the doers of good works, and perhaps as other things I made it a point never to inquire about. I'd known them as pleaders for community projects, as genial hosts at national day celebrations, as abstract factors in predictable electoral equations.

But in a very real—meaning political—sense, their transactions and their reputations, their associations and ambitions, were fundamentally a matter of indifference to me. Apart from the one or two who had scaled the Olympian heights of industry, they were generally at a remove from the real centre of power. For all their money and their sectional influence, they were ultimately on the outside looking in. No transgression, error or lapse on their part could really hurt the government.

But not so Eastlake. Eastlake was on the team, one of the boys, a man publicly identifiable with the standards by which we ran the state. A man with a finger in every pie. The party pie, the money pie, the union pie, the culture pie. And some of these pies, unfortunately, now also contained Angelo Agnelli's finger.

I found Lloyd Eastlake's card and laid it flat in front of me on my desk. I built a hedge of yellow phone message slips around it. I tapped its cardboard edge against the blond timber. I buzzed Phillip Veale, two glass partitions away. 'Hypothetically speaking,' I said. 'What's the score on the director of a public art gallery also operating as a consultant to private clients?'

'Hypothetically speaking,' said Veale. 'Probably legal. Possibly unethical. Definitely unwise.' He didn't ask who and I didn't tell him. I couldn't help but feel that our relationship was on the mend.

Then I called a contact at the Corporate Affairs Commission and asked him to look up the company registration information on Austral Fine Art, Pty Ltd. He promised to get back to me within an hour.

Finally, I called Eastlake. Not the mobile number. If he was in his car or on the hoof, Spider might overhear the call. I rang the number that looked like it might be his direct office line. It was. He picked it up after the first ring. 'Where the fuck are you?' he said. 'I've been frantic.'

'It's Murray Whelan.'

'Oh, hello.' He dropped his voice an octave and changed down to cruising speed. 'I thought it was someone else.'

'Are you speaking hands-free?' I like to know exactly who is listening to my conversations. 'Is there anyone else in the office with you?'

'No. I'm alone. Why?'

'Regarding that matter we discussed yesterday at the Deli. I need to talk to you again.'

Eastlake didn't mind indulging my penchant for the melo-dramatic at the weekend. But, come the working week, he was a busy man. 'Not more of Giles Aubrey's tall tales, I hope.'

'Aubrey's dead,' I said.

'Dead? How?'

'That's what I want to talk to you about. Among other things. Face-to-face and as soon as possible.'

A couple of long seconds went by. 'The soonest I can see you is six.'

Not the most convenient of times, Red-wise, but I was the one doing the asking. 'Fine,' I said. Eastlake gave me Obelisk's address, a downtown office block, and rang off.

Three other people could help me shed light on what was happening. One of them was lying low. One would keep. The other, I decided, might best be caught on the hop.

'Don't worry,' I told Trish's disapproving look as I headed out the door. 'I'm not going far.'

Just across the road and into the trees.

Fiona Lambert was wearing a fire-engine-red, thigh-length tunic that emphasised the paleness of her skin and the indelible-ink blackness of her hair. She was standing at the front door of the Centre for Modern Art watching two men in company work-wear drag a flat wooden crate out of a van parked in the driveway.

I sat across the road in my car, watching her watch them.

A young woman in harem pants and a beehive flitted about, getting in the way. I remembered her from Friday night. Janelle Something. Fiona's assistant. The delivery guys negotiated the crate through the door and Fiona and Janelle followed them inside.

Our Home had a new home.

And Ms Lambert, at a guess, would be far too preoccupied for the next little while to participate in the kind of consultative process I had in mind. *Our Home* would have to be uncrated, examined, gloated over, stored away. Slipping the Charade back into gear, I pulled out from the kerb. I had an idea. Not the best idea I'd ever had. But, at the time, it had a compelling sort of logic.

I drove through pools of shade cast by elms and pines, turned into Domain Road and found a parking spot in a quiet residential side street. Hope Street, said the sign. I left my jacket in the car and walked around the corner.

Domain Road, with its two-storey terrace houses and small apartment buildings, was quiet. A solitary jogger panted along the footpath. I leaned against a parked car and cased Fiona Lambert's pink stucco block of flats. After a couple of minutes, the dowager with the miniature mutt came out the front entrance and carried her schnauzer across the road. She clipped a lead to the benighted animal's collar and led it into the park. Doo-doo time for Dagobert.

When the pair of them had moved out of sight, I went into the flats and walked briskly up the stairs to the landing outside Fiona Lambert's door. I rapped confidently with the little brass knocker, listening for any sound in the flat opposite. There was none. I rapped again, Justin Case. Justin wasn't home, so I angled up the Ming Dynasty pot-plant holder, slid the key from underneath, opened the door and put the key back in place. It wasn't breaking and entering. That would never have occurred to me. I was just dropping around when there was nobody home.

Not that I let myself into people's places on a regular basis. Usually it was the other way around. I'd given a spare key to my place to Faye in case Red ever needed to get in while I was at work and occasionally I'd come home to find she'd left something exotic in the fridge. But this was something new. Just thought I should make the point.

The flat was exactly as I had last seen it. Same Bauhaus chairs, same boxy sofa, same honey-coloured dining table, same pornographic portrait. Out the uncurtained window, the roof of the CMA was just visible between the trees. If Fiona decided to pop home across the greensward, I'd see her coming through the trees.

The object of my search was vague. Anything to corroborate Lambert's association with the bogus CUSS collection. Anything to connect her with Marcus Taylor, to help clarify the mutually contradictory information I had about their relationship. Had

Taylor hated her as the woman who stole his birthright? Or was he providing fake artworks for her Austral Fine Art operation? Was it possible that she had the missing version of *Our Home*? Given what I now knew, Eastlake's line about it being a student copy of a masterwork had taken on a decidedly hollow ring.

The small study opening off the lounge room was the logical place to start. A strictly utilitarian space. Walls bare except for a row of tiny canvases, each no more than four inches square, each a different shade of blue. A ladder-frame bookcase filled with art magazines. A chrome-inlaid Aero desk, tres chic, with matching stainless-steel waste paper basket, empty. A cardboard box containing several dozen brand-new copies of *A Fierce Vision*. A two-drawer filing cabinet. Bottom drawer, stationery supplies. Top drawer, domestic appliance warranties.

On the desk, an Apple computer with a plastic cover. Must learn to use. Postcards. Someone called Vicki saying Budapest was fab. Invitations to exhibition openings. Bills. Gas, electricity, phone. Very ordinary. Visa, Mastercard, Amex. Denting the plastic to the tune of about twenty-two hundred a month. Clothes and restaurants mainly. Mortgage statement. Nine hundred a month, $86,000 left to pay.

On a salary of, what, sixty grand? Fiona Lambert was living beyond her means. Extravagant but, so far, nothing illegal. Nothing relating to Austral Fine Art. Not so much as a sheet of letterhead. Must keep all that over at the CMA.

Scanning the view out the window on my way, I went up the hall to the bedroom.

Heavy drapes, open a chink. Window overlooking a small courtyard. Enough light to see by. Big contrast to the *Vogue* casualness of the living room. Queen-size bed, black sheets smoothed tight. Cotton. Satin would be tacky. Many big plush pillows, red. Pale carpet, low nap, soft like felt. On the wall above the bed was one huge painting. Not Szabo. Thickly laid-on acrylic paint, high texture, chopped like the waves of a starlit sea. Abstract, tactile, sensual. I could smell clean linen and Oil of Ulan. Red lacquer chest of drawers, antique Japanese. Rice-paper lamps. The whole room reflected back on itself from a mirrored wardrobe occupying entire side wall.

An intensely private atmosphere, redolent of the mysterious feminine. Then again, maybe it was just that I hadn't been in a woman's bedroom for quite some time.

I slid open the mirror-fronted wardrobe and saw a great quantity of clothes, all of them either red, white or black. Enough shoes to make Imelda Marcos's mouth water. About a dozen men's business shirts. Top brands. Ironed. No half million dollars. No Certificate of Incorporation for Austral Fine Art.

Nothing for me on the rack. I looked in the Japanese chest. For a moment longer than absolutely necessary, I stood staring down at a girl called Fiona's collection of investment-quality lingerie. Nothing tarty. No reds or blacks here. Shell-pink, ivory, cream. Resisting the temptation to touch, I knelt on the floor and looked under the bed. Nothing, not even dust.

Straight across the hall was the bathroom. The chunky vanity basin was littered with toning lotions and night creams. Princess Marcella Borghese Face Mud. A cupboard held thick towels, folded and stacked. A cane laundry basket contained damp towels and a white t-shirt with two interlocked Cs in gold on the front.

The kitchen was expensively spartan: Alessi kettle, Moulinex, crystal wineglasses, stainless steel Poggenpohl appliances. Japanese crackers on an empty bench-top.

By now I was hyperventilating. 'Right,' I said, out loud. Time to go. If Fiona Lambert was up to no good, the evidence of it wasn't here.

One last getaway glance out the window. Fiona Lambert was crossing a sunlit patch of lawn between two pines, headed for home. She was, perhaps, two minutes away. At the far side of the courtyard were rubbish bins, a rear exit to the flats. I opened the door a notch to reconnoitre my getaway and heard footfalls coming briskly up the stairs towards me, a heavy male tread.

Whoever he was, he'd be on the landing in a matter of seconds. His destination must be the flat opposite. Fiona was still ninety seconds away. It would be close, but an undetected departure was still possible. Closing the door and pressing my back to it, I listened for the man to go into the other flat.

The footsteps came closer. My hearing, all my senses, felt preternaturally heightened. A radio somewhere was broadcasting talkback. Out on Domain Road, a tram clattered by. Somebody's muffler was due for replacement. The footsteps reached the landing. I waited for the jingle of keys or a rapping on the knocker opposite. All I heard was breathing, the wheezing of an unfit man who had just climbed a flight of stairs on a summer day and was pausing to catch his breath. I strained to hear movement, my heart drumming in my ears.

Distantly, the rhythmic click of a woman's heels rapidly ascended the concrete stairs.

The tattoo beat of my pulse became a surf-roar of panic.

The door was about to fly open. My idiotic spur-of-the-moment impulse was about to backfire horribly, to result in my discovery and disgrace. What possible pretext could I find for being in a woman's flat in this way? What would it look like? I'd be taken for a panty sniffer or a petty thief. A pervert, a psycho. How had I got myself into this position? To what idiot impulse had I surrendered my common sense? What outlandish excuse could I invent? I had to think of something and think of it fast.

I did. I hid.

I hid in the first place I found, a louvre-fronted closet beside the entrance to the living room. I took it for a coat closet but found it held brooms and mops and a vacuum cleaner. Shouldering my way between the broom handles, I swung the slatted door shut behind me just as a key snicked into the front-door lock.

A feather duster tickled the back of my neck. The handle of

a broom toppled to rest against my cheek. The metal nozzle of the vacuum cleaner was jammed up my posterior crotch. Standing to rigid attention in claustrophobic darkness, I held my breath and awaited the humiliation of discovery.

'Did you bring it?' Fiona Lambert opened her front door and stepped through.

Two silhouettes passed before the downward sloping slats of the louvred panel. Just as they did so, I realised that the closet door had not swung completely shut behind me. A chink perhaps a centimetre wide remained open. From where I was standing, it looked as vast as the Grand Canyon.

'You have the delivery docket?' said a male voice, a deep rumble.

My senses were so acute that I could feel the hair standing up on the nape of my neck, taste the dust molecules in the air, smell the residues of floor wax clinging to the broom bristles. A spider in the dark behind me exuded the glutinous thread of its web. Heat radiated from my body. Sweat gushed from every pore, cascading down my skin and dripping into my eyes. My heart belted against my ribs like the bass riff from a Maxine Nightingale disco hit. The saliva had dried in my mouth and, when I tried to swallow it, crackled like a sheet of cellophane being rolled into a ball. I felt as if I was about to burst into flames.

Two shapes went past, into the living room. Through the gap, I could see the shoulder of a white business shirt. The man wearing it had something tucked up under his armpit, blocked by his torso. He half-turned and I could see the back of his near-bald skull. He was examining a sheet of light green paper. Satisfied with what he read, the man folded the page and put it in his pants pocket.

'Show it to me,' said Fiona impatiently, just beyond my vision.

A sliver of dining table was within my narrow line of sight. The man took the thing from under his arm and put it on the table. It was a shoebox in the distinctive hot pink and silver colours of the Karlcraft chain. He took the lid off and removed banded wads of banknotes. He built them into two piles, each about fifteen centimetres high. The money was pale, the colour of hundred dollar bills. Even from inside a broom cupboard on the other side of the room, it looked like a great deal of money.

'One hundred thousand dollars,' said the jowly voice of Max Karlin. 'Cash.'

'*One* hundred thousand?' Lambert was outraged. 'That wasn't the deal. Where's the rest of my money?'

Holding my breath, I leaned forward until my eye was almost pressed to the crack in the door. My field of vision widened to include a good part of the living room. Fiona Lambert stood staring down at the money on the table, her expression caught between elation and petulance.

Karlin ignored her outburst. 'Aren't you going to offer me a drink?'

'You think you can short-change me, is that it?' snarled Lambert. 'Our deal was for twice this amount.'

Karlin put his hands in his pocket and moved out of view. 'It's all I can afford.' His attitude was take-it-or-leave-it. 'If I really wanted to cheat you, Fiona dear, I wouldn't be here at all. Be reasonable. It's still a great deal of money.'

'Our agreement was for one third of the purchase price of *Our Home*,' complained Lambert bitterly, her eyes never leaving the money. 'By my arithmetic, that's two hundred thousand dollars.' Karlin had gone in the direction of the couch. Lambert turned to face him. 'You think it was easy convincing Eastlake to pay more than double the market value?'

Karlin chuckled indulgently. 'Oh, I don't doubt you were very persuasive, my dear.'

His crossed ankles came into view. I could picture him on the couch, leaning back, his legs extended in front of him. 'It's just that circumstances have changed since we made our little agreement. A year ago, cash was easier to lay my hands on. I was slinging fifty thousand a month in backhanders to the building contractors alone. But things have changed. The money has dried up. My bankers are counting every penny. The other investors are watching me like a hawk.'

Fiona Lambert swung around to face him, bare arms akimbo. 'Sell another one of your pictures.' She was spitting chips. 'Sell two, sell anything. Pay me what you owe me.'

'Even if I thought I owed you anything, I've nothing left to sell.' Karlin indulged her, but he was unsympathetic. '*Our Home* was the last really valuable picture I still owned outright. The rest were sold long ago. I've been leasing them back, keeping up appearances.' Compared to him, he was saying, she had nothing to complain about.

'Liar!' She actually stamped her foot.

Karlin snorted with amusement. 'Take the money, Fiona.' His tone was fatherly, unprovokable. He'd seen all this before. 'Be happy you got anything at all. I'm walking away with nothing. Time was, I was a shoe salesman who liked to collect pictures. Then I decided to be a big-shot property developer. I sold my shops, hocked my pictures, bet everything on one big project. Now, after fifty years of hard work, all I've got are banks and investors and unions and construction contractors gnawing at my flesh. Jesus, I've even got an art gallery director blackmailing me.' He emitted a dry humourless guffaw, as if this was the ultimate indignity.

'You're breaking my heart.' Little Miss Lambert didn't sound so well brought up now.

'Be grateful you're getting anything, Fiona. I'm only here because of my sentimental attachment to *Our Home*. Because I'd rather see it go to a public art museum than be sold off in a fire sale. And because I'm a man who keeps his word. I used to be, at least.'

'I don't care where you get it,' insisted Fiona sullenly. 'I want my money.'

'Or what? You'll sue me? I can picture the scene in court. I can hear your lawyer explaining how you extorted money out of me.' Karlin came back up onto his feet and gave a sarcastic demonstration. He drew himself up to his full diminutive height and waggled his chubby finger, imitating a lawyer pleading a case. '"They had a watertight deal, Your Honour. She, expert on the works of Victor Szabo, proposed that she would refrain from deliberately raising suggestions that the painting known as *Our Home* was of dubious authorship. He, in return, agreed to sell the work to her gallery and to pay her a secret commission on the deal. Further, Your Honour, she proposed that if he did not comply with her demands she would cast public doubt on the integrity, and therefore the market value, of other art works in his collection. A perfectly normal commercial transaction, Your Honour."' His address to court complete, Karlin wheeled on his feet and headed towards the kitchen door. 'Yes, Fiona, I can just imagine that.'

Lambert was silent, scowling, one foot tapping. Her gaze followed Karlin and flashed across my hiding place like a spotlight playing on a prison wall. I cowered back into the darkness and slowly emptied the exhausted oxygen from my lungs.

Plumbing whined in the wall behind me and water hit a metal sink. Karlin was in the kitchen, running a tap, getting his own drink. Under cover of the noise, I gulped down air and eased the tension in my muscles. My skin was tacky with sweat and my pulse still raced, but the terror of discovery was abating, replaced by a sense of exultation. My instinct in coming here had been vindicated.

This Fiona Lambert was some piece of work. Selling an entirely forged collection of art. Forcing Karlin to sell *Our Home* and blackmailing him into paying her a secret commission on the deal. Inveigling Eastlake into raising the money.

I ran the desiccated rhinoceros of my tongue around the Kalahari of my mouth, cocked my ear for the next amazing revelation and put my eye once more to the crack. So what if I was discovered? Compared with Fiona Lambert's outrageous felonies, cupboard-skulking was a mere social misdemeanour.

Lambert was sitting at the table, staring at the money. Avarice and triumph lit her face. Karlin's voice came from the kitchen. 'Stop squawking and be grateful you got anything. Frankly, my other creditors won't be anywhere near as lucky. The financial empire of Max Karlin is about to collapse into a pile of rubble and I'm not sticking around to see it happen. I'm on my way to the airport. I'm leaving the country. At five this afternoon, bankruptcy papers will be filed for my private holding company. At nine o'clock tomorrow morning, I'll be in Europe. A liquidator will be sitting at my desk. And the dogs will be fighting over Karlcraft's carcass.'

Fiona Lambert couldn't give a damn about Karlin's misfortunes. Breaking the band on one of the wads of cash, she licked her thumb and started counting. Her lips moved silently like a devotee telling her rosary beads. Karlin came out of the kitchen and when he spoke the sound was so close it startled me. 'Don't bank it all at once. Large cash deposits get reported. And don't start spending it either, not unless you want Lloyd suspecting something.'

'You think I'm stupid?' said Fiona rancorously. 'You think I don't know that?' He'd made her lose count and she had to start again. 'And leave Lloyd to me. I know how to handle Lloyd Eastlake.'

Karlin was standing immediately in front of my hiding place, blocking my view. 'Tch tch. Greedy girl, tch tch.' His shape moved towards the front door. 'Goodbye, Fiona.'

Lambert got up from the table. I leaned backwards and held my breath. The front door opened. 'Bon voyage, Max.' Fiona was caustic to the last. 'And thanks for nothing.' Karlin's footsteps rapidly receded down the stairs. The door was pulled shut and Fiona spoke under her breath. 'You miserable little Shylock.'

Charming.

My big moment, I decided, had arrived. Throw open the cupboard door, jump out and spring Ms Director of the Centre for Modern Art with her hands sunk elbow-deep in ill-gotten loot. Bang her up, dead to rights, with the evidence of her sins piled on the Baltic pine dining table of her over-geared pied-à-terre.

Lambert's silhouette passed the louvred door. I pressed my eye to the crack, waiting for exactly the right moment to make my move.

Her mood had improved remarkably. She kicked off her shoes, sashayed her hips, pumped her arms at her side and sidled across the living room. 'Let me look at you,' she cooed throatily. 'You beautiful, beautiful money.'

She picked up one of the packets of bills and fanned it with her thumb. She kissed it. She slowly ran it over her bare arms, luxuriating in its feel. She squirmed sinuous. 'Money, money, money,' she sang. The tune from *Cabaret*.

Tearing the band off with her teeth, she smeared a fistful of bills across her neck and torso. The loose notes cascaded past her swaying hips and settled on the floor around her feet. She reached for another wad and danced a slow silent rhumba with it, pressing the cash to her belly with one hand and describing a slow circle in the air above her head with the other. She was in a trance.

I couldn't believe my eyes. Turned on by a wad of cash. It was a mesmerising sight. And sexy as all hell. She slid the wad of bills slowly down her body, moaning a low guttural tune in the back of her throat. She moved out of sight. Glassware clinked. She segued back into sight, drink in one hand, money in the other. I'd seen enough. Time to spring.

Bang. Bang. A sharp metallic rapping came from the flat door. I nearly jumped out of my skin. I cringed backwards and my line of sight narrowed.

Startled out of her reverie, Fiona dropped her bundle. She went down on her knees, scrabbling for the bills strewn about the floor. Rap, rap, came the knock at the door. 'Just a moment,' she called, scooping up an armful of loose money, dumping it on the table and going down for more. 'Who is it?'

'Me.' A male. Not Karlin.

'Coming.' She disappeared from my sight briefly, then darted back with a piece of cloth, some sort of throw-sheet off the couch. It billowed above the table and fell loosely over the money. She composed herself, smoothing down her clothes and hair. She came towards me, scooping up her shoes on the way. When she reached my hiding place, she paused to slip on her shoes. She leaned against the louvred door. It clicked shut.

My heart shot backwards in my chest, hit my spine and bounced off. My legs requested a transfer to other duties. I braced myself for exposure. Fiona, oblivious to the pulsating tom-tom of my heartbeat, stepped to the front door and opened it. All I could see was a section of carpet, visible through the downward-raked slats of the closet's louvred door.

'Hi.' Fiona was purring, butter not melting in her mouth. 'What brings you here?' Like this was the nicest surprise she'd had all day.

'Just a chance visit.' The voice sounded familiar. When I heard it again, I had no trouble putting a face to it. 'I called in across the road to see if the picture had arrived safe and sound. Janelle said you'd come home for lunch, so I thought I'd join you.' It was Lloyd Eastlake.

Things were getting more interesting by the moment. I hung on Lambert's response. She said nothing.

'Aren't you going to ask me in?'

A moment's silence. 'Um. I'm just on my way back to work, actually.' And not really in a position to do any entertaining, what with the flat all cluttered up with hundred-dollar bills.

Eastlake was undeterred. 'Let's have a little drink first. Celebrate your success. The Centre for Modern Art's first major acquisition. *Our Home*, ours at last.' His tone was more than just chairmanly. 'You look a bit flushed. You haven't been having one all by yourself, have you? You naughty little girl.'

She played along. 'Okay, I admit it. You caught me at it. But

I really must be getting back. The picture has to be stored away properly. You know what Janelle's like.'

'What's the hurry? Janelle will be fine.' The tone was playfully wheedling, but there was a possessive edge to it. 'You haven't got someone in there with you, have you?'

'Like who?' She laughed the idea away, resenting the inference.

'An attractive woman like you,' he said, turning it into a compliment. 'Could be any one of a million men.'

This all had an air of easy intimacy to it. I began to suspect I knew what Fiona had meant when she said she knew how to handle Lloyd Eastlake. 'I just love it when you get jealous.' Playful sarcasm. 'Married man and all.'

'C'mon. How about that drink.' Eastlake didn't want to stand in the door. He was coming inside. Like it or not.

I was breathing through my skin, willing myself invisible. Eastlake's shoes appeared in the louvre-framed square of carpet in front of the closet. Suddenly, the outline of Fiona's red dress pressed back against the door. The louvres bulged inwards and the whole door creaked on its hinges. Fabric rustled against fabric. Fiona had grabbed Eastlake and pulled him against her. Another sound came—part moist sucking, part sibilant inhalation, part low moan. They were going the smooch, the full mutual tonsillectomy by the sound of it.

The vixen! 'Hmm,' she murmured appreciatively. 'I do find it exciting, I must admit. Getting *Our Home* at last.'

Lloyd Eastlake wasn't a man to pass up an opportunity. 'Hmm,' he agreed. Now that she'd started him up, there was no stopping him. The cupboard door bowed inwards. All I could see was the bare backs of Fiona's calves, her ankles, her fire-engine red shoes. Eastlake's shoe slid between hers, the light grey check of his trousered leg rubbing against her bare flesh.

Movement traced the silhouette outline of Fiona's body. Something slid behind her, cradling the small of her back. Through the slats of the louvre, I could clearly see the individual hairs on the back of Eastlake's hand. My mouth turned to a desert. It seemed inconceivable that they couldn't hear my heart beating. I could hear every breath they took, distinguish their individual rhythms. I might as well have been in bed with them.

They might as well have been in bed with each other. The pace of their breathing quickened, the volume of their slurping noises. Eastlake's hand was tugging up the hem of Lambert's dress. Her knickers were pale lilac. His hand slid into them, down into the valley of her buttocks. Her feet eased wider. 'Hmm,' he murmured. 'I'll have to buy you an expensive painting more often.'

She moaned encouragement. Eastlake's hand was out of her knickers. He was down on his knees, tugging at them. Her legs closed. A flash of lilac slid past her white knees. Through the inverted V of her thighs, I saw him shake free of his suit jacket. He reached down and opened his trousers.

All the blood in my body had converged in my groin. I could have got a job as a coat hook. The pulse in my ears was beating a rhythm like the time-keeper on a slave galley. Faster. Faster. Ramming speed. I screwed my eyes shut and tried to think of something else. Anything else. Humpity, humpity, went the door, threatening to burst in. Bang, bang, bang.

I peeked, knowing already what I would see. Fiona's feet had vanished, raised off the floor. Little ridges of red dress were being forced into the gaps between the louvre slats. So too was the bare flesh of Fiona Lambert's arse. One red shoe lay on its side. The other had vanished. Eastlake was still wearing his. I could see their stitching. Four-hundred-dollar shoes. Only the tips showed. His trousers were round his ankles. His calves were braced. His knees were buckled. His thighs were thrusting.

Bang, bang. I closed my eyes and searched my mind for some distracting thought. I peeked again, then squeezed my eyes tight.

Eastlake's trousers were Prince of Wales check. This was the pattern favoured by the sharpies, part of the uniform. Wide

Prince of Wales check trousers and skin-tight maroon knit tops. That's what Geordie Fletcher wore.

Geordie Fletcher and the horrible twins, Danny and Wayne. I was back at the Oulton Reserve. Round and round I was spinning, biffed and bashed at every turn. My life was in the hands of a gang of brain-dead sharpies. Spider, my supposed protector, was in league with the enemy. My hand was curled tight around the neck of a bottle. A potential weapon, but tangled in the folds of my coat.

Suddenly, it came free. I brandished it like a club. Dizzy with vertigo, I staggered sideways and fell. The bottle hit the concrete path. Broken glass scattered in a pool of spilt alcohol. I was on my knees breathing in the acrid smell.

'Fucking idiot. You wasted it.' Geordie Fletcher had me by the collar, hauling me to my feet. This was it. The cat-and-mouse game was over. I was about to be beaten shitless. The twins had stopped their jeering and fallen silent. Big brother was going to show them how it was done.

More fool him. The neck of the bottle was still in my hand, a hard knife-edged cylinder. Slashing sideways, I caught Geordie unawares. My blow sliced across his thigh, opening a gash in his pants. Blood sprayed into the air.

Geordie jumped back. Amazement lit his face. My fear became exhilaration. I thrust the bottle neck in front of me, daring them to try anything. The Fletchers circled, Geordie's surprise turning to rage. Spider Webb elbowed his way between the twins. 'Put it down, Whelan,' he said. 'Don't be a dickhead.' Somewhere in the dusk beyond the tea-tree, car doors slammed and footsteps raced towards us. Every sharpie in town was about to descend on me. There was blood everywhere. 'Come on, you little cunt,' Geordie yelled. 'Have a go.'

I did. I rushed him. Spider grabbed my arm, twisting it. 'Drop it. Drop it.' Pain shot through my elbow. The bottle neck fell from my hand. Broken glass crunched underfoot. Geordie kicked me in the balls. The pain was searing. Spider's face was in mine. 'Fucking idiot.' Bent double, eyes welling, I retched.

The galloping feet arrived. Hands grabbed my hair, jerking my head back. I swung wildly, no longer caring what happened. An adult had me. A police uniform. A sergeant's stripes. I recognised the face. I'd seen it in the hotel, drinking with my father after closing time. Open handed, he whacked the side of my head so hard that I saw stars and my teeth nearly fell out. 'You're coming with me, son.'

'Come! Come!' urged Fiona. 'Yes. Yes.' She said some other things, too. Things I won't repeat here.

The pace of Eastlake's thrusting increased. The closet door quaked in its frame. An anchovy smell tinged the air. Rumpity, rumpity. Casanova let out a plaintive groan. Hissing like a braking steam train, he slowed to a halt. Suddenly, all was still.

Eastlake disengaged with a suction-cup slurp. Fiona Lambert's bare backside separated from the louvres and her feet found the floor. Her dress fell back into place. She let out a long breath. I wished I could do the same. 'You tiger,' she said. 'That was wonderful.'

With a dull thud, Tiger Eastlake slumped back against the wall opposite. He swallowed, caught his breath. 'You came?'

'Uh-huh.' She might have fooled him, but she wasn't fooling me.

'You sure?' His voice was post-coitally dreamy.

'Would I lie to you?' Her real love, I knew, was lying on the dining table. The knee-trembler had kept him out of the living room for a while. But what was she going to do now? Push him out the door? Her back was still pressed against the closet. 'Now I really do need a drink. Be a darling. There's an open bottle in the fridge.'

Eastlake's hands came down and his pants went up. A zipper zipped. He took a step closer. Nuzzling sounds. He was compliant. His shoes swivelled in the direction of the kitchen. As he moved away, Fiona's back came off the door. I sensed, rather than heard, her flit across the living room.

From the kitchen came the rattle of a refrigerator shelf. Bottles clinked. A cork was withdrawn. A cupboard opened.

Glass nudged glass. I could have done with a drink myself. And a cigarette. I like one afterwards.

'I don't suppose Max Karlin personally delivered the painting, by any chance?' called Eastlake. There was a well-practised familiarity at work here. The easy way the switches went on and off. This sex business between him and Fiona had been going on for some time. But the casualness of Eastlake's question was a little too studied. He had something on his mind.

'Max?' Miss Innocence was relaxed. The dough must have been safely out of sight. 'Haven't seen him since Saturday. Why?'

She came over, picked up her knickers, went back into the living room. 'Where's that drink?'

'I've been trying to contact him all day.' Eastlake came out of the kitchen. 'He's not returning my calls.'

I remembered his anxious grab at the phone when I'd rung. Poor Lloyd. His timing was lousy. Thirty seconds earlier and he'd have run into Karlin on the stairs.

'I really should be getting back to work,' Fiona said. Not, of course, with any of her previous door-blocking urgency. They were like a married couple. He wanted her to listen while he complained about his hard day at the office.

'Sorry to burden you with my worries,' he said. 'I know you hate shoptalk. But if you hear from Max, tell him to call me immediately. There's a rumour going around that he's getting cold feet. The Karlcraft Centre is at the don't-look-down stage. The whole thing is in danger of falling over if Max loses his nerve right now. Obelisk has sunk a lot of money into Max Karlin. More than I was authorised to lend him. I've staked Obelisk's whole future, and my own, on Max's success. If he goes belly-up, he'll take me with him. The least he could do is return my calls.'

'You worry too much.' Fiona played the wifey part, smoothing his fevered brow. 'He's probably just in a meeting or something. It'll be okay, you'll see. If he rings to check that *Our Home* has arrived okay, I'll tell him to call you straight away.'

Eastlake was pacing about while Fiona made reassuring noises. I couldn't quite make out what was being said. My whole body ached from the effort of standing to attention. Carefully, I moved my wrist into a position where I could read my watch. Thirty minutes I'd been standing there. It felt like years. I needed to urinate. Suddenly, something jolted my heart back into my mouth. I heard the sound of my own name.

'That reminds me,' Eastlake was saying. 'You don't have to worry about Giles Aubrey any more. That Whelan guy rang me, said he was dead. I knew I shouldn't have told you what Whelan said Aubrey told him. You've probably been worrying about it.'

'Dead?' she said, only mildly curious. 'How?'

'Whelan didn't say. All very enigmatic, he was. I'm meeting him later, so I'll find out then, I suppose. Anyway, there's one less problem.'

'Oh, I was never really worried about Giles Aubrey.'

Yet again, I couldn't believe my ears. But the logic was overwhelming. The story Aubrey told me—whether true or not—had the potential to derail the CMA's purchase of *Our Home*. Lambert had put a great deal of effort into making sure the sale went ahead. She had a lot riding on its successful conclusion. She could hardly just stand by and let Giles Aubrey ruin her plans. A woman as young, fit and ruthless as Fiona Lambert would have no trouble pushing a frail old man down a steep riverbank.

'I'll just try Max again.' Eastlake came closer and I heard a distinct grunt as he bent to pick up his hastily shed suit jacket. Blip, blop, blip. Mobile phone dialling noises. Silence. Glasses tinkled. The kitchen tap ran again. Fiona, clearing up. Eastlake got through, asked for Karlin. 'Still not back? Okay. Same message.'

My bladder was full. If I didn't get out of that fucking closet soon, I'd have to start paying rent.

They were at the door. 'Remember, if Max calls…'

'Don't worry. I'll tell him…'

'I don't know what I'd do without you.' Eastlake spoke in

tones of unalloyed affection. Jesus. The schmuck was in love.

The door closed. Lambert waited a beat, then let out a long sigh of relief. She moved down the hall. Seconds later, the pipes in the wall behind me started up. From the direction of the bathroom came the sound of running water, then of teeth being brushed. Brush, brush, brush. Then the shower started. Above the cascade of the water, I heard the screech of a curtain being tugged along a metallic rail.

Leaning lightly on the cupboard door, I popped it open. Reassuring myself that no-one was coming up the stairs, I drew the flat door shut behind me. My shirt was drenched in sweat and draped with cobwebs. My hands were shaking. I gulped air. My breath came in short pants, dressed for the weather.

I hurried downstairs, gripping the banister.

Droplets of moisture flashed in the sunlight. Sprinklers played across the lawns of the Domain. Children ran between the trees squirting each other with water pistols. Senior citizens at picnic tables poured streams of steaming tea from thermos flasks. After what felt like an eternity trapped in that broom closet, my bladder was about to explode.

Tilted forward at the waist like a particularly obsequious Japanese, I scuttled across Domain Road and cast about for a public convenience of some description. The only facility in sight was a shoulder-high bed of red and yellow canna lilies. Advancing into its leafy interior, I proceeded to irrigate its tuberous root structure.

Below the waist, I sighed with relief. Above the neck, I struggled to make sense of all that I had just observed. Some things were crystal clear. Others were murky and obscure. I had a growing sense of dismay and responsibility.

That Fiona Lambert was some piece of work. And she definitely had Lloyd Eastlake's measure. Our Man in the Arts, puffed up with smug vanity, was a soft target. Particularly by the time Fiona Lambert had finished working her charms.

Scam one was the CUSS set-up. Eastlake, doing his girlfriend a favour, had put the art investment business of the

Combined Unions Superannuation Scheme her way. This entailed a conflict of interest on his part, both as a director of the CUSS and as chairman of the Centre for Modern Art, but he had probably done no more than what a thousand other company directors did every day of the week. His hot-shot lover, however, had taken full advantage of the opportunity to slip the unsuspecting CUSS an entirely fabricated art collection. The sheer scale of her audacity was staggering.

Scam two was the Szabo deal. Eastlake, persuaded that *Our Home* was an absolute must for the CMA collection, had exerted his influence with both the government and Obelisk to fund its purchase. Fiona, meanwhile, had forced Max Karlin to sell the picture and cut herself in for a piece of the action.

My presence within the stand of lilies, I was suddenly aware, had not passed unnoticed. An amorous couple reclining on the lawn nearby were beginning to cast hostile glances towards where my head extended above the leaf line. I turned my back to them, lest they get the wrong idea.

Was it really possible that Lambert could have got away with her CUSS fraud if not for the accidental depredations of a pair of skylarking ten-year-olds? Would Taylor's forgeries have remained undetected in the face of public scrutiny? And why had Taylor been colluding with Lambert? According to Giles Aubrey, he hated her guts. Had the whole Szabo–Taylor story been a product of Aubrey's notorious tendency to misrepresentation? Or had Marcus Taylor eventually become reconciled to his father's ambitious young bit of cheesecake? Or had his broker, Salina Fleet, handled customer relations? Was it possible that he had no idea that Lambert was the buyer of his 'appropriations'?

Did canna lilies, I wondered, benefit from the occasional dose of concentrated uric acid? This slash was taking on the proportions of an Olympic event. Marcus Taylor. Perhaps he, too, tried to piss in somebody's garden. Maybe he thought he'd found the perfect way to avenge himself on Fiona Lambert. Maybe she had unwittingly given him the opportunity to engineer her downfall. Maybe he had wanted his forgeries to be discovered, as evidenced by the stamp on the back of *Dry Gully*. But not for the reasons Claire had postulated—not out of a forger's vanity—but to discredit and destroy Fiona Lambert.

For months he had toiled in obscurity, producing an entire collection of fake art works in his ratty studio at the old YMCA. For months he had bided his time, waiting for just the right moment. For the moment when he could reveal that his perfectly innocent post-modern tributes had knowingly been passed off as the real thing by Fiona Lambert.

But something even better had come along. The CMA's acquisition of *Our Home*. An irresistible opportunity—not just to avenge himself on Lambert—but to strike a blow against his dead father as well. Frustrated by his inability to obtain anything but the most meagre recognition of his own achievements as an artist—a paltry grant can be even more insulting than none at all—Taylor had manufactured a carbon-copy of *Our Home* with the object of compromising the integrity of Victor Szabo's entire artistic output. Oedipus meets Hamlet on the banks of the Yarra.

At long last, the call of nature rang less stridently in my ears. Drained, I parted the broad green leaves of the cannae, stepped back out onto the lawn and gave the scandalised lovers a cheerful wave. Through the trees, I could see the white facade of the Centre for Modern Art. A scenario, part memory, part speculation, began to take shape.

Poor little Marcus Taylor. He really was a fuck-up. He painted his duplicate *Our Home*, but then got pissed and cocky and tipped his hand at the CMA opening. That little performance of his must really have set the cat among the pigeons. No wonder Salina Fleet had looked so nervous when he got up on that table and started waving his arms about. She knew what he was going to say. He'd given her a sneak preview of the notes to his speech a few moments before, out in the back garden.

Fiona Lambert was a cool customer, though. She didn't betray herself, even though she was the one with most at stake.

Later that night, while supposedly home in bed, she caught up with Taylor and sunk him and his troublesome plans in the National Gallery moat.

The sky was blue. Birds were singing. The grass was green and cool underfoot. I walked back towards Hope Street, where the Charade was parked, through a beautiful summer afternoon. I wondered how she had done it. How she'd managed to get Marcus Taylor's unconscious body up over the parapet and roll it into the water. Knocking him out would have been the easy part. He was practically legless the last time I'd seen him, staggering down the Domain Road footpath.

His big moment had come to nothing. But he still hadn't played his trump card. *Our Home* Mark 2 was still on its easel back at the YMCA. His day would come. Just you wait, he said. Just you wait.

Through an intermittent stream of traffic, I could see the very spot where I'd heard him mumble those words. Pausing beside an enormous Moreton Bay fig, I leaned against the trunk and recalled the scene.

Taylor coming one way. Me going the other. Up ahead of me, the Botanical Hotel. Ahead of Taylor, Lambert's flat and, a fifteen-minute walk away, his own room in the YMCA. The disappearing tail-lights of Lloyd Eastlake's Mercedes.

Rewind further. Up in the flat. Fiona on the phone. Out the window, standing less than fifty metres from where I was currently standing, also on the phone, Spider Webb.

The Missing Link. I'd been battling to put Spider into the picture. He and Fiona Lambert were, after all, far from a natural pair. But now that I began to put the pieces together, an alliance between the two of them made a certain sort of sense. Each was working Eastlake from a different direction—Spider looking for the main chance, Fiona needing help to work her gold mine.

Spider. Warning me off. Tidying up the loose ends. Loose ends like the fact that Taylor had gone to the bottom of the moat with his keys in his pocket. So somebody had to go back the next morning and retrieve the duplicate Szabo and dispose of the evidence of the Austral forgery factory. Loose ends like the fact that I'd got there first and had to be locked in the basement with Willy the Whale. Loose ends like Salina Fleet.

I thought again of Salina's reaction at the moat. Those frozen expressions on her face, caught by the flashing ambulance light. Shock, panic, fear. Did she guess what had happened? Was her insistence that Taylor had killed himself a hastily improvised way of protecting herself, of demonstrating that she could be trusted to keep silent? And her appearance at the YMCA? Was she acting on her own initiative, hastening to clear out all evidence of Taylor's work? Or was everyone just after Taylor's version of *Our Home*?

Then I had come along, sticking my bib in. Not content to remain locked in the basement of the YMCA, I'd kicked up a racket. When Salina inadvertently released me, I put her on the spot. She was a fast thinker, but not entirely convincing in the clinches. And, by then, I'd seen the picture on the easel in Taylor's studio. By then, I was starting to make a real nuisance of myself. I sought out Giles Aubrey, a man who could be relied on to grab the first opportunity that came his way to stir the pot, and gone running to Eastlake with what he told me. But Eastlake, in turn, told Lambert. So Aubrey had ended up at the bottom of the nearest riverbank with a compound fracture of the *corpus delicti*. At least Sal had the sense to make herself scarce.

As I stood there, concealed by the grey folds of Moreton Bay fig, contemplating my responsibility for Giles Aubrey's death, Fiona Lambert came out of the block of flats. Hands empty, teeth shining, looking exceptionally pleased with herself, she crossed Domain Road and walked towards the Centre for Modern Art.

It was, I decided, time to blow the whistle on Ms Lambert. Get the cops on the case while she still had the hundred grand stashed in her flat. Detective Senior Constable Chris Micaelis would be hearing from me, I resolved, very soon. Just as soon as I'd made a couple of phone calls.

Once Fiona Lambert disappeared into the CMA, I hurried to the Charade and headed back towards the office. It was getting on for 4.30 and the ebb tide of early rush-hour traffic had begun to flow out of the city. Anybody with half a brain had already clocked-off and was headed for the beach.

Something I'd overheard in Fiona Lambert's flat was exercising my mind. The world of high finance was *terra incognita*. It was time I got hold of a tourist guide. Even as I turned into St Kilda Road, I was pulling up in front of the Travelodge and fishing in my pockets for coins.

I could find only notes. This meant that before I could use the pay-phone, I was compelled to go into the bar and buy myself a drink. A shot of Jamiesons with a beer chaser. I needed to be both alert and relaxed. I fed the change in a phone in the lobby and called the *Business Daily*. 'You're a finance journalist,' I told Faye Curnow.

'If that's a news tip,' she said. 'You're a bit late.'

'Matter of fact, I do have a tip,' I said. 'A scoop. But first tell me about Obelisk Trust. It's like a bank or a building society, right? Government guaranteed.'

'Don't you believe it. High returns, high risk.'

'And what if I told you that Lloyd Eastlake has been sinking large amounts of Obelisk money into the Karlcraft project without his board's approval?'

'I'd say that he might well soon regret it. The rumours are flying thick and fast that the banks are about to refuse to roll over Karlin's loans. If that happens, he'll have no alternative but to file for bankruptcy.'

'How would he go about that?'

It wasn't complicated. 'You lodge some forms with the Federal Court. A court-appointed trustee moves immediately, shuts the doors and starts liquidating your assets. Your creditors howl like stuck pigs. Then they sit around for the next ten years not getting their money back.'

'So what would you say if I told you that, even as we speak, Max Karlin's lawyers are approaching the court, bankruptcy forms in hand? And that, further, I've got my life savings in Obelisk Trust.'

'I'd tell you that if you don't get your money out of Obelisk by close of business tonight, you can probably kiss most of it goodbye. And I'd ask you how reliable is your information about Karlin.'

'Straight from the horse's mouth.'

'Then you'd better get off the phone. I've got a story to break, and you've got a hasty withdrawal to make. Thanks for the tip.'

I didn't get much thanks for my next call. In fact, I got a flea in my ear. 'Murray Whelan here,' I said. 'Calling from Angelo Agnelli's office.'

'What now?' barked Duncan Keogh.

This wasn't going to be easy. The last time I'd rung the finance committee chairman, I'd hung up on him. 'It's about that deposit with Obelisk Trust.'

'Thought I told you I'd done it.'

'You did,' I said. 'Only there's been a bit of a rethink in the strategy department. Angelo wants the funds withdrawn immediately and put back where they were.' Eastlake wasn't the only one who could play at this exceed-your-authority game. 'Like you said this morning, Duncan. No need to get our shirt-tails in a flap.'

Standing at a pay-phone in the lobby of a budget hotel with a finger in one ear to drown out the muzak bouncing off a tour party of Taiwanese dentists' wives was not the ideal location for a conversation of this nature.

'You tell Agnelli from me,' said Keogh. 'That I'm still the finance committee chairman, not some bank clerk, and if he wants something done he should have the courtesy to call me himself, not get his office boy to do it.'

This was great. Keogh had finally decided to grow a backbone. 'Listen, Duncan…' But Duncan wasn't listening. It was his turn to hang up.

This was not good. I went back into the bar and bought

myself another beer. With the option of bluffing Keogh now closed, the only way left to get the party funds out of Obelisk before the balloon went up was to call Agnelli and have him speak to Keogh. That would entail a great deal of explanation. Frankly, given the choice, I'd rather have gone straight back up to F. Lambert's kitchen, stuck my bare hand into her high-speed Moulinex blender and thrown the switch.

I racked my brain for a plausible lie. It was a fool's errand. The truth, or a passable facsimile of it, was my only option. But first I would have to get through to the ministerial hovercraft plying the distant waters of Lake Eildon. I gorged the pay-phone with coins and dialled Agnelli's mobile. 'The mobile telephone you have called has not responded,' said a female robot. 'Please call again shortly.'

Shortly? Just how much time did she think I had? It was exactly five o'clock. If Obelisk kept standard business hours, it had just shut its doors for the day. I hung up. The phone ate my change.

I dialled the Arts Ministry and asked Trish for a precise fix on my employer's whereabouts and contactability.

'Somewhere in transit,' she said vaguely. 'Not due back in town until later tonight. Why, is there a problem?' Trish's discretion was a one-way valve. Nothing came out, but she was always open to input.

'No problem,' I said. 'Any messages?'

My contact at Corporate Affairs had called. Austral Fine Art, Pty Ltd, was an off-the-shelf number with a paid up capital of two dollars, incorporated the previous year. Its sole shareholder was a Lloyd Henry Eastlake of Mathoura Road, Toorak.

This took a moment's consideration. If Austral was Fiona Lambert's company, how come Eastlake owned it? What a sucker. He even had his name on the corporate shell his girlfriend used to doublecross him.

Right at that instant, the structure of Austral Fine Art was the least of my worries. Unless I did something pronto, our campaign funds would disappear into financial never-never land.

Which in turn meant that Angelo Agnelli, rather than being carried shoulder-high through the next election-night victory party, would be lucky if he was allowed to slink away and commit harikari with a blunt raffle ticket.

My meeting with Eastlake was at six o'clock. But if I could get through to him before then, perhaps he could see his way clear to reverse Keogh's deposit. In a deregulated world of round-the-clock electronic banking, surely Eastlake could authorise an after-hours transaction. Maybe there was still scope for some fancy financial footwork. I didn't need to tell him the truth. I could say I'd been tipped off by a *Business Daily* journo.

Eastlake's direct line was engaged. So was his mobile. I looked up Obelisk in the book and rang the number. Yes, said his secretary, Mr Eastlake was in. But no, he couldn't take my call. He was currently in conference and absolutely could not be disturbed.

The 'in conference' bit was a nice touch, spoken with the strained plausibility of a nuclear power plant press officer during a meltdown. Eastlake was either still desperately trying to track down the elusive Max Karlin, or the penny had finally dropped and he was on the phone trying to parley his way out of financial ruin.

My name had nudged the secretary's memory. 'Mr Eastlake just asked me to contact you, Mr Whelan. Regarding your meeting at six. He said can you please meet him at the Little Collins Street entrance to the Karlcraft Centre. He said he wants to show you some of the public art there.'

A building site was an odd place for a business meeting, but I wasn't arguing. Eastlake was perhaps hoping to find Max Karlin there, too. He'd have to settle for me. It had just gone five-fifteen. Enough time to drive back to the Arts Ministry, park the car and walk the three blocks into the city. Calling the cops could wait.

Famous last words.

Thirty storeys of concrete and steel skeleton towered upwards. A construction hoarding ran along Little Collins Street, thick with show posters and aerosoled graffiti. Iggy Pop. Leather is Murder. On the footpath opposite, an endless stream of home-bound shoppers and office workers flowed out of the Royal Arcade, sparing only a passing glance at the big Mercedes parked tight against the hoarding. Construction Vehicles Only, read the sign, 6 a.m to 6 p.m.

The hours were a fiction, a pretext for the council to issue parking tickets. Building industry hours are 7.00 a.m. to 4.30 p.m. and the only remaining evidence of construction vehicles was a powdery sludge in the gutter, the hose-down water from long-departed concrete trucks. A pink slip nestled beneath the Merc's windscreen wiper.

Spider Webb was nowhere in sight. I wondered exactly where he was. If he was lurking about, I doubted he would try anything smart with Eastlake present.

Not that Eastlake's presence was apparent. The building site was deserted. Through a chain-mesh gate in the hoarding, all I could see was a maze of scaffolding, piles of sand, stacks of breeze bricks, the silvery worm-casings of air-conditioning ducting. I rattled the padlock and peered inside, finding only shadows and silence.

Down a side alley was a smaller gate. An open padlock dangled from its bolt. It led directly into an access walkway, a two-metre-wide tunnel of white-washed plywood extending into the interior of the site, its walls streaked and pitted from the casual buffeting of loaded wheelbarrows and the elbows of apprentice plumbers. Safety Helmet Area, said a sign. No Ticket, No Start.

I didn't have a ticket, at least not one from the Building Workers Industrial Union, but I started anyway. I headed along the unlit passageway, breathing plaster dust and the smell of polymer adhesives, hearing nothing but my own footsteps, hoping I was headed in the right direction. Forty metres in, the tunnel doglegged sharply, ramped upwards and opened onto a broad balcony of raw concrete.

An immense atrium extended before me, as vast as the interior of a cathedral. Muted sunlight filtered through a glass ceiling high overhead. A series of galleries lined the sides, ascending three storeys above me. From the floor, two storeys below, a forest of scaffolding sprouted upwards, clinging to the edges of the jutting balconies and wrapping itself around the row of columns that marched down the centre of the great space. The whole place was the colour of ashes.

Lloyd Eastlake was sitting on a pallet-load of ceramic tiles at the edge of the balcony, staring out into the void. One hand was resting on the metal piping of a temporary guard rail. The other was supporting his chin in the manner of Rodin's *Thinker*. Whether this disconsolate pose was deliberate or not, I couldn't tell. But it spoke volumes. Here was a man who had heard the news.

He turned at my approach and slowly rose to meet me. His arm swept wide in a grand, operatic gesture. 'Welcome to the Karlcraft Galleria,' he declared, his voice larded with irony, his words instantly swallowed up in the empty vastness of the place. 'Come. Admire.'

We stood together at the guard rail and gazed at the vista spread before us as if it was some marvel of nature, some wondrous subterranean grotto. 'Over forty thousand square metres of retail space. Nearly a hundred fashion boutiques and specialty stores. Five bars, three restaurants, a cinema.' Eastlake spoke as though offering me dominion over the cities of the world. 'Above us, twenty-eight floors of prime commercial office space. Below us, parking for a thousand cars.'

I remained silent, not knowing how to respond. Eastlake was inviting me to share the loss of his dream. I could hardly tell him that parking for a thousand had never been one of my visions.

'Even as a hole in the ground it was impressive,' he went on, wistful now. 'Sometimes I'd come here and just look for hours on end. Watching it take shape. Imagining what it would be like finished.'

That, at a guess, was about three months away. The finishing-off was well under way. All the essential structure was there. The escalators sat ready to roll, sheathed in protective cardboard. Stacks of plaster sheeting, pallet-loads of tile and marble, plate glass, rolls of electrical conduit lay everywhere, giving the place an air of having been abandoned in haste.

It was not entirely abandoned, though. Across the concrete canyon, on the level below, something flickered at the periphery of my vision. I leaned forward and squinted, trying to penetrate the shadows. All I could see was the doorway of an embryonic boutique, the pitched angle of a sheet of plate glass. Nothing moved. A play of the light, perhaps.

Eastlake was wearing the same Mickey Mouse tie as when I had first met him. He'd pulled it down a little and undone the top button of his shirt. Close up, his eyes were distracted, a little wild. His skin was the colour of putty. His forehead glowed with the slightest patina of perspiration. It was the closest to dishevelled I could imagine him.

'I heard about Karlin,' I said. By that time, it could hardly have been a secret.

'The bastard,' said Eastlake, flat and expressionless, almost without rancour. '"No hard feelings." That's what he told me. "No hard feelings. It's just business." Can you believe that?'

Karlin was right, I thought. Concentrate on the basics. I wasn't there to console Eastlake. I had problems of my own. 'What does this mean for Obelisk?' I said. 'For the funds Agnelli invested last Friday?'

Eastlake seemed not to have heard me. He was leaning out over the edge of the guard rail, looking straight down. 'See that?' he said.

Immediately below us, a drop of two storeys, was a section of mosaic flooring. The newly laid tiles were bright in the half-darkness. The pattern was a cornucopia spilling forth the fruits of abundance. 'Public art,' he said. 'As a major investor, I was able to insist on the inclusion of murals, sculptures...'

His voice trailed off. He turned and picked up a terracotta tile from the pallet behind him. Casually, he tossed it over the balcony. Twenty-five metres below, it hit the horn of plenty and exploded like a grenade. 'So Angelo wants his money back, does he? Well, you tell him that he's not alone. I want my money, too. And I've lost a damn sight more than he has.'

Eastlake threw another tile, then another, flinging them out into the void. Four, five, six he hurled, rapid fire, grunting with the venomous exertion of it. They bounced off scaffolding, struck columns, ricocheted downwards. The harsh clashing of hollow metal and the shattering sound of breaking glass filled the air. Across the reverberating emptiness, well out of range, one part of the shadows seemed lighter. A shape like a man stood immobile, watching.

As abruptly as it began, Eastlake's cathartic rage halted. Taking a handkerchief from his jacket pocket, he placidly wiped his hands. 'Obelisk is finished. As Karlcraft's principal unsecured creditor, it will be lucky to get ten cents in the dollar.' Despite his pretence at composure, he was wound tighter than a spring. 'Obelisk customers, I'm afraid, have done their dough. All thanks to Max Karlin's cave-in to the banks.' He shook his head in disbelief. 'And to think that only yesterday I was concerned about maintaining the value of his art collection.'

We had moved to the reason for our meeting. 'Giles Aubrey died of a fall,' I said. 'Or that's what we're supposed to think. Personally, I have my doubts.'

Eastlake smiled thinly, continuing to wipe his hands. 'And this is why you insisted we meet? Face-to-face, as you put it. So you could share your doubts?' He put his handkerchief away, did up the top button of his shirt, straightened his neck and slid the knot of his tie into place. The obscure inferences of a nutcase were the last thing Lloyd Eastlake needed at a time like this. This meeting, a pit stop in the journey of life, was now at an end. He turned to go.

I could see his point. Time to start getting down to detail. 'I intend to share my suspicions with the police. And, unfortunately, you are involved.'

That stopped him in his tracks. 'Me? How?'

'Because of your ownership of a company called Austral Fine Art,' I said. 'And because of the political implications arising from its dealings.'

'What's Austral got to do with Giles Aubrey? What political implications?'

It was a long story and I had to begin somewhere. 'This afternoon,' I said, 'purely by chance, I discovered that one of the paintings in the Combined Unions Superannuation Scheme art collection is a forgery. A painting supplied by Austral Fine Art. It is quite likely that other works sold by Austral are fakes. Further, I suspect that the person who organised the fraud was responsible for the deaths of both Marcus Taylor and Giles Aubrey. We both know who I'm talking about.' I leaned back against the guard rail and let the implications of my words sink in. 'Don't we?'

Eastlake stared at me with frank amazement. He tilted his head and searched my eyes, as though attempting to discern my motives. He appeared to conclude that I was stark raving mad.

It was a perfectly understandable reaction. Not only had he just suffered a reversal of his financial fortunes. Now he was being told that the woman he loved had been taking advantage of him, and that she was suspected of murder.

'These are remarkable allegations,' he said at last. 'Can you prove them?'

I did my best to look sane. 'The evidence is largely circumstantial at the moment, I admit. But once a proper investigation begins, the outcome will be inevitable. If I felt I could hold off taking my suspicions to the police, I would. But you understand that I can't be party to concealing activities of this nature.'

'Why are you telling me all this?' Eastlake was genuinely perplexed.

'Don't be dense.' Did he want me to spell it out for him? 'Think about the political implications of your little peccadillo. You've set yourself up as Labor's man in the arts. You'll have to immediately resign from the Visual Arts Advisory Panel, the CMA chairmanship and the various other government appointments you hold.'

Eastlake was utterly incredulous. 'Have I got this right?' he said. 'You're telling me that you've held off informing anyone of your suspicions until you had the chance to ask me to resign my official positions?'

Not strictly true, but I nodded anyway. 'I know it's a case of shutting the gate after the horse has bolted,' I said. 'But I think you'll agree that your position will be untenable once this gets out. The sooner you act the better.'

Eastlake seemed to give this suggestion some thought. He bent his head and ran a hand slowly through his hair. We were standing about three paces apart and I could see the bald patch on the crown of his head.

Suddenly, it came towards me. Eastlake's shoulder rammed full-strength into my upper body. His leg went behind my heels and swept my feet out from beneath me. I tilted backwards, off balance, and felt myself pivoting over the guard rail. One arm flew out wildly, scrabbling for equilibrium. The other shot desperately towards my attacker, my fingers raking the air.

'Oumphh,' I said, caught in a wave of vertigo. Then I toppled backwards over the rail and pitched weightless into empty space.

My right hand closed around something soft and smooth. My shoulder joint wrenched violently in its socket, jerking me upright. I was no longer falling. I was dangling in mid-air.

'Urrgh,' said a voice above me. The thing in my hand was Lloyd Eastlake's Mickey Mouse tie. Somehow I'd managed to grab it as I went over the rail. I hung from it, one-armed, swinging like a pendulum. My feet scissored the empty air. My free arm flailed upwards. 'Urggh,' said the voice again.

Lloyd Eastlake's face stared down at me. His lips were purple. His eyes bulged. His windpipe was pinned against the horizontal bar of the rail. My weight was dragging him down, strangling him. The fingers of my left hand found the tie and gripped it. I held fast, two-fisted, and felt the silky noose tighten further around Eastlake's neck.

His arms flew over the rail. He grabbed his rodent-infested neckwear and started hauling it upwards, desperately fighting to relieve the pressure. The thin fabric began to slide from my grasp. My elbows sawed against the raw concrete lip of the balcony. My feet windmilled helplessly, two storeys above the hard floor.

As Eastlake pulled upward, the clenched knuckles of my

right hand struck the bottom pipe of the guard rail. I let go the tie and lunged for it. My fingers wrapped themselves around smooth metal. It took my weight. With my left hand I immediately refastened my grip on the tie. But the pipe was too thick for my fingers to encircle. It was already slipping from my grasp.

All this was happening very quickly. I tried not to look down. I looked up, past the Mickey Mice. Eastlake reared above me, his throat now clear of the top rail. One hand was tugging at the middle of his tie, the other was clawing at the knot. Spit was dribbling from his lips. His eyes were utterly whacko. He had tried to kill me and now both of us would die.

Not if I could help it. I released the tie with my left hand and grabbed the bottom rail. Eastlake flew backwards, out of sight. Now I had the rail by both hands, I began to haul myself upwards. Over-arm chin-up. Never my best event. My bicep muscles quivered. They felt like jelly. My cheek grazed the concrete rim. Then my chest. Then my sternum. It was like trying to climb out of a swimming pool without the resistance of water to push back against. I twisted and jived in mid-air, struggling to swing a leg up over the edge of the balcony.

Now I could see Eastlake. He had collapsed on his backside. His hands tore at the garrotte around his neck. He sucked at the air and wiped his spit-flecked lips with the back of his hand. His palms went flat to the floor and he began to lever himself upright. His mouth was a smear of murderous intent. One swift kick and I'd be cactus.

'Wait,' I wheezed. If I could buy a few seconds, I might get my arm over the rail. 'Fiona Lambert's not worth killing me to protect. She's just using you. She got a cut of the Szabo deal. Karlin was in her flat this afternoon, just before you. Making the pay off. She knew he was leaving the country and didn't tell you.'

Eastlake was back on his feet, dusting off his pants. He took two steps towards me and raised his foot.

'You wanted proof,' I grunted, my knee finally finding the

edge of the balcony. 'Look in her flat. You'll find a Karlcraft shoebox full of cash.'

'Bullshit.' Eastlake's voice was a rasp. His heel came down hard on the knuckle of my right hand.

'Arrgghh,' I screamed and felt my fingers begin to loosen. Scrabbling to shift my balance onto my knee, I heard the sound of running feet. It was coming from below and behind. 'The cops,' I winced through gritted teeth, pain throbbing up my arm. 'I told them I was coming here.'

It was no use trying to bluff him. Eastlake was beyond reason. His face was a blank mask. His eyes were empty. The sound of running footsteps became a high-pitched twittering. Bats, I thought. The squeaking wheel of a supermarket trolley. A choir of heavenly angels come to carry me aloft. The bells of hell.

I had, I realised, got it all horribly wrong. Eastlake wasn't doing this to protect Fiona Lambert. He had his own reasons for wanting me dead. Austral was just as much his scam as Lambert's. Maybe more so. It was he who had killed Taylor and Aubrey. And I was next on his list. That's why he wanted me to meet him here. You stupid idiot, I thought. You've brought this on yourself. You deserve to get yourself killed.

Eastlake's heel came down again. One. Two. Both hands. I was going to die. All I had left was a vindictive lie. 'Your darling Fiona's fucking Karlin, you know.'

'Liar!' He pressed the sole of his shoe flat against my chest. His hands curled around the guard rail. With a great heaving grunt, he pitched me backwards. The pipe slid from my faltering grip.

Once again, I plummeted into the abyss.

My whole life began to flash before my eyes. It's true. It happens. A great soft tit filled my mouth. My mother stabbed me with a nappy pin. My first day at school. Sister Mary Innocent raised the yard-long blackboard ruler and brought it down with a mighty whack on the back of my bare legs. My knees buckled and gave out beneath me. I crumpled into a heap.

I was on a small platform of loose planks. It was the top of a mobile scaffold, the kind painters use to reach really high ceilings. Someone had pushed it beneath me while I was clinging to the railing above. That squealing noise was the rolling of castors. I had plummeted a grand total of perhaps four metres. From above came the sound of running feet. The scaffolding tower began to tremble and sway. Either we were having an earthquake or someone was climbing rapidly up the ladder braced to its side.

Adrenalin surged through my veins. My fight or flee reflex went into overdrive. There was nowhere to flee to. Rolling up into a crouch, I grabbed hold of the nearest cross-piece of scaffolding. Wincing at the jolt of pain in my fingers, I braced myself for action.

A hand closed around the top rung of the ladder. Then another. I saw a chunky gold pinky ring. Spider Webb was coming to finish me off.

Webb's head appeared, sunglasses pushed up on top of his sleek hair. Bobbed down like a Cossack dancer, I kicked out at his head.

I missed. Spider put his forearm up and easily deflected the blow. 'Fuckwit,' he snarled. 'Thought I told you to stay out of this.' He cocked his head, motioning me to silence. Rapidly retreating footfalls reverberated off plywood walls. Eastlake was high-tailing along the access walkway. Spider's head disappeared. He was clambering back down the ladder. It was all very hectic and not at all self-evident.

'Wait,' I blurted. Would somebody please tell me what the hell was going on? Creeping forward on hands and knees, I peered over the edge of the tower. Spider slithered to the floor. Weaving his way between drums of pre-mixed grouting, he sprinted towards a stairway leading to the upper concourse.

Whatever the hell was happening, I had no desire to be left alone. Not with Eastlake still rampaging around the joint. Not this far from *terra firma*. I swung myself down onto the rungs of the ladder and gingerly climbed to the ground.

The ground was good. I liked it a lot. I let its reassuring presence seep upwards through the soles of my shoes. I was shaking like a leaf. The memory of Sister Mary Innocent had always affected me that way. At the bottom of the stairs was a skip overflowing with carpenters' off-cuts. As I went past, I grabbed myself a club-sized length of timber. It was only light-weight pine but it had some tremendously reassuring nails sticking out the end. Nobody was going to mess with me.

Nobody tried. The upper balcony was deserted, the whole site silent as a grave. I loped through the access walkway, headed for the exit. I took the dogleg corner wide, ready for anything. Nothing like being on the receiving end of an attempted homicide to get the old glands pumping.

Spider was in Little Collins Street. Pedestrians were coursing around him. He'd run hard and was doubled up, catching his breath. The back end of Eastlake's Mercedes was barrelling through a green light at the far end of the block, past the flashing No Turns sign. 'Shit,' said Spider, standing erect and sliding his visor back down over his eyes.

I had no idea exactly where this big-eared lug fitted into the scheme of things. I no longer flattered myself that I had any grip at all on the scheme of things. The only thing I knew for sure was that Spider Webb had just saved my life. And that gets you a lot of points in my book. I nearly kissed him.

'Fucking psycho,' I said. 'Your boss is a fucking psycho.' Two approaching women, spotting the cudgel in my hand, veered to the other side of the street. A weapon was now probably super-fluous. I tossed it back down the alley.

'He is now,' said Spider, like Eastlake's behaviour was entire-ly my fault. 'And Christ alone knows where he's headed.'

Christ and yours truly. 'Fiona Lambert's place,' I said. 'Bet you anything.'

'Why there?' Spider didn't find the idea by any means obvious. 'What did you tell him?'

'I told him that his girlfriend's been cheating.' I was begin-ning to get a very bad feeling about having told Eastlake that.

And the other bit. The bit about her and Karlin. I'd been thinking on my feet, so to speak. The lie hadn't bought me any more time. But judging by the expression on Eastlake's face when he stomped my knuckles, it had certainly hit home.

'Shit,' said Spider again. 'No wonder he flipped out.' His neck went up and his head radared about.

'What's going on, for Chrissake,' I demanded. 'Tell me.' I was starting to sound like Claire.

'Later.' Spider took off up the street, head swivelling as he went, like he'd mislaid something. 'Wait,' I yelled, and headed after him.

The rush-hour traffic was beginning to ease, but Swanston Street was still busy. It was the main thoroughfare through the central business district and the route for all cross-town trams. A row of them was banked up at the traffic lights. I was three paces behind Spider and one step ahead of him. Given the rate the motor traffic was inching ahead, there was a better than even chance that a tram would beat a Mercedes to Domain Road. 'Please, Noel,' I pleaded. 'Tell me what's going on.'

Spider didn't answer. He was too busy joining the crowd of pedestrians surging across Swanston Street, weaving through the gridlocked cars towards the green and yellow trams. The foremost was a Number 8. *Toorak via Domain Rd*, read the destination board.

Halfway across the street, Spider stopped abruptly and bent to the driver's window of a black Saab. As I caught him up, he reached inside and snatched a car phone from the ear of the driver and began punching in numbers. The chinless wonder behind the wheel couldn't believe it. Spluttering, he tried to open his door, demanding his toy back. Spider held the car door shut with his foot and clamped the phone to one of his auricular protuberances. 'C'mon, c'mon,' he urged. Then, quickly, 'He's headed for Lambert's place. Get there fast. He's finally flipped.'

He tossed the mobile back into the Saab driver's lap and sprinted for the trams. The lights went green, air-brakes hissed and the front tram lurched forward. Spider swung himself aboard just as the door began to glide shut.

I wasn't so fast. I raced alongside and swung myself up onto the running board. The tram was crowded. Standing room only. It crossed the intersection, gaining momentum, headed for Princes Bridge. Faces peered out at me, some amused, some alarmed. The door slid open and a rough hand hauled me aboard.

'You in a hurry?' the conductor scowled. She had a nose ring and was wearing acid-proof work boots with her green uniform skirt and blouse. 'Ta!' I said and began shouldering my way into the press of hot bodies, pursuing Spider towards the front of the carriage.

My fellow passengers parted before me like the Red Sea. And with good reason. My grime-streaked shirt-tails were hanging out. I was clutching my throbbing right shoulder with a swollen red hand. My half-healed ear had started bleeding again. I was panting heavily. And an aromatic wet patch extended down my trouser leg from crotch to knee. Apart from everything else that had happened in the preceding twenty minutes, I had evidently contrived to piss myself.

Spider had got as far as the front window. He was squeezed between a couple of strap-hanging white-collar types, doing his best to pretend he didn't know me. 'Piss off,' he hissed, squaring his glasses on the bridge of his nose, smoothing his hair and twiddling his jewellery. I pushed myself right up against him. The salary-men cringed back and averted their eyes. 'Persistent bastard, aren't you?' Spider muttered, craning over the heads of the seated passengers, monitoring the passing cars on the road outside.

'You'd better believe it,' I warned. 'And until I get some answers, I'm sticking to you like shit to a blanket.'

Spider shrank back, but he started talking. 'Eastlake's been tickling the till,' he said. 'He syphoned Obelisk Trust funds into his own account and used them to play the stock market. It worked okay for a while. But when the crash happened in October '87 he lost the lot. Ever since then, he's been running a round-robin, paying Obelisk depositors their dividends out of their own capital. Karlcraft Developments was his only hope for a big win, a way to cover his losses. He lent the project every penny he could raise. As long as Karlin stayed afloat, he had a chance of survival. Now that Karlin's folded, the whole Obelisk house of cards will fall over. Eastlake's looking not only at personal financial ruin but prison time for fraud.'

'He's also been selling forged art,' I said, not to be entirely outdone. 'He's been using a front called Austral Fine Art.' The guy had just tried to kill me, so I was keen to sink the boot in.

Spider pushed my head aside, tracking a stream of passing cars. 'We know all about Austral,' he said. 'That's why we suspect he killed Taylor.'

Spider's metamorphosis was happening a bit fast for me. 'What do you mean "we"? Who's "we"?'

The tram was hurtling down St Kilda Road at a steady clip, approaching the war memorial. The greenery of the parkland raced along beside us. It wasn't the only thing. As we slowed to disgorge passengers one stop short of the turn into Domain Road, a blue Mercedes sped by, a grim-faced Lloyd Eastlake at the wheel. Spider began elbowing his way to the door, me right behind him. The conductor blocked our way. 'Fez please.'

I fumbled in my pocket. Spider pulled out a wallet and flipped it in her face. She was looking at it sceptically when I reached past and dumped a fistful of change in her palm. 'Two all-day travel cards, please,' I said. The tram rounded the corner and accelerated up the slight incline of Domain Road. As the connie punched our tickets, I reached up and jerked the communication cord. The tram's clicketty-clack crescendo reached its peak and it began to decelerate. The door slid open.

Eastlake's Mercedes was pulled up on the park side of the road. It was empty, its boot open. Spider hit the bitumen running. Me too.

I ran around the back of the tram and narrowly beat a stream of oncoming traffic to the footpath in front of Lambert's block of flats. When I looked back, Spider was still on the far side of the road. He'd thrown open the Merc's driver-side door and was reaching across to the glove compartment.

Fiona Lambert was not a nice person. But if Eastlake did anything violent to her, it would be because of what I'd told him. I turned and started into the flats, almost colliding with the old chook with the schnauzer. 'Well I never!' she exclaimed, clutching the hapless pooch to her bosom.

'Me neither,' I said, and started running up the stairs.

The door of Fiona Lambert's flat sat carelessly half-open. Behind it, bananas were being gone in no uncertain terms. The sound was coming from the direction of the bedroom. 'Bitch!' Eastlake's voice was shrill with indignation. 'To think that I killed for you.'

The spare key was in the lock. Fiona Lambert's security consciousness was appalling. 'You're crazy,' she was saying, over and over, sounding very convincing.

I was all ears, panting, imagining the scenario, figuring the options. Shivers were running up and down my spine. Eastlake had a lead of, what, five minutes. Time enough to burst in, launch into a truth and consequences confrontation, maybe get rough. A glass container shattered. Definitely get rough.

He was having a busy few days with the rough stuff, Chairman Lloyd. Getting quite a taste for it. The targets were easy. Marcus Taylor, drunk and emotional. Giles Aubrey, frail and disposable. And me. I'd gone to him like a lamb to the slaughter. He'd been showing me some public art and I'd gone too close to the edge. Dangerous places, building sites.

But the motive here was different. With Taylor and Aubrey and me, it had been about money and staying out of prison. This was personal. He'd called me a liar back there at the construction site, but he'd been quick to believe. The seeds of doubt must already have been there, waiting to flower. Deep-seated doubts about his true worth, perhaps. A self-esteem problem. Something to do with the business that transpires between rich men and expensive women.

Money, reputation, ego, sex. If he couldn't have it any more, nobody would. No pre-meditation here, no calculating the odds. Now it was all just cataclysmic rage. 'Take it, take it,' Fiona was crying. 'It's yours. Take it.'

She'd folded, shown him the money. Bad move, sister. It wouldn't satisfy him, only prove the point that the whole world was against him. The deck stacked. The game over.

A shoe box of petty cash wouldn't fix anything. The raw sound of a slap came through the door.

Spider's running footsteps echoed up the stairs towards me. Time for the Coalition Against Domestic Violence to start getting pro-active. I pushed the door open and entered the flat. An ornamental candlestick sat on the hall table, a drooping blob of burnished silver. I snatched it up and began down the hall. 'Don't. Please don't,' Fiona Lambert was begging.

I stepped into the bedroom doorway. What I saw is fixed forever in my mind.

Eastlake had his back to me. He was bending slightly at the waist, one arm thrust out rigidly in front of him. Fiona Lambert was beside the bed, one knee on the floor as if genuflecting. She'd been showering. Again. A very hygienic girl. Her hair was half-dried and she had a pale yellow towel wrapped around her body. One hand was clutching it closed. The other was raised to her cheek, touching a blazing red welt. Her eyes were as big as dinner plates and she was doing her effortless best to look tremendously contrite. A shattered jar oozed moisturising cream onto the carpet.

On the bed was the bright pink Karlcraft shoe box. Its lid was off. The money was back in its banded bundles, neatly stacked. Spread out beside the box was a painted canvas, the edge frayed from where it had been cut from its stretcher. A red-brick suburban dream home. Blue sky.

Eastlake jabbed his extended hand towards it. 'Look at it!' he ordered. 'It's perfect. You'd be a laughing stock if I hadn't done what I did.'

But her eyes were turning towards the door. Eastlake spun around, his arm still extended. In his hand was a gun. The gun from the glove compartment of the Mercedes. He stuck it in my chest.

The gun had crossed my mind as I ran up the stairs. I thought Spider was reaching across to the glove compartment to get it. For some reason, Eastlake and the gun were an association I had simply not made. Guns were for bodyguards, bank robbers, cops. Committee-chairing, well-suited Melbourne businessmen didn't go packing firepower. Not even homicidal ones. Wrong again, Murray.

'You!' accused Eastlake. Me, the guy who kept turning up like a bad penny. Me, the interfering busybody he'd last seen disappearing over a second-storey balcony. He looked at me like I was an apparition. 'You.'

As if to confirm that I was flesh and blood, he prodded me in the chest with the barrel of his Smith & Wesson. His Black & Decker. His Gulf & Western. Whatever the fuck it was, my Daliesque candelabra had met its match. I let it slip to the floor.

Back at the Karlcraft Centre, Eastlake had been hyped-up and homicidal. But his actions had a certain logic. Criminal, but rational. He was disposing of a potential threat. Now, he'd come completely uncorked. The windows to his soul were wide open and the view was not a pleasant one. Like a tantrum-wracked child who could neither believe how far he'd gone nor conceive of how to get back, he was simultaneously thrilled and appalled by his own behaviour. A disconcerting combination of emotions in a man with a gun against your chest at point-blank range.

Even as Eastlake's berserk eyes locked onto me, Fiona Lambert saw her opportunity. She began to come up off her bent knee, backing away. As she rose, she reached out to steady herself against the edge of the bed. Her towel slipped to the floor, exposing her nakedness. Instinctively, she snatched up the canvas from the bed and covered herself. It was an odd moment for modesty and there was an almost coquettish aspect to the gesture, as if she hoped that her vulnerability might offer her some defence.

It didn't. Eastlake, reacting to her movement, swung the gun around. Fiona cowered back, raising the picture in front her body protectively, as if to shield herself from his sight. At exactly that moment, Eastlake fired.

An explosive crack reverberated through the confined space. The bullet punched a neat round hole straight through the front door of *Our Home*. Fiona Lambert staggered and fell backwards onto the bed, the painting draped over her face, covering her head. Her naked body twitched and went limp. It was stark white against the black sheets. Colour co-ordinated to the last.

Eastlake's hand jerked at the recoil and I lunged forward. I caught him in mid-turn and the barrel of the gun twisted upwards. It went off again and blew the top off his head. Blood and brains went everywhere.

The two reports echoed in my ears. The smell of cordite filled my nostrils. Eastlake was still on his feet, the gun still in his hand. He sort of teetered. I was moving backwards, partly reeling from the scene before me, partly being dragged from behind. The gun hit the floor and Eastlake crumpled like a wet rag.

Then I was stumbling backwards down the passageway. Spider Webb was dragging me by the collar. 'Far canal,' he said. He didn't hear any argument from me. Perhaps twenty seconds had elapsed since I'd entered the flat.

From the direction of the street came the wail of an approaching siren. Spider released me and ran into the living room. He looked out the window, cursed, then dashed out the front door. I drooped against the passage wall, shitless.

A low moan came wafting out of the bedroom. With my back pressed against the wall, I sidled up to the doorway and peeked around the corner. The gun came into sight, half covered by Eastlake's inert torso. The moan happened again. It was coming from behind the painting. I stepped over Eastlake, flicked the gun away with the toe of my shoe and raised the punctured canvas.

A gory furrow started at the bridge of Fiona Lambert's nose and ran the length of her forehead, parting her hairline. Her eyelids, caked with blood, fluttered. Her mouth goldfished. She moaned again. The bullet had only grazed her. She'd need a lot of aspirin and a very good cosmetic surgeon, but she'd live. She also had great tits. Pity she wasn't my type.

Sliding an arm under her shoulder, I propped her limp white body upright. The shoe box lay beneath her. A hundred thousand dollars. It didn't look like much any more. I propped Fiona up with a pillow, scooped up the box, dashed into the bathroom and dropped it into the laundry basket. 'Noel,' I called. 'Come quick. She's still alive.'

Footfalls thundered up the stairs. A small dog yapped germanically in the distance. I settled Fiona Lambert's head in my pee-drenched lap and pressed the towel to her brow. Suddenly, the room was full of men, some of them in uniform. The one named Detective Constable Micaelis was calling Spider 'sir'.

I sat in the living room on Fiona Lambert's white sofa in my pissy pants and bloodied shirt and waited my turn, watching sundry coppers traipse through the front door and listening to their cryptic confabs. Apart from the odd glance, most of them paid me so little attention I might as well have been part of the furniture. A couple of classic plain-clothes types wandered in at one point and had a cursory sniff at the fittings and fixtures. 'Now that's what I call art,' one of them said. He was looking at the Szabo above the mantel, young Fiona in the buff.

The real thing was in the bedroom being worked on by an ambulance crew. We'd propped her up and the bleeding had pretty well stopped by the time the paramedics arrived. She was in deep shock, they said. I wasn't feeling too well myself.

I scrounged a coffin nail from one of the dicks and was just lighting up when Fiona was helped out the front door, held up by the armpits. They'd put a bandage around her head and got her into a bathrobe. She was almost walking, but she wasn't talking and she didn't look at all glamorous. Spider and Micaelis went downstairs with her, then came back inside a couple of minutes later. Micaelis did the talking.

'How ya doing?' he said. 'I reckon we'll need a statement, eh?

How about you accompany Detective Senior Sergeant Webb to the station, while I make sure Ms Lambert gets to the hospital, okay?'

'Sure.' It wasn't like I had much choice. 'But I need to call my son first.' Red's flight was at nine-twenty and it was already seven o'clock. Micaelis looked to Spider for confirmation. 'I wouldn't want to be done up for child neglect,' I said. 'Sergeant Webb.'

Spider pointed his chin towards the phone. 'Make it quick.'

'And I'd like to do something about this.' I stood up and framed my crotch with open palms. 'My thighs are starting to chafe.' Micaelis didn't think it necessary to refer that one up the chain of command. I smelled worse than the back of the grandstand at the Collingwood football ground. 'Use the bathroom,' he said. 'Make it quick.'

Tarquin answered the phone at the Curnows'. 'Something's come up,' I told Red when he eventually came on the line. 'See if Leo can find the spare key to our place, pack your bag and wait for me. Sorry about this.'

'No worries,' Red said, the voice of experience. I'd been late before. We'd still managed to get to the airport on time. It was only forty-five minutes away. Thirty-five with a tail wind and a good run at the lights.

Leo came on the line and I repeated what I'd just told Red. 'Can do,' he said. Faye was still at work and he was feeding the kids. 'You don't happen to know where Faye keeps the lettuce, do you?'

I went down the hall and looked in the bedroom door. Eastlake was still on the floor. He wouldn't have to worry about his bald patch any more. A woman cop was standing on the bed with a camera, getting an overhead shot. What with five detectives plus their reflections in the mirrored wardrobe door, it looked very crowded in there.

The bathroom was immediately opposite. Stripping off my pants and underpants, I turned on the tap and started sponging myself with one of Fiona's fluffy towels. I could see the cops behind me in the mirror. Spider looked across and saw me standing there bare-arsed in my shirt-tails. 'What is this?' he said, reaching over to pull the door shut. 'A fucking nudist colony?'

I grabbed the pink shoe box out of the laundry basket and stepped into the toilet cubicle. The box contained ten bundles of hundred-dollar bills, each about two and a half centimetres thick—an inch in the old dispensation. One thousand pictures of a man in a grey ski mask.

My jocks were in a pretty deplorable state. Pulling them back on was not a pleasant experience. I distributed the cash evenly around the waistband. It bulged a little, but at least it was dry. I sucked in my breath, buttoned up my pants and left my shirt hanging out. When I checked the result in the bathroom mirror, I looked like a candidate for Weight Watchers. This would never work.

'Here,' said Spider, half-opening the door. A clean shirt sailed through the air and landed at my feet. 'Found a dozen of these in the wardrobe. The owner won't be needing them any more.' Spider Webb was turning out to be a real gent.

Eastlake was two sizes bigger than me. His crisp white Yves St Laurent fell like a tent over the bulge at my midriff, perfectly concealing it. That's why the rich look so good. It's all in the tailoring. 'Ready,' I told the cops, wiping my face. With my cash assets concealed and my shirt hanging out, I could have been the President of the Philippines.

A small crowd had gathered at the front of the flats, so we went out the back way. A prowl car was waiting in the access lane with a uniformed constable behind the wheel. He was eleven, maybe twelve years old.

The money felt a little uncomfortable at first, but I got used to it. It's extraordinary how much cash you can carry on your person, I thought. Almost as extraordinary as the number of times you put your hand in your pocket and find nothing at all. I got in the back seat and Detective Senior Sergeant Webb got in beside me.

The ride into town was almost nostalgic. The only other time I'd been driven to the station in the back of a police car was the trip from the Oulton Reserve to the Preston cop shop. As the major offender in the affray, I had the prestige vehicle. The Fletcher twins rode in the back of a brawler van. Geordie Fletcher was driven off to hospital blubbering about an unprovoked attack and calling the cops cunts. Spider, who'd managed to weasel his way out of the whole thing, had been sent home.

On the way to the station, they told me I'd be charged with attempted murder, aggravated assault, going armed with an offensive weapon, possession of intoxicating liquor in a public place while a minor, assaulting police, hindering police, disorderly behaviour, offensive behaviour and resisting arrest. At fifteen, it sounded like a lot. I'm not 100 per cent on this point, but I think I may have burst into tears.

But nothing the cops said was as demoralising as the look on my father's face. After an hour's solitary in the lockup, I was ready for anger. What I got was silent, unanswerable disappointment. It wasn't the brawling. That was bad but not unprecedented for a boy my age. It was the liquor. The bourbon could only have come from one place. And that meant guile and deceit.

'I ought to give you a hiding,' Dad said when we got home. I wished he had. There was no getting out of the Brothers, though. I was back at St Joey's before you could say muscular discipline. It was either that or boarding school, so I considered myself lucky. From then on, my rebellious instincts were channelled into joining Young Labor and handing out how-to-vote cards at council elections. The police, needless to say, were never heard from again. This was less out of mercy for me, I concluded, than consideration for the tribulations of a recently bereaved publican. Either that or Geordie Fletcher—guided by some sharpie code of *omerta*—had refused to make a formal complaint. I never saw him or his brothers again.

Spider Webb's mind must have been turning over similar ground. He sat there for a while, chewing his cud and practising his thousand-yard stare. Then, as we passed the Arts Centre, he spoke. 'So,' he said, as if making a commonplace observation for no other purpose than to break the silence. 'Still a fuckwit after all these years.'

The money was sticking into my bottom rib. I straightened up a little and hoped that it didn't look like a summoning of my dignity.

'Remember that night in the park when you tore that Fletcher kid's pants with a piece of broken glass?' said Spider, smiling to himself at the memory. 'Him and his brothers were just fooling around, having a bit of fun, stirring you. All of a sudden, you went ballistic. Tried to take them all on. I'll never forget the look on Geordie Fletcher's face when you ripped his precious strides. If they hadn't been so baggy, you'd probably have cut him.'

You'd think a detective sergeant would have more highly developed powers of recall. 'I did cut him,' I said. 'There was blood everywhere.'

'Yeah,' said Spider. 'Yours. You gave yourself a blood nose when you fell on the ground. You always were a loose cannon.'

'Yeah?' I jerked my thumb back over my shoulder, back the way we'd come. I didn't remember any blood nose. 'I suppose all that was my fault? I suppose it was my fault that Eastlake tried to push me off a balcony?' Actually, it was. I'd practically begged him to do it. But Noel Webb wasn't to know that.

'If you hadn't stopped me talking to the Fleet woman yesterday,' he said, 'there's a fair chance that we'd have questioned Eastlake by today. Possibly even charged him. I doubt if he'd have tried anything under those circumstances. Even if you'd given him the chance.'

Now I was being taken to task for my gallantry. 'How was I supposed to know you were a cop? The way you were coming the heavy, flashing that gun of yours. I thought you were up to no good.'

'If I remember correctly,' said Spider, remembering correctly, 'you were the one throwing your weight about. I merely suggested that you refrain from involving yourself in matters outside your authority. When you refused to take the hint, I emphasised my point by showing you Eastlake's gun.'

'I thought it was your gun.'

'What would a chauffeur be doing with a pistol?'

'Why would I assume it was Eastlake's gun? I thought you were his bodyguard.'

'It's not all that uncommon for rich men to own a weapon,' said Spider, like he was stating a self-evident truth. 'Eastlake had three. All licensed, of course. But he always kept them at home. When I found that one in the Mercedes on Saturday morning, it was unusual enough to make me think he might be getting unstable.'

We were crossing Princes Bridge. A pair of sculls came gliding out from beneath the pilings and raced each other upstream in the direction of the Botanic Gardens, the water flashing at every dip of the oars. I turned my head and followed the rowers' progress until a truck in the next lane blocked my view. 'I thought you were working some sort of scam on Eastlake,' I said.

'Yeah?' Spider shifted his gum from one side of his mouth to the other. 'What gave you that idea?'

'That,' I admitted, 'is a very good question.'

We rode the rest of the way in silence. It was preferable to having Noel Webb tell me how many ways wrong I'd been. As the car pulled up in front of police headquarters, Salina Fleet was coming down the steps. She was back in her serious costume. Beside her was a balding middle-aged man in a dark suit carrying a briefcase. They didn't look like they'd just won Tattslotto.

I got out of the police car, fluffed up my kaftan and wondered what Salina and I might say to each other this time around. We didn't say anything. Salina's mouth was just starting to open when Noel Webb stepped onto the footpath behind me. Salina's jaw snapped shut like a trap. She and her companion executed an almost perfect left turn and the two of them wheeled off down the footpath together.

'You were always wasting your time there,' said Webb. 'I could have told you that all along.'

If I hadn't been standing in front of police headquarters, I might have made some appropriate reply. As we entered the building, Spider stuck his sunglasses in his shirt pocket, screwed off his pinky ring and spat his gum into a fire bucket. His ears seemed less prominent.

'Wait here for the present,' I was told. The present was a long time coming. I waited ten minutes. I waited fifteen minutes. Seven-thirty came and went and it still hadn't arrived. I began to entertain serious doubts that I'd get Red to the airport in time, even with a force-nine gale behind me.

'Here' was an interview room on the fifth floor. It had a little window in the door, a narrow laminex table fixed to the wall, a tape recorder and two plastic chairs. For some reason, I half-expected the door to be locked. Maybe all that padding around my waist was weighing on my conscience.

Next to the interview room was a sort of open-plan office. The sign on the door said Fraud Squad. It was deserted. Except for the tireless DSS Webb and his Hellenic sidekick, the bunco team was clearly a nine-to-five sort of outfit. I picked up a phone. Nobody jumped out of a waste paper basket and demanded to know what I thought I was doing.

Faye answered, home from work. Fresh from chasing her big story on Max Karlin. 'I'm at the cop shop,' I announced. As quickly as I could, I told her that Lloyd Eastlake had committed suicide and that I'd been with him when it happened.

'How awful,' said Faye. 'Can I use this information?'

'Possibly,' I told her. 'But I can't discuss it right now.'

She took that to mean I couldn't speak freely, so she changed the subject. 'The boys tell me you paid a visit to Artemis Prints this afternoon,' she said. 'You sly dog.'

This was not an ideal time for a gossip session. 'Did the boys tell you why I was there?'

'No. But I can guess.'

'I bet you can't,' I said.

'Speaking of Claire,' she said. 'Wendy rang. She tried to call you at Ethnic Affairs and they referred her to Arts. Arts said they didn't know where you were. And you weren't at home. So she called here. Anyway, she said to remind you to make sure to get Red to the airport on time.'

That was thoughtful of Wendy.

At least the subject was back where I wanted it. 'Listen, Faye,' I said. 'Can you do me a favour? If I'm not there by 8.30, do you mind driving Red to the airport?' That way, at least he'd get back to school on schedule, even if it meant that next time I wanted to see him I'd probably have to appeal to the full bench of the Family Court.

'Sure,' said Faye. 'You poor dear.'

I'd just hung up when Ken Sproule arrived. I'd been wondering when he'd turn up. His transition from Arts had been a smooth one. Ken's short-sleeved business shirt and polyester tie were clearly in their element in the hugger-mugger world of the gendarmerie. He was bouncing about on the balls of his feet like a champion full forward angling for a mark.

'Been in the wars, I hear, Murray,' he said. 'Thought I told you to watch out for them cognoscenti.'

He gave me a good looking over, as though appraising my bloodlines for stud purposes. 'You're okay, though, aren't you? No missing limbs? No internal bleeding?' He didn't look in my mouth, but he was only half joking. Clearly, he'd been thoroughly briefed.

'Shaken but not stirred,' I assured him. 'But your mates the rozzers are keeping me on tenterhooks. Eastlake didn't succeed in killing me, but the suspense of hanging around here just might.'

Ken took me back into the interview room and shut the door. 'You got the big picture, right?' He was bouncing around so much the room felt like a squash court. 'Paper-shuffling at Obelisk Trust. Eastlake suspected of knocking off the bloke in the moat.'

I had that much of it, I agreed. 'Plus the Combined Unions Super Scheme art fraud.' I didn't want him thinking I was a complete slouch.

'How'd you hear about that?' He was impressed.

'Buy me lunch one day,' I said. 'I'll tell you all about it.'

He didn't press the point. 'As you can well imagine,' he said. 'The manure has really hit the ventilator. Major construction project goes bust. Mutual fund chief executive dead on the floor. The business community is going to have kittens.' He beamed at the sheer horror of it.

He straddled a chair, folded his arms over the backrest and dropped his voice a notch. 'And to cap it off, the city's finest now find themselves in the embarrassing situation of having left a homicidal maniac on the loose for three days longer than absolutely necessary. They had grounds for questioning Eastlake on Saturday. If they had, most of this shit could have been avoided. They didn't because the fraud squad guys decided their undercover investigation into the Obelisk fiddle took precedence over the Taylor homicide investigation.'

The implications of what he was saying were clear. People were dead because of a police fuck-up. 'If this gets out,' he said. 'The boys in blue will have very red faces.' The fixer's fixer had at last found something worthy of his mettle. If Ken Sproule could square this one away, the Chief Commissioner would be eating out of Gil Methven's lap for years to come.

Sproule jumped up and gave another display of shadow boxing. 'It's going to take some fancy footwork to get our ducks in a row on this little baby,' he said. 'You with me?'

'I don't see why I should be.' Spider Webb might have saved

my life but, if what Ken said was true, only after he'd put it at risk in the first place. I had no reason to want to let the cops off the hook. And Ken hadn't exactly been 100 per cent frank with me last time I'd spoken to him, so I was in no big rush to do him any favours.

Sproule didn't smoke but he had some cigarettes. Was this standard interview-room procedure, I wondered? The informant smoked a hearty cigarette and agreed to co-operate with the authorities. I drew the smoke into my lungs and waited for the phone book around the head.

He straddled the chair again like he was doing the bad cop/good cop routine as a one-man show. 'What's the first rule of government, Murray? The one that precedes and supersedes all others. The *sine qua non* of political power.'

I didn't know Ken could speak Latin. And he was a philosopher as well. It was a surprise-packed day.

'Keep the cops happy,' he said. 'That's the paramount rule of political survival. Cause if the cops are unhappy, life just ain't worth living. Doesn't matter if you're Joseph Stalin or Mahatma Gandhi. It's a universal truth.'

'What do you want me to do?' I said. Ken's logic had an unarguability to it that I just couldn't argue with. And I might, at least, find out what he had in mind.

'Good boy.' He got up and started pacing again. If this kept up much longer, I'd get dizzy and pass out. And then Ken would start to go through my pockets and find what I had in my Reg Grundys. 'Everybody wants the lid put on this thing as fast as possible. The Chief Commissioner has okayed it for you and me to sit down with the cops involved and see if we can't come up with a result that everyone can live with.'

'Two conditions,' I said.

Ken was ready for that. He would have thought less of me if I hadn't asked. 'Gil Methven is prepared to say that Eastlake resigned from all his official Arts positions as of the end of last year,' he said, correctly anticipating my first demand. 'That way, none of this will reflect on Angelo Agnelli as current minister.

What's your other condition?'

'That depends on how long this little pow-wow takes,' I said. 'And it's more of a favour than a condition. I might not even need it. But it's well within your power, if I'm any judge. I'll tell you what it is at the end of the meeting.'

As a matter of principle, Ken Sproule didn't like dealing in the dark. But he didn't have much time to manoeuvre. The press would already be making a beeline for the Domain Road flat. 'Okay,' he scowled. 'Let's go. And try not to give too much cheek. The cops have long memories, you know. Mind your manners.'

It wasn't my manners I was worried about. It was the spondulicks in my dank underdaks. They were beginning to itch. If I didn't get them out of there soon, I'd have a very nasty rash.

We went upstairs to a conference room with venetian blinds on the windows and rings from coffee cups on the tabletop. Webb was already there and two other cops I'd never seen before, both in their fifties, one in a suit, the other in uniform. You could tell the one in the suit was a senior officer by the cast of his face and way Noel Webb approached him on all fours. The one in uniform was an Assistant Commissioner. I knew that because his epaulette insignia consisted of crossed silver batons in a laurel wreath surround. Also because he was wearing a name tag that said *Eric Worrall, Assistant Commissioner—Crime*. Eric was a gaunt, expressionless man who could have got a job walking behind the hearse in a Charles Dickens novel.

The guy in the suit was introduced as Chief Inspector Brian Buchanan. He was all neck and looked like he'd gladly bust Santa Claus for driving an unregistered sleigh.

None of the cops were delirious with joy about me and Sproule being there and they didn't go to a lot of trouble to conceal the fact. Having to share trade secrets with a couple of political flacks was bad enough, never mind that one of them had his shirt hanging out and smelt like he should have been in the care of the Salvation Army. I tried to take up as little space as possible and resist the urge to scratch.

Micaelis arrived just as we'd finished the introductions. Assistant Commissioner Worrall waved us into our seats. 'This is strictly informal,' he said. 'And strictly confidential. The objective is to pool our information and determine a course of action. Agreed?' Ken Sproule and I nodded. Worrall handed the running of the meeting to Buchanan.

'Let's get on with it,' said Buchanan. He had a pencil in his hand and pointed at Micaelis with it. 'What did the Lambert woman have to say?'

'She's on pain-killers, sir, but reasonably lucid.' Micaelis' hitherto pally demeanour was no longer in evidence. 'She says she has no idea why Eastlake attacked her. Claims they'd been lovers for about a year but never quarrelled. She says she'd seen him earlier today and he was agitated about business matters, but otherwise normal towards her.'

Which meant, as I had hoped, that she had enough cunning not to mention the money. She probably wondered why Micaelis didn't ask her about it.

'What about the other one?' said Buchanan. 'Fleet.'

Micaelis had a sheaf of paper in front of him. 'She contacted us this afternoon and came in with her solicitor while I was in attendance at the Lambert residence. She had a statement already prepared.' He shuffled the papers around until he found what he wanted, referring to it as he spoke. 'She and Eastlake were both on the committee that recommends arts grants. Last August, about the time that applications were being considered, she was having a relationship with Marcus Taylor. She recommended him for a grant and spoke highly of his technical skills and his'—Micaelis' finger found the exact phrase—'his postmodernist sensibility in relation to the validity of quotation and appropriation.'

'What the hell's that supposed to mean?' Buchanan pointed his pencil at me. He seemed to think I was an art expert.

'It means he could do good fakes,' I said.

'You can get a grant for that?' For a man who thought he was an orchestra conductor, Buchanan was harbouring some deep cultural insecurities.

'Only a small one, sir,' said Micaelis. 'And Fleet thinks that was only to keep her happy. But, a few weeks later, Eastlake approached her wanting to know more about Taylor. In particular, he wanted to know if she thought Taylor could paint him some pictures in the manner of certain well-known artists. He even produced a list.'

Sproule spoke, addressing himself to the Assistant Commissioner. 'The background here relates to the Combined Unions Superannuation Scheme. Eastlake had persuaded the CUSS to invest hundreds of thousands of dollars in an art collection, using a front called Austral Fine Art. The collection was a fiction. It existed only on paper. He used the money to keep his Obelisk round-robin going. He probably had in mind that when the Karlcraft project eventually paid off, Austral could recommend liquidating the collection. He got away with it for nearly a year, pretending to buy and sell artworks. But then the CUSS board decided it wanted to have an exhibition. Got all excited about the idea. Eastlake had no option but to play along. Suddenly he needed real paintings.'

Micaelis resumed. 'Fleet approached Taylor on Eastlake's behalf. She claims she was never party to any deception he may have subsequently engaged in, but she clearly knew what was going on. Taylor began producing paintings of the kind Eastlake required. The pictures were painted in his studio at the old YMCA building. Fleet informed Eastlake when they were ready. They were then picked up by Senior Sergeant Webb.'

'The sergeant was already working undercover as Eastlake's driver,' Buchanan explained to Worrall. 'Part of a long-term fraud squad investigation of Eastlake's activities in relation to the Obelisk Trust.'

Ken Sproule tipped me a quiet wink. A vision came to me of the Members' carpark at Flemington, of Sproule convincing a well-tanked Eastlake to hand his car keys to Noel, the helpful man from the detailing company.

'Eastlake assumed I had no interest in his business affairs,' said Webb. 'I had access to his home, his office, documents, telephone conversations and so on. We were well on the way to establishing a strong case against him in relation to Obelisk when this business with the paintings began. My instructions were to collect them from Taylor's studio—as many as two or three a week for nearly three months—and store them in the garage of Eastlake's house in Toorak.'

'We suspected these paintings related to some illegal activity,' said Buchanan. 'But our main focus was on the Obelisk investigation and it was only after the events of last Friday night that we began to realise the significance of the art works.'

By then, I'd worked out that Buchanan was the fraud-squad head honcho. He and Webb were very concerned that Assistant Commissioner Worrall adopt a favourable view of their activities. 'And exactly what happened last Friday?' said the big chief.

Yeah, I thought. Exactly what did happen? I leaned forward in my seat and adjusted my underpants under the rim of the table. There was a slight rustling sound.

Noel Webb cleared his throat and worked his jaw as if he wished he hadn't chucked his chewy away. 'About 9.30 on Friday night, I was driving Eastlake along Domain Road when we passed Taylor staggering drunkenly down the footpath. We picked him up and Eastlake had me drive the two of them around while he talked to Taylor about some particular painting. Something special, by the sound of it, in the style of a painter called Szabo. First he tried to convince Taylor just to let him see the picture. Taylor said he had it hidden away somewhere and nobody was going to see it until the time was right. Eastlake had a bottle of scotch and plied Taylor with it, but he wasn't getting much joy. Taylor wouldn't say where he had the painting. Eastlake offered him money for it, sight unseen. Twenty grand. Taylor reckoned that Eastlake was just trying to find out where the picture was hidden. Taylor was maudlin drunk. He kept going on about Fiona Lambert, how he was going to settle the score with her. He had no idea that she was Eastlake's bit on the side. Meanwhile, I was driving around in circles through the Domain.'

Police headquarters weren't centrally air conditioned. The cooler in the window frame kicked in with a whirr like an asthmatic fridge compressor. Noel Webb had our undivided attention.

'After a couple of hours of this, Eastlake told me to park the car and dismissed me for the night. This was across the road from the National Gallery. I hung around for a bit, watching, but all they were doing was sitting in the back seat talking and drinking. I left them to it and went home.'

He paused at this anti-climax, as if offering us the opportunity to ask questions. Assistant Commissioner Worrall had one. 'Can somebody enlighten me on the significance of this conversation?'

Micaelis could. 'According to Salina Fleet, sir, Taylor had a grudge against Lambert. She'd knocked him back for an exhibition of his real pictures, told him they weren't up to scratch. Plus there was some sort of bad blood relating to a dead painter by the name of Victor Szabo. On Lambert's recommendation, the Centre for Modern Art recently purchased a painting by this Victor Szabo. So Taylor got the idea of painting a copy of the Szabo and using it to discredit Lambert in some way. He was getting quite het up about it, apparently. Fleet realised this might cause problems for Eastlake and alerted him to the fact. She also tried to dissuade Taylor. But he got drunk and went off half-cocked at an exhibition at the Centre for Modern Art last Friday night, threatening to blow the whistle.'

I thought it was about time I said something, just so I didn't get taken for granted. 'I was there,' I volunteered. 'Taylor had been drinking, psyching himself up, and he fell over mid-speech. Made me cut my finger on a broken champagne glass.' I held up the damaged digit. Worrall looked at me like I'd just given him further grounds to doubt the wisdom of the Chief Commissioner's information-sharing policy. 'Because Taylor was drunk, nobody paid any attention to what he was saying,' I said. 'But it must have given Eastlake a scare. If Taylor made himself the centre of an art-world brouhaha, the whole CUSS fraud would be at risk.'

Webb took up the narrative from there. 'The next morning, I'd just heard about Taylor being found dead when Eastlake told me to go clear out his studio. He particularly wanted any paintings of a house with a lawn-mower.'

Buchanan held up his hand and stopped him there. 'Sergeant Webb sought instruction at that point,' he told Worrall. 'At that time, on the basis of information to hand, the cause of Taylor's death was still unknown. Eastlake may have been involved, or he may just have been taking advantage of the situation to cover his tracks. So rather than jeopardise a successful ongoing undercover investigation, I instructed Sergeant Webb to carry on as normal.'

'In the meantime,' said Micaelis, 'Salina Fleet had seen Taylor's body being recovered. Her immediate assumption was that Eastlake was responsible.'

The penny dropped. 'Bastard!' I said. Everyone looked at me. '"Bastard!" That's what Salina Fleet said when she saw Taylor's body. She must have meant Eastlake. I thought she meant me.' They all looked at me then like maybe I should explain why she might think such a thing. 'Sorry,' I said to Micaelis. 'Please go on.'

'Fleet panicked. She thought that if Eastlake was prepared to kill Taylor, then maybe she'd be next. She immediately started talking up the suicide scenario, hoping to send a signal to Eastlake that she was no threat to him.'

Noel Webb cleared his throat. 'As instructed by Eastlake, I went to the YMCA and searched Taylor's studio. I found a painting that fitted the description Eastlake had given me and put it, and a number of other sketches and paintings, in the boot of Eastlake's Mercedes.' As he said this, he fixed me in a steady gaze, inviting me not to contradict him or elaborate on his story. Discussions about people being locked in basements for their own well-being, I clearly understood, had no part in these proceedings.

Assistant Commissioner Worrall wasn't interested in fake paintings. He had homicide on his mind. 'How does any of this relate to the Taylor death?' He looked at his watch like maybe somebody should get to the point. I checked mine, too. 8.07 p.m. It was beginning to look like I definitely wouldn't be seeing Red again for some time.

Chief Superintendent Buchanan was all for getting back to the point, too. He wanted it made clear that his decision to keep Spider undercover hadn't resulted in a killer being allowed to run loose. 'At that time, the only evidence to connect Eastlake with Taylor's death was purely circumstantial.' He tapped his pencil on the table, punctuating his points. 'The medical evidence suggested an accident. When we sought to question Fleet about inconsistencies in her original statement, the one suggesting suicide, she couldn't be found.' He gave me a meaningful look. I kept my trap shut. The coppers were too clever by half for the likes of me.

He tapped again. 'It wasn't until this afternoon that more substantial information came to hand. The scotch bottle found with Taylor's body had two sets of prints on it. The second set didn't match any we had on record. Sergeant Webb lifted a set of Eastlake's dabs off his vehicle for comparison, but the match didn't come back until late this afternoon. As you know, sir, they're pretty under-resourced down there.'

Here Worrall looked at Ken Sproule to make sure he took the point.

'Then Fleet turned up,' Buchanan went on. 'She'd spent the night at the Travelodge, she said, thinking things over. Apparently, she was under the misapprehension that Sergeant Webb, acting on Eastlake's instructions, was planning to kill her. She brought her lawyer with her and gave us a fairly detailed statement. Also, as a result of enquiries among taxi drivers working that night, a driver...'

'Stanislaw Korzelinski.' Micaelis must have been hoping for

an A-Plus in note taking.

'...reported seeing two men fitting the general descriptions of Eastlake and Taylor on the moat parapet about the time of death. He says that one was lying down and the other appeared to be shaking him by the shoulders. Either that or banging his head on the stonework.'

Buchanan dropped his pencil and it rolled into the centre of the table. We all looked at it. We all saw the same thing. Eastlake, remonstrating with the drunken Taylor, knocking him unconscious and rolling him into the water.

Assistant Commissioner Worrall waited until the pencil came entirely to rest, studying it down his thin bony nose. 'Very well,' he said, at last. 'Point taken. Now how does all this bear on the current situation, the shootings in Domain Road.'

Chief Superintendent Buchanan pressed his point home. 'Whether Eastlake killed Taylor intentionally or not will probably never be known. What we do know is that the imminent financial collapse of Obelisk Trust was going to both ruin Eastlake personally and bring his fraud to light. So killing Taylor solved nothing. The pressure of this knowledge, and various other factors, drove him over the brink. As evidenced by his unprovoked attack on both Mr Whelan here and on Fiona Lambert, he was no longer in control of his mental faculties.'

'These other factors,' I said. 'Would they include the murder of Giles Aubrey?'

Sproule kicked me under the table.

'Who?' said the Assistant Commissioner—Crime.

'A retired art dealer,' said Buchanan, quickly. He made a drooping movement with his wrist that might, arguably, have been a gesture of casual dismissal. 'Marginal to the case. He died of a fall yesterday afternoon. We have no reason whatsoever to suspect foul play.' The police, too, bury their mistakes.

'As to the business in the Domain Road flat,' said the Assistant Commissioner. 'I have been given to understand that Eastlake, having shot Miss Lambert, turned the gun on himself.'

He looked at Sproule. The other three coppers looked at me.

Nobody said anything. Me least of all.

'That's it then,' said Worrall. 'An open-and-shut case. Suicide brought on by pressure of business. Now it only remains to tie up the loose ends.'

Micaelis was still young. He hadn't quite got the whole message. 'We'd have to prove Fleet knowingly conspired to defraud, sir,' he said. 'Very difficult with her co-conspirators dead.'

'And without a complainant,' said Sproule good-naturedly, doing his best not to take the mickey. 'I've already spoken to our friends at the Trades Hall. The board of the Combined Unions Superannuation Scheme has no interest in further investigation of this matter. Its art collection no longer exists. It never did.'

The westering sun had turned the venetians to burnt sienna. There wasn't anything left to say. Assistant Commissioner Worrall pulled his navy blue sleeve back and looked at his watch. I could have told him if he'd asked. 8.12 p.m.

Worrall stood up, nodded and briskly left the room. It must have been his turn to ride the goat at the Masonic Lodge. Buchanan reached across the table and picked up his pencil. Noel Webb pushed his chair back, blew out a long stream of air and took a packet of gum out of his pocket. Senior Constable Micaelis gathered his papers together and squared off the edges. Ken Sproule cracked his knuckles and looked exceedingly pleased with himself.

'Ken,' I said. 'About that favour.'

The white Commodore V-8 with the chequerboard stripe down the side flashed its twin blue lights, whooped its siren and swung across the path of the metallic green Laser reversing away from the kerb. I jumped out and jerked open the Laser's rear door. 'Out of the car and spread 'em,' I barked.

Tarquin cowered back. Red, faster off the mark, gave an ecstatic grin.

'Tricked ya!' I said.

Faye reached back from the driver's seat and biffed me around the ear. 'Scared the shit out of me,' she said.

Ken Sproule, true to his grudging word, had managed to get a traffic division squad car placed at my disposal. 'It's only to save him the trouble of running his own red lights,' he explained to the despatch officer. Even on a quiet Monday evening, running red lights was strictly the prerogative of the constabulary.

As we raced through the intersection outside the Trades Hall, the caretaker was removing the CUSS art exhibition sign. An unprecedented burst of efficiency from Bob Allroy. One less speech for me to write.

On my lap in the front seat was a black plastic bin-liner.

'What's in the bag?' Ken said as I emerged from the toilet in the police garage, tucking my shirt into my pants. The hundred-dollar bills that had been pressed against my skin were as soft as suede and I had inky smudges like tread marks on my spare tyre. 'Dirty laundry,' I said.

Faye nosed her Laser back into the kerb. The boys got out and extended their attention to the figure in blue behind the wheel of the police car. His sunglasses were the same kind as Spider's. I was beginning to think that the Police Co-operative Credit Union owned shares in Ray-Ban. 'This officer is going to drive us to the airport,' I told Red. 'Hop in.'

Tarquin, green with envy, demanded to be allowed to come along for the ride. 'Next time,' I said. 'But you can sit in the back seat for a minute while I talk to your mum.'

Prompted by my remark on the phone, Faye had successfully grilled the boys on the true reason for our flying visit to Artemis Prints. She'd followed up with a call to Claire. 'She didn't sound very impressed, Murray,' she said. 'She thinks you took advantage of her better nature. She was quite keen on you, you know. For a while. But I'm afraid you've blown it. So what's all this about friends of yours with a forged Drysdale? And what's that smell?'

A proper answer to those questions would take three days, a whiteboard, a flow chart and a breach of confidence. I gave Faye the thirty-second version. 'Wow,' she said, mentally reaching for her keyboard.

'This is absolutely not for publication,' I warned. 'Within the life of this government.' The money in the bag in my hot little hand, of course, I did not mention.

'Look!' called Tarquin. He'd pulled something out of a box on the back seat of the prowl car and was waving it out the window. It was a deep red stick of waxed paper about as long as my arm. 'Extra-length dynamite!'

It wasn't, but it might as well have been. It was an emergency flare. Two kilograms of compacted magnesium with a ring-pull activator cap. I reached over and deftly relieved

Tarquin of its possession. 'My wrist,' he squealed. 'You've broken my wrist.'

In what seemed like no time at all, we were barrelling down the Tullamarine freeway with the roof lights flashing, the siren wailing and Constable Speedy Gonzales of the Accident Appreciation Squad making the rest of the traffic look like it was standing still. 'I'm sorry your visit was so boring,' I told Red. 'Next time, we'll do something more interesting. Go fishing, maybe. And we'll definitely have that pizza, I promise.'

Speedy dropped us at the terminal with ten minutes to flight time. 'Told ya,' I informed Red, although we were too late to get him a window seat. We embraced at the departure gate. 'See you later, Dad,' he said. 'Sorry about busting the picture.'

'Do something for me,' I asked. 'Tell your mother I've got a new girlfriend.'

'You haven't really?' The kid squinted at me dubiously. 'Have you?'

'No,' I said. 'But you never know your luck. And don't mention the dead body. Or the snake. Or the painting. Or the police car. Or the dynamite.' I started to reach into the plastic garbage bag, thought better of it and fished a twenty out of my wallet. 'In case you need a beer on the plane,' I said. 'And your teeth still look fine to me.'

We embraced again. Then he was gone.

If anyone needed a beer it was me. I hadn't eaten since breakfast. I found an airport eatery with a tray-race and a neon sign that read Altitude Zero. I got myself a tray and ate something they claimed was lasagne. Ate it all. Right down to the plate. That's how hungry I was.

It was eleven before I'd got a cab back to the Arts Centre, picked up the Charade, put the black plastic bag under the seat and drove home. Home sweet lonesome home. I stepped inside the front door and reached for the light switch. Intuition stopped my hand in mid-movement. I bent my head to the darkness of the hall and listened. The muted rustle of paper. An infinitely faint flush of light beneath the door into the living room. An electrical charge in the atmosphere. Someone was in the house. My hand went sweaty around the black bag.

Streetlight flowed through a gap in my bedroom curtains. Nothing out of order there. I flicked the money under the bed. The only thing in the room vaguely resembling a weapon was the bedside lamp. It was either that or a lumpy pillow. With the lamp cord wrapped around my wrist, I advanced noiselessly down the hall, put my shoulder to the door and pushed it open.

Claire was lying on the couch, her red hair lit by the feeble fluorescence emanating from the kitchen nook. She looked up over the top of an open book. 'Pretty dense,' she said. *The Rise and Fall of the Great Powers*.

'You'll ruin your eyesight.' I knelt on the floor and plugged in the lamp. 'How did you get in?' Not that I was complaining.

'Your security is abysmal,' she said. 'But your friends are terrific. Faye gave me the key. She also told me what's been going on. I thought I'd save you the price of a lunch.'

The face of Sister Mary Innocent flashed before me and dissolved. 'Don't go away,' I said. 'I've just got to take a quick shower.'

'Not a cold one, I hope,' said Claire.

When I came out of the bathroom, Metternich was on the floor and Claire was in my bed. Luckily, I'd changed the sheets. I do that every time I get a new job. 'I don't know about this, Murray,' she said.

'Me neither.' I dropped my towel to the floor and she could see that I was lying. I lay down beside her and put my head between her breasts, my ear over her heart. It didn't hurt at all.

Few things remain secret for long in the modern office. Even through two plate-glass walls I could read Angelo Agnelli's face like the fine print on a rent-a-car contract. If Ange had got any sun while he was inspecting those mountain lakes, it wasn't showing in his complexion.

My boss's ashen face wasn't the first reading I'd done that morning. Over a two-egg breakfast with Claire, I'd taken in the headlines. The *Age*, doing its best at broadsheet restraint, led with KARLCRAFT DEFAULT PROMPTS OBELISK SUICIDE. The *Sun* concentrated on the human interest angle with LOVE NEST DEATH PACT. Faye's piece on the front page of the *Business Daily* took a more soberly fiscal line. FUNDS SINK IN WAKE OF LIQUIDITY DRAIN.

Agnelli had read them, too. They were spread across his desk in front of him. He'd been sitting there, staring down at them, for what felt like a very long time. I knew that because I'd been watching him ever since he'd arrived. He told Trish he was not to be disturbed, shut his door and sank into his seat like a condemned man assessing the comfort of the electric chair.

A minister is rarely alone and almost never lost in silent contemplation. It was a sight to behold. From time to time, Angelo's leonine head would rise and he would peer over at me. I was pretending to read *Craft Annual*. His hand would extend towards the phone, hover, then withdraw. His fingertips would drum on the desktop. His gaze would again lower.

Eventually, the suspense got too much for me. Undeterred by Trish's gorgon bark, I invited myself into the ministerial presence. 'How was the water?' I said. 'Dam and be damned, as they say in Tasmania, eh?'

Angelo broke off from his self-guided tour of purgatory and regarded me bleakly. 'Damned's the word,' he said. 'Sit down.'

Angelo Agnelli was not a bad man. He was no better or no worse than he ought to be. He was vain and his ambition exceeded his abilities. So what? In a politician these are not failings but the minimum requirements for the job. Why else do it? Angelo was a minister because enough people thought he should be one. Those people, for better or worse, were my people. Perhaps they didn't know Angelo quite as well as I did. But they had not entirely misjudged him. He was occasionally a fool, but he was not an idiot. He could be petty, but he was rarely malicious. Others, perhaps, could do his job as well, or even better. But it was Angelo, not others, who signed my pay cheque at the end of the week.

If there was to be a pay cheque. Just as well I'd taken out insurance.

I did as I was bid and sat down. The glorious morning sunlight pouring through the floor-to-ceiling windows might as well have been acid rain. Angelo stared at it in blank-faced silence for a long moment.

Then he rapped abruptly on his desk as though calling his internal caucus to order. 'About your future here,' he said. 'Things have not necessarily transpired as entirely advantageously as initially anticipated.' He sounded like the freshly-mouldering Hirohito announcing the capitulation of Japan.

'You're not satisfied with my performance?' I asked.

Now that Ange had set his course, he had no intention of allowing himself to be distracted. 'I was going to tell you about something today,' he said. 'Get your input and so forth. But events appear to have overtaken me.'

He slapped the papers on his desk with the back of his hand. He stood up. It was getting momentous. He began to address me as though I was a plenary session of state conference. 'I am responsible...' he began.

His mouth, unaccustomed to this phrase, did not know what to do next. He began again. 'A situation has arisen...' That was better. 'A situation has arisen whereby it may be possible for me to be seen to be responsible for the diminution of a significant component of the party's campaign funds.' There, he'd said it.

'Really,' I said. 'How could a situation like that have come about?'

'Against my better judgment,' he said. 'I allowed myself to be persuaded to become involved in the affairs of the finance committee.' He didn't say who had done the persuading. My preferred candidate was the invisible little Angelo sitting on his shoulder, the one in the red suit with the horns and tail.

'A bad call was made. The long and short of it is that as a consequence of subsequent events, events beyond my control...' He glared down at the newspapers with an expression he'd borrowed from Charlton Heston for the occasion. 'I am no longer able to confirm your ongoing employment. As soon as the implications of this situation become more widely appreciated, my position will no longer be tenable. In fact, I will have no option but to tender my own...' He searched for the word. He didn't have far to look. It was on the tip of his tongue. 'Resignation.'

For the sake of Angelo's finer feelings, I feigned surprise. 'Really!' I said. 'Is it that bad?'

As ideas went, it was worse than bad. Resignation would be an admission of culpability. A free ride for the opposition. A step closer to power for the true grafters. The smug, despicable, self-serving, incompetent, sanctimonious blue-bloods of the old-school-tie brigade. The enemies of the human race. The Liberals. The ice was thin enough beneath the government without the heat given off by Angelo Agnelli sweating over his failures.

'I'm a little confused here.' As I spoke, I reached across Agnelli's desk and drew the phone towards me. 'It was my understanding that finance committee affairs were Duncan Keogh's responsibility.' Agnelli's phone was as state-of-the-art as the desk it sat on. 'Shouldn't we hear what Duncan has to say about all this?'

Before Agnelli could stop me, I pecked out Keogh's number and pushed the hands-free button. The speaker went brr-brr and Keogh's irritable hello came down the line, loud and clear. 'Murray Whelan here, Duncan,' I said. 'Calling from Angelo Agnelli's office.' My call sign.

Agnelli, exhausted from the unaccustomed rigours of self-examination, slumped back into his chair and buried his head in his hands.

Duncan wasn't having a very good morning either. 'Tell Angelo I can't get anybody at Obelisk to talk to me. All deposits have been frozen and they reckon they can't deal with us preferentially just because of our association with their former CEO. Especially because of that. They say everybody wants their money and we'll just have to wait our turn. They don't have any idea how long that might take.' He was talking twenty to the dozen and his sweat was oozing through the phone speaker. 'Rumour is that it wasn't just the Karlcraft collapse that tipped the balance. That chickenshit prick Eastlake stuffed things up right and proper. We might be lucky to get back anything at all.'

He went on and on like this for quite some time, sinking the silent Agnelli ever deeper into the slough of despond. Then, barely pausing to draw breath, he changed tack. 'Okay,' he said. 'I admit it. I should have withdrawn the money yesterday afternoon. But Agnelli should have called me himself.'

At the mention of his name, Angelo shuddered visibly.

So far, I hadn't said anything. Personally, I found Keogh's remarks perplexing. 'I don't know what any of this is about, Duncan,' I said. 'But Angelo couldn't possibly have called you yesterday afternoon as, for some reason, you seem to think he should have. He was out of town on ministerial business. And you're the signatory to the finance committee accounts, aren't you?'

Keogh, sensing slippage in the rug under his feet, switched to the offensive. 'You tell Agnelli I'm not wearing this alone,' he snarled. 'He said at our meeting on Friday that he'd be backing me all the way to Cabinet.'

'What meeting was that?' I said.

Angelo took his head out of his hands.

'You know very well what meeting. The one in Agnelli's office at Ethnic Affairs.'

This didn't sound at all right to me. 'Are you sure about this, Duncan?' I said. 'Angelo hasn't mentioned any meeting to me. You kept minutes, did you?'

'Of course I didn't keep minutes.' Dunc was getting quite snappy by this stage.

'Was there anyone else at this meeting, Duncan?' I wondered. Some good was coming of Eastlake's death already. 'Anyone who can back you up on this?'

A tinge of luminescence had begun to creep over Agnelli's eastern horizon.

'You still there, Duncan?' I said. For a while the only sound coming out of the speaker was the steady bubble of boiling blood and the rustle of the rug beneath Keogh's feet reaching escape velocity. Then Duncan made a manly lunge for the soft option.

'You tell Agnelli that he can tell the Premier that if I can't get our funds out of Obelisk by close of business tonight,' he said, courageously taking it upon himself to do the noble thing, 'he'll have my resignation on his desk first thing in the morning. You can also tell Agnelli to go take a flying fu...'

Fortunately, I'd been keeping count. It was my turn to hang up. The green had by now drained entirely from Agnelli's gills. He looked like he might soon be sitting up in bed, sipping beef tea and receiving visitors. But I could see that he was still somewhat troubled.

'Keogh's a suck-arse little prick,' I told him, hoping to allay any sense of responsibility he might have for the demise of the soon-to-be-ex finance committee chairperson.

But it wasn't his conscience that was bothering Agnelli. That stunted faculty was already slouching back to its cryogenic cave. 'Keogh might take the fall,' he said. 'But the party's still down the tubes to the tune of $200,000.'

'That's quite some tune,' I admitted. 'Would it help if I hummed the first few bars?'

I picked the package off the floor beside my chair where I'd put it when I came in and spilled the contents onto Agnelli's desk. Less reasonable expenses. A packet of fags, two tram tickets, last night's lasagne and the dry-cleaning of a pair of strides.

Agnelli stared down at the small mountain of cash. 'Fuck Jesus fuck.' From Ange, that was high praise indeed. 'You rob a bank or something?' He must have been confusing me with Lloyd Eastlake.

'An anonymous donation from an intimate acquaintance of a former party member,' I explained. 'A strong believer in discretion. You and I are going to be buying a lot of raffle tickets in the next few months.'

Angelo was deeply appreciative. The moolah vanished into his bottom drawer, the newspapers went into the waste basket and my appointment as his cultural counsellor was immediately confirmed.

'I don't think I've got the stamina,' I said. 'Not if yesterday was any indication of the pace.' He really needed someone with the proper background for the job. 'An Italian, perhaps,' I suggested. Machiavelli. Houdini. Alfa Romeo.

But I did agree to stay in place on a temporary basis. 'Only until I've had a chance to put some proposals in front of you regarding retrospective amendments to the National Gallery's policy on the granting of maternity leave,' I said. 'After that, I'd like a chance to spread my wings in Water. If that's okay with you.'

It was, and that's where I've been ever since. The view from the office isn't as good as the one at Arts. And the only openings

I get invited to are new sluice gates. But it's not as stressful here. And it's getting to the point where I can stand up on the skis for nearly fifty metres at a stretch.

Now that the eighties have officially drawn to a close, there's a lot of media rhubarb about what it all meant. Much breast-beating and decrying of all the glitz, the greed, the gullibility. Much calling on us to put the past behind us, tighten our belts and look grim reality square in the eye.

Myself, I don't know that there's all that much wisdom to be found in hindsight. Sure, we learn from our mistakes. But only from the ones we've already made, so the lessons have limited applicability. And whenever I hear that stuff about belt-tightening, I can't help but think how much bigger some people's belts are to begin with. And this is coming from a guy who knows a thing or two about cashed-up waistlines, remember. And about the mad glint in the eye of reality.

Max Karlin's in the belt-tightening business these days. He's living in Gdansk, advising the Polish government on the appli-cation of free-market principles to the footwear industry. Perhaps he can find a place in his operations for Duncan Keogh. At last report, Duncan had let his party membership lapse and was calling himself a freelance management consultant. Not getting a lot of what you might call work, from all accounts.

The Karlcraft Centre was completed only three months behind schedule, although not under that name. It's now called Absolute Melbourne. Current ownership resides with a fluid consortium of Singaporean shipping magnates that Faye tells me are looking to unload it onto a Dutch insurance company as soon as the Foreign Investment Review Board rubber stamp gets back from having its worn-down lettering refurbished. For the opening ceremony, an ice-rink was installed in the Galleria and the Australian Opera performed *Gotterdammerung* in cos-tumes designed by Ken Done.

The shops don't seem to be doing much business, though. And there's so much un-let office space upstairs that you could run a fifty-head dairy farm on some of the floors. Claire and I had a drink in there a couple of weeks ago, in the tapas bar on the second level, overlooking the mosaic floor. 'How's business?' I asked the tapas barman.

'Dropping off,' he said.

The children's wear boutique opening onto the horn of plenty was having a clearance sale. I bought Grace a pair of Osh-kosh overalls marked down from a hundred dollars to thirty-nine ninety-five. Still a bit rich, I know, but nothing's too good for my Gracie.

Claire is back at the National Gallery. One of the recommendations of the Human Resources Policy Review Committee was that former employees whose termination was the result of discriminatory industrial relations practices be given hiring priority if positions became available due to natural wastage. When one of the conservatorial staff was pensioned off with prostate cancer induced by chronic cadmium yellow exposure from handling too many French Impressionists, Claire got his old job.

Not that she goes near the Monets. She's in the Australian section. From what I can tell, she spends most of her time with a pair of tweezers and a magnifying glass, sticking ochre blobs back on Aboriginal dot paintings with Aquadhere general-purpose wood glue. But she feels her professional skills are much better employed than they were at Artemis Prints and Framing. Plus she doesn't have to work Saturday mornings. She sold Artemis for the cost of the stock and cleared twenty grand on the outstanding mortgage, so the property boom was not without its upside, while it lasted. The place is now called Fred's Head Shop and sells extra-width cigarette papers, blown-glass water-pipes and framed posters of Bob Marley. So some connection with the arts remains.

Speaking of art, the real authorship of *Our Home* remains a mystery. To me, at least. Very few other people know or care about its existence. The version with the bullet hole and the blood stains is in the vault at the new Police Museum, along with the bullet-riddled banister from the Trades Hall. The version which belonged to Max Karlin was eventually de-accessioned by the Centre for Modern Art. It now hangs in the collection of the Victa Motor Mower Company, although this is probably more because of its subject matter than its authorship. It was recently the subject of a doctoral dissertation published by the PIT Department of Cultural Studies entitled *(Sub)liminal Penetration in the (Sub)urban Landscape*.

Public interest in the works of Victor Szabo never scaled the heights Fiona Lambert hoped and the planned retrospective exhibition was cancelled due to lack of funding. The content of future exhibitions at the Centre for Modern Art will be determined by its interim curator, Janelle. It was Janelle who phoned Fiona Lambert that night at the flat. She rang to say that Fiona had left her keys behind, yet again. Fiona popped over and picked them up as soon as she'd brushed me and Lloyd off. Then she had an early night.

Fiona is now Assistant Curator of Naive Pottery at the Warracknabeal Regional Gallery. It's a bit of a come-down, I suppose, and a fair way from the bright lights. But that's probably the way she prefers it, given that she looks like she's had a zipper installed in her forehead. She probably still thinks the cops pinched her dough.

Salina Fleet, on the other hand, has gone from strength to strength. The commission she was charging on Marcus Taylor's knock-offs was more than enough to cover the cost of her relocation to New York, where she is now performance art commentator for *Flashy'n'Trashy*, a theoretical journal financed by the Sony Corporation. The name Fleet, it transpired, was a legacy from an early and soon discarded husband. Her maiden name was Fletcher. Makes you wonder, doesn't it.

Obelisk's depositors were eventually paid out at forty-five cents in the dollar. So Agnelli's brief foray into high finance just about broke even—if you count Fiona's contribution. Even better than break-even if you add in the two trips to Bali, the three microwave ovens and the fourteen dinners-for-two we won in raffles and kicked back into the cause.

Red was a bit pissed off that I didn't keep the trip to Bali and take him along. He's been there twice now with Wendy and Richard. He reckons it's cool although he did get embarrassed when his braces set off the metal detectors at the airport. My alarm bells certainly rang when I saw the bill. But I insisted on paying the whole lot, not just half. It's my genes they're designed to compensate for, after all.

Wendy and Richard got married. In a church. Wendy wore white. 'More oyster, really,' said Red. 'Puke-a-rama.'

He's coming down next month and I've got the use of the Water Supply houseboat on Lake Eildon. Tarquin is coming too, just for the first few days. Unfortunately there's very little chance he'll drown. The water level is too low.

The drought has been going on for nearly a year now. Quite a challenge, policy-response wise. Sometimes we pray. Sometimes we dance.

The election will be late next year. We're hoping to dance it in. We definitely don't have a prayer. Not even with *Nea Hellas* behind us, to the hilt.

NICE TRY

To Gary Foley
Dare to struggle, dare to win

In Memoriam Kevin and Aileen

'Athleticism can occasion in
man the most noble of passions
and also the most vile.'
Baron Pierre de Coubertin,
Founder of the Modern Olympics

'Yibbida, Yibbida!'
Rex Hunt,
Australian sporting philosopher

Melbourne, 1956

They confronted him at the Royal Exhibition Building, just before the first lift of the final round. It was safer there, away from all the prying eyes at the Athletes Village, and he did not suspect anything until it was too late.

He was a very strong man, not as big as some of his teammates in the higher weight divisions, but formidable enough to be a medal contender. When he bolted for the door, it took four burly trainers to subdue him and force the gag into his mouth so his cries for help could not be heard by the Australian officials in the warm-up area. Even then, he continued to put up a struggle and the first hypodermic needle snapped off in the muscles of his arm.

That's when the deputy chef-de-mission struck him with the heavy steel lifting bar. The bone snapped immediately. After that, for all his strength, he offered less resistance and the doctor was able to administer the drug.

The Australian volunteer driver had no reason to suspect that the heavy bags of equipment they were loading into the Bedford van contained anything other than the usual sporting gear. He was, however, disappointed to be told that he should immediately drive them to Appleton Dock. It was only fifteen minutes away through the early summer sunshine but the trip meant that he would miss the final of the tournament. As the Bedford pulled into Nicholson Street, the Duke of Edinburgh was already arriving to present the medals, the Olympic standard fluttering on the bonnet of his black Bentley.

The weightlifter did not regain consciousness until he was on board the ship. By then, further resistance was futile.

Despite the speed and secrecy of the operation, the Australian Security Intelligence Organisation was soon aware that something untoward was happening. Officers manning the observation post in the cargo shed across the turning basin became suspicious when they noticed that the official supervising the unloading of the van was far too senior for such a task. The fact that Russians were seen carrying aboard heavy equipment belonging to the Polish team was also considered unusual enough to warrant a telephone call to headquarters.

By late evening, lights were burning in the large Victorian mansion in Queens Road and the Director himself was being briefed. A deeply conservative man, steeped in military culture, Colonel Spry had a face which did not display his thoughts. His subordinates could easily imagine, however, the depths of the dilemma that now confronted him.

The Games of the XVI Olympiad of the Modern Era, the Friendly Games, were rapidly descending into farce, a circus which threatened both Australia's reputation as a sporting nation and the future of the Olympic ideal.

A week earlier, one of the Russians had eluded her escort at the Melbourne zoo and fled through the animal enclosures. A brawl had erupted at the Russia–Hungary water polo final and blood had been spilt in the water. Soviet competitors had been openly jeered at the fencing. President Brundage of the International Olympic Committee, an American and no friend of the communists, had already protested to the organising committee at this lack of sportsmanship. The CIA was busy in the background, attempting to provoke incidents. Emigré groups had invaded the Athletes Village and torn down flags.

It was an informant from one such group who alerted ASIO to the sudden withdrawal of the Polish medal contender only moments before his final lift in the medal round of the weightlifting. Officially he had strained a ligament but, according to the contact, the lifter was planning to defect from the podium during the medal-presentation ceremony.

Two years earlier, Colonel Spry had not hesitated in ordering his officers to assist Commonwealth Police snatch Mrs Petrov from the hands of Soviet agents who were hustling her aboard a plane on the tarmac at Darwin airport. But this time, the interests of the nation were different. The Gruzia was moored under the terms of the Olympic truce. To search it would be a violation of that truce. If nothing was found, the communists would gain a great international propaganda victory. ASIO would be embarrassed and Australia's honour tarnished before the world.

Only one course of action was possible, decided the Director. Three days later, a battery of twenty-five-pounder guns fired the final salute and the Friendly Games concluded in triumph as the athletes danced their way through the Closing Ceremony.

Melbourne, 1990

She was giving me the eye. No doubt about it.

Every time I glanced her way, I caught her looking at me. Her gaze would dart somewhere else, but she was definitely checking me out. She was twenty-two, maybe twenty-three, with a body that looked like it was moulded from fibreglass to a design by Benvenuto Cellini. Smooth. Firm. Flawless.

Too flawless for me, surely, a man teetering on the cusp of his late thirties. A man whose waist measurement was almost as high as his IQ. Not that I automatically assumed it was impossible for a woman like her to be interested in someone like me. But you get to a certain point, you know what's reasonable and what's not. Christ, she was practically a teenager.

She tossed back her blonde ponytail, parted her thighs and thrust her hips forward. 'Come on,' she urged. 'Do it. Do it.'

I couldn't. I just didn't have the energy. Wiping the perspiration from my eyes with the hem of my t-shirt, I lowered my vision to the electronic display panel of my exercise bike and urged my faltering muscles on. For more than half an hour I'd been at it. First the warm-up, then the super circuit. Three sets of leg extensions. The front lateral press and the rowing simulator. The mini-trampoline, the squat rack and the Stairmaster. Thirty-seven minutes of self-imposed agony.

Beyond the window of the aerobics studio, the gorgeous creature had turned away. She was on her knees on the carpet now, extending first one leg then the other, her flanks as fine as a gazelle's. She was inexhaustible, her energy boundless, her body unravaged by time and cigarettes and a sedentary occupation. 'Keep it up, keep it up,' she cried. Her every move was immediately replicated by the twenty women in her class, flexing their lycra-sheathed limbs to the syncopated thud of the sound system. Madonna.

God, I hated Madonna. I tried to think of something else, to force my mind off that taut blue leotard. That pert, peachy derriere. Those surreptitious glances. To find some thought I could use to focus my energy on the last, muscle-quivering kilometre up the computer-generated incline. Concentrating my attention on the liquid-crystal terrain-simulator on the console between the handlebars, I screwed up my determination, bore down and pedalled into the final sinew-searing five minutes of my daily work-out. Every fibre of my mortal being screamed at me to stop.

With a sharp electronic beep, the stationary bicycle announced that I'd arrived at my destination. Ten kilometres at Mark 8, a total kilojoule burn of 250. The calorific equivalent of two cherry tomatoes and a haircut. Responding as surely as Pavlov's dogs salivating at the sound of a bell, my legs went limp. With one last surge of willpower, I forced them to continue for the final minutes of my warm-down.

I was warming down but the gym was hotting up. At the bike beside me, a furiously pedalling endomorph looked up from his copy of the *Financial Review*. 'No pain, no gain,' he muttered. Probably rehearsing his statement to the shareholders.

The City Club was located in the Hyatt Hotel, but few of its clientele were hotel guests. Most, like me, worked in the surrounding office buildings. Many, judging by their furtive eyes and abrasive manner, were members of the finance community. The women tended to be younger and better togged out. The average male was a laterally expanding desk-jockey teetering on the brink of middle age. My kind of guy.

My fellow City Club members, I reflected. Desperate old farts and despicable yuppies. So what did that make me, an AWOL apparatchik, sneaking away from the office to work on his personal downsizing plan? Not for the first time, I reminded myself that I'd chosen the place solely on the basis of its location, a three-minute walk from Parliament House. That, and the incentive provided by its astronomical cost.

It was, I had told myself a month earlier, crunch time. Either face up to my need for constant maintenance or surrender entirely to my inner beanbag. So it had been on with the training shoes and out with the credit card.

At $1500 a year plus joining fee, the City Club was more than I could really afford. On the other hand, I was getting a lot for my money. You name it, the City Club had it. An atrium-roofed swimming pool in chequerboard tiles. Microchip-regulated warm-up bicycles. A front lateral press and a modular triceps extension machine. Rowing simulators, each with an in-built computer-generated opponent. Weight machines, both Universal and Nautilus. A boutique offering a comprehensive range of swimsuits, pedal-pushers and Musashi high-protein snacks. Shiatsu massage. Boxercise. Wet and dry saunas. Slide, step and low-impact aerobics. Complimentary cotton-buds in the change rooms. An attentive staff of chipper young men and perky young women, each with the calves of a Sherpa and the smile of a toothpaste testimonial.

Including, it seemed, the nymph with the wandering eye. My mysterious admirer. I'd first noticed her earlier that week when she started taking the midday aerobics session, replacing a rather fey young man with a taste for Vangelis and a cute little backside that was entirely wasted on his all-female class.

Aside from the body of a goddess, clearly a prerequisite for the job, she had an open, frankly inquisitive face and wore her mandatory smile with a slightly ironic twist that didn't quite match the earnest, professional cheerfulness of her workmates. With a perennial tilt to her head and large, wide-open eyes, she appeared to regard the world with amused scepticism, as though nothing could ever quite manage to surprise her.

Just the expression she used when she looked me over. A cool, appraising look which, while I found it flattering, seemed oddly perverse when directed at a man with trembling knees, a low-slung chassis and the motto 'I'm With

Stupid' printed across the front of his sweat-soaked t-shirt. Perhaps she needed glasses.

The aerobics class was finishing. Twelve-thirty. My cue to start making tracks for my lunch appointment. I climbed down off the bike and waited for my head to stop spinning. Four weeks I'd been a member of the City Club and so far most of the weight loss had been in the region of my bank balance. On the other hand, where else did I get ogled by bodacious young babes? One bodacious babe, anyway.

Now she was staring at me. As I slung my complimentary towel around my neck and staggered towards the locker room, she advanced across the floor, cocking her head and peering dubiously into my face.

'Hey!' she declared, pointing knowingly. Women from the aerobics class looked our way. Shit, I thought. She hadn't really been looking at me. She'd been catching me looking at her. I was about to be banged-up for perving. Denounced as a sexual harasser. 'Your name's Whelan, isn't it?' Her rising inflection was a clear accusation.

'Murray Whelan,' I admitted cautiously.

'Thought it was.' She clapped her hands in self-congratulation. 'Am I good or what?'

I stared at her blankly, not at all sure where this was going.

'You don't remember me, do you?' she said, crestfallen. And what a crest. I made a point of not looking at it. 'Holly. Holly Deloite.'

'Of course I remember.' I racked my brains. As offsider to a politician, I meet a lot of people. More than I could ever hope to remember and quite a few I'd prefer to forget. But this Holly Deloite definitely wasn't in that category. If I'd ever pressed her flesh, I was sure I would've recalled.

'Hadfield High School, Year 10 work-experience program,' she prompted. 'I've probably changed a bit since then.'

Had she ever.

She was taking me back almost seven years. Back to when I was electorate officer for Charlene Wills, Member of the Legislative Council for the Province of Melbourne Upper. Running a shopfront office in a working-class electorate on the northern edge of the suburban sprawl. Keeping the constituents happy, massaging the grassroots of the political process, soliciting campaign donations, that sort of thing.

Every year we'd take a work-experience placement from each of the local high schools. Give bored and slightly bewildered fifteen-year-olds a taste of real life. Teach them to stuff envelopes and make coffee, let them answer the phone if they were exceptionally capable.

Holly Deloite had been a mumbler, if I remembered right. Mouth full of braces, a tubby bubby, pimples. Well stacked for her age and shy about it. Head always down, hiding her face behind her hair. But keen to please. It was all coming back to me. 'The photocopier girl!'

She blushed and her hand flew up to her mouth. 'You bastard,' she grinned. 'You still remember that.'

I liked the bastard. It was a big improvement on Mr Whelan. 'How could I forget?'

Truth be known, I hadn't given the matter a second thought since the day it happened. The day she'd misread my handwriting. Made five hundred copies by two o'clock instead of two copies by five o'clock.

'Got the zeros mixed up with the noughts,' she laughed. 'But you were real nice about it. Even bought me lunch at that Chinese restaurant.'

The Dow Sing. Along with the rest of the office staff, courtesy of the petty cash account. Our standard farewell gesture for work-experience students. Nothing untoward. But clearly I'd made quite an impression on the young Miss Deloite. So, too, had the intervening years. All trace of the dumpy, bashful teenager had vanished.

'You had that little kid, didn't you?' she said, now in the full throes of reminiscence. 'What was his name again?'

Work experience occasionally included the development of child-care skills in the visiting students. With my wife Wendy seconded to the Office of the Status of Women in Canberra, I had assumed the prime parenting role. Which inevitably meant that our son put in a fair bit of time at the office. Keeping a four-year-old amused had been about Holly's intellectual speed, far less demanding than the technological challenges of the photocopier. There were little brothers somewhere in her background, I seemed to recall.

'Red,' I said. 'He lives in Sydney with his mother. We're divorced. I'm on my own now.'

'Aww.' She tilted her head even further to the side and pursed her lips into a sympathetic little frown.

Yes, it was a pity. Red, at least. Not the divorce. Wendy could look after herself. She was Director of Equal Opportunity for Telecom now, tapping away at the glass ceiling on behalf of the sisterhood. And herself. Remarried and doing well, thank you very much.

At this declaration of my marital status, our conversation lurched into an awkward silence. Unnecessarily so. My assertion that I was footloose and fancy-free was not intended as a pick-up line. Young Holly Deloite was a delight, all right, but she was still too young. Even if she was interested, what would we talk about afterwards? Not to mention the potential damage to my reputation. An older woman with a younger man, that was an historic advance. Vice versa, and the belles of censoriousness began to peal.

Still, it was nice to be fondly remembered, especially by a ravishing young thing. And her frank manner reflected well on the employment policies of the City Club. Nothing worse than subservient help, in my opinion. You never know what they're really thinking. 'You like it here?' she said. 'Good, isn't it? Great place to work.'

'Yeah,' I enthused, looking around at the heaving flesh and clanging metal. 'Just started this week, have you?'

'Nah,' she shook her ponytail. 'Been here ages, nearly a year. Just come back from six weeks in Queensland, but. The Hyatt Coolum Beach Resort. The chain has this sort of exchange thing with their instructors. Like I specialise in slide, okay? So I was doing that up there, training their staff, and they sent their low-impact guy down here.'

Mr Bottom, the vanished Vangelis fan. Visiting Fellow in Bump and Grind at the University of Soft Knocks.

'Sounds great,' I said. Holly had clearly found her vocation, gun aerobics coach. Have leotard will travel. I was pleased for her but it wasn't an area I felt qualified to discuss. We were running out of subject matter.

'Still with Mrs Wills?' she said, casting about for a safe topic. 'Out at the office.'

'Charlene died a fair while ago,' I said. 'It's Angelo Agnelli now.' The Honourable Member for Melbourne Upper. Minister for Water Supply and the Arts. My current employer.

Nearly six years Angelo and I had been together, ever since he inherited me from Charlene. Ours was a shotgun marriage of political convenience and, frankly, the relationship was wearing a bit thin. It was one of Angelo's remarks which had prompted me to join the City Club. 'Lucky I'm not Minister for Agriculture,' he told me. 'Or they'd start calling you Beefy Whelan.' This from a man with three chins whose only exercise was running off at the mouth and jumping to conclusions.

Never heard of him, said Holly's face. A politician. Inhabitant of a distant galaxy. Holly's was the world of the here and now. Politics just wasn't in the frame. Life was elsewhere. Anywhere, really. Everywhere. She was young.

'Anyway,' she said. 'Just thought I'd say hello. Really great to see you again, all of that. Anything you need, I'm here ten 'til eight every day.' She flashed me the corporate rictus. 'Maybe you'd like to join a class.'

'Maybe.' I nodded amiably. 'I'll think about it.' Like hell. Nothing more pathetic, in my book, than the sight of a man doing aerobics. Prancing about to infantile music in a room full of mirrors, making a complete dick of himself. If I really wanted to look like an idiot, I'd start riding a bike to work.

Holly Deloite's wandering eye was beginning to wander elsewhere, over towards the front counter where an unattended member was waiting impatiently for his complimentary fluffy towel. Nice girl, Holly. Beautiful body. Mind like a muesli bar. We parted, then, with a nod and a smile, she to customer service, me to the locker room.

In the buff, all men are equal. But, even bare-bummed, class finds a way of expressing itself. No tattoos here, no amputees, no horny hands or industrial injuries. Only the best-bred, corn-fed flesh in the locker room of the City Club. Vivaldi humming quietly in the background. Fresh flowers on the wash stand, limitless conditioning mousse in the showers. Silk ties and tailored jackets. Wooden coat-hangers in ash-panelled lockers. An atmosphere redolent of Eau Sauvage and insider trading.

As I stepped under the shower, the sudden shock of cold water reminded me of the dickheads I'd been dealing with that morning.

Union officials, they called themselves. Back in my day at the Trades Hall, they would've been lucky to get a job with the Amusement Employees Federation, Circus Division. Clowns whose idea of negotiation was to start with a threat and work their way up to personal abuse. Typical Miscellaneous Workers Union bullshit. The Missos were never what you might call Mensa material.

For months I'd been playing umpire in their interminable wrangling with the bureaucrats at the Department of Water Supply. Trying to convince them that the government was in no position to meet their demand for an across-the-board productivity bonus for the entire maintenance division.

A productivity bonus, for Chrissake, as if the water was suddenly getting wetter as a result of their improved work practices. All they had to do was to keep the stuff running downhill, after all. And now these absurd threats of industrial action. 'Such as what?' I wanted to know. 'Putting LSD in the reservoirs? Making the toilets flush in reverse?'

The dipstick drongos didn't seem to realise that it was 1990, that we were in the middle of a recession. Their obscure attempts at intimidation were the last straw. I'd finally lost it, given the miserable pricks a piece of my mind. Not my finest moment, professionally speaking. The meeting had ended in acrimonious disarray.

There has to be a better way to make a living, I thought as I towelled myself dry.

An elderly patrician with a washboard stomach and a mat of grey on his chest combed his temples at the mirror with all the gravity of a Roman senator. Paunchy plutocrats, towels at their midriffs, emerged dewy from the sauna. A consortium of brash young go-getters commandeered the benches, swapping their Florsheim brogues for Nike trainers, self-assured as Olympians.

The Olympics, I thought, pulling on my jocks. My big chance.

Brian Morrison had been insistent but tantalisingly vague when he rang and suggested we catch up. An old mate, Brian had wangled himself a berth with the Melbourne Olympic Bid, Incorporated, the organisation running the city's candidacy to host the 1996 Olympic Games. 'Let's have a bite,' he said. 'I might have a job for a man of your experience.'

I wasn't really in the job market. But I was curious. To exactly what aspect of my experience, I wondered, was he referring?

Surely not my current situation as Senior Adviser to the Minister for Water Supply, formulating policy options on the privatisation of the Mordialloc Main Drain, negotiating staffing levels with maddies from the Missos and making sure that Angelo didn't fall out of the boat while inspecting the catchment facilities.

Nor, I thought, had Brian been referring to my brief sojourn at the Arts Ministry, my employer's other area of current responsibility, where I'd briefly grappled with transgressive postmodern cultural practice. Perhaps he meant my time at Ethnic Affairs, Angelo's previous portfolio.

Yes, I thought, that was it. Athens was Melbourne's main competitor for the prize of the Centenary Games, after all. And five years at Ethnic Affairs, arm-wrestling the largest Greek community this side of the Peloponnesian peninsula, had taught me a thing or two about the Hellenic psyche. Helping to outwit the Athenians, I assumed, was what he had in mind for me.

As I knotted my tie, my face stared back at me from the mirror. Assessing my presentability, comparing it with that of my fellow City Club members. No doubt about it, almost a decade in the antechamber of political power had done wonders for my wardrobe. What would the blokes back at the Municipal Employees Union have said about my Hugo Boss suit, I wondered? Or the electors of Melbourne Upper? Holly Deloite was not the only one who had changed.

Smoothing my shirt front and buffing my shoes on the complimentary shoe-buffing machine, I strapped on my watch. Twelve-forty-five. Well exercised, well presented and on time. An ornament to the Australian Labor Party.

Holly was at reception, sprucing up the motivational books and videos in their revolving display rack. Buns of Steel. Abs of Alabaster. Pecs of Polycarbon. 'Lookin' good,' she said. Just the sort of thing they said at the City Club, but that didn't stop me drawing encouragement from it.

'What's it like?' I nodded at the book in her hand. *The Seven Keys to Eternal Youth.*

Holly studied the object like she wasn't quite sure what it was. 'Um,' she said. 'He's supposed to be really deep. You know. Philosophically.' On the back cover was a photograph of the author, a man in a turban with heavy black-rimmed spectacles and a full beard.

'Is he?' The guy looked like a myopic yak.

'He did this one, too.' From the rack she handed me *Mastering the Forces That Shape Personal Identity*.

'Interesting title,' I said. Refreshing in its brevity.

I scanned a page at random. '*Man is an air animal*,' it said. '*Shed your clothes whenever possible. Take off your shoes, loosen your collar. Sleep in the nude.*'

'Perhaps we could workshop this together,' I suggested.

But Holly wasn't listening. She was staring over my shoulder to where a customer was coming through the glass doors from the elevators. He wasn't one of the regulars, not one I'd seen before. He advanced towards us with the swaggering gait of a man acutely conscious of his physique. And with good reason. He was built like a small truck. Something compact but substantial. A Hilux two-tonner, for example, or a Ford Transit with aluminium dropside tray and dual rear wheels.

'Uh oh,' said Holly. 'Here's trouble.'

He was a very solid piece of work. Medium height, oval face, a neck like a hatbox. Arms like legs. Legs like I don't know what. They were enclosed in voluminous pants made out of what appeared to be parachute silk. His torso bulged beneath a loose sweat-top that must have been a size XXXXL.

He was somewhere in his mid-twenties, although his dark hair had already begun to thin at the forehead. The rest of it was slicked back over his skull and pulled tight into a rat's arse of a ponytail. The loose drape of his clothing seemed to accentuate rather than conceal the solid bulge of his body and he carried himself with the bow-legged strut of a man who has watched a few too many Sylvester Stallone movies.

He'd probably been reasonably good-looking, in an over-masculine sort of way, before the acne got to work on his cheekbones.

He smiled, showing a wide gap between his front teeth. 'Hey, babe,' he said.

I took it that he was not addressing me. Holly's smile snapped shut like a venetian blind and her chin shot up about ten centimetres. 'Excuse me a moment,' she murmured, moving out from behind the counter to block Arnold Schwartzenschnitzel's advance.

'Thought I told you to stay away.' She spoke in an undertone, her irritation unmistakable.

'Holly, babe.' His voice was jaunty, undeterred. 'Don't be like that.'

Holly folded her arms across her chest and glued her feet to the floor. 'Listen, Steve.' She spoke through gritted teeth. 'It's all over between us. Can't you get that through that thick head of yours?'

'Aw, be nice,' Steve cooed, rolling his shoulders, a couple of performance artists trying to get out of a satin sack. His arms hung so far out from his sides he looked like he was doing an impression of the Sydney Harbour Bridge.

Holly tossed an apprehensive glance over her shoulder and dropped her voice to a steely hiss. 'You'll get me sacked if you don't stop coming around like this. And I want my stuff back.'

By this stage, I'd realised that I wasn't witnessing a bad moment in customer relations but a disagreement of a more personal nature, probably romantic in origin. Returning the hairy guru to his place in the wire display rack, I began to edge away, heading for the exit.

'Don't be like that,' Mr Muscle said again. He was trying hard to sound casual but there was a note in his voice that I wasn't sure I liked. Holly didn't like it either, especially when he reached across to stroke the side of her neck. 'I roolly miss you, babe.'

Her arm shot up and brushed his away. 'I'm warning you, Steve.'

As I angled around them, Holly suddenly grabbed my elbow and thrust me forward. 'This is my lawyer,' she declared. 'Stop harassing me or he'll have you in court, dead set.'

Too astonished to contradict her, I cleared my throat, squared my jaw and tried to look jurisprudential. A damsel in distress and all that. The Hulk gave me the slow once-over, not much impressed with what he saw.

'What choo wanna lawyer for?' Now his feelings were hurt. 'They just rip you off.'

I concurred with the general sentiment but resented the specific insinuation. Behind me, I heard a click like the latch falling on a closing gate. Garth, the club's deep-tissue masseur, was emerging from the pool deck with an armful of folded towels. The clicking noise was the sound of his tongue rebounding off the roof of his mouth. He steamed towards us.

'Holly,' he commanded tersely. 'Put these in the stock room for me, please.'

Shooting me a quick look of thanks, Holly grabbed the towels and evaporated.

Garth wasn't quite as hefty as this Steve character, but he had a good half-head on him. And a very butch manner, considering. He inserted himself between me and Steve, arms akimbo. 'Come in here again,' he said, 'I'll call security. This is your last warning. On your bike, Tinkerbell.'

If looks could kill, Garth was a goner. Tinkerbell's lip curled back and his nostrils flared. But he managed to restrain himself. 'Hey, man,' he sneered. 'Call this a gym. This ain't a gym. It's a pussy factory.' He pirouetted on ballerina feet, tiny in comparison with the inverted triangle of his torso, and stalked contemptuously out the door.

'Sorry about that, sir,' said Garth. 'Not our kind of person at all.' On the other side of the glass doors, a balled fist was pounding the lift button, hammering it into the wall.

'No trouble,' I reassured the masseur, glancing first towards the stock room then at my watch. 'No trouble whatsoever.'

Of course, Steve hadn't killed anyone at that stage. Not yet, anyway.

Leaving the Hyatt by way of the food court, I lit a cigarette and strolled up Collins Street, allowing myself to be swept along by the Friday lunchtime crowd. At little tables on the footpath, women in haute couture sat sipping coffee and toying with overwrought pastries. The boutiques of the carriage trade were doing a brisk business in steamer trunks and silk handkerchiefs embossed with little interlocked initials. Yellow and green trams click-clacked past at a dignified pace. It was a long way from Paris, but it possessed a certain well-heeled charm.

The weather didn't hurt, either. Spring arrives in Melbourne as a relief, an end to dismal winter, a harbinger of a summer that might or might not eventuate. Autumn, however, is its own reward. It stands alone, dependable, often glorious, sometimes sublime. The sky is blue and the air invigorating, the canopies of the trees turn to russet and the bounty of the season is upon us. Time to start making provision for the chill days ahead. And chill they would no doubt be, if the polls were to be believed.

It was late April 1990 and the Labor government in whose ranks I served was on the skids. Bankrupted by financial mismanagement and special pleading. Riven by factional shenanigans and two-bob power plays. Skimmed by fast operators and administered by slow ones. Cactus. A political *Titanic* adrift in a Sargasso of lost opportunity. Our credibility was so seriously shot we'd be lucky to survive the two years until the next election. Nothing short of a miracle could save us.

Dream the Dream, read the banners fluttering from every light stanchion. Bring the Olympics to Melbourne. Above the words was a stylised flame, the logo of the Melbourne Olympic Bid, Inc.

Everywhere you turned, there it was. Emblazoned on the sides of trams, plastered to bumper bars, stuck on the doors of stores, dangling from power poles. We wanted this, and we wanted it bad. If the support of the populace counted for anything with the International Olympic Committee, Melbourne had to be odds-on favourite.

At the top of Collins Street stood the Old Treasury Building. Thick with baroque curlicues and neo-classical flourishes, the ornate edifice stared down at the city with all the imperious condescension of one of Queen Victoria's colonial secretaries. It had been built to store the rivers of bullion flowing from the goldfields of Ballarat and Bendigo. But that was more than a century ago. The mines were long exhausted and the wealth long spent. Our hopes were currently invested in new and more magical sources of wealth. Rich foreigners would come from the sky and shower us with gifts. As if in anticipation of their imminent arrival, Brian Morrison stood at the building's front door, staring up into the heavens.

A tall, curly-headed man of my own age, Morrison wore a tailored charcoal-grey suit that must have set him back a good eight hundred dollars. What with his executive tie and his air of self-satisfied affability, he was the very picture of the corporate man. There was certainly nothing about his current appearance to hint at the fact that in his younger days he'd once been the Socialist Left candidate for Mayor of Collingwood, that most mythically militant bastion of the working class.

Once upon a time, Brian had been a lowly ministerial adviser like me. Offsider to the Minister for Planning, responsible for seeing that nobody crept up on his boss in the dark and blind-sided him with a leaked memo or a preselection threat. Before that, back in the dark ages before Labor was in power, he and I sat on the odd committee together. More recently, he had been party campaign director during the last state election, a role roughly analogous to that of Mandrake the Magician.

Now he was an up-and-comer in the corporate sector, Director of Government, Corporate and Community Relations for the Olympic bid. DOG for the MOB, as he put it when he rang and suggested we have lunch. As I ascended the wide terrace of steps towards him, he cackled with pleasure and thrust his forefinger into the air, inviting me to turn my attention skyward.

A born conspirator, Brian was never happier than when he was cooking something up, putting something over. I followed the angle of his finger. Far above, a tiny plane was looping-the-loop, etching great white circles in the otherwise unbroken expanse of blue. 'The Olympic Rings,' he declared, in case I was unfamiliar with the design. 'A welcoming gesture for Don Pablo Cardena, the IOC's representative from Costa Rica. Cost me twenty grand but worth every penny. Don Pablo's very influential with the Latins. Plus it'll make a great front page.'

The pictorial editors would need to move fast. Even as the last of the four-thousand-dollar rings was inscribed in the air, the first was melting away, reduced to a few faint wisps of pallid vapour. We stood for a moment, reverently watching Brian's budget disperse into the stratosphere. Then he grabbed my elbow and propelled me through the front door. 'Take a gander at this,' he commanded.

For most of the preceding century, the Old Treasury Building had housed the Department of Administrative Services in conditions reminiscent of a scene out of *Great Expectations*. But now the public servants had been relocated, the facade scrubbed, the linoleum carpeted, the desks French-polished and the walls painted in heritage colours. An electronic display on the reception desk spelled out the countdown until the IOC made its decision. *142 days*, it flashed, *Welcome Don Pablo Welcome Welcome Welcome*.

Brian nodded briskly to the receptionist and led me along a short corridor lined with earth-toned dot paintings. 'Clifford Possum,' he murmured. 'Turkey Tolson.'

We arrived at an ornate set of double doors, their heavy brass handles buffed to a high sheen. Brian pressed a button on the wall and the portals swung silently open to reveal a darkened chamber lined with black curtains. We stepped inside and the doors closed behind us. A beam of light descended from the ceiling, illuminating a plinth upon which sat what appeared to be a ball of compressed shrapnel.

'The Baron Pierre de Coubertin, founder of the modern Olympics,' whispered Brian. 'Artist's impression.'

He put a finger to his lips, the lights dimmed and we were plunged into pitch darkness. Sounds began, faint at first, rising in volume. Bushland noises—the cackle of a kookaburra, water tinkling over stones, leaves rustling in the breeze. Then, gradually, came the low thrum of a didgeridoo and the rhythmic click of clap-sticks. A voice joined in, an adenoidal Aboriginal chant. '*Manuyangka nyiyarlangurlu, jarntungku marda, yankirrirli...*'

Gradually, the one voice became many, a babel of tongues. French and German, Spanish and Chinese, accumulated into the clamour of a massive crowd. Whistles blew and commentators whipped themselves into a frenzy. The hubbub built to a deafening crescendo. Then, with one final triumphant honk of the didgeridoo, the din ceased and the curtains parted.

A large well-lit room opened before us, its walls covered with glossy images of sporting venues. Glass-fronted cabinets displayed sporting memorabilia. Historic hockey sticks, famous fencing foils. Great moments in sport. Gold medals and team pendants. *Celtius, Fortius, Altius* read a scroll stretched between the beaks of two stuffed fairy penguins.

'The bottom line,' said Brian, indicating a series of architectural models. The Athletes Village, old docklands at the edge of the city transformed into cluster housing with water views. A media centre rising fifty storeys above the railway switching yards. New swimming and diving pools, a baseball diamond, cycling velodrome and soccer pitch. 'Sixty thousand jobs, minimum. A total revamp of our public infrastructure. Revenues of four billion dollars, mostly from American television. That's the beauty of this thing. The fucking Yanks will pay for it.'

It was indeed an inspiring possibility. 'Yeah, but what are our chances?' The question on everyone's lips.

Brian fluttered the palm of his downturned hand. 'We're in the lap of the gods. At the end of the day, mate, it's about kissing arse. And these IOC types are experts at having their arses kissed. At any given time, there are six cities bidding for the Summer Olympics and six for the Winter, each spending upwards of twenty million US dollars. That's nearly $250 million being spent to schmooze ninety people.'

'So it's a bidding war?'

He shook his head. 'It's more subtle than that. Half these guys are princes and dukes. You can't just buy their votes. Not all of them, anyway. You've got to play them individually.' He hunched over and wrung his hands like Uriah Heep. 'Demonstrate your commitment to the sacred ideals of Olympism. Speak of the brotherhood of man and the importance of the athlete. Then wine and dine the bastards to within an inch of their lives. Above all, convince them that you won't fuck it up.'

'What about the competition?' I prompted. 'Athens?'

'Definitely the big risk. Still the sentimental favourite, despite the smog, the chaos and the security problems. Frankly, we're praying that terrorists blow up an airliner on the runway at Athens airport between now and the vote.'

This, I hoped, was not the job he had in mind for me. 'Toronto?' I asked. 'Manchester? Belgrade? What about

Atlanta? Big money, media-friendly time-zones, the ghost of Martin Luther King.'

'Forget Atlanta,' he snorted. 'Everybody hates the Yanks. Personally, I reckon we've got this thing in the bag. Long as nothing happens to dump us in the shit.'

'Such as?'

'Come upstairs,' he said.

We went up an imposing staircase to a broad hallway on the first floor. A conclave of suited men spilled from one of the rooms. Big chiefs, conversing importantly among themselves. I recognised one of them as Hugh Knowles, chairman of the MOB and chief executive of Mincom Resources, one of the country's biggest mining companies. Brian all but genuflected as Knowles passed.

'Thought we might have lunch here,' Brian said, shouldering open a door. 'If that's okay with you.'

The door opened into a small conference room overlooking the Treasury Gardens, a vista of autumnal red and gold. A gilt-framed landscape hung above the marble fireplace and beneath the window was an antique walnut sideboard covered with platters of food. Helping himself to the smoked salmon was a gnarled leprechaun in a tweed jacket and rimless bifocals.

'You two know each other, I think,' said Brian.

Indeed we did. Denis Dogherty was one of my colleagues, senior aide to the Minister for Sport, Recreation, Racing and the Olympics. He looked up from his plate and scrutinised me in an oblique, testing way with the sort of face that could once be found in the front bar of any hotel in Australia, usually topped with a pork-pie hat and tilted in the direction of the racing results. He gave a long, low whistle.

'Very respectable threads, Murray,' he said. 'Was the magistrate impressed?'

'How original,' I replied. 'You old spiv.' Denis was somewhere in his mid-sixties. He was wearing a burgundy pin-corduroy shirt with a button-down collar, a mustard-coloured tie and a pair of tan permanent-press trousers. His hair, a gingery thatch, was brushed forward in the manner of a Roman emperor or an ageing Beatle.

'Go ahead and eat,' urged Brian Morrison. 'I'll be back in a minute.' He disappeared, shutting the door behind him.

Denis Dogherty and I were old friends. I'd first met him more than fifteen years earlier, back when I started work at the Trades Hall and possession of a university degree was regarded as proof positive of homosexual tendencies by many of the older union officials. But not by Denis. A job delegate for the Stevedores Federation, a man who'd spent his formative years digging wharfies out of grain spills and fighting the ship owners over slave labour on flag-of-convenience rust buckets, he had a high regard for the value of learning.

'Always remember who your enemies are,' he told me. 'And never forget your friends.'

The last time I'd seen him was at the quarterly briefing sessions the Premier conducted for the staff of his ministers. Bible class, Denis called it, a bunch of political fixers being lectured on the need for scrupulous standards of probity and professionalism by a man so far above the ruck that his feet never touched the ground.

'All the dough we've given this Olympic mob,' he said, thrusting a plate into my hand. 'Might as well get in for your chop.'

For the previous few weeks, lunch had been an alfalfa sandwich and a glass of mineral water, all part of the concerted attack on my love handles. Maintaining discipline, I forked a couple of slices of smoked salmon and an artichoke heart onto my plate, averting my eyes from the platter of petits-fours and chocolate-dipped florentines. Denis uncorked a bottle of white wine and poured me a glass. It was a fragrant drop, redolent of wildflowers and the fruits of office.

'Off your tucker?' Thin as a rail, Denis was one of those people who never put on weight. 'I'm not surprised. Running messages for that dog Agnelli'd be enough to ruin anyone's appetite.'

Our masters were factional allies, so I was unperturbed by Denis's disparaging remarks. 'I'm in training,' I said. 'Thought I might see if I can get a run with the Royboys this season.'

'Fitzroy?' Denis arrested his fork in mid-air. 'Thought you were a South man.'

His memory was amazing. It must have been a good dozen years since we'd slipped out of the Trade Union Training Authority seminar on Confronting the Issues of Industry Restructuring to listen to the South Melbourne–Fitzroy match in the public bar of the Dover Hotel. Both of us barracking for the Bloodstained Angels. For Denis, to change football teams was tantamount to class treason. Even when the money men threw a net over his beloved South Melbourne, dragged them north of the border and rebaptised them as the Sydney Swans, Denis did not desert them.

That's what I liked about Denis. There was a commendable permanence to his allegiances. For Denis, fidelity was a primary virtue. He might have lacked the formal qualifications that were so highly valued by the lawyers, sociology lecturers and assorted technocrats who inhabited the higher reaches of our administration, but Denis Dogherty had the certainty of conviction it takes to hold a political party together. And a good thing, too. Whenever the Labor Party finds itself in power, loyalty tends to be the one thing in shortest supply.

'Fair go,' I said. 'Fitzroy is the closest thing left in town to the Bloods. They have the same martyred qualities.' Eating irons in hand, we plonked ourselves down at the round six-seater dining table and thrashed out the ethics of my decision to change football teams. Since I lived in Fitzroy, Denis was reluctantly prepared to cut me some slack on the issue.

As the subject moved to premiership prospects and injury lists, I began to wonder what scheme was being hatched here. When Brian Morrison suggested we get together for a nibble and a natter, he made no mention of Denis Dogherty. Yet Denis's presence was clearly no accident. So what was going on? The Ministry of Sport etc. was the point of over-lap between the government bureaucracy and the MOB. Chances were that anything too sensitive or complicated for MOB to handle would get handballed to the minister's office where Denis would deal with it. Or find someone who could. Such as me, I wondered?

'How's Woeful?' I said.

'The Right Honourable the Minister for Sport, Recrea-tion, Racing and the Olympics?' Denis looked past me. 'Ask him yourself.'

Coming through the door, followed by Brian Morrison, was a tall, D-shaped, bald-headed fellow about the same age as Denis. His long, oval face wore a hangdog expression and his broad shoulders drooped as though carrying the weight of the world. As well they might, for it was Douglas 'Woeful' McKenzie's responsibility to see that the government's $15 million investment in securing the Olympics, and its own future, was not wasted.

'G'day, Murray,' he sighed wearily. 'Not talking about me behind my back, I hope.'

I knew Woeful only slightly, a nodding acquaintance from fund-raising barbecues and factional pow-wows. An ex-wharfie like Denis, he was that rarest of anachronisms, a blue-collar worker in the Cabinet of a Labor government. Beyond that fact, about the only other thing I knew for sure about Woeful McKenzie was that, despite appearances, it was not his lugubrious demeanour which accounted for his nickname.

Back in the early fifties, according to legend, young Doug McKenzie was a pretty fair footballer. Not a star by any means, but a league-standard full-back who clocked up a couple of reasonably successful seasons with South Melbourne before buggering his hamstring. Built like the proverbial, he played a solid defence, plugging up the goalmouth with his lumbering body and long arms. But, like many a full-back, he was an erratic kick. As often as not, when he sank the slipper, the result was an absolute shocker. Either a wobbly punt off the side of his boot or a turf-skidding worm-burner of a drop-kick.

'Woeful McKenzie strikes again,' declared a radio commentator one afternoon, coining a tag so apt that Woeful had been Woeful ever since, even to many who knew nothing of his athletic prowess.

Woeful and Denis had always been thick as thieves. Port Melbourne lads, born with seagull shit on their shoulders, they had grown up together in the shadow of the biscuit factory, dived recklessly off the end of Station Pier and eventually slung their hooks in the same work crews. But Denis was no footballer, not even a nippy little rover. The spirit was willing but the flesh never quite made the team. Instead, he settled for the job of trainer. Water bottle in hand, he lurked at the boundary line, waiting for the right moment to dash onto the ground and pass a word of tactical advice to his burly mate.

Despite the disparaging moniker, Woeful's reputation as a sportsman had done him no harm in the years after he quit the football oval and the cargo sheds and began his slow but steady ascent through the industrial and parliamentary ranks of the party. And wherever he went Denis went with him. First into the Stevedores as his branch organiser, then as his electorate officer, finally as his ministerial adviser. Whatever the title or the game, however, their roles remained essentially what they had been on the footy field. Woeful played a dogged defence while Denis monitored the moves and proposed the play.

The Laurel and Hardy of the labour movement, somebody had once called them. Physical and temperamental opposites, the two old operators had been rusted together for the best part of forty years.

'Good afternoon, Minister,' I said, properly respectful.

McKenzie was no great stickler for protocol but there was no point in taking uninvited liberties. If this was a job interview, it had just gone major league. The Minister for Sport, Recreation, Racing and the Olympics hadn't just dropped by on the chance of an open-face sandwich and a petit-four.

With an audible sigh, Woeful lowered his ample frame into a chair. He wore a dark brown suit with a club tie, a presentation number by the look of it. Garden City Bowls Club. When he sat down, his neck sank so far between his shoulders that he looked for all the world like a thumb with a face painted on it. Brian dealt him a hand of cutlery and a plate of sandwiches and sat down.

'Meeting go okay?' said Denis.

'This bloody Evaluation Commission,' grunted Woeful, knocking back a solid slug of chardonnay. 'Hugh Knowles never shut up about it.'

Evidently, listening to Hugh Knowles had a stimulating effect on Woeful's appetite. While the big man laid into his lunch, Denis brought me up to speed.

'Big week next week, Murray. Three IOC high flyers winging into town to run the tape measure over us. Facilities, security, hospitality, you name it. Without the nod from this lot, we're down the gurgler in no uncertain terms. The MOB here have been running round like blue-arse flies, making straight the way. Anything upsets these blokes, it's bye-bye Olympics.'

'Crunch time,' added Brian Morrison, in case the point had escaped me. 'Get the picture?'

Woeful washed down the last of his sandwich and dabbed his lips daintily with a paper napkin. Then he pushed his plate away and turned his full attention to me.

'So, Murray,' he said. 'Brian here tells me you know a bloke named Ambrose Buchanan.'

The change of tack was so sudden I wasn't sure I'd heard right.

'Ambrose Buchanan?' I said. 'The Aboriginal activist?'

'Yeah. The blackfeller.'

'Koori,' said Denis. 'They're called Koories now.'

'Jesus Christ, Denis,' said the big man. 'I know that. They've been Koories for donkey's years. Well, have you, Murray?'

My appetite had gone right out the window. Denis and Brian, too, had stopped chewing and were observing me closely. 'We've met,' I admitted warily. 'But it was a fair while ago.'

Back in less morally equivocal times, back when doing good and doing well were less likely to be confused.

'Go on,' urged Brian. 'Tell them.'

'You tell them,' I said pointedly.

Ignoring my sarcasm, Brian unbuttoned his jacket, put his elbows on the table and eagerly launched into the story.

Hand gestures, facial expressions, the works. Could have got a job on 'Play School'.

'This is back in the late-seventies, right. Ten, twelve years ago. I'm running this federal housing project. Murray here is Charlene Wills' electorate officer in Melbourne Upper, just been kicked out of the Labour Resource Centre.'

I let that one go by. My decision to leave the Resource Centre was entirely voluntary, albeit accompanied by sighs of relief all round. And Brian wasn't in charge of the housing program, he was acting assistant administrator on temporary secondment.

'Anyway,' Brian continued. 'The project involves replacing run-down public housing stock and relocating the tenants. Some of which are not exactly keen to co-operate. Think it's a trick to evict them. There's this one old duck in particular, really digs her heels in. Merle Plunkett. An old Aboriginal woman, originally from up Mooroopna way. She's had a pretty rough time over the years at the hands of what she calls The Welfare and we just can't persuade her that there's a nice new place waiting for her.'

Merle had raised six grandchildren in that two-bedroom Housing Commission box of hers, and filled it with her memories. But the plumbing was rooted, the damp was rising and the entire block was slated for immediate demolition. Her new flat was right beside a community health centre, close to public transport and the rent was lower. Still she wouldn't budge.

'Tried everything we could think of,' continued Brian. 'Including having a representative of her local member of parliament call around, speak to her in person.'

Merle was one of Charlene's few Aboriginal constituents. One of the few locals not indigenous to the greater

Mediterranean. 'Brian was clutching at straws,' I told Denis and Woeful. 'There was no reason to think that I would have any influence at all.'

'Anyway,' persisted Brian, building up a head of narrative steam. 'There's me and Murray, sitting at Merle's kitchen table, attempting to persuade her that we're not trying to pull the wool over her eyes, when her son Reggie barges in. Now Reggie is one cranky Koori and he reckons he's sick to death of white bureaucrats hassling his dear old mum. To emphasise the point, he produces a rifle, sticks it in Murray's face and declares that unless we agree to let Merle stay where she is in perpetuity he'll redecorate the place with gubba brains.'

Denis opened his mouth. Before he could say anything, Woeful stopped him with a look. He knew what a gubba was. The two of them were like an old married couple.

'The gun wasn't loaded,' I said heavily.

We'd agreed at the time that it was best for all concerned if certain aspects of the story remained untold. And I, for one, had stuck to that commitment. But Brian was plainly unconcerned about ancient promises.

'I immediately offered to convey Reggie's demands to the appropriate authorities,' he said. In other words, the chicken-shit coward took off so fast I thought it was a vanishing trick.

Not that I blamed him. Reggie Plunkett was indeed a very angry man, forty going on sixty, one of the walking wounded. A man who'd had it rough all his life. Rough red by the smell of him. And when he cocked that rabbit gun and pressed the muzzle against my forehead, his hands were shaking so badly with booze and rage that I was halfway through the Act of Contrition before I remembered I was an atheist.

'Reggie would never have really shot me,' I insisted.

Denis had picked up on my reluctant tone. 'Black with one sugar, Brian,' he said, tilting his chin towards the sideboard. 'White with two for his nibs. Murray?'

Brian took the hint and busied himself with the coffee pot.

'Nobody's asking you to do the dirty here, Murray,' said Denis. 'We're just trying to get a handle on this Buchanan bloke, that's all.'

I didn't know where this little show-and-tell was going, but now that we'd come this far I figured I might as well go on. Better the truth than Brian's drama-school documentary. Woeful gave me a nod of encouragement.

'Reggie's problem was how to back down,' I said. 'Which became a major problem once the police arrived.'

Summoned by Brian, the silly prick, the cops had the place surrounded within twenty minutes. An entire SWAT team, peeing themselves with excitement at the prospect of what they called a hostage-type siege-situation. When they shouted through a bullhorn for Reggie to come out with his hands up, he yelled back that he'd meet ten of them in hell first.

Which was a pity really, because Merle had just about convinced him to take the gun out of my face and start to think about getting himself sober. 'You've really gone and done it now, Reggie,' his mum said, fetching him a wallop around the ear-hole with a hand the size of a frying pan. At that point, I thought I was one dead whitefeller.

'Fortunately, I had the presence of mind to ring the Aboriginal Legal Service,' said Brian, unable to help himself. 'Who sent a mediator. Ambrose Buchanan.'

Buchanan was originally from Wilcannia or Walgett, one of those shit-awful racist dumps in the backblocks of New

South Wales. He'd been radicalised as a teenager when the Freedom Riders arrived in the mid-sixties, busloads of activists inspired by the American civil rights movement. He joined up and hit the road, helping desegregate municipal swimming pools. By the time he walked through the police lines and into Merle Plunkett's kitchen, he had a national reputation as a firebrand agitator.

'And Reggie knew who he was?' said Woeful.

I nodded. 'He was pretty impressed, I think. But mainly he was sick to his guts at the thought of going back inside. He'd already spent half his life in prisons of one kind or another. But Ambrose gave him his money's worth. Started off by dressing me down, saying how high-handed we'd been.' We being Brian. 'Said we should've worked through a Koori community organisation and that Reggie would be quite within his rights to shoot me where I sat. Then he suggested that I apologise to Merle.'

Which I was not reluctant to do, given that Reggie was still holding the rifle. And because it didn't seem unreasonable, all things considered.

'The gun,' urged Brian, irrepressibly. 'Tell them about the gun.'

'Ambrose eventually convinced Reggie to put it on the table between us. Then he stuck his head out the front door and put the coppers on hold while Merle made us a big pot of tea. Then we spent an hour trying to figure out what to do next.'

'Which was to make me look like an idiot,' said Brian cheerfully.

I didn't bother to contradict him. 'The firearm was the problem,' I said. 'So Ambrose unloaded it and got Reggie to chop the stock into matchwood with his mum's kitchen cleaver. I shoved the bolt and the bullets down my under-pants and the two of us, me and Ambrose, went out and explained to the posse that it was all a misunderstanding. Told them that Brian had misread the situation, that the gun was just a harmless old barrel and that I didn't want to press charges.'

'They buy it?' said Denis.

'Put it this way,' I told them. 'Last I heard of Reggie Plunkett, he was running a very successful twelve-step alcohol rehabilitation program up in Rockhampton.'

'How about Merle?'

I left that one to Brian. 'Died of a diabetes-related illness,' he said. 'Three months after she moved into her new flat.'

Denis exchanged a meaningful look with Woeful. 'Seen much of Ambrose Buchanan since then?'

'Only in the press,' I said. 'Mind telling me why all the interest? I thought you wanted to talk to me about Greeks.'

'Greeks?' Brian was mystified.

'Show him the tape you showed us,' said Woeful.

'What Greeks?' Brian leaned back in his chair and opened the walnut sideboard. Inside was a television set and a VCR. 'German documentary. Just gone to air in Europe. Seen by fifty million people. The PR firm that handles our European lobbying sent it to us. They don't think it's done much for our prospects.'

A long shot of Uluru filled the screen, superimposed with the words *Roter Kontinent—Schwarzer Kampf*. Brian held down the fast-forward button. Images skittered past. Rock art, desert landscapes, talking heads, old monochrome images. Black men chained to trees, mission-station children, Bobbi Sykes in an Angela Davis afro, police dismantling the Tent Embassy outside the old Parliament House in Canberra, Gough Whitlam pouring dirt into Vincent Lingiari's hand, street marches, black babies with flies in their eyes. Brian removed his finger and the tape slowed to normal. Ambrose Buchanan appeared.

The footage was recent and he looked remarkably unchanged by the decade that had passed since he stood in old Merle's kitchen, Reggie Plunkett sobbing in his arms, while I stared down between my feet, speechless with relief, thinking how badly the floor needed wiping. Busting for a piss after all that tea.

He still had the same cocky body-language, the same fine-boned, nut-brown face with its hint that some long-gone Afghan had watered his camels at the gene pool of the western plains. The beard was a new addition, if you could call it a beard. Overgrown designer stubble, flecked with silver. But Ambrose Buchanan was no tribal elder, not yet. He still wore faded blue denims, emblem of our shared generation. I hoped I'd weathered the years as well as he had.

He was standing at a microphone on the tray of a flat-bed truck. Behind him, on a row of plastic chairs, sat a dozen old Aborigines, men and women, as ancient and impassive as the landscape. As Ambrose spoke, he gripped the microphone stand with one hand and punctuated each phrase with an upward sweep of his other, as though gently but forcefully freeing an injured bird.

Brian's finger found the volume control and suddenly we could hear what was being said. Buchanan's voice was reedy with excitement, but the measured cadence of his phrases rose and fell like an irresistible tide.

'They say that our demands are unreasonable. They say that we should be content with all we've been given.

They say that everything that can be done is being done. They say that we must put the past behind us. They say that before the law we are all one nation. That is what they say.'

Buchanan paused here and lowered his head, as if pondering an impenetrable mystery, as if burdened by a sorrow too deep to communicate. As if inviting us to join him in a moment of silent contemplation. Then, emerging almost reluctantly from his reverie, he drew himself up to his full height and once again gripped the microphone stand. 'And what do we say, eh?'

The camera panned across the flags and banners of a huge demonstration, a sea of red, black and yellow, hemmed in by the hard blank facades of city office buildings. 'And what do we say to them?'

The question hung for a moment, then a great chant welled up from the crowd. 'Land rights now! Land rights now!' Buchanan's open palm became a closed fist that punched out the beat. 'Land rights now! Land rights now!'

Brian hit the stop button and the screen turned to snow. 'Brisbane,' he said. 'Two years ago. Quite impressive, don't you think?'

Impressive? It was bloody fantastic. Buchanan was a natural orator, one of the best I'd ever seen. Which isn't saying much, admittedly, for ours is not a culture characterised by public eloquence. Woeful and Denis had turned in their seats, waiting for my reaction.

'Very impressive,' I agreed, cautiously. I was beginning to suspect where all this was leading.

'Ambrose's been in Brussels for the past six months,' said Brian. 'Arguing some case before the International Court of

Human Rights. He arrived here in Melbourne a few days ago. Says he wants to talk to us, got a proposition.'

'Hmm,' I said. 'And?'

'Demarcation dispute,' said Denis, humour crinkling the edges of his foxy little eyes.

Brian explained. 'We've already been through the community consultation process with the local Koories. The full corroboree. Even went up the bush. Echuca, Robinvale, Mooroopna, Eunamit. Explained how there'll be plenty for everyone if we win. Politely requested their assistance.'

'And not just because of the black vote on the IOC,' said Denis, a man whose heart had always been in the right place. On race issues, the Stevedores' credentials were unimpeachable.

'We were advised to employ a Koori liaison officer,' continued Brian. 'Which we did. Bloke by the name of Charlie Talbot.'

The surname struck a distant clap-stick. The Talbots, I recalled, were one of the more prominent families in local Aboriginal matters. Back at Ethnic Affairs, according to hearsay, half the Koori bureaucrats in Victoria were Talbots. Koories, of course, are not ethnics. Laotians are ethnics. Eritreans are ethnics. If we had any Eskimos, they'd be ethnics. But Aborigines aren't ethnics.

'So what's the problem?' I said.

Woeful leaned back, let his belt out a notch and crossed his hands over his belly. 'Charlie's in Nairobi right now,' he sighed, shaking his head. 'On his way to Lusaka for a meeting of the Organisation of African Sport. Hugh Knowles and the rest of the board thought we should have at least one black member on our delegation. God knows what the Africans will make of Charlie Talbot. With the light behind him, he's whiter than I am.'

'Not that the minister's saying you can't have a fair-complexioned Aborigine,' said Denis, tipping me a sly wink. 'You're not saying that, are you Woeful?'

'Murray knows what I mean,' said Woeful irritably. 'This isn't a fucking Rotary meeting, Den.' He started patting his pockets. Denis tossed him a roll of antacids. He caught it without looking, peeled one off and ground it loudly between his molars.

'The point being,' Brian said, moving right along. 'Ambrose and the Talbots don't get on. He reckons they're coconuts.'

Denis cupped a hand around his mouth and leaned across the table. 'Brown on the outside, white on the inside.'

'Piss off,' grumbled Woeful. The days of vaudeville, it seemed, were not entirely dead.

'Ambrose Buchanan said that?' I was surprised. Washing black linen in public didn't sound like Ambrose's style.

'Shit no!' said Brian. 'Charlie Talbot told me. Anyway, the point is, Buchanan's in town and Charlie isn't. And we all know that Buchanan won't be satisfied with a company car and an overseas trip. He'll want something big, something unrealistic, something outside the scope of the MOB to satisfy.'

'What about the Department of Aboriginal Affairs?' I asked. 'Isn't this their jurisdiction?'

'Leaks like a wickerwork basket,' said Brian. 'If the Talbots suspect that we're cutting a side deal with Ambrose, they'll get their nulla-nullas in a knot. Accuse us of reneging on the agreed consultation process, maybe even pull the plug.

Then we'll really be in the shit, indigenous support-wise. So, until we've got a better idea of what Ambrose has in mind, we need to tread carefully, go at the whole thing sideways.' He made a sinuous, inserting gesture. 'Know what I mean?'

At that point, I had an overwhelming urge to make a break for the door.

Before I had the chance, Woeful leaned forward in his seat and put his hands flat on the table. Big shovels of things that once humped sacks of sugar out of the holds of cargo tubs at Swanston Dock and punched footballs thirty metres into the crowd at the Lakeside Oval. He levered himself upwards and fixed me in his melancholy gaze. 'I don't have to tell you how important this bid is to future of the government, Murray,' he said. 'And I know we can rely on you.'

Denis already had his hand on the door knob. 'C'mon, Your Excellency,' he said. 'Let's leave these young blokes to sort out the details. See you later, Murray.'

As the door closed behind them, Brian Morrison slid the plate of chocolate biscuits across the table towards me.

'No way known,' I said. 'No fucking way, pal.'

Brian Morrison stood at the window, backside on the sill, heels angled into the carpet, hands thrust deep into his pockets. Behind him, reflecting the coppery foliage of the parkland, rose the glass wall of a brand-new office tower. A banner hung from its roof, ten storeys high. *To Let*, it read. Brian cast his eyes downwards and took a long draught from the cup of bitter disappointment.

'Thought you'd be in this like a shot, Murray,' he sighed. 'A chance to get yourself out of Water, put your talents to better use. Get in on the ground floor of the hottest project in town. Do your bit for the party's re-election prospects.'

I was looking at the painting above the mantelpiece, a landscape of the old school. One of those bush scenes politicians love to borrow from the National Gallery to hang in the office, impress the constituents. The vision splendid of the sunlit plain extended, the murmur of the river on its bars, the distant smudge of innumerable grazing merinos. Australia Felix.

'Listen to yourself, mate,' I said. 'Next you'll be appealing to my sense of patriotism. If you're going to soft-soap me, at least work up a decent lather.'

'Okay,' he said. 'How much do you want?'

'You offering me a job?'

'Fair go,' he pleaded. 'This should only take you a couple of days. Woeful can talk to Agnelli, arrange a temporary secondment to Sport.'

'You appear to be mistaking me for Mother Teresa,' I said.

'Okay, okay. I suppose I can wangle you a consultancy fee on top of your salary. Say five grand.'

'Five thousand dollars?' I whistled. 'That the going rate for putting down a native uprising?'

'Jesus, Murray,' said Brian. 'Don't tell me you're having an attack of conscience.'

That crack was a low blow, an assault on my integrity. No worse allegation can be levelled against a paid functionary of the Australian Labor Party than the insinuation of morality. My position was entirely pragmatic. Five grand was a tidy sum for a few days' work, but it was scant compensation for what was being asked. Aboriginal politics were just too complex, intractable and thankless. A morass of good intentions gone wrong. The domain of missionaries, mystics and mercenaries. None of which categories included me. For Brian to suggest otherwise was an insult to my commonsense and an attempt to prey on my better nature.

Nor had I forgotten what happened last time I agreed to do Brian a favour. I nodded towards the blank television screen. 'You already know what Ambrose wants—land rights and an end to two centuries of injustice. You reckon your budget will run to that?'

The Director of Government, Corporate and Community Relations hung his jacket on the back of his chair and rolled up his shirt sleeves like maybe he was about to beat some sense into me. He poured two fresh cups of coffee and plonked one on the table in front of me. 'I'm begging you, mate. If Ambrose succeeds in making race an issue in this bid, I can kiss my brilliant new career goodbye.'

'Don't go hysterical on me,' I said. 'Or I'll be forced to slap you.'

Morrison jerked his thumb in the direction of a hypothetical top floor. 'Hugh Knowles is really spooked by this. And, believe me, anybody who underestimates the viciousness of the Australian business class just isn't getting out of the house enough.'

'I can see you've really bonded with the corporate sector,' I said. The coffee had been standing for too long and had turned bitter. Just to cut the taste, I had a biscuit. A cigarette would have been better but I didn't dare.

'Less than twenty years ago, Mincom was burning blacks out of their homes to make way for its bauxite mines. Federal legislation and the land councils put an end to all that but the mining industry will still only deal with indigenous people if the courts force it to. There's a lot of corporate ego involved in this bid and these guys are terrified by the idea that a media-wise Abo might hold them to ransom. Ambrose knows that and he'll play it to the hilt.'

I shrugged. 'More power to him.'

'I agree. I absolutely agree,' said Brian. 'Except this isn't about the mining industry or corporate ego. It's about creating sixty thousand jobs in this city. It's about saving the government that you and I sweated our tits off to get elected. Losing Melbourne's Olympic bid isn't going to eliminate trachoma in the Northern Territory. But if the blame can be slated back to the blacks believe me it will be. And that's not going to do much for race relations.'

'And you think Ambrose Buchanan can do that, single-handed?'

Brian topped up our coffees. 'For Ambrose Buchanan, the Olympic bid is part of a bigger agenda. He knows that the real political constituency for Aboriginal rights in this country is the white population of the south-eastern cities. If it was up to the voters of Queensland and Western Australia, the pastoralists and miners would still be free to chain black-fellers to trees. Ambrose's self-appointed role is to keep the issue of racism to the forefront down here in the south. He's unencumbered by any official position in the Aboriginal bureaucracy, he's well networked internationally and he's got a good local power base.'

'It's all a bit big-picture for me, mate,' I said. 'You want a branch stacked or a ballot rigged, I'm your man.'

'Exactly,' said Brian. 'You have the sensitivity to deal with the issues. On top of which, you and Ambrose have a history. He'll trust you. I'm only asking you to find out whether he's prepared to deal, that's all.'

'You're offering me five thousand dollars just to find out if Ambrose Buchanan can be persuaded that black interests won't be served by an attack on the Olympic bid?'

'More or less.'

'It's not my area of expertise. I'd stuff it up. Honestly.'

'Crap,' he said, vehemently. 'You've just spent five years working with the Greeks. After that, how much of a problem can a solitary Aborigine be?'

He had a point. But I wasn't about to concede it. Not until he played his trump card. 'That son of yours...' He snapped his fingers to jog his memory, back in pantomime mode.

'Red,' I reminded him. Brian's eldest was about Red's age, I seemed to recall. Matilda, Mabel, something like that. Red decked her at her third birthday party. Brian's wife Sandra was something in public advocacy at the time, back when Wendy was executive officer of the Women's Information Exchange. They still kept in touch.

'That's right,' said Brian, confirming my son's identity for me. 'Wendy was saying to Sandra the other day on the phone that Red was one of our junior runners in the *Dream the Dream* Torch Relay.'

The torch relay was a public relations stunt being run by the MOB. Two thousand children carrying an anodised aluminium baton down the east coast of the continent, a demonstration of the commitment of the youth of Australia to the ideals of Olympism. Participants got a free Coca-Cola t-shirt and a McDonald's voucher. Every kid in the country wanted a piece of the action.

'Two hundred metres along Parramatta Road last Sunday afternoon,' I said. 'The banners in the used-car yards lent the occasion a particularly festive air.'

Or so I imagined. Unfortunately, I hadn't been there to see it. After Red made the cut at Little Athletics, I booked a plane ticket to Sydney to witness the big event. But Agnelli insisted I stay in town in case the union dispute went critical.

It didn't, of course, and I missed my first opportunity in four months to see the kid. He was, Wendy made a point of telling me, 'bitterly disappointed' by his father's failure to show.

'What's Red got to do with this?'

Brian adopted a guise of innocence. 'The thing is, a bit of an opportunity has arisen. We're looking for a kid to present the torch to the visiting IOC members at the gala dinner next Thursday night. Hugh Knowles' grandson was lined up for the job—nothing warms the heart of the IOC more than a bit of nepotism—but young Nicholas has come down with the Hong Kong flu. We're thinking of selecting one of the interstate runners at random and flying him—or her—into town especially for the occasion. Good media angle and so on. Anyway, I might just be able to organise it so your boy Red gets the gig.'

Pleading, flattery, persuasion. Now bribery. You had to hand it to Brian Morrison, he didn't rest until he'd found the right button to push. 'Is this the lowest you've ever sunk?' I asked.

'Shit no,' he beamed. 'Back when I was with the Minister for Transport, I started a rumour that a particularly trouble-some secretary of the Railway Workers Union was a closet pixie. Took off like wildfire, it did. He lost the next election by forty-three votes.' He puffed out his cheeks and stared up at the ceiling. 'You'll probably want to discuss it with Wendy,' he said. 'Sandra reckons she'll be thrilled at the idea.'

Bribery buttressed by blackmail. He caught the rush of green to my gills and moved in for the kill. 'Tell you what,' he said. 'Sleep on it over the weekend. Talk it over with the ex. Let me know what you decide. Monday at the latest.' He put his flame-embossed business card on the empty plate in front of me. Somebody appeared to have eaten all the chocolate biscuits.

Brian was on his feet again, staring out the window. 'Beautiful weather,' he exhaled. 'This town's really at its best at this time of the year. Don't you agree?'

When I came out of the Old Treasury, Sir Charles Gordon was standing across the road with a swagger stick under his arm and his gaze fixed on the far horizon, oblivious to the traffic swirling around his feet. He'd been standing there since 1938. *He would not desert those dependent on him* was chiselled into the plinth at his feet. A pigeon was shitting on his head.

Like Gordon awaiting his doom at Khartoum, I was in no great hurry. Agnelli was in Canberra for the annual meeting of Ministers Responsible for Public Infrastructure. There was nothing for me at Water that couldn't wait. My next appointment was still half an hour away. My cigarettes were already in my hand. Twelve left of a pack broached fresh that morning.

'Nine,' I said, out loud. Keep count advised the brochure issued by Quit. Counting contributes to a sense of control.

With a control born of constant practice, I slipped the filter between my lips, made a small flame in the cup of my hand, lowered my head and inhaled. A violent inrush of smoke penetrated to the core of my metabolism. The tension which had been building since my arrival at the Old Treasury broke like the wall of a dam and a calming energy permeated my entire being. I exhaled slowly, tilting my head back and expelling a column of evanescent vapour into the lucid afternoon air. Then I inhaled again, less urgently this time, letting the calm spread within me. God Jesus, I needed help.

Beyond Sir Charles sat Parliament House, the nominal seat of power. Just down the hill were the office towers of the nation's biggest corporations. The companies whose directors had conceived the Olympic bid and raised the money to fund it. Ten million dollars, so far. A grubstake which the government had readily doubled. Small beer, considering the potential pay-off. A marketing bonanza for the corporate sector, re-election for the Labor Party. Someone had to win, so why not us?

Idle speculation. Returning Messieurs Benson & Hedges to my pocket, I set off towards St Vincent's Hospital. The afternoon was at its peak. The sun was spilling its warmth from the sky and the gutters were thick with fallen leaves, a rich yellow-brown, the colour of the finest Virginia tobacco. Once upon a time, council workers would have swept them into piles and burned them, filling the air with the smoky aroma of the season's passing, the exhaust fumes of time's speeding chariot. But not any more. Now, in accordance with Environment Protection Authority ordinances, the incineration of vegetable waste material within the greater metropolitan area was prohibited. The leaves would rot to a mucous mulch and be flushed down the stormwater drains into Port Phillip Bay.

Something similar would happen to me if I didn't start making some serious plans. So far, my career trajectory from union researcher to electorate official to ministerial adviser was less the product of driving ambition than an incremental advance through the ranks of the party. And look where it had led me. Cooling my heels in Water, writing policy analyses for a minister who rarely read them. Spending my working hours in the company of engineers, men whose idea of intellectual stimulation was to calculate the flow-through rate of a sewage tunnel.

Brian Morrison's little consultancy hardly represented a major opportunity, especially considering the task involved. And the idea that my decision might in some way affect the outcome of the bid was, of course, absurd. If anything was going to convince me to accept his proposition, it was the prospect of getting Red down from Sydney, if only for a couple of days.

My intimacy with Red was fading, eroded by the passage of time and the exigencies of absentee parenthood. Intimacy requires habit, the sharing of daily routines. For a time, when his mother was off pursuing her career, Red and I had lived a kind of shared bachelor existence, camping out amid our dirty dishes in the vestiges of the family home. I still missed that time, missed driving him to school, picking his socks off the floor, bickering. I also yearned for the paternal bit, the chance to offer advice and point directions. To swing a bit of fatherly lead.

Wendy would make the big decisions, that was inevitable and accepted. His school, his choice of friends, they were outside my power. But why should everything be that way? If Brian was fair dinkum, if the pay-off for my co-operation was that Red would get bumped to the prize possie in the fun run, then maybe his proposition was worth considering.

Prompted by such thoughts, my ruminations turned to my own childhood. When I was about eight or nine, my father was the licensee of the Carter's Arms Hotel in Northcote. Occasionally, Aborigines would come in off the street, one or two at a time, into the public bar. Not really black blacks like the ones in the Jolliffe cartoons in *Pix* and *Post* at the barber's shop; these were lighter skinned men. But you could see it straightaway, that touch of the tar brush. Half-castes, my father called them, the first time I ever heard the word.

'They make trouble,' Dad said, mouthing the orthodoxies of the age. 'It's not always their fault, but if you let the races mix you get trouble. Just look at America.' And so we did, on television almost every night. Snarling police dogs, night-sticks, water cannon. 'They can't handle the grog like normal people. It's their genes.'

But my father was, in his way, an advocate of equal rights. At least the right to get legless, regardless of race or creed. He wouldn't serve them over the bar but he'd sell them bottles at the back door. Royal Reserve Port, Seppelt's Solero Sherry, tawny muscat. 'Better that than aftershave,' he told the regulars. We didn't stock aftershave.

I felt sorry for them. And, in some obscure way, my pity gave me a sense of superiority. Not just towards the half-castes, poor unfortunates who couldn't help the way they were, but also towards my father. And particularly towards the regulars in the public bar, the men whose way of life Dad was defending. Barstool philosophers with scruples so finely honed they couldn't share as much as a slop-soaked bar towel and a threadbare carpet with men of a different hue.

These reflections got me as far as St Patrick's Cathedral, its steeples aimed at the heavens like a thicket of Gothic missiles. In the forecourt stood yet another statue: Daniel O'Connell, Irish patriot and political agitator. *The Liberator*, read the inscription chiselled into his plinth. Another trouble-maker from a race notoriously incapable of holding its liquor.

Unlike their dark-skinned cousins in more northerly parts of the country, Melbourne's Koories were a tiny, almost invisible minority. Four or five thousand souls in a population of nearly three million. And Ambrose Buchanan, for all his firebrand reputation, was not originally from these parts. So, even if he insisted on playing hard ball, it remained to be seen what local support he could muster. Especially if he went treading on the toes of the Talbots. For all of Brian's big-picture scenarios, an experienced operator like Buchanan would be unlikely to let rhetoric get in the way of a deal, if one was offered. I flicked my stub into a pile of leaves, half-hoping for a tongue of flame and a wisp of smoke.

Reaching Victoria Parade, I crossed to the private consulting rooms next to St Vincent's. The customary cluster of smokers lurked at the entrance. You had to admire them, puffing away, undeterred by the irony of the location. Admire them? Hell, I joined them. I still had ten minutes up my sleeve and might as well spend them exercising my lungs in the great outdoors.

There were four other smokers. A brace of gossiping nurses in plastic smocks and white running shoes, a tradesman in khaki overalls and a sales assistant from the hospital florist with a dusting of pollen on the sleeve of her chunky-knit sweater. She was no more than nineteen, young enough to know better. Gripping her cigarette fiercely between lacquered fingernails, she sucked at it hungrily with fleshy, over-glossed lips. A name tag was pinned to her bosom, the lettering too far away to read. Sharon, I bet myself. Or Krystal.

Patronising bastard, I thought, lighting up one of my own guilty pleasures. What makes you think you're so superior? Just as I lit up, a woman emerged from the building and joined us, energetically hunting in a black leather handbag that hung by a strap from her shoulder.

Somewhere in her mid-thirties, quite a nice temperature for the time of year, she was dressed in a professional but slightly haphazard way, as if she had better things to worry about than her grooming. Her dark maroon pants-suit complemented her tall, slim build, and her disc earrings exactly matched the gold buttons on her jacket, but she wore very little make-up and errant strands kept escaping from the tortoiseshell combs that pinned back her dark brown hair. Hospital administrator, I bet myself. Healthcare professional. Corporate Services. Strategic Planning. Something quite senior.

Lest I appeared to be staring, I averted my gaze. 'Ten,' I said to myself, lighting up.

Reflected in the plate-glass window of the florist shop, the woman continued to ferret in her bag. A look of mild exasperation furrowed her brow. She let the bag drop to her side and turned to leave. It seemed she hadn't checked her supplies before slipping outside for a smoke. Fortunately for her, there was a Good Samaritan in the vicinity. I cleared my throat, thumbed open my gaspers and extended the pack.

She hesitated for a moment. Then, with an apologetic little grimace, she took one. 'Pathetic, isn't it?' she said.

I shrugged. Sure it was. But it was why we were standing there, after all.

Close up, there was something vaguely outdoorsy about her. A slight tan. A hint of muscularity. A definite self-sufficiency. A girl, I could tell, who knew how to change a tyre. A bushwalker, perhaps? A Girl Guide, but one with a vice. The combination was appealing. I made a flame.

As she leaned forward to accept it, she held my gaze, making her own assessment. Her seal brown eyes had little crow's-feet in the corners. There was laughter in them. Not mockery but a wry, playful humour. They were grown-up eyes. I liked them. They'd seen a lot but they didn't give much away. I could've looked into them for a long, long time.

She kissed three little puffs out of her cigarette, just enough to get it burning. She wore, I noticed, no wedding ring. Not that I had any particular reason to notice, but there you are. Nodding thanks, she tucked one of those nomadic strands behind her ear and took a step backwards. Half-turned towards the street, her stance was both casual and slightly self-conscious.

They say you can read a woman by the way she smokes a cigarette. I could read this one like a book. It was called *Woman Smoking a Cigarette*. I wanted to say something, but didn't know what. Certainly nothing banal or obvious or gormless. Nothing that might prematurely reveal my true nature.

A steady tide of pedestrians streamed past, entering and leaving the hospital. The pregnant women and children with plaster-encased limbs weren't so bad, but when a skeletal old geezer with an intercom in his thorax wheezed past in a walking-frame, moving at the speed of an emphysemic snail, I tracked his progress with fascinated revulsion.

Turning to share this cautionary vision with my fellow desperado, she of the Dunhill-coloured hiking suit, I found that I had left my run too late. She was already stubbing her half-smoked cigarette in a planter box of sand. With a brisk nod in my general direction, she hurried into the building.

The nurses and the blokes in overalls, too, were extinguishing themselves and drifting back to duty. So Sharon and I stood there alone, smoking our cigarettes and thinking our thoughts. I can't vouch for Sharon, but I was thinking about love. It was a mystery I'd been contemplating for quite some time.

For most of the previous year I'd been investing my emotional reserves and bodily fluids in what had turned out to be a losing proposition. Claire was my first serious relationship since the end of my marriage, an apparently ideal match who arrived in my life complete with a large libido, a small business and a four-year-old daughter. And when her ex-husband came knocking on the door, wanting to see little Gracie, I encouraged such visits. How could I do otherwise? I, too, was an access father, snatching time with my child only when the opportunity arose and his mother acquiesced.

Claire, however, acquiesced to more than just parental access. Full conjugal relations, it transpired, were also resumed. 'It just sort of happened,' she told me, like that explained everything.

Single again, I was no longer sure who I missed the most, the mother or the daughter. Gracie at least had the sensitivity to shed a tear when I said goodbye. Claire merely congratulated me on how well I was taking it.

So well did I take it that within three months my cigarette consumption had gone through the roof and all my trousers had gone tight around the waist.

Burying my butt in the mass grave, I headed inside. Even as I turned to go, another smoker was taking my place. We brave few, sentries at mortality's gate. As I waited for the lift, I scanned the directory of tenants, a *memento mori* in moveable plastic letters. Gastroenterologists. Urologists. Neuro-ophthalmologists. Colorectal surgeons. A cardiothoracic specialist. I didn't like the sound of that one.

Telling myself I was doing the right thing, I boarded the lift and pressed the button for the ninth floor. Nine. The same number as my total remaining cigarettes.

Dr Bernard Manne, although described on the honour-roll downstairs as a consultant physician, was essentially a general practitioner. The fact that his surgery was located in this hotbed of specialisation was a matter of convenience rather than a claim to professional eminence. Most of Bernie's regular patients worked, like me, in the immediate area and he had built up a lucrative little practice ministering to our many and varied medical needs.

Apart from the usual collection of dog-eared *National Geographic*s and long-defunct *Business Weekly*s, I found the waiting room empty. 'Go right in,' said the receptionist. 'The doctor is waiting.'

Except the doctor wasn't Doctor Manne. It wasn't any kind of man at all, in fact. It was the neglectful smoker from downstairs. She was sitting at Bernie's desk, scanning a file as though looking for something incriminating. Hello, I thought, they've caught up with Bernie at last.

I cleared my throat in the open doorway and the woman looked my way. As she did so, her face broke out in a smile that was both totally spontaneous and utterly infectious. She had a wide, generous mouth and, now that I could see them more clearly, it occurred to me that those creases at the edges of her eyes were sneaky little laugh lines. She recognised me from downstairs but didn't say so.

'Mr Whelan?' she said.

I didn't deny it.

She stood up and stuck out her hand. 'I'm Phillipa Verstak. I'm looking after the practice until Dr Manne has recovered.' Her voice was quiet but authoritative, as though she was accustomed to dealing with your more diffident category of patient.

'Verstak?' I said. A name from my childhood. 'Any relation?' To Tanya Verstak, Miss Australia 1961, famous at the time as the first New Australian to win the title. White Russian, we were told. Whatever that meant.

Dr Phillipa Verstak merely gave a polite shake of her head. It was an obvious question, one she had probably been asked all her life.

Her grip was firm and warm. As I took it, I found myself glancing surreptitiously at her other hand. She still wasn't wearing a wedding ring. Meaning that she hadn't got married in the lift on the way upstairs. Or perhaps that she found a ring inconvenient during certain sorts of medical procedures. Or meaning nothing at all. She probably had a mature and ongoing commitment to a colorectal ophthal-mologist with whom she resided in a mock-Tudor home in

Doncaster with their 3.4 children. If so, he was a cheapskate. Apart from the earrings, she wore no jewellery at all.

'Recovered?' I said. Bernie had given me my annual grease-and-oil change only the previous week. He'd just come back from a Stress Management conference in Noumea and was glowing with the kind of well-being that only comes from five days of tax-deductible wind-surfing.

'He was kicked by a horse.' She'd repinned her hair but a strand had fought its way loose, unnoticed. I wanted to reach over and tuck it behind her ear.

'Not Bijou Deluxe?' I pointed to the framed thoroughbred hanging among Bernie's diplomas and degrees.

Bernie owned Bijou Deluxe in a consortium with three Chinese dental technicians, a copyright lawyer and the shelf company of a master builder. He'd tried to sign me up, rhapsodising from behind the pile of bloodstock gazettes that littered his desk. Twenty grand, plus stabling and training. 'Three wins and two places in seven starts,' he said. 'You'll never regret it.' And nor did I. I passed instead. So did every other horse that Bijou Deluxe subsequently raced.

'I didn't ask its name,' she said. 'All I know is that Dr Manne got a bit too close in the mounting enclosure and his jaw will be wired for the next few weeks. The locum service asked me to stand in for him. Of course, if you'd rather wait until he returns…'

There was no question of that. A team of Clydesdales couldn't have dragged me away.

'I'm sure I'll be safe in your hands,' I said, and lowered myself into the patient's chair.

Dr Verstak sat in Bernie's chair with the big window behind. It faced back towards the city, giving out onto the old watchtower of the Eastern Hill fire station. Any moment, bells would sound and men in red braces would slide down a brass pole, rush across the road and douse my burning desire with buckets of water. 'What seems to be the problem?' she said.

'I'm just here to pick something up,' I said. 'Bernie said to drop by today.' My file was in clear view on the desk. It was the one she'd been reading when I came in. A snatched smoke and a quick bone-up just before the patient arrives. That's why they call it medical practice. I indicated the file. 'Take your time.'

I watched her scan the last page, then smile her wry smile. 'I see that Dr Manne has been treating you for nicotine addiction.'

'Harsh words,' I said. 'From a fellow junkie.'

'According to this,' she said, not looking up. 'You're on twenty-five a day. I only smoke four a day.'

The woman was in deep denial. A four-a-day smoker relishes the special moment. A four-a-day smoker does not stand in a draughty vestibule, tossing off a quick puff. Botting from strangers. Still, who was I to quibble?

'You're doing better than I am,' I said. 'But I must say it's unusual to find a doctor who smokes.'

'Physician heal thyself and all that,' she said, looking up now. 'Doesn't do much for my credibility, does it?'

'On the contrary,' I said. 'I find it refreshing. It probably gives you a more sympathetic appreciation of the patient's situation.'

'Perhaps,' she said, putting a little professional distance between us. 'But we're not here to talk about me, are we?'

'No, of course not,' I agreed. 'How did you start? I mean being aware of the risks and all.'

'You mean that I should've known better?' She sighed, resigned to my curiosity. I'd bought the right to ask, after all. Paid for it with a Benson & Hedges. 'By now, we all should know better.'

'Humour me,' I said. 'I'm interested.' I was interested, all right, but cigarettes weren't the half of it.

She let out a little exasperated sigh, yet I wasn't entirely convinced that she didn't mind the chance to talk about herself. 'I started at university. All those late nights, burning the midnight oil. Actually, I think cigarettes really did help. After I graduated, I didn't smoke for ten years. I started again last New Year's Eve.'

I nodded knowingly. 'A few convivials, your guard goes down.'

'Mortar attack, actually,' she said. 'I thought I was about to die, so I wasn't too concerned about the long-term effects.'

'Mortar attack!' I reeled back in mock horror, assuming she was joking. 'I heard things can get pretty hairy at Western Hospital, but I had no idea it was that wild.' Western was in Footscray. Little Saigon.

'Phnom Penh, actually.' She could see the humour in it, but she hadn't been joking. 'I've been working there for the past nine months. Community Aid Abroad. I've only been back a couple of weeks.'

That explained the tan and the slight otherworldliness. Our esteemed Foreign Minister had recently taken a break from his full-time job of brown-nosing the Indonesian military to bestow his peace-making skills on benighted Cambodia. Phillipa's job there, I assumed, was part of the attendant aid effort.

'Well you've got the best excuse for backsliding I've ever

heard,' I said. 'It must have been fascinating. Not the mortar attack. The whole experience. Are you going back?'

Take me with you, I thought. After twenty years in the Australian Labor Party, mine-infested paddy-fields didn't frighten me. Not with Dr Daktari at my side, borrowing my cigarettes.

'Haven't decided yet.' She tucked the loose strand of hair back and turned again to my file, terminating the subject. 'I see Dr Manne referred you to an acupuncturist.'

'Professor Wu,' I said. 'From Wuhan. It worked fine for three months. When I started again, I went straight to a pack a day.'

'And you tried the ear-clip?'

'Decided I preferred lung cancer to the ribbing I got at work.'

'No luck with the hypnotism? Dr Karpal gets very good results, I understand.'

'High recidivism rate. But I lasted nearly a year.'

'Nicotine gum?'

'Made everything taste disgusting.'

'Yes. It does, doesn't it?'

As we worked our way through my back-catalogue of failed experiments, I got the distinct impression that her interest was not entirely abstract. Cure-swapping is one of the principal by-products of cigarette smoking. 'Transcendental meditation. Cold turkey. Weekend retreats. Herbal mouthwash,' I said. 'You name it, I've tried it. Everything except Smokers Anonymous. I may be desperate and despicable, but I haven't entirely lost my self-respect.'

'Let's hope we have more success this time,' she said. The medical first-person plural.

'Let's. Should I take my clothes off now?'

'Thanks for the offer,' she said. 'But this is something you can do by yourself. Be sure to read the instructions very carefully first.' She slid open a drawer and took out a small cardboard container.

Nicotine patches. Bernie's latest weapon in his war against my recalcitrant metabolism. Cuts out the middleman, he said. Sends the poison directly to the brain where it's needed, reduces the bitumen in the lungs and assists the addict to break the cigarette habit. On top of which, if I volunteered as a guinea pig for the trial program, I'd get them for free. She handed me the box.

'Nicabate,' I read. 'Rate-Controlled Nicotine Patches. Bit wimpy, isn't it? Shouldn't it be something like Decimate or Niceradicate?'

'Nick Off,' she suggested.

'So where do I stick them?'

She ignored that one. 'The dose has been calculated to match your current tolerance level, so it's very important that you don't smoke while wearing the patches. You should be particularly wary of social situations where you might unconsciously accept an offered cigarette.'

'Such as mortar attacks,' I suggested. 'Or while having a drink after work.'

'Yes, exactly.'

'At Mietta's, for example.'

Mietta's was a watering hole in the city. The place to be seen. A place of timeless elegance and ten-dollar aperitifs. The sort of joint where corporate art advisers drank Campari sodas with stockbrokers at one table while a rising soprano displayed her coloratura to the Argentine consul-general at the next. I mentioned it as a provocation, to get a rise. Some of those Community Aid Abroad people had a touch of the hairshirt about them.

'What's wrong with Mietta's?' The woman was being deliberately obtuse. It was driving me wild.

'Ever been there?'

'Of course,' she said primly. 'Makes a change from the Irish Rover in Phnom Penh.'

She rose to her feet, signalling the end of the consultation. 'Please call me if you experience any difficulties. I'd appreciate you letting me know how you get on. Side effects and so on.'

'Side effects?' I said. Bernie hadn't said anything about side effects.

'Disturbed sleep patterns. Headaches. Mild agitation. An itch.'

The itch I already had. Disturbed sleep patterns I could only hope for. 'Headaches and agitation,' I said. 'Sounds like my job.'

'Oh?' She opened the door. 'What kind of work do you do?'

I sucked in my stomach. 'Special consultant to the Olympic bid,' I said. It wasn't exactly brain surgery but it sounded a lot sexier than plumber's apprentice.

As I slipped the Nicabate box into my pocket, my fingers closed around the packet of Benson & Hedges. 'Eleven,' said a voice in my head.

The phone started ringing at eight on Saturday morning, dragging me from the arms of anaesthesia with the voice of an insistent stranger.

'Are you the yellow 1979 Daihatsu Charade auto hatch-back with six months registration?'

'Huh?'

'The one in the paper?'

'Oh, that.' Earlier in the week, I'd booked an advertisement for the Saturday car classifieds. 'I need some work,' I yawned. I swung my feet over the edge of the bed and rubbed the sleep from my eyes. 'I mean *it* needs some work.'

A fair bit, really. The diff had gone, the transmission was slipping, the brakes were soft, one of the tail-lights was kaput and the finish was showing the general ill-effects of long-term on-street parking. But I wasn't telling him that, whoever he was. '$4990,' I said. The market price. 'Or nearest offer. Available for inspection all day.'

He took my address and said he might drop round later. Much later, I hoped. I lay back down and pulled up the bedclothes. The phone rang again. 'Are you the yellow Daihatsu Charade…?'

By nine o'clock, I'd fielded six calls. Despairing of a lie-in, I got up and cooked myself breakfast. Cooked as in toasted. Two slices, dry. An orange juice and a serve of hi-fibre lo-taste cereal. Each bowl had more roughage than a coir doormat. In celebration of the weekend, I spoiled myself and demolished two of them. Tea without milk.

Saturday and Sunday were lay-days on the personal-training front. Apart from lugging the papers home from the corner store, my only form of weekend exercise was a bit of domestic horticulture. And after I'd gone out into the courtyard and fertilised the lemon tree, even that was taken care of.

There was no lawn to mow, no hedge to trim, no path to sweep. Apart from the brick-paved courtyard, large enough only for my well-tended gin-and-tonic tree and a cast-iron patio setting, there was no garden at all. Nor was there anything else requiring more maintenance than could be done with a kitchen knife and a wet rag.

Handy I was not. A lesson it had taken me seven years to learn, at the cost of many a bruised thumb and bent nail. When Wendy and I went our separate ways, the first thing I did was sell our renovator's-opportunity in West Brunswick and move back to already renovated Fitzroy. A modest two-bedroom terrace in a quiet little street at the city end of Brunswick Street, all for a measly hundred and fifty grand.

Worth ten grand less since the real estate market hit an iceberg and sank. But as long as I wasn't planning on moving house, and still had a job that let me keep up the payments, the bank and I were quite content with it.

With breakfast eaten, the papers read, and the first of my potential buyers yet to arrive, I lit a cigarette and rang Wendy. *Choose the right psychological moment to start*, instructed the brochure in the pack of Nicabate patches. *Pick a day when you are less likely to be stressed.* Any day I was required to speak with Wendy definitely did not fulfil that criterion.

I'd rung her the previous evening but found only the answering machine. As a senior corporate executive and the wife of a prominent Sydney lawyer, she obviously had better things to do with her time than return her ex-husband's messages. Even if she did get a substantial staff discount on the cost of the call. 'What is it this time?' she said.

Four years we'd been divorced, no fault all round. Don't get me started.

I told her about Brian Morrison's offer. Not the consultancy bit, just the part about Red presenting the torch to the IOC Evaluation Commission. It was short notice, I knew, but what did she think? Red could fly down on Thursday, do the relay bit, stay on for the weekend. He'd miss out on school, I admitted, but going absent for a couple of days in the sixth grade wasn't going to ruin his chances at a Rhodes Scholarship. Assuming, of course, that he wanted to come.

'He won't want to stay the weekend,' Wendy said. 'He'd miss his rugby game. And that might affect his chances of selection for the state side.'

'Red's playing rugby?'

He'd been living in Sydney for a while, so I should've been prepared for this. Still, it was a disturbing development. My little boy, seduced from his roots, wallowing like a brute in the mud, his nose broken, his head up the arse of some future detective-sergeant in the NSW drug squad.

'Union, of course,' said Wendy. 'Not League.' The distinction was too fine for me. Something about one being a game for thugs played by gentlemen and vice versa. But it got worse. 'Richard thinks Red shows real promise.' Richard was the new husband, a Crown prosecutor with an income in the high six figures, a yacht at the Rushcutters Bay marina and considerably more influence than I had on my son's life. 'He's been very encouraging.'

'So what happened to the cult of the warrior?' I said. 'Changed your tune about the rituals of male bonding?'

'Sport has been very good for Red's self-esteem,' she said. 'Richard doesn't think we should stand in the boy's way.'

'Especially not if he's running through the Hyatt ballroom with a flaming torch in his hand,' I said. 'Can I talk to him?'

She'd have him ring me, she said, when he got home from the junior-league game. But, in principle, she had no objection if he wanted to fly down for a night or two. 'Did Brian Morrison say anything about accommodation?'

'I didn't ask,' I said. 'I assumed he'd stay here.'

'With you blowing smoke all over him?'

'I've given up,' I said, exhaling away from the phone. 'I'm on the patches.' Or would be by Wednesday.

'Bit of a dump, isn't it?' she sniffed.

The inference was unwarranted. Red's Melbourne digs may have lacked the water views of his new stepfather's semi-detached at Darling Point, but they were perfectly adequate to his needs. Red had, in fact, been a prime consideration when I bought the house. He had a room of his own and, on the three or four occasions a year his mother's schedule permitted Red to stay with his father in Melbourne, he found all of his familiar things waiting for him.

Okay, so he'd outgrown the Masters of the Universe doona cover and no longer played with Skeletor and the other inhabitants of Castle Greyskull. But the movie posters from the video rental store were reasonably up-to-date, his skateboard was in perfect working condition and several pairs of clean socks were standing by if required. And, if he climbed onto the window sill and held his head at the right angle, he could see right over the neighbouring rooftops as far as the high-rise Housing Commission flats on the other side of Brunswick Street.

The rest of the house, too, wasn't exactly a slum. Luxurious, even, if you counted the adjustable shower nozzle and the microwave oven. The mortgage was certainly top-class and managed to hoover up a fair whack of my salary, what was left after I shipped four hundred dollars a month north for child support. Not that I regretted a penny of it. It probably paid for the upkeep on Wendy and Richard's new in-ground pool, thereby preventing Red getting chlorine poisoning.

'Ask him to call me, please,' I said to her. 'If he wants to do it, I need to confirm with Brian Morrison asap.' As soon as Wendy rang off, the first of my customers arrived.

The Daihatsu, I'd decided, was not worth the expense of fixing. The arithmetic just didn't add up. More often than not, I trammed it or walked to work. Even with a permit, finding a parking spot was practically impossible. Registration, insurance, repairs, tickets. All up, for a man in my situation, car ownership was a losing proposition. Cab vouchers and an occasional dip in the departmental car-pool would, I'd decided, see to my transport needs. Selling the Daihatsu would be a mutually beneficial congruence of private and public policy.

Three weeks earlier, I'd put a handwritten For Sale notice on the board in the staff lunchroom at Water Supply, and stuck up photocopies around the office. The only expression of interest had come from the shop steward in Faults & Emergencies. He took my details and said he'd ring to arrange an inspection time but never called back. Perhaps I'd have more luck with my ad in the newspaper.

My first callers were a young couple with a newborn baby, looking for a second car so she could take the little mite to the baby health centre while hubby was at work. She was exhausted and the two of them looked like they didn't have two bob to rub together. They stared blankly under the hood, whispered to each other about the broken tail-light and asked vague questions about the mileage. When they left without asking for a test-drive, I was relieved.

Invidious business, selling a car privately. Even before I'd begun, I was having second thoughts.

'Watch the brakes,' I warned the next caller, a young buck in skin-tight stonewash. I had him pegged as a spotter for a dealer, but that didn't stop me talking down the merchandise. He left the keys to his own car in lieu and took the Charade for a quick burn around the block.

'The shockers are shot,' he said on his return. 'Four grand. Take it or leave it.' I may have lacked the killer instinct of a true used-car salesman, but I wasn't that much of a soft touch. I left it.

The rest of the day was spent fielding a steady but tepid stream of shoppers. Fathers with teenage daughters. Wary migrants. First-car buyers on a budget. More spotters. Every time it took off on a test-drive, I broke out in a mild sweat and braced myself for the distant sound of impact.

In between, I pottered around the house, dusting Red's room and listening to the football on the radio. In preparation for *Quit Day*, as the Nicabate brochure referred to it, I cleared away all the ashtrays. More saucers than ashtrays, really. The real ashtrays had been disposed of long ago. As a method of fortifying the intent to give up cigarettes, ashtray removal was, in my experience, far from foolproof.

Nor was the news on the football front encouraging. Fitzroy started behind and stayed that way all day, thrashed by Melbourne out at VFL Park. No joy for Denis, either. The Swans were demolished in the third quarter by a resurgent St Kilda. Not even the home-ground advantage helped.

By five o'clock, I'd had seven inspections, four test-drives and no sale. With each new caller, I felt worse. Not only had I failed to make a sale, I felt like a huckster attempting to palm off an agglomeration of mechanical deficiencies as a functioning automobile. First thing the next morning, I decided, I would shop it around the caryards. The return would be five hundred dollars lower but I'd sleep easier at night. It wasn't as if I really needed the money, after all. Wasn't I about to pick up an easy five grand, courtesy of Brian Morrison and the MOB?

That's when my final caller turned up. A nondescript, rather taciturn bloke with a brown cardigan and a stammer. Undeterred by the vehicle's catalogue of deficiencies, he insisted that he was s-still interested, s-subject to a t-test-drive.

Which he t-took, leaving a single key on a leather plait. 'It's the g-green Camimirra at the end of the s-street,' he said and burbled off in the Charade.

I put on a Roy Orbison album and ironed some shirts and, after twenty minutes, began to w-wonder just how f-far my potential buyer had gone. Perhaps he'd hit a mechanical snag. Or another vehicle. When he hadn't returned in three-quarters of an hour, I started to get toey. I needed cigarettes anyway, so I left a note and wandered down to Brunswick Street.

A few hundred metres down the hill, it was all cafes and patisseries and bookshops. Up my end, close to the housing estate, the tone was still defiantly downmarket. Smelly derelicts in crap-encrusted overcoats dozed on the tram stop outside the Little Sisters of the Poor. The drone of post-match commentary leaked from the Rob Roy Hotel. The crusty whiff of old souvlaki hung in the air. Across the road, at the foot of the flats, Chinese fathers pushed little girls in ornate chiffon dresses on the swings in the playground and turbo-heads with soapy forearms washed their GT-XLs in the carpark.

Cars crawled past anonymously or throbbed by with the windows down and the stereo up. But none of them was a butter yellow Daihatsu Charade with a busted tail-light, *Any Reasonable Offer Considered*. I bought cigarettes at the Asian grocery, lit up in the odour of sesame oil and overripe jackfruit, and went back home.

Nobody was waiting, so I took the key on the leather plait down to the green Camira parked at the end of the street. It was a poor fit and, as I jiggled in the lock, a bloke opened the door of the nearest house. 'Right there, are you, mate?' he said, and I knew immediately that I'd been dudded. That

Mr Stammers had given me a useless key in exchange for my 1979 Japanese hatchback with 67,000 on the clock and a bald spare tyre.

Hardly worth his trouble, really, but not a bad deal from my point of view, considering the piece of shit was fully insured for a replacement value of five grand. If it stayed stolen, was chopped up for spare parts or pushed off a cliff in the Wombat State Forest, I'd be laughing.

The Fitzroy cop shop was near the flats, a cream brick attachment at the rear of the town hall. I waited another hour, then went over and reported my tragic loss. The duty officer, a buzz-cut lug fresh from the academy, gave me some superfluous advice and a piece of paper for the insurance company. It was a story that got me a good laugh at Faye and Leo's dinner party that night.

Faye and Leo were neighbours who lived in a big terrace on the other side of my back lane. Their son Tarquin was the same age as Red, and the two boys had been friends since back when they were in kindergarten together. Faye was a gourmet cook and an inveterate matchmaker. At seven-thirty, I dug up a bottle of Mount Ida shiraz, nicked across the lane and knocked on her back door.

'Only the lonely,' I hummed, knocking on the back door. 'Dum, dum, dum, dewy, dum, dum.'

This time, Faye was well wide of the mark. Wide being the operative word. Her candidate was a generously proportioned children's book illustrator with a laugh like a flock of seagulls being sucked backwards into the engine of a jumbo jet. A real tryer, she insisted on reading my palm over the poached pears and praline parfait. I had, she said, a particularly pronounced love-line. When I finally succeeded in retrieving my hand, I suggested we all walk down to the tapas bars in Johnston Street for a nightcap. Once there, I managed to flee unnoticed by slipping off the end of the conga line during a Gypsy Kings number.

Red rang on Sunday morning, gung-ho for the torch relay. 'All the other kids at Little Aths are spewing,' he said.

Wendy came on the line. 'I've decided to come down, too,' she said. 'I'm due to touch base with the Melbourne office anyway.' Lucky them. 'And Brian Morrison says the MOB will pay for a suite at the Hyatt.'

'You've spoken to Brian?'

'I was talking to Sandra on the phone and Brian just happened to be there.' The woman's presumption was unbelievable. A long time ago she presumed to be my wife. 'He agrees that the hotel is more convenient from a press-availability point of view. And I thought it'd be a bit of a treat for Red. Something different.' From his room at his father's house, for example.

'But...' The word froze on my lips and I conceded defeat.

It would've been petulant to do otherwise. She was right about the hotel being an adventure for the kid. Up there on the sixteenth floor, jumping on the beds, ordering room service, souveniring the Do Not Disturb sign, leaving wet towels on the bathroom floor. Rock'n'roll heaven. If I was Red, I knew what I'd prefer.

'We'll come down Wednesday so Red can visit his grand-parents. He hasn't seen them all year. Richard would like to come, too. But he's got a big case.'

As distinct from a small penis.

First thing Monday morning I rang Automotive & General and explained my predicament.

A form could be mailed to me, I was informed in the cheeseparing tones characteristic of the insurance industry, but my claim would be processed only after the standard thirty-day waiting period applicable in auto-theft cases. Full details of which could be found on my policy document. If I happened to have a microscope handy. In the meantime, should I require the use of a vehicle, interim arrangements could possibly be made, subject to approval by an assessor. Shoot me the form, I said. Hold the assessor. The exercise will do me good.

And so it did, although the most auspicious moment to commence the patch cure had not yet arrived. There were certain formalities to be transacted before I donned the cloak and dagger of MOB's Secret Emissary to the Renegade

Native. The small matter of obtaining the approval of my employer. The man who paid my wages, Angelo Agnelli.

I set off through the mild morning sunshine and walked up the hill past the flats and St Patrick's to the rear entrance of Parliament House. On the way, I detoured via the hospital consulting rooms, hoping for an accidental encounter with the refreshingly candid Dr Phillipa Verstak. Thoughts of her had come to me unbidden on more than one occasion during the weekend and I was disappointed not to find her among the puffers at the portal.

I did, however, find Angelo Agnelli. He was in his parliamentary lair, one of a row of utilitarian, glass-walled cubicles in the vaulted catacombs beneath the Legislative Council. He'd returned from the Canberra confabulation on the weekend, newly conversant with progress on the Perth to Darwin rail link and plans to irrigate the Simpson Desert with overflow from the Tasmanian glacial thaw. Feet on the wood-veneer desk, he was refreshing his memory on a money bill he was about to propel through the Upper House on behalf of the Treasurer.

'As I understand it,' he yawned, displaying his bridgework and the damp splotches in the armpits of his shirt. 'We put the state debt on Visa, which we then pay off using our Mastercard.'

After two terms in office, Angelo's heart was no longer in it. The first flush of his reforming zeal had generated a certain pale incandescence but now even that feeble light was dimming, exhausted by the recognition that his larger ambitions would remain unrealised. He would, he had belatedly come to understand, never be Attorney-General. At forty-five, Angelo was a man with a fluorescent future behind him.

Even his boyish good looks were beginning to go. With remarkable speed, his chubby cheeks had hit the downhill slope to jowldom and his well-cultivated bella figura was beginning to take on the faded aspect of a run-down resort hotel. Angelo, I didn't doubt, remained firmly on the side of the angels but the only song the heavenly host had been singing in his ear lately was the current balance on his parliamentary superannuation.

'Godfather,' I said. 'I've had an offer you can't refuse.'

He leaned back and folded his hands over his paunch. 'It's this fucking fitness jag you're on,' he said. 'Now you've gone and got yourself drafted into the Woeful McKenzie All Stars.'

'Woeful's already spoken to you?' My decision, apparently, was a foregone conclusion.

'Told me at caucus this morning.' Angelo and Woeful were factional allies, each reliant on the other for his place in Cabinet. 'Woeful McKenzie's a fucking idiot. And if the Olympic bid needs your help, we must be in deep shit. But I've told Woeful he can have you for a week. Any longer and he'll have to start paying you out of his own budget.'

'A week'll do it,' I said. Three days, tops.

Ange stood up, took his jacket off the back of his chair and handed it to me. 'What's happening with the union negotiations?'

'Same as usual,' I said, helping him into his jacket. 'SFA. Nothing the bureaucrats can't handle. The Missos are all talk, anyway.'

He did up his button and shot his cuffs. Mr Minister. 'Play your cards right with this one, you might do yourself a bit of good with Hugh Knowles & Co.' Pausing briefly on his way out the door, he laid a fatherly hand on my shoulder. 'Time you were thinking about the future, Murray.'

With that worryingly ambiguous advice ringing in my ears, I strolled the short distance to the Old Treasury Building, soaking up the sunshine and a couple of cubic metres of carcinogenic vapour. General Gordon looked down disapprovingly. What would he know? He was dead.

Brian Morrison's base of operations was on the top floor, up where the heritage carpeting ran out and the real work got done. It was less an office than a command centre, a bunker with a view. A dozen or so grey metal desks squeezed into the room. The paintwork was peeling and the lights hung by chains from the ceiling. Piles of press releases and media kits covered every surface, computer consoles glowed, phones rang and staff bustled. With the exception of Brian, they were all female. But then Brian was always a firm believer in getting the best man for the job, especially if he was in charge.

The man himself was standing at a white-board, the Darth Vader of Community Relations, mapping a media schedule with a woman I recognised as the former political roundsperson for the *Sun*. Blu-tacked to the wall behind them were front-page stories on the progress of the bid. THUMBS UP FROM IOC BOSS, read one, illustrated by a flattering photograph of Juan Antonio Samaranch. In little more than a year, this ancient gnomic Catalan had become a household name to Melburnians, his every utterance divined for evidence of our city's Olympic prospects. The arrival of any of his IOC associates in town was reported with all the solemnity of a papal visit.

Covering another wall was a large-scale map of the eastern seaboard on which the course of the torch relay was traced in thick red marker pen. A cardboard arrow captioned 'Today' pointed to a spot on the Princes Highway halfway between Eden and Disaster Bay.

'Murray,' cried Brian, as if my arrival was a complete surprise. 'Great news, mate. It's all fixed.'

Rummaging briefly among the paperwork littering one of the desks, he thrust a document into my hand. The torch-relay schedule for the following Thursday. Redmond Whelan, 8 p.m., Hyatt Hotel ballroom. Brian instantly replaced it with my letter of agreement, ready for signature. It was one of those vague 'duties as agreed' deals, about as legally binding as the fine print on a chewing-gum wrapper. I signed, using Brian's gold-nibbed Mont Blanc. He hastily pocketed the paper and handed me an engraved entree card.

In Honour of the Visit of IOC Evaluation Commissioners
Pascal Abdoulaye, Kim U-ee and Stansislas Dziczkowszczak,
the Board of the MOB invites
MURRAY WHELAN AND GUEST
to Attend a Gala Dinner
at the Savoy Ballroom, Hyatt-on-Collins,
Thursday 26 April, 1990 at 7:30 p.m. RSVP.

'Two hundred dollars per,' he said. 'I've arranged for it to be deducted from your fee.'

From now on, Brian instructed, I was to liaise directly with Denis Dogherty. As for Ambrose Buchanan, Brian suggested we meet informally. Officially, Buchanan was Visiting Lecturer in Identity and Ideology in the Faculty of Dispossession and Displacement at Footscray Institute of Technology. But he was only ever on campus on Fridays. In the meantime, he could be found at the Stars Cafe in Gertrude Street, Fitzroy, around about lunchtime.

'Welcome aboard, then,' he concluded. 'We're relying on you.' The beeper on his belt began to vibrate and the mobile phone in his pocket started ringing. Two frighteningly efficient-looking women hovered peripherally with items to be actioned.

'Find your own way out, can you?' Brian said.

As I reached the ground-floor hallway, a tottering aristo-crat was being feted into the exhibition room by an entourage of suits. '*Par ici, Monsieur,*' I heard someone say. '*S'il vous plait.*' As the doors closed behind them, a second voice spoke. '*Manuyangka nyiyarlangurlu, jarntungku marda, yankirrirli…*'

It sounded pretty convincing to me. But then I don't speak French.

Lunchtime, by any reasonable estimate, was still at least an hour away. I lit a cigarette and headed for the City Club. After pigging out at Faye's matchmaking dinner and sleeping most of Sunday, I was in need of a solid work-out.

I did a double round of sets on the super circuit, jogged a couple of kilometres on the treadmill and was warming down when Holly Deloite came and stood beside the bike. She was wearing shorts and a polo top with a penguin stitched on the pocket. Even her knees looked fit. 'Um,' she said, sheepishly. 'Sorry about the other day.'

'Magilla Gorilla?' I exhaled, knees pumping, thirty-seven seconds left on the clock, t-shirt plastered to me like a wet Kleenex.

She made a face. 'I used to go out with the guy, can you believe it? His name's Steve Radeski. He worked downstairs at the nightclub. You know, Typhoon. Haven't seen him for ages, then he starts turning up here, pestering me. Wants me to go out with him again. I mean, as if.'

All her sentences seemed to end on a rising note. A phonetic question mark which compelled a response. Which I was in no position to offer. Merely breathing was difficult enough.

'He's a jerk,' she said, shaking her head in disbelief. That she'd ever got involved with him, I supposed. 'And he's getting to be a real pain in the butt. If he keeps coming back, he'll get me fired. Garth reckons he frightens the clients.'

I dismounted, calves trembling, thighs in spasm. Hoping I wouldn't pass out from the sudden rush of oxygen, I sucked in a lungful of air, flexed my arms, and made muscle. 'If he hassles you again, bay-bee,' I exhaled. 'He'll have me to deal with.'

'Gee, that's a relief,' she grinned. A thought crossed her mind, leaving its footprints on her forehead. 'Um,' she said. 'You got a car?'

'Uh-huh.' Being so easily gulled out of my motor, I'd decided, didn't show me in my best light. And, if you don't have a car, people think you're a crank. 'Why?'

Holly smiled again and the crease in her brow went away. 'Just wondering,' she said. 'Need a fresh towel or anything?'

While I changed back into my Hugo Boss, I considered dashing home and slipping into something a little more informal for my meeting with Ambrose. But there was enough bullshit flying around already. Might as well play the part. Besides which, it was already one' o'clock. Time to rock. I caught a Number 11 tram in Collins Street, rode past St Pat's and St Vincent's and was in Fitzroy in less than ten minutes, my hair still wet from the shower.

The flats rose a sheer twenty storeys into the cirrus-streaked sky, throwing a shadow across Gertrude Street. I walked in the shade cast by a row of nineteenth-century buildings, survivors of the slum clearances of the 1950s that had threatened half of Fitzroy with demolition in the name of progress and clean living.

Past the Champion Hotel, a bloodhouse of the more traditional kind. Lingerie Lunches, said the hand-painted sign on the tinted-glass window. Topless Barmaids. Past the Lebanese chicken bar where the chickens were rumoured to come with special herbs for those who knew the password. Past the Tai Lai Unisex hair salon and the Commonwealth Bank, filled with single mothers waiting to cash their pension cheques. Past the Aboriginal Health Service, formerly the inner-metro clap clinic, with its red, black and yellow facade and its perpetual gaggle of Koories on the front steps.

Long ago, long before the Greek man came, all this land belonged to the black man. Now he had claimed it again. Apart from the Macedonians, the Serbs, the Cambodians, the Ethiopians and the Tongans, this end of Gertrude Street was an exclusively Aboriginal precinct. Darktown, all half a block of it.

The Stars Cafe was a high-ceilinged, linoleum-floored corner room with a self-service race and pine tables, part of a mouldering row of ornately decorated Victorian terraces. Presuming such places still existed, it might have been the cafeteria at a country railway station.

A haze of steam rose from a bain-marie, misting the windows and carrying with it the aroma of vegetable water and baked meat. Two women in aprons stood beside a tea urn, buttering bread in the roar of the dishwashing machine surging through the servery hatch from the kitchen. The place was almost full, thick with the rhubarb of conversation and the clatter of crockery. Aboriginality lay lightly dusted across the clientele, as unmistakable as a pinch of cinnamon.

I recognised Ambrose Buchanan immediately. It wasn't hard. He was the darkest man in the room. His beard was a little longer than in the video, the flecks of white more pronounced, but he still wore the same battered denims and the same air of restless engagement. He was holding court at the end of a long table, leaning back casually in his chair, giving the good oil to a bunch of teenage Koories with bad-boy earrings. They stood there, hanging on his every word. Or maybe just hanging, hands thrust deep into the pockets of their Air Jordan windbreakers. A bulging leather valise, crammed with papers, sat on the floor beside his chair.

As I came through the door, he looked across the room and immediately marked me as being there for him. Either that or a lost businessman who'd mistaken the place for one of those gravlax and goats-cheese joints that littered Fitzroy like noxious weeds.

I nodded at him and he nodded back. We held each other's gaze for a moment, then he inclined his head towards the chalkboard menu. I picked up a tray and he returned to his conversation.

The ham salad came with a slice of tinned beetroot and a circle of fresh orange. Bush tucker. At the Stars, even the gastronomic flourishes were survivors. By the time I carried my plate to Ambrose's table, his home-boy disciples were farewelling him with elaborate soul shakes. They leered at me scornfully and loped to another table, all boneless legs and jutting elbows and acquired attitude.

Ambrose extended a leg under the table and pushed out a chair. 'Got a call to say someone was coming. Thought I recognised the name.'

'Ambrose.' I accepted the offered seat, clearing aside a litter of used crockery to make space for my plate. 'Didn't think you'd remember me.'

'Oh, I remember all right.' He tilted back in his seat and scrutinised me thoroughly. 'Never saw a man so scared in all my life. 'Course you've put on a bit of weight since then, eh?'

'You should talk, greybeard,' I said. 'Old man of the tribe now, are you?'

Ambrose scratched his whiskers. 'Last of the old-time cheeky blackfellers. Come to warn me off, eh?'

'Maybe it's to invite you aboard.'

'Your salad's getting warm,' he said. I sawed off a couple of mouthfuls of limp lettuce and he studied me as I chewed. 'Why you?' he said, after a while. 'Any particular reason they sent you?'

Not the reason he thought. I wanted that clear from the outset. 'Just lucky, I guess.'

'Not planning on calling in any old debts, eh?'

'Didn't know there were any.'

'No?' He was sceptical. 'So, you're here to tell me what a great thing it'll be for Aboriginal people if Melbourne gets the Olympic Games, eh? To tell me all about the great contribution Koories have made to Australia's sporting history.' He jerked his chin at something past my shoulder and I turned to look.

I'd been wondering about the Stars. And there they were. One entire wall of the cafe was lined with sporting trophies.

A vast silver array of cups, medallions, shields, pennants and boxing belts. I'd seen engraver's shops with smaller displays. Hung at intervals between the trophies were framed photographs of Aboriginal sporting heroes.

Doug Nichols, rejected by Carlton on account of his colour. And the other magical black footballers who came after him. The great Polly Farmer. Syd Jackson, the best half-forward flanker of his generation. The Krakouer brothers. Maurice Rioli. Nicky Winmar. Derek Kickett. Gilbert McAdam. Boxers, too, of course. Lionel Rose, bantamweight champion of the world. Tony Mundine, titleholder in four separate weight divisions. Plenty of others that I didn't recognise, women as well as men.

More than just a tribute to athletic prowess and an extra-ordinary accumulation of historical mementos, the display was an affirmation of black pride. A collective up-yours to the entire gubba world. When I turned back, Ambrose had taken a manilla folder from his overstuffed portmanteau and put it on the table between us.

'Three,' he said.

'Three what?'

'That's the number of indigenous athletes this country has selected to represent it in the ninety years it's been competing in the Olympics.'

'Point made,' I said. 'But it's the view of the MOB that attracting the Games to Australia will radically increase the opportunity for Aboriginal participation.' I recited the official formula without pretence at enthusiasm.

'Radically, eh?' Ambrose stroked his whiskers.

'Considerably, then.'

'So what do we get? Didgeridoo anthem at the opening

ceremony? Exclusive rights to the souvenir boomerang concession? Bit of this sort of thing?' He opened the folder and pushed a photograph across the table, a glossy 8 x 10 print.

Ambrose Buchanan travelled fast and light but that didn't stop him doing his homework. The photo was a true classic. You could date it immediately from the wide lapels and short haircuts, the smug potato-fed faces.

A group of white men was standing around an Aborigine, grinning at the camera, relishing a joke. The black man was the joke. He had a gangly stork-like build and he was so black he looked like he was chiselled out of anthracite. A white singlet hung pathetically from his bony shoulders and baggy white shorts dangled to his knees. Five interlocked rings decorated the chest of his singlet and he held aloft a sputtering Olympic torch. The white men were slapping his back, urging him forward with mocking enthusiasm. He was staring straight into the camera, his teeth dazzling, his eyes pools of bewildered terror.

'This the sort of thing they've got in mind, eh?' Ambrose made it a high rhetorical flourish, loud enough for faces all around the room to turn our way. 'Well, fuck that shit.'

We were, I implicitly understood, actors in a piece of public theatre. I was the gubba in the suit, the snake in the garden, up to no good. Ambrose was the righteous brother, champion of the community, refusing to be drawn into any backroom treachery.

Playing my role, I did my best to look chastened, waiting until our audience turned back to its lunch. 'No need for the history lesson,' I said. 'You've already got them worried. They want to know if you're just going to blow hard in general or if you're planning something in particular.'

'This is where I'm supposed to issue a demand for land rights over the proposed baseball stadium, eh?'

'Where the Gunditjmara used to assemble for friendly contests of spear-throwing,' I suggested.

'That right? Sounds like we'd better get the lawyers on the job. In the meantime, finish your lettuce and come take a look at this.'

Past the kitchen, narrow stairs led downwards. Sports posters lined the walls, their edges curling. Dusky-skinned ruckmen taking high marks, runners breasting finishing tapes, high-jumpers clearing crossbars. The muffled thud of reggae rose to meet us as we descended into the pong of sweat and leather.

The basement had windowless cement walls, a floor-level boxing ring, a pair of heavy punching bags suspended from a low ceiling, a speedball and a rack of free weights. An Easter Island statue stood in the corner, feeding towels into an antique twin-tub washing machine.

A young man in a singlet and track pants was sitting on the edge of a press bench, curling barbells. He was maybe twenty years old, medium height, slight build, not an ounce of fat. He wore a knitted black beanie, pulled down almost to his eyebrows. He might have been a very swarthy Sicilian but for the angle of his cheekbones, the fullness of his lips and the slight flare of his nostrils. The land-rights slogan on his singlet, too, was a dead giveaway. For a boxer, he was slightly built. Somewhere between bantam and fly, I guessed. Rosella weight, budgerigar weight.

We stood at the bottom of the stairs, checking it out. Ambrose was in a frisky mood. He did a quick dance around the heavy bag. Muhammad Ali. Jab, jab.

The arm-curler ignored him, his face impassive, absorbed in his task. His arms pumped mechanically in time with the rastafarian rhythm emanating from a ghetto blaster. I dawdled on the spot, hands in pockets, taking it in. Such as it was. No atrium-roofed pool here, no fluffy towels, no sauna. Just hungry determination and hard training and rising damp. The tape ended and the curler finished his set and returned the weights to their rack.

Ambrose danced over. 'You're Darcy Anderson, aren't you? Ernest's cousin? I'm Ambrose Buchanan.'

Darcy bobbed his head, nodding listlessly, eyes down-turned. The name Anderson rang a distant bell in the back of my mind. I couldn't quite place it, but I felt for the kid, living in the shadow of some high-achieving relation.

'So how's it going?' Ambrose picked up a barbell, tested its heft.

Young Darcy had the eloquence of· the true athlete. 'Orright,' he shrugged. 'I 'spose.'

The Easter Island statue dropped the lid on the washer and kicked it into juddering action. Ambrose shadow-boxed, beckoning him over.

Maxie was built like Samoa after the cyclone, his brow a solid ridge of ancient scar tissue. He was some sort of islander mix. Part Polynesian, part Melanesian, part brick shithouse. He crossed the gym with the proprietary waddle of a troll in its lair, the subterranean servant of some volcano god. Ambrose danced close and swung wide, knuckles balled. Maxie raised a languid hand and absorbed the punch in his open palm, smothering Ambrose's fist in fingers the size of bread rolls.

'This is Murray Whelan,' said Ambrose. 'Maxie's in charge down here. He used to box with Sharman's.' Taking all comers in a travelling tent show. Five quid to any mug lair who could knock him down.

Maxie let go of Ambrose's fist and extended his massive hand. I took it tentatively and found it as soft as a feather pillow. I pumped it once and let go before it smothered my entire arm. 'Now don't you go disturbing this man's training, Ambrose,' he growled.

Darcy picked up a rope and started skipping on the spot. The rope was taped together at the handles and the spot was worn shiny from a million shuffling footfalls. We watched him get into his stride, his spidery legs flying.

'He's dead keen,' rumbled Maxie. 'In here at lunchtime, nights.'

'What class does he box in?' I said, trying to pretend I knew what I was talking about.

'Box?' Maxie stared at me blankly. 'Darcy couldn't box to save his life. Triathlon, that's his sport.' He mimed the actions—running, cycling, swimming. 'Rated third in the state, seventh nationally. Working himself up for the national titles. Wouldn't hurt a fly. Would you, Darce?'

Darcy pounded on, oblivious, sweat beading on his upper lip. I grinned stupidly, tripped up on a ready stereotype.

'Murray here's from that MOB mob,' Ambrose told Maxie. 'The Olympic bid, y'know.'

'That right?' Maxie looked at me anew. 'What are our chances?'

'You'd better ask Ambrose that,' I said.

'I'd say it's still an open question, eh?' Ambrose nodded towards Darcy. 'Doin' okay, is he?'

Maxie shrugged, a tectonic realignment of continent-sized shoulder blades. 'Reckon he'd have a better chance if that jailbird cousin of his kept away.'

Ambrose frowned. 'Deadly's out, eh?'

Darcy pounded on the spot, mind turned inwards. Maxie gave a disgusted grunt. 'Been hangin' round, trying to buddy-up to young Darce here. Goin' the long-lost cuz. Bad news, that one. I run him off.'

'Yeah, well.' Ambrose started dancing again, sparring backwards, out of Maxie's impassive range. 'Better you than me.'

We went back upstairs and helped ourselves to tea at the urn. The lunch rush was over, the crowd thinning. Our table had been cleared and wiped and Ambrose's folder set back in place. We sat down and I waited for the pitch. Ambrose gazed towards the trophy cabinet and adopted a pensive air.

'I have a dream,' he said at last. 'As they say in Pitjantjatjara. A Koori Institute of Sport. State-of-the-art equipment. Culturally appropriate residential facilities. Scholarships. All tailored to the specific needs of the indigenous athlete.'

For fifteen minutes, without drawing breath, he pitched his proposition. Spoke of how sport had once been a ticket out of the native reserves. How blacks played in a world of white games, white rules, white officials and selectors, never partners in the enterprise. How discrimination persisted. How difficult some found success, particularly when it took them away from their families. How an Aboriginal Sports Institute could maximise the potential of future generations of indigenous athletes.

He didn't need to sell me. If the MOB was worried about Australia's race-relations image among the sporting world's heavy-hitters, an Aboriginal Institute of Sport would be a very smart card to play. Incorporate the idea in the bid prospectus, have the state pitch in a bit of seeding money, talk up the national focus and slide the whole thing sideways to the feds. A bargain, considering the potential pay-off. A win-win situation, I could hear Brian Morrison calling it.

'Well worth exploring,' I said when Ambrose finally shut up. 'If we get the Games.'

'If? You don't sound too confident. We were hoping for a bit more enthusiasm.'

'We?'

He jerked his chin across the room to where his young acolytes were hunkered down at a table of their peers, bullshitting and smoking cigarettes. 'The community,' he said. 'Young people angry and frustrated at the lack of opportunity.' From where I was sitting, the community looked about as angry as a swarm of enraged tree sloths. Not that it mattered. High-pressure tactics wouldn't be needed to sell this idea. It was a stroke of marketing genius.

'It would need to be adequately resourced to work properly,' I said. 'The MOB would need to make representation to Woeful McKenzie, the Sports Minister. Get him to run it up to Cabinet for in-principle approval. Before that, some basic issues need to be sorted out. Funding issues, federal-state issues, management issues. Of course, I'll need some costings first.'

Ambrose was glazing over. 'You're the bureaucrat,' he said. He opened his file and dug out a page of jottings. Big-picture stuff, no detail. 'I see my old mate Pascal Abdoulaye is due in town.'

I stared at him blankly. A newspaper clipping emerged from the file. IOC Chiefs to Receive Relay Torch. Ah, yes, I remembered. The Evaluation Commission honcho. One of Samaranch's point men. As seen on my invitation card. 'You know him?'

'He's the Senegalese ambassador to the European Community. I was on an anti-apartheid committee with him in Brussels. Maybe I could catch up with him at this thing with the kids.'

My heart sank. 'The torch relay?' I said, knowing what was coming next.

'That's the one. How come you haven't got a Koori kid handing over the torch, eh?'

Ah shit, I thought. Can't argue with that. Why hadn't Brian Morrison thought of it? 'Good idea,' I said, unenthusiastically. Red's disappointment, I felt sure, would not be fatal. Yet another fuck-up by good old dad. 'Got someone in mind?'

Ambrose's hand twitched absently, flicking the offer into oblivion. 'Save the tokenism for the Talbots,' he said. 'As they say in Wurundjeri. I'm more interested in this Sports Institute. You think the MOB might buy the idea?'

'I'm just the messenger boy,' I said. 'But, personally, I think they'd be mad if they didn't. Got a number I can call you on?'

'You're in me office now,' he said.

And that was it. A perfectly civilised discussion. Apart from an initial bit of pro-forma chest beating, Ambrose had been a pussycat. His proposition wasn't a threat. It was a golden opportunity. Brian Morrison's hysterics had been entirely unwarranted. If the MOB knocked back a winning idea like this Aboriginal Sports Institute, it didn't deserve to win the bid. All it need do was stick its imprimatur on the thing until seeding funds could be found. For very little money, the country could buy itself a shitload of goodwill with the gnomes of the IOC. And probably quite a few gold medals in the long term, considering the sporting potential of the Aboriginal population.

Maybe even one in triathloning. If synchronised swimming and curling could make the Olympic program, the pedal-run-swim combo was definitely in the race. As I waited at the tram stop on Gertrude Street, the conscientious young Darcy emerged from the side door of the Stars, a sports bag slung over his shoulder. Casually wading through the stream of slow-moving traffic, he headed across the street. Busy tanning my lungs in the sunshine, I paid him little attention. It was the other guys that caught my attention.

They were coming through the screen of trees between the undercroft of the high-rise and the street. It was little more than a scrubby cluster of shrubs designed to enhance the environment a little for the residents of the flats. Mostly it just accumulated scraps of litter. There were four of them, pissing around, kicking a can along in front of them and swearing loudly enough for the sound to carry across the street.

Skinheads were not a common sight in Melbourne. These ones must have bought their outfits from some British bovver-boy catalogue. Close-cropped hair, jeans turned up at the cuff, high-lace Doc Martens, rolling gait. As they burst through the bushes, an Asian woman was coming along the footpath, pushing a child in a stroller. Before she could react, they had her surrounded. 'Ching-chong-chonkie,' sang one, clearly the spokesman of the group.

The woman attempted to ignore them, continuing on her way with as much dignity as possible. The child in the stroller was about eighteen months old. Its tiny cheeks were framed by a furry little hat with bear's ears. The skinheads pranced about making ching-chong noises, trying to get a rise out of the woman, but going no further. Even if they'd had the guts, they wouldn't have dared. Not in this neighbourhood, not in broad daylight.

Already a couple of drinkers had spilled out of the hotel across the road and were watching the show, standing on the footpath with glasses of beer in their hands. The Asian woman turned into the flats just as Darcy cleared the traffic and reached the footpath. Looking for fresh game, the skinheads moved to block his path.

'You a dago or an Abo?' the gang's leading intellectual shouted. He probably lived in one of the leafier suburbs and decided to become a skinhead after the gloss went off train-surfing. Didn't want to waste his Scotch College education.

Darcy shouldered him aside, disregarding the taunts. 'Hey,' yelled the skinhead. 'We're talkin' to you.'

As they started after the Koori, reinforcements joined the jeering crowd at the door of the hotel across the road, waving their pool cues for emphasis. 'Piss off, you wankers,' came a shout. From a safe distance, the skins lobbed a barrage of double-fingered salutes and incoherent witticisms. If not quite good natured, the exchange almost had a sporting quality, like it was a familiar game in which all the players were reprising old moves. Even by the debased standards of local street theatre, it was a sorry spectacle. Maybe this happened every afternoon at about this time.

As quickly as it started, it was all over. Darcy had vanished into the housing estate beyond the flats. The skins clomped back the way they had come. The drinkers returned to the bar. I drew hard on my cigarette and flicked it into the gutter, leaning off the kerb to signal an oncoming tram.

The meeting with Ambrose Buchanan had gone well. The easiest five grand a man ever made, paperwork pending. I was out of Water for the duration and Red's grip on the butane baton was secure. All was well with the world. The tram glided to a halt, brakes hissing, and I climbed aboard.

With one hand I found my Zone One All Day ticket, with the other the box of Nicabate. The psychological moment, I resolved, had arrived. Taking my seat, I undid two shirt buttons, tore open one of the little sealed envelopes and attached a patch to my midriff. This was going to be a piece of piss.

And so it would have been if, less than twelve hours later, young Darcy Anderson wasn't flat on his back on a slab in the morgue.

The ministerial suite at the Department of Sport, Recreation, Racing and the Olympics was a snug berth for a couple of old Port Melbourne lads. Strolling distance to both parliament and the bid headquarters. Nice view across the Treasury Gardens. Comfortably clubbish brown leather furniture. A Skytel dish on the roof to keep the minister appraised of trackside conditions and starting prices. A well-stocked liquor cabinet. The only thing missing was the smell of cigars and the little pictures of bulldogs in derby hats playing snooker.

Denis Dogherty, more terrier than bulldog, raised his head from the paperwork on Woeful McKenzie's desk, pushed his glasses up onto his brow and massaged the bridge of his nose between thumb and forefinger. He looked like a wizened child at a school desk too big for him. 'Park your carcass,' he said. 'Take the load.'

I stood instead at the window. He came around the desk and joined me, nodding north in the general direction of Parliament House.

'Question Time,' he said. 'The boss'll be up on his feet right now, explaining to the opposition why the Totalisator Agency Board found it necessary to pre-purchase a ten-year supply of potato chips for its corporate hospitality box at Moonee Valley racecourse.'

'And why did it?' I asked.

'Invite a few clients around for a drink,' he said. 'Nothing worse than running out of chips.' He spoke with neither humour nor rancour, a man who would rather be somewhere else.

A cool change was blowing in from the south, a smear of grey that herded the stratocumulus before it as it advanced. Down below in the gardens a breeze rippled the leaves and gently swayed the branches. A couple more weeks and the colour would be gone. Woody skeletons would thrust their fingers into a leaden sky. Denis nodded contemplatively down at the traffic crawling along Wellington Parade.

'Mug's Alley. That's what we used to call it. You had to be a mug to park there. A thieves' paradise. Bold as brass, they were. Come back, you'd find your wheels gone. Radio stripped, the works. All in broad daylight, too.'

He shook his head. Not just in disbelief at such barefaced larceny, I suspected, but also at the passing of a more innocent time. Denis Dogherty had seen quite a few seasons come and go, and not all of them from the twelfth-floor window of a Minister of the Crown. He didn't have a political philosophy, at least none I'd ever heard him bother to articulate. He had a memory and he had a class. It made little difference that the class had changed beyond recognition and that the memory, too, was far from reliable.

'Ancient history,' I said affably. 'Which we will be if we don't win this bid.'

Denis came out of his reverie. He marched back behind the desk and sat down beneath a framed photograph of the finish of the 1989 Cox Plate. Stylish Century and Empire Rose neck-and-neck at the post, courtesy of the Bloodstock Council of Victoria. 'So,' he said. 'This Ambrose Buchanan going to be a fly in the ointment?'

'Not unless he's playing his cards very close to his chest.' I gave him a detailed rundown of our conversation at the Stars.

'An Aboriginal Institute of Sport?' He chewed the idea over, nodding to himself. 'You ever see that photo of Lionel Rose as a kid, barefoot beside a tin humpy? When he wins the world title, the bloody hypocrites turn around and give him a civic reception. Like that makes it all right. Criminal the way those people were treated. Maybe we could call it the Lionel Rose Institute.'

'So you agree it's a good idea?'

'It's the sort of thing that floss merchant Brian Morrison should've come up with months ago. Christ knows he gets paid enough.' Deserting the sinking ship had done nothing to endear Brian to Denis.

'Probably,' I said. 'But he should buy this. It's obviously well worth supporting.'

Denis looked at me like I'd arrived with the last fall of rain. 'Unfortunately, mate,' he said, 'merit is not sufficient grounds for making it onto the Olympic shopping list.'

Obviously not. It never is, whatever the list. 'I don't just mean for altruistic reasons,' I said. 'It's also a great selling point.'

Denis rubbed his eyes and tried to hide his exasperation. 'That's what everyone says about their pet project, Murray. And this late in the piece, four months to go till the decision, it's difficult to get the MOB to pick up any new proposal, no matter how marketable.'

By the look of it, my little consultancy was going to be the shortest job in the history of employment. 'So I go back and tell Ambrose Buchanan thanks but no thanks?'

'Not necessarily,' he said. 'But if we want to get this thing up, we'll need a bit of leverage.'

'Leverage? What sort of leverage?'

'This sort.' He picked up the phone and punched in a number. His combative instincts were kicking in. Whatever else he was doing, he was enjoying himself.

'Brian,' he said into the phone. 'Bad news, mate. Got Murray Whelan here with me, just back from talking to Ambrose Buchanan. You were right to expect trouble. Apparently Ambrose knows our African IOC. All part of the international brotherhood of the dusky-hued. Anyway, he's threatening to get into the bloke's ear, piss on our parade if we don't meet his demands. Wants our support for an Aboriginal Institute of Sport...Yeah, not a bad idea in itself...yeah...'

He leaned back in Woeful's big office chair and smiled conspiratorially as he listened to Brian's response. Tiberius on the telephone. 'He mentioned the torch relay, too. High potential there for a media stunt. Just the sort of thing that gets international press coverage...'

On top of Woeful's credenza was a football on a little wooden rack, some sort of presentation number, covered in autographs. My hands found it and started tossing it back and forth between them.

Denis was laying it on with a trowel. 'A very vulnerable time, especially with the Evaluation Commission in town... Ambrose could probably round up a war party of young Koories if he really wanted to make a pain in the arse of himself...Blackmail? Couldn't agree with you more...' He tipped me a broad wink. I flipped the ball end over end, going with the play.

For ten minutes they conferred, mapping out a way to get us off the hook. As I listened, I worked up a good spin. Just as I got the ball to balance on the tip of my forefinger, Denis hung up.

'This is the deal,' he said. 'You write up the proposal for the MOB's consideration. Brian does the spade-work to get it accepted as a matter of urgency. The MOB submits a formal request for government support. We lash it to the raft of projects to be considered by Cabinet on Thursday. If it goes through, Hugh Knowles can announce it at the big dinner that night.'

'You certainly don't muck around, do you?' I said, genuinely impressed.

'You'd better not, either,' he said. 'If we're going to make the Cabinet agenda deadline, I'll need a draft submission by close of business today. Copy to Brian for distribution to MOB management. And he wants you on deck for their breakfast meeting tomorrow morning, in case of questions. Eight-thirty. Broad brushstrokes.'

Given the notice, they'd be lucky to get a thin undercoat. 'Anything else?' I said. Land-speed record? Four-minute mile?

Denis was back on his feet. 'Use my office, save going back to Water. I'll be over at the House, clueing Woeful up. Giving him his post-match rubdown.'

He'd need one. The Liberals had the smell of blood and were cutting up rough, sure that power was about to drop into their waiting laps. Unless we won the bid, of course. All bets would be off if we won the bid. On his way out the door, Denis introduced me to Woeful's private secretary. 'Carmel here'll do any typing you need for this, won't you, love?'

Carmel was one of those public-service perennials, the basilisk at the minister's door. A fifty-year-old Kim Novak who made the trains run on time and the tea for the boys in the backroom with equal equanimity. If she didn't know where the bodies were buried, I was prepared to bet, she had a pretty fair idea where the receipts for the shovels were filed. She was sharp as a tack, gave nothing away, typed 100 wpm and sized me up at a glance. 'I'll stay until six,' she said. 'No later.'

Denis paused in the doorway. 'No longer than two pages. No more than half a million in seeding funds. And, for Chrissake, either kick that frigging football or put it back where it belongs.'

Denis's office was a small, glass-walled work-station just down the corridor. He kept a neat desk, everything shipshape and Bristol fashion. I raided the stationery cupboard for pens and notepads and proceeded to make a mess of it. Tempus fugit, as they say in Walpiri.

For the next three hours, I gave free rein to my most creative bureaucratic faculties. Like an economist, I worked backwards, fabricating arguments to fit my conclusions, bolstering them with statistics plucked from thin air.

Employing the usual organisational models, an occasional phone call, a pocket calculator and a damp finger held up to the wind, I sketched a hypothetical management structure, ballparked a budget and identified plausible funding mechanisms for a High Intensity Training Program for Indigenous Athletes.

Properly speaking, such an endeavour was a federal matter. Properly speaking, a thorough feasibility study was required. Properly speaking, community consultation was the order of the day. But this wasn't a proper proposition. This was rabbit-and-hat territory, a pump-priming exercise. The bells-and-whistles could come later. Even if we lost the bid, the thing would at least get an airing. In the meantime, it was abracadabra rules.

By six o'clock, my little piece of embroidery had been typed and duplicated. The requisite number of copies had been dispatched to the Cabinet office for distribution with the weekly agenda papers, subject to the Premier's approval, and others sat in a neat pile on Woeful's desk. Five minutes after Carmel put the cover over her word-processor and headed for the train home, Denis returned from Parliament House. He reported that he'd had a word with the minister who, in turn, had cornered the Premier and requested that the matter be listed for consideration by Cabinet at its Thursday meeting.

Under the circumstances, Denis thought, it was the best result possible. 'The Cabinet agenda's chock-a-block with budget issues at the moment, what with the Treasurer leaving his wallet in his other trousers. And the Premier's never been keen on last-minute inclusions. But he's agreed to think about it overnight, tell Woeful his decision in the morning.'

Not a bad afternoon's mischief. Apart from the Premier's okay, only one matter remained outstanding. 'Feel like a drink?' I said.

'You'd be all carrot juice and mineral water these days, wouldn't you?' said Denis. 'A man with his sights on the big league.' He took cans and chilled glasses from the well-stocked bar fridge built into the credenza. 'Want a chip? There's plenty.'

Normally, the first sip of beer had me reaching for a cigarette. This time, I realised with astonishment, I felt no such impulse. Cigarettes were a concept, an abstraction, an idea with which I was familiar. But I did not crave one, even mildly.

Four hours had passed since my last cigarette and, until the hops hit my mouth, I hadn't even noticed. Despite the wussy name, these Nicabate band-aids packed a real wallop. I touched the magic patch through the fabric of my shirt, giving it an encouraging pat. 'Nothing on tonight?' I asked. 'Game Fishing Association presentation night? Jockey Club smoker? Dancing the bossa nova with Don Pablo Cardena?'

In our racket, our evenings were rarely our own. Squiring the boss to social functions was all part of the gig, a continuous round of catered dinners and mail-order chitchat, feigned enthusiasms and set-piece speeches. Back at Ethnic Affairs, I'd often found myself at such events four or five times a week, consoled only by the free linguini, too much retsina and the fact that no-one was waiting at home.

Denis loosened his tie. 'Quiet night at home with Marjorie, for once,' he said. 'Cup of cocoa and beddy-byes.'

We sat on the clubby brown sofa, sipped our beers, ate salt'n'vinegar chips from the packet and watched the gloaming settle gently over the gardens.

'You ever drink at the Pier Hotel?' I said, just chewing the fat. 'My old man had the licence there for a while. We lived upstairs.'

Eighteen months at the Pier while I was still in short pants were my sole claim to roots in the Port Melbourne community, a way-station in my childhood migration around the watering holes of Melbourne.

'That right?' said Denis, interested. 'I'll admit to the occasional beer there, although the Sandridge was the wharfies' pub. So when was this?'

'Late fifties,' I said. 'You lot at the Stevedores were in the news all the time. More strikes than a bowling alley, they used to say. I was just a little kid at the time. You remember the Eclipse?'

'The picture theatre? Where the 7-Eleven is now? 'Course I do. Every Saturday, rain or shine. Cowboys and Itchybums, lollies ten for a penny.'

Very ancient history. The wooden workingmen's cottages of the old seaside suburb had long been transformed into the pastel-tinted, marine-themed abodes of advertising executives and fashion designers. The only lollies they still sold in Port Melbourne were individually wrapped Ferrero-Rocher hazelnut truffles. Still, you take your nostalgia where you find it.

'And when it was your birthday,' I recalled, 'they'd put your name up on the screen. Happened to me when I turned eight.'

'No, that was the Port Cinema,' he said. 'They had the upstairs at the Eclipse, the dress circle. Me and Woeful used to meet the girls there. Just after the war, this was. We couldn't go round to the house, pick them up. Old Mother Boag didn't like the idea of her girls going out with a couple of red-raggers. Fearsome pious, she was. Pope on the wall, Mass at Saint Joey's every Sunday. But a real battler. Worked at the Swallow & Ariell biscuit factory after the girls' dad was killed in the war. Burma Railway, just like Woeful's. You got fleas or something?'

One of my hands was running circles around the nicotine patch. The other was scratching my armpit. I desisted immediately, went to the fridge and cracked another couple of cans. 'That's right,' I said, remembering. 'I heard that you and Woeful were married to sisters.'

Beth and Marjorie Boag,' he nodded. 'The belles of Bay Street. There was a third one, Irene. The little sister. Married a migrant, funny sort of bloke. Fell off a ladder and died, she did. Tragic.'

So much for my reminiscences of historic Port Melbourne. We lapsed into silence. Me toying with my can, Denis staring pensively into the night. He drained his glass and stood up. 'Time, gentlemen,' he said. 'Time.'

We rode down in the lift together, me headed for the ground floor, Denis for the carpark. 'See you in the morning after the MOB meeting,' he said. 'We'll have the word from the Premier by then and you can brief Woeful in detail. You all right?'

'Yeah,' I said. 'Why?'

'You seem a bit keyed-up, that's all.'

'I'm fine,' I said, wondering what he meant. Apart from a little tingling in the scalp, I felt buoyant.

'Take care,' he said, as I stepped into the foyer.

'You, too,' I told the gap in the closing doors.

But Denis's course was already set. And, besides, I don't think he heard me. He should have gone home.

A restless energy was jiggling its hands in my pockets. Mild agitation, Doctor Phillipa had warned. A side-effect of the mysterious osmosis at work in my shirt.

The evening rush hour had finished and the darkening streets were almost deserted. I stood for a moment, considering my options. Across the road, in the syrupy dusk of the gardens, a pair of Japanese honeymooners were trying to tempt a possum from a tree, timidly waving bread rolls at the foliage. The Windsor was just up the road, the favoured watering hole of Parliament House staffers and press gallery leak-sniffers. A man would need to be desperate to seek company there. A more compelling alternative suggested itself to me.

I turned down Flinders Lane, the slope of the hill adding momentum to my pace. No hurry, I told myself. The chance that I would find Dr Phillipa Verstak in the lounge at Mietta's at seven o'clock on a Monday evening was a very long shot indeed. Still, nothing ventured. Wire-caged posters at the rear of the *Herald* building carried the latest news. PRINCE EDWARD—I'M NOT GAY. That was a weight off my mind.

Flinders Lane was once the heart of Melbourne's rag trade. But the whirr of the sewing machine was no longer heard there, nor the rattle of wire coat-hangers on garment racks. Now it was all tribal art galleries, pasta bars and the entrances of multi-storey carparks. At Rosati, its tiled interior as vast as Milan railway station and as empty as an Etruscan tomb, bored waiters in floor-length aprons lounged against the bar. A hundred metres down the hill, I turned up a laneway that led towards Collins Street.

Sheer walls rose on either side, punctured only by the service entrance of the Hyatt hotel. Sitting in the loading bay was a garbage skip the size of a shipping container, surrounded by plastic milk crates and empty detergent drums. Fixed to the wall beside the staff entrance was a row of metal benches. Usually, they were occupied by hotel employees who had nicked outside for a quick smoke. Evidence of this fact could be seen in the butts that littered the cobblestones. I looked down at them with the disgust of a reformed man.

The seats were vacant except for a waiter in a dinner suit. He stood up as I approached, shifting his weight from foot to foot and running a finger around the inside of his collar like an impatient bridegroom. He wasn't smoking, I realised, but waiting for someone, peering impatiently up the steps towards the door marked Strictly Staff Only. As I got closer, I recognised him.

It was Holly Deloite's insistent ex, the thick-stemmed Steve Radeski. Dressed not as a waiter, I realised, but a bouncer. A crowd-control supervisor, an event-management security consultant, a chucker-outer. Professional muscle.

But not, in the half-light of the alleyway, the most frightening example of his metier. He was a few centimetres shorter than me and I found something almost comical about the posturing way he held himself, legs bowed, arms dangling. Bulging slightly in a hand-me-down dinner suit, he looked too dumb to be seriously dangerous.

His hair was thinning. His ponytail was greasy and lank. He had a rash of some sort, pinhead pustules which pitted his cheeks and inched up his neck past the over-tight collar of his dress shirt. He looked like he'd been using Manuel Noriega's dermatologist and Clive James's tailor.

What on earth, I couldn't help but wonder, did a gorgeous girl like Holly ever see in a meatloaf like this? With that thought, a sudden wave of irritation welled up within me. Just where did this strutting bonehead get off, thrusting his unwanted attentions upon women? One woman, anyway. One that I knew about. This was the sort of bloke who gave blokedom a bad name. And what was he doing here, lurking about the staff exit? He couldn't by any chance be waiting for Holly to come off her shift upstairs, could he?

'Steve, isn't it?' I heard myself saying. 'Steve Radeski?'

Bigfoot's eyes flicked over me, indifferent. You meet a lot of people in the hospitality industry, you can't be expected to remember them all.

'You know Holly Deloite, right?'

He stared, triangulating the content of the question with known associates. It was a lengthy process. 'Yeah,' he finally admitted. 'Why?'

'Not waiting for her now, by any chance?' It came out as a challenge.

'Could be,' he said, stepping closer. 'Who wants to know?'

'A friend of Holly's,' I said. 'Trying to save you some trouble.'

The penny finally dropped. 'You're that fucken lawyer, aren't you?'

Radeski suddenly seemed a lot bigger, more bulked-up, less pathetic. It was like someone was inflating him with air. His jaw muscles bulged. The veins in his neck were pulsing like compressor hose. I began to have second thoughts. Maybe I should have expressed myself better, made some light conversation, built a little rapport, eased into the issue gradually.

'Where do you fucken get off?' he demanded.

'Now listen here,' I said, hearing what sounded like fatuous pomposity echo up the ominously empty alley. 'I'm just trying to do you a favour, that's all.'

But he didn't want any favours. He stuck his face in mine. His breath smelled of sour milk and the whites of his eyes had a muddy liverish tinge in the stark fluorescent light spilling from the loading bay. 'The fuck you think you are?'

Rational discourse was clearly out of the question. My fight-or-flee reflex kicked in, making my underpants decidedly nervous. Anything to placate him. 'Sorry,' I babbled. 'My mistake.' I began to back away, showing him the palms of my hands. The universal gesture of submission. The international sign of the chicken.

Grovelling cut no ice. This guy had a serious anger-management problem. His ugly mug was contorted with blind rage. He was on a hair trigger and I'd just pulled it. A low growl came from the back of his throat. His nostrils flared. He lowered his head.

I turned to run but it was too late. He charged. The top of his head hit me square in the middle of the chest. 'Oomph,' I said as the air rushed from my lungs. My feet lifted off the ground. I flew backwards and slammed against the garbage skip.

I was boxed in, trapped in the narrow gap between the wall of the loading dock and the side of the dumpster. Radeski took a backward step and lowered his head, preparing to head-butt me again.

My courage—what little I still possessed—deserted me. This was no way to die. Liverpool-kissed to death in a back alley. And for what? For being a meddling busybody. 'Please!' I blurted, the only supplication my breathless lungs could manage. Please don't kill me. Please don't crush the life from my worthless body, O Mighty One. 'Please!'

'Police? Where?' Radeski paused and glanced over his shoulder, checking for evidence of the constabulary.

In that split second, I dived sideways. Agile as a hysterical mountain goat, I clambered up the stack of milk crates and jumped onto the rim of the open dumpster. The metal was thick with grease and my feet skittered out from beneath me. I flew sideways, the heel of my shoe connecting with the slotted lever arm propping open the lid of the skip. A rancid stink rose to meet me and my shoulder hit a bag of garbage. It burst, spewing its contents. A buffeting pillow of fetid air pressed down upon me and a great echoing crash exploded in my ears. The lid of the dumpster slammed shut.

I lay in total darkness, panting, my ears ringing. The dumpster vibrated like a gong. My shoulder throbbed. A disgusting stench filled my nostrils, part table scraps, part toxic waste.

Rolling onto my knees, I groped about blindly for a means of self-defence. Slimy plastic brushed my skin. I gagged on the overwhelming smell. Reaching up into the dark, I felt for the lid. It pressed down, cold to the touch. Shin-deep in bags of trash, I backed into a corner and braced myself for the worst.

Worst? Just how bad was it going to get? There I'd been, strolling peaceably along, minding my own business, en route to a quiet drink in the elegant surrounds of Mietta's cocktail lounge. Now here I was, trapped in a giant garbage bin, about to have my features rearranged by a psychopath in a penguin suit.

Right. Things had gone far enough. Grievous bodily harm was one thing. But being suffocated by the smell of room-service leftovers? That was too much. The laneway was a public thoroughfare. Somebody must have heard the dumpster lid crashing shut. Christ knows I still could, resonating like a tidal wave in my Eustachian tubes.

A place the size of the Hyatt must have hundreds of employees. Sooner or later, one of them would pop outside for a smoke. Or somebody would arrive for work. Night shift on the front desk. A bellboy. Anybody. If Psycho Steve was still there, surely he wasn't mad enough to bash me in front of witnesses.

The silence continued. I crouched motionless, suspecting a trick. Time passed. Palms flat on the lid, I bore upwards. It must have weighed half a tonne. A narrow crack appeared. I peered out into the lane. Steve Radeski was swaggering away, hands dangling at his hips like a gunslinger, ponytail dangling between his shoulder blades. Arsehole.

My strength gave out and the gap closed. I banged the metal with my balled fist and got a futile hollow ring. A dull ache mustered its forces in my frontal lobes. What I needed was a lever, something to prop the lid open while I squeezed through the gap. All this trash, there had to be something that would do the job.

I fumbled in my pockets and found that I still had my cigarette lighter. I flicked it on and looked around. Apart from a scatter of paper litter, the rubbish was bagged up. I tore at the flimsy plastic, spilling out the contents. After I'd gutted half a dozen of the bags, I struck another light and examined the result.

No doubt about it. It was garbage all right. Five-star crap. Evian bottles. Individual pot-sized serves of grain mustard. Cigar stubs, Romeo y Julieta, full coronas. A soup-stained banquet menu: Timbale of Tasmanian Scallops, Rack of Herbed Lamb, A Macedonia of Seasonal Fruits. Wilted gladioli. The foil from a first-class airline ticket: Melbourne–Amsterdam return. An empty condom packet. Top-shelf brand, ribbed for her sensual pleasure. *This Week in Melbourne*.

I searched with my feet, kicking bags open, banging on the dumpster wall as I went, yelling at the top of my lungs. Stomp, stomp. Something hard struck my shin. It felt promising, wooden by the heft of it, about as long as my arm and half as thick. A chair leg. Imitation Regency. Someone had been breaking up the hotel furniture. Thank Christ for rock bands. It was just what I needed.

One hand braced against the lid of my steel sarcophagus, I thrust the lever into the gap. Then, pulling downwards with my right hand, I swung my left leg into the narrow opening and over the rim of the skip. Gradually, I managed to wriggle the rest of my body into the slot until I was sandwiched between the lid and the rim of the skip, my cheek pressed against the greasy metal. One side of me hung inside, the other outside.

'Right there, are you, mate?' said a voice.

Horizontally headlocked, I stared into the night. Not five paces away, sitting on a milk crate on the apron of the loading dock, was a fat guy in kitchen whites, smoking a cigarette.

'How long you been there?' I grunted, my chest compressed between the skip and its lid.

He languidly raised his cigarette and let me see that it had just been lit. Holding the chair leg in place long enough to prevent my fingers being crushed, I swung both legs over the edge and dropped to the ground. 'No, no. Don't get up,' I said. 'I'll be right.'

Dignity is an overrated virtue. I brushed my lapels, dusted off my knees, buffed my shoes on the back of my trousers, detached a cold canapé from my shirt front and adjusted my tie. The pudgy smoker sat with his elbows on his knees, an ironic smile on his face, silently observing my toilette.

'You see that guy attack me?'

The smoker looked at me like I'd been prematurely released back into the community. He said nothing.

I found myself agreeing with him. Let's not mention this to anyone, I suggested to myself. Worse things happen at Party Conference. What I needed was a drink. And a cigarette. Quitting could wait until tomorrow. Fuck the nicotine, I could do with the consolation.

'This hotel is a disgrace,' I said. 'Lousy decor, poor housekeeping and no little mint on my pillow.'

Unbuttoning my shirt, I tore off the adhesive patch and tossed it on the ground.

Collins Street seemed to think it was the Rue de Montparnasse. Fairy lights twinkled in the trees, horse-drawn carriages plied the tourist trade and the baroque facade of the Old Treasury glowed like a honeyed lie in the middle distance. Dodging a steaming pile of manure, I made my way to Alfred Place and the sober facade of Mietta's, the most elegant gin joint in town.

A faint odour of refuse still clung to my apparel and my hands were streaked with grease. Flitting through the deserted vestibule, I ducked under the stairs and into the gents' lavatory. This relic of a bygone era had been preserved intact since before the Great War, its vitreous enamel as crackled as celadon china and stained the colour of hundred-year-old eggs. The water was cold as permafrost and the soap as thin as a communion wafer, but I had the place to myself.

In the bleary glow of the single 25-watt globe, my Hugo looked more like a science-fiction award than a six-hundred-dollar suit of clothes. My tie, flecked with what I hoped was chocolate mousse, was beyond redemption. Discarding it in the used-towel bin, I sponged down my jacket, scrubbed the smear of grease from my forehead, ran wet fingers through my hair and examined myself in the mirror above the chalky marble washstand. Only the manly scent of coffee dregs and wet ashes remained to suggest the nature of my recent misadventure. Presentably raffish, I decided. Devil-may-care. Now for a cigarette.

The vending machine was in the foyer, butted against the payphone at the entrance to the lounge. Tearing the cellophane off the pack with my teeth, I fed the change into the slot and dialled the Hyatt Club, reading the number off my membership card. Smoking Causes Lung Cancer, declared the warning on the pack. Life is a Terminal Condition.

'Is Holly Deloite there?' I inquired. 'Can I please speak to her?' Yes and no, came the answer. Holly was presently taking a class. Could someone else help?

I didn't see how, given that her ex-boyfriend's bad behaviour had already jeopardised her employment. Leaving a message that he was lurking about the hotel, assaulting patrons, could only exacerbate her problems. I said I'd call back later, rang off and went into the lounge.

The house style at Mietta's was *belle époque*. Urns of orchids on pedestals, flock wallpaper hung with over-framed oils, the windows swathed in more washed silk than the bustle on Nellie Melba's wedding gown. The furniture was an eccentric mix of mismatched antiques, all deployed around a concert grand with a vase of hydrangeas on the lid and a marble negro kneeling beside the keyboard with a basket of fruit on his head. The eponymous proprietress was standing by the cash register, surveying her domain with a purse-lipped hauteur more suited to the headmistress of the Presbyterian Ladies College than to a saloon keeper.

Apart from all that furniture, she didn't have much to look at. Scarcely a dozen customers were scattered around the room, the last of the late-working office crowd. Three or four couples, chatting in low undertones or toying silently with their drinks. By the fireplace, a bright little blaze of conversation, two trim women in after-five, three men in dark suits and careful ties, looking like they'd come straight from chambers or the counting house. A solitary drinker propped at the bar, thumbing through a back copy of the *New Yorker*.

No sign of Dr Verstak. And probably a good thing too, given that I was in no fit state to conduct a seduction. The only suit I could see myself pressing that night was the one I was wearing. A tuxedoed maitre d' materialised, looked at me like I was something the cat dragged in, led me to an obscure nook and ushered me into a low-slung wing-back horsehair-upholstered chair last seen in Colonel Mustard's library. I ordered a double whisky, single malt, water on the side, and lit a cigarette.

Every cigarette has its purpose. This one served many. Recompense for injury received. A balm to my bruised ego. A prayer of thanks for deliverance. A reward for a day's work well done. A healing draught from the well of solace. A sensual pleasure. An affectation appropriate to the surroundings. A warranted act of self-indulgence. An existential affirmation.

Try getting all that from a nicotine patch. I downed my drink, straight up, and signalled for another. When I reached for my wallet to pay, I found the invitation card to the IOC dinner. Three courses and a showband in the company of their excellencies Pascal Abdoulaye, Kim U-ee and Stansislas Dziczkowszczak, imminent envoys from the cloud-swathed heights of Olympus. Recipients of the sacred fire, to be carried hither by my own fleet-footed progeny, bearer of the city's fondest hopes.

For which I would need a dining companion. A woman, preferably. I considered the possibilities. It didn't have to be a date, to adopt an odious Americanism. There was no reason I couldn't invite any one of a dozen women. Workmates, past and present. Party comrades. Old flames. Ex-wives. God, wouldn't that be a bummer. I sipped my drink and gave the matter some thought.

You didn't really think that Phillipa Verstak would be here, I told myself. Sitting alone with her legs crossed and an enigmatic half-smile playing across her lips. You didn't really imagine her turning quickly away as you came through the door, then turning back and saying 'Of course I remember' and 'No, I don't mind' as you invited yourself to sit down, reaching across to light her cigarette, your eyes meeting. Of course not. That would be ridiculous. Absurd. Pathetic.

Little gusts of conversation and the tinkle of glasses wafted across from the congenial fivesome sitting by the unlit fireplace. The talk was of European aviation. '*The Flying Dutchman,*' groaned a male voice and the others all whinnied. I envied them their easy sociability and lit another cigarette.

'We'll miss the curtain if we don't hurry,' warbled one of the women. This initiated a bout of general fussing and fidgeting and finishing of drinks. Suddenly they were all on their feet. One of the men, a bony, angular fellow with so much self-regard he didn't even need to show it, beckoned the waiter and whispered pontifically into his ear. Then they were gone.

After a while, my watch told me it was pushing eight. Beyond that, it didn't have much else to say. The booze started doing its job. I gave my lungs a good fumigation. Pretty soon I was feeling quite a bit more chipper. The possibility of dinner canvassed itself. Something Chinese, I thought. One of the more affordable provinces.

That's when she arrived. Appeared in the doorway, just like that. In a skirt this time, knee-length. Black hose, nice calves. A high-collared teal-blue blouse, a fringed Carmen scarf around her shoulders, pinned in place with a silver brooch. Clutch purse. All dressed up for a night out. Make-up, even. Lipstick. Yum-yum. A little breathless, slightly flustered.

She scanned the room. Her mouth tightened with irritation then quickly relaxed into relief. She hadn't noticed me, back there in the corner.

She hesitated, trying to make up her mind. The maitre d' did that for her, leading her to a place not a million miles from mine. She'd scarcely sat down before her hand was in her purse.

Gotcha!

She reached for the book of matches in the ashtray on the little marquetry table in front of her. But I got there first. 'Say something in Cambodian,' I said.

She accepted the offered light, again holding my gaze. Kiss, kiss. Puff, puff. '*Neuv m'dohm nih mian miin reu te?*'

Sing-song tones, rising and falling. Pretty convincing, I thought. Especially the long, vibrating vowel at the tail end. 'What's it mean?'

'Stick out your tongue,' she said. 'And say "Ahhh".'

Then the waiter was at her shoulder. 'Excuse me, madam,' he said. 'But if you're the lady with the opera party, your friends said they couldn't wait any longer.'

'Thank you,' she said. 'I'll have a Glenfiddich, no ice.' A warranted indulgence. 'It's been that sort of day.'

'Mine, too,' I said. Particularly the last half-hour. 'Do you mind?'

She didn't have the energy to resist. 'The man with the patches, isn't it? So, do they work?'

'Murray,' I reminded her. 'Ask me next week.' I lit a cigarette. 'I haven't found the right psychological moment.'

'Pathetic, aren't we?' She eased back into her seat, relaxing now.

I liked the *we*. Nothing medicinal about it, this time. 'Didn't know they played opera on Mondays,' I said. 'Or whatever it is they do to opera.'

'Preview night,' she said, going with it. 'A friend works for a big sponsor, got free tickets. *Tristan and Isolde*. To tell the truth, I'm a bit relieved. Wagner's a bit heavy going, don't you think?'

I nodded sagely. The old fucking Nazi. 'I'm more of a Bizet man myself,' I said, playing to the shawl. 'Puccini. That sort of thing.' Goofy on Ice.

Her drink arrived and she took a decent belt. Hard liquor. Hot dog. Doctor, doctor, gimme the news. 'I was thinking of having a bite to eat,' I said, gesturing vaguely in the direction of the bar. 'Do you feel like…'

'I've already eaten, thanks. Couldn't face three hours of Wagner on an empty stomach.'

She yawned, put the back of her hand over her mouth. 'Sorry,' she said. 'I was on stand-by casualty at the Alfred last night. Worked until 2 a.m.'

'Long hours,' I agreed. I was a very agreeable fellow. Just what the doctor ordered. She hadn't said if this friend with the freebies was male or female. The fivesome was three boys, two girls. Odds were it was a he. But he couldn't be that much of a friend if he left without her.

But let's not talk about him, I thought. Let's talk about her. And me.

'You must tell me all about Cambodia,' I said, searching for common ground beyond operaphobia and cigarette addiction. 'I used to work at Ethnic Affairs. Had a bit of contact with the Indochinese community here in Melbourne.' Angelo opened a festival once. Tet. My job was to see he didn't do anything offensive.

'Perhaps some other time.'

Not quite the brush-off. She *was* dog-tired. I could see it. But there was something I definitely needed to know. 'If you don't mind me asking,' I said, coming right out with it. 'Are you by any chance married or otherwise involved at the moment?'

She took her time, languidly swirling the liquid in her glass. 'Why do you ask?'

'So I won't ask you anything inappropriate.'

'Such as?'

The entree card was in my hand. 'I know it's short notice and all, but there's this big Olympic dinner on Thursday...'

I felt the old visceral clutch. Apart from anything else, there was the doctor-patient ethical stuff. Not that she was my doctor. Bernie was my doctor and I wouldn't dream of asking Bernie out.

But she was smiling. 'I'll see you there,' she said.

'Really?' If I had a tail, I would've wagged it. 'You'll come?'

'I already am. Rodney, the one with the opera tickets, he's something to do with the Olympics, too. I'm going with him.'

If I was your friend, I wanted to say, I wouldn't have left you for *Tristan and Isolde*. Either of them. I'd be here with my magic flute, working up a little *Così fan tutte*. Something to do with the Olympics, eh? Him and half of Melbourne.

She yawned again. 'Sorry,' she smiled, heavy lidded. ''Scuse me.'

'Sure,' I shrugged.

She looked a shade off-colour. 'Can you smell something?'

'I think the water in the flower vases needs changing.'

She finished her drink. 'I think I'll make the most of my reprieve, get an early night.'

'Very sensible.' I was in with a chance. Look at the opposition. One of three chinless wonders. We parted at the door.

'Good luck,' she said. I didn't think she just meant quitting cigarettes.

Dinner was a Hokkien mee at the Nam Loong. Five dollars fifty and you couldn't do it cheaper at home. Strips of red-cooked pork in the window, a melamine bowl and teacup, a bucket of chopsticks on every table and Cantonese caterwauling from the kitchen. Stuffed with noodles and jasmine tea, I waddled back up to the Collins Street tram stop. The footpath was thick with moviegoers headed for *Death Warrant* and *RoboCop 2*. Evidence that, even at eight-thirty on a Monday night, the vibrancy of our city's cultural life yielded to none. As we clattered past the Old Treasury, I noticed that upstairs lights were still blazing.

Work, you bastards, I silently urged. Do whatever it takes. The barbarians are at the gate, nudging it open with the doors of their Rolls Royces. Win us this bid or Labor's fate is sealed. Win it and we will set our house in order. Lose it and in will rush the Liberals, and with them all that is grasping, avaricious, mean-spirited, cynical, arrogant, self-righteous, punishing, hypocritical, pompous and cruel.

Nothing like a feed of Chinese to get the proletarian juices flowing.

I bought milk and bread at the souvlaki joint on the corner and walked up the narrow street to my humble abode, meeting its emptiness with fortitude sufficient unto the day. The red light was blinking on the answering machine. Brian Morrison reminding me of the morning's meeting with the MOB.

I showered off the remnant *bouquet de dumpster* and balled Hugo into a supermarket carry-bag, ready for the dry-cleaner. I'd missed 'Four Corners' and there was nothing left on television, so I set the alarm for seven and hit the hay early.

As sleep's dark pool rose to meet me, laughing picca-ninnies splashing among its lily pads, a faint presence crept towards me through the night, scattering the X-ray barramundi. Wugga wugga, it went. Wugga wugga. Kjuk kjuk kjuk.

The fucking police helicopter. It passed overhead, low enough to rattle the window glass. Then came the sirens. First ambulance, then police. Then more police.

Trouble at the flats. Again. Police over-reaction. Again. You could bet they never hovered above silvertail Toorak at chimney height, setting the cookware rattling and terrifying the companion animals. Nor were they patrolling city laneways, protecting innocent ministerial advisers from the steroid-deranged psychopathic ex-boyfriends of pulchritudinous aerobics instructors. Never around when you needed them. Wugga wugga, they went, interminably.

I buried my head in my pillow and embraced the darkness.

'Say "Ahh",' she said. 'And tell me where it hurts.'

The clock radio woke me at three minutes past seven with what was left of the hourly news bulletin: '...*outside the Fitzroy flats last night. Police have so far been unable to establish a motive for the fatal attack. They believe the man, a local resident, may have been the victim of a gang bashing and are appealing for witnesses.*'

The reporter's voice came at me through the fug of waking. It was not until my feet were on the floor and the news had shifted to Canberra that I fully registered the meaning of her words. A street killing in Fitzroy last night? Well, that explained the police helicopter, I thought, as I groped my way towards the shaving mirror and the low-fat milk.

A bit of a worry, a lethal bashing only streets away. But this was Fitzroy, after all. And thus had it ever been. In a perverse way, there was even something comforting about the persistence of crime in Melbourne's oldest suburb. A victory of tradition over the forces of gentrification.

Today was the day, I swore over my high-fibre cereal. Yesterday was a false dawn; my relapse was due to circumstances beyond my control. It was now or never. I stood naked before the mirror, scraped the remnants of adhesive off my solar plexus and carefully attached a new Nicabate patch. I shaved and dressed. Then, as my tea brewed, I field-stripped my thirteen remaining cigarettes and washed the tobacco down the sink. Take that, you bastards.

Bright-eyed and bushy-tailed, I stepped out into the dawning day. The morning was fresh with promise. The sky above the flats glowed with the first flush of sunrise. Pink, grey and yellow streaked the clouds, marbling them like the layers of some outrageous confectionery. Sunlight struck the dewy lawns of the Exhibition Gardens, transforming them into a carpet of diamonds. The air was crisp and invigorating. I breathed deep and felt it doing me good.

As I walked towards the city, I mentally marshalled my arguments for the Aboriginal Institute of Sport. I also recalled the words of the news bulletin. *The victim of a gang bashing.* What the fuck did that mean?

Fitzroy didn't have gangs. Not any more. This wasn't the 1920s when razor-toting larrikins tore the pickets off fences and beat each other insensible at all-in brawls. Nor was it Bedford-Stuyvesant, or South Central LA with its ethnic warfare and drive-by shootings. We still had our rough edges, our greatcoated winos and barefoot ferals, our ferret-faced teenage mothers and lingerie lunches, our dumb-fuck rev-heads and back-lane chop shops. But these were no more than the embellishments of urbanity, bait for a suburban gentry in search of inner-city authenticity. In reality, the corner pub had given way to the sushi bar and the futon factory. And racial differences were just so much local colour. In contemporary Fitzroy, street violence was rarer than an oven-roasted artichoke heart.

The front doors of the Old Treasury were not yet open for business, so I pressed the night bell and waited on the doorstep, watching an endless flow of commuters emerge from Parliament station. At the kiosk on the footpath, newspaper posters hung in their wire racks. BEATEN TO DEATH. COUP FEARS IN KREMLIN. Both the morning dailies were, by the look of it, leading with bad news about the government.

One of Brian Morrison's efficiency women opened the door, led me upstairs to the first floor, offered me coffee and deposited me in a small conference room almost identical to the one in which I had lunched with Denis and Woeful the previous Friday. On the table was a large, lushly produced book with a cloth-bound slipcover embossed with the MOB logo. It was a copy of the city's formal proposal to the IOC, a paean to Melbourne's pre-eminent suitability to stage the Olympic Games.

Each sport had a chapter, replete with technical specifications, projected attendance figures and unimpeded hyperbole. Even culture got a run: shots of string quartets and white-faced mimes were interspersed with cross-hatched rock wallabies and a bearded Aborigine I was sure I had once seen at the Victoria Market, sitting cross-legged on the asphalt with a didgeridoo, busking for coins beside the hot-donut wagon.

I flipped through the book and drained two cups of coffee. The door-opening woman reappeared and delivered a photocopied memo. The words were mine, but the signature belonged to Brian Morrison. It confirmed that Denis Dogherty's game plan was running exactly to schedule.

The Aboriginal Institute of Sport was now an initiative of the MOB Department of Government, Corporate and Community Relations. The board was urged to commit itself to the project as part of the total Olympic package and to request government endorsement. As I finished reading, Brian opened the door.

'The board is studying it now,' he said. No hello, no nothing. 'I wheel you in, you give it a general boost, answer any questions. Ready to rip?'

As ready as I'd ever be. Talk about a cowboy outfit, this MOB was the original pearl-handled capgun. We went along the corridor and stopped at a door. Brian reached for the handle, paused, furrowed his brow and drew me back a couple of steps. 'What do you know about this killing at the flats last night?'

'I heard the flying pig and lots of sirens,' I shrugged. 'The radio said some poor prick got himself beaten to death.'

'Some poor *Koori* prick.' He paused expectantly. Suddenly I was the resident expert on dead Aborigines. 'No negative fall-out for us, I hope.'

'Well, I didn't kill him, if that's what you mean.'

'Ha. Ha. You know perfectly well what I mean.'

'He wasn't in police custody at the time, was he?'

Brian smirked and eased the door open. 'Let's be thankful for small mercies.'

We went into a room with Victorian-era wallpaper and French windows overlooking Collins Street. A long conference table ran its length. Sitting around it were about a dozen men, each looking like he'd been born wearing a suit.

This was the force at the core of the MOB. The business worthies and marketing experts and superannuated sports officials in whom the city had invested its highest hopes. In whose hands rested the future of the Labor government. Men who regarded spending other people's money as their highest public duty. Men far too important to wash their own socks or iron their own shirts. Pulse-takers and decision-makers. The only woman in the room was taking minutes. It was pretty much as I'd expected.

Hugh Knowles, the big banana, was seated at the far end of the table. He was a flinty-eyed man in his late fifties with a crown of pepper-and-salt hair. According to the finance pages, he possessed an air of quiet authority. For my money, he had all the charisma of an actuary.

Flanking Knowles was one of the men I had seen in the lounge at Mietta's. The horse-faced one who had whispered to the waiter, then bolted for the opera. Phillipa's friend. My rival. He had about him the alertly oleaginous air of a professional courtier.

I adopted a suitably deferential demeanour and stood at the end of the table while Brian introduced me as a special consultant on Aboriginal matters. The room responded with a collective look of such profound sympathy that he might equally have told them I was dying of leukaemia. He sat down and I went into my shtick.

'The proposal currently before you provides a unique opportunity to project a positive international image of Australia's race relations. It will also serve to further enhance support for the bid from the Aboriginal community.' Blah, blah. And so on and so forth, about five minutes' worth, including manicured thumbnail costings. 'Any questions.'

There was a long silence, then Knowles' greasy sidekick leaned forward. 'Downside?' he said.

I sucked my cheeks and gave it a count of ten. Brian had no doubt spread a little quiet terror, talked up the threat angle. My job was to show them the stick but not to wave it about. 'Failure to grasp this opportunity could be construed as lack of commitment to racial justice by a certain member of the Evaluation Commission due in town this week.'

The darkie, not to put too fine a point on it. You could hear the creases falling out of their underpants. There was a minute but distinct shifting of bodies in chairs as attention was transferred from me to the far end of the table. Hugh Knowles cleared his throat. When he spoke, his voice was barely audible. A flat, lock-jaw monotone.

'Thank you, very much,' he said. 'Mr Whelan.'

And that was it. Brian was out of his seat like a rocket, piloting me through the door, easing it shut behind him as gently as if stepping from a nursery.

'Great work, mate,' he declared in a reverential half-whisper. 'It's a foregone conclusion. You can sense the enthusiasm. Call me in an hour.' He slapped me on the shoulder and slithered back inside.

Go figure.

As I stepped outside, I suddenly realised that I hadn't so much as thought about a cigarette since leaving home. It was a realisation that filled me with a pleasure as satisfying as any smoke could provide. A pleasure that lasted just about as long as it took me to cross the street to the news kiosk and read the front page of the *Sun*.

> The unconscious body of a 22-year-old student, Darcy Anderson, was discovered lying in the undercroft of the Gertrude Street flats at about 10 p.m. He was rushed

to St Vincent's Hospital where he died a short time later of severe head injuries. A promising triathlete, Anderson was training at the Stars gymnasium shortly before his death.

The story was illustrated with a photo of the crime scene and rounded off with the 'Crime Stoppers' hotline number.

Jesus Christ. So this was the dead Koori that Brian was wondering about. Darcy Anderson. The kid in the gym. This wasn't just some anonymous punch-up at the flats. This was somebody I could put a face to. Somebody I had spoken with, if only to say hello. This was also a death with wider implications.

The nearest phone was a hundred yards down the street in the glass-roofed plaza at Collins Place. I waited my turn, thinking that maybe it was time I got myself a mobile. Became a proper wanker.

Ken Sproule was senior adviser to the Minister for Police. Our respective masters did not exactly see eye-to-eye but Ken didn't hold that against me. Ken was a crafty little fixer with a keen sense of the nuances and a man who tried not to make more enemies than absolutely necessary. If he saw any mileage in it, he could even be helpful.

'You know I can't talk about police operational matters,' he said. 'Even if it did happen in your front yard.'

I wasn't calling on behalf of the Fitzroy branch of Neighbourhood Watch, I explained, but because I was doing a spot of Koori cajoling for the Olympic bid. 'Not a convenient time for young Aboriginal athletes to start getting themselves killed,' I said. 'Just tell me it wasn't racially motivated.'

Under the circumstances, Ken was prepared to be a tad more forthcoming. 'Sorry, mate,' he said. 'But I'm afraid that's exactly what it looks like. A gang of skinheads were seen trying to pick a fight with him in the street yesterday afternoon, very close to where he later had his head smashed against a concrete pillar. Homicide are out there now, trying to track them down. Unfortunately, our informants aren't what you might call the world's most reliable witnesses. Piss-heads from the Royal Hotel across the road. All of them well tanked, most with prior convictions. Apart from the haircuts, none of them can describe these alleged skinheads for shit.'

'I can.' I told him what I'd seen the previous afternoon.

'Why didn't you fucking well say so,' he said. 'Hold on a tick.'

While I was standing there with the phone in my hand, I looked across the plaza and saw Hugh Knowles striding manfully towards the entrance of one of the office towers. His briefcase bearer, Dr Phillipa's friend, trotted at his heels. Knowles, not missing a beat, fed himself into one of the revolving doors. His hoplite was not so adroit. The rubber edge of the door hit him in the face and he reeled back, clutching his nose.

'What's so funny?' said Ken Sproule. He'd been onto the cops. They wanted a contact number. I told them they could get me at Woeful McKenzie's office and he rang off, telling me to expect their call.

It was ten o'clock. Time to connect with Denis. I headed back towards Spring Street. Up ahead, some sort of press conference was happening in front of the Old Treasury, a knot of cameras and notebook-toting hacks milling at the foot of the terrace. As I reached the corner, the ruck parted and I saw the object of their attention.

A hand-painted banner had been unfurled across the front of the building. NO OLYMPICS WITHOUT JUSTICE, it read. Lined up behind it, arms folded in an attitude of truculent militancy, stood a row of young Koories. In front of it, speaking into a megaphone, was Ambrose Buchanan. He was in full oratorical flight, his words ringing across the intersection.

'If racist thugs believe they can attack Aboriginal people,' he declared, 'it's because institutions like the one behind us are prepared to tolerate their activities. Until we get justice for Aboriginal people, how can we be expected to support this country's bid for the Olympics?'

He thrust his fist into the air and began to chant, his slogan echoed by the bumfluff brigade behind him. '*No Olympics without Justice. No Olympics without Justice.*'

My heart, never reliably buoyant, sank.

But I knew immediately what I must do. What any reasonable, thinking, politically aware member of the Labor Party would do under the circumstances. I left the scene. Quickly. Concealed in a thicket of pedestrians, I continued on my way towards the Sports Ministry.

By the time I reached the next corner, the banner was being rolled up, the Young Panthers had stuck their clenched fists in the pockets of their windbreakers and the hacks had closed their notebooks. Having made the media deadlines, Ambrose and crew clearly had no intention of hanging around the Old Treasury steps all day.

Keener than ever to speak with Denis, I hurried upstairs to Woeful McKenzie's office. The minister was closeted with his departmental head and Denis was nowhere in sight. According to Carmel, he hadn't arrived at work yet. While I waited for him, I borrowed his desk and rang Brian Morrison.

Brian came down the line at me with the unstoppable enthusiasm of a fire hose. 'We got the green light,' he crowed. 'Soon as Cabinet okays the funding, Knowles'll make the announcement. Great work, mate.'

'Looked out your window recently?'

'Buchanan?' he said. 'Plus two men and a dog. The only thing that little tantrum will achieve is to undermine his credibility. We kept our part of the bargain and Ambrose Buchanan has no legitimate reason to go bitching.'

'You don't think this killing in Fitzroy could make us look bad? The cops think race was a factor.'

'Crime happens everywhere, mate. The IOC members understand that. Christ, the IOC from Uganda used to run the army for Idi Amin. What's one killing more or less to someone like him? Our job is to demonstrate that such things are an aberration. To counter any residual perception that this is a racist society. Which this institute project will help achieve. A project that we now own, thanks to you. Soon as Charlie Talbot gets back from Africa, the local community can add its stamp of approval. You've stitched up Ambrose Buchanan beautifully, Murray.'

Not an achievement in which I felt I could take much pride. It didn't seem the ideal moment to confess that Denis and I had somewhat overstated Ambrose Buchanan's negotiating stance on the institute matter. Fabricated it, actually. 'So what should I tell Buchanan?'

'As of now, he's out of the loop, irrelevant. And your job is to work with Denis, advance the proposal through Cabinet so Hugh Knowles can announce it at the dinner on

Thursday night. Far as I'm concerned, you can tell Ambrose Buchanan to go to buggery.'

Instead, I called the Water bureaucrats to get a progress report on the union negotiations. Progress was not progressing. It was, in fact, regressing. After months of bluster, the union had called a snap strike. Effective as of midday, all maintenance crews were off the job.

Being the first strike ever in the history of the metropolitan water utility, this was embarrassing news for Angelo Agnelli. Fortunately for me, it had not happened on my watch. For the next few days, at least, it was not my problem. And, with any luck, it would all be over by the time I returned. Leaving a few well-chosen words of encouragement for the minister, I pleaded pressing Olympic business and rang off.

By now, it was past ten-thirty and Denis still hadn't clocked on for the day. I rang around Parliament House, thinking maybe there'd been some misunderstanding about where we would meet. He wasn't there either. I was trying to make up my mind whether or not to wait when Woeful's door opened. His departmental head emerged, carrying a bundle of files, and disappeared down the corridor.

'Due at the Premier's in ten minutes,' Carmel warbled.

Woeful lumbered out and stood at her desk. 'Where's Denis?' he demanded.

Carmel shook her head and shrugged. 'I've just had Marj Dogherty on the line, wanting to know if he had to go up the bush or interstate or anything on short notice.' She handed Woeful a sheet of paper, his copy of my Cabinet submission on the Aboriginal Sports Institute.

Woeful pushed his eyebrows together, scanning the page. 'Not that I know of,' he grunted. 'Why?'

Carmel's confidential secretary eyes slid across to me. They slid back to Woeful. I must have passed the credentials committee. But only just. She lowered her voice. 'Apparently he didn't go home last night.'

'How do you mean, didn't go home?'

'Didn't go home,' she repeated. She tapped the face of her watch. Chop, chop.

Woeful hesitated, suspended between two demands. 'Well,' he growled. 'How am I supposed to know where he is?' The sheet of paper became a cylinder in his hands. He slapped it against his open palm a couple of times, deliberating.

Then he noticed me. 'Thought you were supposed to be squaring things off with that Ambrose Buchanan. I look out my window this morning, there he is, across the road, shitting on the MOB's doorstep. Bloody big help you turned out to be.'

True. 'This kid getting killed last night didn't help.'

The big man sighed gloomily. 'Terrible business.'

Poor old Woeful, I thought. The last vestige of that vanished era when the ranks of the Labor Party were filled with such men. Shearers, engine drivers, coal miners. A time that still informed our collective mythology. But a time long gone. Only accident and inertia and the obscure functioning of factional hydraulics had allowed Woeful to rise as far as he had. And the talents of his trusty henchman, Denis Dogherty.

Nobody, least of all Woeful himself, ever pretended that managerial talent had anything to do with it. By rights, he belonged in a museum. Either that or serving out the twilight of his career lunching with the trustees of the Tennis Centre and appointing his cronies to the Bookmakers Registration

Board. Not bearing the full weight of the party's hopes and the people's Olympic expectations.

'According to Ken Sproule, the cops think it was racially motivated.'

Woeful's shoulders sank another inch. 'Just what we need.' He peered at me suspiciously. 'Mate of Sproule's, are you?'

'Strictly business,' I protested, hand on heart. The Minister for Police, Ken Sproule's master, was Woeful's most powerful adversary in caucus, Gil Methven. 'Wouldn't trust him as far as I could throw him.'

'Bloody well hope so,' said Woeful, apparently mollified. 'Haven't seen Denis this morning, by any chance?'

I shook my head. 'Not since we left here last night. Said he was going home. I'm looking for him myself, check progress on the Cabinet item.' I indicated the paper in his hand.

Woeful nodded absently, like he'd already forgotten the question. He looked down at the cylinder of paper and gave a resigned shrug. 'Suppose I'd better do what I'm told, then. Go give the Premier a nudge.' He set off, bear-like, towards the lifts.

'What'll I tell Marj?' called Carmel after him. He vanished around the corner, making no reply.

'Denis ever done this sort of thing before?' I asked her. 'Not go home?'

She stared at me across the rampart of her desk, blank-faced. What she saw was a person of uncertain status. A man who trafficked with the minions of Gil Methven. As far as she was concerned, Denis Dogherty's domestic arrangements were not the subject of office gossip. And she was right. It was none of my business. A man might not go home for any number of reasons.

At that point, the phone rang. It was for me. The police. Carmel arched her eyebrows and switched the call through to Denis's desk.

The voice identified itself as Detective Senior Constable Carol Sonderlund who stated that she was calling in relation to the incident in Fitzroy overnight. While the police appreciated my offer to help identify possible offenders in the matter, my assistance would not be required. Adequate descriptions of the individuals concerned had been subsequently obtained from a number of people who had seen them in the vicinity the previous afternoon.

This dose of wary legalese suggested that I was getting the full benefit of Ken Sproule's clout at police HQ. 'You really think the skinheads killed Darcy Anderson?' I said, fishing for information. 'They didn't strike me as being up to it.'

'We'll determine that when we interview the persons concerned,' said Sonderlund.

So they hadn't picked them up yet. 'Any other suspects?'

I didn't really expect an answer and I didn't get one. Denis's desk diary was sitting beside the phone. I flipped it open and checked the previous night. No appointment was listed. Inquiries were continuing, Detective Sonderlund advised me, and the police were optimistic of an early arrest.

When I went back to the minister's office, Carmel was speaking softly into the phone. 'I'm sure there's a simple explanation, Marj.' As I came in, she put her hand over the mouthpiece. 'I'll let him know you called,' she told me. She took her hand off the phone and waited for me to leave.

Fair enough. The punctuality of a member of Woeful McKenzie's staff was hardly my affair. My actual employer, *pro tem*, was the MOB. And, so far, I had met my contractual obligations to them. Nobody was paying me to sit around twiddling my thumbs waiting on a missed appointment. An appointment which was now unnecessary since I'd spoken to the minister myself and confirmed that the matter was in hand.

I went to the gym.

Holly Deloite was wiping the glass display cabinet behind the reception desk. The electric blue of her leotard exactly matched the colour of the window-cleaning fluid. Her eyes were a slightly paler tint. She opened them very wide.

'You're kidding!' She put down her pump-pack of Windex. 'Steve Radeski threw you in a dumpster?'

'Not threw,' I said. 'Shut. After I threw myself, trying to get away. Soon as I opened my mouth, he went absolutely batshit. Tried to kill me, I swear. If he's not on steroids, I'm Mr Universe.'

'He's definitely on something,' she confirmed. 'Must be. In the six weeks I've been in Queensland, he's really bulked up. Stacked on, like, thirty-five kilos. Which is, like, crazy. I mean it's not like he's competing any more.'

'What would he compete in?' I said. 'The pan-galactic dickhead titles?'

She got all defensive then, probably because she could tell I was wondering what she'd ever seen in the guy. 'Believe it or not,' she said. 'Steve Radeski used to be an Olympic athlete. Almost, anyway. He was in the national weightlifting squad. Not one of the really big ones, either. Eighty-kilo class.' I currently weighed slightly more than that. 'He used to be a pretty nice guy.'

'Well, he isn't any more,' I said. 'He's a maniac. And, if I were you, I'd be worried about him hanging around this place.' Suddenly I was back *in loco parentis*. 'And not just because he might get you fired.'

Holly drew back her shoulders and fired a rapid volley of cleaner onto the counter top. 'Don't worry about me.' Squirt, squirt. Wipe. Wipe. 'I can handle Steve Radeski.'

'Excuse me,' called an American accent from behind a rack of pedal-pushers. 'Do you have this in my size?'

'You be careful,' I warned. 'Or I won't join your aerobics class.'

Holly darted a quick glance around the gym, then leaned across the counter and gave me a peck on the cheek. 'You're very sweet to worry,' she said. 'Coming!'

Sweet? I didn't want to be sweet. I wanted to be feared. I wanted to be desired. I wanted the body of a twenty-year-old. I changed into my shorts, set the resistance dial on the exercise bike to Tour de France and climbed aboard. I took a deep breath and filled my lungs with air. It was fourteen hours since my last cigarette and I wanted to see what those babies could do.

The patch on my midriff was definitely working, foxing my nicotine receptors with its surreptitious hex. The thought of cigarettes had scarcely entered my brain all morning. Cigarettes were a thing of the past. For cigarettes I felt nothing at all. Perhaps a slight nostalgia, a remembrance of things past. But, beyond that, nothing. *Nada. Niente.* What I did feel, by the time I'd run to the top of the Empire State Building on the Stairmaster and rowed the length of the Amazon on the rowing machine, was gut-churning sick.

All morning, ever since my song-and-dance routine before the MOB bigwigs, a teensy jitter had been creeping up on me. A faint standuppishness at the nape of the neck. A slight cerebral pulsation. Now, my bloodstream pulsing with nicotine and lactic acid, I definitely needed a little lie down.

I staggered into the sauna and fell naked onto the top row of roasted cedar planks. A purging heat enveloped me, rich with the koala-fart aroma of eucalyptus oil. Sweat gushed from my pores, sluicing away the toxins in a great, cleansing torrent. Gradually, my stomach settled. I lay there, my brain twitching, thinking about Ambrose Buchanan.

He had been pretty fast off the mark. Even a pissy little demonstration like the one on the Old Treasury steps took a bit of organising. Paint the banner. Find the megaphone. Round up the usual suspects. Which suggested that he'd been planning all along to come out against the bid at the first opportunity. Which made it look like he'd been jerking my string with his Aboriginal Institute of Sport idea. If so, he'd shot himself in the foot, handing a great PR opportunity to the MOB even as he planned to attack it. Not a smart move, on the face of it.

Perhaps he didn't expect us to deliver. The white establishment didn't usually fall over itself in its haste to implement suggestions from black activists. As far as Ambrose knew, the MOB hadn't yet even considered his proposal, let alone snapped it up and taken it over. Quite possibly, he had simply assumed he would get the customary run-around and acted accordingly.

No Olympics without Justice. Was that an ambit claim, a coverall slogan that encompassed the entire wider agenda? Or did it refer specifically to the Darcy Anderson case? Ambrose's sound bite blamed racist thugs. Was he referring to the skinheads, or making a general polemical point? With the police hot on the trail of the suburban bovver boys, how could Brother Ambrose justify his inference that the MOB was somehow complicit in Darcy Anderson's death? Surely that was just polemic.

By the time I got under the shower, my bones had turned to rubber. As I wafted back through the gym, Holly hailed me. 'Um,' she said, tentatively. 'I was wondering if you could do me a favour.'

'Sure,' I said. 'Name it.'

Unfortunately, she did. 'It's just that there's some CDs and stuff, a cassette player, that I left at this person's place when I went to Queensland. Anyway, I really need them back for this new aerobics routine I'm working on. Only I haven't, like, got a car at the moment and I was just wondering...'

'You need a lift?'

'It's not far. Heidelberg.'

A twenty-minute run, hardly a major excursion. On the other hand, I didn't actually have a car. 'Um.' I prevaricated, thinking that my stolen car story would sound like a bullshit excuse.

'Of course, if it's not convenient.'

It was all I could do not to laugh. I'd seen better pouts on a two-year-old. 'Somebody else is using my car at the moment,' I said. 'But I could probably borrow one from the pool at work.'

'Great.' She brightened immediately. 'Is tonight after work okay?'

What the hell, I thought. It wasn't every day that a gorgeous young gym bunny tried to twist me around her little finger. And it wasn't like I was expecting Michelle Pfeiffer around for a candle-lit dinner, after all. Or even

Doctor Phillipa Verstak for that matter. And Heidelberg wasn't Wheelers Hill or Hoppers Crossing or Patterson Lakes, some godforsaken suburban dormitory an hour away.

'You finish at eight?' I said. 'Right?'

Downstairs in the food court, I sat at the bar with a bowl of rabbit food and a bottle of Evian. My personal contribution to the national current-account deficit. 'See that,' said the barman. The picture on the big-screen television showed a pillar of water gushing high into air, a great white geyser exploding from the middle of a residential street. 'Some idiot driving around town, running over fire hydrants.'

I cocked my ear to the voice-over. Over two thousand homes were currently without water in the western suburbs and emergency tankers had been rushed to parts of Hampton and Glen Waverley.

For a moment, I was tempted to call Water Supply and find out what was going on. I dismissed the thought. For a few days at least, they could get along without me. I lingered over my lettuce, sipped my spring water, then set an unhurried course for the nearest blackfellers' camp.

It was one of those days when you can almost see the point of golf. A day not to be stuck indoors, chained to a desk.

I headed down the sunny side of Exhibition Street and into the Carlton Gardens. The Ideal Home Show had just opened and young couples on their lunch-break hurried past, hand in hand, in hot pursuit of fresh kitchen ideas and new bathroom solutions. Their destination, the resplendent cupola of the Exhibition Building, floated above the treetops like a Valkyrie's bra cup. The sky was a cloudless vault, but in the deep shade of the Moreton Bay figs there was a damp chill in the air that sent a shiver down my spine.

I broke back out into the sunshine and turned down Gertrude Street towards the Stars Cafe. At a piss-drenched phone booth outside the Champion Hotel, I rang Sport for a word with Denis.

Still no show. But there was a message from Woeful. The Premier had okayed the agenda inclusion request. And could I come to Woeful's office at Parliament House at five, no reason given.

Further down the street, the perennial cluster of malingerers on the steps of the Aboriginal Health Service eyed me impassively as I walked by. Across the road, the flats looked exactly as they had the previous day. Nothing suggested that a young man had been beaten to death there less than eighteen hours earlier. I half-expected signs of police activity. Doorknocking uniforms, latex-gloved forensic pathologists, homicide dicks with narrow ties and gruff manners. As it was, nothing out of the usual marked Darcy Anderson's passing.

Almost nothing. The Stars was closed. Black crepe paper was taped around the windows and a hand-printed notice was pinned to the door. 'In memoriam Darcy Kevin Anderson. Closed until Thursday.' Somebody back up the road at the Health Service could probably point me in the general direction of Ambrose Buchanan, but I wasn't inclined to ask. Under the circumstances, it wasn't a good time to go pushing a bureaucratic wheelbarrow around the neighbourhood.

Ambrose Buchanan would keep. I bought a takeaway coffee and a copy of the city edition of the *Herald* and walked them up to the tram stop opposite St Vincent's consulting rooms. There was nothing for me at Sport, I was avoiding Water and I still had some time to kill before Woeful wanted me at Parliament House. Sooner or later, Phillipa Verstak would come outside for a cigarette and I'd catch her in the act, pretend I just happened to be passing. In the meantime, I sat in the sunshine, ate my lunch and read the paper.

So far, the press spin on the Olympic bid had been unanimously positive. Today was no different. Ambrose Buchanan's little demo on the Old Treasury steps didn't rate a mention, despite the photo opportunity. The *Herald* led instead with a full-page piece about fuck-ups in the public transport ticketing system. Millions Wasted Shock Horror. To compound the damage, the story was a leak from the Transport Workers Federation, a factional game-play by our comrades in the union movement. Yet another of the thousand self-inflicted cuts from which we were slowly dying.

The Labor Party, I thought. It's a great life as long as you don't weaken. Across the road, shifts of smokers came and went. I regarded them with benign condescension. I, too, used to do that. Filthy habit.

Darcy's death got a spread on page five with a photo of the flats and a picture of the victim on a surf-ski, courtesy of the *Warrnambool Advertiser.* They were running the sportsman angle, first Aboriginal to compete at national level in a triathlon, great future cut tragically short. An act of random violence, the nature of the injuries indicating that he had been slammed backwards with considerable force, striking his head against a concrete pillar and dying almost instantly.

A sidebar canvassed resident reactions, playing up the mean-streets angle. A real little morale-booster for the local residents. The Fitzroy flats were no Shangri La, apparently. Shades of the Bronx. Made you wonder why their looming presence never managed to put a dent in local real estate prices. It got to be three o'clock and I'd read the dismal rag from cover to cover twice and still there was no sign of Phillipa.

Now that I thought about it, as far as I could recall, I'd never met a doctor socially. A couple of bulldozer nurses at the Health Employees Federation was as close as I'd ever come, but they didn't count. Doctors and nurses were not in the same class, not by a long calcium carbonate.

Medicine was more a caste than a profession. Socially incompetent alcoholics, most of them. Higher than normal suicide rate. The most lucrative of the money-harvesting professions. Only the law came anywhere near it. Forget Ms Verstak, I told myself. You'd need to be a barrister earning a minimum of two hundred grand to stand any hope at all. Or a mining company executive, holder of the key to the executive washroom, chief pocket pisser to Hugh Knowles.

Feeling like a love-struck schoolboy, I ambled back towards the city. As I passed St Patrick's I was tempted to go inside, examine the architecture, make sure Daniel Mannix was still in his crypt. Instead, I turned down Cathedral Place, cut across an empty building site and tapped on the door of the portable site office in the middle of the pot-holed asphalt expanse which was the government carpark.

Theoretically, ministerial advisers were entitled to the use of a fleet vehicle, if, as and when required, subject to availability and ongoing priorities. As often as not, getting a car was like drawing teeth. I knocked more in hope than certainty.

Fortunately, the dispatch officer recognised me. He'd been Angelo's driver for a while back at Ethnic Affairs, a military type in the agreeable sense. A bit of a finagler. He was bored out of his brain and it took very little persuasion to get him on the phone and initiate proceedings for the issuance of telephone approval from the transport wallah at Water. He probably thought I was headed out to hunt the hydrant kneecapper or direct a tanker run to dehydrated pensioners at the Maidstone old folks home. He was right. I should have been doing something. I just didn't know what.

In due course and the fullness of time, approval was obtained and I was issued with the keys of a white Toyota Corolla with red government plates. The previous user had left a tape in the cassette player. *The Eagles' Greatest Hits*. A powerful argument for the need to downsize the public service. The radio was tuned to the ABC and as I pulled out of the lot the announcer crossed to the newsroom for an update.

Gorbachev was threatening armed intervention in response to Lithuania's unilateral declaration of independence. KGB troops were moving into Vilnius. Ambrose Buchanan made the number two spot, warning that the bid would draw international attention to high Aboriginal mortality rates. This was followed by a police appeal for witnesses in the Darcy Anderson case, a sure sign they weren't making much progress. Dermott Brereton was up before the tribunal on a striking charge, cited on video evidence. Again. The weather outlook was fine and mild.

City traffic was at a crawl. It took me fifteen minutes to get to the underground carpark at the Hyatt and another ten to find a spot. There was a fifteen dollar minimum charge, daylight robbery. By the time I'd argued the toss with the carpark attendant and walked back up the hill to Parliament House the sunshine was all but gone.

Woeful's office was a glass-walled cubicle in the arched

vaults below the Legislative Council. It was a small, functional space with barely enough room to swing a chihuahua. Especially when there were visitors.

Woeful had two of them. The lanky one with the dour face, perched on his chair like a praying mantis, was Gil Methven, the Police Minister. The short one, backed against the bookcase, hands deep in his pockets and doing his best to conceal his glee, was his aide, Ken Sproule. Woeful was hunkered down behind his desk, cornered, looking even more dismal than usual. He saw me arrive and beckoned me inside.

The atmosphere was poisonous. Ken inched to one side, making room for me beside him. Methven ignored me. You could have cut the air with a knife. Woeful was doing the talking.

'He told her he'd be working late last night, so she didn't wait up. She thought he might've been trying to ring but couldn't get through because one of the grandkids knocked the phone off the hook and she hadn't noticed. She's frantic with worry. Called all the hospitals. Been ringing the office every five minutes to see if he's turned up.'

Gil was a hard man of the right and not noted for his sense of compassion. He spoke with a hoarse, sandpapery rasp that made him sound like he'd been screaming at his subordinates all afternoon. He probably had. 'We can give it to Missing Persons,' he said bluntly. 'But there's nothing they can do until the morning.'

'What are you saying?' grumbled Woeful. 'That I should go back to his wife and tell her not to do anything?'

'Gil's just laying it out for you.' Ken spoke soothingly. 'Once it's official, it's out of our hands. Word goes around. Lots of different people start shaking the tree, you never know what might fall out. You've got absolutely no idea where he might be?'

Woeful spread his palms and shrugged morosely. Going to Gil Methven for help must have required considerable effort. The pair had been bitter factional foes since the dawn of time and Methven had publicly questioned Woeful's fitness as a minister on more than one occasion.

'Hasn't got a girlfriend, has he?' rasped Methven.

Woeful bristled. 'He's been happily married for thirty-five years.' As if that had anything to do with it.

'We're not trying to pry,' said Ken.

Woeful fixed his jaw. 'Definitely nothing on the side. I'd know if there was.'

'Nervous breakdown?' said Methven. 'Out of his depth at work?'

Woeful snorted contemptuously. Nervous breakdowns were for nervous Nellies. 'What you're really saying is that he's been promoted above his level of competence. Like me.'

Again, Ken hastened to pour oil on the waters. 'You've got a lot on your plate, Woeful, that's all. This Olympic business, we're all hanging on the outcome. A conscientious bloke like Denis, it'd be no reflection on him if it all got a bit overwhelming. And these things do tend to happen out of the blue, no warning.'

Woeful looked a long way from convinced. 'Put it like that,' he said, grudgingly.

Gil Methven looked at me sideways. 'You're Agnelli's bum boy, right, Wheeler, something like that?'

A lifetime in the Labor Party had inured me to such childish name-calling. After the last election, Agnelli had helped marshal the caucus numbers to deny Gil the deputy premiership, so I knew his remarks weren't personal. I rose above them.

'You must be mistaking me for somebody else,' I said. 'Someone easily intimidated by a pompous arsehole.'

'Now that we've got all that off our chests,' said Ken cheerfully. 'Woeful says you were the last one to speak to Denis last night.'

'We left the office together,' I said. 'About seven.'

'He say where he was going?'

'Home,' I said. 'And I'm no expert, but he didn't look like a man on the brink of a nervous breakdown.'

Woeful shot me a grateful glance and I realised why I was there. In Denis's absence, Woeful wanted a witness to his dealings with Gil Methven.

'Orright,' said the Police Minister. 'Either the wife reports it now, or she waits until the morning. If she decides to wait, Ken here can have a few discreet inquiries made.'

Woeful made a noise in the back of his throat. 'What's that supposed to mean?'

Methven slowly unfolded his legs and stood up. 'You were the one came to me,' he said. 'You don't want my help, fine.'

The bells began to ring for a division. A continuous, insistent jangle, penetrating as a dentist's drill. It filled the tiny office, on and on. When at last Woeful spoke, he all but choked on his words. 'I appreciate this, Gil. I really do. I'll talk to Marjorie, suggest she waits.'

We in the Victorian branch of the ALP may have lacked the viscous cohesion of the NSW Right, but we were not entirely without a sense of solidarity. Factional differences were sharp in our decline, but they were not yet cut-throat. If one of the boys goes missing, you send out a friendly search party.

The two ministers went upstairs, each taking a different route. 'Nice work,' I said to Ken.

He agreed. 'When you've got 'em by the short and curlies.'

'So what are you going to do about finding Denis?'

'Fucked if I know,' he shrugged.

Holly looked edible. An absolute muffin. Thigh-length V-neck sweater over her lycra work-out suit, her ponytail threaded through the back of a suede-billed Nike baseball cap. She brought an empty sports bag with her, tossed it in the back seat, and we headed north through the suburban night. Her effervescence filled the car like a well-shaken bottle of Gatorade.   .

'I really appreciate this,' she said.

'My pleasure. Beats sitting around the old folks home, dribbling in my rocking chair.'

'C'mon. You're only as old as you feel.'

I didn't feel a day over a hundred. But we old codgers must take our pleasures where we find them. I couldn't help but notice that, every time we stopped at a red light, I copped envious glances from men in other cars. Holly's buoyant mood was infectious. I told her about the Charade and we laughed like drains. 'I mean, why bother to steal a car like that?' she said. 'No offence.'

As we conjured up the possibilities—getaway car for a poor-box robbery, a criminal mastermind with low self-esteem—I was thinking what a good idea this had turned out to be. Like a kind of chaste date, I told myself, sneaking guilty sideways looks. Fun, until I asked about our destination. 'So who's this friend?' I asked. 'The one with your CDs?'

She didn't bat an eyelid, the little vixen. 'Steve, of course,' she said. 'Who else?'

'Steve Radeski? That fucking steroid-deranged lunatic?' My foot hit the brake so hard we almost went into a tailspin. 'No way.' I flicked the indicator on.

'Chill out, Murray,' said Holly. 'He won't be there. I made sure of that. He's at work. Some shitty disco in Northcote. I checked. Honest.'

'You sure?'

She crossed her heart and hoped to die.

I flicked the indicator off. 'You must really want this stuff.'

'It's not that. It's, you know, the principle. I want him to realise it's totally over between us. So he stops hassling me.'

I could see her point, sort of. 'Yeah, but what if he's home?'

'He won't be. I rang the place, The Climber. Checked he'd be there. Eight till two, they said.'

'Yeah, but just say he's there.' A hundred kilos of chemically fuelled aggression.

'He won't be,' she insisted. 'Anyway, I can handle him.'

'It's not you I'm worried about,' I said. 'I'm not trained for this sort of work. Maybe you should have got somebody else to drive you.'

'Like who?'

'I don't know. One of those guys I see hitting on you all the time in the gym.' Young blokes with well-defined pectorals. Old blokes with access to private security firms.

'Maybe I prefer to do the hitting.'

What could I say to that? It had to be bullshit, but she knew she had me. 'Okay. He's not there, but ten of his muscle-bound ape mates are.'

'No mates,' she said. 'It's his father's house.'

'Don't tell me,' I said. 'A sweet-tempered four-foot rose enthusiast who cries when he has to kill an aphid.'

'A crabby old tyrant who used to run a weight gym,' she said. 'And thinks the world's out to get him. But don't worry. He won't be there either. He had a stroke and Steve put him in a home.'

'What a great family. How did you get mixed up with this lot?'

She set her heels on the edge of the seat, tucked her knees under her chin, hugged her shins and gave me the full ball of wax. How she met Steve at his father's gym while touting her résumé around the suburban sweat shops, looking for casual work. 'Across the road from the Rosanna railway station, it was. One of those old-style places, just free weights and crash mats and a few ratty old pressing benches. Didn't even have aerobics. Real Charles Atlas stuff.'

The historical reference surprised me. Charles Atlas was back there with Bob Menzies and Queen Victoria.

Holly saw me smile. 'Amaze your friends,' she said. 'You ninety-pound weakling. Anyway, the gym's not there any more. Got taken over by Fit'n'Well before they went bankrupt. I don't think old Rudy Radeski was much of a businessman.'

Although there was no opening for newly registered aerobics instructors in the Radeski family gymnasium, Steve soon found other ways of making himself useful to Holly. 'He was a very good lover.' She tucked one knee under her chin, hugging her shin. 'You know.'

I told her I could vaguely remember the concept.

'This was, like, before the steroids, right?' she hastened to reassure me. 'Back when he was normal.'

I found it hard to imagine Steve Radeski as normal but I took her word for it. 'A normal weightlifter?'

'A better than average weightlifter. You're just prejudiced. It's a perfectly legitimate sport.'

'Like aerobics?'

'Aerobics isn't a sport,' she said. 'It's an activity.'

Anyway, she continued. It was Steve who alerted her to the vacancy at the City Club. This was when he was working downstairs at the Typhoon nightclub. They might have even moved in together if it hadn't been for Steve's father. 'They were, like, pretty close-knit because his mother died when he was little and his dad brought him up after that, just the two of them.' A widower, his business overtaken by new trends, the old man had become possessive of his son. 'He reckoned I was a distraction. Probably thought I was sapping Steve's strength or something.'

I could see old man Radeski's point. 'Were you?' I said. 'Sapping his strength?'

'Let's just say I gave as good as I got.'

Together the Radeskis concentrated their energies on getting Steve into the national weightlifting squad. Both were ecstatic when he finally made the cut. But their satisfaction was not long-lived.

'Steve reckoned he'd been victimised, that it was all politics. That everybody was using steroids and the federation just needed a scapegoat. After he was kicked out, he didn't know what to do. Just sat around all day feeling sorry for himself, arguing with Rudy, losing condition. That's when things between us started going off the rails. He just didn't care any more. Lost his job at Typhoon. Even lost interest in you know what.'

I nodded sympathetically. To lose interest in you-know-what with Holly Deloite a man would need to be in a bad way. To compound the situation, the father had suffered his stroke. 'Steve wanted to look after him at home but it was hopeless, so he had to put him in a home. He's pretty old anyway,' she explained. 'Sixty-something.'

Geriatric. Just as she told me this, we drove past the Olympic Hotel where my father took the licence after the Carter's Arms. We lived there for nearly five years, all through my adolescence. Unexpectedly, I had a sudden sense of fellow-feeling for Steve Radeski. I, too, was the only son of a widowed father with lousy business acumen. The carpark of the Olympic was now occupied by a Kentucky Fried franchise. Too late for us, the Colonel.

Unlike Rudy Radeski, fortunately, my father had projected none of his own displaced ambitions onto me. The life of a hotelkeeper left him with few illusions, scant time and even less energy. And I took care to do as little as possible to excite his expectations.

And, unlike old man Radeski, my father was not mouldering in some hospice bed. He was living on Bribie Island, fishing every day from his aluminium runabout and studying the stock market with the eye of a man who has finally cracked the code. From a publican who had managed to go broke in five different hotels, he had transformed himself into a late-blooming Midas, parlaying the proceeds from the sale of his last pub into a healthy little nest egg. First it was macadamia nuts, then avocado farms, then resort development. The old fox had even contrived to unload his Qintex shares before the crash of '87, after doubling his dough.

Eventually, I supposed, there would be full-care retirement villages to think about. But later, not now. At seventy-seven, he was showing every sign of living forever.

Sympathy, Holly was explaining, has its limits. Hers ran out when Steve tried to clobber her. 'That was a big mistake. He should have known better,' she said, setting her jaw.

So she'd cut her emotional losses, changed the lock on her flat and left him to wallow in self-pity. When the job-exchange opportunity came up, she jumped at it. Used the six weeks in Queensland to make a clean emotional break. But now, Steve suddenly reappears, acting like he's got some prior claim. Fronting up at her workplace, demanding you-know-what. Almost getting her the sack. Understandably, a girl decides she wants her things back, wants it understood that what's past is past.

Traffic was thin on the divided road, fast moving, and we had the run of the lights. We passed indoor cricket centres and discount furniture showrooms and warehouses lit like nuclear power plants. Heidelberg wasn't much further, two, three kilometres. As the road dipped and narrowed to cross the Darebin Creek, I asked for directions. 'Next left,' said Holly. 'Liberty Parade.'

'Thought you said he lived in Heidelberg?'

'West Heidelberg,' she said. 'Same thing.'

Not where I came from it wasn't. Heidelberg was a leafy middle-class neighbourhood where famous landscape painters once daubed masterpieces *en plein air* on the wooded banks of the Yarra. West Heidelberg, on the other hand, was an experiment gone wrong.

Originally built to accommodate the athletes at the 1956 Olympics, it was hailed at the time as a model of modular housing. A vision of the future where those displaced by inner-urban slum clearances could breathe the life-giving air of suburbia. Within ten years, it was a wasteland of broken fences, ravaged lawns and teenage thuggery.

That, at least, was how I first encountered it, back when it peopled my adolescent imagination with terrors such as the Fletcher brothers who carried knives to school, set fire to Preston Town Hall while the mayoral ball was in progress and eventually graduated to the exercise yard at Pentridge prison, five minutes up the road.

Things had changed, of course, in the two decades since I lived just across the Darebin Creek. A more house-proud ethos had taken root. As we continued past streets named for half-forgotten battlegrounds in far distant lands—Tobruk, Narvik, Wewak—we found ourselves in a working-class neighbourhood as respectable as any in the city, all picket fences and native gardens. But, despite the applied decoration, the houses were still near-identical boxes, biscuits from the same cutter. Three or four standard designs, street after street, varied only by the occasional three-storey walk-up.

We passed a row of shops set back behind a lawn, the approximation of a village square. All were closed but for the hamburger joint, some battling immigrant's grim purchase on prosperity. Holly directed me down a cul-de-sac and I pulled into the kerb.

The Radeski residence was unlikely to rate a feature in *House & Garden*. One of the standard boxes, it squatted behind a rectangle of neglected lawn, the windows dark. The untended lavender hedge had grown woody with neglect and the flowerbeds were choked with weeds. Even the houses on either side were dark, with not even the flicker of television to betray life inside.

'How are you going to get in?' I said.

'Easy.' Holly grabbed her sports bag. 'Back in a couple of minutes.' She bounded up the short path towards the front door.

White-painted rocks about the size of bowling balls lined the path and, as I watched, she picked one up and lobbed it through the frosted glass panel of the front door. With an abrupt clatter, the panel collapsed into a pile of shards. She turned, brushed her palms together, tossed me a smirk and let herself into the house.

Ah, the course of love gone wrong. Doubtless she planned to break every ornament in the place. Nothing to do with me, of course, I was just the wheel man. I slid down in my seat, waiting for the neighbours to appear, alarms to sound. Nothing happened. I unsnapped my seatbelt and twiddled the dial of the car radio. A panel of academics was discussing the future of the Warsaw Pact. Madonna was living in the material world.

No more noises emerged from the house. Smashing down the front door had, it seemed, satisfied Holly's vengeful urges. I stepped out of the car and stretched my legs. The night was cool and very dark. Two streets away, a rev-head gunned his motor and laid rubber. A dog barked. As a kid, I wouldn't have been caught dead in this neighbourhood after sunset. Now the idea seemed just plain silly. Even the animal population had lost its feral edge. A sleek-furred cat appeared from nowhere, mewing expectantly. I reached down and it ran its tail through my hand. 'What's your name, kitty cat?'

The moggie arched its back with pleasure and rubbed itself against my leg. Obviously not a female. It went up the driveway and I went with it, following it around the side to the backyard, killing time.

Along the side fence, tomato stakes were splayed against each other in disarray. A screened porch had been added to the back of the house, its rafters extending to form a pergola shrouded in a tangled mass of overgrown passionfruit vines. A carpet of rotting leaves squelched damply underfoot and the stem of a rotary clothes hoist loomed out of the murk. The driveway extended back to an old zincalum garage, half-buried under creepers, the buckled metal doors sagging on their hinges. I could just make out a small white sedan, the same model as the one I was driving. A jungle of overgrown shrubs swallowed the cat.

Something smacked against my forehead. An old hanging basket, suspended from the pergola. As I backed away, an arm snaked around my neck, squeezing my windpipe and jerking my head backwards. 'Gotcha,' a voice hissed in my ear.

Jesus, I thought. It's on again.

Reflexively, I drove both my elbows backwards, hard.

'Oomph.' Breath rushed past my ear and the choke-hold slackened.

I wrenched free and ran, glancing backwards over my shoulder. Whoever he was, he was definitely not Steve

Radeski. This bloke was much less solidly built. He was wearing a black tracksuit with the hood up and the drawstring pulled tight around his face. That was as much as I could see. A ninja, I thought. Some martial arts dickhead.

He came at me fast, shoulder down. My feet skidded and I slammed into the metal post of the clothes hoist.

'Take it easy,' warned a voice, another shape in the darkness, black on black. He wasn't talking to me.

The two shapes circled, indistinct presences in the darkness. The ninja had something in his hand. He swung wide and it whistled through the air. A blow hit my ribs, a jolt of electricity. He swung again and I dodged sideways. Something struck the clothes hoist and a dull wooden note sounded.

You let your guard down, I thought. Get taken in by a bit of crazy paving and some potted geraniums, start thinking that you can just go wandering around West Heidelberg at night, devil-may-care. This is what happens.

I reached up and grabbed the radial bar of the Hills Hoist, kicking out. My heels connected and I swung backwards, recoiling from the impact. The clothes line spun on its axis and I felt a shudder run through the crossbar. 'Fucken hell,' yelped the voice.

My feet hit the ground running and I darted for the side of the house. Not fast enough. A blow struck the back of my knees and I pitched forward through the air. It was a short flight, no frills. No movie, not even a cup of coffee. When I hit the screen door of the porch, it splintered off its hinges and thwacked flat on the ground, me sprawled on top of it.

I was going to suffer. It was going to be brutal and ugly. I went foetal, arms curled around my head.

'Murray!' shouted Holly from somewhere inside the house.

A white radiance seared through my clenched eyelids. I opened my eyes. Two dark shapes loomed above me, staring down. One of them, his head surrounded by a halo of light, was Darcy Anderson.

'Hey,' he said, irritably. 'You're not Steve Radeski.'

I was staring upwards into the unshaded globe of the porch light. One hundred watts, its sudden incandescence sent hallucinatory worms wriggling across my field of vision. Darcy Anderson's face came in and out of focus.

Not Darcy Anderson, I realised. Similar face, but older and harder. Unmistakable Aboriginal features, burning with malice. Whoever he was, he held a fence picket in his hand and spoke in a staccato burst. 'Where is he? Where's Radeski?'

Standing next to him, staring down in disbelief, was Ambrose Buchanan. He scratched his whiskers. 'Murray Whelan?' he said. 'The fuck you doing here?'

'Murray!' shouted Holly, somewhere close. 'Stop mucking around.' I scrambled to my feet. As the back door flew open, the two Koories melted back into the darkness. Holly appeared in the doorway, her eyes wide with alarm.

'Come quick,' she said. 'There's a body in here.'

The back door opened directly into the kitchen, a fifties laminex job that had seen better days. Vinyl floor tiles and a flickering fluorescent tube. Radeski was a man of simple tastes and prodigious appetite. Either that, or he was doing the catering for the Mormon Tabernacle Choir.

Bulk foodstuffs were piled everywhere. Twenty-five-kilo sacks of rice, hessian bags bulging with potatoes. Cardboard boxes of tuna in brine, plain label. Plastic pails full of something called Megamix 5000, whey protein isolate. Cartons of eggs. Innumerable bottles, vials and jars. Amino acids, creotone monohydrates, ginseng, mineral extracts, an alphabet of vitamins.

Holly charged ahead, through swinging doors, into the lounge room. Not that Radeski had been doing much lounging. Apart from a row of built-in shelves, there was no furniture. Bolted to one wall was a slotted metal frame, some sort of home-made gym equipment. On the floor beside it lay a pile of round weights, like a collection of oversize phonograph records, heavy metal favourites. A press bench sat under the frame, the lifting bar fully loaded. At a glance, Radeski was pressing something in the vicinity of 450 pounds. The air reeked of sweat and the parmesan tang of dried vomit.

We kept going. On the faded floral axminster beside the front door, surrounded by broken glass, lay a cheap boom box and Holly's blue bag, spilling audio tapes and dog-eared paperbacks. Bruce Springsteen. *The Power of One*. Past a telephone table, a short hallway led to the bedrooms, one front, one back. Holly stopped at a door. 'It's Rudy's room. I was on my way out when I thought I heard something.'

The matrimonial bedroom. Neat, musty, old-fashioned, the curtains drawn, dust showing on the glass top of the triple-mirrored dressing-table. The double bed was covered with a cream candlewick bedspread. Hanging above it on the wall in a cheap gilded frame was a picture of the Sacred Heart of Jesus.

'Jesus Christ,' I said.

Jesus didn't say anything. Surprised, probably. He and I hadn't been on speaking terms for quite some time. He merely bared his inflamed aorta and stared down with his long-suffering eyes. What he beheld was a sight to see.

'Jesus,' I said again. 'Denis!'

Denis Dogherty was lying immobile on the bed, his dark tie knotted at the collar of his corduroy shirt, his shoes neatly laced. His spectacles, neatly folded, peeped from the breast pocket of his jacket. A dark stain leaked from his right ear and crusted on the pillow beneath his head. Pink foam flecked his lips. His skin was pallid and waxy. His eyes were closed. I sank to my knees beside the bed and peered into his face. The hair on the back of his head was matted and sticky with blood.

'Denis,' I said, taking him by the shoulders. 'Can you hear me?' His eyelids fluttered and his cheek twitched. The foam on his lips bubbled and he emitted an almost inaudible groan.

'He's alive,' blurted Holly in a gush of relief. 'I thought he was dead. Scared the shit out of me.' Then, confused, 'You know him?'

'I work with him.' But not for much longer, by the look of it. He did not respond to my voice. I shook him gently, powerless, not knowing what to do. His breath was so faint I thought it had stopped.

Holly was back in the hall, furiously jiggling the receiver. 'Shit,' she yelled. 'Cut off. Steve mustn't have paid the bill. Typical.' She reappeared at the door. 'There's a phone booth at the shops.' She took off, tossing her voice behind her. 'I'll get an ambulance.'

'Take the car.' I called after her but she kept going, her feet crunching glass, her footfalls receding down the path.

You didn't need to be Dr Kildare to see that Denis was in a bad way. I withdrew my hand, sticky with blood. He'd been lying there for some time, that much was apparent. I thumbed back an eyelid. The white was a filigree of ruptured capillaries, the pupil fully dilated. Whatever that meant.

Snatches of first-aid crowded my brain. Immobilise the patient. No problem there. Keep the victim warm. I laid the back of my hand on his cheeks, found them cool to the touch, tugged the bedspread across his chest and legs. Clear the airways. Don't let the patient choke on his own tongue. Remove dentures, if applicable.

Sticking two fingers between his teeth, I probed his mouth, chanting his name over and over like a mantra. 'Denis. Denis. Denis.' His head felt as fragile as an eggshell in the palm of my hand.

Something moved at the door. Ambrose Buchanan's face appeared. 'What's happening, eh?' He crept into the room and stared down at us.

'You tell me,' I said sharply.

He took umbrage at the accusation. 'We don't know anything about this,' he protested. 'Do we, Deadly?'

He moved aside and the ninja sidled into the room, pushing back his hood. Deadly. The name suited him. Early thirties, a bandanna tight across his skull, pirate-style. Medium height, lithe, slippery. Orangy-brown freckles smeared across his cheeks. A red, black and yellow stud in one lobe. Reform-school tats on the back of his sinewy hands. Three shades lighter than Ambrose. Good-looking in a careless, surly sort of way. But speedy, jittery. Deadly.

He jerked his chin at Denis, excited, delighted. 'See,' he bragged. 'Told ya.'

'Told him what?' A dull ache spread through my side where the picket had connected. 'If you did this, I'll kill you. I swear I will.'

Deadly sneered. 'Think I'd still be hangin' round if I done this?' He didn't mind if I thought he was violent, he just didn't want anyone thinking he was stupid. Anyway, my good opinion was irrelevant. He was more intent on proving some point to Buchanan, citing Denis as evidence. 'Told ya Radeski was fucking crazy,' he said.

My fingers were still in Denis's mouth. As far as I could tell, his teeth were all his own. Not bad for a bloke of his vintage. His generation often had them all pulled out by the time they were twenty-one, rotten or not. Save trouble later.

'Urghhl.' Denis dry-retched, coughing bile. His hand came up, ropy-veined, and pawed at my chest. 'Stevie?' His voice was a faint whisper, his eyes open but fighting for focus. 'That you?'

'It's Murray.' I put my hand in the nape of his neck. 'Murray Whelan. Hang in there, mate. You'll be right. Ambulance on its way.'

He winced and something like panic crossed his face. 'You won't mention Woeful, will you?' Fresh blood dribbled from his nose and he started to cough.

'Okay,' I nodded. Anything to calm him.

He was no child to be so easily placated. His fingers became a claw, grabbing at my shirt, drawing my face down to his. 'Promise me you'll keep Woeful's name out of this.'

'Promise,' I swore, startled at his vehemence. 'I won't mention Woeful.'

He relaxed his grip and subsided onto the bed. His body went limp and his eyes closed. 'It's up to you now, Murray,' he whispered.

'I understand.' I didn't have the foggiest idea what he was talking about. Neither did he, probably. He must have been in shock. 'What happened, mate?'

'Stevie.' His mouth went slack and he slipped again into unconsciousness.

Ambrose and Deadly were standing at the foot of the bed. 'See,' said Deadly again. 'Told ya.' He prowled, a simmering presence, teetering on the edge of violence. He slid open a drawer and started prodding around inside.

Ambrose nudged him away and shut the drawer. 'Woeful?' he said. 'Is he talking about Woeful McKenzie?'

'He works for him.' I put my ear to Denis's chest. I didn't know what else to do. His heartbeat was faint, slow, distant.

'You a mate of Radeski's?' demanded Deadly. 'So where is he then?' He was a madman, bouncing all over the place, cranked up. The bedroom felt crowded, as claustrophobic as a Christmas sale.

I ignored him, staring up at Ambrose Buchanan from my knees beside the bed. 'What's going on, Ambrose? Why are you here? What do you want with Steve Radeski?'

Running feet thudded in the street, approaching fast. Beyond them rose the distant wail of a siren. Deadly backed into the doorway, tugging Ambrose's sleeve. 'C'mon, bro. Let's get out of here.'

Ambrose looked down at me, his face a plea for forbearance. He raised his open palm, swearing an oath. 'This isn't down to us, dead set.' He backed away reluctantly, drawn by Deadly's insistence. 'Later, eh? I'll explain later.'

A hollow gurgle came from deep in Denis Dogherty's chest. His breath was infinitely faint. The back door slapped softly against its frame. Holly's feet pounded up the hallway. A siren moved closer, rising and falling in the distance.

'On its way,' Holly gulped, flushed from the sprint. Lolly legs, the fat tongues of her white trainers sticking out above the laces. 'How is he?'

The ambulance woop-wooped into the street and she again dashed off. I could hear her at the front door, hastily clearing away the broken glass. Then the paramedics arrived. Well-practised young men who had Denis in a spinal brace and out of the house on a gurney in under two minutes.

He had sustained his injuries, the ambos estimated, quite some time before. Perhaps as much as twenty-four hours. His skull was fractured and he'd lost great deal of blood from a gash at the back of the head. When they lifted him off the bed, we found that blood had saturated the pillow and soaked down into the mattress.

I told them what I knew. Which, apart from his name, wasn't much. It was all there in his wallet, anyway.

My request to ride to the hospital in the back of the ambulance was politely but firmly refused. Nor should I follow in my own car, I was told. We were to wait there for the police. They were definite about that.

It all happened very quickly. Holly and I stood on the footpath and watched the flashing light disappear around the corner. The cluster of curious youths which had materialised as if by magic at the sound of the siren vanished just as abruptly. Suddenly everything seemed remarkably quiet, as though the planet had been struck by some inexplicable catastrophe and we were the sole survivors.

As the burst of activity ended, shock gave way to bafflement. My hand went into my pocket, looking for a cigarette. We don't do that any more, I told it. But it wished we still did.

'This is really weird,' said Holly, the mistress of understatement. 'Steve's a fuck-up, I know, but I can't believe he'd do something like that. Who is that old guy, anyway? Why was he here? Did he tell you what happened?'

Very good questions. 'His name is Denis Dogherty,' I said. 'He works for the Minister for Sport.'

That exhausted my supply of answers. And did nothing to explain how he had come to be lying, unconscious and bleeding, in the deserted house of a rubbed-out ex-weightlifter. But at least his whereabouts were no longer a mystery. In less than five minutes they'd be wheeling him into the emergency room at the Austin Hospital. Holly was looking considerably chastened. She chewed her bottom lip. 'What now?'

'We wait for the cops.' And take a quick squiz around the house. Seek enlightenment there.

'Uh oh,' said Holly, as we reached the shattered front door. 'What about this?'

'Wilful damage,' I said, sternly. 'Breaking and entering.'

She took me literally. The colour drained from her cheeks.

'Lucky you've got a good lawyer,' I said.

She still didn't get it. 'Lawyer? You really think I need a lawyer? What lawyer?'

'You gave me the job,' I reminded her. 'Remember?'

'You think this is funny, do you?' Shirty now, she began brushing crushed glass off the doorstep with the side of her shoe. Touchy, touchy. She was embarrassed, I realised. Not just at her gullibility but at the whole situation. At having lured me here with assertions that all would be well.

'Tell the police the truth,' I reassured her. 'Under the circumstances, I don't think a busted window is going to upset them.'

She said nothing, more interested in picking up plate-sized fragments of broken glass. I went down the hall. There were two doors. The master bedroom where Holly found Denis was on the right. I opened the door on the left.

Little Stevie's bedroom, outgrown but never abandoned. Steam locomotives on the wallpaper and dirty socks on the floor. The bed was seriously unmade, the sheets long unwashed, the greasy pillow flecked with shed hairs, dark pubic curls. Pages from body-building magazines were stuck to the walls, all straining sinews and triangular torsos. Hanging from a nail above the bed was a lifting suit and a truss, a wide leather belt emblazoned with the word 'Buffalo'. Spilling from beneath the bed was a lurid fan of stick books, DIY gynaecology.

An overfilled wastepaper basket lay on its side amid the dirty laundry, spilling its trashy contents. Perforated blister packs, empty pill bottles, snap-top glass ampoules, blood-smeared tissues, used hypodermics. Methyltestosterone enanthate. Finaject. Androl 50. Venabol. One of the packets had the outline of a chess piece on it. The knight. Equipoise, long-lasting veterinary steroid, said the label.

Back in the front door, Holly was fussing with a broom, unwilling to meet my gaze. I went into the lounge room and took a good look around.

Apart from the gym equipment, there wasn't much to see. Heavy black drapes hung over the windows, making it even more rank and dank than the bedroom. A row of shelves was set into a recess beside the oil heater, collecting dust. On the wall opposite the pressing bench was a full-length mirror. Dead centre, about head height, the glass was shattered. A sunburst of cracks radiated from a dark smudge that could only have been blood. It didn't take Einstein to work out whose.

I took a closer look at the shelves. On the middle shelf was a row of photographs, family sporting triumphs. A teenage Steve in a striped jersey, a soccer ball tucked under his arm. Not a bad-looking kid. An old black-and-white shot of a stocky weightlifter in the classic strong-man stance, legs braced, upraised arms holding a hugely weighted bar above his head. Beside it, a group shot. Thirty or so men in blazers staring soberly at the camera. *Polska Druzyna Olimpijska XVI* read the banner hanging behind them.

'Steve's father,' I called to Holly. 'Was he in the 1956 Olympics?'

'That's how come he came to Australia,' she called back. 'Never went home. Well, you wouldn't, would you?'

The bottom shelf held books, propped in place by a chipped plaster statuette of the Virgin Mary. I scanned the spines. Not big readers, the Radeskis. *The Guinness Book of*

Records, 1979 edition. Half a dozen brown-covered Reader's Digest condensed books. A James A. Michener paperback, *Hawaii*. I remembered the movie. Max von Sydow and Julie Andrews. *Stalin's Crimes against Poland* in hard cover. I flipped open the title page and read the publisher's imprint. The Council of Captive Nations.

Old soldiers of the Cold War. Men from eastern Europe with dubious war histories and questionable sources of finance. Self-proclaimed community leaders who cultivated their grievances in suburban social clubs with portraits of dead fascists on their pine-panelled walls. Compulsory folk dancing for the young people. The women out in the kitchen doing things with pickled herrings. I'd spent years at Ethnic Affairs avoiding just such characters. Not that it was difficult. Most of them thought the ALP was a communist front.

But Rudy Radeski was no intellectual cold warrior, I could see that, and I read into the presence of *Stalin's Crimes* no more than an exile's rough obeisance to the history of his benighted homeland. Steve's reading, by the look of it, was limited to *Beaver Monthly*.

The top shelf held a row of sporting trophies. Most were towering plinths of gilded plastic, but some were more modest. I reached up and took one down, a small figurine of a woman tennis player frozen in mid-serve. *St Joseph's Social Club, Mixed Doubles, 1955. Irene Boag.*

Could this be right?

'Steve's mother,' I called to Holly. 'Do you know how she died?'

'What?' she snapped back, irritably.

I repeated the question. I wasn't sure why I was asking it. The answer was in my hand. One of the belles of Bay

178 NICE TRY

Street, racquet poised. The little sister, Denis called her. Married a migrant, funny sort of bloke.

'Accident,' called Holly. 'Fell off a ladder. Why?'

'Jesus fucking Christ,' I muttered, returning the dusty trophy to its place. Denis had pruned a twig off the family tree.

Well, at least one thing was now clearer. Denis Dogherty was Steve Radeski's uncle. Which meant that so too was Woeful McKenzie. Amazing how little I knew about the two of them. Related by marriage to a right-wing reffo.

'Promise you won't tell them about Woeful,' Denis had pleaded. And I'd promised. Tell them what? Fucked if I knew. He was probably brain-damaged, picked up by little Stevie and thrown against the mirror. Christ. As if Woeful didn't have enough on his plate without a berko nephew.

Rudy Radeski and Irene Boag. Immigrant lad and local lass. Battlers, hence the West Heidelberg address. Not far from Rosanna, site of the struggling family business. The mother devoutly Catholic, the father carrying it as cultural baggage from the old country. Steve, the only son. First a mummy's boy, then the focus of his father's expectations.

Enough of the pop psychology. Somebody else could sink their forensic scalpel into this little lot. I went through the kitchen and into the backyard, wondering if Ambrose Buchanan and Deadly Deadshit were still lurking about.

But nobody came out of the shadows, not even when I squinted into the darkness of the overgrown garage and confirmed that the white shape was a government-issue Toyota.

Car, mirror, syringes. The scenario was falling into place. Some time after work the previous evening, Denis had driven here to visit his nephew Steve, an immature young man with a short temper, big muscles and a bloodstream full of elephant juice. Steve had decked Denis, then laid him out in the master bedroom. To recover? To die?

Those weren't the only things that remained unclear. What had set Steve off, for example? And why had Denis come calling in the first place? And what about Steve Radeski's more recent visitors, an Aboriginal activist and a petty-crim Koori? My little brown brothers had clearly not popped around for a glass of sherry and a chukka of cribbage. The ache in my ribs told me that much.

I looked at my watch. Ten minutes since the ambulance's departure. Holly returned the white rock to its place beside the front path and swept the broken glass into a pile. She found a pile of newspapers in Steve's bedroom and I squatted beside her, prising jagged fragments out of the old putty of the door and laying them on the paper for her to wrap. We worked in silence, crouched on our haunches. As I carefully laid each piece flat on the newspaper, Holly folded a page over it as precisely as if she was wrapping a birthday present.

The papers were more than a month old, their news as stale as flat beer. Olympic items dominated. The official start of the torch relay, the Prime Minister handing the flaming firebrand to some beaming tacker in a MOB t-shirt. Plans for the proposed new Aquatic Centre praised by a Finnish architect. IOC CHIEFS TO RECEIVE RELAY TORCH, the same story that Ambrose Buchanan had shown me, breathless prose about the upcoming Evaluation Commission visit. This item was circled in black marker pen, and the rest of the page was scrawled with hammers and sickles.

'Was Steve using steroids when the two of you were an item?' I said.

'Sometimes.' She inclined her head in the direction of the bedroom. 'But nothing like that.'

'You hear things.' I was openly nosy.

She grinned bleakly, emerging from her shell. 'Make you a regular stallion, they do.' She balled her fist and flexed her forearm.

'That explains the horse on the pack,' I said. 'Think I should give them a try?'

'Not unless you want your hair to fall out and your nuts to shrivel to the size of raisins.'

'That really happens?'

'Acne, mood swings, memory loss. Steve, he'd come out of training, not be able to remember where he left his car. Does wonders for your motivation, though.'

I thought of Denis, doctors working on him. I wanted to ring Woeful, wondered how long before the police arrived. 'What do you think motivated this?'

'This?' said Holly, sombre again, kneeling, wrapping. 'Who knows? Nothing probably.' The voice of experience.

As I reached up to the top of the door for the last chunk of glass, somebody stuck a red hot poker through my side. Holly saw me wince. 'Are you okay?' She stood and put her hand on my arm and looked at me with such sweet concern that I was in immediate danger of trying to take advantage of the situation.

'Indigestion,' I said. An old man's complaint. The sort of thing you get eating tagliatelle primavera in the Hyatt food court, watching the seven o'clock news on the television above the bar, lip-reading Ambrose Buchanan as he goes on about No Olympics without Justice.

Holly was looking through the missing panel in the door.

'This should be interesting,' she said.

First came the uniforms. One male, one female. All clipboards and torches. Aggregate age thirty. They took our names and listened to our explanations and we gave them a guided tour of the premises. Then the second lot arrived. Detectives, this time.

The top dog was a Detective Sergeant named Hendricks. He wore a drab-olive suit and a put-upon manner and had more lines around his eyes than usual for a man in his mid-thirties. Another five years and he'd be out of the force, running his own business, something with plenty of scope for the long lunch. His offsider was much younger, an up-and-comer who looked at Holly a little too wolfishly, in my opinion, for a man on the public payroll in pursuance of his duties.

Either it was a very slow night at the West Heidelberg station, or Denis was in a pretty bad way. Just how bad, the dicks weren't able or prepared to say. They asked us to wait, separating us to avoid the possibility of collusion. Which was fine by me because I didn't have anything to collude in. Not with Holly at any rate.

I did my waiting in the backyard, edgy and tired at the same time, queasy with apprehension and the slow drip from the nicotine teabag taped to my abdomen. A wooden picket lay on the ground beneath the clothes line and as I looked down at it a string of names uncoiled itself in my mind, connections from which I could draw scant comfort. A story from the papers, a name that fitted a face. Deadly. Deadly Ernest. Ernest Anderson.

It was back in the early eighties, if I remembered right, a couple of years after the incident with Reggie and the gun in Merle's kitchen. A prisoner by the name of Ernest Anderson barricaded himself in the maximum-security division of Goulburn Gaol, along with three other serious offenders. Claiming the NSW Armed Robbery Squad had stitched them up, they articulated their demands for a retrial by mutilating themselves with broken glass and setting fire to their mattresses. The prison authorities took their time finding the right key and, by the time the doors were unlocked and the fire doused, Anderson was the only one still alive.

Ambrose Buchanan was prominent in the campaign for a retrial, arguing that Anderson was a victim of institutional racism, that his original conviction had been based on planted evidence and police perjury. Eventually, the courts were compelled to concur that the coppers had shaved a few too many corners in their haste to make a case. In due course, Anderson walked. Not that anybody seriously doubted he was capable of the crime. With a string of priors running all the way back to primary school, Ernest Anderson was unlikely ever to be confused with Nelson Mandela.

It seemed reasonable to assume that this was the same Deadly who had just belted me in the ribs with a picket. None of which explained why he was looking for Steve Radeski. Or why he'd taken such apparently perverse delight in finding Denis bashed insensible. Or why Ambrose Buchanan was squiring him about. And the name Anderson, was there a connection there?

A cigarette, I felt sure, would help me answer these questions, help get the mental processes working a bit more efficiently. I plucked a blade of grass and gnawed it, but somehow it wasn't the same.

Out the front, radios were crackling and car doors slamming. Several more representatives of the law enforcement community arrived. A clot of curious onlookers assembled on the footpath. After they'd poked about inside the house for ten minutes, the detectives got around to talking to us. Hendricks came out into the yard and stood under the clothes hoist and listened while I repeated what I'd already told the uniforms—who I was and how I knew Holly and what I was doing there, about knowing Denis and how he'd been missing all day.

'I understand the victim spoke to you,' said the cop when I finally paused to draw breath.

'He only regained consciousness for a few seconds. I asked him what happened and he said, "Stevie." Then he passed out again.'

'He didn't say anything else?'

This was the tricky bit. 'He was pretty far gone,' I said. 'Incoherent. But he definitely said, "Stevie." Apart from that, nothing else made sense. I'm afraid I can't be much more help to you.'

That's not quite the way Hendricks saw it. 'Anyone else here when you arrived?'

'Far as I know, the house was empty.' I did my best not to sound evasive.

'You know where we can find this Steve Radeski?'

I shrugged, just wanting it all to be over. Dreading the prospect of having to ring Woeful, wondering if he was still at the House. 'He's a bouncer at some club. The ex-girlfriend knows all about it.'

Hendricks sucked his teeth and rubbed the back of his neck. 'Can you believe this shit?' he said. It wasn't a question, not even a rhetorical one. Just another night on the job.

'What happens now?' I said.

We went back to the kitchen where Holly was sitting across the table from the wolfish dick. He was wearing a cashmere overcoat and laying on the charm with a silver trowel. 'The Climber?' he was saying. 'That dump in Northcote, just near the railway line? Bit of a come-down after Typhoon, isn't it?'

This was all getting a bit pally for Hendricks. 'We'll be requiring a full statement in due course. And the homicide squad will probably want a word.'

'Homicide?' I said, knowing already. Not wanting to know.

'The victim is not expected to recover,' said Hendricks.

'Wow,' said Holly. 'That's terrible.'

Detective Lothario stood up and pushed her sports bag across the table. 'Don't forget your things, Ms Deloite.'

The boom box was one of those Taiwanese knock-offs, already falling apart. Sixty bucks at K-Mart. A lot of trouble for the price.

'What about the front door?' she said.

'We'll let you know.' Meaning she'd never hear about it again.

'When?' She missed the point.

'C'mon.' I drew her chair back. 'I'll drive you home.'

But first a cigarette. Just the one. This sort of situation, a surrogate nicotine-delivery system just didn't cut the mustard. This sort of situation, intimations of mortality were essential, burnt offerings were demanded. Even as I asked Holly where she lived, hoping it wasn't Keysborough or Park Orchards or some other twenty-kilometre haul, I was already turning the Toyota into the West Heidelberg shops. The hamburger place was still lit, still empty, the rack of cigarettes visible through the plate-glass window.

Also visible, waiting on the bench at the deserted taxi rank, were Ambrose Buchanan and Deadly Anderson, his hood back up.

First things first. I pushed open the door of the take-away, inhaled the smell of fried onions and rancid cooking oil. *Come to Where the Flavour Is.* I named my brand. A filter was between my lips, a burning match in my hand, before I was back on the footpath. It had been almost twenty-four hours, but some things you never forget. As the flame bit into the tobacco and the first rush of smoke hit my exultant lungs, Ambrose Buchanan got up and walked towards me.

Tears welled in my eyes and a cough exploded in my chest. Head spinning, I staggered to the edge of the footpath and spat the lining of my throat into the gutter. I was feeling better already.

'Those things'll kill you, man,' said Ambrose. He took out one of his own and lit it. Twenty metres away, his bruiser mate was watching us over his shoulder, one arm draped nonchalantly across the back of the taxi rank bench. 'You tell the cops?' he said.

I got my breath back. Used it to inhale some more smoke. 'What do you think?'

Buchanan thought I'd behaved pretty much as he'd expected. He acknowledged the fact with a small nod. 'So what was that all about?' he said. 'Back there.'

'Thought you might be able to tell me.'

'Nothing to do with us,' he swore.

'Yeah, right,' I said. 'So I just imagined that your dickhead mate over there decked me with a lump of four-by-two.'

'That was just a misunderstanding,' he said. 'Nothing personal.'

'Well that's a fucking relief,' I said. 'What about Denis? Was he a misunderstanding, too?'

He shifted uncomfortably and picked a speck of tobacco off his bottom lip. 'Who's Denis?' he said.

'Denis Dogherty. The old bloke bleeding all over the bed.'

Buchanan showed me the pale skin of his palms. 'Nothing to do with us,' he repeated. It was a line I was getting sick of hearing.

'So you said. You also said that you'd explain what you were doing there. Well, here's your big chance. Enlighten me.'

Buchanan kept glancing back towards the bench. He was impatient to go. 'Not now,' he said. 'Later.'

'Try telling that to the Homicide Squad,' I said, fed up with being taken for granted.

Buchanan stopped in his tracks. 'What do you mean?'

'Denis Dogherty is expected to die. If that happens, all bets are off. I'll scream like a stuck pig.' I looked past him to the taxi stop. 'That's Ernest Anderson, isn't it?' I said. 'Unless I get a pretty convincing explanation, right now, I'll have no choice but to tell the cops he was there.'

Ambrose did not like what he was hearing. He chewed his cigarette and scratched his beard. Eventually, he conceded to my point of view. 'Ah, shit,' he said. 'Give us a minute.'

Holly was sitting in the car, wondering why I was taking so long to buy a packet of cigarettes. I went across to her window and asked her to wait while I talked to these men. She started to ask me something but I turned away. Let her do the wondering for once. Ambrose was bent over Deadly, giving him the word. Deadly was reluctant. Listening, resisting, listening some more. As I approached, he shook his head. I couldn't tell if he was refusing or capitulating.

'Murray Whelan,' Ambrose said stiffly. 'This is Ernest Anderson.'

The intricacies of Koori kinship were beyond me. Big Maxie at the Stars gym had talked about Darcy having some jailbird cousin. Deadly had ten years on young Darce and a lot more wear and tear, but there was a definite resemblance. Similar height and build. But something else as well. Something intangible, familial.

Deadly radiated hostility like a three-bar heater on full power, yet his deference to Ambrose was total, so tangible that I felt no fear. What I did feel was a little light-headed, as if the cigarette I was smoking was my very first. I extended my hand. When he shook it, he made sure I knew he was doing me a favour. 'They call me Deadly,' he said.

'You wouldn't be related to Darcy Anderson, by any chance?' I said. 'Deadly.'

Buchanan answered for him. 'Darcy and Deadly are cousins. Were cousins.'

'I'm sorry for your loss.' I stripped off my tie, stuffed it into my jacket pocket. 'And for some reason I've just lied to the police for you. Dunno why. Must be the company you keep.'

The pain in my side had subsided to a dull ache. It only really hurt when I coughed. So I coughed for a bit, wincing at the pain. Deadly smiled. 'Thought you was Radeski,' he said. 'Sneakin' round like that.'

'A fence picket wouldn't be much use against Steve Radeski,' I said. 'Is that why you brought Ambrose along? Reinforcements?'

Ambrose was the real puzzle. What was he doing in the murky milieu of he-men and petty crims? Ambrose Buchanan did not strike me as a man given to cruising the night in such company.

Deadly's attention was focused on the parked car. 'Who's the chick?' he said, appreciatively. He pushed his hood back to reveal his corsair bandanna.

'Radeski's ex,' I said, starting to get the wheels of reciprocity turning. 'She asked me to drive her out here to collect some stuff she left behind when they broke up. That's what she was doing when you jumped out of the shrubbery and went into your Don Bradman impersonation.'

Holly stared back at us, expressionless, then turned away. The three of us in a row, Ambrose Buchanan in the middle.

The Good, the Bad and the Ugly. All of us hyper as buggery, acting cool. Holly tilted the Toyota's rear-view mirror and began studying the skin around her lips.

'So,' I said. 'Somebody going to tell me what's going on?'

Nobody spoke. A cab cruised into the parking area and approached the rank. The driver craned across his steering wheel, took one look at Ambrose and Deadly, turned off his roof light and kept going.

'You've got to appreciate Deadly's situation,' said Ambrose. 'He's on a suspended sentence. Any problems with the law and he's straight back inside.'

Perry fucking Mason, beard and all. No, that was Ironside.

Whatever. I cleared my throat and hawked into the gutter. An irritable, impatient gesture. Also a necessary one. Bits of my lung kept falling off. I pitched my cigarette away with a grimace of disgust. It was past ten and I still hadn't called Woeful. Holly had finished with her lips. She closed her eyes and tilted her head back, neck like a swan. The silence grew longer.

'I've got things to do,' I said, starting to get up.

Ambrose put his hand on my sleeve. 'There was this session at the Royal earlier tonight, on account of Darcy. First time I've seen Deadly here in quite a while. Anyhow, he takes me aside, says he knows something. He's prepared to tell you what he told me but only on condition that he doesn't have to talk to the police.'

'Something about what?'

'No police?'

In for a penny. I was already withholding information, fuck knows why. An ethical loophole could always be found later, if I needed to renege. 'No police.'

Ambrose held my eye. The last time he'd given me that look was in Merle's kitchen. Ah shit, I thought. I raised my right hand, three fingers. Scout's honour.

'Tell him,' he said.

Deadly Anderson motioned for a cigarette. I gave him one and lit another myself. At the first hit of smoke, a red mist swirled behind my eyes. The veins in my forehead ticked like an alarm clock. Deadly leaned forward, forearms on his thighs. He flicked invisible ash off the end of his smoke. 'Got this mate, right. Works at this stud farm up Lancefield. They use these steroids, right.' Flick, flick. 'So anyway, we've got this line going. He brings the stuff down at the weekend, I deliver it to the buyers.' He took his eyes off Holly long enough to check me out, make sure I was keeping up.

These buyers were not, I took it, certified practising veterinary surgeons. 'So you're Radeski's horse steroid connection?'

'Silly prick can't get enough. Joke is, he thinks he's getting the stuff they put in them million-dollar racehorses. Only that shit's not easy to get, even if you work in the stables. Last few weeks, it's been impossible. So me mate gets the labels. Sticks them on this other stuff. They use it to stop pizzle rot.' Flick flick.

I had a bit of a flick myself. 'Pizzle rot?'

'That's when rams' dicks go rotten and fall off. Happens in wet weather.' Flick, flick.

'That's the secret information?' I said, incredulous. I'd stumbled on a phoney steroid trafficking ring run by Koories. 'What's this got to do with anything?'

'Shut up for five minutes and I'll fucken tell you,' said Deadly. I did as he suggested. Flick, flick. Mollified by my silence, he continued. 'I'm supposed to meet Radeski last night, right. Nine o'clock, under the flats near the Royal. Only I'm an hour late. When I turn up there's jacks everywhere. Blue lights flashin'. You name it. So, only natural, I disappear, right.'

'And?'

'And then today he heard what happened to Darcy,' said Ambrose. 'So he came to me.'

'You think that Radeski killed Darcy?'

'That sheep shit can't be doing his brain cells any fucken good. Maybe he decided to pay out on Darcy 'cause I wasn't there.'

Okay, there was a certain degree of logic in the supposition. Darcy finishes training, shuts up shop at the gym, crosses the road to where hair-trigger Radeski is waiting for a man of a similar build and complexion. Some kind of interaction takes place, Radeski goes batshit, Darcy winds up beaten to death.

'So you decided it's payback time?'

Ambrose jumped to his feet and started pacing in front of us. Addressing the jury. 'You got it wrong, Murray. Deadly here just wants to talk to Radeski, ask him where he was last night.'

'Why not just tip the cops? Ring them anonymously or something?'

'And have Darcy's name connected with steroids?'

'You think that being killed by a drug-crazed maniac might be bad for Darcy's posthumous reputation?' I said, incredulous. 'That's fucking crazy.'

'Not just Darcy. Think about it, Murray. Sport is one of the few places Aboriginal people are allowed to be high achievers in this country. Ask the average white person to name an Aborigine, who do you get? An athlete, right. And so far, no Aboriginal sportsman or woman has been associated with steroid use. See what I mean?'

'But nobody's saying Darcy was on steroids,' I protested.

'Not yet. But when the cops get involved, things take on a life of their own. Say Radeski didn't do it. But say the cops talk to him and find out where he gets his shit. You see my point. The crap starts flying around, who knows who it sticks to.'

'Darce was clean,' said Deadly, vehemently. 'I never done the wrong thing by Darce. Dead set.'

'So, rather than risk your parole, you decided to run your own private homicide investigation?'

'Looked Radeski up in the phone book,' asserted Deadly, a man perfectly within his rights. 'Waited for him to come home, have a quiet word. Ask him where he was last night. What's wrong with that?'

Except it was me who'd got the quiet word. 'Phone book?' I repeated dully, feeling like I'd been hit with one.

If Deadly's suspicions were right, the steroid-crazed nephew of the Minister for the Olympics had not only possibly killed a member of his own family but also a promising young Aboriginal athlete.

'I can fucken read, y'know,' muttered Deadly venomously.

'Deadly here can get a little emotional at times,' said Buchanan. 'That's why I came along with him. But instead of Radeski we found you.'

'And Denis Dogherty,' I reminded him. 'In a state that seems to confirm Deadly's hypothesis about Radeski being homicidal.'

'Looks that way. And very convenient for the cops if they can pin Darcy's death on Radeski. Do wonders for their clear-up rate.'

'Jesus, Ambrose,' I said. 'Make up your mind. This morning you claimed that Darcy's death was racially motivated. You said so on television. What about those skinheads?' I kneaded my temples between thumb and forefinger.

'We're talkin' different issues here.'

I was in no mood to argue the toss. Deliberately misleading the cops is rarely wise, particularly for someone in my position. Now I was sworn to secrecy. I needed time to think, to give matters more tranquil consideration.

Tranquillity was in short supply at that point. Holly got out of the Toyota, yawned and looked ostentatiously at her watch. Deadly stood up. Holly tilted her head to one side quizzically, then started towards us.

Explaining these two blokes would be hard enough. Introductions were absolutely out of the question. I needed to get rid of them. Just then, another cab turned into the parking area.

I stood and raised my arm, a white man in a suit. As the cab drew into the rank, I jerked its door open. 'Radeski's a bouncer at some joint in Northcote called The Climber. Better hurry if you want to beat the cops.'

Deadly didn't need to be told twice. He dived into the cab, dragging Ambrose with him. I swung the door shut and the cab pulled away.

'One minute,' I told Holly.

I dropped a coin into the payphone, dialled Parliament House, got put through to the party room and listened while the phone rang off the hook. Then I called directory assistance. The only D. McKenzie listed for Port Melbourne was a silent number. I tried, I told myself. At least I tried.

'Who were those two?' said Holly when I got back in the car.

'Clients,' I said brusquely. 'A work-related matter. Where are we going?'

She didn't believe me, but let it go at that. We were going to Carlton, she informed me, where she had a flat in one of those courtyard blocks opposite the cemetery in Lygon Street. She'd been there for a couple of years. Before that, she lived at home with her parents and younger brothers in Pascoe Vale. Her dad was a mechanic at Essendon airport, where he worked for a firm that maintained corporate jets. Her mother was part-time at Qantas catering at Tullamarine, putting individually wrapped Anzacs on in-flight meal trays.

My mind was working overtime, trying to get an angle on what I'd seen and heard over the previous hour. 'Promise you won't tell them about Woeful.' Denis had been adamant, made me swear it. Were his words simply the delirious wanderings of a concussed brain? Or had he summoned up some lucidity from the brink of his battered condition?

Buchanan's role was now easier to figure. He was keeping Deadly on a short leash, trying to ensure he didn't make things worse than they already were. Deadly was clearly unlikely to wait around for the formal processes of the law to take their course. If he didn't have revenge in mind before, he was almost certainly looking for it now.

And, for expedience sake, I had just told him where to find it. Shit, Murray.

Maybe Radeski wasn't at this Climber joint, after all. Even better, maybe the police were there already. The cab driver would probably take his time, stop at every yellow light, try for the maximum fare. I was pretty sure I knew where the club was. If I stepped on the gas, we could probably get there first.

I tossed up telling Holly what I was doing, decided against it. It was all too complicated. I wasn't sure what was going on myself. Fortunately, she had lapsed into morose silence. And the most direct route to Carlton lay through Northcote. We practically had to drive past the place.

At one time, the area had specialised in textile and footwear manufacturing, back before wiser heads than mine decided that the country needed fifteen-dollar Indonesian running shoes more than it needed jobs. Most of the factories now lay idle, stripped to a shell. Some operated as samples'n'seconds outlets where busloads of bargain hunters from Shepparton spent their social-security cheques on Chinese jim-jams and Taiwanese tea-towels. Others had been converted to new roles in the leisure and entertainment sector of the service economy.

The Climber was characteristic of the trend. When I first noticed it, maybe two years earlier, it was painted matt black and called Klub Funkk. Next time I drove past, the name had changed to Silver's, a clear pitch for the more sophisticated end of the blue-collar market. A scalloped awning over the front entrance, Bacardi and Coke by the jug, Chris de Burgh on the turntable.

The facade was now a muted green with a sinuous pattern of darker leaves spelling out the name. The street outside was deserted, no sign of the cops. Ambrose and Ernest were standing on the little strip of carpet under the awning, arguing with the tuxedo-clad doorman behind his loop of red rope.

'Hey,' said Holly as I pulled into the carpark across the road, behind the Voularis Emporium. 'That's where Steve works. And there are those guys again. What's going on?'

'Back in a minute,' I said.

She was beginning to regret recruiting me as a chauffeur. 'Think I'll get a taxi the rest of the way home.'

'Suit yourself,' I said. I knew I was acting strangely but she was the one who got me into this situation, after all. I left her sitting in the car and crossed the street.

The doorman was shaking his head. 'Nothink personal, fellers,' he was saying, a great big side of halal beef, another

live-at-home boy. 'Private function. Hens' night. Chicks only.'
He reached down to adjust the hang of his tackle, then
jerked his thumb over his shoulder at a poster beside the
ticket-office grille. A chorus line of oiled beefcake, bare
torsos in leather posing-pouches, bowties at their naked
necks. *The Chessmen.* Seeping through the double doors
beyond came the steady throb of a bass line. *The Climber
Welcomes Food Barn Social Club.*

'Then fuckenwell get him to come out here,' said Deadly.

I grabbed Buchanan by the elbow and waltzed him
backwards along the footpath. 'This is insane,' I hissed. 'The
cops'll be here any minute. C'mon, I'll drive you back to
Fitzroy, anywhere you like.'

Deadly swung a leg over the stupid little red rope. The
doorman put the flat of his palm on the Koori's chest, 'I'm
warning you, mate,' he said. The two of them went eyeball
to eyeball. Shit, I thought, this thing's about to go thermo-
nuclear. Without shifting his position, the doorman extended
his free hand towards an intercom on the wall. Just as his
hand reached it, it spoke. 'Security to rear exit. ASAP.'

Indecision flashed across the bouncer's face and he
swivelled his head, looking past the box office towards the
closed double doors, then back at Deadly. The squawk box
sounded again, even more urgent. 'Security to rear exit.
Steve's flipped out.'

A wide grin creased Deadly's face and he was over the
rope and through the vestibule. The doorman took off after
him. Buchanan and I gaped stupidly at each other, shrugged
simultaneously and raced after them, my stomach churning
at the sudden burst of activity, the rush of adrenalin, the
dread of anticipation.

We hit the swinging double doors at a trot and burst into black. Black walls, black ceiling, black floor. A million swirling fragments of light speckled the darkness, thrown by spinning mirror-balls. The thump of amplified music, the raucous clamour of a hundred cheering women standing on their seats or banging their glasses on tables. At their centre, a male body in a jockstrap and coconut oil and nothing else, gyrated in a pool of light on a circular stage, mechanically thrusting his groin into the face of an off-duty checkout chick in a sequined cashmere sweater. She squealed with hysterical laughter.

'Macho, macho man,' they chanted to the pump of the music. Secret women's business. Christ, no wonder they didn't want any witnesses. All this on a Tuesday night.

Deadly and the bouncer were ploughing through the crowd, headed for the back wall where an exit sign glowed. A knot of male bodies crowded into the gap of a broached doorway. Waiters in cut-off jeans and shredded t-shirts, their bum cheeks hanging out. Barmen in boxer shorts with matching red braces. A fussy little man in shirt sleeves issuing futile instructions.

We fought our way through the scrum and out into a concrete stairwell. A Chessman in an American sailor suit was bent double, spitting broken teeth into a cupped hand. Sprawled on the stairs beside him was a girl with an emerald green miniskirt pushed up around her waist. In one hand she held a shoe. The other hand was pressed to her nose. A torrent of vivid red blood streamed down the front of her blouse into her bare thighs. Her drop-earrings jerked in time with the sobs that racked her body.

Beyond her, Deadly was shouldering open a door into the night. Buchanan took the steps three at a time, me right behind him. We exploded into an empty laneway, a brick wall rearing before us. To the right was the street. To the left, beyond a row of rubbish bins, the alley took a dogleg.

Panting, the pulse in my neck beating a wicked tattoo, I pulled up short. As Ambrose disappeared around the corner, still in hot pursuit, I put my hands on my knees and coughed. Barked like a blue heeler. A voice shouted in my ear. The voice of reason.

Fuck this, it said. Whatever they're paying you, it isn't enough. And it certainly isn't for this kind of crap. Not for chasing psychopathic maniacs through lunatic ladies' lounges. This is none of your business. Get out of here. Immediately. Before even more complications arise. Before the cops arrive and explanations become necessary.

It was good advice. I took it, starting up the laneway at a trot. Deadly and Buchanan could chase Steve Radeski all the way to hell and back if they liked. Not my affair. The dull ache in my chest had become a sharp stitch. Jogging into the carpark, I threaded my way between the rows of cars. Floodlit on the rear wall of the Voularis Emporium was an advertising hoarding. Milka Full-Cream Swiss Chocolate. Purple cartoon cows in an alpine meadow. Black spray paint covered the cows' udders. Milk is Murder, read the graffiti.

The lesbian vegans strike again, I thought. Eyes on the billboard, I didn't see Radeski until I collided with him.

He was crouched at the door of a low-slung Celica, trying to fit a key into the lock. I bounced off him, tripped on a concrete traffic bolster and went down on one knee. In the instant I recognised him, he was looming above me, hugely square-shouldered in his dinner jacket and bowtie. Pumped for action. Mad as a cut snake.

My feet found themselves and I steadied myself against the dented mudguard of the Celica, cornered at a half-crouch. Radeski stared down. Baffled recognition spread across his features. This was it. Again. I was dog meat.

'Why don't you pick on someone your own size?' It was Holly, behind him. He turned. I began to back away.

'Hey, babe,' said Radeski. 'Wha cha doon here?'

'Don't you "Hey, babe" me,' Holly snarled, coming closer. Suddenly, she rose vertically into the air.

For a long second she hung there. Then she swivelled, half-turning. Her leg shot outwards and her heel slammed into Radeski's solar plexus. There was an audible thud and he teetered on the spot. She landed, light as a feather, and closed the gap between them, her clenched fists pistoning in a blur of flying punches. Radeski reeled backwards past me, forearm up, as a swift succession of blows and kicks rained down on him.

An Amazon! I was out for the evening with Sheena, Queen of the fucking Jungle. And thank Christ she was still there, not in some cab, halfway home. She grabbed my arm and hauled me in the direction of the Toyota. 'C'mon, cowboy,' she yelled. I didn't need any encouragement. Radeski was right behind us, roaring like a bull. No, a ram.

We wrenched open the doors and threw ourselves into the Toyota, my elbow snapping down the lock button as I jammed the key into the ignition. Radeski's forehead pounded into Holly's window, shattering the glass. I gunned the engine and slammed the t-bar into reverse. Rubber screeching, we hurtled backwards. I spun the wheel, found drive and floored the pedal. We thudded across the gutter and roared down the street.

'Wow.' Holly pummelled the air, buzzing from the action. 'Did you see that? Did you see that?'

What I saw was a police car, coming towards us. I slowed and it passed us. Through the rear-view mirror, I watched it pull into the kerb at the Climber. At the same time, Steve Radeski's Celica emerged from the carpark and burned off in the opposite direction.

'That's the first time I've ever done anything like that outside the ring.' Holly tore off her Nike cap and shook her hair loose. 'I didn't think I still had it.'

'We'd better go back,' I said. My vice-like grip on the steering wheel was easing and colour was returning to my knuckles.

'What for?' she said. 'They'll pick him up soon enough. There's nothing else we can do.' She was on a high, flushed with victory.

And she had a point. The cops probably already had an APB out on Radeski. If he went home, they'd nab him there. If he was headed elsewhere, it surely wouldn't be too difficult to spot a rusted bronze-coloured Celica with a peeling vinyl roof and a demented gorilla behind the wheel.

'What *was* that back there?' I said. 'Karate? Tae kwon do?'

'Kickboxing. I used to be the northern region Under-17 champion. I'm a bit out of practice, but.' She glowed with false modesty, pleased as Punch. Or Judy, I supposed.

'Wow.' Now I was saying it. 'You saved my life.'

'Probably,' she said. 'You think I'm a real idiot, don't you? For ever getting involved with a guy like that.'

'Drugs change people,' I said, offering the solace of a meaningless cliché. Although in Steve Radeski's case it might well have been true. The long-term effect on humans of merino penis enhancer had probably not yet been clinically tested.

The dashboard cigarette lighter popped. As I lit up, Holly drew her hand up into the sleeve of her pullover and punched out the shattered passenger-side glass. A trail of crystal scattered behind us, discarded jewels. Wind tore through the car, cold and exhilarating, sending her hair swirling in a halo around her face. 'Hope it's insured,' she grinned.

We turned into St George's Road where a wide median strip separated the north-south lanes. Across the divide, a yellow Daihatsu Charade passed us, speeding in the opposite direction. 'Wow,' said Holly.

She was staring straight through the windscreen. Just up ahead, an immense column of water was gushing from the median strip, towering high into the air and dropping a curtain of water across the road. We hit it and burst out the other side, our hair wet, the cigarette sodden in my mouth.

'Wow,' said Holly, droplets glistening on her hair and skin. 'What was that?'

'The hydrant bandit strikes again.' As I began to explain, Holly half-turned in her seat and studied me. 'You're a bit of a dark horse, aren't you?'

'How do you mean?'

'Going into the Climber like that. Trying to capture Steve, single-handed.'

If that's what she wanted to think, I wasn't going to contradict her. I shrugged self-effacingly.

'And those guys back at the club, the ones you were talking to at the shops. They looked part-Aboriginal to me.' This non sequitur was somehow also a question.

'Which part?' I said.

'Come on,' she said. 'What's the story?'

'Like I told you. It's work-related. They're helping out with the Olympic bid. Community relations.'

'You work for the Olympics?' She narrowed her eyes and regarded me with profound scepticism. 'You're bullshitting me, right?'

The closest thing I had to proof was the invitation card to the gala dinner. I wrestled it out of my wallet and handed it over. She read it out loud. '*In Honour of the Visit of IOC Representatives Pascal Abdoulaye, Kim U-ee and Stansislas...*' She hit the Pole, the twelve-letter jaw-breaker. 'How do I pronounce this?'

'It's hard to say,' I said.

Impossible. Quite beyond me, anyway, a man who'd spent four years at the Ministry for Ethnic Affairs, bending his mouth around all kinds of phonetic contortions and alien nomenclature. Running up and down to the Translation and Information section, making sure that the minister did not utter an inadvertent obscenity when addressing the Khmer Retailers Association or opening the Turkish Senior Citizens Centre.

Just one glance at this IOC joker's name and all I could think of was Mr Mxyzptlk, Evil Genius from the Fifth Dimension in the Superman comics. Or all those unpronounceable Russians in Tolstoy and Turgenev—General Zherkwilkzlovskayachikov and Madame Shlyapnicwitz-Dzhibladze. At least in a novel, you didn't have to try to say them out loud. And Polish was even worse than Russian. All those strzs and cyzks. It was as if successive waves of invaders and occupiers over the centuries had plundered the country of its vowels, leaving only tangled piles of consonants in their wake.

Holly studied the card like it was a priceless artefact. 'Mr Murray Whelan,' she read. 'Wow. So what are our chances?'

'Pretty good,' I told her authoritatively. 'Apparently.' Something else occurred to me. 'You doing anything Thursday night?'

She looked at me sideways, the ironic look. 'You're asking me to this?'

'I know it's short notice.'

She shrugged. What was the harm? 'Sure.' She'd have to find somebody to take her last aerobics class of the day, she explained, but otherwise there was no problemo. 'Could be fun. Ta.'

She turned on the radio and nodded along. That fucking Madonna again. She was everywhere. My fingers drummed a beat on the steering wheel. My mind churned. What an eventful excursion this was.

Holly's flat was on the ground floor of a three-storey block of units. Mid-sixties, by the look of it. A white-painted, bagged-brick place behind a thick screen of acacias. All very Costa del Sol. Most of the tenants, she said, were visiting academics at the nearby University of Melbourne. Despite its location near a major freeway feeder, the place had a quiet, almost secluded atmosphere. Straight across the road, behind its stand of raddled cypresses, the Melbourne General Cemetery was as quiet as a graveyard.

I asked if I could use the phone and we went inside. The front door opened directly into the lounge, a cheerful little room with coir matting on the floor, a cane sofa with hibiscus-patterned cushions, a couple of Bangalow palms, a scatter of covers on the CD player—Prince, INXS, Toni Childs. Two half-empty bottles sat on the cane bookcase, Midori and Galliano. A beaded curtain led to the kitchen. Through the bedroom door I could see a double bed piled with folded laundry, a framed poster of a dolphin on the wall. It was a tidy, lived-in little flat with the smell of apple shampoo in the air.

While I used the phone, ringing around Parliament House until I got an answer, Holly put the kettle on. It had just gone ten-thirty and Woeful, I was eventually told, had been called away about an hour before. Some sort of emergency, his current whereabouts unknown. I called the Austin Hospital and learned that Denis Dogherty was in intensive care. No further information was available.

As I was finding this out, Holly thrust a cup of steaming liquid into my hand. 'This'll help you relax.'

Give up cigarettes, she meant. *Smoker's Infusion*. A half-empty packet of the stuff had been sitting in my pantry for nearly a year. Red clover and dandelion root. The only root I'd had in six months. Useless. Like Holly's front-door lock, a standard Yale-type. Useless, even taking into account the security chain. Radeski would only have to lean on it. She saw me looking. 'Why would he come here?'

This from a woman who had just smacked 130 kilograms of concentrated lamburger repeatedly in the chops. 'Because he's out of control, Holly, that's why. The guy's a maniac. He's already put one person on the critical list. Plus he just thumped someone back there at the Climber.' Not to mention Darcy Anderson. 'God only knows what's going on in his mind, what scores he might get it in his head to settle. One thing's for sure, I'd hate to be in his bad books right now.'

She stared at me over the rim of her herbal infusion. 'You trying to scare the shit out of me?'

'Got anything proper to drink?' I said.

She had Stolychnaya, pronounced vodka, a half bottle of it in the freezer. I tossed down a bracing shot and leaned back on the hibiscus cushions, closed my eyes and pricked my ears to the lizard slither of my bloodstream. Insects crawled under my scalp. A whole fucking zoo of baboons howled in my ears. I ground my teeth and clenched my diaphragm and forced the gastric reflux back down my oesophagus. I felt like shit on a stick.

Holly's hand rested on my shoulder, then gently took the cup from my hand. 'You look about ready for bed,' she whispered.

My hand went into the crook of her neck, her hair silky between my fingers, and I drew her towards me. Her lips met mine, cool and impassive. A terrible shame welled up within me, the realisation that I had betrayed myself as a sleaze. Burning with humiliation, I drew away.

But she followed, maintaining the gentle pressure of the still unbroken kiss, refusing to relinquish it. Her lips softened and opened, drinking me in. She sighed. Our breaths mingled, hers smelling of freshly laundered towels and tasting of Lite'n'Low. The kiss went on and on forever.

Instantly, magically, we were in the darkened bedroom, hands roaming hungrily, mouths locked together, devouring each other. She wrenched at my shirt, tearing it open. Buttons ricocheted off the walls. My hands went under her sweater, gliding up her sides and over her breasts, slippery smooth beneath a skin-tight sheath of lycra. A sheath in which there was no breach or opening. My fingers caressed her bodysuit, searching for a means of entry, a point of insinuation. Her firm body moulded itself to my touch, at once accessible and inviolable. My hands moved ceaselessly, exploring every slope and mound, every cleft and indentation. I was as long and hard as a Polish surname. No zipper or button, no buckle or clasp could I find. It was like trying to make love to a seal.

Not a seal, a python. Her limbs wound themselves around me. A pythoness, squeezing the breath from me, shedding her skin. In one deft, invisible movement, she peeled off her leotard and was naked. 'How did you do that?' I wanted to ask, speechless at the sight. Her breasts, lovely beyond description, filled my hands. I pressed my lips to a ruby nipple and sucked. Smoke filled my lungs.

I exhaled, savouring the exquisite sensuality of it, and reached to suck again. She laughed, leaning back out of my reach, and drew provocatively on her own cigarette. Mine was in a glass ashtray, a cold circle on my bare stomach, the terminus of a sinuous white thread reaching down from the ceiling. Another cigarette, somehow, was already burning between my fingers. She straddled me. Swirling wraiths of grey surrounded her head. She bent low and inhaled, drawing me inside her. A force welled deep in me. I teetered on the brink of eruption.

Stars spun before my eyes. An immense spasm racked my body, expelling all air. Daggers stabbed my chest, jack-knifing me upright. Head in my hands, feet on the floor, I began to cough. Cough upon cough shook my body, a pounding surf inside my lungs. My ribcage was a concrete mixer. Oysters flew from my mouth and nose.

Slowly, the attack abated. I wiped my nose on the back of my arm and rolled back beneath the bedclothes, dragging the sheet up beneath my chin. The digits on the clock radio said it was six-thirty. I believed them. The pale light of dawn was already sneaking around the curtains.

Jesus, was that a dream or what? I was alone. My bed had the same number of people in it as when I had climbed in, seven hours before. After I had said goodnight to Holly and driven home. My chest ached. Likewise my heart. A man could die and nobody would be any the wiser.

The patch on my midriff was smooth to the touch, its toxic cache leaking imperceptibly into my bloodstream. The brochure warned of disturbed sleep patterns. Now I knew what that meant. That mouth, those filter-tips, I could still taste them. Was it really only a dream? Memory darted before me, eluding my grasp.

I dozed until seven. When the alarm sounded, it met no resistance. I hurt too much to sleep. The pack of cigarettes was still in my jacket pocket. They whispered to me from across the room. Just the one, they said. To start the day. After that, I'd be fine.

I went into the bathroom and stood under a scalding shower for as long as the water stayed hot. An ugly purple-black bruise covered the left side of my ribcage, tender to the touch. Replacing the nicotine patch with a fresh one, I shaved, dressed, ate breakfast and still felt ratshit.

The radio was reporting more attacks on water mains. Three during the night, all in the northern suburbs. Despite suggestions of sabotage linked to the current industrial dispute, the union had denied responsibility. Bullshit, I thought. It looked like the Missos had finally figured out a way to make water run uphill. There was no mention of the Darcy Anderson case.

Those damn cigarettes just wouldn't shut up, so I broke them in half and stuffed them down the plughole. All but the last one, which I smoked. It didn't make me feel any better. It was going to be one of those days.

The red light was flashing on the answering machine. I had forgotten to check when I came home. I punched the button and listened to Wendy remind me that she and Red were arriving at noon and would be at the Hyatt if I wanted to see Red. I liked the 'if'.

I looked up Holly in the phone book. Despite my best efforts to persuade her otherwise, she'd insisted on sleeping at her flat. 'I can handle Steve Radeski,' she maintained. Having witnessed her combat skills, I found it hard to contradict her. But in the cold light of morning, I thought I should touch base. When I rang her number there was no answer. Don't panic, I thought. Not yet. Maybe she was out jogging. I'd call again later.

I rang Ken Sproule. It took a while to run him to ground but I eventually found him on his mobile. He sounded like he was speaking from the halls of purgatory. 'Denis Dogherty died on the operating table at 1 a.m.' he said, straight up.

I wished I'd saved those cigarettes.

'They tell me you were on the scene when he was found.' It was both a question and a statement. In a case like this, the violent death of a senior government adviser, Ken would take a close personal interest. We compared notes. I told him what I'd told the police. He told me what the police had told him. That Radeski was Denis's nephew. That it looked like a family argument gone wrong. That Woeful had gone straight from Parliament House to the hospital. He was waiting there with Marj Dogherty when they wheeled Denis out of emergency surgery with a sheet over his face.

'Denis Dogherty was quite a character,' said Ken. 'Despite our political differences, I had a lot of time for him.'

Only the first part of his statement was true, but I appreciated the sentiment. The platitudes would soon be flying thick and fast.

'They don't make them like that any more,' I said.

'Amen.'

For the next ten seconds neither of us said anything.

Then we got back down to it. Steve Radeski was still at large. The squad car sent to pick him up at the nightclub where he worked had missed him. According to the club manager, Radeski was in an agitated state all evening. He fled the place after indecently assaulting a customer and roughing up a male dancer, and had not returned home. 'Apparently he's been using some sort of veterinary shit,' Sproule said. 'Extremely high testosterone content with unknown psychological effects. The homicide boys are scouring the body-building scene, trying to pick up his trail.'

Until they collared Radeski, the cops were playing it low-key. 'The press might be prepared to cut Woeful some slack. Family tragedy and all that. But the Olympic minister's chief aide being killed by his steroid-abusing nephew is too good a story for them to sit on forever.'

'Let's just hope they catch this prick before he does any more damage,' I said. 'Finding Denis like I did, I feel like I've got a personal stake in the outcome. I'd appreciate knowing about it as soon as he's arrested.'

'You got it,' said Ken. 'Comrade.'

'Before you hang up,' I said. 'Any developments in the Darcy Anderson case?'

'Apart from those blackfellers of yours going on the warpath about the Olympics?' said Ken. 'Nothing so far. You wouldn't credit it was so hard to find a handful of skinheads.'

'No other suspects?'

'Such as?'

I was almost tempted to share my secret intelligence. But with the police already looking for Radeski there was no immediate reason to break my promise to Deadly. Anyway, I didn't intended to speak to anyone until I had a chance to talk with Woeful. I rang Phillipa Verstak's consulting rooms and made an appointment for my aching chest. Ten was the earliest she could fit me in, the receptionist told me. Then I rang Holly's place. Still no answer. As I hung up, the phone rang in my hand. It was Carmel, Woeful's private secretary. 'I don't know if you've heard,' she began.

'I have.' My tone was more brusque than I intended.

There was an embarrassed silence and when Carmel spoke again it was in her most officious voice. 'The minister would like to see you as soon as possible, to brief him on the Aboriginal Institute of Sport matter listed for tomorrow's Cabinet meeting.'

Given the situation, it seemed a strange request. 'I didn't think he'd be at the office today,' I said, surprised.

Carmel softened a little. 'I'm not sure it's completely sunk in,' she confided. 'I don't think he's been to bed yet.'

'I'll come straight in,' I said.

On the way, I returned the Toyota to the car-pool, blaming the destroyed passenger window on vandals. The dispatcher, a different one this time, couldn't have cared less if the Huns and the Visigoths had also had a hand in the matter. He took the keys with a grunt and shoved a damage-report form across the counter at me.

When I got to Sport, Carmel told me to go straight in, her red-rimmed eyes wide with caution. Woeful was behind his desk, brooding like a caged animal. Or so it seemed; the vertical slats of the blinds behind him looked like bars against the brushed-metal sky. 'Shut the door,' he ordered, his face haggard and unshaven.

I did as I was told, nodding sombrely and reciting the stock phrases of condolence. He ran his hand backwards over his scalp. I was one of the first. Soon the whole world would be coming at him with such courtesies. 'You were there,' he stated bluntly.

For what felt like the hundredth time, I told my story. Woeful listened impatiently, cutting me off when I got to the part where Holly ran to the shops to phone for the ambulance. 'I was told he spoke to you.'

It sounded like an accusation, like I'd stolen something from him. Which I had, in a way. His dying mate's last words. 'Well. Out with it.' He stared at me intensely, like he was prepared, if necessary, to wring the information out of me. 'What'd he say?'

'He mentioned your name.' There was some small comfort in that, I hoped.

'What exactly did he say?'

'He was in shock,' I said. 'But he said, "Promise you won't tell them about Woeful."' Or words to that effect.

Woeful tensed. 'Tell them what about me?'

'He didn't say. He was in shock. I'm not sure he knew what he was saying.' I felt defensive, a trespasser. 'I didn't even think it was worth mentioning to the police.'

Woeful's eyes narrowed in his big, sad face. If he knew the meaning of Denis's last words, he made no attempt to explain them. 'What else did he say?'

'When I asked him what had happened, he said, "Stevie." That's all, just "Stevie".'

His expression was impassive but his body could not conceal the slight tremor that ran through it. 'Stevie,' he said, in a voice so low he could have been talking to himself.

Then, abruptly, he swivelled his chair, turning his face to the window. For a long time neither of us spoke. Eventually, the silence grew too uncomfortable. 'If there's anything I can do,' I said, backing towards the door. 'For you. Or for Mrs Dogherty.'

'Marjorie.' The word was a sigh, tinged with infinite regret. 'She'll never forgive me.'

'You did everything you could.' Another trite formula.

He spun in his seat. 'What would you know about it?'

Weeping politicians were all the rage in those days. The Prime Minister would blubber into his hankie at the first sight of a camera. But Woeful McKenzie was a man of the old school, uncomfortable with the overt expression of deep emotion. I took his belligerence as a sign of grief.

'Denis was a good man,' I said. 'According to his ex-girlfriend, your nephew had been having problems adjusting to his father's stroke. I guess Denis went out there hoping he could help.'

Woeful's tension ebbed a little. 'Yes,' he said, fastening onto the explanation as though it had just occurred to him. 'That accounts for it.'

Carmel tapped lightly and put her head around the door. 'I've told them to bring your car around.' She spoke in a tone that brooked no contradiction. 'And cancelled your appointments for the rest of the day.'

The Aboriginal Institute of Sport had never been more than a pretext. The real reason Woeful had summoned me was to recount Denis's final moments. He could have said so, rather than treating me as an outsider. But, I supposed, that's just what I was.

'Yes,' Woeful repeated, turning again to the window. 'He was helping Stevie adjust to the difficulties of Rudy's stroke. That explains why he was there.'

But not why he'd gone there without informing his wife. Or why Steve Radeski had thrown him against a mirror, put him on a bed and left him to die.

'If there's anything I can do,' I said, backing out the door. 'Anything at all.'

One thing I could do, short term, was my job.

I went downstairs and headed for the Old Treasury. As I approached, a party of MOB officials emerged from the front door and rushed down the steps to where three identical white Fairlanes were just pulling up. Judging by the solemnity of the fuss, I was witnessing the arrival of the IOC Evaluation Commission. Suppressing the urge to rush forward and fling myself at their feet in supplication, I leaned against a balustrade and cast an appraising eye over the three men whose good impression of Melbourne would decide the outcome of the bid.

The first to emerge from his car was a tall, middle-aged African in an elegant pinstripe suit. He wore an amiably diplomatic expression and carried himself with all the cultivated arrogance of a graduate of the Ecole Nationale d'Administration. Pascal Abdoulaye, no doubt, representative of the International Olympic Committee in Senegal.

His associate, Mr Kim of Korea, was a squat, muscular man with hooded, predatory eyes and a subdued manner. According to what I'd read in the papers, he was a key player in preparations for the Seoul Olympics. You know, the ones with the persistent background odour of tear gas.

Finally, there appeared a thin, elderly white man with wavy grey hair, a clipped moustache of the same colour and heavy square spectacles. He drew himself upright and looked around expectantly, as if for a guard of honour to inspect. Stansislas Unpronounceable, the jaw-breaking Pole.

In a flurry of fervent handshakes and hearty welcomes, they were swept up the steps and through the front door of the MOB HQ. After a respectful pause, I followed. *Welcome to Melbourne*, said the electronic banner in the empty foyer. '*Manuyangka nyiyarlangurlu, jarntungku marda, yankirrirli…*' said a voice from down the corridor.

Pressing the cosmopolitan flesh was not part of Brian Morrison's job. I found him upstairs in the war room, getting an update on the torch relay. He'd already heard the news about Denis. Shaking his head solemnly, he led me into the office kitchen. Despite his move to the greener pastures of the corporate world, he still retained all the sentimentality of a true Labor man.

'Bloody Denis,' he said, prising the lid off a can of instant coffee. 'He's really left us in the lurch, going and getting himself killed at a time like this. Who's going to look after Woeful McKenzie now?'

'He's really taking it hard,' I agreed. 'Seems to blame himself.'

'Woeful's done all right for an old wharfie,' said Brian. 'But he wouldn't have got off the docks without Denis and everybody knows it. Denis was the one with the brains.'

'You think this has adverse implications for the bid?' It was an angle I hadn't yet had time to consider.

'Without Denis, Woeful is dead weight,' said Brian, handing me a cup of truly terrible coffee. 'Which is the last thing we need this close to the big decision. Unless we can find somebody to hold his hand, there's a real danger he'll drop the ball.'

I didn't like the way he looked at me when he said that. 'Surely Woeful isn't so central to the bid.'

'Maybe not,' he said. 'But it's a risk we can't afford to take. He's been a prominent part of our lobbying. Personally kissed the arse of nearly half the IOC. That sort of thing is not to be underrated in the Olympic family. Plus, he's got a crucial role in the funding and political side of things. Woeful was never the best choice in the world for the job but he's done reasonably well so far, thanks to Denis. What we've got to do now is find the right person to step into Denis's shoes.'

Nature abhors a vacuum, they say. The Labor Party relishes one. Denis Dogherty was barely cold and there we were discussing his replacement. But, if Brian Morrison thought he could induce me to volunteer as Woeful McKenzie's new minder, he could think again. 'The Aboriginal Institute of Sport...' I said.

Brian got the message. 'Listed for Cabinet tomorrow. In the meantime, your brief is to concentrate on Ambrose Buchanan.'

'You told me Buchanan was out of the loop.'

'And that's where I want him kept. Apart from a couple of mentions on the bloody ABC, he didn't get any publicity out of that demo yesterday. So now he might decide to pull some stunt with the Evaluation Commission. I want you to stick to him like glue, make sure he keeps his distance.' He reached into his pocket and handed me a small booklet, the Evaluation Commission itinerary: *Visit to Melbourne Olympic Bid, Inc. River Cruise of Proposed Olympic Village at Docklands. Luncheon with Lord Mayor. Tour of Museum of Sport. Inspection of Main Stadium. Sailing on the Bay. At Home with the Australian IOC member. Cocktails with the Foreign Minister.*

Etcetera and so on. The full schedule for a three-day, red-carpet, chauffeur-driven, fully escorted, all-expenses-paid tour of the world's most livable city for Messrs Abdoulaye, Kim and Dziczkowszczak.

'And I'm supposed to make sure that Buchanan doesn't buttonhole these blokes as they inspect a cocktail party?' I snorted. 'Don't you have guys in dark glasses with suspiciously bulging jackets to handle this sort of thing?'

'Matter of fact, we don't,' said Brian. 'Apart from Samaranch, these IOCs are virtually unknown. A couple of bodyguards at the more public events, that's about the extent of their security requirements. Which also happens to suit our terrorism-free visitor-friendly image.'

'Ambrose Buchanan isn't interested in disrupting the Evaluation Commission visit,' I said.

'Yeah?' He couldn't stop himself smiling. 'That's not what you suggested when you addressed the board yesterday morning.'

Shit. Hoist on my own petard. By conspiring with Denis to inflate Ambrose's connection with the African IOC into a threat, I had hastened the MOB's endorsement of the Aboriginal Sports Institute. But I had also played straight into Brian Morrison's hands.

Building up Ambrose Buchanan as a threat to the bid, I now realised, had simply been a bit of professional game playing on Morrison's part. Create a problem—or the perception of a problem—then save the day by solving it. And choosing me for his stalking horse had been a way of massaging his relationship with Woeful and Denis.

But then Ambrose had gone and fulfilled his dire predictions by staging a demonstration on the Old Treasury steps. Which was a bone I had yet to pick with the bewhiskered Buchanan.

'Other duties as directed,' Brian reminded me. 'That's what it says in your contract.'

'What do you suggest? Chaining him to a tree for the duration?'

'I'll leave the method to you.' Brian tossed the dregs of his coffee into the sink. 'You're a very inventive person, Murray.'

Also an uncomfortable one. Every time I coughed, a sharp pain pierced my side. And I seemed to be coughing a fair bit that morning.

The white Fairlanes were gone when I went outside. According to the itinerary booklet, our VIPs had just been whisked down to the river for a water-borne inspection of the proposed Docklands Olympic Village. As I made my way down the steps, the temperature suddenly dropped five degrees and a squally shower blew across town, turning the sky into a miserable grey stew. With characteristic Melbourne timing, the run of decent weather was ending in the first hour of the Evaluation Commission visit.

A tram was coming up Collins Street. I ran for it, clutching my side, and in less than fifteen minutes was standing in front of Phillipa Verstak, unbuttoning my shirt.

'Playing squash.' I sucked in my stomach and displayed my bruise. 'Copped a whack from my opponent's racket.'

Squash carried the right sort of social connotations, I thought. Business-class combat. The idea of telling Phillipa Verstak that I'd been bashed with a fence picket in West Heidelberg never entered my mind. Irrelevant to diagnosis. Inimical to prospects.

She wore a fawn linen jacket, the sleeves rolled once at the cuff. Scrubbed for action. Still no luck with the recalcitrant hair. 'Anything else?' she said. 'You look a bit wrung-out.'

Perceptive, I thought. 'I've just had some bad news. Friend of mine died last night.'

'Oh,' she said. Polite but distanced. Fair enough. She nodded in the direction of my heart. 'I see you've started the patches. How are we doing so far?' Back to the Hippocratic we.

'Very little desire,' I lied.

'Any side effects?'

'Been having these dreams,' I said.

She nodded knowingly. 'Nicotine stimulation at a time when the brain wouldn't normally be getting any. Not unless you smoke in your sleep.'

I shook my head. 'They're very explicit.'

'Anyone I know?' She stuck a freezing cold stethoscope against my chest. 'Cough. And again.' Long cool fingers explored my tender regions. 'Put your shirt back on.'

'Anything broken?'

'If it was, you wouldn't be standing here dropping Freudian hints. But we'd better make sure you haven't damaged your pulmonary lining.' Like it was my fault, or something. 'Third floor, Suite B.' She handed me an X-ray referral chit and told me to come straight back afterwards.

As befitted one of the most lucrative branches of subsidised medicine, the pathology lab operated on the principle of maximum throughput in minimum time. A quick swipe of my Medicare card, a signature, a lead apron over the gonads, rapid irradiation with high-velocity electrons and I was out of there with my snapshot under my arm before you could say Wilhelm Konrad Roentgen, winner of the inaugural Nobel Prize for Physics, 1901.

Back in Bernie's anteroom, I waited for a break in the traffic. A business-bureaucrat with the sniffles. A woman in a bankteller uniform on early lunchbreak. Typical Bernie clientele. I absently flipped through the pile of magazines and found the most recent issue. *Newsweek*, a month or so old. It had a feature story on the fate of the Eastern bloc sports machines, post-perestroika.

In the six months since the fall of the Berlin Wall, the whole shebang had come unglued. Regimes seemingly as imperishable as concrete had evaporated like the morning dew, undone by the Home Shopping Channel and reruns of 'The Beverly Hillbillies'. Everywhere, the shoe was on the other foot. In some cases, the fit was less than comfortable. Lech Walesa, hangdog candidate for the presidency of Poland, looked like he'd rather be back in prison. Gdansk for the memories.

Gone forever, too, were all those East German women shot-putters with their deep voices and baffled chromosomes. All those amenorrhoeal Romanian gymnasts and ox-shouldered Czech swimmers. For forty years, the East–West conflict had played itself as gladiatorial combat in the Olympic arena. Boycott and counter-boycott. Now it was all just sport, mere stopwatches and scoreboards, no longer Good v Evil.

But my mind was not on Manicheism. It was more concerned with deciding whether to use this opportunity to ask Phillipa out. Dinner perhaps? No, too obvious. And what if her professional ethics precluded her accepting a dinner invitation extended by a patient during a billable consultation? What if her flirtatiousness was no more than comfortable banter? And what if her excuse the other night at Mietta's had been just that, a polite rebuff?

My name was called and I handed Phillipa the big envelope containing the X-ray. 'Know anything about steroids?' I asked as she opened it. 'This friend of mine, his nephew's a bit of a body builder. He's become very aggressive lately.'

'Not the sort of body building I've had any experience with, I'm afraid.'

Her sort used spare parts. I could see her in a tin-roofed ward, fitting prosthetic limbs to children with stumps. Little kids who'd stepped on a landmine while running after a ball. And here was I, a grown man, come bleating to the doctor with my pathetic little bump. She held the transparency up to the window. She could see right through me.

'If you feel uncomfortable,' she said. 'Take a couple of aspirin. And no squash for a while. But there's no real damage. You should be right for tomorrow night.'

'The Olympic dinner?' Oh, that. Like I'd practically forgotten it. 'I guess I'll see you there with your friend. Rodney, isn't it? Something to do with the Olympics.'

'Rodney Elderton. Executive assistant to the chairman.' Her tone was almost mocking.

'Hmm,' I said, appreciatively. 'Sounds important.' Catty. But then the Nicabate instructions did warn of increased irritability.

'Try not to exert yourself too much, Murray,' she said, opening the door.

The brief autumn squall had exhausted itself by the time I stepped back onto the street. I stood for a moment on the footpath, considering my options. It was not yet eleven, so there was no point in heading for the Stars. Buchanan would not be there yet. Red and Wendy would be arriving soon. I decided to check on Holly.

At the swank pharmacy in the arcade at the Hyatt, I bought a packet of Panadeine Forte and swallowed two of them dry, bringing on another jag of coughing. The shop assistant, terrified that I might crop-dust her display of Diorissimo, almost fell over her false eyelashes in her haste to fetch me a glass of water. When I'd regained my composure, I went upstairs to the health club.

To my immense relief, Holly was there. Hale and hearty as ever, she was just starting her eleven o'clock aerobics class. As I glimpsed her thrusting pelvis and heaving bosom, I felt my ears catch fire. Prurient images of nocturnal congress flashed before my mind's eye. Taking a deep breath, I pushed them away. It was just a dream, I reminded myself. The involuntary by-product of biochemical processes. Lest my thoughts were somehow visible on my face, I hurried into the locker room.

For half an hour, I lounged in the sauna, excusing myself from exercise on doctor's orders. Drenched in a miasma of heat, I pondered a number of things that had been lurking in the back of my mind since my appointment with Woeful.

There seemed something odd in the big man's reaction to the situation. The urgency of his need to know exactly what Denis said to me, extending to the use of a pretext to summon me to his office. That line about Marj Dogherty never forgiving him. The eager way he fastened onto my suggestion that Denis had gone there to comfort Steve Radeski in his time of emotional need. Even his lack of anger towards Radeski.

I thought, too, of Denis. And I remembered that the last name he spoke was not Woeful's but mine. '*It's up to you now, Murray,*' he'd said.

But what was up to me?

When I emerged, none the wiser, I found Holly on desk duty. She cocked her head sideways, inviting me into the comparative privacy of the boutique. 'You really got me worked up last night,' she said, sotto voce.

Christ, I thought. It wasn't all a dream, after all. Blood rushed to my face in the nanosecond it took to realise the thought was absurd. Holly didn't notice. She was busy with the news.

'You got me really worried,' she went on. 'So I rang a cab straight after you left, went home to mum and dad. Spent the night there. The police think it's a good idea if I stay there until they catch Steve. He didn't go home last night and they don't know where he is. And that old man, Denis, he's dead. Awful, isn't it? But you'll never guess what. He was Steve's uncle. That's how come he was there.'

'You've talked to the police?' I said.

'I rang up that one who gave me his card,' she said. Detective Senior Constable Casanova. 'But don't worry, I didn't tell him about us going to the Climber. Not without talking to my lawyer first.' Now she was the one cracking funny. 'Anyway, I thought about what you said, how Steve might be out to settle a few old scores. So I told him how I remembered hearing Steve talking to his father one time, saying he was going to fix this guy if he ever got the chance, rip him limb from limb.'

'What guy?'

'Cheech somebody.'

'Cheech?' I wasn't sure I'd heard right. 'As in Cheech and Chong?' She stared at me blankly, no idea what I was talking about. 'Comedians,' I explained. 'Big in the early seventies.'

Of course she hadn't heard of them. She would've been all of five years old at the time. 'I don't think he's a comedian,' she said. 'More like some kind of weightlifting official. Maybe the one who got Steve kicked off the squad. Anyway, he said he'd look into it.'

It sounded like a nickname. Another turbo-charged meatloaf who'd got into a contretemps with Radeski at the free-weight rack. Fallen out with him for monopolising the shoulder press.

'You still want me to go with you to the Olympic dinner?' she said.

'Of course. If you want to.' Turning up with Miss Gorgeous on my arm, I'd decided, would not do my image any harm. 'Did I mention that my son Red is presenting the torch to the visiting IOC members. He's eleven now. My ex-wife will be there, too.'

'In other words,' she grinned mischievously, 'you'll be too busy to jump me.' She took a green and yellow windbreaker off the rack and held it in front of me, appraising the result. 'Jeeze, you're a goose.'

A goose was better than a lech. 'I'm glad we've got that clear.'

'The other thing I was going to ask,' she said. 'Those Aborigines, the ones you said are helping with the bid? Are they going to be there?'

I chuckled at the thought and shook my head. 'Not their scene. How much are those Adidas water bottles?'

'Twelve dollars,' she said, taking one down from the shelf.

'Bit expensive, aren't they?'

She went into sales mode. 'They *are* non-slip. And you're paying for a prestige brand, don't forget.'

'I'll take it,' I said. Nothing worse than losing your grip.

In the palaces of ancient India, the walls were tinted pink with the blood of slaves killed expressly for that purpose. A similar effect had been achieved in the lobby of the Hyatt Hotel although, at the insistence of the Building Workers Union, by a different means. The whole place was clad in marble the colour of raw veal.

The large abstract paintings above the reception desk, on the other hand, looked like they were executed in egg custard and butterscotch sauce. It was past twelve-thirty and I guessed I was getting hungry. At least I wasn't thinking about a cigarette.

When Red and Wendy came up the escalator from the motor court, I sat watching from behind the floral display.

Wendy was a handsome woman and it wasn't difficult to appreciate why I'd married her in the first place. She had the makings of a fine husband. The life of a corporate high-flier clearly suited her. Long gone was the perpetually harassed air of a member of the Women's Industrial Research Collective. Wendy had come up in the world. So had her hair. Her wardrobe and personal grooming were exemplary. What with the understated power suit and the dark hose, she exuded all the unassuming authority of an SS *Obersturmbannführer*.

Redmond, I was pleased to see, hadn't changed too much since his last visit. A little taller, perhaps, but I'd got used to that over the years. Just turned eleven, he'd shed his baby fat and his frame was reaching upwards in the general direction of adolescence. That dubious destination remained, thankfully, some distance away. In the meantime he was still just a kid with his shoelace undone and his bomber jacket tied around his waist. While Wendy signed the register and frightened a room key out of the desk clerk, he cast a curious eye over his luxurious surroundings, doing his best to look blasé. Eventually, he spotted me.

He dropped his backpack beside Wendy and sloped over, smiling crookedly. This was partly because of the amount of stainless steel in his mouth and partly because these encounters were getting to be as difficult for him as for me. 'Nice place you've got here,' he said.

'It's modest,' I said. 'But it suits my needs.' We embraced in a properly awkward way, all very manly, breaking the clinch even as it was formed. 'Sorry I missed you on Parramatta Road,' I said. 'Ready for the big re-run?'

Red gave me the thumbs up and we ambled across in the general direction of his mother. 'Murray,' she said, punctiliously neutral.

'Wendy,' I said, somewhat less effusively.

The family reunion complete, we headed upstairs to their room. In the lift, Wendy took the opportunity to outline her proposed arrangements for the next two days. Proposed as in brooking no argument. Taking into account quality time with the maternal grandparents, Red's social visits with his old friend Tarquin and preparations for the torch relay, there would be scant opportunity for father-son bonding. 'You're probably very busy anyway,' said Wendy. 'God knows, winning the Olympic bid is the only hope this town's got.'

For the sake of the child, I desisted from prising open the emergency telephone hatch and bludgeoning his mama insensible with the handpiece. Instead, I offered Red the Adidas water bottle. 'Won it at the gym,' I said. 'Most Improved Father of an Olympic Torch Bearer. I thought you might like it.' It wasn't much of a gift, I knew, but it's the thought that counts.

As thoughts went, this one didn't go very far. Red wrinkled his nose. 'Adidas is for losers.' Nothing personal, you understand. Just setting me straight, brand-consciousness wise. As we started down the hallway, I dumped the deficient object in a housemaid's laundry bin.

Their room was on the fifteenth floor, a suite with a wrap-around view that extended all the way to Antarctica. Clouds roiled and boiled and sprinted across the sky. Red went through the room like an infectious disease, testing the beds, counting the pillows, ferreting through the minibar and loading up his knapsack with the free toiletries. 'Sealed for your protection,' he called from the bathroom. Unlike his mother's mouth.

'I see the weather hasn't improved,' she said. Like it was my fault. Like she hadn't lived in Melbourne for the first thirty years of her life. Like the climate should have got its act together, knowing she was about to arrive.

While Wendy was looking for something else to complain about, the porter knocked with the luggage. Dressed in a green monkey suit and built like a pretzel, he took approximately forever to insinuate one suitcase and an overnight bag from the hallway into the room. Then he took even longer to leave. 'Don't just stand there,' commanded Wendy. 'Give him a tip.'

'You want a tip?' I said. 'Join the union. Begging demeans a man.' I gave him a dollar a bag, more than fair and less than the recommended rate. Wendy's parents were picking Red up at two o'clock, which meant the boy and I had time for lunch together. I suggested McDonald's.

'Richard says no Maccas while I'm in training,' announced Red.

McDonald's was Red's oldest vice, one I'd long given up trying to fight. Now it appeared that my competitor for the boy's affection had succeeded where all my lectures about the Amazonian rainforest had failed. 'Don't be so cheap,' said Wendy, off to a free feed with her Melbourne management.

For a special treat and the sake of convenience, I took Red downstairs to the restaurant in the lobby, a small forest of potted palms. When the waiter pulled out the chairs and flapped the napkins, the kid took it all in his stride, quite the sophisticate. But then he lived higher on the hog in Sydney than had ever been the case with his old man in Melbourne.

The place was running a special bush-tucker promotion. Fillet of emu with quandong chutney. Wallaby sausages in a lilly-pilly coulis. Glacé of bush tomatoes. I opted for the braised hump of Nullarbor camel with a witchetty-grub cappuccino on the side. 'Yuk,' said Red and ordered a burger with fries.

So much for Richard's training regime, I gloated secretly. 'It's a pity you can't stay until Saturday,' I said. 'We could go to the footy.'

'If I start missing games, I'll lose my place on the team,' said Red.

I knew the score. It was the same in the Labor Party. 'Pretty strict for Under-12s,' I said.

'Under-13s,' he corrected me. 'I'm playing above my age. And you've got to be strict if you want to go all the way to the top.' He had it figured.

'Sounds like you really like this rugby thing,' I said, fascinated by this hitherto unrevealed side of my son's personality. Red was once so easy-going, so laid-back, that he would have scoffed at the idea of such discipline. Apart from a passing passion for Batman merchandise or Star Wars figurines, he had never before displayed such commitment to anything. 'What do you like about it?'

'Winning,' he stated flatly. 'What else is there?'

'Are you winning at the moment?'

'Killing 'em,' he said, fiercely and without a shred of humour. 'Absolutely murdering them.' He threw out his chest, awaiting my approval.

'Oh,' I said. 'That's good.'

It was the age, I supposed. That last year of primary school when a certain bravado was bound to emerge in a boy. Top of the heap in the schoolyard, yet secretly apprehensive of the imminent move to high school and instant demotion back to little-kid status. In sport, he had found a place to match himself against his peers, to find the potential of the present.

I empathised but I could not identify. Ruthlessly relegated to the bench by the match-hardened Sisters of the Good Shepherd, I had by Grade 4 reconciled myself to watching from the sidelines. A spectator rather than a participant, I had done little to encourage Red into an on-field role. Standing on the boundary line on a Saturday morning, screaming my tits off at the Under-7s, had never been part of my parenting experience.

Little Athletics. Rugby Union. Sailing. These were all part of Red's life without me, part of his growing-up, his inevitable declaration of independence. Part of his life with Richard, I thought darkly as I threw myself onto my fricassee of dromedary. Richard was the source of all this competitiveness, I was prepared to bet. A certain degree of competition was a good thing. Sport would be impossible without it. But I wasn't sure I liked the relish with which Red appeared to have embraced the concept. It smacked of the motivational lecture.

My first wife's second husband was reasonably okay, as far as I could tell. Red could probably have found a worse stepfather. Ambitious and slightly oily in that Sydney way, Richard was not actually a Liberal Party member to the best of my knowledge. He was, however, from a privileged background. Cranbrook School, father a judge, independent income. In that context, a tendency to nurture competitiveness had the whiff of ideology about it. If we were talking about a proper game, Australian football, I might have felt different. But rugby! Jesus.

I spent the rest of the meal big-noting myself, knowing I was doing it and not being able to stop. Talk about competitive. It was pathetic. Fortunately, Red was too busy to notice, preoccupied with trying to fit a triple-decker Hyatt burger into his mouth without getting the decorative toothpick up his nose.

By the time I'd finished my witchetty-grub cappuccino—a frothy farrago of beige milk and wet sawdust—our conversation had flagged out to a series of long silences. I'm losing him, I thought. This is the way it will be, more and more, from now on.

As we rode back up to the room, the elevator doors opened at the gymnasium level. Holly was standing in the lift lobby, chatting with a customer. She beamed and waved cheerily, a cross between Margaux Hemingway and Jamie Lee Curtis. 'My date for the big dinner tomorrow night,' I whispered as the doors slid shut again.

Red's head turned and he perused me slyly. 'You've got a date with *her*?'

'Sure,' I shrugged modestly. 'She's my personal trainer.'

Red's eyebrows went up and down like a yo-yo and he gave a low whistle. Redmond T. Firefly. 'Lookin' good,' he said. 'Dad.'

The Stars Cafe was open for business again but there was no sign of Ambrose Buchanan among its late-lunching clientele.

'Think we're running a secretarial service, do you?' said a woman in an apron behind the roast of the day. But her bark was worse than her bite and she pointed her electric knife through the front window, towards the hotel across the street.

The Royal was one of the last unreconstructed watering holes in Fitzroy, a reminder of the days when no member of the working class need be more than staggering distance from alcoholic oblivion. *Happy Hour 10 a.m.–12 p.m.* read the chalked sign at the door of the front bar. I stepped across the threshold and squinted into the gloom.

The atmosphere was not what you might call inviting. Tired paintwork, ratty carpet, the stale fumes of a million dead beers. About twenty drinkers, early starters. Koories, mainly, and a few paunchy Yugoslavs. Voices echoed off hard tile walls. A juke box thumped away in the murk at the back of the room. Merle Haggard, by the sound of it. The snick of balls came from a pool table on a step-up in the crook of the bar. Two men were playing: Ambrose Buchanan and Ernest Anderson. Ambrose had shaved his beard off, a definite improvement. Deadly's appearance, by contrast, had grown even more deadly. He'd shed the bandanna and his caramel-coloured skull was as bare as the ball of a roll-on deodorant. The tight skin was covered with scars, a tonsure of cross-hatching. The sort of handiwork you do on yourself in a cell with a broken bottle during lock-down. He must have really looked like something when they finally got around to opening those doors. He glowed with a patina of unhealthy sweat and, in the wait between shots, his fingers knotted and unknotted themselves at his side.

I took a stool at the bar. Whatever the deficiencies of the decor, the pipes were clean and the beer was crisp. Buchanan was playing the low-numbered balls. He potted three in a row and dropped the 8-ball into the side pocket. A dark-skinned indigene of indeterminate age with a soft rubbery face and no teeth leaned against the wall muttering unintelligible encouragement. Deadly racked them again and broke. The impact was as loud and abrupt as a gunshot.

Buchanan played a couple of strokes then handed his stick to the spectator. Flashing the barman two fingers, he lowered himself onto the stool beside me. Up close, his skin was raw from shaving and his eyes were exhausted. He looked like he hadn't been to bed. Deadly, it appeared, took some keeping up with. He put his elbows on the bar and waited.

'Found Radeski yet?' I said. One possible reason why the police hadn't.

Buchanan shook his head. 'Never been much of a black tracker, myself,' he said. 'But Deadly's been making inquiries.' He nodded towards the payphone. 'Currently awaiting developments.'

'Then what?' I said. 'Rough justice?'

Buchanan stared down into his beer. 'Justice,' he said softly. 'That's Deadly's special subject. He's been studying it since he was nine years old. That's when they first put him in a home. Told him that's what little black bastards get for breaking school windows. Picked him up in a paddy wagon and handcuffed him to the seat, just to help him get the hang of things.'

'Save the violins,' I said. 'Eraserhead over there isn't the only one with dibs on Steve Radeski. That old bloke, Denis Dogherty, was a friend of mine. He's dead now and I want to know why. If Deadly knows something, he should go to the cops and tell them. If he's worried about incriminating himself, tell him to take a legal-service solicitor with him.'

'You tell him,' said Buchanan wearily. 'I'm sure you'll have more influence than me.'

We contemplated the issue, sipping our beers. The brown man's burden. What I really needed was a cigarette. I thought about the idea, long and hard, using my entire body. Deadly went to the payphone and jabbed at the keypad. Waited for an answer, jaw grinding. Snapped a question. No joy. Repeated the procedure. When he picked up his cue again, my hand moved to my side, feeling the tenderness.

'Pretty close to Darcy, was he?' I said.

Buchanan snorted into his beer. 'That's what you might call the irony of the situation.'

Deadly and Darcy were proper cousins, he explained, but Darcy was born long after Deadly was taken away. What with one thing and another, Deadly being in and out of prison, the two of them never met. But Deadly heard about his young cousin, his closest living kin, the rising champion.

'He's real proud, eh? So when he gets out this time and hears that Darcy's here in Melbourne, he turns up, wanting to party. But Darcy's a bit freaked out, not sure if he wants to know. Maxie tells Deadly to piss off, not come around. Naturally enough, he's pretty cut up. Then this happens.'

'In other words,' I said, 'Deadly's desire for revenge is some sort of attempt to make right his family obligations to Darcy.'

Buchanan examined the inch of beer in the bottom of his glass. 'You're not one of them anthropologists, are you?'

'Fuck you, too,' I said. 'Want another drink?'

I ordered again, three this time, and held one up to Deadly. The cops weren't having much success in finding Radeski. Maybe Deadly, his nose closer to the ground, would have better luck. 'He'll get himself back in strife,' I said, 'if he does anything stupid.'

'He's never been out of strife,' said Buchanan. 'More strife than Jacky-Jacky, that one.'

Deadly laid his cue on the table, came over and downed his beer in a single contemptuous tilt of his head.

'Know anyone called Cheech?' I said.

Last night, for Ambrose's sake, he had tolerated me. But he'd said too much and he resented me for it. Now I was in his pub, asking fucking stupid questions. I could get stuffed.

'Word is, Steve Radeski is looking for someone called Cheech. Find this Cheech and you might find Radeski.'

He didn't even look at me. Just wiped his mouth with the back of his forearm and went back to his game. But he had to be thinking about it.

'Cheech?' said Buchanan. 'As in stoned hippy comedy duo.'

'Same name. Different bloke. Unless Radeski is looking for an Hispanic-American with a black moustache and a string of lousy movies.'

'I thought he was a Mexican,' said Buchanan.

I wasn't buying into that one. 'This Sports Institute. Big wheels are already in motion.'

Buchanan grinned. 'So our little protest yesterday did the trick.'

'That piss-poor effort? You've got to be joking.'

He shrugged. Okay, so the demo hadn't been the most brilliant example of his work. 'Not up to my usual standard, I admit. Some of the younger generation felt they should express their justified anger. I thought a demo was better than other options being discussed.'

It was plausible, I supposed. 'The MOB had already decided to back your proposal. Now they think you'll try to disrupt this IOC visit.'

'Why would I do that?'

'Because you're a trouble-making agitator who's prepared to destroy the nation's hopes for a bit of cheap self-promotion.'

'That's true.'

Buchanan was smoking roll-your-owns. So was I. It must have happened when I wasn't looking. 'So I'm supposed to make sure you behave yourself while these VIPs are in town.'

'Is that right?' The tips of his fingers tested the smoothness of his chin. 'How do you intend to do that?'

'I was thinking of threatening to go to the cops about this Deadly–Radeski business unless you agree to co-operate.'

Responding to some unseen signal, the barman put another round of drinks on the bar. My shout, apparently. 'As they say in Arunta.' Buchanan raised his glass in a toast. 'Looks like you got me over a barrel.'

I started telling him how I'd fleshed out his concept for the institute, how it might be structured, funded. Koories kept coming to the bar. Buchanan would introduce them and I'd buy another drink, bat the breeze. Every now and then, Deadly would hit the phone again, Buchanan never missing a move.

By five o'clock, I was slurring my words. My life was going to hell in a handbasket. Midweek afternoon, working hours, I was pissing on in a low-life dump with men named Dikko and Toad. Colluding with a known criminal. Cigarettes were smoking themselves in my mouth. My son was turning into a rampant rugger bugger. I hadn't had sex with another person for months. The Righteous Brothers were on the jukebox. They'd lost that loving feeling. It was gone, gone, gone.

Time I was, too. I no longer had the body for this sort of thing. I walked, squinting into the low afternoon sun, past the flats, across Brunswick Street and through my own front door. The light on my answering machine was flashing, calls backed up since late morning. I took the phone off the hook, swallowed a handful of painkillers and went out like a light.

I was woken three hours later by a knock on the door. Bang, bang. Thanks a lot. It was the tyro flatfoot from the Fitzroy cop shop, the one who'd taken my report on the stolen Charade. It was in relation to that matter, he said, that he was there. 'You'd better come inside,' I told him, standing in my suit pants and bare feet, smelling like a brewery. 'Quick.'

He sat at the kitchen table while I answered nature's call. More of a bellow, really. All that beer. 'Turned up, has it?' I said, zipping my fly. 'I was just about to send in the insurance claim.' The form was sitting there on the table with the junk mail and threatening letters that had come in the afternoon post.

'You are aware, sir,' he said. 'That there are penalties for making a false insurance claim.'

Hello. What was this? 'You suggesting this is a put-up job? That I nicked my own car for insurance?'

He took out his notepad. 'I understand you work for the water department.'

'Not currently,' I said. 'I'm on secondment to the Olympic bid.'

'Yeah?' He wrote it down. 'What are our chances?'

'Pretty good,' I said. 'If our water holds out.' He wrote that down, too. 'What's my job got to do with my car?'

'Your vehicle has been identified as involved in the current spate of incidents involving fire hydrants. You wouldn't happen to know anything about it, would you, sir?'

'You're telling me some prick is using my car as a battering ram to knock over fire hydrants?' I said. Those pricks at the union. Probably their idea of psychological warfare. I'd give them warfare all right.

'We were hoping you might be able to assist us in this matter, sir.' They were on to me, he was letting me know, big time. Now was the time to confess.

'I suggest you interview all members of the Miscellaneous Workers Union,' I said. 'The man you're looking for has a brown cardigan and a stutter. When you find him, tell him from me that if this little stunt affects my insurance claim, I will personally cut off his water supply.'

The copper closed his pad and got to his feet. 'If you do happen to remember anything, sir.'

'That Aboriginal kid, the triathlete?'

He perked up immediately. 'Yes?'

'I was just wondering if you've caught whoever did it? Shocking, something like that happening just around the corner.'

'A random attack. Not much we can do to prevent that sort of thing, sir.'

So much for the efficacy of the constabulary. Changing into track pants and a sweatshirt, I sloped down to the corner shop and bought a frozen lasagne, no cigarettes and a copy of the *Herald*.

Denis's death rated eight paragraphs on the inside front cover. He was described as 'a government consultant and former union official', the circumstances of his death 'probably a domestic dispute'. Police were reported to be seeking a former member of the national weightlifting squad who they believed would be able to assist them with their inquiries.

In a separate item, a spokeskoori for the Aboriginal Legal Service, Graeme Talbot, expressed dissatisfaction at the lack of police progress in the Darcy Anderson case. He suggested that such foot-dragging presented a poor picture of Melbourne to the international community.

I put my Papa Giuseppe in the microwave, rang Ken Sproule on his mobile and learned that Radeski was still at large. That, he said, was all he knew.

'I wonder how the media will react when they learn that Gil Methven recommended not reporting Denis as missing?' I prompted. 'If he'd been found earlier, he might still be alive.'

'You wouldn't dare,' said Ken.

True, but he got the idea. Ken was a man who didn't respect you unless you threatened him from time to time. He told me, strictly not for attribution, that a neighbour had seen Radeski move Denis's car off the street and into his garage late on Monday night. And that Radeski's own car, an early model Celica, had been found abandoned in Preston, not far from his house.

'Looks like he spotted them waiting for him and did a bunk.'

Associates in the iron-pumping fraternity claimed not to have seen Radeski for several weeks. Described him as a loner. Nobody, particularly the bigger guys, knew anything about any steroids. Checks on planes, trains and ferries had drawn a blank, suggesting he was still in town somewhere. The closest thing to a lead was a report that two men had been looking for him at the nightclub where he worked shortly before he disappeared.

'Dark-skinned,' said Ken. 'Whatever that means. Nobody was paying much attention at the time considering he'd just been disturbed trying to rape one of the customers on the fire escape. Apparently the type of shit he's been using really puts lead in your pencil.'

Maybe they should've been searching down at the stock-yards, catch him humping a ewe. I kept that suggestion to myself.

'Speaking of which,' continued Ken. 'This ex-girlfriend of his, your little friend, reckons he might be gunning for somebody called Cheech. As in Cheech and Chong? Those dopey American comedians from back in the seventies?' Ken's range never ceased to amaze me. 'I can never remember which was which.'

'Cheech was the wetback,' I said. 'Chong was the chink.'

'You'd know,' said Ken. 'Being the ethnic expert.'

Which reminded me. 'How about the father? Any joy there?'

'Totally ga-ga. A cerebral haemorrhage six months ago, compounded by early-onset Alzheimer's. Sonny boy is a regular visitor, every weekend, so the place is under surveil-lance, but the old bloke himself is a write-off. Half the time, according to the staff, he thinks he's on a ship. Keeps muttering in Polish. They got a translator in, but he accused her of being a member of the communist secret police.'

Despite their lack of success, the coppers were optimistic that Radeski would soon draw attention to himself. 'The way he's behaving, he's bound to clobber someone else sooner or later.'

'Let's just hope it's a Liberal next time,' I said. 'Any progress on the Darcy Anderson case?'

'Operational confidentiality,' he said.

'Come on, give.'

'Interesting developments,' he said.

But that was all I could get out of him. He promised he'd call again as soon as they collared Radeski but I had the feeling I'd exhausted my goodwill. The oven bell rang, so I hung up and demolished the lasagne in record time. While I was shovelling, I checked the phone book and found a Deloite in Pascoe Vale.

One of Holly's kid brothers answered the phone, bellowing her name over a background of television noise. 'It's a man,' he jeered.

'No it's not,' I reassured her. 'It's just me, Murray, calling to report still no sign of Steve. Had any other ideas?'

Not really, but she appreciated my calling to check on her welfare. 'Was that your son in the lift today?' she said. 'He's a good-looking kid.'

'Takes after his father,' I said. We let it go at that.

I popped a couple of Panadeine Forte—it wasn't a cigarette but at least it was a drug—and spent another hour on the phone, clearing the backlog off my answering machine. Detective Senior Constable Sonderlund had rung, inviting me to attend the Fitzroy police station at nine the next morning to provide my written statement in relation to the Denis Dogherty matter.

Sonderlund was the one who'd called the previous day about my offer to identify the skinheads. First the Darcy Anderson case, now Denis. Either police resources were stretched or a crossover was happening in the investigations. Had they already made the connection, rendering Deadly's information redundant? Or was Sonderlund simply the homicide housekeeper, fielding the public and attending to the paperwork? I guessed I'd find out soon enough.

In the meantime, the news about my walk-in role in the discovery of Denis had been making rapid progress along the grapevine and various of my party cronies had thoughtfully taken the time to ring. Before I spoke to any of them, however, there was one person I felt deserved a call. I rang him at Parliament House, where he was piloting a raft of money bills down the legislative rapids.

'Poor Denis,' said Agnelli. 'He'll be a great loss to the faction. And to the party and Woeful. And to his family, too, I suppose.'

The funeral was to be private, no flowers by request. The Labor Party had more than its fair share of Denis when he was alive, Marj Dogherty had complained. And she knew her husband's opinion of certain people only too well. The sight of them shedding crocodile tears over his coffin would be too much to tolerate. A proper wake was being organised for later in the week, details TBA.

After Agnelli, I made another half-dozen calls, passing on my version of the event and taking general soundings. Woeful had been out of the picture all day and there was already talk that he would soon decide to pack it in. The implications of a ministerial resignation were dire, given the fragility of the deals which cemented together the precarious architecture of the government. The factional balance hung on a knife edge and any attempt at a reshuffle would inevitably erupt into public brawling. Gil Methven, with characteristic sensitivity, had been heard doing mental arithmetic out loud in the corridors of Parliament House. The Premier, concerned for both the general stability of the government and the tenability of his own position, was a pillar of support to Woeful in his hour of bereavement.

My boundary-riding done, I turned on the television and caught the tail end of the late news. While I was at the Royal Hotel, doing my bit for race relations, the Evaluation Commission had been inspecting the Docklands, proposed site of the Athletes Village.

The footage showed them under umbrellas, boarding a luxury cruiser, the MV *Dream the Dream*, admiring the city skyline for the benefit of the viewers. Although this was the first visit to Australia by the African and Asian delegates, said the voice-over, it was a sentimental journey for the Polish delegate, bringing back memories of his time in Melbourne during the 1956 Games.

In a related report, the Olympic torch had reached Westfield Shoppingtown in Melbourne's northern suburbs. Shoppers had lined the mall to cheer on participating local schoolchildren. The torch was now on the final leg of its journey to be presented to the visiting representatives of the IOC tomorrow evening.

By now, it was nearly eleven o'clock, too late for a goodnight call to Red. Too late and too strange. The kid's bedroom was empty while he slept in a hotel only a few kilometres away. He might as well still be in Sydney. According to Wendy's schedule, we would next see each other at the rehearsal for the torch handover. It had come to this, I thought gloomily, that I should count myself lucky to get an appointment with my own son.

As I brushed my teeth, I surveyed my battered and Nicabated chest in the mirror. My little sachet of poison potion. So far, so good. A permanent headache, some crabbiness, a tendency for the concentration to wander, the odd instance of backsliding, a tender throat. Twenty-four hours since my last cigarette, not counting one for breakfast and three greyhounds in the pub.

To stay patched overnight or not, that was the question. To chance waking in a nicotine-starved state, a pushover for the first fag that came along. Or to wrestle with the sandman, drenched with chemical stimulants. To sleep, perchance to dream.

I'll have a dream, I told myself, and hit the hay.

But the vision that visited me that night was no succubus with a stethoscope or smoke-wreathed nymph. It was a leprechaun with rope-veined fingers and fading breath. '*It's up to you, now, Murray*,' Denis kept repeating. '*You promised. You promised.*'

'Hard night, Mr Whelan?'

On the face of it, Detective Senior Constable Carol Sonderlund was a netball dyke with a bad haircut and a personality like a clenched fist. On the other hand, maybe I was just having a bad morning.

'I'm giving up smoking.'

Barely through the door of the cop shop, I was already pleading mitigation. Sonderlund pretended to be sympathetic but she wasn't fooling me. In her line of work, the customers usually had worse things to worry about.

'We'll get this over and done with, then, shall we?'

She opened the security door and ushered me into an empty office with a computer on a bare desk.

My dreams had been complex and troubling and not at all erotic. Twice or three times I had woken in a cold sweat, pursued by a hulking green figure in a torn shirt, Denis's dying words echoing in my ears. On top of which, I'd arisen to find myself out of milk and muesli and was forced to stagger, bleary-eyed, to the shop for my breakfast necessities. By the time I read the papers, picked up Hugo from the dry-cleaners and made myself presentable, it was just on nine, time for my appointment.

'Rounded up Steve Radeski yet?' I asked. Bad choice of words. Didn't mean to sound critical.

'We will,' said the detective. 'Believe you me.'

She took the cover off the keyboard.

'What about Darcy Anderson? The skinheads still your main suspects?'

'We usually ask the questions,' said Sonderlund, thin-lipped.

Despite the NO SMOKING sign, cigarette burns pitted the floor and the air smelled of stale smoke. The walls were bare but for a Police Credit Union calendar and a loudly ticking clock. Welcome to the home of the third degree. 'Fire away,' I said.

'Tuesday night,' she said. 'West Heidelberg.'

Detective Sonderlund was a pretty good touch-typist and my statement took less than fifteen minutes to dictate, print out and sign. I'd had plenty of time to rehearse it and in the interest of brevity and consistency I didn't add any new revelations. Once all the paperwork was in order, I was thanked for my assistance and shown the door.

Which left me pretty well at a loose end. According to the schedule, the Evaluation Commission was currently inspecting the proposed equestrian facility at Werribee. A cow paddock, fifty kilometres away. Well out of Buchanan's reach, even if he wanted to make a nuisance of himself.

Which, I believed for a certain fact, he did not. With Radeski still at large, Ambrose had his hands full riding shotgun on Deadly.

And Deadly, presumably, was attempting to cherchez le Cheech. Fishing in the same water as the cops. I wondered who would land Radeski first.

Just because I was being paid to do nothing, there was no reason to get myself into a lather. My ribs weren't too uncomfortable, the day had dawned fine and mild and the rehearsal for Red's torch presentation was still two hours away. I caught a tram into the city and went into one of the little arcades running off Collins Street.

A wise man approaches the tasks of government, according to Lao Tzu, as he would the cooking of a very small fish. Sardines on toast, in this particular instance, prepared by a woman named Magda Lipsky.

Unlike the Italians and Greeks, Melbourne's Polish community was neither large nor conspicuous. Poles formed no visible subculture and colonised no suburbs. Polish Jews, to be certain, could be found in the borscht belt extending from St Kilda back into the hinterland of Caulfield and Balaclava. But that was a different matter, modern European history being what it was. Apart from a minor influx of refugees after the declaration of martial law in 1981, most of the city's Poles were ageing postwar immigrants, models of assimilation whose children had vanished without a trace into the wider community.

In my four years at Ethnic Affairs, only once had a Polish issue come to my administrative attention. Two old codgers turned up one day, referred by their local MP. Men with a dream.

During World War II, Piotr Lipsky and Jerzy Melnyk were members of the Free Polish forces fighting in the North African desert. After the war, they refused repatriation and opted to settle in Australia. Both had done modestly well in business, Jerry in sheet metal and Peter in real estate. Restless in retirement, they had decided it was time to reaffirm their roots.

Not only was the famous author Joseph Conrad born a Pole, they explained, but he had actually visited Melbourne in the 1880s as the captain of a trading ship. Would not a statue of the author of *Heart of Darkness*, prominently located, preferably with a marine outlook, be an ideal way to celebrate the historic links between Poland and Australia? Funds were not an issue but an appropriate site needed to be found and official sanction obtained.

Statues were for the birds as far as Angelo Agnelli was concerned. But Peter and Jerry were likeable and persistent old bastards and for two years I conspired with them to get their monument afloat. We sometimes met at the Do Duck Inn, a small coffee shop in Howey Place owned by Peter Lipsky and run by his daughter Magda.

The Arts Ministry showed some initial interest, especially when somebody there realised that it was Conrad who had written the first draft of *Apocalypse Now*. But by the time the Harbour Trust found a site in the carpark of the new container terminal, cultural priorities had shifted. Couldn't we do something in postmodern pre-contextual dance, Arts asked? When Jerry died at seventy-seven of a coronary occlusion, Peter's enthusiasm for the project waned. Eventually the whole thing ground to a halt and he returned to getting under Magda's feet at the Do Duck Inn.

It was one of those narrow old-fashioned places, once common but now rarely seen, where ladies enjoying a day's shopping in the city could rest their tired feet beneath a bowl of tomato soup and an asparagus roll. In a world gone mad for radicchio focaccia and sushi negri, it was a bastion of buttered crumpets and apple crumble. I found Peter in the tiny kitchen, slicing ham for the lunch-order sandwiches.

At that time of the morning, there were few customers and Peter took off his apron and joined me, leaving Magda to get on with it. A pinched, avaricious woman of my own age, she seemed to regard my friendship with her father as a ploy to cheat her of her inheritance. But she made the best sardines on toast in town.

Peter Lipsky was always a spare man, but I was shocked at how much weight he'd lost since I'd last seen him. His black turtle-neck sweater and grey permanent-press slacks hung loose off his rake-like frame and the strut was gone from his cavalry-officer tread. 'The Big C,' he said, answering my unasked question. 'Lungs. Let's not talk about it.'

We talked ancient history instead, sitting in a chintz-cushioned booth beneath a poster of Jemima Puddleduck.

'Rudy Radeski? Now there's a name I haven't heard in yonks.' After five decades of speaking English, Peter Lipsky's idiom was perfect but he retained a distinct accent. Deliberately, I suspected. Part of his hand-kissing continental-gentleman persona. 'Not pestering you about a statue, is he? These New Australians can be such a nuisance.'

'You should know,' I said. 'But I'm not with Ethnic Affairs any more. I'm working for the Olympic bid.'

'So what are our chances?'

'Very good, apparently,' I said. Magda put a plate of sardines in front of me. Comfort food. Wedges of lemon. Little points of toast on the side. 'Best in town,' I told her. 'What's your secret?'

She tapped the side of her nose. Classified information. 'Horseradish,' Peter whispered when she was back in the kitchen. 'It cuts the oil. I remember 1956. Biggest thing ever happened to this city.'

'You were saying—Rudy Radeski.'

'The defector? Yes, whatever happened to him?'

'That's what I was hoping you might be able to tell me. Background for something I'm working on. Former Olympians, that sort of thing.' Less than frank but entirely necessary unless I wanted to spend the rest of the day in the Do Duck Inn. Peter Lipsky was a born talker. In his current condition, I could see, it was also a form of therapy. One that simultaneously exhausted him and sustained his vitality. 'How do you mean, defector?'

'One of those who stayed behind after the Games. Quite a lot did, you know. Some Czechs, Romanians, even a Russian. Mostly Hungarians, of course.'

The reason for this was too well known for him to bother explaining. The 1956 Olympics opened only days after Russian tanks poured into Hungary to smash the liberalising regime of Imre Nagy. When the Hungarians and Russians met in the final of the water polo, the match quickly degenerated into an all-out brawl. Blood in the water, screamed the commentators, and the crowd would have lynched the Russians if they hadn't been rushed from the building.

'Almost the entire Hungarian contingent refused to return home,' said Peter. 'Most of them went straight to America where they had been offered jobs and money. Only two Poles stayed, even though the situation in Poland, too, was pretty grim. A girl from the track-and-field team. Anna, I think her name was. Stayed to marry a Polish boy in Adelaide. And Rudy Radeski, of course. Don't tell me he's trying to sell his story again. All this fresh interest in the Olympics gave him the idea, I imagine. You want something else? Magda! Bring some apple pie and ice-cream.'

'No ice-cream,' I said, patting my stomach. 'I'm trying to lose weight. How do you mean, sell his story?'

'I should be so lucky,' said Peter, skin and bone. 'His dramatic defection. How The Communists Stole My Medal. You haven't heard this?'

'Not yet,' I said. 'He was a weightlifter, that's all I know.'

Magda brought the pie. It was nothing to write home about, not a patch on her mashed Santa Marias. She put a plate in front of me and a large glass of green slime in front of her father. 'Extract of wheat grass,' he explained. 'It's supposed to regenerate the cells. Tastes like frog shit. Tell you the truth, I don't know what's worse.' Magda stood, arms crossed, until he'd taken a mouthful.

'Very boring,' he said. 'Weightlifting. Circus strongmen. Grunt, lift. Grunt, lift. Not very interesting at all. I preferred the fencing. We won a medal there. Poland, that is. But I did go to the weightlifting, I admit. In those days I was still hungry for the sound of my mother tongue.'

As soon as Magda's back was turned, he tipped the slimy liquid into a potted plant. It had very green, very shiny leaves.

'Radeski got through to the final but he withdrew before the deciding lift. I forget who won in the end. Nothing more was seen of him until after the Games. Suddenly he reappeared, waving a bandaged arm, telling the most dramatic story. He said the communists broke his wrist to stop him making a big public defection at the medal ceremony. He said some teammate had informed on him, so the commissar made sure he wouldn't be able to compete. He claimed they made a prisoner of him on the Soviet ship, the one they used to transport the Russian and Polish and Czech teams, and he escaped just in time, right as it was about to sail away.'

'Claimed?' I said. Actually, the pie wasn't too bad. 'You weren't convinced?'

Peter turned a ring on his long, thin, nicotine-stained index finger. 'I believed that the communists were capable of such a thing. So did some of the émigré groups. They wanted to make a hero of Radeski. He wanted to sell his story to the newspapers, just like the Hungarians did with the Americans. He even thought the Australian government would give him a job.'

A self-made man, Peter took a dim view of those he suspected of chasing a free ride.

'But it was all too fantastic. Even if they wanted to, the communists would not have dared do such a thing. They were too far from home and everybody was watching them. There was a lot of fraternisation. The Russian athletes even used to go over to the American section of the Athletes' Village to see Frankie Laine singing. The commissars couldn't stop it, even if they'd wanted to. In the end, they just went along with it.'

'You mean there were easier ways to defect than jumping off a ship?'

'These were the Friendly Games, remember. It was made very clear that there were to be no political demonstrations or nationalist outbursts, and émigré groups were warned not to make trouble. But it was well known that nobody from the communist bloc would be forced to go home against their will. They just had to wait until the Closing Ceremony. The only person who defected during the Games wasn't an athlete at all. She was a stewardess on the Russian ship. Some local communists took her to the zoo. She said she wanted to go to the toilet, then slipped away. That's how easy it was. She went to Myer's and declared to the lady behind the counter in the millinery department that she wanted political asylum.'

Poor woman must have been on tenterhooks. You can stand in Myer's for hours before the staff even notice you. 'What about the broken wrist?'

'Very convenient. Maybe he knew he wasn't going to win the medal, after all. Better to be a hero of the war against communism than a has-been strongman coaching high school students in Lodz. Maybe he hurt himself by accident, ruined his medal chances, invented the story to console himself.'

'But at the time,' I said. 'The height of the Cold War. The whole anti-communist atmosphere. Why didn't he get more publicity?' Why hadn't I heard this story before? It should have been a sensation, on par with the blood in the water-polo pool.

'You were just a child,' he said. 'You don't remember how proud everybody was about the Olympic Games. It was bigger than Ben Hur. The greatest thing that had ever happened to this town. Nobody wanted to think anything bad had taken place, even if the communists were responsible for it. It would have left a sour taste in people's mouths. The newspapers knew that.'

It was certainly true that the Melbourne Games belonged to that golden era when the Olympics were unsullied by politics or violence. Back before Mexico City with its machine-gunned student protesters and Black Power salutes. Before the Munich massacre and the era of boycotts. An era for which the current IOC must yearn. Apart from the money, of course. There was no money in it, back then.

'So what happened to Rudy Radeski after that?'

Peter shrugged his shoulders, sharp triangles inside his turtleneck sweater. 'Last I heard, he married an Australian girl. This is more than thirty years ago. More apple pie?'

'I've had about as much as I can digest for the moment,' I said. It was past eleven, time I was elsewhere. Peter Lipsky's story was fascinating but was it relevant? And relevant to what? Was my curiosity about Rudy Radeski no more than a blind groping into the unknown?

You bet it was.

Murder is never a private act. The death of Denis Dogherty was already having political repercussions, still subtle but potentially significant. More to the point, the man had reached out in his final lucid moment and exacted a promise from me. A promise which, so far, I had kept. But which I might not be able to keep indefinitely. Not unless I understood what it meant.

If there were clues here, they were successfully eluding me. Too many missing pieces. Too much history. The women could probably fill the gaps, the Boag sisters, Beth McKenzie and Marj Dogherty. And Carmel, she'd know a thing or two. But they had no reason to speak to me. Nor I to presume to interrogate them. Even if I knew what to ask. Which I didn't. Any answers would have to come from Woeful. At the right time, I would ask the right questions. In the meantime, I had an appointment.

'See you later, Peter,' I said.

'Only if you're quick.'

Apart from a minor mishap on the outskirts of Wangaratta when a member of the support team was inadvertently sprayed with hot asphalt during an animated discussion with a municipal road-repair crew, the 2000 kilometres of the *Dream the Dream* Torch Relay had been unmarred by accident or incident.

Hundreds of children had proudly carried the hopes of the nation and the logos of the sponsors through town and country, shopping precinct and rural municipality. Tens of thousands of names had been added to the petition to award the 1996 Olympics to Melbourne. Acres of newsprint and hours of television had been devoted to the spectacle, raising national awareness of Melbourne's ambitions.

Now, the peripatetic flame was nearing its date with destiny. Soon would come the final leg, its ceremonial passage down Collins Street from the Old Treasury, its progress into the Hyatt Hotel and its formal enthrustment into the waiting hands of the visiting representatives of Olympism's highest body. By my boy, Redmond Evatt Whelan.

I found him in the hotel motor court with a half-dozen of his fellow relayists, a collection of bony little knees in flame-motif t-shirts and running shoes. They were hunkered down in the lee of a logo-bedecked minibus, sheltering from the wind while they awaited further instructions from the relevant authorities. Red advanced to meet me with a self-deprecating grin, flexing his muscles and showing off.

'Lookin' good,' I told him. He looked like an albino flamingo. This rugby thing couldn't possibly last. 'What's happening?'

'Hangin' loose,' he drawled. 'Freezin' our butts off.'

'How were Roger and Iris?' The maternal grandparents.

'Same as usual.' The toe of his runner probed a crack in the artificial cobblestones. Wendy's parents were an ordeal to be endured, Liberal voters from Camberwell who insisted that Red visit whenever he was in town, then spent the entire time fretting about the furniture.

The motor court was a hive of activity. Taxis came and went, air crews and group tours arrived and departed, MOB logistics people buzzed about, going into huddles with the hotel doormen. Wendy materialised at my elbow. 'About time,' she said. 'I've rescheduled. When the rehearsal's over, you can have him until four.'

'Great,' I said. An improvement of two hours on the prior arrangement. Now all I had to do was figure out how to entertain him on a Thursday afternoon on zero notice. Being short on practice and all. Red kept anxiously swivelling his head back towards the other kids, afraid of missing some vital directive. The boys were hoppo-bumping each other, acting the goat, while the girls maintained an air of superior indifference.

As Wendy vanished, an official with a walkie-talkie appeared and called the runners to attention.

I hung at the fringes with the other adults, listening as orders were issued. The minibus would distribute the runners to their allocated places along the last section of the route, from the Old Treasury to the Hyatt. Red and a girl called Amber would await the arrival of the baton at the hotel before proceeding upstairs to the ballroom. In the interest of gender equity, the torch would be carried up the escalator by a runnerette. Lest I cramp Red's style with my presence, I headed upstairs to await his arrival there.

Preparations were in full swing. Workmen swarmed about the ballroom foyer, erecting an exhibition of Olympic paraphernalia. The place looked like a sports store clearance sale. Badminton racquets, javelins, baseball bats, boxing gloves, fencing foils, bows and arrows, ski stocks and judo suits were being hung on every surface in sight. A rowing scull was suspended from the ceiling, volleyball nets draped the walls, and store dummies dressed in historical costumes stood in glass cases on either side of the ballroom doors.

Inside, roadies were setting up a sound system on a temporary stage. Technicians wearing headphone mikes fine-tuned the focus on Olympic rings thrown against the walls by a bank of projectors. Members of Brian Morrison's innumerable staff moved around the tables, checking place cards against seating plans and conferring with the banquet staff.

Morrison himself was standing on the stage, hands on hips, casting a proprietary eye over the proceedings. He spotted me lurking in the doorway, beckoned me over. He was not a happy man.

'Your mate Buchanan rang the hotel early this morning, asked for Pascal Abdoulaye. Some idiot put the call through. Buchanan told Abdoulaye he'd like to catch up, discuss issues of mutual concern.' He puffed his cheeks and slowly exhaled. 'Abdoulaye says sure thing, brother. I'll see you at the official dinner. Then he asks Hugh Knowles to make sure Buchanan gets a ticket.' He shook his head glumly and radiated disappointment in my direction. 'Just the sort of thing you're supposed to stop happening, Murray.'

'Gee, mate, I'm sorry,' I said. 'Ambrose must have gnawed through his bonds.'

He thrust an invitation card into my hand. It was made out to Ambrose Buchanan and Guest. 'I'm putting him on your table. And I'll hold you personally responsible if there's any trouble. Knowles will be announcing the Aboriginal Institute of Sport initiative during his speech and the last thing we want is heckling from the only blackfeller in the room.'

'The institute was Ambrose's idea in the first place,' I said. 'He's hardly likely to object to it.'

'Yeah, well,' admitted Brian grudgingly. 'You never know.'

At that point, we were joined by an immaculately besuited man carrying a clipboard. He had a buttonhole rose, a sly twinkle in his eyes and manners that had been buffed to a mirror sheen. Brian introduced him as the MOB Director of Protocol. He was looking for volunteers, he explained, to act the part of the dignitaries who would formally accept the torch. 'Come on, Murray,' ordered Brian. 'It's about time you started earning your pay.'

Along with the other conscripts, I was seated at the high table and briefed on my role. 'You three are the members of the IOC,' the protocol man told us. 'When you hear your names announced, step to the front of the stage.' He handed each of us a name tag. A roadie named Gus was Pascal Abdoulaye, Brian was Kim U-ee and I was Stanislas Dziczkowszczak. 'As the most senior member of the delegation, the gentleman from Poland will accept the torch.'

The head honcho relay official appeared at the doorway and signalled that the arrival of the torch was imminent. Seconds later, Red appeared, holding aloft a rolled cardboard tube. Framed by the doorway, he paused for maximum effect. 'Ladies and gentlemen,' announced the protocol chief over the PA. 'Please welcome Redmond Whelan, representing the aspirations of the young people of Australia that Melbourne play host to the Games of the Twenty-sixth Olympiad, the Centennial Games of the Modern Era.'

Red looked tiny, dwarfed by the pharaonic scale of the hotel. He'd got the gig by dint of finagling, but my heart swelled with pride anyway. 'Applause, applause,' said the protocol director. 'Rhubarb, rhubarb.'

The house lights dropped away and Red began his circuit of the empty room, tracked by a spotlight. His face was a mask of such intense concentration that it was hard not to laugh. It was the same expression he'd used as one of Santa's elves at the kindergarten Christmas pageant. Moving at a slow lope, he twice orbited the dance floor. Finally, reaching the steps leading up to the stage, he again paused and held the torch aloft.

'And to accept the torch on behalf of the International Olympic Committee,' intoned the voice over the PA. 'Please welcome the Chairman of the IOC Evaluation Commission.' This was my cue. As Red mounted the stage, I readied myself to step forward.

The protocol director spoke slowly, at pains to pronounce the difficult name correctly. 'Mr Stanis-las Zitch-kovs-chuck.' He peered closely at his clipboard and said it again, enunciating every syllable. 'Zheech-kovs-chuck.' The ch was a soft buzz.

I stepped into the circle of light and Red thrust the rolled cardboard into my hand. 'Cop this,' he whispered. We turned to face the darkened room, shoulder to shoulder. 'Shake hands,' instructed the voice through the PA. 'And please don't hold the torch in your armpit, sir. Photo. Snap, snap.' Red wheeled briskly and left the stage. 'Now hand it to the African gentleman.'

The light widened to include Gus the roadie. 'And what do I do with it?' he said. Smoke it if he had the chance, by the look of him.

'Hand it to the Korean,' sighed the protocol director.

Gus passed the torch to Brian. A track-suited relay official then reached up from the side of the stage, took the object and followed Red through the door into the kitchen. Where the real thing, presumably, would be doused in a Waterford crystal tureen of turtle soup.

The ultimate destination of the torch was not my problem. My energies were otherwise engaged. I was warming up for a shot at the world record in jumping to conclusions.

While Red changed back into his civilian clothes, I sat on the edge of the bed with the phone in my lap and picked the salad out of his room-service lunch. Waste not, want not. Ambrose Buchanan wasn't at the Stars, so I left a message that his invitation was waiting at the Hyatt reception desk. Not exactly personal delivery, but the best I could do. Short of an exploratory probe into darkest Fitzroy, scouring the known haunts of Deadly Anderson, there was no guessing where Ambrose might be.

Then the kid and I stood together at the window and looked out over the vast amorphous sprawl that is Melbourne. Through the windows of nearby skyscrapers we could see empty offices, fruit of the busted building boom. Below us flowed the Yarra, green-flanked and segmented by bridges. And Jolimont railway yards, one of the finest collections of scrap metal still in public hands anywhere in the world. On the far horizon sat the faint smudge of the Dandenong Ranges. The bay extended vastly, gunmetal grey and dotted with ships idling for a berth. We played spot the familiar landmark and Red pointed out the brick-red bowl of the Melbourne Cricket Ground, light towers poised around its rim.

'They look like giant fly-swatters,' he said.

They did, too. 'I've got an idea,' I said. 'Let's go to the Gallery of Sport.'

We could just make it out, stuck to the rear wall of the MCG Members' Stand. A shrine to sporting history. A collection of artefacts, records, rolls of honour, statistics and team lists. 'It's like a museum.' I realised my mistake. 'But good.'

And only a few minutes away. If he didn't like it, I said, we could always take in a movie. Fair enough, he agreed. I left Buchanan's invitation at the front desk and let the doorman hail us a cab.

Five minutes later we were standing beside the walls of the venerable old stadium. Through an open gateway we could just glimpse the green expanse of the playing arena, the city's most sacred site, holier than any cathedral. A row of identical white Fairlanes was drawn up at the entrance to the Gallery of Sport, each with the customised number plates of the Melbourne Olympic Bid.

As we paid our admission, an entourage of navy-blue blazers with flame motifs on their breast pockets came down the stairs from the upper level. At its centre were the three gods of the Evaluation Commission. Asia, Africa and Europe. 'See that man,' I nudged Red and discreetly pointed. 'He's the one you'll be handing the torch to.'

At close range, Dziczkowszczak looked to be in his mid-seventies. He was chatting with his hosts, the relaxed elder statesman of sport. But I thought I could detect a definite wariness behind his apparent ease. Wariness and weariness. Occupational hazards for a member of the International Olympic Committee, no doubt. Another day, another city, another pestering army of sycophants.

An apparatchik, I thought. But that was an obvious guess. Nobody got to be the most senior office-bearer in one of the old Iron Curtain sports machines by bucking the system. He descended the stairs with care, gripping the banister with bony arthritic fingers. Like the system he represented, his best days were behind him. 'Gee, he's old,' said Red, a little too loudly.

'Shuddup.' I clapped a hand over his mouth. 'You'll fuck up our chances.'

In 1956, Dziczkowszczak would have been almost forty. No spring chicken by athletic standards. I wondered what his sport had been. Something for the longer in tooth. Horse-riding? Yachting? Shooting? We waited in respectful silence while the official party passed, then went upstairs.

The entire top floor of the museum was dedicated to the Games of the XVI Olympiad, Melbourne 1956. All the usual stuff—the sacred objects and blown-up photos, continuous-loop videos and push-button commentaries. Betty Cuthbert hurtling open-mouthed down the track. Murray Rose and Dawn Fraser blitzing the pool. Vladimir Kuts on his last lap of the stadium, the cheering crowd on its feet. Ron Clarke lighting the cauldron. Red picked up on that one, so I told him the story. How Clarke stumbled in the final stretch of a big race, I couldn't remember exactly which, and how his rival John Landy paused to help him up before continuing.

'Yeah, yeah,' said the kid, rolling his eyes. The lives of the saints. 'So winning isn't everything, right?'

'Except in politics,' I said.

The exhibit was deserted but for a lone attendant. His boredom was palpable, a groundsman relegated to indoor work for the off-season. A man who knew where to place the screens and when to roll the wicket and who harboured serious doubts about the durability of some of the newer ryegrass-fescue blends. Keith, according to his name tag. 'I see you've just had the IOC in here, Keith,' I observed, chatty. 'They said on TV that the Polish bloke was here in '56.'

'Oh, yes indeed,' said Keith, stirring to life. 'We've even got a picture of him from back then. Part of a special display on Poland's participation. Did the same for South Korea. Do it for all of them, we do. Not that he was here in '56, the Korean fellow. Actually, there were only seven Koreans here, as against more than a hundred in the Polish team. Which is not to say that Korea didn't do well, considering. Won a silver in boxing. Bantamweight. Song Soon Chung, I believe.'

Keith believed right. A captioned photograph of the man was right there behind glass, along with the names of all other participating Koreans. More Parks than an urban design manual. 'Beaten by a German, Wolfgang Behrendt. The Germans fielded a combined team in those days, East and West together. Came eighth in the medal tally. Just behind Britain. Germany, that is. Poland was eighteenth. Bad luck for the African chap, of course. His country didn't exist back then.'

I had misjudged Keith's vocation. He was, in fact, a

torpid encyclopaedia. A Friend of the Gallery of Sport, lying in wait for an unsuspecting visitor to whom he could demonstrate his boa-constrictor grasp on the minutiae of Melbourne '56. Quite possibly, he was just what I was looking for. If only I could get him to shut the fuck up. 'Not too many African teams at all in those days. South Africa, of course. This was back before the boycotts. They were still in the Commonwealth Games at that stage as well.'

'The Polish IOC member,' I said, talking right over him. He didn't seem to mind. 'What sport did he play?'

'One gold, four silver, four bronze,' he recited, though I hadn't asked, and marched me to the relevant array of photographs. Fencers in white, visors under their arms. Women gymnasts poised on the Roman rings. Shooters holding armfuls of flowers. A formal group portrait, entire delegation, names listed. 'Third from the right, bottom row. Deputy chef-de-mission. Originally a cyclist, apparently. Never made it to an Olympics as a competitor. The war and all that, probably. Although you'd be surprised how few of these IOC actually competed at an Olympic Games. Some, on the other hand, did very well. The Dutchman, Geesink, beat the Japanese at judo in Tokyo '64. We had him in here a few weeks ago. And the Guatemalan.'

'Deputy chef-de-mission?' One figure among a hundred, Dziczkowszczak's face was no bigger than a speck of confetti, a metre away behind a sheet of glass. No clues there. 'That's like assistant team manager, right?'

'Exactly,' said Keith. 'As I was saying…'

'Rudy Radeski?' I found the name in the caption, looked in vain for the face. 'The weightlifter, right? Wasn't there some controversy there?'

Keith sensed a piss-take. 'Fair go, mate. There were 3,342 competitors from sixty-seven nations. You can't expect me to know about every last one of them.'

'Hey, Dad,' called Red, fingers jabbing a touch-screen display. 'Guess what city holds the record for the largest crowd at an Olympic opening ceremony?'

'Los Angeles?'

'Wrong,' he whooped. 'Loser.'

'It was Melbourne, wasn't it, son?' said Keith. The two of them ganging up on me. What sort of an idiot was I?

The sort who'd probably gleaned as much useful information as any Friend of the Gallery of Sport could provide. The question I now wanted answered was beyond Keith, beyond even the library in the basement. It related to the exact function of the deputy chef-de-mission of the Polish team. Was Dziczkowszczak's role, I wondered, exclusively sporting? One of the team managers, it was reasonable to assume, was responsible for political matters. Somebody must have had the job of keeping the boys and girls on the straight and narrow. Of seeing to it that they did nothing to embarrass the socialist motherland.

'How did he like it?' I said. 'The display?'

'Tickled pink,' said Keith.

Red had pushed every available button and his interest was waning fast. I thanked Comprehensive Keith for his assistance and took the kid down to the next level, a sideshow alley of hands-on interactive opportunities to test our physical skills. A basketball hoop, a long-jump pit, a rowing machine, a golf tee. This time I pulled no punches. Despite my sore rib, I beat the little bastard every time I could. 'Not fair,' he bleated.

'Sore loser,' I said. As we left, we passed the open gate into the stadium and couldn't resist a quick look inside. Red ran ahead, down the tunnel beneath the Members' Stand, all the way to the fence. The vast green of the playing surface spread out before us, framed by the curved lip of the grand-stands, silent and empty, lidded with a perfect ellipse of sky.

The last time we had both been there, so had forty thousand other people. Melbourne versus Essendon, three years before, on one of Red's term-holiday visits. A lousy, scrapping game of football. Not much in it for anyone, let alone a little kid dragged along by his sometime father as an exercise in intermittent parenting. We threw in the towel at three-quarter time. The rain had set in and Melbourne was so far ahead it didn't matter. It was more aversion therapy than cultural education and I feared it had done nothing to endear the game to the boy.

'You remember?' I said.

'We had pies,' said Red. 'It was good.'

The lure of the majestic oval was too much to resist. Peeling off my suit jacket, I vaulted the low fence and crossed the boundary line. Red was right behind me. An unspoken dare passed between us and we sprinted for the centre, expecting at any second a challenging shout from one of the custodians of the temple. When none came, we slowed to a jog and turned for the white posts. 'And it's the Whelans into attack,' I yelled. 'Heading into an open goal.'

Shoulders forward. Once bounce, two bounces. I feinted to avoid an invisible opponent and passed an imaginary ball to Red. He marked it on his chest, played on and ran for the sticks. Twenty yards from the goal-mouth, he steadied and took a ping. A huge kick for a kid of his size, a high torpedo punt that sent him reeling backwards from the effort. Up, up, it arched, spiralling overhead. Straight through the high-diddle-diddle. The crowd she roared.

Suddenly, he had the ball again, tucked under his arm this time, rugby style. Head down, he charged me. 'Wrong game.' I sprinted for the back pocket. 'Kick it. Kick it.'

He pulled up sharp and snapped me a pass. It came high and I had to jump, plucking it double-handed from the air above my head. I fired it back, too short, and Red ran to meet it, swerving to follow the bounce, scooping it one-handed off the ground in a tight circle. He drew back and took his time, tugging at his socks. His run-up was long and again the kick was tremendous. 'Woof,' he exhaled as his foot swept through the empty air, the sound of boot on leather.

In the distant past, when he was much smaller, Red and I occasionally bandied a thin plastic ball around the backyard, constantly breaking off play to retrieve its dented shell from beneath the shrubbery or off the roof. This new, invisible model was infinitely better. Especially when used on hallowed turf with the inaudible murmur of a capacity crowd in our ears. Every grunt and shout echoed back from the circling stands, every kick unerringly found its target, every mark was a screamer.

Red revelled in the pretence, running all the way to the Punt Road end of the oval, a 150-metre dash that scored him an uncontested goal and left me coughing my lungs out at centre half-forward. Fortunately, before I could pull a hamstring or die, a groundsman appeared and told us to piss off.

As I put on my jacket and wiped the flecks of grass from my shoes, I gazed back across the arena and tried to imagine what it must have looked like in 1956, the flags of sixty-seven nations fluttering above the grandstands. Tried to imagine, too, the climate of the times. Russian tanks in the rubble-strewn streets of Budapest. Witch-hunts and blacklists. Petrov and the ALP Split. Fascist hyenas and fellow travellers. Blood in the water.

I thought about Rudy Radeski and his broken wrist and events alleged to have taken place in the Olympic city some thirty-four years before. Wondered, too, if they might have any bearing on the intentions of a certain psychotic young man currently eluding capture by the Victorian police force. And what role, if any, Denis Dogherty might have in such a scenario. Or the current Minister for Sport, for that matter.

We headed back into the city on foot, going leaps and bounds through ankle-deep drifts of fallen leaves. At Captain Cook's tiny stone cottage in the Fitzroy Gardens, we stopped to wonder aloud that a continent as big as Australia had been discovered by a man the size of a midget.

At the Hyatt Hotel, I put my arm around Red's shoulder and reminded him not to drop the torch when he came through the ballroom door. Then I handed him back to his mother.

'You're late,' she said.

'It's not his fault.' Red flew to my defence. 'The game went into extra time.' A rugby expression, I took it.

'Time-on, mate,' I said. 'That's what we call it in proper football.'

But Wendy was right. There were things to be done. I was beginning to have a theory. On the way downstairs, I stopped at the City Club.

'That name, Cheech,' I said to Holly. 'Do you think it could've been Zeech? Think hard.'

She could see that I was agitated, jiggling up and down beside the pec-deck like a man with a urinary tract infection. 'Excuse me, madam,' she said to the petite Japanese tourist trapped inside the padded cage. 'Sumimasen.' She bowed slightly, then grabbed my elbow and dragged me over to the glute isolator. 'Can't you see I'm working?' she hissed.

'Sorry,' I whispered. 'But could Cheech be Zeech?'

'Like I told the police, I really can't remember. I'd already decided to give Steve the flick and I wasn't much interested in listening to him bicker with his father. It only stuck in my mind because he said he'd rip the guy limb from limb if he ever got the chance.'

'And what did Steve's father say?'

'He said he'd believe it when he saw it. Something like that.'

'Did Rudy Radeski ever talk about the 1956 Olympics?'

'Steve told me not to ask him. Said it was still a sore point, that he was cheated out of winning a medal. Said not to get him started or he'd never shut up. Why? What's going on? It's Steve. He's killed someone else, hasn't he?'

'No, no,' I said quickly. 'Not that I know of.' Not yet. 'Pick you up at seven, okay? Your parents' place. Better give me the address.'

'Make it my flat,' she said. 'That's where I keep my party dress.' She swivelled her hips and made with the cha-cha-cha. 'Seven-thirty, right?'

It had just gone five. I went up to Parliament House and found Ken Sproule in the Police Minister's office, feet on the desk, conspiring on the telephone. He put his hand over the mouthpiece and shook his head. Nothing to report. Steve Radeski was still at liberty. I backed out, leaving Ken to his dirty work, and went upstairs to the public gallery of the Legislative Assembly.

With only a few sitting days remaining in the autumn session, a considerable backlog of legislation still to be cleared and a majority no bigger than a bee's dick, the party whips had been cracking. Bereaved or not, Woeful McKenzie was in his usual place, propped between the Minister for Agriculture, a town planner by trade, and the Minister for Education, poor woman.

Although he had been prevailed upon to buck up and stand to his post, it was clear that Woeful was feeling the weight of a considerable burden. The big, bluff man of the previous week appeared inwardly drained, a diminished version of his former self. Oblivious to the Treasurer's plaintive ramblings, he stared absently between his feet, his sad caterpillar gaze fixed on the oak-leaf pattern of the carpet.

When the going gets tough, some politicians turn brittle and bite the head off anything that moves. By the look of it, Woeful was going the other way, spinning a cocoon of silent introspection, sharing his burden with the pixies. His eye was definitely not on the ball.

I mentally marshalled my evidence. The newspapers in Steve Radeski's room. The obsessive training for no apparent purpose. The threatening talk overheard by Holly. The pronunciation of a name. It didn't amount to much. Chances were that I was wrong. But if I was right, only halfway right, the stakes were too high to risk hesitation. The clock was ticking. Time to do a Denis. Dash onto the oval and have a word in the full-back's ear.

I got out one of my business cards and wrote on the back. Block capitals, headline style. OLYMPICS MINISTER'S NEPHEW IN IOC REVENGE PLOT. It seemed just too bizarre. I hoped to Christ it was. I added a question mark, scant extenuation, and asked the sergeant-at-arms to hand the folded card to the Honourable Member for Melbourne Docklands.

The fuse lit, I stood in the empty hallway outside the door of the chamber and waited for the explosion. I needed a cigarette like a cigarette had never been needed before. A wave of nausea rose in my throat. Panic. What if I was wrong?

When Woeful emerged, it was with a look of such utter defeat that I knew immediately I wasn't. Not entirely, anyway. 'So they've got him, at last,' he said, wearily.

'Not yet,' I said.

He jerked upright, chins quivering. 'So what's this crap?' But the cat was out of the bag. The question now was how to skin it.

'Somewhere a little less public,' I suggested. 'Let's go outside.'

We went through the side door into the rose garden and walked together beneath a sky the colour of aluminium, the gravel path crunching at every step. 'Who else knows?' said Woeful.

'Nobody who heard it from me.'

'You worked this out yourself?' The idea made him look even more depressed.

'A stab in the dark,' I said. 'But it's bound to come out eventually. And when it does you'd better be ready.'

He squinted at me warily. 'Who are you working for, pal?'

A good question. I looked back the way we'd come,

towards the seat of government. 'Us?' I shrugged. We true believers, clinging by our fingernails.

You've got to hand it to Woeful. When push came to shove, he was every inch a Minister. 'Tell me what I should do,' he said.

'I'd like to know what I'm buying into,' I told him. 'If I'm buying into it.'

We stopped at a rose bush, the last of the late blooms. I could hear Woeful breathing in the silence between us. 'It's a long story,' he said.

I had the time. And when it came right down to it, Woeful didn't need all that much persuading. He seemed relieved.

'Talk about the dead weight of history,' he said. And so he did.

This is the story he told me, hands thrust deep in his pockets, the pathway of the Parliament House gardens crunching portentously underfoot.

Woeful and Denis were children of the Depression, beasts of burden by birth, fighters by temperament. Never actual members of the Communist Party, but not ill-disposed towards its militants who ran the union. Who in turn appreciated the occasional gesture of support from a local sporting identity. And, when the Communist Party turned on a bit of fraternal hospitality for the socialist athletes in town for the Olympic Games, Woeful and Denis were happy to help make up the numbers.

Their girlfriends, too. The Olympics were just about the most exciting thing that had ever happened and Beth and Marjorie had no intention of being left out of the festivities. For two weeks, there was sport by day, music and beer in bohemian St Kilda flats by night. That was how they came to be aboard the *Gruzia*, the Soviet liner moored at Appleton Dock, home base and hospital for the socialist bloc teams.

It was two days after the Closing Ceremony, after the athletes had created a new Olympic tradition by breaking loose from their national teams and mingling freely across the arena in one exuberant, youthful mass. Even Irene was there, a raving Catholic like her mother, caught up in the mood of the moment, prepared to risk her immortal soul for one last taste of Olympic glamour.

The ship was scheduled to sail the next morning and the hosts were relaxed, all the more since the police had cleared the anti-communist demonstrators from the wharf at sunset. As well as Russians there were Czechs and Poles and Bulgarians. The boisterous Australian comrades crowded into the staterooms, the vodka flowed freely and many toasts were drunk to the undying friendship of the sport-loving peoples of the world.

Too many toasts for Denis, never much of a drinker anyway. Head swimming, he found his way through the throng and out onto the open deck. Summer had arrived, but the breeze was cool and the sea air went straight to his stomach. In the darkness between two lifeboats, tossing his pickled cucumbers into the water below, he felt a tugging at his sleeve. 'Please, friend,' whispered an urgent voice. 'You help. You help.'

It was pretty clear what kind of help was wanted. Others among the Australians might, perhaps, have been less responsive to such a plea. Others might have seen the man in hospital pyjamas with the bandaged wrist as an enemy of socialism and a traitor to his homeland, might have drawn attention to his overtures. But he had, by luck, chosen the right person to ask. Denis Dogherty was ever a friend of the underdog.

'When Denis sidled up to me and wanted to know what I'd done with my hat and coat, I thought it must have been time to go,' said Woeful. 'I didn't know what he was talking about.'

But Irene did, and it was on her arm that Rudy Radeski was smuggled down the gangplank when the party finally ended and the Australians were poured ashore. On Irene's arm, in Woeful's coat and hat, at the centre of an apparently well-tanked party of friends. Reliable friends of reliable friends, wharf labourers and proletarians.

'You ended up brothers-in-law,' I said, cutting to the chase. It was a good story but not the one I wanted to hear. The history that interested me right then was much more recent. 'And now his son Steve is out for revenge against the man who did his father wrong.'

'Rudy's a prick. The way he treated Irene, I used to wish we'd left him on that fucking ship. He saw sport as a way out of Poland. And he played his cards well enough until he got here. Except he couldn't keep his mouth shut, started telegraphing his punches. Let it be known that he intended to defect. Decided he was going to be world-famous. But it all blew up in his face. And since Rudy would never dream of blaming himself, he passed his grievance down to the boy.'

'Did you know this Stansislas Dziczkowszczak was the one who broke his wrist?'

'No idea. Not until Stevie rang me at home last weekend. Said he was going to make the bastard pay.'

The tendency to telegraph punches seemed to run in the Radeski family. 'Did he say how?'

'He didn't say. But he was quite het up about it. Enough to get me worried.'

'But you didn't inform the MOB or the police of the threat.'

'Denis reckoned he could hose Stevie down. He was closer to the boy than I was.' Woeful faltered at that thought and put a hand to his face.

Denis's discretion was more than family loyalty. It was not the possibility of violence that was the problem. Protecting Dziczkowszczak from Steve Radeski would be a relatively simple matter. Just employ a few men with bulging armpits and tell them to be on the lookout for a demented dipstick with a body like a bag of potatoes. The real problem lay with Steve's motive. That's what needed to be kept under wraps.

If word ever got out that a serving member of the IOC had deliberately injured an athlete at an Olympic Games, the ensuing scandal would blast Melbourne's bid right out of the water. The IOC closet was probably standing-room only with skeletons. All those dukes and generals and third-world potentates certainly weren't going to thank us for bringing to light the misdeeds of one of their members.

But there was also a more immediate political matter, one much closer to home. To inform the police about Stevie would put Woeful in the hands of Gil Methven. Apart from the humiliation this would entail, there would be a price to pay for the Police Minister's discretion. Sooner or later, sooner probably, Methven would want his pound of flesh. When Denis went to see Steve Radeski, to talk him out of acting on his threat, it was to protect Woeful from the possibility of political blackmail.

'So Denis went out to West Heidelberg on Monday night?'

'When he didn't show up on Tuesday, I thought he

must've taken Stevie somewhere. You know, convinced him to leave town while the Polish IOC was here. Gone along to keep an eye on him or something. Never occurred to me that Stevie would do anything like what he did.'

'Anyone else know why he went out there?'

Woeful shook his chins. 'We were playing this one close to the chest. With Denis dead, I decided to keep it that way. Telling anyone wouldn't change the fact of what happened. And Marj would never forgive me for letting him go out there alone.'

'Because Steve's been violent before?'

He bristled. 'Who told you that?'

I let it go. We were back where we started. 'For what it's worth,' I said. 'I think you've done the right thing, keeping it to yourself.'

It wasn't like Woeful hadn't been pondering the issue. 'Yeah, but what happens when the police get hold of Stevie?'

'At the rate they're going, that could be weeks,' I said. 'With luck, Dziczkowszczak will be long gone. Anyway, Steve'll have zero credibility. A homicide suspect out of his tree on veterinary steroids. You can plausibly deny knowledge of any threat he might have made. If he wants to make an issue of it, we'll get Brian Morrison on the case, massage the media. In the meantime, sit pat. Don't lose your nerve.'

He was still holding my business card. I took it back, tore it into small pieces and scattered them around the base of a rose bush. 'That's what Denis would want, don't you think?'

Woeful didn't look too convinced. But as I walked him back into the House, I flattered myself that I had braced up our back line at least a little. That I had, in part, acquitted my promise to Denis.

My dinner suit hadn't seen service for nearly eighteen months, not since I'd escorted Angelo Agnelli to the Our Lady of Lebanon dinner-dance. Removing the mothballs and leftover pistachio baklava from the pockets, I discovered to my surprise that it fitted like a glove. All that work on the Stairmaster was finally beginning to pay off. And what man does not feel debonair in a tux?

'Whelan,' I told the mirror. 'Murray Whelan.'

At seven-fifteen, I took a cab to Holly's flat. While the driver waited out front, I walked around the side and knocked on the door. The peephole flickered cyclopically. Suddenly, rough hands seized me from behind and threw me to the ground. My arms were wrenched up violently behind my back, a shoe bore down on my lumbar declivity and a cold metallic object which I registered instinctively as a gun was jammed into my ear. 'Police,' barked a frenzied chorus of voices. 'Freeze.'

It sounded like good advice. I did as I was told.

The door to Holly's flat flew open. 'Wrong one,' hissed a female voice. 'This guy's the new boyfriend.'

'Dinner suit,' insisted the foot connected to my kidneys. 'He's wearing a fucking dinner suit.'

Who were these guys, the Sartorial Standards Squad? Since when was possession of formal wear grounds for police brutality? The Victorian wallopers had a reputation for excessive zeal, but this was ridiculous. It wasn't like I was wearing a pink shirt or a velvet bowtie.

'Go. Go,' urged the woman. Grunting something unintelligible, the foot and gun obeyed. A hand grabbed me by the cummerbund, hauled me upright and propelled me into the flat. The door slammed behind me.

'Sorry about that, sir,' said Detective Senior Constable Carol Sonderland. 'They thought you were Steve Radeski. We believe he's in the vicinity.'

Apparently, I had stumbled into some kind of stake-out. As I stood there, indignantly brushing down my lapels, Holly wandered out of the bedroom, busy attaching an earring. 'That you, Murray?'

Her hair was up and she was wearing a shrink-wrap, strapless, red vinyl dress that clung to her tighter than a shipwreck survivor. The full front yard, hem up around the nature strip, no visible means of support.

'Wow,' I said. A man could get arrested just for being in the same city. Sonderlund scowled at me like she was keen to lay the charges.

Holly finished fiddling with her ear and straightened up, offering herself for scrutiny. 'It's not too…you know?'

Definitely. But somehow she carried it off. 'Apart from the

risk of pneumonia,' I said, 'you look fantastic.'

'You, too,' she reciprocated. 'That style's coming back into fashion.'

The flat was a disaster area. Dirty dishes and discarded food containers were strewn everywhere. The fresh, girlie bouquet had been replaced by a rank, zoological fug. The bottles of Midori and Galliano, now empty, lay discarded on the floor along with an exhausted blister pack labelled *Animal Use Only*.

'Found it like this when I arrived to get changed,' explained Holly, wrinkling her nose. 'Bastard ate everything in the place. Shed hairs in the bed. Pissed in the sink. Lucky for him he wasn't here when I turned up, eh? Ready in a minute, okay? We're not late, are we?' She darted into the bathroom.

While Holly was doing whatever it is that women do in the bathroom, I prised an update out of Detective Sonderlund. Steve Radeski, the police now believed, broke into the flat through a side window early on Wednesday morning, soon after Holly left for her parents' place. He'd probably been holed up there ever since. According to an upstairs resident, a man in a dinner suit quit the place shortly before Holly returned. Acting on the assumption that Radeski, still in his bouncer's uniform, was out refreshing his supplies of food and drugs, the coppers had placed the joint under close surveillance.

Holly emerged, lusciously lipsticked, hot to trot. 'Make yourself at home,' she told Sonderlund. 'Sorry I haven't got any k.d.lang CDs. And if Steve does turn up, kick him in the nuts for me, will you?'

'No Lana Cantrell?' said the detective as we went out the door. 'Dusty Springfield?'

The taxi was still waiting, engine running, twenty dollars on the meter already. As Holly climbed aboard, she peered quizzically at the cabbie. 'Did you write *The Seven Keys to Eternal Youth*?' she asked.

'I am a Sikh, madam,' he said. 'We all look like this.'

Leaving the constabulary lurking in ambush, we headed past the proliferating pasticceria of Lygon Street, bound for the Hyatt. For a woman whose domestic space had been violated by a psychopath and commandeered by the Keystone Cops, Holly was extraordinarily chipper. 'There'll be, like, sporting personalities and that?'

'Sure,' I said. She wouldn't have any trouble finding somebody not to talk to.

Barricades had been erected across the motor court of the Hyatt and a small army of *Dream the Dream* Youth Relay officials swarmed about, clad in identical artificial-fibre flame-motif tracksuits. According to the head honcho, Red was currently posing for press photographs and I should await his arrival in the ballroom with the rest of the guests.

The vast, pink-tinged lobby was a sea of dinner suits and silk bodices as the blue-ribbon crowd sailed across the marble floor and up the dual-carriageway escalator to the ballroom. Checking at the front desk, I was told that Mr Buchanan had not yet picked up his invitation. I wondered if he'd got my message. If he hadn't, I decided, there was nothing I could do about it.

Ambrose Buchanan, of course, was not the only one whose presence interested me. Was there, I wondered, a Doctor Phillipa in the house? Only one way to find out. We went upstairs and threw ourselves into the thick of it.

The Olympic bandwagon was gathering speed and everybody, it seemed, had jumped aboard. Society wives and advertising gurus. Radio motor-mouths and former Lords Mayor. Property developers, of course. Brewery CEOs and Merton Hall old girls and Liberal Party bagmen. One-time Davis Cup seeds and third-generation scions of retail fortunes. Poultry heiresses and former swimming greats. Half the Cabinet. People I should have been gladhanding. Some I was keen to avoid. Clutching flutes of Domaine Chandon Vintage Brut, they percolated through the display of sporting memorabilia, bubbling with confidence at Melbourne's Olympic prospects. The thing was in the bag.

The fox on my arm was an ornament to my masculinity. But she was only costume jewellery. While I scouted for the sight of Phillipa, Holly was busy playing Spotto the Celebrity. 'Hey,' she whispered. 'Isn't that whatsisname?'

No, it wasn't. It was Angelo Agnelli. 'I can see why you've been so hard to find, Murray,' he said, casting a knowing Latin eye over my companion.

'I'm his personal trainer,' said Holly, right on the program.

'Then I hope you have more success than me,' sighed the Minister for Water Supply, allowing himself to be sucked back into the swirling current.

Brian Morrison gravitated our way, caught between working the room and inspecting the merchandise. 'Aren't you going to introduce us?'

'This is Ms Deloite,' I said. 'From the Australian Kickboxing Federation.'

Brian chuckled nervously. 'Any sign of Buchanan?' he muttered out of the corner of his mouth.

Before I could answer, an electric ripple of excitement ran through the room and the crowd parted like the Red Sea. One by one, the members of the Evaluation Commission appeared at the top of the escalator and advanced towards the ballroom doors, objects of undisguised curiosity.

First came Stansislas Dziczkowszczak, escorted by Mr and Mrs Hugh Knowles. The chairman's bird-like wife was so petite that the tall Pole had to stoop to hold her arm. Next came Kim U-ee, flanked by Woeful and Beth McKenzie. Finally there appeared Pascal Abdoulaye, locked in animated conversation with a figure in faded denims.

Brian Morrison stiffened. 'Holy shit!' he muttered.

But Brian didn't know the half of it. Trotting alongside Ambrose Buchanan was Deadly Anderson. He was wearing a ruffled apricot shirt and a spangled green tuxedo, boob tattoos peeking from the cuffs. The bandanna was back. Thank Christ, or they would've had to clear the exits with a crowbar. As it was, Deadly looked like the emcee at a Bandidos bingo night.

Brian started hyperventilating. 'Do something,' he ordered.

Abdoulaye and Ambrose were sharing a joke, laughing as they made their way towards the high table. Then, shaking hands, they broke off contact. As the Senegalese took his place with the other dignitaries, Ambrose turned and scanned the room.

'Something like this?' I waved, catching Buchanan's eye. Brian put a couple of steps of distance between us.

'It's those guys,' said Holly brightly. 'Your clients.'

As Ambrose and Deadly came my way, heads turned to follow their progress. Buchanan had seen this sort of gig a

thousand times before and regard it with faintly amused indifference. Deadly strutted, both relishing the discomfort he was
clearly causing some of the snootier elements in the crowd
and also a little intimidated by the unfamiliar surroundings.

'He's cool,' Buchanan reassured me. 'He's had some sleep
and calmed down a bit. Just about given up on Radeski.' He
was definitely a lot calmer than last time I'd seen him,
punching numbers into the payphone at the Royal Hotel.
'How about the cops?'

I shrugged. 'Hopeful of an early arrest.'

'They're with the band,' I heard Brian tell somebody. Pass
it on.

'Aren't you going to introduce us?' said Holly.

I did the honours all round. 'I see you got your entree
card, then,' said Brian, somewhat redundantly.

'Deadly's my date,' Ambrose told him. 'I asked Miss
Advancement League but she's washing her hair tonight.'

'Nice outfit,' I said to Deadly. 'Brotherhood of St
Laurence?'

He copped it sweet, entirely focused on Holly. She looked
like about ten million dollars. 'Seen youse the other night,' he
mumbled, bashful all of a sudden.

'Saw you, too,' she said, coy itself. Now here was a girl
who really knew how to pick them.

'Brian Morrison?' said Ambrose, dredging his memory.
'Not the Brian Morrison who called the cops on Reggie
Plunkett?'

Waiters erupted through the kitchen doors, laden with
plates.

'You'll like this,' blurted Brian, nervously herding us
towards one of the tables, well away from the top brass. 'It's

bush tucker. Shovel-roasted breast of emu for the ladies. Paperbark-wrapped loin of kangaroo for the men.'

Wendy was there to meet us. In keeping with her SS theme, she was wearing a silk pyjama-suit the colour of bruised avocados. She'd probably bruised them herself. 'Pleased to meet you,' she told Holly unctuously. Me, she fixed with a look of dick-shrivelling contempt.

'Neil,' said a voice, and I nearly did.

It was Wendy's escort, introducing himself. He stared at Holly's tits like they were scoops of vanilla ice-cream. 'Regional Director, Privatisation.' I bet you are, I thought.

Phillipa Verstak materialised at my elbow. 'Hello, Murray,' she smirked. 'I see you found yourself a date.' She was decked out in a natty little gold-frogged bolero jacket. Ole!

'My niece,' I said, tongue stuck firmly in cheek. 'And this must be Rodney. Executive assistant to the chairman.'

'We sort of met the other day,' he nodded. My star turn before the MOB management team, I assumed. He eyed Deadly charily.

'My squash partner,' I said. 'Rod.'

We found our seats and sat down. Boy, girl. I had Holly to my left and Phillipa to my right. Holly was already deep in conversation with Deadly. 'Aerobics isn't a sport,' she was telling him. 'It's an activity.'

'I work out a bit meself,' he said. Their heads were almost touching. Some kind of weird chemistry was definitely brewing. Beauty and the Beast stuff.

Brian Morrison's better half, Sandra, waved at me across the floral centrepiece. Her husband was watching Ambrose Buchanan like a hawk. Ambrose was seated beside Wendy. Judging by the way she was squirming in her seat, he was running her to ground on Aboriginal representation in the higher reaches of Telecom management. At the head table, Pascal Abdoulaye was engaged in the customary pre-prandial bonhomie with Woeful and the other high-ups.

As I turned to Phillipa, the first course arrived. Fillet of Barramundi in a Macadamia Crust. All prospect of conversation was immediately lost in the gnash and clatter of a thousand knives and forks. 'Fish?' said Deadly. 'Where's the chips?'

Between bites, I stole a closer look at this Rodney joker. Call me biased, but I couldn't see the attraction. Neither, it seemed, did Phillipa. Compared with the animal heat now emanating from the general direction of Holly and Deadly, their relationship struck me as a very low kilowatt affair. They showed more interest in their nut-encrusted fish than they did in each other.

Phillipa saw me looking and leaned over. 'Rodney's an old friend,' she said. 'We go back a long way.'

Back before Cambodia. Before she realised that she wasn't all that keen. Or I hoped that's what she meant. 'That's nice,' I said, letting her know that I knew.

The wine was a sauvignon blanc. It had a big herby nose and plenty of zest to the finish. Head tilted back, savouring the aftertaste, I noticed that the ballroom ceiling was mirrored. You could see everything, upside down. The white circles of the tables. The chrome domes of the trucking magnates. The ant-farm teeming of the black-clad waiters.

I'd never done banquet work myself, strictly bar, but as the descendant of three generations of hotelkeepers I always took a semi-professional interest in the organisational side of such matters.

Harry Hyatt ran a tight ship. Commis-waiters clearing. The service door flapping on its hinges. Captains at their stations. My plate was whisked away and I tracked its inverted progress across the room. Piled onto a tray, it disappeared through the service door where a stout, ram-headed supervisor stood sentry. He bounced on his toes, scoping the scene, engine ticking over.

Steve Radeski.

I felt a hand on my sleeve. 'How long now?' said Phillipa.

'Eh?'

'How long since your last cigarette?'

'Thirty-seven hours and fifty-two minutes,' I said. 'Approximately.'

Radeski's attention was fixed on the stage, raking the head table. His eyes, manic raisins in his doughy cheeks, alighted on Stanislas Dziczkowszczak.

Phillipa reached for her purse. 'I'd better find another partner in crime, then.'

This quitting business sucked. My criminal confederate, Deadly, shifted his concentration from Holly for a moment. Just long enough to see what I was seeing. Holly followed his stare. 'Steve?' she exclaimed. 'What's he doing here?'

'Distinguished guests,' boomed the public-address system. 'Ladies and gentlemen.'

Deadly was out of his seat, rocketing headlong across the room, elbows flying.

'Please welcome, representing the young people of Australia, our *Dream the Dream* torch-bearer, Redmond Whelan...'

'Murray!' shrieked Wendy. 'Where do you think you're going?'

The lights dimmed. The ballroom doors swung open. A small figure in white appeared, a guttering flare in his outstretched hand. Suddenly, the entire crowd was on its feet, applauding wildly, craning for a view.

'And to accept the torch on behalf of the International Olympic Committee...'

As Stanislas Dziczkowszczak stepped forward, the concentrated hormones of a hundred rampant jumbucks surged though Steve Radeski's bloodstream. This was the moment he had waited for, trained for, longed for. These arsehole officials would soon know better than to fuck with the Radeski family. He lowered his head and charged.

Deadly Anderson, swerving to avoid the husband of the MOB Director of Facilities Planning, collided with him. Head-on, with all the force of a runaway divvy van. Completely unexpected, the impact of the collision threw the would-be assassin sideways, back through the swinging doors.

Apart from Holly and me, who had bolted after Deadly, nobody else seemed to have noticed. With the house lights down and the room echoing with applause, all eyes were focused on the torch and its bearer. Looking upwards to the ceiling, I tracked the bobbing ball of light that was my son's progress around the dance floor.

For about three seconds.

Then the kitchen doors flew back open. Radeski's hands were wrapped around Deadly's throat, throttling him. The Koori's legs were off the ground, writhing and twitching. Holly flew forward and threw herself at Radeski in a mad melee of punches and kicks.

Heads were beginning to turn. Red's big moment was about to be upstaged. The success of the torch relay, the Olympic Gala, possibly even the entire bid was in jeopardy. Denis Dogherty's killer was on a berserk rampage. Somebody had to do something, and soon. Somebody did. Me.

I played the man. Grabbing Radeski's ponytail, I dragged the flailing cluster-fuck of bodies back into the kitchen.

We burst into a bedlam of steam and stainless steel, a forest of freaked-out faces in tall white hats. Radeski's feet flew from beneath him and his oily hair slipped from my grasp. As he hit the tiles, he flung Deadly aside as if he were a rag doll.

Shimmering like a green tree python in his iridescent tux, Deadly ricocheted off a brace of tray-laden commis-waiters and collided with a vat of bubbling brown liquid. It toppled over and a steaming mud-coloured wave cascaded across the floor.

Radeski staggered upright and turned towards the door,

apparently still fixated on his mission to dismember Dziczkowszczak. Holly blocked his path. 'Hey, babe,' yelped the berko bully-boy, bewildered by the sudden turn of events. 'Where you been?'

Holly went into a kung-fu stance. The Bunny Confronts the Wart-hog. The Vixen Transfixes the Mullet.

Up to my trouser-cuffs in a melange of marsupial morsels, I grabbed a giant stirring paddle and smashed Radeski over the head. The wooden spoon snapped in half, making no impression whatsoever on Muscle Man's armour-plated skull.

Deadly slithered around on the floor, attempting to find his footing on the gravy-soaked tiles. An imperious presence in a towering toque barged through the astonished cluster of onlooking sous-chefs. 'My wallaby jus!' he roared, beetroot-faced with rage. 'What are you doink in my wallaby jus!'

Two security men burst in from the ballroom. Beyond them, through the flip-flop of the swinging door, I caught sight of Red just as he handed the torch to Dziczkowszczak. He turned, took the plaudits of the crowd and jogged towards us.

'You pissed in my sink,' screamed Holly. 'You killed that old man, you mongrel.' She kicked out, aiming for her former flame's face. A red, high-heel shoe detached itself from her foot, flew through the air and struck the chef de cuisine in the mouth.

Swivelling on their toes in the spilt sauce like a pair of twist aficionados, the two protective services personnel stared first at the green Aborigine, then at the scarlet virago, then at the bloated bodybuilder.

'Nobody move!' they shouted, reaching for their under-arm bulges.

Word was finally reaching the deep-fried recesses of

Radeski's brain that his plan had come unstuck. His insane yellow eyes darted about, desperately searching for a way out.

The door swung on its hinges and Red burst into the kitchen, adrenalin pumping. 'Hey, Dad,' he beamed. 'Did you see me, huh? Did you see me?'

I was standing there with my bowtie on sideways and the stump of a stirring paddle in my hand, ankle-deep in potaroo ragout, facing off a maniacal meatloaf with a skin problem. 'Yeah,' I said. 'You were great.'

Radeski saw his chance. He grabbed Red, effortlessly tucking him under his arm. 'Back off,' he bellowed. 'Or I'll fucken snap the little fucker's neck.' His words resonated with a tremulous bleat, as if amplified through a wa-wa pedal.

A tracksuited relay official burst through the door. The torch-disposal specialist. He was attempting to switch off the gas-flow valve at the base of the flaming object. The two security men drew their walkie-talkies and started waving them around in a commanding manner. Deadly hauled himself upright. 'Leave the kid alone, you prick,' he yelled, and lunged forward.

Radeski swatted him off with a forearm jolt and began backing away, bearing Red off into the deeper recesses of the hellish kitchen. 'Put me down, you piece of shit,' cursed the boy, flailing and squirming, vainly attempting to writhe free. 'Dad! Dad!'

I stood there, frozen with horror.

'Hey, kid,' hollered Holly. Wresting the torch from its astonished custodian, she darted forward and thrust the still-burning baton into Red's hand. He waved it like a sparkler, slapping it ineffectually against Radeski's tree-trunk thighs.

Then he jabbed it up over his shoulder, blindly stabbing in the direction of his demented kidnapper's face.

With an audible whoosh, Psycho Steve's hair caught fire.

Emitting an animal cry, he dropped Red and began furiously slapping at the flames. Talk about a bad hair day. Trailing smoke like a blazing oilfield on legs, he turned and ran.

I hoisted Red off the floor. 'You okay?'

Apart from a bit of gravy on his knees, the lad seemed none the worse for wear. 'Did you see me? Did you see me?'

'That's MOB property,' the tracksuited official reminded us, prising the torch from Red's grip. 'It's not a toy, you know.'

Herr Meisterchef clapped his hands. 'To verk, to verk,' he commanded. 'Begin plating ze emu.'

Toques bobbed. Crockery clattered. Steam rose. A mop slopped across my shoes. Waiters swarmed like extras in an Errol Flynn movie. The head pirate, Deadly, took off after Radeski. 'Where's my shoe?' demanded Holly. The security men jabbered into their walkie-talkies. Hustling Red back into the ballroom, I ran slap-bang into Wendy. 'Sweetie,' she cried, clutching the mortified warrior prince to her loins. 'Mummy was so proud.'

Hugh Knowles was at the podium. 'The important contribution of our indigenous people to the sporting achievements of the entire world...' he was saying.

Woeful McKenzie glanced down from the high table and I caught his eye. 'Steve,' I mouthed, index finger inscribing a corkscrew in the air beside my earhole. Woeful's eyes widened in alarm.

'Guess what just happened?' said Red to Wendy.

Moral coward, I turned tail and ran back into the kitchen.

Holly came at me, triumphantly brandishing a vermilion Salvatore Ferragamo slingback. Beyond a freight train of warming cabinets, the crash of shattering glassware indicated the direction of Steve Radeski's retreat. Holly and I joined the stampede, thundering down a carton-lined corridor, tracking the telltale vapour of freshly incinerated coiffure, led onwards by the verdant shimmer of Deadly's diabolical duds. Doors loomed, the concrete changed to carpet and we were suddenly in the ballroom foyer. It was deserted.

Almost.

Radeski, still batting at his spluttering scalp, was dodging and weaving through the exhibition of Olympic memorabilia. He was heading for the escalator. For a man of his size, he was moving remarkably fast. Deadly, twenty steps behind, was moving even faster.

A crack appeared in the ballroom portals and a security man sidled from the hushed interior, his cufflink pressed to the side of his head. Spotting Radeski rocketing towards him, he wrestled a gun from his jacket and levelled it.

'Freeze,' he ordered. Another fucking movie buff.

He might as well have been talking to a herd of elephants. Radeski's momentum was unstoppable. He careered headlong into Dirty Harry, sending him backwards into a massed arrangement of native orchids. The security man's gun skittered across the floor. With an agility born of a million knee-bends, Radeski scooped it up and waved it wildly in the air, still headed for the escalator.

Pulling up sharp, Deadly Anderson wrenched something from the array of sporting accoutrements attached to the wall. It was the aluminium javelin with which Glynis Nunn won her heptathlon gold medal in Los Angeles. Bracing his legs, he tested its heft. He opened his stance a little and marked his target. Then, in one single, fluid movement, he drew his arm back and pitched the missile forward with all his might.

The long shaft flashed through the air in a high wobbling arc and embedded itself in Radeski's thigh.

Radeski didn't know what hit him. He staggered forward a step, twisted around and wrenched the spear from his perforated flesh. Gushing blood, he teetered at the top of the escalator. Then, his mouth gaping in a silent scream, he pitched headlong between the moving rubber banisters and vanished from sight.

Deadly stood rooted to the spot with astonishment.

As did we all. 'Wow,' said Holly. The spell broke. She rushed to Deadly's side, squeezed his spear arm in both hands and pressed her cheek against his shoulder in abject admiration. 'Wow.'

The three of us hurried towards the escalator, arriving at the same time as the florally rearranged security man.

It was the up-escalator. Like a harpooned whale, beached by the waves of an incoming tide, Radeski's unconscious body advanced to meet us. Carried upwards on the relentless machinery of the metal steps, his twitching carcass was dumped bleeding at our feet. As we stood there, stunned, staring down, Woeful McKenzie shoved me aside.

'Stevie,' cried the minister, falling stricken to his knees. 'My son.'

'We have seen demonstrated here tonight the profound sentiments which sport engenders in the heart of our city.' Hugh Knowles paused meaningfully, looked up from his speech notes and fixed the Evaluation Commission with his most sincere expression.

Navigating the maze of tables at an apologetic half-crouch, I crept across the ballroom. 'Psst,' I whispered into Phillipa's ear.

'Not yet,' she whispered back. 'But I will be if this speech goes on for much longer.'

'Medical emergency.' I tugged at her sleeve.

'Thank God for small mercies,' she murmured, allowing herself to be drawn out of her seat.

Wendy looked daggers at me across the table. Sabres. Foils. Epees. Small bore pistols. Double-trap 12-gauge shotguns. Red was perched beside her, oblivious, wolfing down a plate of handmade, chocolate-coated Kakadu plum pralines. Brian Morrison also gave me a dirty look. Ambrose Buchanan had slipped into Woeful McKenzie's vacant seat at the high table. A knowing smile creased his lips as Pascal Abdoulaye whispered, tête-à-tête, into his ear.

'Bring your napkin,' I told Phillipa.

While I was in the ballroom getting expert assistance, the security bloke must have got onto his cufflink and signalled red alert. The woodwork had come alive. Men with shoulders the shape of bricks were swarming all over the scene like a rampant dose of whispering psoriasis.

Phillipa and I arrived in time to see four of them extract Radeski from the escalator mechanism and roll him onto a tablecloth. He lay there, inanimate, all colour drained from his velcro-textured face except for the zebra stripes of cinders where he'd smeared himself with cremated ponytail. His zit-infested forehead was split open and bright arterial blood was gushing from the slash in the seat of his trousers.

'What happened?' said Phillipa.

'Payback.' I indicated the red-tipped javelin lying on the carpet. Sorry business.

Before I could say more, she was hunkered down, stuffing her serviette into the haemorrhaging hole in Radeski's thigh. 'Tourniquet!' she said, tugging at my cummerbund.

There was no sign of Holly, Deadly or Woeful. The only civilians in sight were the hotel manager and a diminutive Hispanic cleaner. The morning-suited manager was reinstating the deranged orchids with the composed imperturbability of a senior instructor at the Neville Chamberlain School of Ikebana. Manuel was at the top of the escalator, wringing his mop into a bucket of pink-tinged water.

As soon as Phillipa got the bleeding staunched, four of the security detail grabbed the corners of the tablecloth. They hoisted Radeski off the floor and ran into an open service elevator. Phillipa trotted beside Radeski's sling and I went along for the ride, down two floors, out the elevator and onto the apron of the loading bay.

As we arrived, a *Dream the Dream* Torch Relay transit van backed into the dock and the rear doors flew open. Radeski was bundled inside and the vehicle zoomed away, orderlies and all. 'Clear, clear,' the remaining security man shouted into his personal communication device.

'What was that all about?' said Phillipa.

A fat guy in kitchen whites was sitting Buddha-like on a milk crate, smoking a cigarette. 'You again?' he grunted.

I snatched the cigarette from his mouth and took a long, deep drag. Then Phillipa took it out of my hand and did the same. 'Hey,' said the slob on the milk crate. 'Gimme me smoke back.'

Reaching into my shirt, I tore the Nicabate patch off my tit and slapped it onto his forehead. 'Try one of mine,' I said. 'You'll live longer.'

I conferred briefly in an undertone with the security guy and he gave me leave to step down into the lane. Phillipa jumped down beside me and we walked slowly towards Collins Street, security trailing a discreet distance behind. As we passed the cigarette back and forth between us, I told her as much as I could about what had just happened. It was as clear as mud, but it covered the ground.

We reached the fairy-lit trees of Collins Street and had turned towards the hotel entrance when a loud shriek suddenly rent the air. There was something oddly familiar about it. A butter-yellow Daihatsu Charade was heading down the street from the direction of the Old Treasury, its brakes emitting a characteristic telltale whine. The car's radiator grille was severely dented. Accelerating suddenly, it mounted the kerb and rocketed towards us.

I pushed Phillipa into the doorway of the Louis Vuitton boutique and pressed myself against her. The screeching yellow rattletrap streaked past, continued down the footpath another twenty metres and slammed into a fire hydrant, shearing it off at ground level. As it came to rest, water surging from beneath its chassis, the driver's door flew open. A man in a brown cardigan clambered out and fled down the street.

My body was still pressed against Phillipa. In relief at our narrow escape, I kissed her softly on the mouth. She didn't resist.

'Ah, shit,' I said, when we broke for air. 'I'm sorry.' In the glow of the street-light, her frogging was streaked with Steve Radeski's blood.

'I suppose I'd better get it off,' she said. 'Give it a good soaking.'

As we stepped back onto the footpath, the force of the water welling up beneath the Charade tilted the small sedan onto its side. A great foaming geyser exploded upwards. A torrent of cold water fell out of the sky, drenching us to the skin.

'You think this hotel has any rooms?' I said.

'Nice try,' said Phillipa. 'Let's find out.'

Two days later, the Evaluation Commission gathered up its notes and left town. Three months later, Melbourne learned that it had failed in its bid to host the 1996 Olympic Games, crossing the finishing line well behind Atlanta, Athens and Toronto.

It was a humiliating rebuff, considering the millions of dollars the city had spent whipping itself into a frenzy of anticipation. There is, after all, nothing more demoralising than coming fourth in an arse-licking competition.

As far as Brian Morrison was concerned, the responsibility fell squarely on my shoulders. 'If you'd done your job properly,' he complained bitterly when he rang Water Supply to arrange for the disposal of the *Dream the Dream* luxury launch, 'we wouldn't have lost black Africa.' Given that it was a secret ballot and he was in no position to know how Botswana and Burkina Faso voted, I thought the accusation a tad unfair.

Especially knowing what Ambrose Buchanan told us when Brian confronted him after the gala dinner and demanded to know what he'd talked about with Pascal Abdoulaye.

'Family matters,' he said. 'As they say in Olympic circles. Pascal was telling me about his sons. All seven of them have just won scholarships to Georgia Tech. He's a very proud man, considering that one of them is still in primary school. He said he's planning on being there for their graduation in six years' time.'

With the loss of the bid, Buchanan's idea for an Aboriginal Sports Institute hit something of a brick wall. He plans to take up the issue a bit later, after he's finished his current work with the Black Deaths in Custody Royal Commission.

Under the circumstances, no charges were laid against Deadly Anderson. In fact, I haven't seen Deadly since that night, standing there in the ballroom foyer with a satisfied look on his face, Holly Deloite nestled into him, the sole of his foot resting on the side of his knee.

I asked Holly about him when I saw her the next Monday at the City Club. 'He's a wild man,' she said, smiling enigmatically as she handed me my complimentary fluffy towel.

Deadly's out there somewhere, a model of successful assimilation, blending inconspicuously with the general petty-criminal population. Selling pigeon steroids to high-flying ruckmen, probably, and frightening the hell out of the hairdressing fraternity.

Radeski was dead by then. He expired shortly after arriving at St Vincent's Hospital. Cause of death was a combination of shock, blood loss and an adverse reaction to the drugs administered during emergency treatment. Apparently, they did not combine well with the concentrated cocktail of veterinary products already flowing through his bloodstream. His natural father was at his side when he passed away, holding the perforated power-lifter's limp hand and confiding into his comatose ear the long-concealed circumstances of his conception.

According to the Health Minister's adviser, who was told by the Hospital Employees Federation assistant secretary, who heard it from the St Vincent's workplace delegate, who was living with the charge nurse from intensive care, who overheard it while changing Radeski's IV-drip, it was a piteous tale. Not, perhaps, particularly extraordinary but made both tragic and ironic by the events which flowed from it.

It was the story of a family secret. Of how Steve's mother, Irene, had always been keen on her older sister's boyfriend. How even after the young footballer and Beth Boag were married, Irene had continued to carry a torch for Woeful McKenzie. And how eventually she had appealed to him for help when her own husband, the disgruntled Rudy Radeski, began to slap her around. How that succour had become guilt-ridden adultery.

Irene had long been praying for a child but all that God had sent her were miscarriages. So when her shameful intimacy with her brother-in-law resulted in pregnancy she took it as a sign that she should dedicate herself to making good her marriage. Unaware of the infant's true paternity, Rudy Radeski duly mended his ways and stopped beating his wife. And when, in young Stevie's seventh year, Irene went to meet her maker while changing a light globe, Rudy insisted on raising the child himself. By then, there was no question of telling him the truth.

Beth McKenzie, too, remained oblivious to her spouse's brief episode of infidelity. The revelation that he had been romancing her little sister would hardly have gone down well with the mother of two young girls. Daughters upon whom Woeful doted and could not bear the thought of losing. 'But Stevie,' he told the recumbent form in the hospital bed, his voice choked with fatherly grief. 'You were my only son.'

I still don't know if Woeful has got around to confessing the situation to his wife. What with one thing and another, I haven't really had the opportunity to discuss the matter with him. In the immediate short-term, I was tied up dealing with the security people.

Despite Brian Morrison's assurances to the contrary, there were quite a few of them in the ballroom that night, maintaining a discreet but heavily tooled eyeball on our distinguished Olympic guests. Dziczkowszczak in particular, whose name had rung a bell with the old cold warriors who continue to haunt the higher reaches of our national intelligence apparatus. All things considered, it was deemed advisable to keep the entire incident well under wraps as in '56.

The hush-hush boys were certainly faster off the mark than the Victoria Police homicide squad, who spent the entire evening fruitlessly staking out Holly's hacienda. Steve, of course, had no intention of returning there. He planned to go down in a blaze of glory.

Familiar with the backstairs byways of the Hyatt from his time at the Typhoon nightclub, he had slipped unnoticed through a side door behind the motor court concierge's desk. For three hours, he'd remained hidden in the room-service storage hold, mentally rehearsing his next move and working out with two magnums of Veuve Cliquot he found stashed beneath a pile of linen tablecloths. Only when he felt sure that the Olympic gala was in full swing had he risked taking the fire stairs up to the banquet kitchen, where he passed unremarked through the bustle involved in plating six hundred edible portions of the nation's coat-of-arms.

Not that I can be too disparaging about the boys and girls in blue. They did, at least, catch Darcy Anderson's killers. Or so it would appear, pending outcome of the trial. We read the story in the next morning's complimentary newspaper, Phillipa and I, over a tray of room-service croissants and a presumptuous young filter-tip cigarette.

In a combined Victorian–Tasmanian operation, all four members of a Launceston-based gang of white supremacists were arrested and charged with the manslaughter of Darcy Anderson. The officer in charge stated that a large quantity of literature had been seized, most of it foreign in origin. Lacking hometown opportunities for the expression of racial pride, the skinheads had travelled to the mainland to conduct what they described as a 'training exercise' in expectation of the imminent outbreak of a global race war.

According to Ken Sproule, the coppers had a watertight case based on a confession from one of the skins and the testimony of a steward on the *Princess of Tasmania* who overheard the crop-top hoons discussing their mission during a feed of dim sims in the after-deck cafeteria.

As to the Daihatsu, I'm still dickering with Auto & General. The vehicle was a write-off, of course, but they seem to think that my being there when it was recovered smacks of complicity in its original disappearance. Insurance company logic. They may pay up eventually, but I'm not holding my breath. And, since my MOB consultancy fee was exactly ten dollars more than the price I was asking for the car, I figure I ended up slightly better than break-even for the week.

So, too, did the staff of the Water Supply maintenance department. Rather than cop the political flak engendered by all those ruptured water mains, Angelo caved in to the Missos and granted them their pay rise.

Another nail in the coffin of fiscal rectitude and the straw that broke the Premier's back. Shortly after the Evaluation Commission left town, he announced his resignation. The resulting Cabinet reshuffle also disposed of Woeful McKenzie. The big feller is spending a lot more time with Beth and the girls these days and can sometimes be seen sitting beside Denis Dogherty's grave in the St Kilda cemetery.

Angelo Agnelli got the Transport portfolio and he took me with him. It's a step upwards and in the wrong direction. Compared with the good old Missos, the Transport Workers Federation is the Mongol fucking hordes. Our new Premier is a woman, which should not be misconstrued as an expression of commitment to gender equity. It just means the boys are losing their grip.

Wendy and Red returned to Sydney as scheduled and I'll need to eat a lot of crow before I see the kid again. We do talk on the phone, though. He rang last Saturday after the Swans beat Fitzroy. 'Nyah, nyah,' he said. 'We beatcha.' But at least he's stopped playing rugby. After he told Wendy what he did to Steve Radeski in the kitchen, she decided that all this sport was making him too aggressive.

Meanwhile, Phillipa and I are thinking of opening a mattress-testing laboratory. And applying for a productivity bonus. I find I have lots of stamina these days, even though I don't go to the gym so often. The sex is great, but the part we both like best is the cigarette we share afterwards.

THE BIG ASK

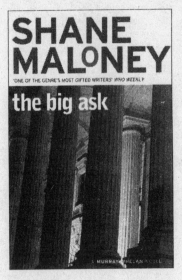

Murray Whelan should have been asleep in bed. That's where the smart money is at 4.30 on a wet winter's morning. Not loitering among the truckies at the fruit and vegetable market. Not picking fights with a gun-toting kid in a cashmere coat. Not tasting forbidden fruit in the back of Donny Maitland's rig.

But what's a lonely political minder to do? His son Red has disappeared, and his boss Angelo Agnelli has sent him on a mission to infiltrate the toughest union in the country.

With an election looming, a homicide cop on his heels, adultery in the air and a gun buried in the backyard, the triumphantly futile hero of Shane Maloney's acclaimed thrillers is crunching the numbers once again.

Now Murray Whelan faces his biggest ask yet.